# THE THINKING
# WOMAN'S
# GUIDE TO
# REAL MAGIC

*Emily Croy Barker*

# THE THINKING WOMAN'S GUIDE TO REAL MAGIC

PAMELA DORMAN BOOKS
VIKING

VIKING
Published by the Penguin Group
Penguin Group (USA) Inc., 375 Hudson Street,
New York, New York 10014, USA

USA | Canada | UK | Ireland | Australia | New Zealand | India | South Africa | China

Penguin Books Ltd, Registered Offices: 80 Strand, London WC2R 0RL, England
For more information about the Penguin Group visit penguin.com

A Pamela Dorman Book / Viking

Copyright © Emily Croy Barker, 2013
All rights reserved. No part of this book may be reproduced, scanned, or distributed in
any printed or electronic form without permission. Please do not participate in or
encourage piracy of copyrighted materials in violation of the author's rights.
Purchase only authorized editions.

LIBRARY OF CONGRESS CATALOGING-IN-PUBLICATION DATA
Barker, Emily Croy.
The thinking woman's guide to real magic / Emily Croy Barker.
pages cm
ISBN 978-0-670-02366-0
1. Magic—Fiction. I. Title.
PS3602.A77548T45 2013
813'.6—dc23
2013013095

Printed in the United States of America
1 3 5 7 9 10 8 6 4 2

Book design by Francesca Belanger
Set in Fournier MT Std

This is a work of fiction. Names, characters, places, and incidents either are the product of
the author's imagination or are used fictitiously, and any resemblance to actual persons,
living or dead, businesses, companies, events, or locales is entirely coincidental.

ISLAND PARK PUBLIC LIBRARY

*To my father, the best of magicians*

# ACKNOWLEDGMENTS

I am enormously grateful to those who were intrepid enough to read early versions of this novel: Catherine Aman, Michael Barker, Maggie Rosen Briand, Shelton Crocker, Roger Devine, Kathy Fitzgerald, Alison Frankel, Susan Hansen, Pam DiRubio Hegarty, Dimitra Kessenides, Sally Rosen Kindred, Patricia Krebs, Anthony Paonita, Emily Allen and Trever Talbert, and Vivian S. M. Wang. Their comments were incredibly helpful, their encouragement even more so. Thanks to Roland Greene for kindly serving as my technical adviser on English departments and in the dissertation process; any errors are mine alone. Thanks to Pascale Retourné-Raab for moral support and to Matt Siegel for the tale of a mouse.

I couldn't ask for a better agent than Emma Sweeney, not only for her wise counsel but also for the brilliant suggestions that helped tame and transform a sprawling early draft. Huge thanks to Pamela Dorman for her belief in this book, and to her and Beena Kamlani for their magical editing powers. Thanks to Clare Ferraro, Hal Fessenden, Leigh Butler, Dick Heffernan, Norman Lidofsky, Carolyn Coleburn, Nancy Sheppard, Andrew Duncan, Dennis Swaim, Kathryn Court, Patrick Nolan, John Fagan, Maureen Donnelly, Roseanne Serra, Francesca Belanger, Kiki Koroshetz, and Julie Miesionczek at Viking and Penguin for all they've done to make this book a reality.

Finally, thanks to my parents for all that they taught me, by word and example, about the joy of making things.

PART
ONE

# Chapter 1

Much later, Nora would learn magic for dissolving glue or killing vermin swiftly and painlessly or barring mice from the house altogether, but that morning—the last normal morning, she later thought of it—as she padded into the kitchen in search of coffee, she was horribly at a loss when she saw the small brown mouse wriggling on the glue trap in front of the sink.

At the sight of Nora, the mouse froze for an instant, then tried to bolt, but only succeeded in gluing another paw to the sticky cardboard.

"Oh, crap," Nora said aloud. "I can't deal with this. Not on top of everything else."

She was angrier at her roommate Dane, than at the mouse. Almost certainly he was the one who had set the trap, and then hadn't had the decency to handle the result himself. Besides, the mouse problem was Dane's fault in the first place. If he had not let Astrophel out—by accident, he claimed—Astrophel would not have attempted to cross six lanes of traffic, and would still be alive and keeping the house mouse-free. The ashy remains of Nora's cat now resided in a small cardboard box on Nora's desk, and the mice had become a scrabbling, bold presence in the house.

She thought about simply letting the trapped mouse remain there for Dane to clean up, but she would have to step over it to fill the coffeepot, and what if the mouse got loose while she was still in the kitchen? Before she could lose her nerve, Nora picked up the glue trap with her thumb and forefinger, and moved toward the garbage can.

But the mouse was still alive. That was disturbing. After a second's thought, Nora took a bottle of olive oil from the cabinet. The good stuff, Tuscan gold, encased in a tall bottle with a sprig of rosemary suspended inside, and she was fairly sure it belonged to Dane.

Outside, a block from her house, in a sliver of park, she carefully poured olive oil on the mouse and the glue board. The smell of the oil filled her nose; she was suddenly hungry. The mouse, its fur now sleek and dark with oil, rolled back and forth on the glue board. All at once it was loose. Nora jumped back, and the mouse scampered away, leaving shiny drops on the pine needles to mark its trail.

She walked back to the house thinking automatically that she had a good story for Adam, and then remembering that she wouldn't be telling it to him.

On her way to the English department, she kept an eye out for him anyway. He was still in town, probably, unless he'd gotten an earlier flight. She might bump into him on campus. It would be awkward. Then maybe not so awkward. And he would realize what a terrible mistake he had made.

Instead, when someone spoke her name outside the department lounge, it was her adviser.

"Nora. I haven't seen you all week." Naomi smiled, showing an unnatural number of teeth. Nora braced herself, trying as always to find Naomi's presence empowering instead of terrifying. Naomi was carrying her eight-month-old son in a sling on her chest: Last fall, in a single semester, she had produced both the baby and a book on sexual ambiguity in Dickens. Following Naomi into the lounge, Nora wiggled her fingers at the baby, who gave her a somber gaze out of bottomless dark blue eyes. "Where are the rest of the papers from your Gender and Genre section?" Naomi demanded. "I have only half of them."

Nora unslung the backpack from her shoulder. "Here they are," she said.

"I wish you'd finished them sooner. I want to look them over before I turn the grades in."

"I'm sorry. I had to grade the Modern Drama exams, too. It's been a busy week."

"Yes, it has. That's why I wanted to see those papers earlier." Naomi leafed through her mail, flicking most of it into the trash and then sliding a thin envelope with Italian stamps into the lustrous leather jaws of her slim briefcase.

It was not the best time to bring up any kind of request, Nora saw, but she had no choice. "Actually, I wanted to mention," she began, "I decided to apply for that travel fellowship, the Blum-Forsythe grant? I was wondering if you could write a recommendation for me."

"I thought you weren't going to apply for that. Can't you ask Marlene to send out the recommendation that's on file?"

"I realized there's some work I could do at Cambridge." The idea had come to Nora two nights before, as she lay awake at three a.m. The inspiration had less to do with John Donne, her thesis subject, than a sudden need to escape. "The form asks some questions that aren't covered by the rec-

ommendation you wrote for me before. If you tweaked the old recommendation, it should be fine. It just has to be postmarked by Monday."

Naomi pivoted, a wrinkle of annoyance visible between her strong
brows. "You know, I'm boarding a plane Sunday to fly to London. I don't
know if I'll have time."

"Oh," Nora said awkwardly. "I didn't realize you were leaving so soon."

Naomi sighed and ran a hand through her hair, which was growing
long, Nora noticed. Naomi usually had it cut on one of her frequent trips to
Europe, one of the side benefits of having a boyfriend in London. "Come
into my office, Nora. I want a word with you."

As Nora lowered herself onto the steel-and-leather chair in front of
Naomi's desk, Naomi shut the office door. Nora's stomach tensed. "I should
tell you that if I do write you a new recommendation," Naomi said, "I don't
know that I'd have anything very positive to add."

Nora blinked. "Really?"

"I haven't seen very much from you this year, just the one thesis chapter. It was fine, but you finished it back in November, and here it is May."

"I wrote that Dickinson paper. 'Wild Nights: The Erotics of Evasion.'
One of the journals was interested, so I've been revising—"

"It's a good paper, and I'm sure you *could* publish it. But you shouldn't
be spending time trying to publish a paper so removed from your dissertation topic. I was hoping that I'd see at least one more chapter from you before the end of this school year."

"Well, I've been working hard. I'm just not making much progress."
Nora paused, but Naomi said nothing, so she plunged on. "I'm starting to
think—I'm just not sure I can say much that's new about gender politics in
Donne."

"Nora, when you chose your topic, we discussed the pitfalls of writing
about a canonical author like John Donne. It can be difficult to find un-
plowed ground."

Hundreds of authors to write about, and yet it seemed that every single
one had already been chewed over by packs of other hungry doctoral students. Even poets who had written only a handful of decent poems in their
entire lives were the subject of lengthy, arcane, lovingly argued disserta-
tions. And someone good, like Shakespeare or Brontë or Dickinson or
Dickens—or Donne? They were mobbed by grad students and professors
alike, like pop stars surrounded by screaming groupies.

"Yes, I know," Nora said. "So I'm wondering whether it might be fruitful to look at another writer, too. I have some ideas about Donne and Dickinson, their comparative poetics, that I'd like to outline for you—"

Naomi held up her hand. "If you really want to write about Dickinson, the emphasis needs to be more American or early modern. Otherwise, you'll get killed on the job market."

"But I really am just—" Nora searched in vain for a way to describe the vast, barren desert of thesis research where she had been wandering without a compass. "Just stuck."

The baby had been fidgeting inside the sling, his starfish arms and legs waving in the air. Now he opened his mouth and began to wail. Nora suppressed an urge to do the same.

"I need to feed him," Naomi said, unsnapping the pouch, "and then I have a meeting with the dean, and then I'm going home to pack. So I'm sorry, I don't have time to finish this conversation. We'll talk after I get back in July."

Nora nodded. "Sure."

"If you want to e-mail me that Donne and Dickinson idea while I'm away, I'll take a look at it." She sounded less than enthusiastic about the prospect.

"Okay, I will. Thanks." Nora stood up, picking up her backpack. "Enjoy London."

Naomi looked up from behind her immaculate desktop. "Nora, I agreed to be your adviser because you're very, very good—in some areas. You're one of the best close readers of poetry I've ever worked with. You have a real knack for understanding the life of a poem. Fifty years ago, that would have gotten you a doctorate, a job, and tenure at any English department in the country. But today that's not enough. You have to be able to address a big question—something to do with aesthetics, or colonialism, or philosophy—*what* it is doesn't matter so much, but you need to play at that level. And that's where you're having problems."

"I know, I know. Big questions aren't my strong point." In fact, Nora had plenty of questions, just less and less assurance that she could ever formulate answers to them. She added, a little desperately: "No ideas but in things."

"Well, that has to change," said Naomi, unbuttoning her linen blouse.

Nora closed the office door, but not before getting a glimpse of the baby's mouth closing urgently on Naomi's brown nipple.

Heading for the library, she checked her phone and found a message from her mother. "Nora, I was hoping you might be able to drive up this weekend. We're going to the beach, and then to a fellowship dinner that you would really enjoy—"

She skipped to the next message, from her father's number in New Jersey. Nora's youngest sister's voice, high and cheerful: "Hi, Nora, how are you? It's me. Teacher shirk day, I have to go with Mom to her work, boring boring. I looked for those books of yours you said were in the attic, but I couldn't find them. Do you know where else they might be? I need something to read. Bye."

Ramona wasn't looking hard enough. Nora could picture the box, left of the attic stairs, near EJ's things. She was in the middle of leaving her own message when she walked smack into Farmer Dahmer, literally collided with him, right in front of the library.

Farmer Dahmer—as in Jeffrey—wasn't his name, but almost everyone on campus, even the senior faculty, knew whom you were talking about if you mentioned Farmer Dahmer. He was a small man, around sixty, with a stiff, gray-brown beard like the wire pads used to scrub out sinks. He usually wore a faded plaid shirt, which Nora assumed was the origin of the agricultural portion of his nickname. Rumor had it that he was a superannuated grad student who had gone crazy after being unable to complete his thesis. Nora no longer found this story as amusing as she once had. He spent most of his days hanging around the library, where she had often seen him bent over a sheaf of papers in a carrel, swaying back and forth, mumbling to himself.

Farmer Dahmer looked even more stunned than Nora at their collision, and for a moment she was afraid that he would topple over. "I'm so sorry," she said, clutching his arm. "Are you all right? I can't believe I didn't see you. I'm really sorry."

"Oh, it's you," he said to her, blinking his small eyes.

"Um, yes," Nora said uncertainly. "It's me, all right. Are you okay?"

With a jerk of his arm, he shook himself free of Nora's grasp. "Oh, I'm fine. Thanks to you. I very much appreciate it."

"There's no need to be sarcastic. I really do apologize."

"No, I blame my own carelessness. You see, I was very hungry, and when I smelled the peanut butter, I simply forgot to be cautious."

She nodded, unable to think of a proper response.

Farmer Dahmer's head swiveled from side to side, as though he were reading something in the figures of passing students or the grass and oak trees of the quad. Then he looked back at Nora. "I suppose you want the usual reward. Is three enough for you?"

"Oh, I'm fine. Don't worry," she said, shaking her head vigorously so that there would be no mistake. "I'm just happy to know that you're okay."

"Oh, it's no trouble at all," he said. "Let's do the thing properly, shall we?" He squared his shoulders and gave her a brisk nod, then turned and marched away, disappearing around the side of the student union.

What a day, Nora thought, rubbing her head. She noticed for the first time the rich smell of olive oil mingled with rosemary hanging in the air. Hell, she must have spilled that stuff on her clothes this morning. She must reek. What had Naomi thought?

She went into the library and spent a few hours finishing up the Blum-Forsythe application. In the air-conditioned quiet of the stacks on the twelfth floor, where she had her carrel, the scent of olive oil and rosemary faded, much to her relief.

Heading home, she took the long way, past Adam's favorite coffee-house, the one where he used to hold his office hours when he was a teaching assistant because he couldn't smoke in his assigned cubbyhole in the English department. Of course he was not sitting there now. Why would he be? Not running into him was a clear sign from the heavens that whatever had existed between her and Adam was over, finished for good, the invisible karmic connection between them severed and tied off forever.

She said aloud, but softly: "I wish I could see him again, though."

Maggie picked her up at four for the drive to the wedding in the mountains. That was a relief. Someone to tell about this nightmare of a week.

"Oh, you're kidding," Maggie said, when Nora had gotten only part-way into her story, as they shot into the I-40 traffic. "He flew all the way back here just to break up with you? And you really thought he was going to ask you to marry him. That's so awful."

"He said he had something big to tell me, and he wanted to tell me in person."

"Well, that's big."

"And he is getting married. Just not to me," Nora clarified.

"And who *is* this woman?"

"Another assistant professor there. An art historian. The French baroque—"

"Oh, God."

"—and they got to be friends, and it was all very casual, and then they went away for the weekend, an art exhibition in New York—"

"You don't just go away for the weekend with a casual friend!"

"I know," Nora said miserably. "He told me all this right after I picked him up at the airport. He wouldn't shut up about her. As though I cared. And then he apologized and said he'd been meaning to tell me, but he didn't want to do it over the phone. And he said he had other friends in town to see. So that's when I said, well, maybe you can stay with one of them. I haven't seen him since." Maggie nodded her approval, but Nora grimaced. "Well, I kept thinking I'd see him and somehow we'd work it out, but he hasn't called, nothing.

"Oh, and then just to top it off," she added, "this morning my adviser gave me the something-has-to-change talk. One step away from the what-are-you-still-doing-here talk. My career and my love life, both going up in flames."

"Oh, honey." Maggie leaned over suddenly to give Nora a hug. The car veered toward the median for an instant, which made the gesture less reassuring than she intended. "Well, fuck it. So what if grad school doesn't work out? There are plenty of other options. You should open your own restaurant and be a celebrity chef. I mean it. That toffee soufflé you made, my God."

Nora was silent, thinking again about her morning's conversation with Naomi. Unofficial probation, that's what she was on, even if Naomi hadn't used those words. All at once she missed Adam more than ever. He had brilliant political instincts; he knew exactly how to soothe and beguile the most implacable thesis adviser. Nora wasn't sure how she'd get by without Adam's coaching, not to mention his protective aura. He'd been such a star in the department that some of his prestige had invisibly accrued to her, too. She wondered suddenly how far news of their breakup had spread. Did Naomi know? Yes, Nora thought, or she would have asked me about him this morning. She always did before.

"You sure you want to go to this thing?" Maggie was saying. "Weddings are no fun when you're newly single, not by choice—that's my experience."

Nora shrugged. "It's okay. How can I not go to Luca's wedding, anyway?"

"Any chance that Adam will be there?"

"No, he's flying back tonight. He wanted to spend the weekend with his *fiancée*." Nora grimaced as she spoke the last word.

"Bastard. Well, maybe you'll meet someone this weekend. And there'll be lots to drink. Forget about Adam."

"Just what I'm planning to do."

Which made it all the more disconcerting, at the party following the re-hearsal dinner, to turn and find Adam standing a few feet away. He had a beer in his hand, and he was having a desultory conversation with a couple of law students, friends of Maggie's. He looked vaguely ill at ease even before he saw Nora.

"What are you doing here?" he asked her.

"I was going to ask you the same thing," she said. "I thought you were back in Chicago."

He shook his head. "Couldn't change my flight. I'm going back Sunday."

"So you decided to come to this thing after all."

"Well, yes. I was invited. Is that a problem?"

"No, I'm just surprised to see you here."

"You shouldn't be. I've known Chris and Luca a long time. About time they got married." He took a swig of beer.

Nora bit her lip. "They started dating a month after we did."

"Really? I thought they'd been together longer."

"No, I remember. We saw them at that French movie, *Amélie*."

"God, that was a terrible movie."

"I liked it."

"Really?" Nora knew the expression on his face well: Adam enjoying the sense of his own superior judgment. Other, more benighted people had always inspired that look—never her. Then he seemed to recollect himself: "Well, good for you. How are you doing?"

"Very well, thank you."

"Good." For an instant, his eyes practically shone with sincerity. "I'm glad. I was a little worried, you know, after the other night."

Nora wanted to believe him. A man may smile and smile and be a villain. "No, you weren't. You would have called me if you were."

"I did call you. Couple of times."

She shook her head. "I would have seen your number."

They went around and around, until it emerged that Adam had dialed the wrong number, manually. He had a new phone, the kind that knew everything, but he had not bothered to enter her number.

"I see," Nora said grimly. "Well, as you can tell, I'm just fine."

"Good." He started to turn away, then swung back. "You know, I still care about you."

She closed her eyes for a moment. "I care about you, too."

"You may not want to hear this right now, but I mean it in the best possible way, believe me. When Celeste and I get married this fall, I hope you can be there. I mean it. October sixteenth."

A few days ago, waiting for Adam in the airport, Nora had been thinking about wedding dates, wondering if October would be too soon. It wasn't as though she'd want a huge, elaborate wedding. "Thank you, Adam," she said now, smiling, with as much dignity as she could muster. "That's awfully"—she considered and rejected a number of words, settling for a relatively bland and obvious choice that she hoped would trouble Adam anyway—"*stupid* of you."

She turned and plunged into the crowd. The party was a large, loose affair: It flowed through the house, which belonged to one of the bride's relatives, and onto the rambling cedar decks wrapped around the outside. Plenty of room to retreat.

Nora refilled her wineglass, then topped it up again and again. The alcohol began to make her feel blurry as she drifted from one group to the next, never quite finding her way into the conversation. But the recollection of her encounter with Adam remained razor-sharp. She kept looking for him—to avoid him, she told herself. Once she looked up and saw him looking at her from across the deck. He turned away without acknowledging her.

They flee from me that sometime did me seek, she told herself. Ducking away, she found herself in a room where a cluster of partygoers were watching an old episode of *The Avengers*. She plunked herself on a couch—grateful for its solidity, although her surroundings continued to wobble slightly—and watched John Steed and Emma Peel battle evil, he in a morning coat, she in a catsuit, exchanging arch bons mots. Why can't real love be debonair and *fun?* she wondered.

After a while, she noticed that the man in the chair next to her was looking at her more than at the television. He addressed an occasional remark to her, and laughed when she did. When someone turned the lights up for a moment, she saw that his eyes were a bright green, like traffic lights. She took it as a good omen. They kept talking after someone turned the TV off. His name was Dave, he was in the history department, but he wanted to know about her life outside of grad school. She told him about being a cook after college. An organic café with locally sourced, seasonal menus; Nora made it to sous-chef. "It was fun for a while. But, God, so much work."

"I hear you," he said. "I waited tables in college. Whenever I get fed up with sitting in a library, I make myself remember what it was like to be on my feet carrying trays until midnight. So you decided to do something more intellectually challenging, huh?"

"For some reason I thought that would be grad school." He laughed at that, and they started kissing soon afterward. Dave's lips were softer than she liked, but that was okay. It was the first time she had kissed someone else besides Adam in almost four years. She hoped hazily that he would come into the room and see her with Dave. Doing just fine, thank you.

Dave's phone rang. The ring tone was Rod Stewart: "Do Ya Think I'm Sexy?" Dave jolted away from Nora. Putting the phone to his ear, he turned, moving toward the door, but Nora still heard more of the conversation than she wanted to.

"Your girlfriend?" she asked when he came back.

He nodded, looking uncomfortable. "Sorry, we just broke up. But she keeps calling me."

Looking at him, Nora was fairly sure he wasn't telling the whole truth to someone—Nora, his girlfriend, or himself. "Well, fuck," she said, hitting the arm of the couch. "Call her back. She wants to talk to you."

He made a face. "She's just emotional."

"Maybe she has a right to be."

"Don't be that way, Norma. It's not that big a deal."

"*Nora,* and yes, it is a big deal."

She had to wait around for a while until she could get a ride back to the house where she and Maggie were staying. That meant having to avoid both Adam and Dave. She skulked on the deck in the darkness with a Coke, pretending to look at the invisible view over the mountains.

Back in her room, Nora undressed quickly. In the mirror, she saw her brown roots were showing. On some women that was sexy. Nora was not one of them. She tried not to imagine what Celeste looked like.

October 16. How extraordinarily dense of Adam to invite her to the wedding. And Adam always so careful—even calculating—about everything he said. That was what really hurt. He wasn't even trying. He had written her off.

She slid under the sheet. My life is a catastrophe, she thought, shutting her eyes.

Lately, for reassurance, Nora had taken to reminding herself of John Donne's own checkered employment history—his unfinished legal training; the government job he was fired from; the long search for preferment—before he finally found success and security in holy orders. But even at the beginning he had been writing those intricate, intimate poems of passion and thought. Nora was almost thirty, and what did she have to show for herself?

Turning restlessly in bed, she thought: Naomi is right, I don't fit in, I'm all wrong for this. I can't do anything right. Well, maybe saving the life of that mouse today. And it's probably already back in my kitchen, eating my food. I wish my life were different. I don't care how.

She woke early, her mouth dry from all the alcohol she'd drunk the night before. In the other bed, Maggie was still asleep. Nora pulled on a T-shirt and jeans and went quietly out of the room.

The cabin that she and Maggie and four other wedding guests were renting for the weekend perched on the mountainside, at the end of a long gravel driveway lined with rhododendrons. She peered out of the living room window. It had rained during the night, but the sky was clear now. The wedding was not until five. People had talked about driving to Asheville for brunch. So far she was the only one up. Nora made herself some coffee and ate half a bagel, then stepped onto the deck outside. Chilly for May. She thought she might walk down to the road for some exercise, but then she noticed the trail leading up the mountain. She went back inside for a sweatshirt. Out of habit, she stopped by the bookshelf in the living room to see if there was a paperback that she could stuff into her pocket for emergencies—you never knew when you might need a book to entertain and comfort and distract you in the day's empty places.

There was not much to choose from. She passed on the Robert Ludlum and a couple of the *Dune* books in favor of a yellowed paperback edition of *Pride and Prejudice* that had originally cost fifty cents. Privately Nora agreed with Charlotte Brontë that Jane Austen's world was too manicured for sustained interest, but on the other hand you could always dip in and find something amusing on almost any page. Besides, she had to teach the novel in summer school next month.

No reason to leave a note. She would be back in half an hour. Nora went outside and started up the path. At first it tunneled through more rhododendrons, but the forest brightened when she reached a stand of hardwoods, skinny gray poles, newly leafed out. There was almost no undergrowth at this time of year, only dead leaves covering the ground as far as she could see.

After the novelty of walking somewhere that wasn't a street or a campus path had worn off, Nora began to find the upward-sloping, dun-colored landscape monotonous. She was wondering whether to head back when suddenly the path leveled off and she stepped out of the woods onto grass.

A fragment of conversation from the party last night came back to her. So this was what Chris's cousin meant by the Bald. The crown of the mountain was an immense green meadow. A few steps forward, and Nora had a 360-degree view of the undulating horizon, mountains rising in all directions.

She walked across the meadow, feeling her heart lift in spite of herself. Ye visions of the hills, and souls of lonely places. Nora found herself smiling. She had the absurd thought—she squelched it quickly—that she could bring Adam up here to show him this place.

Nora turned back when she reached the other side of the hilltop. It was going to rain again, she saw with regret; gray clouds were looming in the west. Otherwise, she would have been tempted to sit down and read for a while. She retraced her steps across the meadow. There was no sign of the trail where she thought it should be, but she reasoned that if she followed the edge of the woods, she was bound to come across the path, even if she had to circle the entire mountaintop.

The first raindrops hit her face as she walked along. Still no path. She walked faster. After a few minutes, she saw a gap in the trees and what looked like the beginnings of a path.

But was it the right one? There might be several paths. A disturbing thought crystallized: If she took the wrong trail down, she could wind up on the other side of the mountain, miles from where she wanted to be.

Oh, well, she thought as the rain began to pelt down, I can go a little way and see whether it looks familiar.

She started down the path. Had the trail been this slick, this steep before? Almost immediately she slipped and fell in a patch of cold mud. Her right ankle protested when she tried to get to her feet. Nora cursed herself. Accidents like this were precisely why she should have left a note at the cabin. Well, someone—Maggie, perhaps—would eventually notice if she didn't show up for brunch *or* the wedding *or* the reception. After a minute, Nora tried again to stand, and this time she was able to pull herself upright. So far so good. The ankle was sore, but it would take her weight. Well, she thought, I wasn't planning to do much dancing tonight anyway.

She found a stick to lean on, and began limping down the mountain. The forest here was full of spindly young trees like the ones that she had passed on the way up, but she couldn't tell whether they were the same trees. It was darker here than on the mountaintop, and the woods were full of soft pattering noises, rain smacking leaves. After ten minutes of slow progress, Nora had to admit that she still had no clue as to whether she was on the right path or not.

She had just about decided to turn around and retreat when something ahead caught her eye. Instantly she knew that she had taken the wrong trail. I would have remembered *that*, she thought.

# Chapter 2

It was a graveyard, a small one. Through the trees she could make out the white glimmer of tombstones; a rusted iron fence surrounded the graves like a border of tattered lace. The path led to an arched entrance, also iron, with a gate that was not so much hung from the fence posts as propped up against them. With some effort, Nora wrenched it open and stepped inside.

Nora had a weakness for country cemeteries. She and Adam had spent one summer crouching on overgrown graves and risking Lyme disease as they copied down Victorian funerary verses for one of Nora's papers, "Voices in the Grass: Strategies of Faith and Subversion in the Post-Romantic Epitaph." Here, the most recent graves were just over a hundred years old. The oldest dated back to the 1830s. About half of the tilting, lichen-spotted stones bore the same surname, Clement. A family burying ground, filled over a few generations and then abandoned. Out of habit, Nora stooped to read one of the inscriptions, a few lines of verse written in the slanting pothooks of the time.

> Read this, take heed, and gain from my sad fate.
> For you the way is open. I must wait,
> Condemned for centuries long to guard this gate.
> Make haste, pass through, the hour is growing late.

Strange, rather creepy. What was this about watching and guarding? The usual Protestant dogma of the period taught that the dead would sleep quietly until called for, when the Last Trump blew. The meek members of the resurrection, Dickinson said. Yet the speaker in this poem spoke as a restless ghost, spying on the living, guarding the gates of death. Of course, Nora thought, the nineteenth century was the heyday of the ghost story, but it was strange to find this view of the unquiet dead expressed on a tombstone.

She looked at the name on the stone: Emmeline Anne Clement. Died May 11, 1833, AE 18 years, 3 months.

May 11, today's date. The coincidence wasn't spooky as much as sad, that Emmeline Anne had died so young on a spring day that was the match to this one. "Poor Emmeline," Nora said aloud. "I'm sorry you had such a short life. I hope it was a happy one." Happier than mine, she thought morosely.

She decided that she might as well make a note of the inscription, in case she ever got around to revising her tombstone paper. She put her hand on her back pocket, intending to sacrifice the flyleaf of *Pride and Prejudice*— but she had nothing to write with. Well, she could memorize the verses and write them down later.

Nora read the poem aloud, then again to make sure that she had memorized it—she was secretly proud of how easily she could learn poetry by heart; none of the other grad students seemed to bother—and then straightened. The rain had stopped. The forest looked lighter.

"Emmeline, I have to leave now," Nora said. Having spoken to the dead woman already, she felt a dim obligation to say good-bye. She wondered what had happened to Emmeline Anne Clement on that other May 11. Fever, consumption, childbirth? There was no shortage of ways for young women to die in 1833. "I'm sorry that you had such a short life," she added, "and that you've been waiting here for so long. I wish—"

But, she reflected, what could you wish for the dead? Wasn't that really the essence of death, to be beyond the power of hopes and wishes? Still, Nora had the urge to leave this lonely grave with some sort of blessing.

"I wish that you were free of guarding that gate, if that's what you want, Emmeline," she said haltingly. "I wish you could move on to the next thing, or stage, or place, and be happy."

Edging among the stones back to the gate, Nora was a little surprised at herself. She remembered trying to talk aloud to EJ in the months after his death, telling him she missed him, but the one-sided conversations had never been much comfort. It wasn't as though he could hear her.

Nora closed the gate behind her as best she could, then set off back along the path. Thankfully, she noticed, her ankle felt better. The rain seemed to have stopped for good, and she caught glimpses of blue sky between the thick leaves overhead. It was warmer, too—almost hot—despite the shade in the forest. The ground had already dried. After a few minutes, the trees in front of her thinned out, giving way to an expanse of sunlit grass. She must be coming back to the mountaintop. All she had to do now was circle around the Bald until she found the path back to the cabin.

But at the edge of the forest, she came to a dead halt. Stretching before her was a lush green lawn surrounding a long reflecting pool. In the center of the water a satyr embraced a nymph, carved in some honey-colored stone. Pouting, the nymph was pushing the satyr away, but not very hard, and meanwhile her draperies were sliding advantageously down her breasts and thighs. The satyr seemed to wink at Nora over his partner's shoulder. On the other side of the lawn was a tall privet hedge with an oval gateway.

Puzzled, Nora stepped onto the grass. She couldn't quite work out where she had gone astray. Perhaps this was another part of the mountain-top that she hadn't seen before.

She crossed the lawn and looked through the opening in the hedge. On the other side were gravel paths and a profusion of rosebushes in full bloom. Their scent was overpowering. Nora hesitated for a moment, then followed the path, stopping now and then to bury her nose in the blossoms.

An arbor with a white lattice gate waited at the far end of the rose garden. Nora pushed it open and discovered an allée of elm trees leading to a folly shaped like a small Greek temple, which turned out to be an entrance to another walled garden, where narrow paths snaked around overgrown beds of lilies and more roses. A small green door in the wall led to a Japanese garden of pines and knobby stones.

Nora sank down on a bench in the diminutive teahouse beside the pond, where fat red koi were swimming. This garden is incredible, she thought. It must be part of some grand mountain estate, like Biltmore in Asheville. She wondered why no one at the party last night had mentioned it. She watched the rippled reflection of trees in the pond and felt an unusual sense of calm. Normally, she'd be nervous about trespassing on someone else's property, especially property that obviously belonged to someone very rich. But it was hard to feel ill at ease in the middle of this lush, well-ordered beauty.

Sooner or later, she would come across a groundskeeper and ask for directions home, or to use a phone. All the plantings looked well tended, and the paths were raked clean. Remarkable that the trees here were in full leaf while those on the mountain still had the gauzy, pale-green foliage of early spring. Perhaps these grounds were situated in some sort of sheltered microclimate that allowed the trees to leaf out and summer flowers to bloom early.

It was certainly warm enough to be summer already. Nora found, suddenly, that she was very thirsty. She stood up and resumed her walk, wondering if it would be safe to drink from one of the fountains. The garden seemed to have no end to it. She passed through a cobble-paved herb garden; a topiary menagerie of green dragons, unicorns, and other mythological beasts that she didn't recognize; an enclosure where all the flowers were such a dark purple that they looked black. Finally, after what could have been an hour or just a few minutes of wandering—her watch seemed to be alternately halting and skipping—she turned a corner to find herself facing a brilliant blue swimming pool, surrounded by more of those high, clipped hedges. At the near end of the pool was a pink marble sculpture, something abstract that reminded Nora of an anatomical model. At the other end of the pool were a pair of white lounge chairs and a matching table with a glass pitcher and a couple of glasses.

The pitcher, dewy with condensation, drew Nora's attention. Coming closer, she saw it was full of some drink that looked like cranberry juice or iced Red Zinger or even cherry Kool-Aid. Anything cool and liquid was fine with her. She poured herself a drink, ice cubes chiming in her glass, and took a long swallow. Some sort of punch. She couldn't quite describe the flavor. Draining her glass, she poured herself another.

"You must be very thirsty," said a woman's voice behind her, throaty, amused.

Nora spun around. The woman standing on the pavement was smiling, but it was hard to see her face beneath the oversize Jackie O sunglasses. She wore a white silk scarf over a glossy pile of chestnut hair. Her dress was also white, a sleeveless, tailored sheath that ended just above her knees. She had the sort of delicate, never-ending legs that movie studios used to insure for their starlets. Around her neck was a choker of pearls so large that Nora thought that they had to be fake, but she wasn't entirely sure, because everything about this woman screamed money. Nora was too young to remember the Sixties, but this woman looked like her idea of the Beautiful People, what the jet-setters looked like back when jets were still glamorous. On someone else the clothes and hair might have looked campy; on this woman they looked only chic.

Horrified, Nora began to apologize. "It must seem incredibly rude for me to help myself this way—well, to be here at all. I got lost on the mountain." She offered a nervous smile. "Your grounds are so lovely—and I was hoping to meet someone who could show me the way back. I'm very, very sorry to intrude like this. I don't know what got into me."

The woman laughed. "But you were thirsty. Go ahead, drink the rest."

She waited expectantly, so Nora raised the glass to her lips. She drank as quickly as she could without gulping.

"Do you like it?" the woman asked. "A friend of mine gave me the recipe."

"It's delicious," Nora said politely. "What is in it?"

"Blood oranges, hibiscus nectar, moonlight!" she said, laughing again. Not quite sure what the joke was, Nora smiled anyway. "But tell me about yourself. You came from the mountain, you say. So far! You must have passed the little graveyard?" The woman drew the last word out, searchingly. Nora could hear the trace of an accent in her voice. Something Italian in the way she caressed her vowels. But there was also a clipped undertone that sounded British, posh, authoritative, making Nora think of nannies and boarding schools and country houses. "It has been so long since I was up there. What is it like now? All the little stones in good order? The fence still standing?"

"It's a bit run-down, but everything is still basically upright. A strange place," Nora said uncertainly. Would this woman think it peculiar if she mentioned Emmeline's grave and the odd verses on the stone?

The other woman nodded. "Yes, it is so lonely, in the middle of the woods. There are still woods? And you? What is your name?" Nora gave her name, and the woman smiled. "It is a pleasure to meet you, Nora," she said.

"And yours?" Nora asked. She had a sudden, unnerving intuition that the answer would be "Emmeline." That was silly; she was talking to a flesh-and-blood woman; there was no such thing as ghosts. But she was relieved when the other woman said, with a moment's hesitation, "You may call me Ilissa. It's what you'd call a nickname. My full name goes something like this—" She rattled off a rapid string of syllables that Nora couldn't quite follow. "But that's too long and boring to say. I make my friends call me Ilissa."

"It's a lovely name."

"You're too kind! But please, sit down. You must be tired with walking so far this afternoon."

Nora demurred, apologizing again for her intrusion. She had already imposed enough on the other woman's good manners. But Ilissa insisted. She had been feeling bored and lonely all day, she said with a brilliant smile. It was wonderful good luck for her that Nora had appeared, and she refused to let her new friend leave—"I'm sorry, I'm just unreasonable!"— until they had had a good long chat. Nora found herself sitting on one of the recliners, sipping another glass of the red punch, and answering Ilissa's questions. The punch must have had some alcohol in it—maybe that was what Ilissa meant by moonlight—because Nora began to feel a light buzz, and was talking more than she had expected to, trying to make a joke out of some of the things that had gone wrong lately: the problems with her thesis, Naomi's disapproval, her dead cat, the mouse in the kitchen. Ilissa listened, apparently rapt.

Although Nora hadn't meant to mention anything terribly personal, even the details of last night's humiliating encounter with Dave came spilling out.

"Oh, but what an idiot," said Ilissa, clucking her tongue. "Ignoring that other poor girl, toying with your feelings—and then not even seeing to his own pleasure or yours! No one has any fun! Everyone is unhappy!"

Nora laughed. Last night, she hadn't considered the situation in exactly that light, but Ilissa had a point.

"I'm surprised, though, that a beautiful girl like you is unattached. Or did you leave your young man back at your university?" Ilissa said, smiling. She leaned forward and studied Nora's face. "Wait, I see you have had another disappointment in love recently. This one is more serious than that boy who was so silly last night."

Nora gave a feebly dismissive wave of her hand—her litany of woes, she thought, must be getting tedious for this elegant creature. But Ilissa would not be put off. So Nora told her the story of her breakup with Adam and then, because the other woman still seemed so interested, the whole history of their relationship, starting with their flirtation in Renaissance Lyric, when Adam had been impressed with Nora's knowledge of Elizabethan sexual puns; his specialty was the modern novel. That was almost four years ago. Adam became her ally in that seminar, taught by the ruthless Naomi Danziger, and by the end of the semester, they were a couple.

As Nora went on talking, Ilissa took off her sunglasses to reveal her own eyes: a deep blue-green, slightly aslant. She looked older than Nora had expected. Not that there were any lines around those clear eyes, but her face had a honed, decisive look, as though she were used to being in charge.

"Oh, he wasn't good enough for you," Ilissa said dismissively, when Nora paused after describing Adam's move to Chicago. "He didn't know his own mind. Most men don't, of course—I've learned that all too well. He got scared and lonely and he grabbed the nearest woman, this Celeste person. Men! What can you do?"

Nora couldn't imagine Ilissa ever having trouble with men straying or not knowing whether they were in love with her or not. She said so, and Ilissa burst into a fit of giggles. "You're so funny! If you only knew!" she said.

Then she looked more seriously at Nora. "But the important thing now is to enjoy yourself. A broken heart doesn't heal until you lose it to someone else. You need diversion. You should simply play, play, play—surround yourself with men until one of them makes you forget all about this poor, childish, confused Adam."

"Surround myself with men?" Nora smiled wryly. "As though it were that easy."

Ilissa arched her perfectly plucked eyebrows. "As it happens, I am having a party this very night, and I can assure you there will be all sorts of delightful male creatures there. It is exactly what you need. My parties are famous. Everyone always has a marvelous time, they dance, they laugh, they fall in love—sometimes twice or three times in one night. People ask me, 'Ilissa, what is your secret?' I tell them, 'There is no secret. I simply invite my friends, the most beautiful and charming people in the world.' "

No party was ever so perfect, in Nora's experience—obviously Ilissa was a bit vain about her gifts as a hostess. Nonetheless, Nora felt tempted. Then she remembered that she was due at the wedding at five. Probably she had already missed brunch. What time was it? Her own watch said 2:38 a.m.—hopeless.

Ilissa wasn't wearing a watch. Smilingly, she shook her head when Nora explained that she needed to get back for the wedding. "I forbid it!" She laughed. "I tell you, you have never been to a party like one of mine. You cannot miss this for the world."

Nora considered for a moment—this way, she'd avoid both Adam and

Dave—then smiled daringly. "All right! I'd love to come. But I should call my friend Maggie, so that she doesn't think I've fallen off the mountain. Would it be okay if I used your telephone?"

A beat passed before Ilissa answered. Then she raised her hand and made a lazy gesture in the air, indicating something in the distance behind Nora. A jewel on her finger flashed in the sunlight, making Nora blink. "Please, make yourself at home," Ilissa said.

Nora twisted around to look in the direction that Ilissa had pointed. "Oh, I didn't see the house before," she said. It was a low-slung, modern structure half-hidden behind the tall hedges. She could make out sliding glass doors under a jutting slab of roof. The style complemented Ilissa's outfit, Nora thought.

"If you don't mind, I think I should call now," Nora said, getting to her feet. To her relief, she wasn't as unsteady as she had feared. The glass pitcher was empty now, she noticed abashedly. She couldn't remember whether she had seen Ilissa drink any of the punch. Then Nora looked down at herself and cried out in dismay.

"I'm sorry, I can't go to your party!" she said. "I'm a mess." Her jeans were still muddy from her fall on the path. She could feel patches of damp in her T-shirt, while her hair must be a haystack after getting soaked in the rain. "I look like a refugee," she said. "What must you think of me?"

"That's easily remedied," Ilissa said. "I'd love to lend you a dress, and of course you can freshen up inside." She touched Nora's shoulder lightly, guiding her toward the house. "I'm so thrilled that you can stay for the party," she added. "I promise you, you'll have a wonderful night, and I'm sure that you will find plenty of admirers. Perhaps even my son," she said, with a half smile. "He will be there tonight, and I should warn you, he's very susceptible to beautiful women."

Then I'm safe from him, was Nora's first thought. Aloud she said, "I'm sure he's a little young for me. You can't have a son who's more than eight years old."

Ilissa gave Nora a little squeeze around the shoulders. "You are too kind! No, I assure you, he is quite grown up. Of course, I was much, much younger when he was born. I will introduce you to him, and you must tell me if you can see the resemblance."

"Oh," said Nora awkwardly, as they passed through the sliding door into the house, "if he's anything like you, I'm sure I'll like him very much."

## Chapter 3

Silver fish with trailing fins hovered and flickered behind a wall of glass tinted the cool, reassuring green of a dollar bill. Nora regarded them thoughtfully as she rinsed her hair, thinking of the bathroom in "The Diamond as Big as the Ritz." The slate tub was so large that she could lie back and float full-length without touching the sides. As she sat up again, a few of the rose petals drifting in the warm water clung to her body, a crimson stippling against her skin. It was undoubtedly the most luxurious bath she had ever taken.

Now that she was alone again, she felt a little puzzled, if flattered, by Ilissa's kindness. "Why me?" she asked herself. Why would a woman who looked as though she should be sunning herself on a yacht off Capri or going up against Audrey Hepburn for the Holly Golightly role—Nora's money would be on Ilissa—take it upon herself to befriend a bedraggled stranger who appeared unannounced in her backyard and spent an hour grousing about her love life? Perhaps Fitzgerald was right about the rich being different from you or me. If I lived like this all the time, Nora thought, I might be a nicer person, too.

Finally, reluctantly, she got out of the water, wrapped herself in a towel so large it trailed on the ground, and went into the dressing room next door. Her stained, wrinkled clothes were gone. On a hanger on the wall was a short red dress with a plunging neckline. Nora was examining it uncertainly when Ilissa entered. She had changed clothes, but her new outfit, a minidress made of gold disks stitched together, still looked like something from a mid-Sixties issue of *Vogue*.

Ilissa held the red dress under Nora's chin and leaned back to consider the effect. "No, no. Too—how shall I say it?—lurid. For you, something with more grace, more sophistication. I have exactly the dress. Just wait." She disappeared with the red dress and came back with a long black one. "Much better," she said, putting it up against Nora's body.

"It's really very sweet of you to lend me your dress," Nora said, "but are you sure—"

"I have so many clothes, I can't wear them all!" Ilissa pulled the dress over Nora's head, tugging the fabric here and there to adjust it. "There!" she said, turning Nora to face the mirror. "I told you—perfect!"

As a general rule, Nora hated trying on clothes in the company of saleswomen or friends who poured her into outfits that she couldn't afford and didn't like, and then pronounced the effect ravishing. But there was something disarming about the way that Ilissa clapped her hands triumphantly at the sight of Nora in the black dress. And the dress was stunning on Nora, there was no doubt about that—flowing over the lines of her body, somehow making her look taller, thinner, and curvier at the same time.

"It might have been made for you," said Ilissa. "Consider it yours, my little present to you. Now, let's do your hair."

Nora protested on both counts, insisting that she couldn't accept such a generous present, that she could fix her own hair. But she found herself sitting in front of the mirror with Ilissa running surprisingly strong fingers through her hair. "Such a pretty color," Ilissa said.

"Well, my natural color is brown," Nora confessed. "You can tell from the roots. I need to do another rinse soon."

"You have no roots," said Ilissa. She began to comb out Nora's damp hair.

Watching Ilissa work in the mirror, Nora was reminded that she still knew almost nothing about her. "What do you do most of the time?" she asked, trying to phrase the question carefully. It seemed out of place to ask someone like Ilissa what she did for a living.

Ilissa laughed. "Oh, I am always busy!" First of all, she said, there was her devotion to beautiful things. "This house, these gardens, all my own design. You like them? I thought so!" Then she had various interests to look after. Nora assumed that meant investments of some sort: Nora had never quite understood why people with money had to spend so much time managing it, but then she herself had little experience in that area.

"And then it is funny," Ilissa continued, "but you know, so often my friends look up to me to help them and guide them. I give them advice, a little encouragement. I don't know why they think I know anything, but they come to me afterward and say, 'Thank you, Ilissa, you were absolutely right!' So I really feel responsible for them! And that takes up my time, too."

Gathering up Nora's hair into a thick strand, Ilissa began to pile it on top of Nora's head. "I'm going to fix your hair the same way as mine," she said. "I love this style."

"My hair's not long enough," Nora said. But somehow Ilissa had managed it, a luxuriant golden tower balanced on Nora's head.

"Now, your face," said Ilissa. "Shhh, you must keep perfectly still when I make you up. I am an artist at work."

As she daubed away at Nora's face, it suddenly occurred to Nora that this was a seduction. Of course, Ilissa had a son, but that didn't mean anything. Nora had gotten a few passes from lesbians over the years—she wondered if it had something to do with looking younger than she was. If she makes a move, Nora thought, I'll let her down as nicely as possible. I'd hate to hurt her feelings.

"Relax!" Ilissa said. "You are going to be even more lovely." It was a promise and a command. Something in her voice reminded Nora of her mother's old wine-colored velvet dress, the one she'd wear on the rare evenings in Nora's childhood when her parents hired a babysitter and went out. Her mother would come in to kiss Nora good night, redolent of Chanel No. 5, and Nora would contrive to rub her cheek against the softness of her dress, as though it were a sort of pledge, an assurance that someday Nora, too, would grow into confident grace and beauty.

Ilissa leaned close to her, smiling. "Close your eyes." Nora obeyed, and Ilissa rubbed something delicately over her eyes and onto her eyelids. "Open them."

Nora gazed into the mirror. "Do I really look like that?" she asked. There had been agreeable moments in Nora's life when she had looked into a mirror and found herself to be just as pretty as she felt, as well as less pleasant moments when she glimpsed some plain or unkempt woman out of the corner of her eye and then realized that it was her own reflection. Being startled by her own face because it was so much lovelier than she expected— that was new.

"Now you're ready for my party," Ilissa said.

Nora stood up, her eyes still on the glass. "Ilissa, thank you," she said. "I've never had a makeover like this. It's a transformation." Maggie had always been after her to wear more makeup, to dress better, to take more pains with her appearance. Maggie had been right.

That reminded Nora of the call she had not yet made. "Oh, I have to use your phone before the party starts," she said. Ilissa pointed through a doorway into a bedroom, where a pink Princess phone sat on the table beside the bed. Nora dialed Maggie's cell. The phone rang and rang without an answer. Funny that voice mail didn't pick up, she thought, replacing the receiver.

A pair of silver sandals was waiting for her in the dressing room. She tried them on and found that Ilissa had guessed exactly the right shoe size. Balancing on heels three inches higher than those she normally wore, Nora felt as easy as though she were wearing her sneakers. Are all really good, expensive shoes this comfortable? she wondered.

Voices and music were beginning to filter in from outside. The party had begun.

Nora had imagined that the evening would be much like the big student parties she normally attended, where it was up to the guests to find their own way in a crowd of unfamiliar faces. If anything, she reckoned, she was more likely to be invisible among Ilissa's guests. But tonight, before she could even stop to survey the crowd, Ilissa was at her side.

"Darling, you must meet Vulpin, Lily, Boodle, Moscelle," she said, leading Nora up to a nearby group, a man in a blue velvet jacket and three women laughing together. "My newest friend, Nora," Ilissa announced. "I found her in the garden today." The four turned to stare at Nora for an instant, wary as birds. Then, with a shared exhalation (of welcome? of relief?) they clustered around Nora, talking to her and past her.

"Leave it to Ilissa to come up with such a beauty."

"Ilissa helped you dress, I can tell. She has the most perfect eye."

"Such a thrill to see someone new, we've been dying of boredom."

Their voices blew around Nora like soft breezes; she could practically feel the compliments brushing her skin.

"What would you like to drink?" asked the man (was he the one called Vulpin?).

"She wants champagne—no, a kir royale," said one of the women (Moscelle?), who wore a vinyl jumper and matching ankle boots. She winked at Nora.

Nora had been on the verge of asking for white wine, but instantly changed her mind. "That sounds lovely," she said. Immediately a glass was in her hand, rich and dark, a real French kir royale, not the pallid imitation that you get in American bars.

The others tossed questions at her, smiling playfully. Was she married? Engaged? Not even in love, at least? Impossible. Perhaps she was just about to fall in love and didn't know it yet; perhaps this very night. . . . Where did she live? How did she get here? How did she spend her days, when she wasn't getting lost? Her companions seemed much amused at the notion of graduate school.

"Four years already?" asked the woman in a top hat, who Nora decided must be Boodle. "How exhausting! You must know everything by now!"

"Well, no. And I don't study all the time," Nora said.

"Of course not," Vulpin said. He caught her gaze and held it. "You don't strike me as a woman who'd be satisfied spending all her days in the library. I can tell you have a taste for adventure, you have a warm, passionate nature, you live life boldly."

He sounded a bit like a fortune cookie, but Nora nibbled at this flattering description of herself and found that she liked it. "How can you tell that?" she asked.

"You're here with us, aren't you?" Moscelle said, giggling. She took Nora's arm. "Come on, I want to introduce you to more people."

The party was in full swing by now, dusk thickening into night, the terrace around Ilissa's swimming pool thronged with people. Nora could hear music, bossa nova, coming from somewhere else in the garden. A girl in go-go boots and silver leather waved them over. Moscelle air-kissed her, once on each cheek, and introduced Nora—"Ilissa's latest find."

"I love your outfit," said Nora to the girl in the boots, whose name sounded something like Oon. "Theme parties are so much fun. I went to a Sixties party at school last year, but the costumes weren't half as good as this."

"Oh, Ilissa likes to do different things," said Moscelle vaguely. "Where is Gaibon? I'm dying for him to meet Nora."

Oon, if that was her name, gave a languid sigh and rolled heavy-lashed eyes upward. "He's hiding right now. From Amatol. Ever since she heard about last night."

Moscelle laughed. "Is she still upset about that? I'd better stay out of the way, then."

She steered Nora over to a loose-knit circle near the pool and began more introductions. By now Nora knew that it was going to be impossible for her to keep names and faces straight tonight. There were more names that sounded familiar but slightly out of context—Nora could have sworn she met someone named Pixel, could that be right?—while every person she met seemed to share the same exotic, slightly feline good looks. Perhaps it was the period makeup, the creamy lips and the huge, astonished eyes, that made the other women seem to blend together, although that didn't account for the men looking so similar, too, as though they had all ordered their sculpted cheekbones from the same catalog.

"Everyone here is beautiful," she said to a man with a lock of dark hair falling into his eyes. "Not just pretty or handsome, but beautiful. Are you all models? Movie stars?"

The dark-haired man thought that was tremendously funny. "No, but I was wondering if you were," he said.

She lost track of Moscelle, but others took her in hand and kept her circulating. She picked up a lot of gossip about people that she hadn't met yet and some that she already had. Rapid coupling and uncoupling seemed to be the norm. In spite of all the kir royales she'd downed by now, she was deliciously clearheaded, just more buoyant than usual. After a while, the people she met started to say things like, "So you're Nora! I've been hearing so much about you all evening!" She felt as though she were moving through the party like the silver ball in a pinball machine, hitting every corner just right, setting off noise and lights, racking up points.

Nora was on the dance floor, doing the twist with one of Boodle's friends, when she saw Ilissa again, talking to a blond girl who had a boa constrictor wrapped around her shoulders. Her eyes kept a steady bead on Nora's gyrations. When the music stopped, Nora went over.

"Nora! You're the hit of my party," Ilissa said, giving her a peck on the cheek.

"I'm having a wonderful time! I'm not tired at all, and it must be almost midnight," Nora said. Something struck her, and she laughed. "Oh, will the magic wear off at midnight? Will I turn back into a pumpkin when the clock strikes?"

Ilissa smiled and reached out to tuck a stray wisp of blond hair behind Nora's ear. "No, the magic doesn't wear off at midnight. It's much more powerful than that. It comes from you. You wanted something, and so it came to be."

Nora was puzzled by the seriousness in Ilissa's voice. "It's that easy?"

"Yes, of course! Look at yourself. You're already a lovelier, happier, more confident woman than the miserable little girl who turned up in my garden this afternoon. It's because you dared to laugh and be beautiful."

"I think you had something to do with it. I can't thank you en—"

Ilissa made a dismissive gesture. "A dress, a little chitchat, a party—it's nothing. I love it when I can help someone. And this is just the beginning, my dear." She looked appraisingly at Nora again. "Pearls, I think, next time. Your skin has such a lovely golden tone. We ought to do more to set it off. I should have thought of pearls tonight. What a scatterbrain I am!"

I *would* look nice in pearls, Nora thought happily, then realized with some regret that she wouldn't be here for the next party. Ilissa seized her arm.

"I am even more scatterbrained than I thought," Ilissa announced. "Did I not introduce you to my son?" She called out a long name that seemed to include some vowels and consonants that didn't occur in English, and out of the crowd Nora saw a dark head set on a pair of broad shoulders turn and move toward them.

"Like me, he has a terribly long and confusing name," Ilissa said. "Raclin is what we call him for short. Darling," she said to him, "this is Nora. You remember I mentioned her earlier."

"But we've met already," Raclin said, holding out his hand to Nora, a lock of hair falling into his eye. "Nora asked me if I was a movie star." His hand felt very strong as it closed around hers.

"And you said no, but I'm sure I've seen some of your films," Nora said, smiling. James Bond, the Sean Connery years.

"Well, if I were in a movie, it would have to be one with some very beautiful woman in it," he said. "Perhaps we could read through a few scenes together."

On second thought, maybe a little *too* charming, Nora thought.

"And I would direct!" Ilissa said. "It would be so much fun! I can already tell you two have, what is it called, screen chemistry."

"Then it's all set," he said. "Now, if you'll excuse me, I'm wanted over there. Lolly insists on getting into a grave misunderstanding with Carnassus, and I think I shall have to peel them apart."

"Oh, the wretch," said Ilissa, watching him move away. "Not Raclin—Lolly. I may have to—but that's not important. So you've met my son. Do you like him? I can tell he likes you."

"He's the best-looking man at this party," Nora said. It was true.

Ilissa looked pleased. "That's what I always think, but then, I am his mother. I see Moscelle coming this way—she's looking for you."

The night flowed faster and faster. Nora had a long, earnest conversation with Moscelle about Gaibon and whether he loved Moscelle or Amatol more. "Really, the way it started out, it wasn't that serious between us," Moscelle said. "But she's so possessive, she's driving him away." Nora squeezed into a snub-nosed red Ferrari with four or five others and they went racing down narrow roads lined with poplar trees, until they had drunk all the champagne that Vulpin had brought and had to go back to the party. More dancing, then Nora wound up talking to the girl with the boa constrictor, whom she realized after a while must be Moscelle's rival, Amatol. "I'm Nora," she said. "Lovely to meet you," said Amatol. "Charmed," said the snake, lifting its head from the girl's shoulder and showing its fastidious, forked tongue.

Nora wandered out by the swimming pool with Amatol and a tall, bald black man. He had small, round Lennon glasses, and he was telling them, in great detail, about a love affair that he'd once had on the planet Jupiter with one of the gaseous women there, whose skin felt like silky smoke, whose kisses were explosions. What has he been taking? thought Nora. She looked down into the pool and saw a naked couple making love at the bottom. They moved rhythmically, wrapped around each other like eels. Nora marveled at how long they could hold their breath.

Someone started a game of hide-and-seek in the garden. Nora hid behind a palm tree until the girl who was It went past; then she ran laughing down the dim paths, skimming the gravel in her high heels until, in the shadow of a bronze centaur, someone grabbed her arm and pulled her to a halt. Nora almost fell, but the person pulled her upright and kissed her, roughly. "Good night, my dear," he said. Raclin's voice.

"Hey!" she said warningly. She felt too good to be really angry, she understood the kiss was all part of the night's game, but still, you could take a game too far.

He kissed her again, more smoothly this time, and then the gravel crunched as he moved away.

It was a very good kiss, she realized too late. "Good night," she said uncertainly.

She walked across the grass toward the house. It was almost dawn. The lawn was flattened, littered with crumpled napkins, wineglasses, a pair of lace panties. The pool was empty of lovers, but the man who'd had the affair on Jupiter was sleeping on one of the recliners, his glasses askew. In the brightening air, Nora noticed vaguely that his skin was not actually black, or brown, but dark green.

# Chapter 4

From under the covers, Nora groped for the ringing telephone. Maggie's voice in her ear, clear but faint. "Nora? Is that you?"

"Maggie?" Blinking, Nora sat up in bed. It took her a moment to realize where she was. "My God, I missed the wedding, didn't I? I got lost in the woods, and I just—I just forgot about it." What on earth had she been thinking? "Luca and Chris must be furious."

"Oh, no, no, no." Maggie laughed, sounding tinny. The phone was the old-fashioned kind, squat and black. "No need to apologize. I hear that you went to a fabulous party last night. I'm so envious! I mean, the reception was fine, but compared to one of Ilissa's parties—?"

"You've heard of her?"

"You never heard of her? I'm shocked! She's famous!"

Nora lowered her voice. "Who is she, exactly? She has the most extraordinary friends. Last night was like something out of Fellini."

Maggie laughed again. "She's one of those people who's famous for being herself."

"Nice work if you can get it," Nora said. "She's been super sweet to me, I must say. I can't wait to tell you about my adventure. How did you track me down here? Could you come pick me up?"

"There's no hurry. The person I just talked to said Ilissa is completely happy to have you stay. Why not take a few days to enjoy yourself? How often do you get to be in a Fellini film?"

"True," Nora said, considering. "But you're driving back tonight, right?"

"Oh, maybe, I'm not sure. Seriously, you don't get a chance to meet someone like Ilissa every day. People like that are magical. For once in your life, Nora, you should spend some time with people who can appreciate how wonderful you are, and show you how to really live."

"Well, last night *was* kind of magical. I felt so different."

"It's exactly what you need," Maggie said. "Oops, I have to run. Have a wonderful time, darling."

"Maggie, wait, I left my phone at the cabin, I don't have your number—"

"Have fun!"

She was gone. Nora hung up, slightly puzzled. It was unlike Maggie, always hyperorganized, to be so cavalier about her own schedule, and she couldn't repress a faint feeling of hurt that, for some reason, Maggie seemed to be trying to keep the conversation brief. Then she saw what must have happened: Maggie had met someone at the reception, and had changed her own plans as a result.

And what she had just said was true. This was an opportunity, an open door, of a kind Nora had never come across before. What had Maggie said? These people could show her how to live. Live all you can, it's a mistake not to. After just a few hours with Ilissa and her friends, everything looked different: softer, brighter, rich with possibility.

The clock on the mantelpiece chimed two o'clock. She realized with a start that she'd slept half the day away. Getting out of bed, Nora approached the mirror tentatively, remembering how she had collapsed into bed without even taking off her makeup; she must look like hell.

But the face that looked out at her was still as luminous and assured as when Ilissa had shown it to her the night before. Nora ran her tongue along her lips, thinking that she had never really noticed how full they were, or how long her eyelashes were, or how elegantly her cheekbones caught the light. Her face smiled back at her, calmly amused that anyone would even doubt its beauty.

A knock at the door. Moscelle, trim and pretty in a riding habit, asking if Nora would like to go riding this afternoon. "I'd like to," Nora said regretfully, "but I don't really know how to ride." Her experience with horses totaled some pony rides and a few painful hours on a stubborn gelding when she was fifteen. But Moscelle said not to be silly. "Ilissa has a sweet mare you can ride. And there's a spare habit that should fit you beautifully. So no excuses!"

The mare was beautiful, jet black with a single white diamond on her forehead, and once mounted, Nora discovered there was none of the vertiginous jolting that had made her cling to the saddle horn in the past. They took a sun-dappled path that wound through the smooth trunks of beech trees, and the horse seemed to know exactly where Nora wanted to go, stepping like a dancer. This was riding as she had imagined it from the horse books she'd read in grade school. Having the right mount must make all the difference.

Vulpin dropped back to ride beside her. He started by asking her about her studies, but she found that she wasn't interested in talking about school. She asked him about Ilissa instead, and he began to reminisce; evidently he had known Ilissa since he was a small child. Nora gathered that Ilissa came from some sort of wealthy aristocratic family in another country, but he was frustratingly vague as to exactly where. Asked directly, Vulpin shrugged and said that it was hard to explain, they had moved around so much. He dropped a few references to the war, or wars, which Nora found confusing. Apparently Ilissa had played some sort of courageous role in saving a large number of people. There had been great privation and suffering.

"Does Ilissa know Anastasia, by chance?" Nora asked archly, and then felt a little embarrassed. Vulpin only looked amused. She kept trying to think of the right questions to ask, something that would help her sort out the details of Ilissa's past without being rude, but she kept getting carried away in the currents of Vulpin's deep, soothing voice.

They caught up to Gaibon and Moscelle. Gaibon grinned at Nora and asked how she had enjoyed the party last night—had she fallen in love?

"Oh, I'm not ready to fall hard for just anyone," Nora said. "I'm going to take my time to pick and choose."

Gaibon seemed to find this very funny. "Oh, you'll be a prize. Ilissa has a knack, you know. When she takes someone in hand—well, you wouldn't know them afterward. They might not even know themselves. She's done a nice job with you, especially the lips," he added. "Almost too pretty, eh, Vulpin? Our friend's a lucky man."

"Stop teasing Nora, you're making me jealous," Moscelle said. Gaibon laughed and said something else, and Vulpin responded sharply, both of them speaking in long, lilting, incomprehensible syllables. Nora looked from one to the other. Then Vulpin said cheerfully that it was time to head back. He rode ahead with Gaibon, neither of them speaking until they were too far away for Nora to hear what they said.

"What was all that about?" Nora asked Moscelle. Moscelle only laughed and said that Gaibon was flirting too much and that she, Moscelle, would have to keep a close eye on him at the party tonight. Nora was surprised: "Another party?"

"Yes, a big one, not like last night. That was a little quiet, don't you think? I think Ilissa was just a tiny bit embarrassed by how quiet it was. But she's had all day to plan this one."

They started down a long driveway, and at first Nora thought they had made the wrong turn. The house ahead of them, basking in the late afternoon sun, was all slate-roofed gables and rose-colored brick, much older than the house she remembered from yesterday, and she started to say something to Moscelle. But Ilissa was waiting for them, slim and white in a dress that swayed around her legs as though it had never heard of gravity. Next to her was a boxy black car. "We're late, my dear," she said, holding her hand out for Nora.

"My clothes—" Nora began. Someone pushed her into the car, a cave of rich green leather. "Don't worry, darling," she heard Ilissa saying. "You'll be changed before you know it." Gaibon winked. Nora discovered she was holding a champagne flute and that Vulpin was filling it. The car sped through a world of black velvet; Ilissa said there was no time to waste, and wasn't night so much more lovely and romantic?

Suddenly they were going over a bridge; an electric grid blazed ahead of them, the serrated skyline of New York. "How did we get here?" Nora wondered.

"Oh, we drove much too fast," Ilissa said with her fizzy laugh.

There was something odd about the other automobiles they passed—their spoked wheels, their headlights like round-rimmed spectacles—but after a moment Nora decided they looked right, somehow. Their vehicle pulled up next to a striped awning, a length of red carpet.

Nora stepped out, carefully, because of her heels, and smoothed her skirts. The car ride hadn't wrinkled the silk at all; the dress rustled deliciously against her skin.

"You see?" Ilissa said. "I promised you pearls. Like milk and honey, with your complexion."

Nora looked down. The creamy strand fell almost to her waist. "They're beautiful. Thank you so much."

"Ah, at last." A deep voice next to her. "Even prettier than last night."

Looking up, Nora met Raclin's gaze, and felt a sudden confused warmth at the nearness of his white smile, his looming, well-tailored shoulders. She thought of the kiss he'd stolen in the garden the night before, and the sweeter one afterward. *Watch out,* a voice said inside, *something wrong here.* It said other things that she couldn't quite discern. Raclin's dark hair gleamed, combed back more carefully than the night before, but she could tell that the stray lock was still threatening to tumble down onto his forehead.

She was suddenly impatient to see it fall; she wanted to tuck it back for him.

Inside the hotel there was dancing, the crowd moving back and forth to the syncopations of a jazz band tucked behind potted palms. Nora recognized faces from last night, the men in black and white, the women in loose dresses that showed off slender legs in silk stockings.

"Another theme party, isn't it?" she said to Raclin, hoping she sounded more collected than she felt. "How does she do it, your mother?"

"My mother lives to entertain," he said. "It's her art form, really. And she finds this particular setting intriguing. There's something very playful about it. She thought it might appeal to you."

"Oh, I've always had a thing for the Twenties. The clothes. The Algonquin Round Table. *Gatsby.* But why would she want to please me in particular?"

"She's taken quite a fancy to you. Ilissa's good at sizing people up. She can see their possibilities."

"What possibilities does she see in me?"

"They're not hard to see." Raclin put out his hand to steer her toward the dancing. On the small of her back it felt assured, possessive. His touch was a pledge: I'm just beginning with you. Only wait.

Once or twice over the days that followed—or was it weeks?—Nora woke up and wondered seriously what kind of strong drugs she had ingested the night before. There seemed to be no other explanation for the parade of marvels every evening, the dazzling, incongruous things that could not possibly be true.

"Was I really talking to Oscar Wilde last night?" she asked herself sleepily. *No, you idiot, Oscar Wilde died in Paris in 1900,* said some weary secret voice. But there he had been, holding court in the drawing room, tall, corpulent, the clever, mournful face that she knew from postcards and book jackets. Nora almost dropped her fan. He spent quite a long time talking to her, gazing at her with that rapt attention to which she had already become accustomed.

She could tell that Oscar Wilde was not attracted to her, or any woman for that matter, but she had discovered by now that her beauty had a life of its own, that it could arouse a sort of greedy fascination in people, even the people at Ilissa's parties, who were all beautiful themselves. She felt the same way whenever she looked in a mirror now, a mixture of wonder and suspense that sometimes held her in front of the glass for long stretches of time, examining her face at different angles to see if the perfection was real, scanning in vain for some hidden flaw.

There was something sympathetic in the way Wilde spoke to her, as though he sensed her puzzlement. She felt emboldened to confide in him. "I don't think I always looked this way," she said hesitantly. "I wasn't always beautiful."

"I am glad to hear it," he said with a smile. "Natural beauty is always tiresome. It lacks that careless touch of artifice that is the hallmark of true originality. There is nothing so overdone and vulgar as unspoilt simplicity."

She laughed. "But sometimes I look at myself and I wonder, well, if it's real."

"My dear young woman, appearances are the only true reality. I thought you would have learned that by now."

Then Raclin was taking her arm to lead her into the ballroom, and she forgot all about Oscar Wilde. It was the same every time: When she looked into those deep blue eyes, every clear thought went out of her head. And that lovely, lazy smile that he saved for her alone, as though they shared some secret joke. But for the life of her, she couldn't say what the joke was.

On the tennis court the next day, she started to tell Moscelle about her conversation with Wilde, but the details were already fading. She sliced the ball and watched it skim the net to bounce just out of reach of Moscelle's racquet. Wonderful how much her game had improved lately. If only her memory were as good as her backhand. The one other thing she could recall from the night before was Vulpin's friend Lysis complaining that someone had taken his horse. At sword point—that was the oddity that made it stick in her mind.

"Game," said Moscelle, and Nora realized that she had lost track of the score, too. "Darling, you win again!"

"My brain is so fuzzy these days," Nora said to Moscelle as they walked off the court. "I don't know if it's the late nights or the champagne." She balanced the racquet on her shoulder with attempted insouciance. "Maybe I've had enough fun for now. Maybe it's time to go back to the real world."

"The real world?" Moscelle asked lightly.

"Well, school, if that counts as the real world," Nora clarified. "I do have to teach summer school, whenever that starts." Next week? Had it already started?

"But we love having you here."

"I love being here, but I don't want to overstay my welcome." They went up the steps and into the entrance hall. Their white-clad figures floated through the silver depths of the tall mirrors flanking the staircase. Then Nora looked again, puzzled. "Moscelle? I just noticed. My hair is short today. It was long last night, I'm sure it was. I was wearing it up."

"Oh, short hair is the style now, darling."

"But when did I get it cut?"

"You don't remember?" Moscelle smiled at her kindly—almost too kindly, Nora thought suddenly, as though inwardly Moscelle were laughing but trying to hide it. "There was so much going on last night, and you were having so much fun, that it just slipped your mind, that's all."

So much fun. "I'm losing my mind, that's all." Nora tried to sound casual, humorous, and it didn't come out that way at all. She moved a little faster up the staircase, almost running, but Moscelle was right behind her, following her into her bedroom.

"Darling, don't cry!" Moscelle put an arm around Nora's shoulders. "Please! You're perfect!"

That was the problem. "How the hell did that happen?" Nora felt Moscelle stiffen slightly. "I'm sorry. But—what's going on? How did I get to be a natural blonde? Where did I learn to play tennis like that? I can't remember. I can't think straight. My friend Maggie—I was supposed to meet up with her sometime, but I don't even know what day it is."

"Oh, honestly, who wants to remember everything?" Moscelle's voice was calm and friendly in Nora's ear. She smoothed Nora's hair. "You were so unhappy when you came here! After that awful love affair. Do you ever think about that man now?"

"No," said Nora. His name came back to her after a moment: Adam. She turned away from Moscelle and sat down on the bed. "But that's another strange thing. We were together for four years, and now I can hardly remember him."

"Why shouldn't you forget about your old life?" Moscelle said reasonably, taking a seat beside Nora. "You have a better one now. And Raclin—I'm sure he's the real reason you haven't given a thought to that man who treated you so badly. When you find your true love, all the other men, they don't matter anymore."

"My true love?" said Nora dubiously, but it was still an intoxicating thought. She savored it for a moment.

*You don't know a damn thing about him. And if you did, would you even remember it?*

"Also, not to be crude," Moscelle went on, "but you know what a catch Raclin is, Ilissa's heir. And Ilissa simply cherishes you. She's so delighted that you and Raclin are together. And you know, darling, Raclin would never let you go!"

He always arrived a little later than everyone else, but that night Nora thought he would never appear.

Ilissa had promised that this evening would be special, a spectacle that no one would forget easily. "You cannot top this," she had said in the taxi. And standing in the cabin of a dirigible moored high over New York, listening to the big band playing in the corner of what was a surprisingly commodious ballroom, Nora decided that Ilissa was probably right.

She was feeling much better. She always did, as day turned to evening and the music began to play and the air filled with chatter and laughter. The champagne helped, too. She had already drunk several glasses, standing around talking to Vulpin, when she saw Raclin shouldering through the crowd. Moscelle appeared briefly next to him and said something in his ear; he nodded without slowing down. I suppose she's telling him what a baby I was today, Nora thought ruefully.

"Sorry to be late, my dear." The band started a new tune. They began to dance, Raclin steering her in a smooth orbit around the dance floor.

"I thought I'd have to find a new dancing partner," she said, pouting a little. "Where have you been?"

"I was helping my mother with her duties. Too dull to bore you with."

People alluded to Ilissa's duties casually, without really explaining what they were. At some point it had become too embarrassing for Nora to admit that she didn't know. Her original hypothesis, that Ilissa managed a large fortune, seemed too dull and technical for someone as graceful and sophisticated—and quite frankly, as frivolous—as Ilissa. For a while, Nora theorized that Ilissa was a clothing designer, producer of some rarefied European line that an impoverished graduate student like herself would never have heard of. Then the nightly spectacles made her decide that Ilissa must be involved in something theatrical. Now she was tending back toward the financial theory, with the revision that Ilissa must be directing some large-scale charitable endeavor that she was too modest to acknowledge openly.

"What is it you do, exactly?" Nora asked.

Raclin smiled at her. "Whatever Ilissa needs me to do. I help her carry out her inspirations."

"So you handle the business side?" Nora hazarded.

"More or less," he said. "You might not think it to look at me, but I'm rather good at that kind of thing."

"Mmm, I'm sure you are." *He hasn't explained what he does, has he?* Nora ignored the faint inner voice—its cheap cynicism—and angled her face upward to put her mouth closer to Raclin's, in case he might kiss it. Raclin looked down at her, his eyes hooded.

"Let's go outside." Taking hold of her arm, he led her onto the outside deck. Through the railing Nora could see the illuminated quilt of city streets, over a thousand feet below, and the spoked silver crown of the Chrysler Building nearby. They were tethered to the Empire State Building. The deck rocked slowly underfoot as the dirigible swayed in the breeze.

"It feels good out here. It was so stuffy inside," she said.

His strong hands slid around her waist. Above the pale blur of his shirt front, his face was in shadow. "Moscelle said you were a little upset this afternoon."

Nora thought she had never heard anything as tender as the concern in his voice. "I was being silly," she said. "It was nothing. I was just a little worried."

"Ah, but we agreed that you wouldn't worry about anything."

"Oh, that's right." She laughed. "Well, I realized that I should think about getting back soon."

"Why? You're not getting tired of us, are you?" As Nora shook her head, still smiling, he pursued: "Getting tired of me?"

She hated that he would even think such a thing. Raclin was so vulnerable—she could sense it—under that princely self-confidence, those dark, sculpted good looks. "Darling! I love it here. But I do have obligations. My life. School."

"School?"

For the first time, something in his tone didn't quite satisfy her. She almost detected a hint of mockery. *You can't hear how he's making fun of you?* "Yes, school," she said. "I've got to get back to teach summer school. And my thesis—I need to get to work on it again."

"That doesn't sound so important."

"Well, it is," Nora shot back. Whatever her private reservations about the worth of her graduate school career, she didn't like the ripple of condescension that was suddenly plain in Raclin's voice.

He laughed quietly. "I've ruffled your feathers, my dear."

"No, it's just—" *Just that he's being a patronizing jerk.* She bit her lip.

Reaching down to touch her chin, Raclin tilted her head back, aligning it just so. Then his mouth melted onto hers.

At last. This was the part of each night that Nora looked forward to most. Throughout the evening, as they danced and circulated, Nora's impatience would build, minute by minute, so that by the time Raclin turned to her, a faint smile on his face, and pulled her toward him, her body would be throbbing with anticipation. And then—it was always hard to remember exactly what happened next, a sort of thrilling blur that felt as though all the circuits in her nervous system were blowing out at once. Afterward she always felt damply exhausted and happy but still wanted more.

The odd thing was that they had not yet made love. Of course it was true that some of Ilissa's events required wearing clothes—costumes, really—that were hardly designed for quick shedding. But even setting aside the hindrances posed by Nora's clothing, Raclin always went just so far and no farther, even when Nora, nearly fainting, begged him—this happened more than once—to keep going. He seemed pleased, almost amused to see how eager she was, but he had never yet taken her up on the invitation that she pressed on him.

Now, as they kissed, Nora thought that this might be the night. Raclin's mouth pressed down on hers, hard, almost the way he had kissed her that first night in the darkness of the garden. Her irritation vanished, and right on cue, her mind and body began to fill up with that familiar, blissful haze. She leaned backward into his arms.

"You see?" Raclin murmured in her ear. "I'll teach you. Isn't this better than anything you could learn from a book?"

His words pricked, even as she was losing herself in his embrace. Nora hesitated, then pulled away to look Raclin in the face.

"Darling, when I go back to school, it doesn't mean that we won't see each other. I just have to—"

"We'll talk about that later." His kiss consumed the words that Nora had been about to speak. As he pressed against her, she could feel the wooden deck railing against her bare back. Now she had bent back as far as she could go. Still he would not let up.

*Enough,* she wanted to say. *That hurts. I'm losing my balance.* But there was no time, as her weight shifted and her high heels slid on the metal deck. She felt herself toppling backward, falling. Her legs kicked through empty space. Nothing but a quarter of a mile of air between her and the New York City sidewalk. Overhead the bulk of the dirigible shrank as she plunged. Nora screamed, but she was falling so fast that by the time she heard it, even her scream seemed far away.

Then she was standing upright on the dirigible deck, with Raclin's arms tight around her.

Nora took a deep breath, then another, waiting for her heart to stop pounding. "My God, I was falling." Her voice shook. "What happened?"

Raclin lifted a hand to stroke her hair. "Are you all right?" he asked calmly.

"Yes. No. What happened?

"Oh, you had a little scare," he said. "You thought you were falling. But you were perfectly safe. I had you in my arms the whole time."

"But it was real. We were kissing, and then I was falling, I could feel it. I could see the—I thought I was going to die. What did you do?"

He pulled her tightly against him. Nora rubbed her cheek against the black cloth of his dinner jacket. This close, he seemed to blot out everything else, even the memory of fear. "Do you think I would let anything happen to you?" he asked. "Don't you know how precious you are to me?"

Nora looked at him and read nothing but loving sympathy in his eyes. "No, I know you'll always take care of me," she said slowly. "I must have had a little too much to drink tonight. I was dizzy. I lost my balance."

"It's a long way down. You got a little panicky."

"I panicked for a moment. We're so high."

"Poor darling." He took hold of her chin and gave it a tweak. "Feeling better? You're not afraid to stay out here and kiss me again?"

"Try me," she said, closing her eyes.

Their lips met. As they kissed, again Nora felt herself dropping. She was still in Raclin's arms, and yet there was nothing to hold on to. She tumbled through the air, wind whistling in her ears, whipping her dress. One of her pumps came loose and was gone.

She closed her eyes, refusing to look at the ground that was coming closer, faster, about to slam her body into jelly.

Eyes shut, Nora could feel Raclin's lips on her lips, his tongue probing her mouth. She moaned, pressing herself against him. If she could just hold on to him, if she could somehow will herself into believing that she was safe in his embrace, she might be able to pull herself up out of this sickening dive.

"Relax," he whispered. "Just kiss me. There's nothing to fear."

Obediently, she clung to him, trying to ignore the vertigo. It was as though she had become two different people, with two different fates. She knew that she was crashing toward earth. She could feel the suck of gravity in her bones. Any instant now, it would all be over. But at the same time she was kissing Raclin.

"Please, hold me," she whispered. "Please."

"You have to trust me," he said. "All you have to do is give yourself to me. That's all. That's all I want. Just relax. Don't keep anything back. Open up, give it all to me."

There were two Noras, one who was about to die, and one who would live and be happy, blissfully happy, because she had surrendered all pain and terror to someone who was stronger than she was. She wanted frantically to be the second woman.

"Yes," she said. Deep inside her, something that had been tight suddenly loosened, and then, with a sigh, it was gone.

The world steadied. She could feel the solid metal of the dirigible deck beneath the soles of her shoes—both shoes, including the one that had blown off her foot in midair.

"Good, that's it. Come on, give it all to me."

"Yes, please, take it. All of it." Nora felt light and fresh, as though she had just been reborn.

"Lovely. That's perfect. See how easy that was, darling?"

"Yes, darling, it's easy. It's—" Nora searched for the right words. "It's good."

"Of course. You're going to be very happy. No more worries."

"Darling," she said. "All yours."

"I know," he said. "That's my brave girl. You did just fine. You were a little jumpy at first, but you did just fine."

"You took care of me."

"Yes, yes," Raclin said, smiling down at her. "All right, that's over with. What next? Shall we get married now? Will you like that?"

Nora nodded. It was almost funny that he would have to ask her. Of course she wanted to marry him. It was all she wanted. "Oh, yes, darling."

"Ilissa will throw us a big wedding. She'll outdo herself. It will be a bother, but I expect you'll like it. You'll have a new dress to wear. Of course you have a new dress every day as it is, but this will be special."

"Pretty?" Nora knew she needed more words to say what she meant, but she was too tired to think of them, and Raclin understood, as he always did.

"Yes, the dress will be pretty, you'll be very pretty. No worries about that. Ilissa will make sure of it." He laughed. "She'd better."

"So happy," Nora said.

"That's a good girl." Raclin studied her face for an instant, then kissed her, carelessly. "All right, enough for now. What do you say we leave this inflatable rattrap and go see the city? It's a beautiful night. June, I'd say. A good time to be in Paris. We could take a cab over to Montmartre and find a café and drink red wine all night. You'd like that, wouldn't you?"

"Paris?" Nora looked over Raclin's shoulder and saw a familiar-looking triangular silhouette picked out in lights against the night sky. She looked down and saw more lights: the S curve of a river flowing through the city, the glowing lines of the boulevards. But she couldn't recall the name of the river or the tower. "I came here once," she said with an effort. "Paris."

"Did you, my dear?" asked Raclin. "You'll have to tell me all about it, once we're at the café. Well, you won't be able to tell me very much, I'm afraid, but do the best you can."

# Chapter 5

The wedding plans were in Ilissa's hands, for which Nora was hugely grateful. Ilissa was very scrupulous about consulting her on various points, and Nora did her best to help, but sometimes it was all she could do just to understand what Ilissa was saying. "Darling, would you prefer pink or white lilies in the silver vases?" Ilissa might ask, and Nora would be a million miles away, thinking about nothing but how blissfully happy she was. Her love for Raclin seemed to stretch on and on, and she could only contemplate it with awe, the way you might gaze at distant mountains. "Pink," she said finally, taking a stab. Ilissa would laugh and give her a kiss and tell her what a great help she was, thank goodness that Nora was so decisive.

Then there was the wedding dress to be fitted, a blizzard of white satin that fell to the floor in gleaming drifts. But then, Nora wore long dresses all the time now, and so did the other women. The men wore long coats and breeches or sometimes tunics and tights. They carried elegant swords with filigree handles almost as lacy as their collars. People arrived at Ilissa's parties in carved and gilded coaches drawn by matched teams of horses, and they danced in the warm, wavering light of hundreds of candles. One day Nora realized that the telephone was gone from her room. She hadn't noticed when it disappeared, and now she couldn't even find the jack in the wall.

She tried to ask Ilissa about the change. "Everything looks so—" she started to say, and then frowned. It was frustrating, because she knew that precisely the right word existed for what she was trying to say.

"Yes, darling?" Ilissa said. They were riding along a bridle path— sidesaddle, because of their skirts—after a day spent hunting in the forest.

"Everything looks different," Nora said. "Old." That wasn't the right word, but it would have to do.

Ilissa understood what she meant. "Yes, I suppose this all may seem a bit archaic to you." She smiled, as though she knew it was exactly that word that Nora had been searching for. "You gave me so many good ideas! But I know you have other things to think about now. And this is a nice change from having everything so modern, don't you think? I do love the old ways. Like the hunt today. Wasn't it a delight? It makes one feel so alive."

There were dark bloodstains on the green brocade hem of Ilissa's skirt, but even while jamming a spear through the entrails of the wounded stag, she had looked exquisite.

"Wait until we go hawking," she added. "You will love that, darling. Watching the hawks and falcons dive for their prey—I never tire of it. And of course, it's very stylish. We always make such an elegant picture when we go hawking."

"I'd like to see the hawks," Nora said.

"We'll go tomorrow, my dear," Ilissa said.

Ilissa, though, stayed behind, as Nora, Vulpin, Moscelle, and a few others rode out the next day. "I have some very dull business affairs to see to, my dears," Ilissa said, seeing them off. "And some wedding matters, which I like much better. Give my regards to the falcons, Nora!"

The hawks had fearsome golden eyes, and their claws dug into your arm, Nora found, even through heavy leather gloves. But Ilissa was right, it was exhilarating to feel the bird leap from your arm, wings pumping, and to see it flash through the air after its prey. The next part Nora found less enjoyable, but the whole process was undeniably exciting. By the time they stopped for lunch near a brook, Vulpin had a brace of rabbits and a couple of doves swinging from his saddle.

Moscelle had brought a picnic hamper, but one of the men, Leptospeer, scoffed when she opened it. "I'm in the mood for some fresh meat," he said. "Let's put some of this rabbit on the fire."

"I'm not sure we should stay out that long," Vulpin said.

But Leptospeer persisted. "What's the harm? It's early yet."

As the meat was roasting, Leptospeer flirted with Moscelle, and Nora and the other two women made daisy chains. Nora listened to her companions gossip, but the conversation went too fast for her to join in. After a while, she got up to hunt for more blossoms of a small, blue, starlike flower that she had taken a fancy to. It was relatively rare, compared with the masses of daisies and bachelor's buttons and poppies that filled the meadow.

Nora crossed the brook, balancing on water-worn stones, and climbed the far bank and the little rise just beyond. She spied a promising patch of blue not far away. Kneeling to pick the flowers, Nora could still hear the murmur of her companions' voices on the other side of the slope, but she could not see them.

She felt an unexpected sense of release, as though she had stepped outside after too long in a cramped room. A white butterfly danced across her view. The sunlight touched her face and bare arms, and she thought wistfully about lying down on the warm turf and taking a nap, peacefully alone, just for a few minutes.

Then a shadow fell between her and the sun. Just as she registered the figure in front of her—she could not see its face—someone else grabbed her arms from behind. She was jerked to her feet.

"Looky what I got, will you?" said a male voice behind her.

"Don't be greedy, boy," said the one in front of her. "I saw her, too." Nora blinked as the sunlight danced off a slim steel blade pointed toward her throat. The blade was as long as her arm, longer.

"Careful, now," said a third voice, also behind her. "They may not look dangerous, but they're fast and they're mean." It wasn't easy to understand him. His voice, like the others, was thick with some sort of guttural accent.

The blade moved up and down in the air, now pointing at her face, now her heart. "No tricks, now. Stay still," the man holding the sword said to her. With the sun in her eyes, she still couldn't make out his face, but she could see that he was wearing a helmet like a stocking cap and a dented metal breastplate.

"Does she understand what we're saying?" asked the man holding her from behind. Glancing down, she could see his hands—meaty knuckles, covered with reddish hair—pinning her elbows.

"She understands well enough. They're not stupid." The owner of the third voice stepped in front of Nora. He, too, was carrying a naked sword, and he wore the same kind of helmet and breastplate. Most of the lower half of his face was covered with a brushy blond mustache that did not appear to have been washed recently.

"Please let me go," Nora faltered.

"Be quiet, you," said the other man with a sword. He moved a little, and now Nora could see that he had a red face and long, grizzled hair under his helmet.

"I never saw one before," said the first man, right in her ear. "Are they all this pretty?"

The red-faced man snorted. "Like you never saw before, and dressed in silk and satin, like this one."

"She smells good, too," said the man holding her. "I wouldn't have known what she is, except maybe for her being so pretty."

"Oh, you can usually tell," said the man with the mustache. "Something about the eyes." Warily, he came a half step closer to Nora and looked hard into her face. "Yes, they have a nasty look, like an animal that's cornered. They may look just like us, but they're not like us."

"The master will want to see her. Get her moving."

"I say we have some fun first. Three against one, she can't be that dangerous."

"Listen," Nora spoke up, summoning all the confidence she could muster. "My friends are nearby. They'll be angry that you're bothering me."

"More of them?" said the man holding her.

The man with the mustache looked to the left, then the right. "The wizard's spell is supposed to protect us all the way to the creek."

"The creek's right over there," said Nora quickly. "My friends are on the other side."

"Oh, hell." The red-faced man coughed heavily and spat onto the ground. "That's too close."

"Please let me go," Nora said again.

"Shut up and start walking," said the red-faced man. They bound Nora's wrists in front and forced her to walk, the red-faced man holding one arm, the third man—a big, round-faced youth—holding the other.

As they walked, it dawned on Nora that the landscape around her had changed. The green grass had bleached to a withered gray-brown, crusted here and there with patches of glassy snow. A winter sun sat low in the sky. She felt the frozen ground crackle under her riding boots, and the wind bit her all the way to the bone, plucking and tearing at her bright silk dress. She began to feel a little envious of her captors, who wore thick leather tunics and layers of wool underneath their armor. Their clothing was grimy and patched, but at least it looked warm.

They had been walking for about ten minutes—she was already thoroughly chilled—when a pair of horsemen appeared in the distance. After a moment, they veered toward Nora and her escort.

"There," said the man with the mustache, sounding relieved. "The master's seen us now."

The two riders pulled up, and the lead rider swung down from his horse. He was wearing a fur-trimmed cloak and the same sort of helmet and breastplate as the soldiers, although his armor was covered with fine, sinuous engraving and polished to a brilliant silver sheen. He had longish brown hair and straight, well-balanced features, but when he came closer, she saw that he had only one clear blue eye. The right socket was scarred and empty.

"Well, Sergeant, what do we have here?" he asked the man with the mustache.

"We were patrolling, sir, near where those cattle disappeared, and we found this one by herself. So we brought her in. She said she has friends nearby."

"Is that true? How many?" the horseman asked Nora sharply.

"I'm not going to say," she said. She hoped that he could tell she was shivering from cold and not from fear.

"Don't be foolish, girl. We can make you tell us." He spoke lightly, but his hand went to his sword hilt.

Nora looked at his face and saw no softness there. After a moment, she said, "I don't remember exactly. Not many. A hunting party."

"Hunting on *my* lands," he said. "If you're not stealing my cattle and my horses, you're hunting my deer and my quail. I'm tired of all the games your people play. We're supposed to have an agreement, but I've lost four cows and a dozen sheep in the past year, and just yesterday, you people killed a deer from my preserve. Next thing, you people will start stealing children again. I'm inclined to make an example of you, just to send a message to that queen of yours. Yes, you may have your magic, but I have a wizard here, and he could make you feel real pain. Any reason why I shouldn't tell my friend to make you howl for mercy?"

Nora's head felt tight as she tried to make sense of this. "I don't know anything about any cows. The deer—I didn't know it was your deer."

"Whose deer did you think it was, then?"

"Wait a moment, Lukl." The second rider, a man in a black cloak, with long black hair that blew in the wind, had been listening from the back of his horse. Now he dismounted and came over to where the others were standing. He was taller than his companion, and he walked with a limp that made his body twist slightly as he moved. He stooped and gave a swift look at Nora's face, and then turned to the other man. "She's human, this one. She's not one of them."

"Human?" The other man, the one called Lukl, looked disbelieving. "Where did she come from?"

The second man shrugged and looked to Nora. "Where are you from?"

She had to stop and think. "New Jersey," she said tentatively.

Lukl shook his head impatiently. "New Jersey?" He pronounced it *Now Jarsey*. "I've never heard of it. This is one of their tricks."

The tall man in black looked thoughtful. He had a lined, battered-looking face—it came as a shock, Nora thought, to see people who looked old and ugly or had an injury like the one-eyed man's. Everyone in Ilissa's circle was young and beautiful. "What's your name?" he asked her.

"Nora." Less confidently: "Nora Fischer."

"Nora is your given name?" he asked, and she nodded. "Are you living with Ilissa now?" the other man asked. She nodded again. "How long have you been there, Mistress Nora?"

She could not say, exactly. "A little while." To impress them, she added: "I'm going to marry Ilissa's son. They both must be very worried about me by now. You should let me go."

"You're going to marry Ilissa's son," the tall man repeated, curling one side of his mouth. "Raclin."

"Yes." She tried to return his smile, if it was a smile. "Raclin."

The tall man turned to his companion. "Well, it's clear enough what's going on."

Lukl nodded. "She's found another wench to breed her cub to. I wonder where the cold hell she got this one."

"You haven't lost any women from your villages?"

"I would have heard about it," he said, shaking his head. "There was that girl from Orimist village who disappeared last summer. But then we heard that she was living in Bruekl market town with a cavalry officer.

"Anyway, you can tell from her speech that this one isn't from anywhere nearby," he continued, gesturing at Nora. "Now Jarsey. That could be the other side of the world."

The tall man grunted deep in his throat and looked back at Nora. "When does this marriage take place?" he asked.

"It's—um, soon," Nora said.

Lukl sighed and rubbed his chin. "Well, I don't see why we should keep her," he said to the other man. "It's one thing to work over one of their females and send her back. It's another thing to take Ilissa's prospective daughter-in-law with us. That's tossing the rock in the beehive."

Frowning, the other man said: "What if he gets an heir on her?"

"They've tried before, and nothing. And it would take years for them to multiply."

"If they did, you'd have far worse problems than a few lost cattle."

"That may be, but if we keep her, Ilissa and her people will be swarming out of their lands and into mine in a day's time. This girl's a tempting little thing, but I'm not prepared for a war just now."

"You'd have my assistance, of course."

"Yes, I know." Lukl folded his arms across his breastplate. "And I'm grateful for your help today and every other time you've come. But no, I won't risk it. Let the Now Jarsians come rescue their own girl. She wants to go back to her damnable bridegroom, anyway. You heard her."

"I doubt she understands the reality of her situation."

"They never do," Lukl said with a shake of his head.

The tall man wheeled around and came back over to Nora. Taking hold of her chin and tipping it up, he looked at her steadily for a long minute. His eyes, meeting hers, were pale as ice water; Nora wanted to look away, but couldn't. Still holding her chin, he pulled her head from side to side, glancing into each of her ears, and then pushed her head up and looked quickly into her nostrils, too. It was like being examined by a doctor, but there was something disturbing about it, too, as though he were seeing things that no doctor could see. Taking off his right glove, he touched his finger to her temple and held it there until Nora suddenly had to close her eyes, the light was so bright. Nodding as if satisfied, he removed his finger, and Nora could see again.

"What did you do to me?" she demanded, still squinting.

"How many legs does a horse have, Mistress Nora?" he asked.

"What?" she said, incredulous.

"A horse. Like those horses over there," he said, with a jerk of his head.

She spat out the answer. "Four."

"What color is your dress?"

Nora looked down at her skirt. "Blue."

"How many legs does a horse have?"

She opened her mouth to speak, then closed it when she realized that there was nothing to come out. "I don't know," she said finally.

"How many legs does a horse have?"

Nora looked over at the horses, who were standing side by side, their reins held by the youngest of the soldiers. "I don't know."

"How do you feel now, Mistress Nora?"

She felt helpless and scared, and any minute now she might burst into tears, but she was trying her hardest not to let these men see that. "I'm cold, I'm very cold," she said as loudly and fiercely as she could. "Why is it so cold? It's summer."

The tall man fixed her with his nearly colorless eyes. "It's cold because it's the middle of winter. The eighth day of the second month, to be exact. So you want to go back to Ilissa and your fiancé?"

"Yes. *He* said I could go," she said, nodding toward Lukl.

"Do you realize that you have several very powerful enchantments on yourself? That your mind and body—and your heart," he said, raising one black eyebrow, "have all been reshaped and rearranged and adapted to someone else's liking? I discern at least four major spells on you strong enough to bind a regiment, plus a half-dozen smaller ones—which are probably just to make you sit up straighter or to turn your eyes a different color or whatever happened to strike Ilissa's fancy."

"That's absurd! What are you talking about? I feel fine. Except a minute ago, when you confused me somehow. I don't know what you did to me, but if I'm under any kind of spell, you must have put it there.

"Of course, there's no such thing as magic spells, anyway," she added.

The tall man smiled, his mouth as taut as a wire. "I have put no spells on you, other than performing a few simple tests for enchantment. I have no idea, Mistress Nora, what manner of person you were before you were put under these spells, but if you're a girl of any cleverness whatsoever, you might wonder why people who profess to be your friends would subject you to their magic—and so much of it."

Nora shook her head. "I feel fine," she said again. "Nothing's wrong with me. In fact, I feel better and happier than I ever have been in my entire life."

"That's what Ilissa wants you to think. But that much magic is dangerous. Eventually it will wreck your health, or drive you out of your mind, or both." He paused for a moment, watching her narrowly. "And your prospective husband—"

"What about him?" said Nora.

"How much do you know about him?"

"What kind of question is that?"

"It's usually a good idea to know more about the man that you're going to marry than that he has a handsome face and a charming manner."

"Raclin is none of your business." Obviously he knew something of Raclin, even if only by repute, but these insinuations were stupidly misguided. She and Raclin had a bond that couldn't be explained to a rude, prying stranger or put into words at all. There are things that you know about a person as soon as you look into his eyes or touch his hand, and what more do you really need to know? she thought.

Deep inside her mind, another thought stirred feebly. *This man is right, though. Just how long have I known Raclin? Weeks? Months?* Long enough, she told herself.

"Raclin is very much my business, unfortunately," said the tall man. "I don't know how much of this will make sense to you, in your befuddled state, but let me tell you this. Raclin has a much less attractive side, a very dangerous side. No woman in her right mind would want to be married to him."

His tone was so serious that Nora felt a chill in spite of herself, but she drew herself up, shaking off her momentary doubt. "I don't know what you're talking about."

"He didn't accompany you today, did he? Do you have any idea why?"

"Raclin has a lot of responsibilities. He helps Ilissa. Sometimes he's very busy." Her words sounded childish and inadequate. She tried to be stinging: "He has to protect all of us. I didn't know before today what kind of enemies Ilissa and Raclin have, but now I do."

"Indeed," the tall man said. Even in that one word Nora could hear the cold edge of anger. One of his shoulders, a fraction higher than the other, twitched under the black cloak.

"That's enough," Lukl said suddenly. "It's hopeless. You heard her. We might as well let her go."

The tall man took a step away from Nora, raised his head, and looked around, scanning the sky and the horizon. Strands of long dark hair blew across his face as he turned his head. "One of Ilissa's people is walking this way," he remarked. "He's on the other side of that hill. He's coming to parley for her release."

"I thought you said you had a protection spell up," Lukl said irritably.

"Oh, it's taking everything he has to make his way through my spell. He's in no condition to fight."

"Well, he can take her," Lukl said. "Good riddance."

"Thank you," Nora said to him. Lukl looked at her and then away again.

The tall man said to her, "You don't know what you're going back to."

"I don't know who you all are, except that your men kidnapped me, and then you insulted me and my fiancé and kept me here against my will!" she said.

"My apologies," he said. "We failed to introduce ourselves properly. This is the Lord Luklren, the twelfth earl of the Northern Border, the master of these lands. It was his soldiers who met you and, as you say, kidnapped you. And I am the magician Aruendiel." He paused as though his name would have some meaning for her, but she looked at him blankly.

"If you're determined to go back to Ilissa and her brood, then by all means, go," he went on. "Obviously, you're in no state to listen to reason. But I will tell you two things that might be of some use to you, if you can contrive to remember them. First, Ilissa and her people can't tell lies to you. Not directly, anyway. They can refuse to answer your questions, they can distract you, they can fob you off by saying something that's completely unrelated to what you asked, but they can't tell you a deliberate untruth."

The information was not what Nora had expected. She tried to make sense of what he had said. She couldn't remember Ilissa or Raclin or any of the others ever lying to her. But why would they want to? "I don't believe you. They don't lie because they have no reason to lie."

"I didn't say they don't lie," he said with a harsh laugh. "I said they can't tell you lies. Words are the only way that they *don't* lie. Second, I'm giving you a token that may be of value." Opening his cloak, he pulled something small and gray from inside his left sleeve and handed it to Nora.

She took it and looked at it curiously. A tiny feather. "If you find yourself in danger, you can use that to call on my assistance."

She opened her fingers. The wind caught the gray feather and twirled it away.

Aruendiel dipped his head in an ironic half-bow. "As you will. Well, your ordeal is almost over. I see your friend approaching."

Nora turned to see Vulpin walking slowly toward them, his green cloak a fresh daub of color against the dry, frozen grassland. He looked very pale and seemed a size smaller than when Nora had last seen him. She ran over to him, calling his name.

"Nora, are you all right?" Vulpin grasped her hand and looked into her face, squinting a little.

"Yes, I'm fine, now that you're here. These awful men kidnapped me, but they say I can go now. I think they're afraid of Ilissa."

"That's good," Vulpin muttered. "I have a message to deliver first, though." He walked over to the other men. Nora followed, keeping a little behind him.

"The Most Gracious Lady Ilissa, Queen of the Faitoren, sends her greetings to the Lord Luklren and Lord Aruendiel," Vulpin said, his eyes slightly glassy. "It is her understanding that Lady Nora, a guest in her home and the intended bride of Lord Raclin, has become subject to a most brutal and unwelcome seizure and made an unwilling prisoner by Lords Luklren and Aruendiel. Lady Ilissa is highly displeased. She demands the immediate return of the Lady Nora, unharmed in every way, accompanied by no fewer than five hundred cows and one thousand sheep, as recompense for this heinous crime, which is a serious violation of the truce between her people and yours.

"If the Lady Ilissa's conditions are not met, she will take this as a sign for the commencement of hostilities, and the people of the Northern Border will be destroyed, their children enslaved, their crops burned, their houses smashed, and their animals seized by the armed fury of the Faitoren." Vulpin bowed deeply and then straightened, swallowing hard. He looked as though he were trying not to throw up.

Aruendiel laughed shortly and was about to speak when Luklren cleared his throat and folded his arms.

"Greetings to Lady Ilissa," Luklren said, narrowing his one good eye.

"I am returning, ah, Lady Nora to her, unharmed, untouched in every way, as I'm sure her appearance and testimony will bear out. She was found wandering on my lands and was taken into custody purely as a precaution. I regret any unease that her absence might have caused, but I would like to remind Lady Ilissa that the Faitoren themselves are in serious violation of the truce by their repeated theft of cattle, sheep, and deer belonging to myself and the people of the Northern Border. I trust that Lady Ilissa will commit herself to better abiding by the truce in the future, including respecting our mutual border and ceasing these raids on my livestock."

"Finished, Lukl?" Aruendiel asked. When the other man nodded, he stepped forward with an awkward twist of his body and touched Vulpin lightly on the cheek.

Vulpin drew back. Nora gasped as his face changed—his nose and mouth thrusting forward to form a blunt, wrinkled snout, yellow tusks erupting along his lower jaw. His ears were suddenly larger and more pointed, covered with a reddish down. More fur—thicker, bristly—sprouted on his forehead and cheeks. His head sank as his frame collapsed a foot in height; Nora found herself looking down at him.

Vulpin's eyes—pathetically, she thought—were still a clear, mild hazel in his hideously transformed face.

"Lord Aruendiel sends his regards to the Lady Ilissa," said the magician. "And good fortune to you in your wedded life, Mistress Nora. Remember that the Faitoren are not always as handsome as they seem." He gave a swift bow and then turned to limp back toward the horses. Luklren took a moment longer, staring at Vulpin in evident fascination, then shook his head and followed his companion.

"My God, Vulpin, what did he do to you?" Nora said in a low voice, as soon as she thought the men were out of earshot. "Are you all right?"

"I'm fine," Vulpin said. His voice sounded different, thick and clumsy, his words garbled as he tried to shape them with his new mouth. "Let's go now. Ilissa will fix everything when we get home."

The two horsemen watched them move away. "I admit, it does seem like a waste to let a girl with pitchers like that go back to those monsters," Luklren said.

"None of it's real," Aruendiel said. "Breasts, face, the rest of it. She could have a harelip under there, or leprosy. You saw the Faitoren."

"What a piece of filth. Ugh. I'm not sure that was a good idea, though, Aruendiel. I don't need you making extra trouble with Ilissa."

"She stirs up plenty of trouble on her own without my encouragement," the other man said. "It's good to let her know that we won't stand for her nonsense."

The air darkened slightly, as though a cloud had moved over the sun. Both horses whinnied uneasily.

Ducking slightly, Aruendiel flung up a hand, fingers spread. A shadowy mass passed high overhead, then flew into the long, low rays of the sun, so that they had to look away.

"The girl's fiancé," Aruendiel said, lowering his arm. Luklren cursed with feeling.

A piece of down blew lazily in front of Aruendiel, tracing a slow spiral around his horse's head. Aruendiel followed it with his eyes. "Yes," he said under his breath. "Go."

The wind carried the feather away, along with his words and the dust raised by the horses' hooves.

"What did you say?" Luklren asked.

"Just a precaution," Aruendiel said. "It's rare for our friend to come out this far, isn't it? I'll sharpen the protective spell tonight."

"It was because of that girl. Good that we sent her back." Luklren paused, as though waiting for Aruendiel to contradict him, but the other man said nothing, so he went on: "Well, let's get going. I want to stop at the sheepfold and the Longcrick watchtower before it gets dark. And I'm famished. Chicken for dinner tonight. We killed a rooster this morning for you."

Aruendiel gathered up his reins with a dry laugh. "The last time I came, it was a stringy old ram—now a winter chicken. You don't believe in spoiling your guests, Lukl. Or maybe you just don't think my magic merits much in the way of hospitality."

"It's been a hard winter. We were fattening up a yearling calf for your visit, but the Faitoren stole it."

"Ah! Too bad," said Aruendiel, spurring his horse. "Well, I will have to exercise greater vigilance against them in the future."

## Chapter 6

Walking back across the fields beside Vulpin, Nora tried hard to keep her eyes fixed ahead. She wanted to be polite, the way she'd avoid staring at someone with any kind of deformity, but Vulpin's transformation had been so unexpected, so impossible, that she felt an almost physical compulsion to turn and look at him again. Finally she did shift her eyes toward him, intending to look just for a second, but Vulpin immediately met her gaze. He nodded and opened his big, tusked mouth, which was the saddest part of all, as she realized that he was trying to smile.

"Poor Vulpin," she said. "Are you in pain? Did he hurt you?"

He shook his head without saying anything, and they kept walking.

It was colder than ever. Nora's teeth chattered, and the tips of her fingers were blue by the time they reached the stream that she had crossed so unthinkingly a little while before. Now, she discovered, it was almost frozen over, ice glazing the stones that stood out of the water. Vulpin had to help her across.

Then she was standing on the other side, and it was summer again—blue sky overhead and tall, green grass waving in a warm breeze. Moscelle and the rest of the hunting party were waiting, along with a dozen horsemen, men she knew from Ilissa's parties, now wearing helmets and a close-fitting, metallic garb that reminded her of the feeted pajamas that small children wear. She realized after a second that it was chain mail.

Moscelle and the others crowded around Nora, asking whether she was all right, exclaiming how naughty she had been to wander away, how frightened they had been, how cold her hands were, how lucky she had been to escape from the soldiers and the evil wizard. Nora was more concerned about Vulpin. It occurred to her that no one could recognize him. "I'm fine, really I'm fine," she said at last, for the fifth time. "But look what they did to poor Vulpin!"

The others, though, seemed reluctant to look at him directly; Nora could hardly blame them. "What happened to you, Vulpin?" Moscelle asked finally, an edge in her voice.

Vulpin shrugged his shoulders. "Lord Aruendiel's little joke," he said thickly. He switched to the other language, the one that they used when they thought Nora wasn't listening. It sounded harsher and wilder in his changed mouth.

"I see," Moscelle said finally, with a glance at Nora. "How unpleasant. Well, you'd better ride ahead and ask Ilissa for help. Tell her we'll be there shortly."

One of the other men led Vulpin's horse over to him. He was too short to climb unassisted into the saddle, so the others had to help him up and shorten his stirrups for him. He dug his small heels into the side of the horse and disappeared at a gallop.

"I'm sorry to cause all this trouble, Moscelle," Nora said. "I only crossed the stream to pick some flowers, and then the soldiers came."

"Oh, darling, we're just so thankful you're safe. None of us realized that we were so close to the border, or we would never have let you out of our sight. Was it terrible for you, sweet?"

"Oh, those men were horrible," Nora said passionately. "They kept looking at me in this awful way. I was afraid they wanted to—well, you know—but they didn't. They were afraid of Ilissa and Raclin, I think."

"They should be afraid. She's very, very angry," Moscelle said, with a little shudder. "How many were there?"

"Three soldiers and two men on horses. A man with one eye, and a crippled man they said was a wizard. I didn't believe it, but he did something to me and made me confused, and he did that terrible thing to Vulpin."

"What did he do to you?" Moscelle said quickly.

"I don't know, exactly," said Nora, "but I couldn't tell how many legs a horse has."

"Is it a riddle?"

"No, I just didn't know."

"Oh, darling, you know how many legs a horse has, don't you?"

"Four," Nora said carefully. When Moscelle said nothing, she went on with more confidence: "I did know it at first, and then I looked at my dress, and it was as though part of my brain had shut off."

"What an awful feeling. Are you all right now?"

"I think so." In fact, Nora reflected, her head felt a bit clearer than it had for a long time. At least, the slippery words that had become so expert at eluding her now seemed easier to grasp. Standing up to the wizard and the soldiers had forced her to gather her wits, it seemed. She felt some pride for not breaking down in front of them. "Moscelle, who were those men? Why did they kidnap me?"

Moscelle had plenty to say on the subject of the one-eyed man and the crippled wizard. The one-eyed man lived nearby and called himself a lord, Moscelle said, but he was only lord over a crumbling pile of stones and some mangy sheep and cows. He was always trying to pick fights with Ilissa—it was very annoying. The other man was a cruel and dangerous wizard—the Black Wizard, Moscelle called him. He'd had been to hell and learned his magic from the devils there, people said.

"You were lucky to get away. He hates us, and there are terrible stories about him." Moscelle lowered her voice. "He murdered his wife. She was a beautiful young girl, much younger than he was. He stabbed her in a fit of rage. But don't worry. Ilissa is a match for him."

"Why do these people hate us?" Nora asked, frowning, a little surprised at this talk of wizards.

Moscelle sketched a vague gesture. "There was a war once, and now we have a truce, but we still have to be on our guard. Someday we'll defeat them for good. Ilissa can explain it better."

"Why didn't anyone tell me this before?"

"Oh, darling, no one wants you to worry about such things. And it's really not that important. You just have to be a little careful so that you don't go too close to the border by accident. I hope Ilissa's not too furious with us. Leptospeer was supposed to keep track of where we were, but all he could think about was lunch, the pig."

"Well, it was me who wandered off."

"It's sweet of you to say that, darling. Do you think you could remember to mention that to Ilissa? I know that she could never be angry with you."

Ilissa was waiting for them on the terrace, looking collected and lovely in a full-skirted white dress embroidered with pearls and gold thread. Nora had seen pictures of Queen Elizabeth I in something similar, although on Ilissa the dress looked less like something you would wear to face off with the Spanish Armada and more like something to go dancing in. Smiling, Ilissa held out her hands to Nora and kissed her on both cheeks.

Only then did Nora notice the change in the rose garden below the terrace. All of the bushes were blackened and leafless, as though they had been scorched with a blast of flame.

"Nora, what a terrible experience for you," Ilissa said, still clasping Nora's hand. "Are you truly all right? I know how wicked those men are."

"She's fine," Moscelle said, before Nora could answer. "They didn't touch her."

"Thank you, Moscelle," Ilissa said tightly, still smiling. Moscelle was right, Ilissa was very angry indeed.

"It's true," said Nora. "They didn't hurt me. They were afraid of you and Raclin. Where is Raclin?" she added, looking around, wondering why he had not ridden out to meet her.

"Oh, Raclin is patrolling the border, making sure that those men don't try to attack us," said Ilissa. "Don't worry about him," she added, seeing the apprehension in Nora's face. "He'll be back before you know it, darling. He was very upset to hear what happened. I would have expected Moscelle and Vulpin and the others to have taken better care of you."

Beside Nora, Moscelle stiffened slightly. Nora noticed Vulpin a few feet away, the grotesque snout and tusks still protruding from his face.

"Can't you help him?" Nora asked. "The wizard did that to him—it's so horrible."

"Yes, it is, isn't it?" Ilissa said. "Well, we could change him back to our dear, handsome Vulpin right away. But Vulpin and I have been discussing it, and much as it pains me, we've agreed that it might be better to let him stay this way for a bit longer. A little reminder to him and everyone else to be more cautious next time."

Nora looked over at Vulpin, and he nodded, his changed face unreadable. "But it wasn't his fault I got lost," she said. "And then he came for me, even though I could tell he felt horrible."

Ilissa's laugh was like a champagne flute breaking on a marble floor. "I'd expect no less of Vulpin!" she declared. "He did only what he should have. But why, darling, did you get lost? Were you trying to leave us? Are you not happy here?"

As Nora met Ilissa's gaze, so endlessly sympathetic and concerned—so impossible to evade—she again began to feel as though her tongue and brain were numbed, as though words and phrases would refuse to combine into anything but the simplest of meanings. (That didn't matter, though, because Ilissa would understand everything perfectly.) "Happy, I'm very happy," she began.

Then, unbidden, Nora remembered the cold winter light and the brown fields and how she had faced the tall wizard in black and found the words she needed.

"I just went to pick some flowers," Nora said, a little sharply. "No one told me there was any danger."

"Of course, I understand," Ilissa said. "So you encountered Lord Luklren and Lord Aruendiel. What did you think of them?"

"I didn't like them. The way they talked about me, and you and Raclin, was very, uh—not respectful."

"They are very coarse, rude men. I use their titles simply as a courtesy. But you have nothing to worry about. Luklren is a nuisance only, and Aruendiel—well, I have defeated him before." Ilissa's eyes narrowed, and suddenly she did look as though she could face the Spanish Armada.

"Under the circumstances, though, I think we should change our plans slightly," she continued. "Darling, I hope this won't be a disappointment, because we've been having so much fun planning the wedding—but I think we should go ahead and have it tonight, even though not everything is quite ready. Once you and Raclin are married, they wouldn't dare do anything to hurt you. Darling, what do you think?"

When Nora had heard the word "disappointment," she'd had the sudden fear that Ilissa was about to say that the wedding was off, the engagement broken. With a surge of relief, Nora said, "That sounds wonderful!"

"Ah, you see, Moscelle!" Ilissa said. "Nothing stands in the way of love."

There was something odd about Nora's bouquet, a lush cascade of white lilies and peonies bound with a white silk ribbon. But if she happened to glimpse it from the corner of her eye, the bouquet was a bundle of black sticks. This was distracting; Nora kept glancing down to see whether she was holding sticks or flowers.

"I'm sorry, darling," Moscelle said, noticing her confusion. "I did the best I could. *She* should have realized that we'd need flowers for tonight before she blasted every plant in the garden. It's going to take at least a day to grow them all back."

"It's all right," Nora said. "They look beautiful. Is Raclin here yet?"

"Oh, he'll be here soon," said Moscelle absently, adjusting Nora's gown. "It's getting dark."

"Do you think anything could have happened to him?"

"Darling, nothing happens to Raclin that he doesn't want to happen to him."

"That's right," said Raclin, coming through the door. Moscelle stepped back just in time to let Nora rush into his arms.

"I was so worried!"

Raclin's lips brushed Nora's mouth. "My dear, there was absolutely no danger. Those cowards know better than to tangle with me. My mother's in a panic that they'll launch some sort of attack, but honestly, I don't think we'll have any more trouble." He looked even more handsome than usual, Nora thought, with his eyes bright and a light flush of color on his perfect cheekbones. "And once the wedding's out of the way, we'll have a marvelous opportunity to launch a counterattack."

"But I don't want you to go off and fight just when we get married," Nora protested. "We need some time together."

Raclin looked down at her curiously. "Did you find your tongue again? That's the longest sentence I've heard you utter for weeks, my dear."

Nora laughed with a tinge of embarrassment. All this time, fogged with happiness, she hadn't realized how distracted she must have seemed, even to dear Raclin. "Oh, you would have been proud of me, the way I talked to that wizard and those soldiers. They kept trying to scare me, and I wouldn't back down."

"You didn't, eh?" Raclin said. "Well, that's good, I suppose. My brave girl."

"Anyway, you shouldn't be thinking about fighting. We're about to get married."

"Look at her! We're not even married yet, and she's already telling me what to do."

"You'd better do what I say, or maybe I'll change my mind about marrying you," Nora said daringly. (*It's not too late to change your mind*, came an echo somewhere deep inside her.) A threat she would never dream of carrying out, of course, but Raclin gave her a sharp look.

In fact, the ceremony went so quickly that Nora would have been hard-pressed to find time to change her mind. A blare of trumpets, and she and Raclin passed through a vast crowd even more splendid than usual. Then they were standing in front of Ilissa, who spoke to them in that strange, sinuous language. Raclin answered in the same language, and Nora chimed in with the response that Moscelle had made her practice a hundred times. (Nora promised herself that she would master this second language of Raclin's, whatever it was, as soon as possible.)

Raclin put a golden ring on her finger. It was tight, almost painful at first—perhaps there had been a mistake, and it was the wrong size—but then it felt fine. She slipped its twin onto Raclin's finger. Ilissa crowned her with a jeweled tiara. Raclin was already wearing a circlet of gold around his head. At the wedding banquet, almost all of the toasts and speeches were in that same mysterious language. Nora smiled through it all, her hand linked with Raclin's. There was dancing, and then Raclin pulled her upstairs to a din of applause and whistles from the guests.

They were finally alone, Nora and Raclin, in a vast new bedchamber that was all gilt-and-whipped-cream rococo, as though the décor had been entrusted to a team of pastry chefs. Raclin swung Nora into his arms as if she were a doll and laid her on the bed, under the billowing canopy embroidered with crowns and cupids and peacocks.

"Well, that's over with, finally," he said. "How's my brave girl?"

"Darling!" Nora said, sitting up and reaching out for him. She suddenly felt she could not wait another second to feel his naked skin under her fingers. He laughed and began taking off his coat.

When Nora awoke the next morning, adrift like a small boat in the big bed, all she could really remember from the night before was the sense of a fierce, delicious frenzy that lasted seemingly for hours and then became indistinguishable from sleep. A few clear impressions remained: the sleek coolness of Raclin's flesh even when his body moved faster and faster against hers, and the look of what might have been amusement on his face as he watched her writhe and pant beneath him.

Lying among tangled sheets in the morning light, she felt drained, frail, happy, with a pleasant trembly feeling in her legs and arms. Only when she rolled over and saw that Raclin was not lying next to her did she feel a stab of disappointment.

"Darling, he had to go on patrol!" Ilissa said, after Nora, venturing out to look for Raclin, found her new mother-in-law instead. "I know, how awful of him to leave you alone on your honeymoon. But he does this every day, and of course, now that we're on a special alert, it's even more important."

"Oh, I didn't know," Nora said, deflated. "Is it really that dangerous? I only saw a few soldiers yesterday."

"We don't want to take any chances, my dear!" Ilissa said. "Raclin will be back by evening, and in the meantime, we'll have a wonderful day. What do you think, a ramble in the park? A musicale in the garden?"

That was the pattern every day, Nora found. Raclin was always gone when she awoke, even though she tried waking earlier and earlier to catch him before he left. Then there was the long day to get through, hours and hours, before she could see him again. Ilissa always thoughtfully organized some entertainment, but the revelries ran together after a while, an endless round of picnics and hunts and rides. Moscelle was generally brimming over with the latest gossip—who had fallen in or out of love, who had quarreled, who had cheated on whom    yet even those salacious bulletins seemed less diverting than they once had.

There was a brief frisson of excitement when Vulpin reappeared, his height restored, the tusks and snout gone. Nora was hoping to find out more about what had happened to him, but he seemed embarrassed to talk about the experience. "It wore off soon enough," he said.

"Nora dear, you look a little blue," Ilissa said one afternoon. They were picnicking at the edge of the forest, she and Nora and a few others, in a grove of saplings that had somehow been teased into a suite of spindly, delicate chairs and tables.

Nora was startled by the comment. Perched on one of the tree-chairs—more comfortable than it looked, fortunately—she had been nibbling a small, pink-frosted cake and contemplating the gold ring on her left hand. "I'm just wondering what Raclin is doing," she said.

"Darling, that's the sweetest thing I ever heard!" Ilissa said, although she did not offer any thoughts about Raclin's whereabouts. "But you know you'll see him tonight."

"I wish he were here now."

"Yes, it would have been marvelous to have him come along today," Ilissa said regretfully. "He's so busy, poor sweet."

Her reply set off a faint echo in Nora's mind, a flicker of déjà vu. It was the Black Wizard's voice she remembered, harsh, urgent. The memory flitted just out of reach.

She said to Ilissa: "Perhaps Raclin would come on a picnic if his wife *and* his mother asked him." Ilissa only smiled. Nora pursued: "Tonight, will you ask him with me?"

The silver thread of laughter that always seemed to run through Ilissa's voice turned suddenly steely: "No, it's not possible."

"Why not?" Nora asked.

"Darling, you don't want to pester him, do you? You don't want to be a nagging wife!"

"No," said Nora, the very idea striking fear into her heart.

"Then don't be," said Ilissa, smiling. She rose, gathering her skirts in her hand, and walked over to speak to Amatol, who straightened noticeably when she saw Ilissa coming.

After a moment, Nora stood up, too, her face warm. She wasn't sure exactly what had just transpired, but she felt as though she had been slapped. What was the harm in asking Raclin—just asking him—to come out with them one day? She paced slowly under the trees, trying to sort it out. Ilissa had not even deigned to answer the simple question: Why was it impossible to ask Raclin to join them in the daytime?

*They can't lie to you. That's what that man said, the one who was supposed to be a wizard.* The thought fluttered through her mind like a falling leaf.

I never said Ilissa lied, Nora thought impatiently. She just didn't answer my question.

*Exactly.*

Nora looked up and saw that she had moved a little farther into the forest than she'd intended. She had a sudden dread of doing anything that might provoke Ilissa's annoyance again. As she turned back toward the picnic grove, a flash of yellow caught her eye.

"Oh!" she said aloud.

There was the iron fence, the slanting gravestones, the abandoned cemetery plot that she had come across in the forest on that day—how long ago now?—when she had first come to Ilissa's. With some curiosity, she walked closer. It looked different. The ground around the tombstones was muddy and uneven, raw orange clay scarred with boot prints and the tracks of some large animal, probably a dog. The startling yellow she had seen was a ribbon of shiny plastic with black letters: POLICE LINE DO NOT CROSS.

A crime scene? Nora came up to the fence and craned her neck for a better view. As she brushed against the iron railings, a stab of pain went through her abdomen. Not that she felt any real hurt, exactly, but she felt the proximity of pain, like an electric shock, inside her body. She staggered backward a couple of steps, then sat down heavily.

"Get her away from there!" someone cried out, behind her. It was Ilissa.

The pain was gone, but it had left a sense of inner agitation in Nora's belly. Food poisoning, she thought. When I can throw up, I'll feel better.

Someone was helping her up—Vulpin, coming to her rescue again. Where was Raclin? "I'll be fine in a minute," Nora said. She hoped that she would not vomit in front of everyone, but then it was too late.

Ilissa, white-faced and furious, swiped at Nora's mouth and chin with a tiny lace handkerchief. "Poor darling," she said. "We'll have to take very good care of you from now on."

That was Nora's first indication that she was pregnant.

## *Chapter 7*

Nora stared blankly at the night sky, where her own face and Raclin's exchanged immense and brilliant smiles, framed by a tangle of golden vines and flowers. There was a ragged cheer from the watchers outside the palace. Slowly the images faded to dim lines of smoke. Another rocket boomed and sizzled, and the sky lit up with a fountain of pink fire.

"Is he still talking to her?" Nora asked.

"No, darling, he's moved on," Moscelle said. She leaned on the balcony railing for a better look at the crowd on the lawn. "He just stopped to say hello to her, that's all."

"What's he doing now?" Nora tried to keep her eyes anywhere but on her husband, afraid she had not imagined the way Raclin looked at the woman with the auburn curls.

"I can't see. Oh, wait, there he is again. He's standing next to Gaibon. He just said something to Gaibon, and Gaibon is laughing. Idiot."

"Raclin's probably complaining about his fat wife." Nora tried to make a joke of it, and almost succeeded.

"Darling, you look perfectly sweet, absolutely adorable."

Nora sighed and put her hand on her stomach. The baby was not due for a long time yet, as far as she knew, but her waist had already thickened out of recognition. She was wearing something loose and shapeless in purple velvet but she still had the uncomfortable sensation that she was about to burst out of her clothes.

Meanwhile, the other women at the party were in long, clinging gowns with trailing sleeves, yoked tight at the bust and waist. Nora turned away from the fireworks to glance into the ballroom behind her, where dancers galloped across the floor in glittering lines. Long as a mast, lively as a colt. The phrase was a fragment from her previous life, Nora knew, but she couldn't say exactly how she knew it or where it came from. She was used to the blanks in her memory now; they did not seem to matter much, not compared with a baby on the way and a husband who paid her less and less attention every day.

At first, Raclin seemed as happy about the baby as she was. She treasured the slow smile that had spread across his face when she and Ilissa gave him the news, after Nora had almost fainted at the old cemetery. "That's my good girl," he said, exchanging a look with Ilissa. Nora would have preferred to tell him herself, the two of them alone, but Ilissa was obviously burning with excitement, and she had a sort of authority in the matter: It was she who, laying a long-fingered hand on Nora's abdomen, had declared definitively that Nora was pregnant.

Nora herself had been startled by the discovery. Somehow, during all those nights in Raclin's arms, she had put out of her mind how babies are made, had never once thought about using protection, although she had always been so careful in the past. Of course, she and Raclin were married, but this was so quick to be having a baby; she and Raclin had hardly had any married life together yet.

She almost said something along those lines to Ilissa, but when she met Ilissa's gaze, the words vanished. Ilissa's blue-green eyes were so full of anticipation, even hunger, that Nora felt a shock of concern. Then it came to her how thrilling to be carrying Raclin's baby inside her body, how wonderful it would be to raise his child. That was why she had married him, wasn't it? So that their lives would be intertwined, so that they could take on the intimate, important work of creating a family. She was content—no, blissfully satisfied to be carrying out her appointed function.

But meanwhile, even before Nora started to look pregnant, there was a sudden end to lovemaking in the big, canopied bed. Raclin now went to sleep immediately, or worse, he let Nora retire early—she got sleepy well before midnight now—while he stayed out for most of the night. In the morning, there would only be the imprint of his head in the pillow to show that he had been there at all.

At first Nora pouted, then she dropped hints, and finally one night she told him point-blank that she was lonely, she missed him, and she was sure that sex during pregnancy wouldn't hurt the baby. Raclin took a long swallow of wine, tilting the goblet up so that she couldn't see his expression.

"Darling?" she entreated.

Raclin lowered the goblet and licked his lips. "Such a pretty face," he said, leaning closer to her. "A pretty, pretty face. I wonder what our baby will look like?"

"Just like you, I hope, darling," Nora said. "In every way."

He laughed. "I should warn you, I was not an easy child to raise. A complete hellion." Nora imagined a small Raclin, face and hands dirty, eyes bright. She laughed, too.

"My mother hopes that it will take after you more than me," he said. Nora felt a stirring of indignation—how could Ilissa be so critical of her own son?—but Raclin only laughed again. "Good night to you and the baby, whoever it looks like."

"You're not coming up now?"

"No. There will be other nights, my dear. I promise not to shirk my marital responsibilities, when it's time for me to fulfill them again."

"What do you mean?" she said. "When will that be?" He was already moving away. He looked back to wink at her, then raised his arm to hail someone across the room.

Slowly her fears crystallized: He was having an affair. She watched him as he mingled with Ilissa's guests, or had Moscelle watch him when she could not stand it anymore. It was true that Raclin didn't seem to single any woman out for special attention, but perhaps that was a subterfuge. Moscelle proved to be an unexpectedly sympathetic ally. Without unduly encouraging Nora's suspicions, she did not dismiss them, either. Infidelity was part of the natural order of things, Moscelle gave Nora to understand, so it was better to face facts and be realistic instead of trying to pretend that one's beloved, no matter how perfect, would never stray. Gaibon, for instance, had been crazy for Moscelle not so long ago, but then he had gotten himself entangled with that little black-haired slut Tinea.

Everything would be fine once the baby arrived, Nora told herself. Raclin would adore the child, and his old passion would return once she got her figure back. And she would have the baby to console her.

Now Raclin was nowhere to be seen, either on the lawn or in the crowded ballroom. Nora shifted her weight on her small gilded chair, trying to find a more comfortable position and spot her husband without being too obvious.

"Darling, I brought you some ice cream. It's strawberry, your favorite!" Moscelle said, handing her a small golden bowl.

*I don't even like strawberry.* Nora spooned the ice cream into her mouth and tried to remember what her favorite flavor was. "I don't see Raclin anymore. Did you happen to see where he went?"

"Well." Moscelle pursed her lips. "I wasn't sure whether to tell you, but since you ask, I just saw him standing on the terrace with Oon."

Oon—Nora had seen her not so long ago, twirling neatly in the dance, light as a leaf in a green dress that was cut a shade tighter than the other women's.

"They were standing *very* close together," Moscelle said.

Nora stood up. "You mean—what?"

Moscelle shrugged gracefully. "Men can be so awful."

"I have to see him," Nora said, taking a deep breath. "Right now." She gathered up her skirt and turned to leave the balcony.

"Nora, darling, where are you going?" Ilissa was standing in the door, looking at Nora with a half-smile.

"Oh, Ilissa, I—" Nora floundered. "It's lovely to see you, but I have to go."

"What's wrong, darling? Your pretty face is all pink. Calm down, sweet. It's not good for the baby for you to be so upset."

Thinking about the baby made it all the worse. Nora burst into sudden, violent tears. Behind Ilissa, a few dancers looked at her curiously.

"Nora, darling!" Ilissa clamped an arm around Nora's shoulder. "Let's not make a scene."

Sobbing, Nora felt a mild jolt, like a hiccup, and the ballroom music and the noise of the crowd abruptly ceased. When she looked up, she and Ilissa and Moscelle was standing in the white-and-gold splendor of her bedroom. "How did we get here?" Nora asked, bewildered.

"You need a little time to recover yourself," Ilissa said firmly. She looked inquiringly at Moscelle.

"Nora's feeling a bit emotional—" Moscelle began.

"I can see that. What set this off?"

Moscelle hesitated, and then said quickly, "I saw Raclin kissing Oon on the terrace, and I thought Nora should know."

Nora launched into a fresh round of sobs. "Raclin doesn't love me anymore," she gulped. "He hates me. He never talks to me, he never touches me, and now he's with Oon!"

"Darling, calm yourself." Ilissa's voice was as soft as cat's fur. "I know you're upset, and Raclin really has been a bit naughty, but there's no sense in getting hysterical over a silly little flirtation. You mustn't take this so seriously."

"But he's my husband!"

"Exactly!" Ilissa said, patting Nora's cheek. "He's your husband. He's married to you, not to Oon."

"He shouldn't be kissing her, then."

"Well, he's certainly not going to kiss you if you're a sopping, hysterical mess, will he, dear? Men get distracted sometimes—and women can never keep away from my Raclin, anyway. But he'll always come back to you in the end. I wouldn't let him do otherwise."

"I don't want him to be distracted."

"Darling, I know, but please be reasonable. It's not good for you to be so emotional right now. We all want this baby to be healthy and happy and perfect, don't we?"

"Oh, the baby—" Nora said, choking back a sob. "You just care about the baby! It's like what those men said, the soldier and the wizard, what they said about breeding—"

"What did they say?" Ilissa asked sharply.

"Something about you breeding your cub. I—I don't know."

Ilissa gave a small, impatient exhalation. "You need to get some rest, Nora." She went over to the bed, turned down the covers, and patted the sheets in a way that reminded Nora of how one might show a dog where to curl up. "Here. It's time for bed." Nora didn't move. "I said, it's time for bed," Ilissa repeated.

Reluctantly, Nora settled herself onto the mattress. She was already wearing her nightgown, she noticed without caring much.

"Get some sleep, darling," Ilissa said. "You'll feel better in the morning." The room dimmed abruptly, although no one had made a move toward extinguishing the candles.

"I'll stay with Nora for a while," Moscelle murmured, edging toward the bed.

"No, you'll come with me," Ilissa said smoothly. "Moscelle, I'd like to know what you were thinking—?" The door shut behind them.

Lying rigid in bed, her mind still agitated, Nora hardly expected to sleep. Surprisingly, though, almost immediately she slid into deep, velvet unconsciousness.

Only to wake up, some hours later, with the pressing need to urinate. She got up to relieve herself and then went back to bed, but her capacity for sleep had vanished. For a while she kept hopelessly picturing Raclin and Oon in a series of torrid embraces, until she reflected that Ilissa was right, she should try to be calm for the baby's sake.

Then she began to worry about how much her anxiety and panic might already have affected the baby, setting its small heart racing, teaching it too soon that there was such a thing as fear in the world. "It's all right, it's all right," she said softly, her hand on her belly. Presently, as though the baby had heard her, she was relieved to sense a flutter deep inside; it was only the second time that she had felt the baby move. Nora lay still so as not to miss a flicker of movement.

Less reassuring were the faint, sharp pains, like pinpricks, that came and went so quickly that Nora would have thought she had imagined them, except that they happened over and over again. She would have to ask Ilissa about them. Perhaps she should see a doctor. It occurred to her that she had not seen a doctor since getting pregnant. Something else to worry about. She sighed and burrowed more deeply under the covers.

The bedroom door opened. Raclin's broad-shouldered figure was silhouetted in the doorway. "Raclin!" Nora said, sitting up in bed. In spite of everything, the sight of him sent a grateful thrill through her.

He came into the room, and the candles on the mantelpiece flared into luminescence. His handsome face was smiling exactly the way that it had always smiled at her, but somehow it was not reassuring. "I heard about your little exhibition tonight, darling. Did you have to pitch your hysterics where everyone could see you?"

"How many people saw you and Oon?" Nora said, half-surprised at her own boldness.

"One too many, obviously," he said, laughing to himself. "Moscelle won't be carrying tales any time soon."

"Raclin, how could you do this to me? I wanted to die, when Moscelle told me."

He stopped laughing and came over to sit on the edge of the bed. He stroked her hair, watching her face. "Oon is nothing to me, darling. Just a diversion."

"Is she the only one?"

"Darling, don't be silly!"

"Answer me!"

"That's too ridiculous to even answer."

"I know you can't lie to me. Tell me!"

"Where did you hear that?" Raclin's voice lost some of its controlled, affectionate tone. "Very well, I'll tell you the truth—see how you like it. Is Oon the only one I've kissed and undressed and made love to these past few months? No, she's not."

Nora found it hard to breathe. "I love you so much, and you just ignore me and neglect me. I'm your wife, I'm going to have your baby."

"Yes, very admirable of you. You've fulfilled everyone's expectations beautifully."

"What does Oon give you that I can't give you? You think I'm ugly because I'm pregnant?"

"You're always beautiful, my dear, pregnant or not. Thanks to my mother. No, since you want the truth, I get a little bored sometimes. And Oon, well, she may not have much of a mind, but it is a mind of her own, which makes things a bit more interesting. No offense, darling."

"What do you mean?" Nora felt suddenly ashamed, without under- standing why.

"I thought that might fly right over your pretty head. Well, you can rest assured that you will hear no more reports of my dallying with other women."

Nora thought hard, trying to understand why his promise didn't sound completely satisfactory. "Does that mean you'll stop seeing other women, or you'll just make sure that I don't hear about it?"

"Ah, that's my clever girl! Sometimes you surprise me. Sometimes."

"Raclin—" She tried to be reasonable. "I wouldn't mind so much about Oon or anyone, if I could see more of you. We need to be together for the baby's sake. We're a family now."

"Oh, I've done my part," Raclin said. He stood up and moved a few steps away from the bed. "I've given Ilissa a grandchild—incidentally, she believes it will be a grandson—and now I'm free to pursue my own interests. You and I will appear together in public when it's appropriate, naturally."

"What do you mean?"

"I mean I'm moving to other chambers, and I will see somewhat less of you until my son requires a sibling. I'm sure you'll find ways to keep occupied. I think you'll be an excellent mother. Ilissa thinks so, too."

He was talking about a sort of separation, a marriage that was empty except for the begetting of children, and he sounded so casual about it, as though he cared nothing for her. Nora felt suffocating panic sweep through her. Clambering out of bed, she caught hold of Raclin's arm. "But darling, you don't understand. I love you. The baby isn't enough. I need you—you! I'll die if I can't be with you."

"No, you won't." Raclin sounded bored. "You just think that. I made you think that." He walked over to the window and looked out. The sky was a pearly gray. "This conversation is dull, my dear, and I must be going. It's almost dawn. I suggest you get some sleep before the rest of the house wakes up."

"Where are you going?" she asked. Raclin only smiled. "You're going to see Oon, right? That's what you do every day. You're with Oon or some other slut!"

"Believe what you like," he said, turning toward the door.

"You've been cheating on me all along," Nora cried, flinging herself on him. "You stay here with me, with your wife!"

"Let me go," he said. "It's late. I lost track of time." He pushed back, trying to disentangle himself from her embrace. She slid to her knees, locking her arms around his legs. "Nora, this is tiresome. You'll hurt the baby."

"I don't care," she said, sobbing. "I want you to stay."

"Let me go, you idiot!"

"Stay with me! Or tell me where you go every day. I want to know the truth."

"Is that what you really want?"

"Yes, I want to know!" said Nora, gripping his thighs. "Tell me!"

He didn't say anything for a long moment, and then she felt a fierce shudder run through his body. She looked up. "Darling?" she started to ask.

The first thing she saw was the jagged line of teeth, two separate rows of them in a long narrow jaw. Then there was the yellow eye, crossed by an oval, elongate pupil, looking down at her. Something was unfolding above her, big as a tent but not a tent, it was shaped wrong. Not a man, either, although there was something manlike in the muscled torso and hard, scaly legs that she was still clinging to.

All Nora could do was utter a little moan of disbelief. It was a dragon, a dinosaur, a monster from a nightmare. Raclin was gone—where? The monster had done something to him. A claw raked her cheek. Letting go of the creature's legs, she scrambled away, crablike, until she came up against the bed. She gripped the bedpost and pulled herself upright.

At first she thought that the creature filled the room, but then she saw that she was mistaken, its body wasn't much larger than a man's. It was the leathery wings, brushing the ceiling's plasterwork, that gave the impression of great size. Snapping its jaws, the thing dropped down to all fours, the joints of its legs protruding into the air, like a lizard's. Almost lazily, it took a few steps toward Nora, and then reared on its hind legs again. The creature turned its long, vicious head back and forth, fixing her with first one yellow eye, then another.

As she faced it, Nora had a terrible intuition. This outlandish, impossible monster that had made Raclin disappear—it *was* Raclin. Impossible, but the idea would not go away. She took a deep breath and cried out as loudly as she could: "Raclin! Raclin! Help me!" He must be nearby— perhaps hurt or stunned by the monster, but if he could hear her, he would surely come to rescue her. The creature opened its jaws again, showing the double row of teeth, as though it were laughing.

"Raclin?" she said fearfully, then bolted for the door. The thing was too quick, leaping in front of her. She could feel its claws on her body, tearing into the flesh of her arms and belly. Oh, no, the baby, she thought.

She struggled free and then slipped and went sprawling flat on the floor, so hard that the breath was knocked out of her. But she kept going, scissoring her legs, moving every limb like a swimmer.

Then she was through the door and in the hallway. She had the wild hope that the creature was too big to fit through the door frame, but it simply folded its wings and slipped through. Nora ran as fast as she could, the streamers of her torn nightgown flying. It was a long corridor, the walls painted with cherubs playing cat's cradle with pink and blue ribbons; they grinned at her as she fled past. She could hear the reptile thing loping along behind her, its claws clicking on the floor.

The hallway divided. Nora took the left-hand turn and found herself at the top of a marble staircase that curved downward into dimness. There were tall windows to her left, light just beginning to filter through them. It was the same ballroom where a few hours ago she had been watching the dancers and worrying about where Raclin might be; she wished that Raclin's indiscretions were all she had to worry about now. She started down the steps as fast as she dared, her body just bulky enough now to make her feel off-kilter. She couldn't hear the monster anymore; perhaps it had taken the other turn.

Then she looked up. The dragon creature swooped just over her head. With a scream, she dodged, and then screamed again as she lost her footing on the polished marble. Slipping, then tumbling, she rolled over and over down the cool, smooth stairs, and as she hit each new step, she thought, Now I can stop, but she kept falling anyway.

At the bottom, she rolled once more and lay still for a minute, panting. It hurt to breathe. She saw a flash of dark wings in the corner of her vision, and she tried to get up, but her right ankle refused to take any weight. She didn't want to think about what the fall might have done to the baby.

She lay back, clutching her stomach, listening to the sound of voices and running footsteps.

"Oh, Raclin." Ilissa stood at the top of the staircase, her hair fanning out loose over her white dress. She called out to the monster crouching on the ballroom floor, her voice shaking with fury: "What have you done?"

Nora was in her own bed again, staring up at the silk canopy, willing herself to believe that everything she remembered from the past few hours was a bad dream. The pain told her otherwise. There seemed to be half a dozen different kinds of hurt warring over her body. The one that was hardest to ignore was the paralyzing cramp that kept seizing her lower abdomen. The bedsheets were soaked, sticky.

People were crowded around the bed. Ilissa's face appeared, white and angry. She was shaking her head. "She's going to lose it."

Nora knew instantly what she meant. "No," she said feebly. "Please, no."

"Be quiet, you ungrateful, stupid girl." Someone leaned over to whisper to Ilissa. "No," she said harshly. "There's nothing to be done. We've failed again. *Again.*"

Other faces hovered over her and disappeared. Then Nora was alone. Time passed, measured in waves of pain.

Two voices that she knew, near the bed.

"Vulpin, what are you doing here? Ilissa will be looking for you. She's insane today. Insane."

"Moscelle?" There was surprise in Vulpin's voice. "Oh, I see. She's taken it out on you."

"She got the idea from what happened to *you.*"

"You don't look so bad. I got used to it. I sometimes wonder whether we should show our own faces more often."

"Ilissa will make you wear your own face forever, if she finds you here."

"My orders were always to look after Nora. Yours, too."

"Oh, you can't do anything more for her. Look at all the blood. How horrid." Moscelle came over to the bed and looked down. "Oh, Nora," she said in a different voice. "You're awake. How are you feeling, darling?"

Nora thought that the fog of pain must be affecting her vision. Three or four pairs of blue eyes seemed to be peering out of Moscelle's face. She tried to ask Moscelle about the baby, but none of the eyes showed any signs of understanding what she was attempting to say.

"She looks terrible," Moscelle said to Vulpin in an undertone. Nora couldn't hear his response. "Well, I liked her, too," Moscelle went on. "But we can't help her now. Come on."

Her light footsteps retreated across the floor, followed by Vulpin's heavier ones.

Nora lay there for a long time. No one else came. Everything was very quiet, except when the cramps made her groan. She felt weaker than she had before. It must be afternoon now, but the room seemed drained of color. Words drifted into her mind: And then I could not see to see. If Nora had had the strength, she would have howled in frustration, but now even the thought of doing something like that made her tired.

A small piece of dust floated across her sight. Ashes to ashes.

Not dust, a tiny gray feather, a piece of down from the pillow or the mattress. It hung stubbornly in the air over her face. Her breath made it tremble, but it only shifted its position in the air slightly.

Making an immense effort, Nora lifted her hand and took hold of the gray wisp between her thumb and forefinger. She looked at it carefully. Just a random feather.

What was the name? She couldn't even remember the name.

"Help me," she whispered. "You said you would help me."

She opened her fingers and let the feather go. Caught in an air current, it whirled away.

It would be nice to have some hope, gentle as the tickle of a feather against your skin, but it was hard to feel anything at all but the rhythm of pain. She closed her eyes, waiting for it to end.

## *Chapter 8*

The magician Aruendiel had a headache. The night before, he had worked late on a spell involving two of the constellations in the southern sky, the Weaver and the Goose, but the results were poor, the stars frustratingly unresponsive. Then he had slept poorly, the old injuries in his back giving him pain as they often did when he was tired. Shape changing gave him some relief, so before dawn he rose and flew into the forest. The exercise helped his back, but he misjudged the time, and by the time he got back to the castle, the morning sunlight had given him the beginnings of a headache, which persisted even after he changed himself back into a man and ate his usual breakfast of oatmeal and ale.

Despite the headache, he spent the morning reading in his study, the shutters half-closed against the midsummer sun. A friend had sent him a scroll that purported to be the autobiography of the ancient wizard

Rgonnish. It was certainly written in a very old dialect, which took a long time to read, but as Aruendiel got deeper into it, his initial suspicion that it was not Rgonnish's own work hardened into certainty. You could tell that the writer did not understand all the magic he was describing. Certain details were left out; in other places, the writer had included extraneous, useless information or crude shortcuts. Rgonnish would no doubt have been infuriated if he had known that his own name would ever be associated with such trash. Aruendiel was massaging the bridge of his crooked nose between two fingers, wondering if he should give in and use magic to dispel the headache, when a small gray feather drifted across his line of vision. He brushed it aside. Dodging his hand, the feather settled on the page in front of him and quivered meaningfully.

Aruendiel picked it up and studied it carefully. Then he sighed.

"I warned her," he said aloud. "She wouldn't listen. And now I'm expected to drop everything and rescue this fool of a girl because it turns out I was right all along." There was probably not much that he could do for her, anyway, he reflected. Years ago, Aruendiel had helped Lukl's father rescue one of Raclin's previous brides. She had gone mad and died anyway.

He let the feather go, but it remained suspended in the air. He blew on it. It refused to budge. Aruendiel's mouth twitched, and the feather turned into a pebble and dropped to the tabletop. He tossed it toward the window, but the pebble bounced off something and came skittering back to land next to his boot.

"All right," he said. "All right." He *had* promised to help, after all. And a good, rousing piece of magic would help his headache. He already felt a little better, thinking of how much his intervention would annoy Ilissa. He rose stiffly, went over to the fireplace, and threw a log onto the bare grate. Instantly it kindled, burning brightly. Ignoring the heat, Aruendiel lowered himself onto a chair and bent over the fire, gazing intently into the flames.

In the park around Ilissa's house, a breeze picked up, moving quickly through the trees, tossing leaves and limbs with more vehemence than breezes ever did in Ilissa's well-mannered domain. Ilissa, walking in the gardens with an uneasy entourage, was too busy scolding everyone within earshot to notice.

"—no appreciation of what I did for her," Ilissa told Oon. "She's a peasant, an animal! But you're worse. You're even stupider, and you don't even have the excuse of being human. This would never have happened if you had kept your hands off Raclin, or at least had the sense to behave with some discretion."

"Yes, ma'am," said Oon miserably. "But it was Raclin who—"

"Never mind what Raclin did. You should have known better. Oh, stop your crying, you despicable girl!"

A drop of water was trickling down Oon's cheek, but she shook her head. "I'm not crying," she said. "It's raining."

Ilissa looked up. The sky had blackened, and big drops were falling, leaving dark splotches on bright silks. What had been an energetic breeze was suddenly a gale, crashing through the trees like a wild animal, scattering leaves, breaking off branches. It swept past Ilissa and her companions, pawing at their hair and clothing, and then careened toward the house.

"Nora! Is anyone watching Nora?" Ilissa cried above the wind. "Moscelle? Vulpin? What are you doing here? Why aren't you watching Nora?" Obediently Vulpin turned to run, but checked himself as a tree smashed down on the path in front of him.

Dully, Nora listened to the rising wind and the clatter of rain against glass. It's been so long since I felt rain, she thought. Since I came here, nothing but sunshine. Her mouth felt as dry as paper. She wished that she could get out of bed and open the window and feel cool rain on her face, just once more.

The window frame creaked, first one corner, then another, almost as though the wind were deliberately testing it. Nora did not turn her head; it was too much effort.

There was a roar, then breaking glass. All at once the room was alive with rain and swiftly flowing air. Nora gasped and struggled to sit up, as the bed's canopy ripped away. The wind found her. It nudged, pushed, shoved her, so forcefully it felt as though she could touch it. The bedsheet wrapped itself around her, firmly and methodically, as though she were a letter being sealed into an envelope.

Someone pounded at the door and shouted, but the door did not open.

The torrent of air moved restlessly around the room, breaking chairs and tables into kindling, then into matchsticks. With another roar, it exited through the window, and Nora, gasping, went with it.

At first she thought she was falling. The upturned faces in the garden below her were startlingly close—Ilissa's among them, her mouth open and eyes brilliant with rage. Then they receded; Nora arced upward, higher and higher, skimming the treetops. So this is flying, she thought, strangely calm because this was too incredible to be real.

She had flown in dreams, but never so far or fast. Ilissa's palace dwindled. In a few minutes, Nora had left the rain behind, and she was moving over pastures flecked with small white and brown dots that were no doubt sheep and cows, perhaps the same animals that Ilissa had once demanded as reparations for Nora's capture. A village of huts with thatched roofs. A wide, shallow river, its bed full of round stones. More forest, then fields striped green with young crops. Fierce gusts of wind hurried her along, flinging her up and down like a ball. The fresh air made her feel better for a time, but the cramping and the other pains continued, and after a while she began to feel airsick. She closed her eyes wearily. Maybe flying was always unpleasant, even if you weren't on an airplane.

An hour or more had passed when she felt herself dip suddenly. Startled, she opened her eyes. The current of air that carried her had slowed, as though it were casting about, looking for something. Please, please don't drop me, she thought. There was another thatched-roof village below, surrounded by fields. A man driving a cart saw her and gave a cry. Farther ahead, she saw tree-covered hills out to the horizon.

The wind picked up speed again, shifting course toward a hilltop crowned with a stone structure. She had the confused impression of thick gray walls and towers; of smaller, gabled buildings inside the walls. A couple of dogs ran across the grass below, barking.

She swept toward the stone wall. She was going to hit it. No, she cleared the wall, then found herself dropping—too fast—into a dusty courtyard. Someone was waiting for her in the middle of it, a dark-clothed figure with a pale, dour, upturned face. The wizard.

He reached up and yanked her out of the air. The ground felt blessedly still and quiet after her flight, but when she tried to put weight on her injured leg, she screamed.

With a grunt, he hoisted her in his arms and carried her across the courtyard and through an open doorway, into a large room that was pitch-black after the sunshine outside. Even if he was trying to be gentle—which was not at all certain, Nora felt—she couldn't help groaning; it was fiercely painful to feel any pressure against her torn body.

"Mrs. Toristel," he called out, "I shall need you upstairs."

Nora felt herself jolted through the shadows, upward. Then she was lying in a bed again. "Drink this," someone said, and she drank thirstily, something milky, warm, and sweet.

There were two voices in the room, rising and falling, a man's and a woman's. Vulpin and Moscelle, debating what to do with her. Feebly, Nora rolled her head on the pillow, trying to get their attention. "Don't leave me," she tried to say. She had no idea whether they heard her.

Nora opened her eyes grudgingly. It seemed unfair to be wakened by her own cries, but there seemed to be no help for it. Her throat was sore. There were candles burning nearby.

By their light she made out the wizard stooping near the foot of the bed. His hands were glistening red. She heard a frail, high-pitched cry.

"What is it?" she asked, with a mad surge of hope: Ilissa had been wrong, her baby was alive. Struggling to sit up, she stretched out her right hand. "Oh, give it to me!"

The wizard glanced at her. She felt herself being pushed backward against her will. It was as though a large, powerful, invisible animal were sitting on her chest, keeping her pinned to the bed. She could still breathe, though, and she could scream.

She was tired, very tired of screaming and pain. None of it did any good.

The two voices were discussing her again. This time she could tell that they did not belong to Vulpin and Moscelle.

A gray-haired woman leaned over the bed, holding an earthenware cup. Nora could see every wrinkle in her face. It must be day now. Tasting the sweet liquid on her lips again, Nora swallowed.

A candle flared, and she saw the wizard standing beside the bed.

"Where's the baby?" she asked.

Without responding, he lifted her arm and felt her pulse. She shifted slightly in the bed, and realized that what was binding her body was only a series of bandages, on her leg, her torso, her hand, even her face. "Mind the wrappings," he said. "You were badly clawed."

She understood that by not answering her question, he had answered it. "The baby is gone, isn't it?"

The wizard's countenance was stony. "Count yourself fortunate."

She closed her eyes so that she wouldn't have to see his hateful face, so that she could be alone to cradle her grief.

Nora dreamed that she had had the baby after all, but somehow it had crawled away and gotten lost. She went searching for it, wandering through stone castles and the high-ceilinged ballrooms of Ilissa's palace and the corridors of the English department. Finally she found the baby, wrapped tight in blankets, in Ilissa's arms. "Give it to me," Nora demanded. Smiling, Ilissa refused: "This is my baby," she said. Nora reached out to take the baby back, but all she grasped was an empty blanket. The baby had vanished. "Now see what you've done," Ilissa said.

Daylight again. It was the gray-haired woman again, back with the cup. Nora took a sip and then pushed it away.

The woman shook her head and said something. She had to repeat it twice before Nora understood. "The master says you're to drink it all."

"I will. In a minute." Nora had to grope for the words. It was almost— not exactly—the way she had felt sometimes at Ilissa's, as though she had just run out of language. Brain damage, she thought, some kind of aphasia. So much for my career as an English professor.

"Where am I?" Nora asked carefully, and then listened hard to make sure that she understood the response.

"At Lord Aruendiel's house."

"The wizard?" Aruendiel, that was the name she hadn't been able to remember.

"Magician," the woman said. "He prefers 'magician.' "

"Are you his wife?"

The woman's face stiffened, as though she were shocked by the suggestion. "No, I tend house for him."

"What's your name?"

"My name is Mrs. Toristel."

"I remember. He called you when I came."

"Yes, that was me. Now, drink. It will help you rest."

Nora nodded. The short conversation had utterly exhausted her.

Mrs. Toristel came back in the late afternoon with another cup, but this time Nora refused to drink any of it.

"I don't want to sleep," she said. "I want to talk to the magician."

Mrs. Toristel frowned and set the cup on the wooden table next to the bed. "The master's not here. He probably won't return until late."

"I can wait."

"I'm leaving the house soon to make dinner for my husband. There won't be anyone here for you to call if you need help."

"I'll be fine."

Mrs. Toristel shrugged her thin shoulders. "I'll leave your draft here. You'll want it soon enough."

The housekeeper was right: As the hours passed, the soreness in Nora's body grew more persistent. She took inventory. Her right ankle was bound and splinted. The pain in her side whenever she took a deep breath must mean a broken rib. Carefully she felt the bandages on her stomach, right hand, and face. The flesh beneath was tender and hot.

The cramps were gone, and her belly was flat again. Well, as flat as it ever got. She was wearing a long, coarse nightshirt of what looked like unbleached linen. Idly she wondered what had happened to the clothes she had been wearing when she arrived—some silky, embroidered blossom of a nightgown.

The room she lay in now was small, with a ceiling crossed by wooden beams, ornamented with crudely geometric carvings of leaves and flowers. More flowers were painted in a frieze on the walls, much faded; in one corner water damage had washed away the paint and left a brown stain on the plaster. There was one window, a checkerboard of small panes. A mirror hung on the wall opposite the bed. The few pieces of furniture in the room—the bed, a trunk, a small table, and a chair—were made of wood, dark and heavy, and looked very old.

The light faded and the sky outside turned to bluish purple. Nora was almost ready to give up and take the draft when she heard the clop of a horse's hooves in the courtyard. More time went by before she saw a light through the crack under her door and heard footsteps outside.

The door opened and the magician came through it, carrying a candle in an iron candlestick. When he saw Nora looking up at him, he paused. "You're awake," he said, not sounding particularly pleased. "Did you not take the draft?" She had to concentrate to follow his words, just as with Mrs. Toristel.

"No. I want to talk to you."

"Ah." Putting the candle on the table, he pulled up the chair and took Nora's pulse, then probed the wrapping on her ankle. Apparently satisfied, he asked, "How are the bandages? Any leakage?" Nora shook her head. "Good. Mrs. Toristel can change your dressings tomorrow. Except—let me see to this one on your face right now." He reached over and unfastened the bandage, pulling it carefully away from her cheek. Then he produced a small square mirror from inside his black tunic and held it at an angle, evidently using it to look at her face.

"What are you doing?" Nora asked, raising her hand.

"Don't touch your face." From a drawer in the table he took a round clay jar and fresh bandages. He smeared something from the jar on Nora's cheek—it stung, a little—then checked the mirror again and began to fasten a new bandage, tying it around her head.

"What is the mirror for?" Nora asked.

"It's to let me see the cuts on your cheek."

"What do you mean?"

He finished knotting the bandage. "You had a fine collection of rather powerful enchantments on yourself, as I told you once before. I've been taking them off over the past few days, a few at a time. This last spell is one of Ilissa's glamours, rather deeply ingrained by now. It's meant to modify your appearance. In addition to bringing you up to Ilissa's own standard of beauty, the spell also camouflages your wound. Hence, the mirror. This particular mirror has certain properties that allow it to reflect what the eye cannot ordinarily see."

Nora thought about this, framing her next question. "What kinds of spells?"

Aruendiel shook his head. "The whole sorcerer's cookbook, although of course Ilissa doesn't use that kind of magic. There were several different glamours. Confusion spells, forgetfulness spells. Love spells. It looked as though she kept adding more magic, spells on top of spells, whenever she wanted to." He added severely, "Very sloppy—I would have expected better craftsmanship from her."

"Confusion spells?" she asked carefully, not sure that she had understood everything he had said. He nodded. "Forgetfulness spells? Love spells?" He nodded again.

That would explain a lot. That is, if there were such things as confusion spells or forgetfulness spells or love spells. "Did you take them all off?" she asked.

"Yes," he said. "All except this last glamour. If you prefer to retain your current appearance, you can, although I recommend against it. You've been exposed to more than enough magic for the present. Too much enchantment sickens the body."

"I'm still—" She stumbled and had to start again. The magician's cool gray stare didn't help her confidence. "I have trouble speaking. I can barely understand what you say."

Aruendiel shrugged. One shoulder moved more than the other. "She put a translation spell on you, too. Otherwise you wouldn't have been able to understand her or the other Faitoren. They speak a version of our common tongue, Ors—in addition to their own language, which I'm sure Ilissa did not permit you to understand. I removed the translation spell last night."

"We're not speaking English?" As soon as she said the word "English," she knew it was true. Her mouth had to reshape itself to pronounce the word, which came out sounding familiar and foreign at the same time.

"No," he said. "It's no wonder that you're having difficulty with Ors now. It's strange, in fact, that you can speak it at all. You must have picked up some knowledge of the language while you were speaking it under the spell."

"I've always been pretty good at languages," Nora said.

"Indeed," he said. He sounded skeptical.

There was a long pause. Nora sighed and looked down at her bandaged body. "So I dreamed it all? It wasn't real?"

"Oh, it was real enough. It wasn't exactly as you believed it to be, though. That is Ilissa's specialty. She traffics in illusion."

"The baby was real?"

"Yes."

She looked up directly into his eyes. "That was a terrible thing you said to me the other night."

Another uneven shrug. "It was true."

"But I wanted that baby so much."

He frowned. After a moment he said, his voice cold: "I know what it is to lose a child. But this baby would have killed you." There was another long silence. He pushed the chair back and stood up. "Well. Shall I remove the glamour, or are you content to remain as you are?"

"Oh," she said slowly, "take it off."

Aruendiel touched her chin with his finger, tilting her head back slightly. It seemed to Nora that his face darkened as he watched her, but she was more interested to find that she could feel a change in herself at once. The skin of her face seemed cooler, freer, despite the bandages. "That is better," she said.

"Good," he said, eyes narrowed. "Now drink your sleeping draft."

Nora raised herself on the pillow and reached for the cup with her left hand. "Is it magic?" she asked, sniffing the cup suspiciously.

"Poppy juice and honey and some herbs. No magic. Except—" He took the cup from her, held it for an instant, then gave it back to her. The cup was warm now.

For an instant the idea of drinking from it made her faintly alarmed, almost queasy, but she fought back the unease and took a sip, feeling the heat of the drink against her tongue. She shivered.

"Thank you," she said doubtfully.

He waited until she had finished, and then took cup and candle out of the room. In the darkness, Nora listened to the magician's footsteps moving away, one foot dragging a little, and then she was asleep.

## *Chapter 9*

Several days passed quietly. The housekeeper appeared at intervals at Nora's bedside, bringing more cups of the poppy-juice draft and, after a while, small meals on a wooden tray: broth, brown bread, stewed cherries. Nora ate obediently, but without any real enthusiasm. The food felt heavy and strange in her mouth. She had to remind herself to chew and swallow it.

Mrs. Toristel volunteered little on these visits, except for some terse commentary as she changed the dressings on Nora's torso. "You were lucky these didn't go deeper. Still inflamed."

Nora looked down incuriously. The raw red lines etched across her stomach, sewn with coarse thread, were like a map of some alien terrain. "Should I see a doctor?" A real doctor, not a magician.

Mrs. Toristel seemed faintly surprised at the notion. "There used to be a doctor in the market town, old Farcap, but he died of the dry plague two years ago."

Afterward, alone again, Nora went over in her mind what they had said. She still found it hard to believe that she could have learned a foreign language, the tongue the magician called Ors, without knowing it. Experimentally, she spoke to Mrs. Toristel in English the next time the housekeeper came into the room, but Mrs. Toristel gave her a blank stare. She tried some of the foreign languages she knew—French, German—but the other woman shook her head. "I don't know what you're saying," Mrs. Toristel said.

Giving up, Nora responded in the same language, the words assembling themselves slowly in her brain: "It was nothing. Never mind."

The poppy-juice drafts were smaller now and came only once a day. When Mrs. Toristel changed her dressings again, she seemed satisfied with how the wounds were healing. "Still hurt?" she asked, applying a new bandage.

Nora's body was still sore, but the pain was duller, more familiar. "It doesn't bother me," Nora said, truthfully enough. After that, the poppy juice stopped altogether.

Time passed more slowly. She stared at the painted walls. Someone had taken away the mirror on the opposite wall and hung a picture for her to look at: a portrait of a pretty black-haired girl in a blue dress. The style was flat, a little crude, but the painter had managed to capture something of the sitter's individuality. Her brown eyes looked into Nora's, sometimes with pity, Nora thought, sometimes with mocking amusement.

She listened to sounds from outside: the barking of dogs; the fussing of chickens; the thunk of horses' hooves; Mrs. Toristel, dry and quiet; the magician's deep tones; other people whom she could not identify. Early in the morning, when it was still gray outside, she heard owls calling. One afternoon Mrs. Toristel stood directly under Nora's window with another woman for half an hour engrossed in a disquisition on the current price and quality of flour, and Nora was hugely grateful for the diversion. The magician most often addressed his dogs, but she also heard him calling for Mrs. Toristel or her husband, who seemed to be in charge of the stables.

Nora had not seen Aruendiel since the night when he had rebandaged her face, which was something of a relief. Whenever she thought of how he had taken the cup into his hand and given it back to her steaming hot, she felt uncomfortable. The quick, casual gesture, replayed in her mind, frightened her because she understood only that it was impossible. Then there was her flight through the air, also hard to explain. In fact, her mind shied away from even trying. Either there was a rational explanation—or not, Nora thought.

Remembering the poppy juice, she had a refreshing inspiration. She had emptied some dull opiate to the drains, had she not? And dreamed a storybook world for herself. Flying through the air—a hallucination. So was the monster that attacked her. The man she had married. Ilissa, and all those strange, beautiful people. The wonderful clothes. Having a baby. Some element of wish fulfillment fueling the fantasies, probably. (How pathetic was that?)

At the thought of the baby, though, she felt sadness deep within her body, like the slow fatigue of illness. There was no baby, it was just a dream, Nora thought resolutely, but her flesh said otherwise. Then there was the gold ring on her left hand. Still, what did a ring prove, one way or the other? She tried to pull it off with her other, bandaged hand, but she couldn't get a good grip, and the ring refused to budge.

She found herself unexpectedly slipping into long crying jags. One day Mrs. Toristel, passing outside the door, came in to see what was wrong. Nora only shook her head mutely, overwhelmed at the idea of even trying to explain. Then she noticed what Mrs. Toristel was carrying.

"Oh, you have some books!" she said, sniffling, sitting up. "May I see them?"

"Oh, no, they're the master's—" Mrs. Toristel said, but Nora had already taken a book out of the housekeeper's hands. It was a small leatherbound volume, the covers embossed with two dragons facing each other across an oval seal. Sitting upright on their hind legs, they resembled two small dogs begging for scraps.

Nora leafed through the book greedily. Strings of elegant brushstrokes climbed the pages, an unknown alphabet that made as much sense to her as a handful of broken twigs. "Another one?" she asked. After a second's hesitation, Mrs. Toristel opened up a second volume, holding it out of Nora's reach. The same as the first book, except this one was printed, the cryptic letters roughly carved into woodblock.

"This is Ors?" Nora demanded. Mrs. Toristel nodded, frowning. "I can't read it. I can't read at all," Nora said. "I'm illiterate." She began to laugh, then to weep again.

Later the same afternoon, Mrs. Toristel came back with some clothes and spread them out on the bed for Nora to see. A pair of jeans, a T-shirt, some underclothing. "Losi in the village, that does the wash, she had quite a scare." The housekeeper's tone was faintly accusatory. "I gave her what you were wearing when you came, a nightie. Losi said she put it to soak and when she came back, it had changed into these things."

Nora recognized her Eno River festival T-shirt. "How did these get here? I wasn't wearing them when I came."

"No, you wore a nightie. Silk, with little pearls. Losi said to me, 'I hope you don't think I stole that nightie, ma'am. I swear I didn't. I didn't leave it for five minutes, and it was gone and these other clothes were in its place.' She felt terrible, she knew that nightie was valuable, but the master said it was nothing she did, the clothes must have changed back when he took those spells off you."

"What does he mean? That my nightgown was really jeans and a T-shirt?" The same jeans and T-shirt that Nora had put on that far-off morning in the mountain cabin, just before she went walking in the woods and met Ilissa.

Mrs. Toristel shrugged. "You look different now than when you came. It's the same with your clothes, I expect."

"How do I look different?" Nora asked quickly.

"Well, your hair. It was yellow when you came. Now it's brown, mostly. Still yellow at the ends."

Most of Nora's hair was bound to her head by the bandages on her face. Now she pulled a thick strand loose. The hair fell past her shoulders. "It's gotten so long," she said, surprised. "Could I have a mirror? There was one in this room before, where that portrait is now."

"That portrait? I didn't take away the mirror," the other woman said, looking puzzled. "You can't see much of your face anyway, with all those bandages."

And under the bandages? "Mrs. Toristel, these cuts, how bad are they?"

"They're healing nicely," she said. "And they'll heal faster if you don't worry yourself sick about them. Anyway, I thought you'd want to know what happened to your clothes. Losi worked hard to get them clean. They were very dirty," she said with a sniff, "in addition to all the blood-stains. She mended the rips, too."

After Mrs. Toristel was gone, Nora spent a long time turning the clothes over in her lap. Yes, Losi had done a good job. Surely no one had ever mended a T-shirt with such care. Nora spread her fingers into a claw and placed her hand over the places that had been torn. Her hand was too small to cover them. There were more of Losi's neat stitches along the inside seams of the jeans. At some point, someone must have ripped out those seams. Were they too snug to accommodate an expanding belly?

If the magician was right, she had been wearing the same jeans and T-shirt for months. Ilissa had simply recycled them into dozens of delecta-ble, extravagant outfits, one after another.

Or, Nora thought—getting a grip on herself—wasn't it more logical to assume that she had simply been wearing jeans and a T-shirt when she ar-rived here, at this place? She'd had an accident on the mountain. Now she was recuperating in a hospital or rehab facility. The man she'd imagined was a magician was really a doctor; Mrs. Toristel was a nurse. Brain dam-age would explain why she couldn't read, why she had trouble understand-ing speech; the whole idea of this foreign language, Ors, might be a self-protective fantasy she'd contrived to shield herself from knowledge of her new limitations.

Why this particular fantasy? Nora wondered. She had never much cared for fiction in the swords and sorcerers vein. When she'd had to read *Lord of the Rings* for Goldstein's Modern Myths, she thought it was a bad joke, some of Tolkien's falsely archaic language was so painful to read. A flash of bittersweet memory: EJ playing Dungeons and Dragons in the den on Sat-urday nights with his friends, a bunch of guys huddled around the coffee table, utterly absorbed. All geeks—Nora could tell, even at twelve—though some of them were cute and didn't know it. D&D was the one interest of EJ's that she couldn't get. That and physics. Maybe, she thought clinically, her injured brain had hurled her into this magical, medieval-style hallucination as a long-delayed expression of grief for her dead brother. But in that case, wouldn't she have come across EJ himself by now?

I wish I were in a fantasy with real bathrooms, at least, she thought. Even Ilissa had indoor plumbing.

She looked closely at Mrs. Toristel the next time the older woman came into the room, trying to see the nurse within. It was not easy. Mrs. Toristel was old for a nurse, stiff in the joints, with the kind of yellowish gray hair that meant she'd once been a redhead. As hard as Nora stared, the house-keeper's ankle-length dress refused to resolve into a nurse's scrubs. When Nora asked her directly whether this place was really a hospital, the woman looked at her incredulously. "Nothing like that around here. I never heard of such a thing."

"You'd think they'd be encouraging me to abandon this fantasy, wouldn't you?" Nora demanded of the girl in the portrait, after the door closed behind Mrs. Toristel. The black-haired girl's half smile was especially mocking today. "Maybe you're not real, either," Nora continued, switching into English. "You don't look like something that would be hanging in a hospital room. Or maybe you are a mirror, but my mind won't admit it because I'm afraid to look at my scarred face."

It was late afternoon, and sunlight streamed through the window's thick panes, throwing a bath of light on the wall where the portrait hung. And the portrait in turn reflected an oblong of light onto the ceiling.

But the picture was unglazed, Nora noticed; there was no glass in the ornate black frame. She watched the patch of reflected light until the sun moved on and it faded.

When Mrs. Toristel came in that evening, bearing a tray of food, Nora was ready. "Where am I?" she asked. "I mean, what is the name of this place, this area?"

Mrs. Toristel pursed her thin lips as she settled the tray of soup and brown bread on Nora's lap. It seemed to be a question that she hadn't considered previously. "When I lived in Pelagnia as a girl, we called this the Northlands," she said finally. "But that would mean a very large territory, from the sea all the way to the Ice. Right around here, they call this area the Uland, after the river Uel. Most of the master's lands fall inside the Uland."

None of these names meant anything to Nora. "What cities are near here?"

That was Red Gate, the market town, Mrs. Toristel said. Three hours away on foot. Barsy, where her daughter lived, and Stone Top, the next market town. "I don't know what comes after that," she added. "I haven't traveled beyond Barsy myself since coming to live here. The king's seat is at Semr, but that's a long way away. Several days on horseback."

"There's no king," said Nora. She now felt on solid ground. "There's no king, I bet there are no towns called Barsy or Stone Top or Red Gate, and I don't think that man Aruendiel can do magic. This is all bullshit." Apparently the word for bullshit was a lot worse in Ors than in English, because Mrs. Toristel looked genuinely shocked. But then there was no such language as Ors, Nora reminded herself. "Can't you just tell me the truth?" she went on. "Where are we? How do I get to I-40 from here? Or Asheville?"

But Mrs. Toristel disclaimed all knowledge of I-40 or Asheville or—upon further questioning—even the United States of America.

"You're lying or you're crazy, then," said Nora. "Or maybe you don't know anything about geography. Maybe you really believe there's a king, or that your precious master is a magician. I don't have to believe it, though."

"You should calm down."

"I'm sorry, you've been kind to me, and I don't mean to insult you. But this is all insane."

Mrs. Toristel said nothing, the wrinkles around her eyes deepening as she looked at Nora.

"I want to go home!" Nora cried out. "Where things are real, where they don't change. Nightgowns don't turn into jeans, or—look," she added, pointing. "That picture on the wall, it's not a picture. It's a mirror. I'll prove it." Picking up the spoon, she aimed it at the portrait and sent it spinning through the air. There was the sound of breaking glass, and a web of black cracks shot across the girl's pale, fine-boned face. A triangular shard containing most of the girl's left shoulder fell to the floor.

"You see?" Nora said triumphantly.

"There was no call to do that," Mrs. Toristel said. "You're overexcited. You need some rest. Give me the tray, and you can lie down again."

"Take it. I don't want it, anyway." She gave the tray a great shove just as Mrs. Toristel bent to take it. A second crash, crockery hitting the floor. The front of Mrs. Toristel's brown dress was several shades darker, soaked with hot soup.

"Oh," Nora said, frozen with shock, her hand stopped in midair.

"Excuse me," Mrs. Toristel said through folded lips. She looked down at her stained skirts, then turned and left the room.

Nora looked at the shattered bowl and the puddle of broth on the floor, surprised by her own sudden talent for destruction. Some minutes passed, and Mrs. Toristel did not reappear. Was she burned? With a feeling of guilt, Nora pushed aside the bedclothes and tried to swing her legs onto the floor. At least she could clean up part of the mess she had made. She was surprised by how weak she felt, how hard the floor was.

"Stop that this instant." It was the magician, or whatever he was. For an instant she wondered seriously whether he might have materialized out of thin air. But no, the door was closing behind him.

"I was going to clean it up."

He came closer to the bed on uneven steps. "Very considerate. After throwing a bowl of soup at my housekeeper, you decide to tidy up."

"I didn't throw it on purpose. It was a mistake."

"I see. Was throwing the spoon a mistake, too?"

From her perch on the edge of the mattress, Nora had to tilt her head back to look Aruendiel in the face, but she refused to be intimidated. "I meant to do that."

"That's how you like to amuse yourself, is it? Breaking things? Abusing my housekeeper?"

"Is she all right?"

"She is not injured, no thanks to you. She is not accustomed to having her veracity or her sanity questioned, however. Personally, I would never dream of doing so. I have known few people in my life to be as completely reasonable and truthful as Mrs. Toristel."

"Well, what she was saying didn't make sense. I want to know what's going on. I want to see a real doctor, and I want to call my friends and my parents. Or am I a prisoner here?"

"You're no prisoner," he said irritably. "The sooner your family and friends can take you off my hands, the better. Where are they?"

"My mother lives near Richmond. My father is in New Jersey."

The magician looked even more annoyed. "Are those cities south of the Middle Lakes?"

"They're in the United States of America," Nora snapped. "You've never heard of that, either, I suppose. Well, either you and Mrs. Toristel are lying to me—or you're crazy—or I am."

"Given your behavior—"

"—and I'm not crazy," Nora said. "I know I'm not. *Something* happened to me at Ilissa's, and I wasn't in my right mind then. But I am now. I feel like me again. Everything feels ordinary. Except it's not. Like that picture. It's really a mirror. There's some kind of trick here. That's why I threw the spoon."

"Ah, so that was your logic." Aruendiel raised an eyebrow.

"You see how it broke?" She pointed at the damaged picture. "It's made of glass."

"How do you know it was not painted on glass?"

"Oh," said Nora, discomfited. "But I saw the picture reflect light, like a mirror. Painted glass wouldn't do that."

"Is that what you saw?" Aruendiel asked absently. He walked over to where the picture hung and picked up the broken piece from the floor, then fitted it into the empty space in the portrait. As he worked it back into position, the dark crackling disappeared from the girl's face, until the portrait was whole and unblemished again. The black-haired girl's red lips curled with more amusement than ever.

"You fixed it!" Nora said. "What did you do?" She knew already, though; there was a sick sensation in the pit of her stomach.

"I could tell you, but you wouldn't believe me," Aruendiel said. "It's what you would call a trick." He lifted the picture from its hook on the wall and regarded it with care. It was hard to read the expression in his battered face.

"If you mean magic," Nora said awkwardly, "there's no such thing. How can there be? It's not logical."

Aruendiel made an impatient noise deep in his throat. "You're a fool," he said after a moment. "But you're right in one respect. This is not a portrait, exactly—it only looks like one."

He turned the frame in his hands and showed it to her. The black-haired girl was gone. The silver skin of a mirror caught the light and gave Nora a glimpse of her own bedraggled figure sitting upright on the edge of the bed. "Until a few days ago, this was a mirror. Then I thought it might be better not to have a mirror in this room, so I made it look like a portrait—doing a rather clumsy job of it. It was clever of you to notice that reflection and re-alize what it meant. It's too bad you're not clever enough to see and under-stand some of the other things in front of your eyes." His voice was quiet, flat with contempt.

Nora swallowed and said the first thing that came into her head. "Who was the girl?"

"What?" Aruendiel looked puzzled.

"The girl in the portrait."

"Oh," he said, with a shake of his head. "My sister. I suppose I remem-bered an old portrait of her. This was her room." His face settled into harsher lines. One side had been scarred somehow, seamed and roughened. It was hard to see the resemblance between him and his pretty sister, except for the dark hair and something about the tilt of the head. He spoke with-out emotion, but from the way he said this was her room, Nora understood that his sister was dead.

"Why did you get rid of the mirror?" Nora said. "No, I know why. Because of my face." Odd that he would be so considerate, but then obvi-ously he had no reason to like mirrors himself. "Could you give it to me, please?" She reached for it. Aruendiel hesitated, then walked over to hold the mirror in front of her.

At first, it wasn't as bad as she had feared. No sign of the shimmering blond goddess that she'd been, but that was all right. Under the bandage, she could see the contours of her old face again: hazel eyes and straight brown brows, a wide mouth, a squarish chin. The skin of her face had a mottled, yellowish look, a tracery of fading bruises. And the great white slash of the bandages hiding her cheeks and nose.

"I'm taking this off," Nora said, scrabbling at the bindings behind her head.

Aruendiel hesitated, then said: "As you will."

Nora looked into the mirror again. Mrs. Toristel was right, the wounds were healing, but the two long cuts across her cheek still had a raw look. Garish and pitiful, they made the rest of her face invisible. "Huh," she said finally. "Will they scar?"

"I don't know," he said. "But the flesh is healthy. You can leave the ban-dage off now."

Looking up at the broken places in his face, she wondered whether her question about scarring had been rude, but he gave no sign of offense. He returned the mirror to the wall.

"What happened to the portrait of your sister, the real one?"

"I haven't seen it for years," he said. "Now, what was the name of the last place you mentioned?" He garbled the name. "Is that near a place called Galifornia?"

"California!" Nora said with a delighted gasp. "Yes, California is one of the states, the United States. You know California? Are we in California?"

"I have been there, many years ago," he said. "From there—let me think—I went to a city called Chigago."

"Chicago, yes," she said. "I have a friend there."

"And eventually I went farther east and sailed across the ocean to another country whose name I can't recall now."

"France, England? That's wonderful. I knew I didn't just fall off the end of the earth."

Aruendiel gave her a tight half smile. "But I'm afraid that's exactly what you've done. Galifornia and Chigago are not in this world at all. I traveled there and came back by very strong magic. As you must have come here by magic, Ilissa's magic or some other kind."

Nora stared at him. She shook her head. "What?"

"Now I see why you are so skeptical of magic. Before I visited your world, I had never been to a place whose inhabitants were so abysmally ignorant of magic."

Was he trying to be insulting? "Well. It's not something I've ever had any use for."

Downstairs, Aruendiel pushed open the door of the kitchen, where Mrs. Toristel was kneading dough. On the table in front of her, he set the glazed bowl that Nora had broken. It was whole again, filled with the soup that she had spilled on the floor.

"You may disregard what I said earlier, Mrs. Toristel," he said. "My guest will remain with us for now, although I must apologize again for the way she mistreated you." He brooded for a moment. "The girl is from a different world, I gather. It would be remiss to turn her out of doors without friends or connections."

Mrs. Toristel acknowledged his apology with a slight bob. "A different world, sir? Well, that goes a long way to explaining the odd things she says. She's been very quiet in general, so today when she threw the bowl I thought I'd better let you know."

"She seems rational enough now, but it's hard to say how these things will go," Aruendiel said with some exasperation. Saving the life of an innocent was all very well, he thought; the aftermath of a rescue was often tedious and less satisfying. "I took enough Faitoren spells off her to make a cat bark. Just to be safe, you should get someone from the village to help you with the girl," he added. "Who was that tall girl who was helping Toristel with the shearing? She took a firm line with the old ram. Very impressive."

"That's Morinen, Corlil's daughter. Four brothers and she's bigger than any of them."

"That's the one. Get her to handle the trays and such," Aruendiel said, turning toward the door. "Again, I'm sorry for the extra trouble this has caused you."

"Oh, this one's easier than some of the folks who've come to you for treatment," Mrs. Toristel said, covering the dough with a cloth.

"Oh? Do you mean the fellow who sang all the time?"

"No, he had a pleasant voice. I was thinking of the lady with the snakes in her hair."

"Lady Asnoria Ulioran, with the Medusa syndrome? My dear Mrs. Toristel, you realize that none of those snakes were actually poisonous."

"Ah," said Mrs. Toristel. "They could still bite."


# Chapter 10


**D**ear Maggie," Nora said aloud, but speculatively, as though she were uncertain of how her voice might sound. She was crouching in the reddish brown soil of the vegetable garden, pulling weeds among the long rows of turnips, beets, and parsnips. The back of her linen dress and the inside of her straw hat were already damp with sweat. It was chilly at night, though, even when the days were hot.

*Maggie, it's Nora. I can't mail you a letter, so I'm just going to speak it aloud, well, because I wish I could talk to you. Also, I miss speaking English. I don't even really know how long it's been since I saw you. Six months? Longer?*

*I'm living in the country. Which country or how I got here—that's complicated.*

Somehow she had begun to get used to the idea that she was living in a world different from the one that she'd been born in—even if she still didn't see how that was possible. Maybe EJ and his physics-loving brain could have explained it to her.

*The place where I'm staying is a castle. Yes, I know, it sounds romantic.*

Nora raised her head to look up the hill toward the high, windowless stone wall that wrapped tightly around the towers and buildings inside. The castle's utilitarian function—keeping enemies out—was starkly clear, even though now, at midday, the heavy gates stood open.

To the north, she could glimpse the edge of the cliff on which the castle was built, and if she listened hard, she could hear the sound of the small river that flowed two hundred feet below. She turned to look in the opposite direction, at the unpaved road that wound from the castle gates past sloping fields and pastures to a small village, a collection of thatched roofs.

When Nora had first been able to walk again, after hobbling around for some weeks with a crutch, she'd had the notion of going to the village to try to find someone or something that might help her get home. A car, a telephone, might be too much to hope for, but there was no harm in seeing for herself whether she was as far from all modernity and civilization and rationality as she seemed to be. She gave that idea up the first time that she walked down the muddy lane that served as the village's main street, passed a line of barefoot children waiting to draw water from a well, and caught a whiff of the latrines behind the whitewashed huts.

*When you go through the castle gates, you find yourself in a courtyard with a big stone tower to your left. Straight ahead is the manor house. Go through the doors and you're in the great hall.*

It was the sort of cavernous gray space that Nora usually associated with parking garages or old train stations. The trussed roof was high enough for a second-floor gallery to crouch darkly at one end of the room.

A long table ran almost the length of the hall, with benches on either side and a single tall, heavy chair at one end. On the wall parallel to the table was an enormous fireplace, big enough, Nora imagined, to give a convincing impression of the mouth of hell when it was in use.

*The kitchen is next door. Stone flags, copper pots, a fireplace, a huge farm table. It would look spectacular in a decorating magazine. All it needs is a Viking refrigerator, an Aga, maybe some recessed lighting—and a good scrubbing.*

Flies made graceful, unhurried sweeps through the open windows, as though they felt very much at home. In one corner was a red-and-white ceramic stove. Fresh straw on the floor, mixed with feathers and a few gnawed bones. Wrinkled sausages hung from the ceiling beams, as well as some strings of dried, fleshy things that looked very much like human ears and fingers. Mushrooms, Nora hoped.

*My room is upstairs, along a hallway with other bedrooms.*

One of the rooms must be the magician's; she had heard his footsteps passing at night. Nora had an irrational fear that at some point she would be walking along the corridor and a door would open and he would come out, a long shadowy figure with pale eyes.

*There are stables and barns behind the manor house. Yes, horses—you'd like that! And then there are the towers along the wall. Most of them are empty, with leaky roofs, except for the big one. But I haven't been inside it yet.*

Something about the construction of the tallest tower, the way its unmortared stones fit together, made Nora think that it must be the oldest part of the complex. It served the magician as some sort of workspace, judging from things that Mrs. Toristel had said.

What sort of room a magician might do his work in, Nora had no idea. She pictured, at random: a telescope, smoldering incense, one of those lacquered cabinets in which beautiful young ladies vanished, candles with pentagrams carved into them, the dried mushrooms from the kitchen. Then one night, getting ready for bed, she glanced out her window and saw a light in one of the tower windows. It was close enough, just across the courtyard, that she could see clearly what the tower room contained.

Books. An entire wall of books, their bindings rich and lustrous in the light from unseen candles. Nora stared hungrily for long minutes. It did her no good to remind herself that she could read none of them. Once she saw the magician's lean figure shamble across the window; his hand plucked a book from the shelves and he disappeared. What was he reading?

Perhaps something incredibly dull. It didn't matter; Nora still felt the bite of envy. She used to be able to do that—sit in a clean, well-lighted room, choose a book from hundreds, start reading, and effortlessly take herself to another world. And now she was actually in another world, and she might never read another book again.

*I've been here for a little over two months, as near as I can figure, given that the months here are different and the weeks have six days. But I'm still very much an outsider here. I've only gotten to know one person who's even close to me in age.*

A tall girl with wide shoulders had started bringing Nora her meals after the soup incident. She spoke Ors with an accent so much broader than that of either Mrs. Toristel or Aruendiel that it took several tries before Nora was sure that she had grasped the girl's name correctly: Morinen. It was clear enough why she had replaced Mrs. Toristel. Once Nora asked for a knife to carve a piece of mutton, but Morinen shook her head. They did not trust her with sharp objects, evidently.

But Morinen had a ready smile and, unlike Mrs. Toristel, she had a propensity to linger, happy to talk to Nora in her near-incomprehensible speech about her brothers, her neighbors in the village, the goats she looked after, the weather, the crops, what Mrs. Toristel had said to her that morning. Nora's Ors vocabulary included far more words having to do with dress, dancing, and court etiquette than with agriculture; listening to Morinen, she began to pick up other things—like the twelve different Ors words for sheep and the apparently inexhaustible number of ways to indicate whether it was likely to rain.

Morinen was curious about Nora, too. Her arrival in a gust of wind had been discussed widely in the village. Still distrustful of her own memories, Nora said only that she was far from home, that she had been a captive, and that Aruendiel had helped her escape.

That shut down further inquiry: The one subject that Morinen was reluctant to discuss at any length was the magician. "I don't exactly know," she said when Nora asked how he had acquired his limp or his scars or even how long he had lived in the castle. Once Morinen mentioned the handsome blacksmith in the next village; part of his attraction seemed to be that he was the only single man for miles around taller than she was. "There's the magician," Nora pointed out teasingly. Morinen didn't laugh; she looked anxious. Nora tried to smooth over what was obviously a bad joke by saying, "He's rather old for you, though," and then Morinen seemed even more uncomfortable.

*Right now I'm weeding the vegetable garden. Earlier I mucked out the chicken house. There's not much in the way of indoor plumbing here. No electricity, either. I have exactly two changes of clothing, hand-me-downs from the housekeeper. I would kill for a shower, but I've gotten used to smelling riper than I used to. There is, at least, a kind of communal bathhouse near the river, with a couple of big hot tubs, except they're not hot. I'll go there this afternoon to get rid of any lingering essence of chicken shit.*

Nora calculated that if she went to the bathhouse late enough so that the villagers would be fixing or eating supper, there would be no one to see the scars on her face and body. She was tired of being stared at. Every time she went to the village, even with Mrs. Toristel, she could feel the eyes of the villagers on her and hear occasional whispers as she passed.

"What are they looking at?" she asked Mrs. Toristel once, as they walked back to the castle.

"They hardly see any strangers, dear, and they know you've come from another world."

"What is there for them to look at, though?" Nora protested. "I don't look that different from them." She was dressed the same, in shabby wool or linen dresses; she was only a little taller; she wasn't much cleaner. True, her teeth were straight, and she had all of them, but that hardly seemed like a reason to stare.

"There is something different about you, though," Morinen said when Nora brought up the same point to her.

"What do you mean? Is it the scars?"

"Oh, no, everyone has seen scars." Morinen thought for a while. "No, it's something about the way you move or the way you look at things. It's different."

"How different?"

"Ah, it's so clear, but it's hard to put it into words. You seem so bold."

"Bold?" Nora was pleased, but had to admit: "That doesn't sound like me."

"Well, you don't act like a woman. You act like you're not afraid of men. You look them right in the eye, and you don't drop your voice, and you speak to them like you're a man."

Nora was speechless for a second. She always said hello to the village men she passed. "You don't act as though you're afraid of men, either."

"Well, I'm not," Morinen said with a laugh. "Most of the men are afraid of me, 'cause I'm so big. Ma is always after me to be more ladylike, not to talk so much in front of the men."

"Why shouldn't you talk in front of them?"

"Yes, well, Ma isn't known for holding her tongue, either. But she talks this certain way. Sort of quiet and respectful and cautious, like I said, and that makes it all right."

"So I act too much like a man, is that right?"

"Not like a man. More like a little boy."

Nora laughed out loud. But in the bathhouse, naked among the other women, she still felt self-conscious about the long, rough scars on her torso. Some version of her stay among the Faitoren had circulated, that was evident. Some of the other women looked sympathetic; others seemed almost amused by the marks on her body. "What did you expect?" their sly glances seemed to ask. In all the stories in literature and mythology about women being offered as tribute to beasts or monsters, no one ever spelled out exactly what that meant, or what it might be like for the woman afterward.

*This place belongs to a person named Aruendiel—excuse me, Lord Aruendiel. He's away right now, on some kind of job.*

Helping a merchant in Leorica get rid of the sea monsters that were wrecking his ships, Mrs. Toristel had said.

*He's a curious character. Um—*

Nora pulled a couple of weeds as she considered what to say next. If she said straight out, "He's a magician," Maggie—even imaginary Maggie—would doubt her sanity.

She thought about the last time she'd seen Aruendiel, the day he left. She'd been sitting in the great hall when Aruendiel came in, Mrs. Toristel trotting behind him. "—a few weeks at sea," he was saying. "I expect to return before the harvest. It's probably the work of a sea hag, but the ocean turns up all kinds of quirky magic. We shall see."

"Yes, sir, I'll pack some of your winter things, for the damp," Mrs. Toristel said distractedly. "You'll want the new boots that Cobbler just sent over. And before you go, Big Faris and Lumper from the village came here, saying there's grasshoppers in the wheat."

Aruendiel groaned. "Grasshoppers! Can they not raise a single crop without my aid?"

"They were wondering, sir, if you would be so kind as to send some birds to eat the grasshoppers, the way you did last year."

"I can do that, but then what? Last year, they complained about the birds after the grasshoppers were gone. How about this: I'll turn the villagers into crows, and they can eat the damned grasshoppers."

He turned and walked straight into the wall. The gray stone engulfed his frame like water, and he was gone.

After Mrs. Toristel had gone upstairs, Nora went over to the wall where the magician had disappeared and touched the freckled granite. It was solid and cool beneath her fingertips. She put her ear to the wall and thought she heard a distant, retreating footstep.

Into the silence that followed, Nora said quickly: "Open Sesame." Then, louder: "Open Sesame!" She waited.

The wall waited with her, quiet, impermeable. Nora gave the granite an experimental smack with the side of her fist. Then she rubbed her hand ruefully. It stung.

Later that day, after Aruendiel had ridden away, she brought herself to ask Mrs. Toristel whether she, too, ever found the magic unsettling. "I saw him walk straight through the wall! Doesn't that bother you? And I heard what he said about turning the villagers into crows."

"Ah, yes, the wall, that's the entrance to his tower," Mrs. Toristel said, unperturbed. "There used to be a door there, and then he had it sealed up, and now you can only get into the tower by magic. Safer that way, he says. I've gone through that wall myself many times. It's like walking through smoke. But that's only if he wants to let you in."

"Would he really turn those people into crows?"

"That was his jest. Although, it's true, the villagers would not think it funny."

Actually, there seemed to be surprisingly little magic in daily use in the magician's household. "Why doesn't he actually do something useful with his magic?" Nora asked. "Why do *you* have to do any work? Why doesn't he just do some magic and poof, the castle would be clean?"

"He would love that as much as killing grasshoppers. Now that you say it, I do remember, when I first went to work for him, I thought it would be an easy berth, with him being a magician. I thought there'd be all kinds of, oh, spirits and demons to do the hard jobs, or maybe I'd learn some spells and my work would be done. It wasn't that way at all. Same old sweeping and scrubbing as at home. But there was a bigger staff in those days, at Lusul."

*Maggie, I guess I'll tell you more about Aruendiel later. I've been spending most of my time with the housekeeper, Mrs. Toristel. We had a rocky start, but now we get along okay.*

*You did tell me that I should go back to cooking.*

True, Mrs. Toristel had looked a shade alarmed the first time she came into the kitchen and found Nora holding a knife, slicing plums. With a deliberate movement—hoping to impress the housekeeper with her sanity—Nora put the knife down and said mildly that she had smelled the vinegar syrup on the stove and seen the baskets of fruit on the table, only some of it peeled and sliced, and would it be all right if she helped make the preserves?

Mrs. Toristel watched Nora closely at first and did not hesitate to offer precise directions on how plum skins should be removed, but by the end of the afternoon she had unbent enough to fill Nora in on the state of Mr. Toristel's rheumatism, the two or three most misguided ways of making preserves, and Morinen's prospects of marrying the blacksmith. (Poor, according to Mrs. Toristel. The miller's daughter had her eye on him, too.)

"You're not slow with the knife," Mrs. Toristel said, with approval. "You must have done this kind of work before."

A whole set of questions was folded into that statement. "I worked as a cook, a couple of years ago," Nora said. "Before I was, um, a fairy princess."

"Ah," said Mrs. Toristel, as though this were a well-established career progression. "Well, I can always do with some help in the kitchen. As long as you don't strain yourself, now," she added severely. "I don't want *him* blaming me if your leg won't heal properly."

It was clear who *him* was. Nora remembered the way the English department secretary always referred to the department chair simply as "she": "Oh, hello. You'll have to wait. She's running a little behind."

And *I'm back to the magician again*, Nora thought, twisting a stubborn root out of the earth.

*I still don't know much about Aruendiel—Lord Aruendiel. Mrs. Toristel has told me a little. No family. A widower. I'm not sure how old he is. She's worked for him her whole life, I gather.*

Morinen would never have lasted a day at Lusul, she was a good-hearted girl, but far too careless, Mrs. Toristel observed irritably one day, after Morinen let the bread burn.

"What's Lusul? A city?" Nora asked. She had heard Mrs. Toristel mention the name before.

"Lusul was his estate," Mrs. Toristel corrected her. "Very grand it was, with good farms all around, not like this place. Plenty of staff to keep it up. My job was to keep the fires going and the rooms swept and dusted in just one wing of the house. There was another girl for the other wing, and another for the bedrooms. And I had to keep all the vases filled with fresh flowers. Her ladyship was so fond of flowers. That was the first magic I ever saw his lordship do, growing roses and such in the middle of winter." Mrs. Toristel's wrinkled face brightened. Nora asked how she got the job. "Ah, that was a kindness of his lordship and his wife's. My father had died, and I was the oldest, twelve. We had an old connection with his lordship's family, and when we heard that he would be getting married and living at Lusul, my mother wrote to him and asked if there might be a place for me in the household.

"Well, she didn't write to him," Mrs. Toristel corrected herself. "She had one of our neighbors, who was in trade, write to him and read the letter to her when it came back. It was her ladyship who wrote back to say yes. I said to my mother how funny it was to think of a woman writing a letter, but she said that great ladies learned how to read and write, some of them."

Nora couldn't help saying that she could read and write, but Mrs. Toristel only looked sharply at her. "When I showed you those books, you said you couldn't read them."

"I can read perfectly well in my own language. I've spent years in school, in fact."

"I thought you said you'd been a cook."

"I've done that, too."

"Well, I know how to read, too, a bit," Mrs. Toristel said with a sniff. "The master taught me, so that I could keep the accounts for him. But there's no call to read or write unless you're a magician or a lawyer or a merchant, maybe."

Job opportunities for English professors: zero. What did it signify, Nora reflected grimly, that she would wind up in a place—real or imagined—where she could not practice the occupation for which she had spent years preparing? But something else that Mrs. Toristel said had caught her attention. "So his wife—the Lady Aruendiel—"

"Lady Lusarniev Aruendielan." Mrs. Toristel embarked on a brief explanation of family names and titles among the aristocracy. "All right, I see," Nora said when the other woman was finished. "What of her? Is she—" She paused politely, but with something wriggling urgently at the back of her memory. Something she'd heard back in that hazy time among the Faitoren.

"Ah, well," Mrs. Toristel said, a little stiffly, "sad to say, their marriage didn't last long." Nora looked at her inquisitively, but Mrs. Toristel pressed her lips together, as though to keep the answer from tumbling out. "I don't like to gossip about his lordship's private affairs."

"Oh, no, of course not," said Nora.

"It's not what he pays me for."

"Certainly not."

"There are some who'd tell you all kinds of terrible stories about him."

"That's too bad," Nora said sympathetically. "Of course, if there are terrible rumors out there, it's good to know the truth."

"Well, all I'll say," said Mrs. Toristel with a nod, "is that some people take their marriage vows less seriously than others. It causes a lot of heartache, but that's the way of the world."

"I know it," Nora said. She pulled at the ring on her finger, as she had gotten into the habit of doing. As usual, it stayed put—this was starting to be seriously annoying. "So he—?"

"No, *she*," Mrs. Toristel corrected. "Devastated, he was. He came home and she wasn't there. Gone. Off with another man. One of his closest friends.

"I remember how his lordship walked into the house that day, never suspecting a thing. He'd been in Semr, I think, at court. The other servants made themselves scarce. No one wanted to tell him she was gone.

"I didn't know any better. I was just a child myself, and I didn't quite realize what it meant, that Lady Lusarniev had ridden away the day before with that young man. Oh, I knew it wasn't quite right, but I couldn't believe that her ladyship might be unfaithful to *him*." She lowered her voice slightly. "To such a famous magician. Think about it. How would you even hope to keep something like that a secret?"

"She did, evidently," Nora observed.

Mrs. Toristel nodded. "Lord Aruendiel asked if I'd seen her ladyship and when I told him that she had gone away with the knight, his own friend, I saw his face change. I saw the anger building in his eyes—oh, I never want to see that again. I'd been dusting the woodwork, and it came to me that he would turn me into dust, too. But he just said, very courteously, 'Thank you, Ulunip,' and then he left the room."

"Ulunip?"

"That's my given name," Mrs. Toristel said. "A good Pelagnian name. It means 'Little Rabbit.' You don't hear it around here very much."

"Then what happened?"

"There's not much to say. He left Lusul that day, and I don't believe he ever went back."

"Did he go after his wife?'

"All I know is that he left, the estate was closed up a few months later, and I lost my job there. We heard he'd gone into the wars. There were all kinds of dreadful rumors floating around—that she was killed, he was killed—but when he asked me to come work for him here, it was obvious that he wasn't dead, even if he'd been terribly injured in the war. I never put much stock in rumors."

"But what did happen to his wife? Maybe she actually was"—Nora cleared her throat—"dead."

"Well, yes, she went to the gods, poor lady. He told me that when I arrived here, the first day. I could tell he didn't want to say anything more, so I didn't ask. It was none of my business, anyway."

"Still, I would think you'd want to know what happened to her. For your own peace of mind."

"That's what Toristel said. He wasn't happy to come here at first. He was like you, mistrustful of the magic, and he'd heard those stories about the master. But I told Toristel," she added with a dry chuckle, "that I'd be perfectly safe as long as I didn't marry his lordship and then run away with someone else. Toristel had to admit there was small chance of that, since I was already married to him.

"We didn't have much choice but to come here, anyway. My daughter was on the way, and there was no work for us near Lusul. People held it against me that I'd told his lordship about his wife leaving. As though he wouldn't have found the truth in the end, anyway. This place seemed like the end of the earth after Lusul, and the winters are terrible, but you can get used to anything."

"And he never married again?"

Mrs. Toristel seemed surprised at the suggestion. "Oh, no."

"It's a sad story," Nora said.

"Yes, well, it's an old story now. But I'm telling you this because you might hear worse from others, and you should know the truth."

"How long ago was this?"

"Oh, it's been many, many years."

"How many?" Nora asked, doing the arithmetic in her head. Mrs. Toristel couldn't be younger than sixty, surely. Sixty-something minus twelve? Surely not. But the housekeeper confirmed it: "It must be four dozen years or more. Yes, I married Toristel four years later, and we've been married forty-seven years."

"So, fifty-one years ago this happened? How old is *he*?" Maybe the magician had married very young. She made a hesitant guess: "Seventy?"

Mrs. Toristel gave a gentle snort and shook her head. "Seventy? Ah, he's older than you'd think."

"Eighty? No. Impossible." Nora was incredulous. "He looks old, but not that old." The housekeeper only smiled. "Is this more magic?" Nora demanded.

"What do you think?" Mrs. Toristel said.

*I think something very, very bad happened to Mrs. Aruendiel, Maggie. But maybe I'm projecting.*

*I should have told you this before: I got married. Before I came to this place. It was a disaster. My husband cheated on me and almost killed me. I left as soon as I came to my senses.*

*Some other things happened, but I don't want to talk about them right now.*

One of the village women was heavily pregnant, and every time Nora saw her, her round belly drew Nora's eyes like the moon. That could have been me, Nora thought wonderingly. By now, she estimated, she would have been maybe seven months along, big and slow, no doubt getting tired of being pregnant but quietly happy, feeling the baby grow stronger—

"Enough," Nora told herself severely, but it was useless, she couldn't stop thinking about it. She missed the child she might have had with a longing that she could not put a shape to, even if there was a horrific suspicion lurking in the back of her mind that the baby was not exactly a baby, just as its father was not exactly a man. What she also missed, she realized now, was the baby's mother, the hopeful, joyful—deluded—Nora who was now a phantom, too.

"It came too soon," Mrs. Toristel said with a sigh, when Nora ventured to ask her about the baby one day as they were packing dried plums into boxes. "There was nothing to be done. He told me the next day, after he stayed up with you."

"He told me that it was a good thing that the baby was gone. A good thing." Nora paused. "Was there something wrong with it?"

"You were lucky to live, that's all I know. Take this from someone who lost two of her own before they were born. Some things weren't meant to be. This batch is all wormy, Nora, didn't you notice when you were sorting it?"

Deciding what next to tell Maggie, Nora found that her eyes were wet. She squeezed her lids shut and felt the tears burn.

*I'm depressed a lot, yeah. But there's a lot to be depressed about.*

*I try to keep busy and be useful, and I've learned how to do things like milking cows and goats. Cooking on a woodstove. I get distracted for a while, and sometimes I'm kind of proud of just surviving in this place.*

*Then I think, What am I doing here? Nothing I've done in my entire life matters now.*

*I mean, yes, I was having problems in grad school—but when I think I'll never have the chance to even try to finish my Ph.D., it just feels hopeless. Like I'm trapped.*

*And I miss—well, everyone in my life. Maybe not Adam. But everyone else. Even Naomi. It's still sinking in, that I might not see you or my parents or my sisters or anyone else again. I remember that awful night, the party after the rehearsal dinner, wishing my life were different. I didn't mean like this.*

This letter to Maggie was not turning out well, Nora thought. She wasn't telling enough of the truth, or maybe she was telling too much, and now she felt worse instead of better.

She pulled one more weed, then stood up slowly, stretching her cramped legs, and half considered going to the bathhouse now, stares or no stares. But she had promised Mrs. Toristel to help her clean some of the unused rooms on the ground floor of the manor house.

Some of the rooms were quite grand, except that the tapestries on the walls were moth-eaten and most of the furniture was missing. Mrs. Toristel said that Aruendiel had sold it off years ago.

"If he's such a great magician, why he does he let this happen?" Nora asked Mrs. Toristel, as she surveyed the wreck of a drawing room. The naked frame of a solitary armchair stood in the middle of the room, reflected in the cracked mirror propped against the wall. "Why can't he at least keep up his own house?"

Mrs. Toristel came as close as she ever did to rolling her eyes. "Can't or won't," she said. "His purse is never very full, that's the truth, but he does find the money for things he likes, books or horseflesh or what have you."

"It wasn't like this at Lusul, was it?" Nora asked slyly. She had discovered that Mrs. Toristel loved to talk about Lusul—not the scandal around Aruendiel's wife, which she had not mentioned again, but the opulent, bustling life of the estate itself.

"Yes, but that was his wife's house, you know. This place was always his family's seat. It's a very old line," she added. "Not as prominent as the Lusars, but much older."

"Does that mean better?" Nora asked. Mrs. Toristel only gave her a reproving look.

The next room was almost empty except for a pile of broken furniture. Surely there was no need to clean here, Nora thought, peering through the door. Then she saw the books, piled haphazardly on a shelf.

She couldn't resist. One look.

Halfway across the room, she had the sudden intuition that she was not alone. Mrs. Toristel was still in the hallway. This was something closer. She looked around, puzzled. It was almost as though she'd heard her name called, in happy recognition, by a voice that was somewhat familiar to her. She felt warmed suddenly. Was it only being in the presence of books again?

A clatter like a small rockslide drowned out any imagined voices. The heap of broken furniture rushed toward her. Nora recoiled.

No, it was just one chair. A high-backed oak chair that managed to be mobile, thanks to the four small wheels attached to the legs. A rickety-looking wooden framework was affixed to the scrolled arms.

The assemblage rolled rapidly after Nora and, thankfully, stopped just in front of her.

"I'd forgotten that was here," Mrs. Toristel said from the doorway. "My goodness, it moved quickly."

"Yes, it did," said Nora, backed up against the wall, wishing she had something large between her and the chair. With a noisy shudder, part of its framework unfolded; it was composed of several jointed poles, each with a different attachment at the end: tongs, a cup, a nasty-looking hook. "What is it?" she asked, dodging, as the tongs reached toward her.

"That was the master's. He could wheel himself around the castle—the ground floor, anyway—and reach whatever he wanted with those long arms. When I first came here, that was the only way he could get around, unless someone carried him, and he never liked that." Mrs. Toristel shook her head. "Oh, it was a shock to me when I came here and saw him all crumpled up in that chair. And his face so scarred, that had been so handsome—I wouldn't have known him, except for his voice."

"What happened to him?" Nora tried not to sound as curious as she felt.

"He was injured in the war that was fought all over the country when I was young. Toristel and I were hired to look after the house, but at first it really meant looking after *him*."

"I bet he was a difficult patient."

"He never threw soup at me," Mrs. Toristel said, giving Nora a significant look. "Anyway, he had his books here, and he managed to do his work, even though he was in a chair all the time. He put a spell on it to make it move, you see. I didn't know it would move without him, though."

"It certainly does," Nora said. The chair crouched in front of her like a huge insect, its wooden joints creaking. As she tried to sidle away, the arm with the tongs took hold of her wrist. "Stop that!" Nora said fiercely.

To her surprise, the arm obeyed. It hovered, as though waiting for a command, and then stretched toward the shelf with the books. With a pawing motion, it made a couple of passes at the books until it pulled one down. "Stop," Nora said again, and the chair stopped moving.

Strange, she thought. Carefully, she took the book from the motionless tongs. "What does it say?" she asked Mrs. Toristel. With some hesitation, the housekeeper read: "*On the Selective Breeding of Fruit-Bearing Trees, with the Aim to Increase Both Yield and Vigor.*"

"That doesn't sound very interesting," Nora said. "Are they all like that?"

"Heavens, it would take me all day just to read the titles. This one I know, though," Mrs. Toristel said, slipping out the book that had been next to the horticultural guide, an oversized volume with a leather binding that was turning to powder. "It's for children. I learned to read from it myself."

Nora opened the book. On the first page, a complicated curl of ink next to a picture of what seemed to be a sheep. A is for *ama,* she guessed—the most common of the twelve Ors words for sheep.

"Would it be all right if I borrowed this?" she asked hopefully.

## *Chapter 11*

The brave warriors are ready for battle. Their long swords are eager to spill blood and carve the flesh of the enemy."

Nora flipped back in the book to check something—that knot of brushstrokes, was it an *r* or long *e?*—then sounded the words out again slowly. The first sentences she'd managed to read in Ors.

Nice reading for little kids. She could hardly wait to hear what happened next.

By habit Nora pulled on the ring on her left hand—still stuck there—and looked up, trying to guess the time from the sunlight filtering through the tree branches. Four o'clock? Five? Back at the castle there were beans to shell and a kitchen floor to scrub. Mrs. Toristel would be back from Red Gate soon. Nora stretched, thinking that she should get up, not really wanting to.

Some weeks back, cutting through the orchard, she had discovered a path in the tall grass that led through the sloping fields, threaded a grove of birches, and emerged on the banks of the river below the castle. Since then, Nora had gotten into the habit of walking down to the river when she had a free hour. It was always cool by the water, although no one else ever seemed to take advantage of that fact. There was one place where you could cross on stones to a small island, really just a slab of rock with a pine tree growing out of it. A good place for sitting and trying to read a book in a foreign language. The stepping-stones on the other side of the island were fewer and the water looked deeper; Nora had not yet attempted a crossing, although she could see that the path continued, carving a narrow passage through the wild black firs on the far bank.

Now, as Nora stood up and tucked the book into her basket, she looked across the water and felt a pulse of curiosity. Why not? she thought. The beans can wait. She put the basket down and walked to the water's edge.

She stepped to the first rock, then leaped to the next one. The ankle that had been broken felt perfectly sound, Nora was pleased to note. She launched herself at the next rock.

"What are you doing here?" someone asked testily, directly ahead.

Nora checked herself in midspring, and discovered that both the rock she had left and the one she was aiming for were equally out of reach.

The water was not as deep as she'd feared, but colder. She thrashed around, fighting the current. The person on the bank had extended a hand. She grabbed it. Pulling herself upright, she recognized the magician. His black tunic was only a little darker than the forest shadows.

Nora scrambled out of the water. "You startled me."

She thought she saw his mouth twitch. "My apologies," he said, more cordially than before. "I did not intend for you to throw yourself into the river."

"Neither did I." Nora looked down at herself ruefully; her dress was completely soaked. "I don't suppose you have any magic to dry clothes?"

"Certainly," he said, with a lift of his eyebrows.

The water trickling out of her clothes picked up momentum; she watched the dampness recede down the length of her dress. She felt a little queasy and much warmer. "Thank you," she said.

"I thought you didn't believe in magic," the magician said.

"I don't know," Nora said. "I just find it somewhat—unexpected."

"That is not a bad thing," Aruendiel said, surprisingly. "Magic is not something one should take for granted. Not at all." Briefly, he seemed to be thinking about something else. "You haven't answered my question yet," he said, more sharply. "What are you doing here?"

"I come down here sometimes to see the river. I wondered where the path leads."

He studied her through narrowed eyes. "Indeed. It is a long climb up and down the hill, no small exertion for a mending ankle."

It was hard to tell whether the sharpness in his voice was from concern over her leg or something else. She told him that her ankle was fine, that she walked everywhere now.

"Show me," Aruendiel said, and watched as Nora walked a few paces along the riverbank and returned. "No pain?" Kneeling, he ran a hand over her shinbone and palpated her ankle joint. "It has healed well," he said finally, sounding more cheerful than before. "Of course," he added, rising, "it is not so hard to set and mend one bone at a time. Mending several dozen, that is more complicated."

Nora looked at him curiously. A war injury, Mrs. Toristel had said. He held himself with more ease and vigor than she remembered from their previous meetings, and he seemed younger, closer to forty than to seventy. She could even see a certain resemblance to that portrait of his sister. On one side of his face, the planes of cheek and brow and jaw were smooth, strong, intact. The other side was rough and broken. He might have been handsome once. But overall, there was a sense of dilapidation about his lean face and frame, an impression of odd angles, joints that were out of true, a great disorder patched together and animated in an act of unlikely improvisation.

She wanted to ask him exactly how he had broken dozens of bones at once, but instead she said, "How was your trip? I didn't know you were back."

"I returned today, a few hours ago," Aruendiel said. "The voyage itself was damp. But all was resolved satisfactorily. A matter of reversing a sea god's curse."

"A sea god?"

"A local deity," he said dismissively. "Now, can you cross the river without falling in again? These woods are not the proper place for an afternoon stroll."

She turned and jumped to the island, conscious that she was making a little show of her agility. He came behind her. "Where does the path go?" she asked, picking up her basket.

At first she thought Aruendiel was not going to answer, but then he said: "Into the hills. It used to run up to the sheepfold, when we grazed sheep on these slopes."

"But this is all forest."

"So it is."

To her chagrin, her foot slipped on the opposite bank, and she had to grab a root to keep from falling. Despite his limp, Aruendiel navigated the stepping-stones with a nonchalance that Nora found ever so slightly irritating. His legs were longer, she reminded herself, and he had probably crossed here a thousand times.

"I've been wanting to talk to you," she said as they started up the path to the castle. "About how I can get out of here—that is, go home. Back to my own world."

Aruendiel cocked an eyebrow. "Well, how did you get here?"

*He* was the magician—why couldn't he tell her? "I don't know," Nora said. "But the last completely normal, ordinary, nonmagical thing that I remember is going to the mountains with some friends, for a wedding." She described that weekend, her walk in the woods alone, then finding her way to Ilissa's gardens.

"You believe something happened to you on that mountain," Aruendiel said.

"Maybe some kind of accident. I've wondered whether I might have hurt my head and become, well, confused. Or maybe—" This possibility had come to her in a black moment; she had tried to dismiss it, and failed. "Maybe I died."

To her secret terror, and also relief, Aruendiel took the idea seriously. He frowned for a moment. "Perhaps. It is unlikely, however. A ghost remains a ghost in any world, and you are certainly alive in this one. There is no sign that you have died even once."

She could not help laughing a little at that. "The graveyard, though. It could have been a sign of my death." He wanted to know more about the graveyard. "It was just a few old headstones in the middle of nowhere," she said, and recounted how she had gone into the cemetery to read the inscriptions on the graves.

"You read the words aloud?" Aruendiel asked. When she nodded, he said: "Some kind of spell there, cloaked in the poem."

"Really?" Nora asked, dubious, fascinated. She ducked under a low-growing branch, trying to keep up with him.

"It's clear enough—there's a gateway in the graveyard that goes from one world to the next." In a quickened tone, he asked: "Does Ilissa know about it?"

"Well—" Nora was not sure how to answer the question. "She knew about the graveyard."

"I thought she might know of such a door to another world. She's not from this one, we know that. But then why hasn't she used this gateway to escape?" Aruendiel turned to look hard at Nora, as though she might actually know the answer.

"That first day, she talked about the graveyard as though she hadn't seen it for years. And then the second time—" Nora tried to piece the memory together. "She was angry. She didn't want me there. I remember throwing up. I was pregnant then," she added, the last few words in a subdued voice.

"Morning sickness."

"I guess. I never really had any, except for that one time."

"You were fortunate," Aruendiel said. "Well, Ilissa would not want you wandering back to your world while you were carrying her heir."

They were coming to a subject that she preferred not to think about. But his words had triggered another memory. "Actually—" Nora said. "I could see, inside the fence, that the ground was torn up, and there was one of those yellow ribbons that they use at crime scenes. Do you know what I'm talking about?" Aruendiel shook his head uncomprehendingly.

"Never mind," she went on. "The point is, it was from my world. I was looking through the fence at a piece of my world. Why the police tape, I don't know." No, she did know. It was because of her own disappearance. At some point searchers must have tracked her, probably with dogs, to the graveyard. And then what? Her trail ended. No doubt the police had never once thought to look for magical gateways to alternate universes. More likely they considered other, more reasonable explanations for Nora's disappearance: wild animals, serial killers.

And her parents must be—Nora shoved that thought down quickly, unwilling to imagine what they must be thinking. First EJ, now this.

"The fence around the graveyard," Aruendiel said. "Was it made of iron?" Nora nodded, and he looked very pleased with himself. "Of course. The Faitoren cannot abide iron. It is like poison to them. That was how we were first able to defeat and confine them, with weapons of iron and steel."

It all sounded highly unlikely, this antipathy to iron—except that she had heard something like this before. "Wait, *fairies*! Do you mean to say that the Faitoren are fairies?"

Aruendiel shrugged. "Is that what they are called in your world?"

"Yes, except there's no such things as fairies! They exist only in folklore, stories." Nora added: "There is an old theory that fairies were actually a Bronze Age people in Britain who went into hiding to escape invaders with iron weapons, but that's just a historical explanation for the legend. In my world, if you call something a fairy tale, by definition it's not true."

Aruendiel rubbed his chin—touching his hand to the good side of his face only, Nora noticed. "I never came across any Faitoren when I was in your world. Although that doesn't mean that they weren't there, or that they had not been there before."

Nora seized upon the one notion that seemed to have some relevance for her. "This gateway, though. To get back to my world, all I'd have to do is go back into the graveyard again, right? Would you help me go there?"

A flash of interest kindled in Aruendiel's face, but then he shook his head. "Nothing would give me greater pleasure than to take on Ilissa," he said. "And I defy you to find another magician who could have extracted you from her castle. But it would be suicidal to battle her on her own turf."

"What if I took, oh, a sword and just marched in?" Nora said. "That's iron—steel. She couldn't touch me, could she?"

"She could still enchant and bemuse you," said Aruendiel with a dark smile. "As she did before, as she has done to people much older and much wiser than you."

"Well, how else could I get back home? How did you get there?" Nora demanded.

"I was traveling, passing through the thin places between worlds, and when I tried to return home, I found myself in yours. It was no great catastrophe. I only had to wait until another thin place opened up in the skin of your world and then slip back into my own—a matter of a year or so."

Nora was dismayed. "That long?"

Aruendiel shrugged his shoulders. "I passed the time tolerably well. It was intriguing to see how a world can be organized without magic. There was magic there, of course, but the inhabitants might as well have been blind or deaf, they were so unaware of it. Of course they were ingenious in other ways," he added, as though making a belated attempt at politeness. "Those great ships, and the swift carriages that run on iron roads, and the mechanical devices for sending messages—telegroms, they were called—were very impressive."

"Hmm," said Nora. "When was this? Never mind—this thin place you used, is it still there?"

He shook his head. "It knitted up long ago. But other thin places will develop. They come and go, like little bruises, as the different worlds touch one another. My friend Micher Samle has made a study of them. He is away in another world right now—your world, very possibly. I spoke to his former apprentice, Dorneng Hul, when I was last in Semr, and Dorneng expects a way back will open within the next ten years or so."

"*Ten* years? What will I do for all that time?"

"Do?" He seemed puzzled.

"Yes—earn my living, pass the time, whatever."

Aruendiel took a minute to turn this new problem over in his mind as they walked along the stone wall that marked the edge of the upper pastures. "In your own world, what is your station?" he asked finally. "Despite your alliance with the Faitoren prince, it seems to me that you are not originally of the nobility."

Nora smiled tightly. "Oh, can you tell?"

"But you are not a peasant, either, I think. What is your father's livelihood?"

"My father is in IT," Nora said, using the English abbreviation. "Don't ask me to explain what that is. As for me, I was in school, studying various books, preparing to become a teacher."

There did not seem to be an Ors word for "literature," and she had some trouble making the magician understand that it was a legitimate field of study in her world. At first he had the idea that her studies consisted of memorizing long epic poems, just as, early in his education, he had had to commit to memory great swathes of works such as the magical chronicles of the *Nagaron Voy* and the saga of the Six Kings' War. When he finally gathered that her work consisted merely of reading books and writing about them, he could not hide his incredulity that this was considered a fit occupation for adults.

"These are simply poems or fantastical tales that you studied?"

"Not always fantastical. The most highly regarded stories have fairly ordinary subjects—daily life, people trying to get married, and so forth."

"But you did not read these things to extract magical spells or history and laws from them?"

"Not in my program. We study poems and stories for their own sake, to understand them better, to appreciate their craft." At least, Nora thought, that is the theory.

Aruendiel shrugged his crooked shoulders. "You will not be able to earn your living in the same fashion here. The nearest equivalent would be the bards, who travel from castle to castle to sing the old poems and songs, but it takes years of training to learn the verses. And of course, it is not a job for a woman."

"What does that mean?" Nora asked sharply. Aruendiel looked blank, so she went on: "Do you mean that women aren't smart enough to learn the poems? Or they're not allowed?"

"I'm only stating a fact. A lone woman traveling through the country-side is likely to be raped or assaulted, if not to suffer a worse fate."

"I've never had any problems walking alone around here."

"Few would dare interfere with anyone who is under my protection."

"I don't need protection." They were climbing into the orchard now, facing almost directly into the light of the lowering sun. Up ahead, in the direction of the castle, the dogs were barking. On an impulse, Nora stooped to pick up a fallen apple, and then let it fly with a snap of her wrist, the way she used to pitch to EJ in the backyard. It squelched dully against a nearby tree trunk.

"Everyone in my household and on my lands is under my protection," Aruendiel said flatly.

They walked in silence for a few minutes, the castle in sight now, and then Nora spoke again. "I was a cook once. There's always a need for good cooks."

"Yes, some lords in Semr keep an entire staff of cooks. It's very hard work, I believe."

"I don't mind hard work," she said, even while remembering how her feet used to ache at the end of a night at the restaurant. On a sudden impulse, she said: "Or—I could be a magician." She wanted to see what he would say. "Whatever it takes, I could learn it."

Aruendiel snorted, then appeared to be thinking. "We could always marry you off," he said musingly. "There's young Peusienith, who holds one of my manor farms. He's a widower and a decent fellow." The magician's eyes flicked over her face, and she knew that he was appraising her scars, trying to decide whether they might put off a potential bridegroom.

"You must be joking!" Nora said, afraid that he wasn't. "Marry me off! It's been tried before, let me remind you." She gave the ring on her left hand an angry, futile pull.

"I meant no disrespect," Aruendiel said mildly. "It would be an easier life for you than cooking in Semr."

"No, thanks."

After a moment, Aruendiel said: "Well, you may remain in my household, if you wish. Mrs. Toristel would be glad of your assistance."

"Well, it does seem to be my only choice. I mean, thank you." She tried to make her voice register more enthusiasm. "I don't mean to sound ungrateful. But this world is not what I'm used to. Where I come from, women can get educations and jobs and live where we like and travel where we like. It's not like that here, from what I can tell."

"No, it's not," he said levelly. "I have always thought it's much better to be a man."

Nora was about to respond that there was nothing wrong with being a woman, that it was all about how society treated women—there was a lot she could say on this subject—when Aruendiel seized her arm and jerked her to the side. He pulled her into a run, jolting her with his clumsy gait.

"What?" she got out. Just as suddenly, he pulled up. Something large plummeted out of the sky, landing on the path a hundred feet ahead of them.

A gigantic black umbrella, bent, broken by the wind, Nora thought. A limp, whitish shape dangled under the dark folds: the forequarters of a dead sheep. Then she recognized the long, narrow head; the stocky, reptilian body; the flapping, leathery wings. She shrank back.

"Your husband has come to pay us a visit," Aruendiel said.

Under her sudden fear, Nora still found his dry, sarcastic tone irksome. Shut up, she wanted to tell him, that's not my husband.

The monster had settled on the ground to eat the sheep, its jaws tearing lovingly at the carcass. After only a few bites, the dead animal was gone, hooves, head, and all. The creature reared up on its hind legs, beat its wings in the air, and emitted a long cry as raucous as a gull's. Dropping to all fours, it paced back and forth, as though looking for a way through an invisible barrier. Then it settled on its haunches again and exhaled a shower of sparks and a puff of smoke. The weather had been dry lately. A bright flame sprang up in the grass.

"That's quite enough," said Aruendiel. He unfolded his arms and held his hand up, fingers flexing with a quick, compressed energy that made the ordinary movement seem like an obscene gesture. Instantly—without moving its wings—the creature went straight up into the air, trailing smoke, until it was so high that someone might take it for a bat or a crow.

A faint screech filtered down, and then the black speck was swallowed up by a pile of sooty clouds that had suddenly appeared in an otherwise clear sky. Thunder sounded as the clouds moved rapidly off to the north.

A splattering of rain fell, extinguishing the fire in the grass. Aruendiel was saying something with great concentration, staring after the clouds that had engulfed the creature. At first Nora thought it was another spell. Then she realized that he was swearing, with considerable fluency and detail.

She looked down at the ring on her finger, twisting it with a sense of unease.

"That sheepfucker, that woodlicker, that pus-ridden son of a slack-bagged whore shouldn't have been here at all," the magician said. "He shouldn't be able to leave Ilissa's domain, let alone come into the heart of mine."

Nora made herself meet his pale eyes. She didn't want to say anything, but she felt obligated to. "I wonder if this has anything to do with it." She held up the hand with the ring.

"What is it?" Aruendiel demanded.

"It's my wedding ring. I've been trying to get it off. But it seems to be stuck."

He seized her hand and looked at the ring without saying anything. Then he touched the gold band with the tip of one finger.

Immediately Nora gulped in pain, jerking her hand away. "It's like fire," she gasped.

Aruendiel did not seem sympathetic. He took her by the wrist and blew lightly on the ring. This time the ring squeezed her finger a little tighter and then relaxed, almost like a living thing. She felt a twinge of nausea. He stared at the ring for another long moment, then gave it a long, hard wrench, without success. "Ow," Nora said.

"There is certainly a spell there," he said. "As far as I can tell, it is what keeps the ring on your finger. But why is it there?"

"I don't know. You can't take it off?"

"Did your husband put it on your finger?"

She nodded yes. "He's not my husband."

"Why do you think Raclin"—Aruendiel pronounced the name with emphasis, as though to test Nora's reaction—"came here today?"

"I don't know."

"I don't know, either. But when I find you wandering at the edge of my private forest, where I do much of my work, where great power rests, without a satisfactory explanation, and then not an hour later, we encounter your husband, who makes himself so free as to devour one of my sheep and has the temerity to threaten me, the magician Aruendiel, a stone's throw from my own castle, I wonder exactly what is going on. Did you summon him?"

"Never! That thing almost killed me once."

"True," he said musingly. "But it would be a cunning trick, enticing an otherwise prudent and experienced magician to take a stranger into his household by making her appear Raclin's victim. A very clever way for Ilissa to introduce a spy into the stronghold of her most powerful enemy— don't you agree?"

"I'm not a spy," Nora said, hearing the menace in his tone and fighting the temptation to take a step away from him. If she did, she feared, she would not be able to stop herself from taking another step, and another, until she was running away as fast as she could.

"You might not even realize that you're Ilissa's tool. The ring could direct your actions at some future time, or right now." As though to himself, he said, "I can't believe I was such a fool as to leave you here in my castle, with my people, while I went away for weeks at a time. I should have turned you into a donkey or geranium for safekeeping or at least locked you up in the dungeon. Only the sun knows what kind of mischief you worked in my absence.

"And you even said just now you wanted to be a magician. What secrets of mine are you trying to steal?"

"Nothing," Nora said, trying to surpress her panic. "Listen, I don't know what this ring is, but it's not controlling me. You would know it, the way you could tell Ilissa put those other spells on me. *I* would know it—I remember what it was like to be enchanted, and I'm not enchanted now."

Aruendiel's expression was stony. Nora added suddenly: "Besides, she's not clever enough to come up with a scheme like that. I mean, she wouldn't do anything that would make Raclin look bad, or ever admit that he's less than perfect."

"You're underestimating her. She has carried out devious and complex schemes before."

"I'm not her spy," Nora said again, with some desperation. "I wasn't trying to steal your secrets. I had no idea that your forest was private, or that it was full of, um, great power. How would I? I don't know anything about magic."

"No," he said, no warmth in his voice. She could feel his eyes on her, probing, distrustful, all the way back to the castle.

PART

Two

# Chapter 12

Aruendiel sat up that night reading everything he could find about the various kinds of enchantments that could be affixed to or expressed in jewelry. He considered it a rather old-fashioned branch of magic, but there was no shortage of spells and commentaries, including many accounts of necklaces, earrings, bracelets, or rings that had been endowed by wizards with specific charms, powers, or curses. Baubles to make the wearer invisible, stronger than a dozen oxen, more beautiful than any other woman alive, uglier than death, or richer than seven kings. Trinkets that conferred eternal youth or a lifetime of pain.

None of the wizards and magicians who had written on the subject mentioned a spell that served only to hold a ring on a person's finger. Aruendiel did not find this reassuring. Most likely, he thought, the girl Nora's ring would not leave her finger because it contained a spell that was still somehow hidden. And yet he was familiar enough with the traces of Faitoren magic—powerful stuff, but cloying, much like Ilissa herself—that he should have been able to detect such a spell. All the more galling that he could not remove the ring.

In the morning, while he was still eating breakfast in the great hall, there was a delegation from the village. In addition to the sheep, Raclin had helped himself to a goat and three chickens, and set three thatched roofs on fire. Aruendiel listened as patiently as he could. Without promising to replace the lost livestock, he pledged to repair the burnt roofs and assured everyone that he would increase the valley's magical defenses immediately.

After they had left, Aruendiel observed to Mrs. Toristel: "If a raiding party came through the village, burned buildings, and stole an equal quantity of livestock, no one would expect me to make them whole. But if an obviously magical creature wreaks havoc here, it automatically becomes my fault."

"They're used to your protection, sir," Mrs. Toristel said. "I'm not saying it isn't ungrateful of them."

"Well, no doubt they assume that if not for my presence, we wouldn't have been blessed with this particular visitor. I suppose they're right," he added, with a glance at Nora, who was gathering up the used dishes from the table. "He came only because I decided to harbor his runaway spouse. Come over here," he called to her. "I want to take another look at that ring."

But after half a dozen of the most potent spells Aruendiel knew for separating objects or undoing magic, the ring was still fast to her finger, which was now black and blue. The girl herself said little, only bit her lip and blinked hard when he tried the Tulushn fire. (Well, he stopped as soon as he saw it was doing no good, and conjured a bowl of water from the kitchen to soak her hand.) A shame that she hadn't listened to his advice about not marrying the Faitoren monster in the first place. "You should always be careful about whom you accept jewelry from," Aruendiel said, as Mr. Toristel came in from the courtyard to say that there was a gentleman to see his lordship.

Nora, who remembered hearing similar advice from her grandmother, felt she was in no position to contend this point with the magician. She took the goblets into the kitchen; then, at Mrs. Toristel's bidding, she went out to the garden to dig some carrots. As she pulled them up, her eye kept coming back to the ring's smooth gleam on her now-grubby, still-smarting hand.

Ilissa's tool? She could not shake a nagging sense of doubt. Despite what she'd told Aruendiel yesterday, would she really know if someone was slipping thoughts into her mind like cuckoo's eggs? It had happened before, after all.

"But if Ilissa were controlling me," Nora argued internally, "would I even be wondering about this?"

Back in the kitchen, Mrs. Toristel informed her, snappish and excited, that Aruendiel's visitor had come from Semr. "That's the king's livery. Put those carrots down and take him out some ale. He'll want it after talking to the master."

Nora took the pitcher of ale and went out into the great hall, where Aruendiel was speaking with a man in a red-and-gold coat. Mrs. Toristel was more correct than she knew. "But His Serene Highness requires the Lord Aruendiel's counsel," the messenger was saying, his voice frankly desperate.

"Then he should have asked for it more civilly," Aruendiel said. He rolled up the scroll he was holding and placed it on the table. "I will look forward to seeing His Majesty next year, at the Assembly of Lords."

The messenger licked his lips. "His Majesty will be sadly displeased."

"Then I am sorry for His Majesty's ill humor. He is not the first king that I have sadly displeased, however, and perhaps he will not be the last. Will you have some refreshment before you leave? There are some hard-boiled eggs here, and"—Aruendiel turned and caught sight of Nora, holding the pitcher—"yes, my housekeeper has sent out some ale."

Nora did not move forward with the pitcher. She was staring at the dish of eggs. She had boiled them herself earlier that morning. So why was one of the eggs rocking madly back and forth? She could hear the tap-tap-tap as it knocked against the others.

Aruendiel followed her gaze to the egg. His eyebrows lifted.

As they watched, the shell cracked, then broke in two. Something bright emerged, a tangle of tinsel. A bird the size of a sparrow, fluffing out silver feathers. It took flight over Aruendiel's head, a glittering streak in the bars of morning sunlight, and then perched on a rafter, throwing a faint radiance onto the smoke-blackened roof beams.

"You brought another message for me," Aruendiel said to the man in the red-and-gold coat.

"Me? No. I'm no wizard!" said the messenger, blinking.

"That's very obvious," said Aruendiel. "But it doesn't mean you didn't bring some magic with you." He pursed his lips and whistled; the bird chirped back.

"What is it saying?" Nora ventured to ask.

"I have no idea. I'm trying to lure it down. Then we'll find out what this is about."

The bird spent several minutes preening itself, burnishing its silver feathers. Finally, it flew down to alight on the table in front of Aruendiel. Now Nora noticed a small roll of paper tied to one of the bird's legs with blue ribbon. Aruendiel's long fingers pulled on the trailing end of the ribbon to free the paper. He picked it up and read it.

"Well, well," he said reflectively. "Why didn't you tell me that the magician Hirizjahkinis is in Semr?" he asked the messenger.

The messenger seemed flustered. "Yes, I believe the Lady Hirizjahkinis is currently a guest of His Majesty."

"If he has Hirizjahkinis, why does he need me?" Aruendiel inquired, apparently of himself. "But she says I should be there, too. She says that I would want to be there. Merlin's folly, she could have squeezed another line of explanation onto that paper." He gave an exasperated sigh and crumpled the paper into a ball. For a moment, he stared into space, considering, and then he turned to the messenger. "All right, your master the king gets his wish. I'm going to Semr—at the invitation of the Lady Hirizjahkinis, not because he ordered me to come."

"His Majesty will be very pleased."

With a snort, Aruendiel turned to Nora. "You there, find Mrs. Toristel and tell her that I'm leaving. I'll start today." He gave her a hard, rather appraising look that she found unnerving. "And shoo this bird out of here, will you?" The silver bird had found a new perch on the railing of the gallery at the far end of the hall. "Otherwise it's going to make a disgusting mess. Even magical birds leave their droppings everywhere."

It was true, Nora saw, glancing at the floor.

In the end, it took both Nora and the castle tabby to get the silver bird out of the house, although that was precisely not the cat's intention. It meowed angrily at Nora as the bird flew out the door and disappeared, bright as thought, into the sky.

Carefully Nora uncrumpled the tiny ball of paper that she had retrieved from the floor. A few lines in the undulating, enigmatic Ors script went up and down the page. The first word was easy—Aruendiel. Decoding the words one letter at a time, she laboriously found her way to the end of the note. "I know you're going to say no to the king, so I'm telling you that you shouldn't. Trust me, you don't want to miss the excitement. I will see you in Semr. Soon, please."

When she went back into the great hall, she found the magician talking to Mrs. Toristel near the kitchen door. There was a leather bag at Aruendiel's feet, and he had changed his clothes: The rough linen shirt he had worn earlier had been replaced by a fine black wool tunic embroidered with gold thread; his cuffs and collar were freshly crisped into a myriad of minute pleats; and his boots looked almost new. Even his ragged black hair had been trimmed, and now fell in a neat curtain just above his shoulders. Perhaps because of the unusual finery, Nora thought his tall figure looked more angular and crooked than usual.

Mrs. Toristel was shaking her head, her arms folded. "No, sir," she was saying, most uncharacteristically. "You cannot do that. Not after yesterday."

"I don't like to go, but something is up in Semr," he said with an impatient exhalation. "I've put on a new spell of deep protection; the other safeguards are in place."

"That's not enough, sir."

"I'm only going away for a few days at most. Perhaps I should make the valley invisi—"

"That's all well and good, but that's not what I mean. What I mean is her."

Nora realized two things: That Mrs. Toristel was talking about her, Nora, and that her entry into the hall had gone unnoticed. Aruendiel had his back half-turned, and he was blocking Mrs. Toristel's view. In such a situation, Nora thought, one can be honorable or one can be practical. She stepped discreetly into the shadow of the great door.

"You won't have to worry about her," Aruendiel said. "She'll be safely restrained while I'm away."

Restrained? What did that mean—transformed into a donkey? Or a geranium? Nora debated whether to make a run for it right now, before Aruendiel or Mrs. Toristel noticed her.

But the housekeeper was shaking her head again. "No, sir, however well she's hidden, and I know you'd hide her well, she'd still be here. She's what drew that thing here last night, and she'll draw it again. That might not be her fault, but there it is. And how are we supposed to fight off that creature with you gone? The villagers won't stand for it."

"I don't care what the villagers think," he said restively.

"You can't just go off and leave her here. It's only chance that we weren't attacked while you were away before."

Aruendiel swore, a long, muscular sequence of profanity. "You mean, take her with me? What on earth would I do with her at court? And it's impossible. I must travel fast and light. I can fly to Semr under my own power, but she can't."

"I'm sure you can find some other way to get there, sir."

Silence. Did that mean Mrs. Toristel was winning the argument? Nora made a swift calculation and decided to take no chances. "I'll go," she said loudly, stepping out of the door's shadow. "I don't want to put anyone at risk."

She walked forward composedly, meeting both Aruendiel's chilly stare and Mrs. Toristel's worried one. Aruendiel was clenching his right hand, as though to grasp and crush thick hunks of air—a gesture of frustration, or was he about to transform her into a geranium?

"If I really am Ilissa's tool," Nora said, "wouldn't it be better to keep an eye on me?"

Aruendiel emitted a sound of disgusted assent. "If it will relieve your mind, Mrs. Toristel, then very well," he said. "We leave in a quarter hour."

"She needs time to get ready," Mrs. Toristel said.

"A quarter hour."

It took less time than that for Nora to throw her only other dress and a change of linen undergarments into a cloth sack. As always before leaving on a trip, she had the nagging feeling that she was forgetting something, but there seemed to be nothing else to forget.

When she came downstairs, she found Aruendiel standing over several large tree branches in the center of the courtyard. Mr. Toristel was nearby, holding a saw. The magician bent to pull the branches into the form of a rough cross, one short piece flanked perpendicularly by two long ones. He put something on the end of each of the longer branches. Nora edged closer to see. Chicken feathers. After surveying the arrangement critically, Aruendiel pulled a penknife from inside his tunic and jabbed it into the tip of one finger. Grimacing, he quickly touched all three pieces of wood, leaving a red print on each, then wrapped a handkerchief around his finger.

"How did it go?" he muttered. "No, that's not it." His lips moved silently as he rehearsed something to himself. Finally he nodded curtly, apparently satisfied. But as he moved his hand over the wooden cross, it seemed to Nora that there was something uneasy in his demeanor.

She had little time to reflect on this observation, though. The wooden branches were stretching, growing into one another; each of the cross's two side arms curved and lengthened; and then suddenly both arms of the cross were covered with a thick coat of feathers, lining up as neatly as shingles. The central piece of the cross was still recognizable as a tree branch, but attached to it now were two stubby-looking wings, fifty feet across. They gave a single, stately flap, stirring up a curtain of dust, and then lowered again, quivering slightly.

"No!" said Nora, horrified. "We're not going to fly on that thing, are we?"

Mrs. Toristel had come out of the house, carrying Aruendiel's cloak. "Ah," she said quietly to Nora. "It's not as bad as it looks. He had one at Lusul, with a saddle on it, specially made."

"I wish this one had a saddle. It looks dangerous."

"Not as dangerous for you as staying here."

The magician came over to them and took his cloak from Mrs. Toristel. "We're ready to go." He gave Nora a sweeping glance, taking in her dusty clogs, the dress that was either a dingy brown or a rusty gray (Nora had given up trying to decide), a bit of chicken fluff clinging to her hem. "She's hardly dressed for court," he said to Mrs. Toristel with an air of testy pleasure, as though he had finally found a good reason to leave her behind.

"That's all I've got," Nora said. "My other dress is about the same." Although she could say with certainty that it was several shades grayer than the other.

Not bothering to suppress a sigh, Aruendiel turned to the winged contraption and carefully lowered himself to sit astride the central branch. Nora clambered onto the branch behind him. There was just enough room to hook her legs in front of the great wings. "I'll have to hold on to you," she said to the back of Aruendiel's head.

"Hold on to the back of my cloak, if you must."

The huge wings began to beat, slowly at first, then faster. Dust rose around them. The housekeeper stepped back a few paces.

"Thank you, Mrs. Toristel," said Aruendiel. "I will see you in a few days."

He hadn't said we, Nora noticed. "Good-bye," she said, lifting her free hand. The winged branch lifted off, tilting backward as it rose, and Nora felt herself slide rearward. Uttering a little shriek, she tightened her grip on Aruendiel's cloak with one hand and grabbed at his shoulder with the other. He tensed slightly under her clutch, but seemed to be too occupied with guiding their flight to protest.

The white speck that was Mrs. Toristel's face, the slates of the roof, the yellowing fields outside the castle walls, all revolved under Nora's feet as she and Aruendiel circled, gaining altitude. But not too much altitude. The immense wings, she could somehow tell, were ready to test their power, to keep climbing until they were miles above the earth, but the magician was leaning forward, holding the branch with both hands and fighting to force it down onto a level path, not much higher than the treetops. That was fine with Nora. She watched the village pass below, with more white dots looking up at them, and then more fields.

They were headed southwest, Nora guessed from the angle of the sun. It was hard to enjoy herself, exactly, but overall this was an easier flight than the one from Ilissa's castle, if only because this time she could see and feel what was keeping her aloft. The great wings pumped away in a rhythm that she began to find almost restful. She was also relieved to note that Aruendiel seemed to have no interest in flying especially fast.

By midafternoon, they had passed half a dozen villages and one good-size town, but the only people who seemed to notice were some children who ran along below, trying to outrace them. Despite the breeze, the sun was warm on her face and shoulders, and it was beginning to make her squint as it sank lower in the sky. Nora yawned.

They were flying roughly along the course of a river that looped through a marsh, leading to a lake just visible ahead. On the river a man fished from a rowboat, the brim of his conical hat tilting as he looked up at them. He was close enough that Nora could tell his mouth had opened in a small O of surprise. But as they flew over, she noticed, the fisherman's gaze did not follow them. He was looking back at the way they had come.

With sudden disquiet, she twisted back to scan the air. A movement above registered as familiar even before she consciously identified it: The powerful sweep of leathery wings, less than a hundred yards away and gaining.

Nora shook Aruendiel's shoulder. "It's Raclin!" She had a quick, irrational fear that the magician had fallen asleep, but no, he had turned his head. She felt his shoulder tighten. Raclin was diving straight at them.

Wings thrusting, their flying contraption torqued upward and to the left, so abruptly that Nora thought she might slide off. The Raclin monster missed them. At once it recovered, turning to climb.

Aruendiel urged their mount into a sort of roller-coaster maneuver—arcing up, dropping down—but Raclin clipped one of their wings as he rocketed past. The wooden mount did a vertiginous half roll before regaining its equilibrium. Now Raclin swooped over their heads, so close that Nora instinctively ducked.

It was painfully obvious that Raclin was both faster and more agile in the air than they were.

"Can't you do something to him?" Nora cried in Aruendiel's ear. "The way you did yesterday?"

He snorted. "If I raise a thunderstorm, we'll be in the middle of it, too."

"Just make him stop!"

Aruendiel pulled his flying contrivance into a steep climb, trying to outrun Raclin. They were already at least a thousand feet above the ground. But Raclin kept up easily, baring his teeth at them as he flew.

Flying to Semr was a complete mistake, Nora thought savagely. Aruendiel should have realized that Raclin would attack them in the air—he had the advantage there. Raclin was just playing with them now. She thought briefly of how lovely it would be to be a geranium, safely anchored in a big pot in a sunny corner of the castle courtyard.

Apparently deciding that they had climbed high enough, Aruendiel changed tactics. They headed into a dive almost as sharp as their previous ascent. Raclin sped after them, claws out. Every time she looked back, he was closer. And so was the ground, crazy-quilted with bright green marshland and golden fields and deep green forest.

"Where is he now?" Aruendiel shouted, his eyes fixed on their downward path.

"Right behind us." Surely it was time to pull out of their dive now—right now—

"Good," Aruendiel said, jerking the branch upward with a sudden effort. With a jolt that almost unseated Nora, they straightened into a fast, level flight path that skimmed the treetops.

Nora looked over her shoulder. If Aruendiel had hoped to outmaneuver Raclin, he had miscalculated. The creature swooped after them, dipping its wings with a flourish. Nora had the distinct impression that Raclin was enjoying himself.

"He's still there," she said. Aruendiel didn't answer. Now they had run out of trees and were flying low over water: the lake that Nora had seen earlier. The wooden wings kept touching the water, throwing up white sprays of foam. Perhaps Aruendiel was preparing for a water landing—another terrible idea, Nora thought, since the Raclin monster looked as though he'd be nearly as comfortable in the water as in the air.

To her alarm, she realized that their speed had slackened. A look back: Raclin was no more than thirty feet behind.

Nora had opened her mouth to warn Aruendiel—couldn't they go any faster?—when she noticed an agitation in the lake dead ahead. She had the impression of shadowy movement under the surface of the water, something long and black and supple. As they flew over it, on an impulse she raised her dangling feet.

She heard a loud splash behind them, as though Raclin had dipped a wing in the water, too. She twisted to look back.

But there was nothing to see, just a white churning in the water. Raclin had vanished. She twisted around in her seat, looking around the lake and up at the sky. It must be a trick; any minute now he would drop out of the air from some unexpected angle or surge up from the lake water.

"Is he gone?" Aruendiel said after a while.

Nora exhaled. "Yes."

They reached the other side of the lake and flew on for about a mile. Then Aruendiel guided their mount to the ground, landing with a bump near a small stream.

"A rest," he said.

"Shouldn't we go on?" Nora objected. "We're not far enough away yet. Or is he dead?" she asked hopefully.

"That would be nice," Aruendiel agreed. "More likely, he is only distracted."

"With what?"

"Something larger than he is, although less ill-tempered." The magician untangled himself from the flying contraption and walked over to the stream. He cupped his hands, gulped down some water, and then stood up. He rubbed his shoulder, then regarded his hand with mild curiosity, as though checking for a tremor or some other sign of weakness.

Nora's mouth and throat were dry, a little sore. Had she been screaming the whole time? She couldn't remember. She went over to the stream, too, and drank until her hands were chilled from ladling up the cool water.

Aruendiel was rummaging in the leather bag lashed to the branch. He came back with a couple of hard-boiled eggs, the last of the batch from the morning. He tossed Nora an egg and sat down cross-legged to peel the other. They ate in silence.

"Is he a dragon?" she asked finally.

Aruendiel wiped his mouth with the back of his hand. "The lake guardian? No."

"Raclin."

"Ah. It's hard to say what he is." He seemed disinclined to go on, but she looked at him expectantly until he spoke again. "There's no such thing as a pure Faitoren. Raclin might have some dragon in him. If so, it's weak. Raclin can't make fire when he's flying—fortunately for us." He added, after a moment's thought: "Ilissa never said anything to you about Raclin's father?"

"No. I never even thought to ask. Who was he?"

Aruendiel shook his head. "She's always been coy about that. Probably with good reason."

"But it would be impossible, a dragon and a human—"

"Ilissa's not human."

"I am, though," Nora pointed out. "The baby I lost. Raclin's baby. What would it—?"

"Children tend to resemble their parents. In your case, as I told you before, you would have been dead before you could notice the resemblance," he said, standing up. "We'd best be moving along. I don't want to have to fly this thing after dark."

She got to her feet as a harsh chorus of bird calls began to sound in the forest bordering the meadow—the scornful, furious accents of blue jays and the hoarse alarms of crows. Then, just as suddenly, the birds fell silent. A long, winged shadow appeared over the treetops.

Nora thought: I knew we shouldn't have stopped. She took a few steps toward the forest, as though that would do any good. Aruendiel stood unmoving, his lifted face pale—frozen with fear, Nora decided, her own hope draining away.

Raclin bulleted toward them, back and wings still slick with lake water. There was no more circling or swooping now, no idle threats, no wicked playfulness in his flight. Only as he closed in—thirty yards, now twenty yards away—did he unsheathe the reptilian grin, allowing himself a jaw-snap in Nora's direction.

She dropped to the ground, shielding her head with her arms. Against the rush of jagged wings, Aruendiel's lean figure looked as frail as a twig.

The magician gave a slight, decisive nod, as though, after long consideration, he had finally made up his mind on a difficult point.

The huge wings wilted. The yellow eyes closed. Raclin dropped to the ground.

For a long, stunned moment, Nora waited, still prone, her eyes on the creature's slumped bulk. One of its wings was flat on the ground, while the other poked upward, askew, like a collapsing tent. A muscular forelimb was flung outward, the claws relaxed, looking almost like a human hand, if you ignored its inhuman size.

Aruendiel walked around the creature slowly. Taking care not to step on the outstretched wings, he tilted his head to view the monster critically from different angles, like a workman inspecting a finished job.

Shakily, she scrambled to her feet. Now she could see that the long, toothy jaw hung slightly open, letting a thread of saliva descend toward the ground. The eyelid facing upward was not entirely closed, either, but the eyeball underneath was as still as glass. Only the surface of Raclin's torso moved up and down in a sluggish rhythm.

"He's asleep!" Nora said. "He's not dead."

Aruendiel gave a short bark of laughter. "You sound disappointed. Anyone would think you didn't love your husband."

"I don't love him, and he's not my husband," she snapped. "Why don't you just kill him?"

The magician grinned darkly at her. "It's not so easy to kill Raclin, as you may have noticed. Especially in this form."

"But he could wake up at any time," she said. "You said that iron could kill the Faitoren. If we only had a knife or something, couldn't we simply stab him?"

By way of answer, Aruendiel went over to the leather satchel tied to the flying branch. Nora heard the scrape of metal against metal as, somehow, from a sack that seemed only large enough for a lunch and a change of clothes, he produced a sword as long as his arm. It was doubled-sided, with a plain grip of black-hued steel, and looked heavy, but Aruendiel handled it comfortably enough. He walked back to the sleeping monster and aimed a sharp blow at Raclin's torso. The tip of the sword bit straight at the heart, but as it touched the lizard hide, it bounced off harmlessly, with a metallic groan.

"Let me try," Nora surprised herself by saying. Aruendiel looked even more surprised, but after a moment, with an odd smile, he handed her the sword. Lifting it with two hands—it *was* heavy—she slashed at Raclin. The sword recoiled violently; her stinging hands dropped it.

Aruendiel smiled again, off-kilter. He picked up the sword and ran his finger along the blade to make sure that the steel was undamaged. Raclin stirred uneasily.

"He's waking up," Nora exclaimed.

Aruendiel shook his head. "Not with that spell. It's the hundred years' sleep—at least, it would be for a human. Raclin might sleep as little as a day. A week or two, more likely.

"The problem, of course, is that when he does wake up, he'll be extremely well rested and eager to exact revenge. It would be prudent to ensure that he doesn't wake up."

"So you are going to kill him."

"Not exactly. It would not be honorable, while he is sleeping." Aruendiel was quiet for a moment, motionless. Only when Nora felt butterflies in her stomach, the momentary giddiness that she was beginning to associate with magic, did she realize that he was doing a spell. She looked more closely at Raclin. His grayish green skin had turned darker and had taken on a dull, matte texture. The wet gash of his mouth, the black, serrated rows of teeth, the shining crescents of his partly closed eyes—all were now the same leaden color. She counted to ten, twenty, thirty, but the muscled torso was no longer rising and falling.

She shot an inquiring glance at Aruendiel. He waved her forward impatiently. "Go ahead. He won't hurt you."

Nora put her hand on the creature's unmoving shoulder. It seemed to her that at first there was a flurry of panicked, angry movement under her fingers, as though she had laid her hand on a door behind which a trapped animal was scuffling, and then she felt only the quiet roughness of the stone, barely warmed by the late-afternoon sun.

"How long will this spell last?" she asked, straightening. "A week? Five minutes?" She wished that Aruendiel were not quite so scrupulous about his honor.

"In theory, until the bones of the earth crumble, the seas go dry, and the power of the sun is no more, as the old wizards used to say," Aruendiel said, sounding more cheerful than he had all day. "In reality, until Ilissa finds him and frees him. Long enough for us to finish our journey in peace, at any rate."

Nora touched the rock again, reassuring herself that it was dead mineral matter. Turning away, she felt taut muscles in her shoulders and neck begin to relax, although—she reminded herself—there was still the rest of the flight to Semr to endure.

"Why didn't you turn him to stone before? When he was chasing us?" she asked Aruendiel.

Aruendiel had already settled himself onto the branch, whose wings were beginning to beat in a slow cadence. "I was occupied with flying," he said shortly. Nora climbed on behind him, twisting slightly as she tried to find a comfortable spot on the tree limb. After a second's hesitation, she took hold of his shoulder again.

The sprawling form of Raclin-turned-statue dwindled beneath them, dark against the yellowing grass. It looked like a broken toy. Nora watched it steadily until the meadow disappeared behind them. Aruendiel did not look back once.

# Chapter 13

By the close of the day, they had reached the sea. Aruendiel guided their craft along a coast of craggy rocks and narrow beaches, until they came to the mouth of a broad river.

The far side of the river bristled with the masts of ships at anchor. More ships headed for port, their colored sails fat with the evening breeze. Beyond the docks Nora could see a crush of roofs and domes and a few slender towers. It was a city, a real city, although it was difficult, in the fading light, to estimate just how large. The wind brought the smell of smoke, dried fish, and sewage to her nostrils.

Aruendiel followed the coast past the river and the lights of the city, then veered sharply inland. They flew over dark ground, and then a lighter strip appeared below. Aruendiel jerked the branch downward, and they landed with a bump, cobblestones under their feet.

"Where are we?" she asked.

"We're outside the main gate of Semr," Aruendiel said. "I see from those torches that the gate is still open, so we will have no trouble entering the city, and yet we have arrived a little too late to wait upon His Majesty at this evening's palace banquet. Our timing could not be improved upon."

Nora stood up, clutching her bag. "Actually, I'm a little hungry."

"Then a palace banquet is the last place you would want to be. No one can eat until the king is served or after he has stopped eating. We'll do what the courtiers do and stop at the palace kitchens." He clapped his hands, and the flying contraption collapsed into three rough branches lying on the cobblestones. Aruendiel kicked the wood to the side of the road. "I'll travel home by different means," he added.

Again, no mention of taking her back with him. "How?" she asked, but he had already turned toward the gate, moving quickly despite his limp.

The city gate had studded bronze doors, set in a limestone wall and topped with an enormous bas-relief that showed a strapping beast with two heads—a wolf's and a lion's—standing upright. It held a sword in one paw and a sheaf of grain in the other. Part of the majesty of the entrance was lost, however, because of the mass of shanties, built of wood and animal hide, that huddled at the base of the wall. The same pungent mix of smells that Nora had caught before was overpowering here, although now she could also discern notes of rotten vegetables and beer.

The soldiers at the gate were occupied with a group of farmers who had evidently come into the city earlier to sell their goods at market and now were leaving. Each had to present his cart or pack for inspection. It took some time. Aruendiel seemed grimly amused. "They stayed too late," he said to Nora.

"Too late?"

"If they had left earlier, the gate would still have been manned by the first watch—which already took its cut this morning. Now the second watch wants its share." Nora wondered whether she and Aruendiel would have to bribe their way into the city, too, but the sergeant obviously recognized the magician's name. Waving them in, he dispatched a runner to notify the palace of their arrival.

The narrow streets of the city were still busy, although most of the small shops they passed were already boarded up for the night. There was no shortage of inns, one on almost every corner, spilling light and noise from their doors. In the streets were other late travelers; beggars, all with more than one limb missing—it took a lot to get sympathy here, Nora thought; drunkards; buskers playing drums or pipes; and small clusters of women and girls—some mere children—wearing low-cut dresses and purple ribbons in their hair. Nora saw instantly what the purple ribbons meant. Some of the women called out to Aruendiel as he passed. He nodded back with surprising graciousness, without breaking stride.

They had been walking for about ten minutes when a young man in red-and-gold livery came running up with a torch to light their way. After that, they made faster progress, as the other pedestrians gave them a clear path. Eventually, the streets sloped upward and the crowds thinned. The buildings uptown were larger, made of stone and brick, their tall windows gated with iron shutters.

"Take us into the palace by the side entrance, I pray you," Aruendiel said to their guide.

"His Majesty still holds court in the main hall," the young man objected.

"All the more reason for us to enter quietly."

The torchbearer led them down several narrow streets to an arched gate guarded by soldiers in red-and-gold tunics. On the other side Aruendiel threaded his way expertly through a series of courtyards until they reached the kitchens, where a skinny boy in a dirty apron served them fish pastries and the palace chamberlain found them a few minutes later. He informed Aruendiel that, regrettably, His Majesty had just retired and would not be available for an interview until the following morning. Aruendiel took the news with equanimity and asked that they be shown to their rooms.

For the length of several corridors and two staircases, the chamberlain spoke fluently about the unusually warm weather the capital had been enjoying, the state of the palace lawns, and the prospects for the king's annual *ben* tournament, an Ors word that Nora had not encountered, but which seemed to denote a game played on a grassy court, something like bowling. The chamberlain smiled at her at intervals, but his eyes constantly flicked back to Aruendiel, as though he were nervous about letting the magician out of his sight for an instant. Eventually they arrived at a large bedroom where a fire was already burning cozily in the fireplace. The chamberlain said something to Aruendiel that Nora couldn't quite catch.

"Certainly not!" Aruendiel said, with a sideways glance at Nora. "Please find Mistress Nora lodgings elsewhere." He swept into the bedroom and closed the door behind him.

The chamberlain led Nora up several more staircases, each narrower than the last. He seemed to have run out of comments about the *ben* tournament. The bedroom he brought her to was very small, almost completely filled by a large canopied bed. "You will be sharing the room with Lady Inristian, Countess of the Valley of the River of the White Boar and Chatelaine of Inris House."

"I hope she doesn't mind having me as a roommate," Nora said.

"I am sure she will not mind sharing with such a charming young lady as yourself," said the chamberlain. "The palace is so crowded at this time of year." He bowed and disappeared.

Nora considered waiting up for Lady Inristian, to introduce herself, but she fell asleep almost as soon as she got into bed. She was awakened sometime later by voices in the room. Someone else slid into bed with her. Then, she noticed sleepily, another person.

Afraid that she was about to know more about her roommate's romantic life than she wanted to know, Nora sat up and cleared her throat.

"Oh, for shame, Daisy, you've wakened our bedmate," said the person next to Nora.

"Lady Inristian?" Nora asked. "My name is Nora. I'm so sorry—the chamberlain put me in your room. I hope I'm not disturbing you."

"No, not at all," said her neighbor in an accent that Nora had not heard before, a slushier version of Ors. "I hope that you do not mind that my maid sleeps with us. They did not have a proper bed for her, and besides, when one is in Semr, I always think that it is safer to sleep with a chaperone. The palace can be very busy at night, if you know what I mean."

"Oh," said Nora. "Well, no one will disturb you on my account." The other women only giggled. It took some time for Nora to fall asleep again, but in the end she slept better than she would have expected. Lady Inristian wheezed, but very softly.

In the morning, Nora awoke before the others and dressed quietly. She glanced at the sleeping Lady Inristian and noticed that the pale skin of her otherwise pleasant face was lunar-rough with pockmarks. Either she'd had the worst case of acne ever, or they had smallpox here; Nora wondered somberly whether the magician could cure smallpox, if she happened to contract it. She went over to the bedroom's small window and peered out.

There was a view over the palace gardens, which, as the chamberlain had remarked, were lush and green—the grass still fogged with dew. She was just letting her gaze wander over the curving paths and the lines of neatly trimmed beeches when her eye fell upon the slender figure of a woman dressed in white, walking by herself. The woman had her back turned, but there was something about her posture—defiantly, almost aggressively graceful—that made Nora catch her breath. How many women walked just that way, and had chestnut hair exactly that shade?

Lady Inristian was shaking her maid's shoulder. "Daisy, get up and fetch a fresh chamber pot, I need to make water." She called over a greeting to Nora.

"Oh—good morning," Nora said, trying not to appear rattled. She glanced out the window again. The woman in white was just disappearing behind a hedge.

Daisy stumbled out of bed, yawning, and disappeared into the corridor. Lady Inristian began to chatter about last night's banquet. She seemed to assume that Nora knew the people that she was talking about. Nora, trying to keep an eye on the garden in case the woman in white returned, made distracted sounds of agreement.

When she finally turned away from the window, Lady Inristian gave a little gasp. "You poor thing, that must have hurt!"

"What? Oh, *that*." Nora raised her hand to her cheek. "It was just a scratch. From an animal." She did not sound as casual as she wished to.

"How awful." Lady Inristian pursed her lips in a little pout. "I have some marvelous face powder that can hide almost anything. Just tell me if you'd like to borrow some."

She meant it kindly enough. Nora felt her cheeks grow warm, and wondered whether the scars stood out more vividly when she blushed. It had been some time since she had really looked in a mirror. "Thank you, I appreciate the offer," Nora was beginning to say, when someone knocked at the door.

Instead of Daisy and the chamber pot, it was a servant in the red-and-gold livery. "My apologies for disturbing you, ma'am, but I have a message for Mistress Nora," he said. Nora indicated that he had found the right person. "The Lord Aruendiel would like to see you at once in the minister's council chamber."

"The Lord Aruendiel!" From the bed, Lady Inristian was all alertness. "I didn't know that he was here in Semr." She looked hard at Nora, as if demanding an explanation.

"We arrived just last night," Nora said to her.

"You came with him! And you are—"

"I've been staying in his castle," Nora said. She went to put on her shoes, conscious of Lady Inristian's unblinking gaze upon her—taking in the gold ring, the scar, the worn dress that had been Mrs. Toristel's, the peasant clogs, the plain, braided hair. "Well," said Lady Inristian, sinking back onto the pillows, her eyebrows raised. "How interesting."

Nora smiled at her and fled after the servant.

After ten minutes of corridors, he delivered Nora to a round room, domed with frosted glass through which a pale, oyster-colored light filtered down. Although the table was littered with a variety of maps, a couple of goblets, and a half-eaten loaf of bread, there was no one in the room. The servant directed her to wait.

Nora helped herself to a hunk of bread, then looked at the maps with interest. Sounding out the Ors names carefully, she eventually identified Semr, a dot on the coastline of a large western ocean, at the mouth of a long river that wound out of a mountain range to the east. At the bottom of the map were several very large lakes, completely landlocked. The far northern and northeastern parts of the map seemed virtually blank—perhaps unexplored? She was trying to work out where Aruendiel's castle was located—somewhere in the hilly country to the northeast of Semr, she thought—when she heard footsteps come into the room, a quick tread followed by a slower one.

"Aruendiel!" she said, looking up. "I think I saw Ilissa this morning, in the garden."

"You did," he said with a grave face. "She's here in Semr."

"Why is she here? I thought she couldn't leave her own lands."

"Normally, she can't, under the terms of the treaty. There are exceptions, though. She has the right to leave her domain for diplomatic missions. And now," he said, inclining his head, "she is here in Semr to treat with the king. In fact, I learn, they have been sending messengers back and forth these past two months. It is a remarkable piece of royal folly."

"What is it about?"

"I intend to find out. This misguided affair is most certainly what Hirizjahkinis was referring to in her note yesterday. She could have been much clearer, I have to say. If I had known exactly what she meant, I would have come—oh, faster than I came. And I would not have brought you with me, into the presence of your enemy. I apologize deeply for that miscalculation."

Nora's heart sank a little to hear how serious he sounded. "But you're a match for her, right?" Aruendiel had stopped Raclin—eventually. "Is that how Raclin got out, because of the mission?"

"Yes, he is considered part of the mission. It's an outrage that I was never consulted about this."

"I wonder if Ilissa knows yet that Raclin is now a piece of statuary."

"I doubt it. That piece of information may be useful in our discussions today. As will an account of Raclin's recent attacks on us. In fact," Aruendiel said, with a lift of his eyebrow, "you might be a valuable witness yourself."

"Me? Why?"

"Kidnapping young women as brides for Raclin is expressly forbidden by the treaty. Ilissa will say, no doubt, that the clause does not cover visitors from another world, but I think we can argue that she has violated the spirit, if not the letter, of the agreement."

"Would I have to be in the same room with Ilissa? Because I don't want to see her."

"No, perhaps that would not be wise." His face hardened, and she guessed that he was considering again whether Nora might be Ilissa's agent, unknowingly or not. "And the ring?" he added in a colder tone.

"No change that I've noticed."

"You wouldn't necessarily notice anything," he said. "Let's see it." After a moment's scrutiny, he dropped her hand with a grunt. "The question then is how to keep you away from Ilissa this—ah, Hiriz, there you are!" His voice warmed noticeably with the last words.

"So you did answer the king's summons, Aruendiel." There was a quicksilver hint of mockery in the voice that spoke from the doorway. Nora turned to see a small but very straight figure step into the room, a dark-skinned woman who looked distinctly different from anyone she had met so far in this world. Hirizjahkinis wore a kimono-like gown of finely pleated linen so thin that the outline of her body was clear beneath it. Her dress did not look particularly warm, now that summer was ending, and perhaps for that reason she had fastened a leopard skin over her shoulders with an immense golden clasp, the leopard's head resting companionably on her breast. There was more gold around her neck and on her arms, and she wore a tight-fitting cap completely covered with rows of pearls, under which her hair fell down in neat, crimson-tinted cornrows threaded with gold and ivory beads. It was hard to estimate how old she was. Her compact, square-shouldered body moved quickly, giving an impression of health and vigor, but when she came closer, Nora could see sharp lines around her smiling mouth.

"You could have told me what was afoot," Aruendiel said. "And you could have told me sooner."

Hirizjahkinis laughed and took Aruendiel's hands in hers by way of greeting, then let them fall. "But I only arrived here two days ago myself. Imagine my surprise when I went to pay my respects to your King Abele and discovered him in eager discussions with our Faitoren friend. You should keep a better watch on matters in your part of the world, Aruendiel."

"Well, what are they discussing so eagerly?"

"What do you think? An alliance. Ilissa has offered to help your king in his next war. He is eyeing some territories to the east; the rights are in dispute. Ironically, it's iron-mining country, I believe."

"The Meerchinland—and the ownership is *not* in dispute," Aruendiel snapped. "Abele's great-grandfather traded it to the Pernish in exchange for the entire Sirknon River valley. Now Abele has the notion of taking it back. He floated the idea at the last Assembly—surprisingly, the lords wouldn't go along. Either they remember that last disastrous adventure of his, or they're worried about their tributes going up."

"Well, now he's found someone who will help him."

"And what does Ilissa expect to get in return?"

"The treaty with the Faitoren will be torn up, the spells binding the Faitoren lands will be dissolved, the Faitoren will be allowed to come and go as free as wind and rain."

"They could not dissolve those spells without my consent, and I would never give it."

"No doubt that is why you were not invited to take part in these very private talks. Your king was not eager to hear from me, either, especially when he heard what I had to say. But I did persuade him that he should consult you, and I sent my own messenger with his to make sure that you actually came."

"You didn't say a word about Ilissa in your message."

"My dear Aruendiel!" She threw up her hands. "Ilissa sat glowering at me across the table the entire time that I was doing the magic. I didn't dare be more specific. The important thing, I thought, was simply to get you to Semr, so that you could see for yourself what was happening."

"What about Bouragonr?" Aruendiel demanded. "He's been chief royal magician for, what, two dozen years now. Bouragonr's no friend of the Faitoren. Surely he's counseled the king against this alliance?"

Hirizjahkinis shook her head with a rueful smile. "I think Bouragonr is senile! He said almost nothing, except that we could learn much from the Faitoren magic. I said that there was already a magician in the kingdom who knew more about the Faitoren magic than possibly even the Faitoren themselves—that's you, Aruendiel!—and that you had never found anything particularly useful in it for anyone who does not happen to be Faitoren. But Bouragonr harrumphed and said it might be time for a fresh look, by magicians who are not prejudiced against the Faitoren, as he put it."

"He said that? Bouragonr fought against them, too, with the rest of us."

"I thought it was very odd. But I haven't seen him for years. He's not looking well."

"I wonder how much magic he actually practices anymore," Aruendiel said musingly. "All those younger magicians working under him—he may be getting lazy. Is he hoping to shore up his own powers by allying with Ilissa? By the way," he added, with a quick half bow, "you're looking well yourself, Hiriz."

"As are you. You must have been doing a lot of magic lately."

Aruendiel made a dismissive gesture. "We crossed paths with Ilissa's son on the way here."

For the first time, Hirizjahkinis looked directly at Nora, although Nora had the feeling that the other woman had been carefully observing her the entire time. There was a moment's pause, as though Hirizjahkinis was making one final appraisal, and then she smiled so warmly that Nora felt unreasonably elated, as though she'd passed a test and met an old friend in the same instant.

"We—?" Hirizjahkinis asked, glancing back at Aruendiel.

"This is Mistress Nora, who accompanied me—for safekeeping," he said. "She is Ilissa's daughter-in-law."

"Former daughter-in-law," Nora said.

Hirizjahkinis raised her chin slightly, but otherwise showed no trace of surprise. "I am Hirizjahkinis," she said, extending her hands to Nora, as she had done to Aruendiel. "I am very happy to meet you. Are you here for a reunion with your former husband's family—"

Nora shook her head. "Oh, no—"

Aruendiel broke in: "Mistress Nora has been a guest in my household for some months, ever since she fled from the Faitoren."

Now Hirizjahkinis did look surprised, her eyes widening. "You escaped from the Faitoren, Mistress Nora! Well, that would explain something Ilissa let drop yesterday."

"What was it?" Aruendiel asked.

"Not worth repeating," said Hirizjahkinis. "But you obviously managed to provoke her, Aruendiel."

Aruendiel made a sound deep in his throat indicating a lack of concern with Ilissa's displeasure. "I want to talk to the king as soon as possible. Where is he?"

"At this hour, I imagine he is still engaged in the morning's ceremonial reveille. You could go and join in, as a peer of the realm."

"Thank you, I have no desire to help my sovereign pull on his breeches."

"But you could talk to him without Ilissa being present. You might not get such a chance for the rest of the day."

"Is she spending so much time with the king?"

"As much as she can. He does not seem to be averse to her company."

"Very well," he said reluctantly, with a twist of his mouth. "I'll go now, and hope His Majesty does not ask me to demonstrate my loyalty by washing the royal buttocks. But we need to find a place to stow Mistress Nora, out of Ilissa's way," he added. "The easiest thing to do would be to turn her into a buckle or a necklace or some other small ornament, and one of us could wear her for the rest of the day."

Nora stared at him, incredulous. "No! Absolutely not."

"Do you want to fall into Ilissa's hands again?"

"No, but I don't care to be transformed into anything, either." It would be so easy—and convenient—for Aruendiel to forget to change her back.

"Perhaps the Kavareen could watch her for a few hours," Hirizjahkinis interjected. "Ilissa wouldn't dare try to get past him."

At this suggestion, Aruendiel looked even more irritated. "It's absurd that you're still carrying that thing around with you," he said. "You don't need it—you have plenty of your own magic. And, you know, it's not entirely safe."

"He's been a good servant, very useful at the most unexpected times. Right now, for instance."

Aruendiel seemed ready to dispute further, but then he checked himself. "As you like. There's no time to argue. You will join me in the king's presence as soon as he is washed and dressed, Hiriz?" At her nod, he went out of the room without another word.

"Well," said Hirizjahkinis to Nora, "let's find a comfortable place for you to wait."

"Excuse me, but what is the Kavareen?"

Hirizjahkinis unfastened the gold clasp that held the leopard skin around her neck, and then shrugged the hide off her shoulders. Carefully she spread it on the floor. The black-spotted fur had a rumpled, worn look, as though Hirizjahkinis had been wearing the skin for many years. The eyeballs in the dead cat's head gleamed a dark yellow—glass, or some semiprecious stone like topaz, Nora thought. Hirizjahkinis stepped quickly onto the hide and then off it.

The leopard skin quivered, collected itself, and then got to its feet with a hiss. The hide was obviously covering a body—a leopard-shaped body—but in the gaps where the skin didn't reach, Nora had a glimpse of roiling darkness, shadow that churned like thick smoke.

The resurrected animal stretched lazily, curving its back and flexing its claws, and then hissed again, looking up at Hirizjahkinis. Its eyes looked just as glassy as before.

"This is the Kavareen," Hirizjahkinis said.

"Was it—is it a leopard?" Nora asked.

"No. He happened to look like a leopard when I killed him," Hirizjahkinis said, a hint of pride in her voice. "He has been with me ever since, as my slave." She spoke to the Kavareen rapidly in a singsong language, and the animal responded with a snarl and a lash of its tail. Hirizjahkinis spoke again, more sharply. The Kavareen snarled a second time, not as loudly. It stalked a few steps away and settled into a watchful crouch that reminded Nora of how her cat Astrophel used to sulk when feeding time was delayed.

"Don't mind his crankiness," Hirizjahkinis said.

"Um, did he say something?"

"It was not very polite. He didn't appreciate being awakened, and he's a little hungry. But don't worry, you'll be fine with him. He is under strict orders to keep you safe, and I have told him that he may eat Ilissa if she makes any effort to take you."

When the Kavareen had snarled, through its open mouth Nora had again seen that agitated blackness, coiling in secret currents. Now it came to her that the interior of the beast was larger—perhaps much, much larger—than its exterior would indicate.

"I thought Aruendiel said he wasn't completely safe," Nora said.

"Aruendiel is my dear friend, and when it comes to natural magic, he knows more than any other magician alive," Hirizjahkinis said. "But, if you haven't noticed, he does have very strong prejudices. He doesn't trust ghosts or demons. Cannot abide them!"

The amused incredulity in her tone implied that Aruendiel's view in this area was one of those incomprehensible eccentricities that one tries to overlook in one's close friends—the way that Nora used to tolerate Adam's ridiculous aversion to tomatoes. On ghosts and demons, however, Nora felt that Aruendiel was on solid ground. "He doesn't?" she said politely.

Hirizjahkinis shook her head emphatically. "No! He thinks it's a lazy way of doing magic, summoning spirits to do your work. Come along, I must find a safe place to leave you."

Outside in the corridor, Hirizjahkinis commandeered one of the red-and-gold-liveried servants, who, after a cautious glance at the Kavareen, led them by a circuitous route to a small room where several divans, covered with brightly colored pillows, made a semicircle in front of the fireplace. Over the mantel hung a tapestry that showed a young woman riding on the back of the two-headed animal that Nora had seen on the city gates.

"This is the unfashionable end of the palace now. No one will stumble across you here," Hirizjahkinis said to Nora. She addressed a few more remarks in the singsong language to the Kavareen, who merely yawned, and then she followed the servant out of the room.

Nora sat down on one of the divans and watched the Kavareen move restlessly around the chamber. She couldn't help wishing that Hirizjahkinis had picked a bigger room, so that the Kavareen would not pace endlessly like a zoo animal in a too-small cage; she thought about how cats hated to be told what to do and wished that Hirizjahkinis had happened to kill the

Kavareen when it was in the shape of a wolf or, better yet, a dog; and she wondered exactly how hungry the Kavareen was and what it usually ate and what happened to the things that fell into its dark interior.

She was trying to imagine exactly how Hirizjahkinis might have killed the creature, and whether it could be killed a second time, when the Kavareen came over and stood directly in front of her. Its dead golden eyes stared into hers. She sat very still while it sniffed her knee. And then suddenly, with a light jump, the Kavareen was on the divan with her, its head level with her own. Nora gasped. The creature made a half turn and lay down on the cushions, curling its lithe body tight against Nora's.

"Aw," said Nora, in spite of her fears, remembering how Astrophel used to settle down to sleep in exactly the same way. Whether it was a ghost or a demon—or both—the bulk of the creature was warm and solid. She raised her hand to stroke the spotted fur, and then thought better of it.

After a while, the Kavareen began to snore.

## Chapter 14

We're making no headway at all," Hirizjahkinis said.

"Worse than that," said Aruendiel with a sort of dark satisfaction, as though he enjoyed having his worst suspicions realized. "The more we argue against the alliance, the more deaf the king seems."

They were standing in the middle of a colonnaded courtyard, next to a pool where a bronze statue of the river god Semisl sent fat jets of water into the air. Although it was technically forbidden to work magic in the palace without permission from the chief royal magician, Hirizjahkinis had cast a discreet spell to amplify the sound of water splashing as a precaution against eavesdroppers.

"It would help if you could keep your temper. Your king didn't appreciate being called a fool and a puppet."

"I didn't call him those things. I only said that one would have to be a fool to even contemplate an alliance with Ilissa, and that his grandfather was no Faitoren puppet."

"I think your meaning was very clear. You should be more careful, Aruendiel. They're trying to provoke you. It was dangerous to say that you would never, under any conditions, support a Faitoren alliance."

"It would be a lie to say otherwise."

"But, because you said those words, it will be easier for them to paint you as a rebel and a traitor, if they wish."

He frowned, narrowing his eyes. "Do you think that is what they are driving at?"

"I do," Hirizjahkinis said slowly. "Both Ilissa and Bouragonr looked very smug after you made that declaration, and the king was colder. Think about it from your king's perspective, Aruendiel. If the most powerful magician in the kingdom refuses to support him, Abele will have all the more need to ally with Ilissa."

"If he did ally with Ilissa, I would not hesitate to stand against him," Aruendiel said matter-of-factly. "I have defied other kings for less reason." After a moment he shook his head. "But how tiresome it would be. The game grows old, very old. Yet another greedy, dunderheaded king—"

Hirizjahkinis's mouth tightened slightly. "There doesn't have to be a war, if we keep our heads."

"You're right, though, they are baiting me. When Bouragonr had the temerity to suggest that my opposition to the Faitoren stemmed from personal hurt and animosity—"

"But, my dear old friend, he was quite right."

"Ah, he doesn't know the half of it!" Aruendiel said with a humorless grin. "But there's plenty of other evidence to damn Ilissa and her people. Look at the record of promises broken by the Faitoren, the lands seized, free people enslaved, women kidnapped—which they are still doing, by the way. You should have seen that girl Nora in Ilissa's hands. Enchanted to the ends of her hairs, brain like a cabbage."

"She seems normal enough now."

"Oh, she's made some sort of recovery. The point is, if you can't trust Ilissa to abide by the existing treaty, it's supreme insanity to enter into an alliance with her."

"Here comes Bouragonr's secretary. The king must be back from his ride, ready to receive us again."

"This is going to be an utter waste of time, do you realize that?"

"Just don't let them push you too far."

"And how far is that?" Aruendiel demanded, but the secretary was already within earshot.

Ilissa was the last to arrive in the chamber allotted for the discussions, a long room with a wall fresco showing the sea battle that had placed the current king's great-grandfather on the throne. It had been painted some years after the fact; Aruendiel, who had been present at the battle, had given up trying to count all of the historical inaccuracies. The others were already seated—the king in the canopied chair at the head of the table, waxy-faced but resplendent in a scarlet robe; Bouragonr at his side, his hair streaked with gray, his cheeks purpled with a network of fine veins (Hiriz was right, Aruendiel thought, the court magician was not looking well); Visonis, the king's chief military adviser; on the other side, Hirizjahkinis and Aruendiel. Hirizjahkinis had taken the seat immediately opposite Ilissa's, on the theory that it would be imprudent to let her face Aruendiel directly.

While they were waiting for Ilissa, Visonis spoke lovingly of the advantages to be gained from an invasion of the Meerchinland—how easy it would be to seize the Lower Meerchin River—how the Pernish could be distracted with a second, Faitoren front. Aruendiel offered up a series of counterarguments, citing the Autumn Campaign of the Third Pernish War, but the king listened with a perfunctory air, as though his mind were already made up.

After half an hour, Ilissa arrived, with a rustle of trailing white silk and a delicate furrow of concern in her otherwise flawless brow. "I am devastated to be so late, Your Majesty," she said. "I was detained by some urgent family matters." There was a throb of unusual emotion in her low voice that was impossible to miss.

The king did not miss it. He turned his pale broad face toward Ilissa and regarded her carefully as she took her seat. "I hope there is nothing wrong, my lady," Abele said.

"It is probably nothing at all," Ilissa said. "Only, I had expected to hear from my son before now. He was due to arrive at Semr last night. He has probably been terribly careless and simply forgotten to let me know that he has been delayed, but you know, as a mother, I can't help but worry."

"It is very unlikely that any harm would come to your son in our kingdom," said the king, "especially if he stayed on the main roads."

Ilissa nodded, with a quick, worried smile. "I know, Your Majesty. But he was traveling alone, and, you see, it has been so long since we have ventured abroad that I'm afraid he may have lost his way."

"We will do all in our power to see that he is soon found. The Royal Horse Guard will begin searching the roads around the capital. And my chief magician is at your disposal."

"Of course, of course," Bouragonr said, bobbing his head. "I will be happy to help."

"Thank you, Your Majesty. I'm grateful for your thoughtfulness."

"We would be sad hosts indeed if we did not do everything in our power to ensure safe conduct through our domain for such valued guests," the king said with a gracious nod.

Aruendiel said calmly, "Allow me to set the Lady Ilissa's mind at ease. Her son, the Lord Raclin, is half a day's ride from here, just south of Lost River Lake."

"Excellent news," the king said. "How do you know this, Lord Aruendiel? You met him on your journey here?"

"I did," Aruendiel said, with a long look at Ilissa. "He attacked me repeatedly, and my peasants as well. In our last encounter, since he refused to let me continue my journey in peace, I turned him to stone."

Ilissa stood up, hands flat on the table in front of her. "You did what to my son?"

"I turned him to stone," Aruendiel repeated.

The king said nothing, but his face was as hard as though he had turned to stone, too. Bouragonr, with a glance at his sovereign, got to his feet. "Lord Aruendiel," he said, "if this is true, it is a serious breach of the safe conduct promised to the Lady Ilissa and her party on their diplomatic mission to Semr. It is a serious embarrassment to the monarchy."

"A safe conduct granted to an emissary does not include the right to steal livestock or burn houses or launch unprovoked attacks—all of which Lord Raclin has done," Aruendiel said.

"As you may know," said Ilissa, turning toward the king, "my poor son suffers from a debilitating condition—a very unpleasant transformation— during daylight hours. During that time, it's quite possible that he might make a perfectly friendly overture that could be seen as hostile."

"Madame, there can be no doubt that Lord Raclin's intentions were hostile," Aruendiel said easily, leaning back in his chair.

"Lord Aruendiel, we spent all morning discussing whether to form an alliance with the Faitoren. Why did you not mention these supposed attacks before this?" Bouragonr demanded.

"I did not wish to introduce any personal animosity into this debate."

The king finally spoke, folding his hands on the table. "Lord Aruendiel, can this spell be removed?"

"It can."

"Well, then, the easiest solution to this matter is for you to remove the spell and restore the Lady Ilissa's son to his previous condition."

"I will not."

"Would you defy a direct command from your sovereign?" Bouragonr asked.

"Sire, simple prudence makes it impossible to agree to your request. I turned Lord Raclin into stone to save my own life and that of a fellow traveler. If I removed the spell—and I would have to travel back to the site to do so—Lord Raclin would only resume his attack. I would have to counter with another spell, possibly something that would cause even more harm to Lady Ilissa's son."

Sinking back into her chair, Ilissa uttered a small, anguished moan and clenched a fist to her breast. "Lord Aruendiel, you are most unkind."

Hirizjahkinis spoke for the first time. "It's possible that someone else besides Aruendiel could remove the spell."

"Why, yes," Aruendiel said. "Most competent magicians could take it off." He smiled mockingly at Bouragonr. "Of course," he added, "there would still be Lord Raclin to contend with, but perhaps he would be better disposed toward another magician besides myself."

"And why, exactly, is Lord Raclin so ill-disposed toward you?" Bouragonr asked. "Perhaps because his wife is currently residing under your protection?"

"Lord Aruendiel, is this true?" the king asked sharply.

Before Aruendiel could answer, Ilissa broke in. "It is true. My daughter-in-law disappeared from my home almost three months ago. We learned that she was abducted by Lord Aruendiel's magic and that she has been living in his castle ever since. I cannot tell you how my son has been heartbroken by this betrayal.

"I did not want to mention this sad affair before now," Ilissa added, casting her eyes down. "Since it involves a stain on my family's honor. And as Lord Aruendiel himself said, it would be a shame to taint state business with personal animosities."

The king looked curiously at Aruendiel, taking in the magician's battered face afresh and perhaps remembering the old stories that were still circulating around the court when Abele was a child. "Lord Aruendiel? What do you have to say about this?"

Aruendiel had been exchanging a look with Hirizjahkinis, but now he turned back to the king with an air of new alertness. He said: "The Lady Ilissa fails to mention that she and her son kidnapped and enchanted the woman who became his wife; that Lord Raclin savagely attacked his wife, to the point that she lost the child that she was carrying; and that the woman left her husband's household willingly. Since then, she has stayed in my household as a respected guest."

"I see," said the king. "Well, there seems to be no shortage of personal animosity to go around."

Hirizjahkinis was the only one to laugh. Ilissa gave her a look of composed dislike, to which the other woman only smiled, straightening her pearl headdress and plucking a small, stray gray feather from her white linen robe. Absently, Hirizjahkinis twirled the feather between her thumb and forefinger, then rubbed it lightly against her earlobe.

"Lord Aruendiel," Abele continued, "you must know that abducting another man's wife, whether she comes willingly or unwillingly, is a very serious crime."

"I am aware of that."

"Men have been killed for this offense."

"Yes," Aruendiel said, with a touch of annoyance.

"This is not a court of law, and I am not sitting in judgment, but I must tell you that I cannot condone it, and that in my view it explains and to some extent justifies the attacks that you claim Lord Raclin has committed."

From the corner of his eye, Aruendiel glanced at Hirizjahkinis, who nodded slightly.

"I would strongly advise you," the king went on, "to return the lady to her husband, no matter how charming she may be."

"Sire, you misread the situation." Now Aruendiel had fully unsheathed his impatience. "There is no liaison. I helped the lady leave her husband's home because she was in danger, and because the Faitoren had—once again—kidnapped a human woman as a bride for Lord Raclin. They show no respect for the treaty that we struck with them almost fifty years ago. Do you think they will respect the treaty that you are negotiating now?"

"My son's wife married him willingly," Ilissa interjected. "She was not coerced."

"She was enchanted," Aruendiel shot back.

"Furthermore, she is not even one of—" Bouragonr said, then caught himself. "I'm sorry, I interrupted the Lord Aruendiel."

"I believe the Lord Aruendiel had finished speaking," said the king. "Please go on."

"I was just going to say, Your Majesty," said Bouragonr, "that we have only the Lord Aruendiel's word that the Faitoren took this lady against her will."

"There is the woman's own word," Aruendiel said quickly.

Bouragonr snorted. "That has no legal weight."

"We are not in the law courts!"

"Your Majesty!" Ilissa said, lifting one slim hand in a gesture that gracefully begged for quiet. "I would like to thank you for suggesting to Lord Aruendiel that he return my son's wife to her lawful husband. We would welcome her back. No matter what tragic mistakes she has made, she is still a member of my family."

The king gave an approving nod. "A very enlightened view. Lord Aruendiel, what do you think now?"

"Why not consult the woman herself?" Aruendiel said, although he did not meet Abele's gaze. He glanced at Hirizjahkinis, who was toying with one of her bracelets with an air of slight distraction.

"That is easily done," said Ilissa smoothly. "She is here at court. I understand that she arrived with Lord Aruendiel last night."

"Well, that does make things more convenient," Abele said. "Bouragonr, will you—?"

"Let us send for her at once," Bouragonr said, raising his finger. At once the door at the far end of the room opened, and his secretary appeared, tablet and stylus at the ready. "Once this side matter is settled," he said severely to Aruendiel, "I trust that we can return to the main issue at hand."

"I would be pleased to do so," Aruendiel said, looking levelly at Bouragonr.

Bouragonr opened his mouth again, presumably to address the secretary, who was hurrying closer. "Pel—" he started to say. The word dissolved into a gasp. Bouragonr's hands flew to his face, groping at his cheeks.

Bouragonr's mottled skin had grown clear and taut; his hair was sleeker, the gray streaks gone; his mouth and jaw line were newly firm; his stooped shoulders filled out. Decades had dropped away in a matter of seconds: The aging courtier was a straight-backed young man. He looked terrified.

"Bouragonr?" said the king, a note of uncertainty in his voice.

Still clutching his face, the young man who had been the old Bouragonr shuddered violently. Then he seemed to fall forward, but that was an illusion; his body was sagging like a falling tent, until he was only three-quarters the height he had been. The fingers covering his face became longer and skinnier, and there were more of them, six fingers on one hand, seven on the other. When he lowered his hands, the others could see that his mouth now wrapped around the side of his head, like a frog's. His lips and nose had disappeared. He looked up at them from round black eyes that had no whites at all.

There was a clatter. The secretary had dropped his tablet on the floor. "Bouragonr?" the king asked again.

"That is not Bouragonr," said Hirizjahkinis.

"That is a Faitoren, in its natural state," Aruendiel said.

Abele's gaze slid to Aruendiel. "My chief magician is a Faitoren?"

"No, not originally. There has been a substitution—probably in the recent past. Sometime after the Lady Ilissa arrived in Semr," Aruendiel said.

"That is an outrageous suggestion, Aruendiel!" Ilissa said. "Your Majesty, I must protest. I will not be insulted by one of your subjects!"

"Do you deny that this is one of your people, Ilissa?" Aruendiel asked. "Hirizjahkinis took off not just the spell that made the Faitoren look like Bouragonr, but the spell that made him look human in the first place."

"Then where is my chief magician?" the king asked, looking at the Faitoren with distaste. "You, sir, what have you done with my chief magician?"

The Faitoren opened its wide mouth, giving the others a glimpse of a long gray tongue, but it said nothing.

"Lady Ilissa, is this indeed one of your Faitoren?" Abele asked. "I had always thought that your people were, well, more pleasing to the eye."

Ilissa hesitated, but finally she nodded. "Yes, Your Majesty. That is one of my people."

"And why was he disguised?"

"Oh, it's the custom among us Faitoren to wear faces of our own devising, Your Majesty," Ilissa said with a wistful smile, "much the way you or any other human might choose an elegant garment to wear. It is a bit of a game with us. We take pleasure in the art of it, in seeing who can make themselves the most beautiful, and in the end we grow so used to our chosen faces that we forget that we are even wearing them. These magicians"—she threw a scornful look at Hirizjahkinis and Aruendiel—"have taken it upon themselves to tear away the face that poor Gaibon made for himself. It is an act of both rudeness and cruelty, like stripping someone naked in a public street."

"Yes, I see," said Abele. "But why would your subject want to make himself look like Bouragonr? Bouragonr is no beauty. An excellent chief magician, but not a handsome man."

"A very distinguished man," Ilissa insisted sweetly.

"Yes, perhaps, but even so, I can't permit one of your subjects to simply insert himself in the place of my chief magician. There are all sorts of security and confidentiality issues here. And what has become of Bouragonr?"

"Oh, I am sure that Gaibon has done nothing to harm Bouragonr. Isn't that right, Gaibon dear?"

Gaibon said something in muddy Ors that could have been an assent.

"You, Lady Ilissa, what have you done with Bouragonr?" Hirizjahkinis spoke up suddenly. "Gaibon is not lying—"

"He can't lie," Aruendiel muttered.

"—but can you deny responsibility for Bouragonr's disappearance?"

"I don't need to," said Ilissa. "It is a preposterous accusation."

"But it's not preposterous at all. You came here to persuade this king to lift the restrictions on the Faitoren. You knew that Bouragonr, his trusted adviser, would not favor such a plan—Bouragonr was one of the magicians, like Aruendiel, like myself, who defeated you half a century ago. But there was a way for you to turn Bouragonr's suspicion to your advantage. If he supported the alliance, despite his known distrust of the Faitoren, it would make your cause more credible. Bouragonr's support would not only help sway King Abele, it would make the alliance more palatable to many lords as well."

"Lady Hirizjahkinis, I'm terribly flattered that you would think me capable of such clever scheming."

"When I arrived here in Semr," Hirizjahkinis continued, "I was surprised by how little opposition Bouragonr raised to the proposed alliance. Today, in fact, he seemed to advocate frankly for the Faitoren side. But I did not think that Bouragonr was not actually Bouragonr, until Aruendiel suggested it to me a little while ago."

"Lord Aruendiel?" the king asked, his voice sharpening. "How did you discover this substitution? Some of your famous magic?"

"No," said Aruendiel. "I simply found it odd that Bouragonr would know that the human woman who had escaped the Faitoren was living in my household. I had done nothing to advertise the fact. But the Faitoren knew. So I asked Hirizjahkinis to investigate while Your Majesty and I continued our conversation."

"I heard no such request," said the king.

"That is some of my famous magic, Sire," Aruendiel said, unsmiling.

"Your Majesty," said Ilissa to the king, with an air of appealing to the only sensible person in the room, "I'm afraid I'm losing patience with this absurdity. Your subjects, these magicians, have insulted and attacked me and the members of my legation. I demand an apology—and I demand that Aruendiel reverse the terrible magic that he has worked on my son."

"I will do it," said Aruendiel, his mouth curling, "I will even apologize—if you tell us where Bouragonr is."

The king coughed and looked down at the table. "Lady Ilissa, if you can offer any help in locating my chief magician, it would be taken as, as—a gesture of great goodwill," he said at last.

"Enough." Ilissa rose from her chair. "I will hear no more of this. King Abele, you should know that those who slight me always regret it. The magician Aruendiel can tell you that." Her lips curved in a fragile smile as sharp as a scythe. Her dress seemed to be made of white flames.

Turning on her heel, she walked swiftly down the length of the long council table to the double doors. They flew open for her without a touch. Gaibon scuttled after her.

"Regrettable," said the king musingly after the doors had closed behind her. "Extremely regrettable." He did not specify exactly what he was referring to, Ilissa's angry departure or the disappearance of his chief magician or the end of the alliance negotiations or the fact that he had opened negotiations in the first place. Quite likely he was not sure himself.

"When did you learn how to undo that Faitoren masking spell?" Hirizjahkinis demanded of Aruendiel, once they were in the corridor. They had left the king and his military advisers to plot out the invasion of the Meerchinland without Faitoren aid.

"I worked out a method and tried it for the first time last winter," he said. "Interesting results, don't you think? Although you took your time getting it to work."

"Your directions were a bit sketchy."

"There's only so much one can say with a feather. You figured it out eventually."

"Now, can we use the same method to find Bouragonr? Could she have used the same kind of masking spell to hide him away?"

"It's possible. Although it's more likely she killed him outright."

"You always believe the worst of that woman, don't you?" Hirizjahkinis said, chuckling. "All right, we will try to find his body then. We'll start by following Ilissa's trail, visiting the places that she has visited."

"How do you propose to do that?" he asked, shaking his head. "By asking the walls what they saw? By wood and water, that will take forever. Once walls start talking, they never shut up."

"No, no. You will be annoyed to hear it, Aruendiel, but this is exactly the kind of situation where the Kavareen can be very useful."


## Chapter 15

Nora was scratching the Kavareen behind the ears when the two magicians came into the room. Aruendiel looked disquieted at the sight, but Hirizjahkinis only smiled. "I see you have become friends."

"More or less," Nora allowed. "After I realized it wasn't going to eat me."

"You'd be too small a meal," Aruendiel said. "The Kavareen prefers to consume cities, or whole armies."

"Enough, Aruendiel! Now, we need the Kavareen for another task, Mistress Nora, so we must ask you to come with us." Hirizjahkinis spoke quickly to the Kavareen in the singsong tongue. The animal jumped off the divan and stalked out of the room.

"Now, the Kavareen has a very keen nose," Hirizjahkinis told Aruendiel as they followed. "Especially for magic."

"Isn't that how it tracked you down and almost killed you, that time in the desert?"

"Luckily, I killed it first. He can tell us exactly where Ilissa has been in the palace and—what is even better—where she did magic."

They came to an enormous hall, forested with octagonal pillars. A crowd was milling around the base of the pillars, the women in luxurious trailing gowns, the men in equally lavish long coats or tunics. The Kavareen growled and sat down. "Ilissa was certainly here, and worked some magic," Hirizjahkinis said, glancing around.

"Not surprisingly—this is the main reception hall," Aruendiel said. "She was probably in and out of here every day of her visit."

They made a slow circuit of the hall. Several people hailed Aruendiel, but he gave only the most perfunctory of responses. Hirizjahkinis, by contrast, made a sort of dignified progress around the room, a small, erect figure who smiled warmly at those who greeted her, without showing the slightest inclination to halt her steps for anyone.

"I can't find anything," Hirizjahkinis said when they had finished.

"Nor I," he said.

"What exactly are we looking for?" Nora asked.

"Some evidence of recent magic," Aruendiel said dismissively. "Nothing that you would know about."

He had said harsher things to her before, but for some reason this offhand remark stung especially. Nora frowned and asked: "Is there any chance that we'll run into Ilissa herself?"

Aruendiel studied her for a moment. "Ilissa would like to see you," he said. "She told us so today. She said she would welcome you back into her family."

"I hope you told her I'd rather die! You're not going to send me back to her—are you?"

"Don't torment her, Aruendiel," said Hirizjahkinis. "Mistress Nora, Ilissa is about to leave Semr, but not with you. We spent quite a long time talking about you this afternoon—I know, you are probably distressed to hear this—but in the end it helped us discover that Ilissa had been sly enough to put a Faitoren in place of the king's magician, and even King Abele was not blind enough to overlook her little trick."

"Hmm," Nora said. "I'd like to hear more about this."

"Yes, yes, yes," said Hirizjahkinis. "Now, where next? Ah, the Kavareen thinks we should go to the east wing."

They went to the east wing, and then the old east wing. Then the queen's pavilion, the queen's gallery, and the queen's drawing rooms. The summer banquet hall, and the two winter banquet halls. It almost seemed to Nora that she was back in the endless splendor of Ilissa's castle.

"Is there any room in the entire palace that she didn't visit?" Aruendiel groaned as they left the long gallery where the king's armor was on display.

The north tower. The king's private reception hall. The buttery. The wine cellar.

"Is Ilissa much of a drinker?" Hirizjahkinis asked.

"She served oceans of wine at her parties," Nora said before Aruendiel could answer.

"That wasn't real wine," he said dismissively. "I wonder if she came down here to poison a bottle for Bouragonr?"

"Or to lock him up in one of these bottles."

Nora moaned inwardly. There were thousands of dark and dusty bottles lying on racks in the cellar. She waited in the semidarkness while Aruendiel and Hirizjahkinis went slowly up and down the narrow aisles, occasionally running a finger along the curved side of a bottle. They found nothing.

The central courtyard. The library.

"The library?" Aruendiel stopped short. "The Kavareen is playing games with us. Ilissa has no interest in books. The Faitoren are magical beings; she's never had to read a spell in her life."

The Kavareen twitched its tail and emitted a long, snarling whine.

"No, she was here," Hirizjahkinis insisted. "The Kavareen says she did some very strong magic here, too."

Nora was looking around with interest. It was a long room, full of light from a row of high windows along one wall. The other walls were lined with bookshelves or wooden compartments designed for scrolls. There were a few reading stands, and a table strewn with oversize books, some of them open to show graceful lines of brushstrokes and bright touches of illustration. At the far end of the room, through an arched doorway, were more shelves, evidently the beginning of the stacks. Nora tried to spell out some of the Ors titles on the shelves nearest her. *History of the Victories of the Sun's Own Anointed Mirle IV. Of the Glorious Founding of the House of Semr.* This must be the history section, or maybe propaganda was more like it. *Record of the Pernish War, Including a True Account of the Southern Campaign, the Suvian Regency, and the Treachery of the Wizard Aruendiel.*

Nora reread the last title, puzzled, wondering if she had read it correctly, and then looked around quickly for Aruendiel himself. He and Hirizjahkinis were disappearing through the arched doorway. She pulled the book off the shelf and scanned the pages for Aruendiel's name, but she could make almost nothing out of the thicket of ink that filled the page. "I hate being illiterate," she muttered.

She followed the others into a second room of bookshelves, half-lit by a single small window, where they were watching the Kavareen pace up and down the aisles. The creature kept looking up at the books and making a faint snicker-snicker sound that seemed to Nora to indicate some degree of frustration. But perhaps, she thought, she was only projecting her own feelings.

"He says it's here," Hirizjahkinis said.

"This room is where the books of magic are kept," Aruendiel objected. "You don't think he could be reacting to them? Some of the books themselves are enchanted, of course."

Both of the magicians were speaking more softly than usual, Nora noticed. Library behavior must be the same in all worlds.

"Let's take a look. We will need more light."

Hirizjahkinis's tangle of gold necklaces suddenly gleamed brighter, much brighter, to yield a flickering yellow light that illuminated the bookshelf in front of her. She began to examine the array of books, touching the spine of each. Aruendiel cupped his hand, and flames blazed up inside his palm, so close to the nearest shelf that Nora feared the books would catch fire. Then she saw how pale and thin, almost watery, the flames were. Like the ghost of a fire, she thought.

As the magicians worked their way through the stacks, Nora drifted along behind Aruendiel, trying to stay close enough to see by his light without being obtrusive. She felt some envy of Hirizjahkinis—Aruendiel treated her as an equal, someone whose opinion he obviously respected, even if he complained about the Kavareen. How long did it take Hirizjahkinis to become a magician? How long had it taken Aruendiel, for that matter? Or were magicians born, not made?

With some wistfulness, Nora ran her fingers over the gilt seal—a snake twined around a crescent moon—stamped on the frayed black spine of a volume as big as the unabridged dictionary.

"Stop that," said Aruendiel, glancing back at her.

"Eh?" Hirizjahkinis called from another aisle.

"Not you."

The magic books were a greater distraction for the magicians, though. Aruendiel kept stopping to yank books off the shelf and leaf through them, balancing them awkwardly in the crook of his elbow while cradling his handful of fire. Judging from the sounds coming from the other aisle, Hirizjahkinis was also browsing.

"Pogo Vernish's book on transformations. I didn't know they had a copy here."

"Isn't it completely out of date? . . . You're right, Aruendiel, some of these books are enchanted. This spell is meant to drive the reader mad."

"I know of that book. In my great-grandfather's time, the crown prince sent it to his father, Harnigon II. He hoped to force the old king to abdicate."

"And did he?"

"The king went mad and had his son killed. Does it still work?"

"The spell? You'll have to tell me," Hirizjahkinis said, chuckling. "I don't feel any different. . . . Ah, Aruendiel, here are some of your notebooks! Let's see, a collection of siegecraft spells, and an essay on magical landscape gardening."

"Oh, yes. I laid out some of the palace gardens here in Semr, years ago." He turned into the next aisle. "This is the end of the magic collection; the last two rows are the foreign books."

"Let me see," Hirizjahkinis said, following him. "This library used to have a good collection from my country, the only copy of the Book of the Five Stones outside of Hajgog—"

Nora wished sharply that she could join in. "I thought we were supposed to be looking for this person Bouragonr," she said under her breath. Aruendiel must have heard, because he frowned. Nora went past them into the last aisle, next to the window. The books in this row were more eclectic in manufacture. On the lower shelves were clay tablets and engraved metal plates; the upper shelves held bound volumes and scrolls. Nora found a myriad of alphabets: one that was all concentric circles; pictograms of running animals and birds; signs that reminded her of Sanskrit or Arabic or Greek without looking exactly like any of those languages. Except that the lettering on the tag for one of the scrolls, lying by itself in a bin, did look very much like Greek. Nora picked up the brittle paper and unrolled it slowly. The first lines of a long poem. Yes, in Greek. She had translated these lines herself, the first year of graduate school, in Dr. Decker's Homeric Greek seminar: μηνιν αειδε θεα.

Nora sang a brief, wordless note of joy. Aruendiel appeared at the end of the aisle. "Look," she said, "Greek. It's Greek! From my world."

He took the scroll from her. "I don't know this language," he said. "You recognize it?"

"Yes, of course! I can read it. A little," she said, wishing violently that she had not dropped Greek after Dr. Decker's seminar.

Aruendiel did not seem to be terribly impressed. "Well, of course, there are books from other worlds in this library," he said with a crooked shrug. "Micher Samle has donated some, I know. You might look around and see if any other books from your world have landed here."

He turned and went back to the end of the aisle. An instant later Nora heard Hirizjahkinis say, "You didn't tell me she was from another world! The things you keep to yourself, Aruendiel." She couldn't make out Aruendiel's reply.

Nora began looking over the shelves more carefully. Ten minutes later, after searching most of the aisle, she had found a clay tablet inscribed with what *might* have been Sumerian cuneiform, and a fat book that was certainly written in Japanese. From the diagrams, it looked like some sort of electrical engineering manual.

"Rats," she said in English, putting the book back. And then, as her eyes traveled along the shelves, a jolt of recognition. Not so much the English words, the familiar title—although that registered quickly enough—but the worn spine, the bright colors: a cheap paperback, the kind you couldn't give away at a yard sale. Not just any cheap paperback, either.

Nora eased it out of the bookcase. It had been wedged in so tightly that the cover almost came off—the same cover that had caught her eye back in the rental cabin. A line drawing of a simpering young miss with a parasol. *Pride and Prejudice*. Jane Austen. Classics Series. Fifty cents. The book was slightly bent down the middle, from where she had jammed it into the back pocket of her jeans.

Nora turned it over and automatically read the blurb on the back, taking pleasure in how easy it was to understand the English sentences. But she was so agitated that she could hardly take in their meaning. The mere presence of the book seemed to be a validation of some sort. She felt like Schliemann unearthing the walls of heretofore mythical Troy. And then a clearer thought: How did this thing get here? It crossed her mind that the book could signal some kind of recovery, that she was about to wake from a long delirium and return to reality.

Aruendiel turned and looked down at her, his gray eyes curious, cool. "What do you have there?" he asked.

"This book, it's from my world," she said, giving him a challenging glance. He showed no signs of vanishing.

"Oh? What kind of book?" Hirizjahkinis said.

"It's a—story," Nora said, searching for an Ors word for "novel," and failing to find one. "A very famous one. A comedy of manners that takes place in England—" The others looked blank; she amended the description quickly. "It deals with love and marriage."

"Really? The whole book? What an interesting idea!"

"The odd thing is," Nora said slowly, "this is my own copy. That is, I had it when I came into this world. But I lost it. I don't know how it got into this library."

Aruendiel's expression was honed with interest. "But you only just now found it again?"

"Yes. I'm sure it's mine, though." Absently she opened the paperback to flip through the pages.

Her first thought was that the book was alive. That was impossible, but if it was not alive, how could it be looking up with that red-rimmed eye, wet and blinking? Just the one eye, roving wildly under wrinkled lids, where there should be nothing but neat lines of type.

She wanted to slam the book shut, but at the same time she had a squeamish fear of crushing the eye and feeling its gelatinous squelch through the thin cardboard of the cover. Then she saw that the eye wasn't resting on the page, it was *under* the surface of the page. She got a glimpse of a distorted face and foreshortened limbs, like the view through the fisheye peephole in an apartment door, except what exactly was she looking into? Lost in a book, lost in a book, she thought—I will never use that expression lightly again.

"I think I found your Bouragonr," she said.

Bent over the open paperback, Aruendiel and Hirizjahkinis experimented with a couple of different spells that had no apparent effect before trying one that made the book grow very large and then very small and finally left a gray-haired man in a brown velvet tunic tottering in front of them. He groaned and collapsed against the bookcase.

Aruendiel half dragged, half carried the newly freed prisoner into the reading room and went to summon help from the palace staff. Hirizjahkinis produced a silver flask from thin air and made Bouragonr drink it. In fits and starts, he told her his story: He had run across Ilissa in the library, and she had shown him a little book in a foreign language, which he had opened with mild curiosity. The next thing he knew, he was shut up in a dark place with no food or water.

The library quickly filled with people: a crew of servants, the palace chamberlain, one of the royal doctors, and a growing cohort of gawkers. The doctor attended to Bouragonr for some minutes, and then the patient was taken away on a stretcher. Nora was relieved to see him go. Unfair as it was, she felt a certain resentment toward Bouragonr. The shock of seeing his agitated eye looking out of the book had slightly tainted her pleasure in finding it again.

"He'll be fine in a few days," said Hirizjahkinis, fastening the leopard pelt around her neck again; she had retired the Kavareen after he snarled at one of the visitors.

"Oh, Bouragonr's health will be restored easily enough. It's his position that will feel the hurt," Aruendiel said sourly.

"The king will dismiss him, you think?"

"His chief magician taken prisoner by the Faitoren within the very palace walls? Abele can hardly keep Bouragonr on after such a blunder. It's too bad," he added. "Bouragonr isn't a bad magician, or at least he wasn't before he spent so much time at court."

Hirizjahkinis laughed. "You won't be applying for his job, I believe?"

"Never! Although I almost wish that you would, Hiriz. It would ease my mind to know that a magician with good sense had taken the post. I want no more talk of Faitoren alliances."

"I'm surprised you wish me so ill, Aruendiel. Never will I subject myself again to one of your terrible winters."

Aruendiel glanced around. The library was almost empty again. "Nothing else to do here. We can be on our way. Mistress Nora!"

Nora was in the history section, looking for the book that had mentioned Aruendiel in the title. She turned with a twinge of guilt. "Yes? Are we leaving?"

"Yes, make haste," he said. "And I want to know more about this book of yours."

"Well, I have a theory about how it got here," Nora said. "Ilissa brought it. It must have fallen out of my pocket at Ilissa's castle, and then she found it. What I don't understand, though, is why she brought the book to Semr. Could she have been planning to use it all along to trap Bouragonr?"

Aruendiel gave a crooked shrug. "Perhaps. It was a shrewd place to hide him, a book in a foreign tongue that no one would likely open for years. Or she may have brought the book with some idea of doing you harm. Since it was your possession, it would give her some limited power over you. That's a very primitive, imprecise form of magic, and not Ilissa's usual style, but it's a possibility."

"But how could she have known that I would even be here in Semr?" Nora objected. "We only decided to come yesterday."

"Perhaps she was reading your book," said Hirizjahkinis. Aruendiel snorted. "No, I am only half-joking," she added. "Mistress Nora says that it is a very famous story, and it is all about love and marriage, very much to Ilissa's taste, I think."

"I don't think Ilissa can read," Aruendiel said stiffly.

"It's really not one of my favorites," said Nora. "But I was going to have to teach it in summer school."

Even if *Pride and Prejudice* wasn't one of her favorites, it left the library with her, tucked surreptitiously inside her sleeve. Finally, something to read.

Leading the way from the library, Aruendiel chose a route through the palace that went through back staircases and side corridors. Nora could guess why. The news of Bouragonr's kidnapping had already spread throughout the court. They got stares and whispers from the people they encountered on their way.

"Ridiculous uproar," Aruendiel muttered.

"Don't pretend you're not enjoying it," Hirizjahkinis said.

The chamberlain waylaid them near one of the winter banquet halls. He expressed a hope that the two distinguished magicians who had just rendered such a great service to Lord Bouragonr and the king were not too fatigued to join the king's other magicians and ministers in the council wing, in order to give a full account of the day's remarkable events.

Before Aruendiel could answer, Hirizjahkinis said they would be pleased to do so. The three followed the chamberlain to a part of the palace where the corridors were smaller and dingier. Through half-open doors, Nora saw clerks filling their scrolls with brushwork or dropping stones into a complicated wooden gadget that, she decided, must be some sort of abacus. This was evidently the palace's back office.

After a few minutes, they entered a long, columned gallery. A knot of men engaged in conversation turned to greet the two magicians; then an older man with a ballooning double chin claimed Aruendiel's attention. Nora could not get close enough to hear much of what was being said. Aruendiel was speaking rapidly, matter-of-factly, the double-chinned man interrupting with what seemed to be a tinge of skepticism. Aruendiel paid no attention to the interruptions.

Hirizjahkinis, closer at hand, was drawn into a technical discussion with a youngish, heavy-featured man about the spell that had imprisoned the royal magician. That was interesting, or might have been—Nora was hoping for some clue as to how this magic thing actually worked—but their talk of edges, stops, seals, and wicks soon lost her.

With some frustration, Nora moved toward the other end of the gallery. Portraits hung between the columns that lined the walls—grave, elderly men, mostly, although there were some grave, young men represented, too. Nora amused herself by noting the change in men's fashions, from layered, vaguely Chinese-looking robes to tunics and knee-length coats worn over close-fitting breeches. The coats seemed to be the more modern note; only a few men in the room now were wearing tunics, the older style. Aruendiel was one. Again, she wondered how old he was.

A fireplace was set into the wall at one end of the gallery, with a pair of ceramic animals guarding each end of the mantelpiece: a wolf and a lion. Nora had seen variations of the two-headed wolf-lion carved, painted, and embroidered all over the palace that day. Some sort of dynastic symbol, obviously—representing the union of two kingdoms, or two ruling families? This was the first time she'd seen the two animals depicted separately. She ran an exploratory finger over the ceramic lion's head. It was clear that the artist was familiar with exactly what a wolf looked like—especially a large, hungry wolf—but was not so sure about a lion. The lion he had shaped had a luxuriant, shawl-like mane of carefully curled ringlets and a round, rather merry face.

"You know, *I* was the one who found Bouragonr," Nora told the lion quietly, slipping into English. She glanced back at the group at the other end of the room. "And it was my book, and hey, I'm from another world. Not that I'm a magician or anything, but you'd think they might want to talk to me, too."

The lion looked at her with wide, amused eyes. She touched the glazed mane again, gently tracing the curve of one clay lock. It really was a lovely piece, she thought, the kind of sculpture that belonged in a museum— if there were museums here. "I don't know anything about art—art in this world, anyway," she said, leaning close to the clay figure, "but I know what I like, and I like you very much. I can tell you're a lion of character."

She raised a finger in a brief, ironic good-bye, and then turned slowly to retrace her steps.

Midway down the gallery, an open archway on the right led into a spacious hall, lightly trafficked, with a grand bronze door at the far end. On the left, another archway opened into a very small, enclosed garden. Nora stepped outside and took a turn around the stone path. After a few minutes, she went inside.

As she stepped into the gallery, Nora had a direct view through the opposite archway, into the other hall. A woman was passing—tall, wrapped in a dark green cloak. She turned and looked at Nora. It was Ilissa.

## Chapter 16

fterward Nora thought that if she had reacted more quickly, if she had called out or run away or done *something*, there might have been time to escape. Ilissa seemed as surprised to see Nora as Nora was to see her. For a moment neither of them moved. But then Ilissa smiled and looked heartbreakingly beautiful and kind, and it was too late.

The truth—Nora felt it come scuttling out from the shadows of her heart—was that when she had told Aruendiel that day that she didn't want to meet Ilissa, she had been lying. Or rather, she both dreaded seeing Ilissa and hoped that she would. It was a kind of bravado: This time, she wouldn't be weak. She'd be strong, wise, adult enough not to fall victim to whatever sweet, suffocating magic Ilissa had worked on her before. Also, she was curious to see whether Ilissa was as perfect—as lovely, as loving—as Nora remembered. Surely there must be a flaw somewhere, a clue that it was all fake. The tip-off would be obvious once you saw it; the trick was to see it clearly for the first time.

But that moment of revelation would not occur now, Nora realized, facing Ilissa. Ilissa's charm was still intact, her face ready to launch a thousand ships or sell a million magazines, and worse, Nora herself had not changed, or at least not enough. Whatever unprotected place Ilissa had found before, she still knew how to find it.

"Nora, you poor darling!" Ilissa's voice was soothing, gentle, impossible to ignore. "Dressed in rags! We've missed you so much, you know," she added sadly.

In spite of herself, Nora's heart was wrung. Without exactly meaning to, she took a step toward Ilissa.

"Are you really happy, darling? You don't look happy. There's something so dissatisfied in your face."

Nora willed her feet to stay firmly planted on the marble floor. After a few seconds that seemed very long, she took another step.

"You look lonely, I think. Are those magicians"—a little purr of scorn underlined the word—"being kind to you?"

Nora looked over at the magicians in question, a few dozen paces away.

Hirizjahkinis had her back turned. Aruendiel's head was visible above the crowd; he was looking down, listening to something the double-chinned man was saying. "Help!" Nora screamed as loud as she could. "Ilissa's here!" Nothing emerged from her mouth except a silent rush of air.

Ilissa gave a short laugh that sounded nastier than anything that Nora had ever heard her utter. This could be the crack in the crystal, the tip-off that she'd been waiting for, but it was a little late. Nora took another step.

"Wouldn't you like to come home with me, darling?" Ilissa held out her hands. "Where we love you so much."

No, you don't, Nora thought swiftly, although part of her only wanted to run straight into Ilissa's arms. Again, she concentrated on staying exactly where she was. The desire to move her foot forward was like an overpowering itch. Five seconds, she could hold back for five seconds. She counted them off. Another five seconds. That was a little worse, but she could stand it. Another five. The desire to move forward was agonizing.

A shade of exquisite disappointment passed over Ilissa's face, and Nora winced inwardly. It was very wrong, she knew, to make Ilissa unhappy—Ilissa, the only person who loved her. And what Ilissa said was so true. Nora was lonely, worse than lonely—she was terrified, lost, worn out from making her way in a world of strangers, from being at the unpredictable mercy of magicians.

Tears filled Nora's eyes. But she did not move.

"They don't care about you, those magicians. What do you matter to them?" Ilissa's voice seemed to be coming from within Nora's own heart. "No one here understands you. This is not your world. You mean nothing here."

Ilissa was false to the bottom, Nora could smell it, and yet there was no resisting the truth of her words. Nora uttered a silent whimper. If she kept standing here, trying to resist Ilissa, she would collapse and lose control of her own body—go sprawling on the floor, helpless as an infant. And even then, perhaps, the magicians over there, absorbed in their conversations, would notice nothing.

She tore her eyes from Ilissa's face and looked frantically around again. Only the round eyes of the clay lion met hers.

All at once, a new emotion rose within her, a calm, spreading exhilaration. Surprised by joy, Nora thought. There was no reason for her to feel this way. Was it part of Ilissa's honeyed enchantment? Why did she suddenly feel so powerful, when she had no power? Then the fear seized her again, roughly.

In the corner of her eye, off to the right, there was a blur of movement. An animal leaping. Something shattered, explosively. The noise splashed against her ears like cold water.

"If what you're saying is true, Lord Aruendiel," the minister said, "we'll have to—" He broke off at the sound of the crash. The murmur of voices halted.

Aruendiel looked up. Broken crockery was sprayed across the floor at the far end of the gallery.

The minister clucked, turning back to Aruendiel. "The servant girl knocked something off the mantelpiece."

"Wasn't that one of the Deriguisian figurines?" said someone disapprovingly. "They're irreplaceable."

Aruendiel saw that the girl Nora was standing near the smashed figurine. Her head half turned, and her eyes met his. Her mouth worked silently. There was a heavy, glazed look on her face that was unusual for her.

"Excuse me," he said to the minister, pushing his way through the group. Nora took a step into the next room, disappearing from view.

She was giving in now because she was too exhausted to do otherwise. The sound of the smashing statuette—poor lion, she felt oddly responsible—had startled both her and Ilissa, had given her a brief respite. But now she was completely out of strength. Weary of desires and dreams and powers, of everything but sleep. Ilissa came toward her, smiling graciously now that she'd won.

Awkward, hurrying footsteps sounded on the marble floor, and Nora sensed rather than saw a dark figure looming at her back. "Ah," said Aruendiel's voice, in a tone that indicated he was neither surprised nor pleased to see Ilissa. He clamped his hand onto Nora's shoulder. She felt a jolt, a backlash surge through her body, trying to repel his grip. His hand only tightened.

"Let her go, Aruendiel," Ilissa said warningly.

"After you do."

Ilissa did not answer. Her eyes moved back and forth, studying him closely.

A smaller figure came up behind Nora on the other side. "Well, if there must be a fight, I don't want to be left out," Hirizjahkinis said.

With an almost imperceptible shrug, Ilissa stepped back. "Very well then, Aruendiel," she said, flashing a radiant smile. "You take her, the poor child. But it's sad, really. Is she the best you can do, these days?"

Aruendiel said nothing as Ilissa turned on her heel and strode down the other hall toward the bronze door. Only when it had closed behind her did he let go of Nora's shoulder. She turned to look up at him.

The girl was pale and drained, he saw, but the dull, preoccupied look in her eyes was gone. "All right now?" he inquired brusquely.

"Thank you," Nora started to say, but no sound would come out of her mouth. She tried again with no better results. "My voice is gone," she mouthed, gesturing toward her throat.

"A silencing spell, eh?" Aruendiel said. He yanked Nora's jaw up and glanced quickly into her nostrils, then into one of her ears. He had done something similar, Nora remembered now, the first time she had met him. Then, frowning, he looked over at the mass of broken crockery.

"What happened here?"

Nora made a hesitant gesture to indicate something jumping. She was almost positive that she had seen the lion leap off the mantelpiece.

Aruendiel smiled sardonically. "You like to break things, don't you?" he said. "Hirizjahkinis, can you get this silencing spell off Mistress Nora? I want to make sure Ilissa has really made her departure."

A faint look of surprise crossed Hirizjahkinis's face. "Certainly. But are you sure? Would you like me to——?"

"No," he said abruptly. "Don't worry. I won't engage her. I'll be back tonight." He turned before she could say anything else and walked quickly through the archway.

Some time later, Nora sat facing Hirizjahkinis in the small salon to which Hirizjahkinis had ushered her. Nora had consumed some cold roast chicken and a glass of rather sweet white wine, and was feeling more like herself again, although her voice was still gone. It was tempting to think that hunger alone—low blood sugar—might have made her succumb to Ilissa.

Nora kept replaying the scene in her mind, thinking of what she should have said to Ilissa, the defiance she would have offered with just an instant's more preparation. But she could not shake the memory of those unwilling, inevitable steps that had carried her toward Ilissa's summons.

"I hope he's back soon," muttered Hirizjahkinis, placing her hands lightly on either side of Nora's neck. "If only because he may be the only one who can take off this silencing spell. He knows a dozen times more about Faitoren magic than I do."

She was talking about Aruendiel; Nora raised her eyebrows in an interrogative way.

"Oh, yes, he has made a deep study of it. It is to keep an eye on Ilissa. Me, I never even think about her anymore, except when I come to this wretched north country. Of course, Aruendiel has strong reasons to, I suppose."

Hirizjahkinis must have caught another flicker of interest in Nora's eyes, because she smiled and gave her a shrewd look. "You must tell me more about yourself, Mistress Nora, while I try to remove this spell. So you come from another world?" Nora nodded, as Hirizjahkinis gently palpated her neck. "And you fell into the hands of Ilissa and her horrible son." Hirizjahkinis touched the scars on Nora's cheek. "Then you escaped from the Faitoren. Aruendiel helped you?" Nora nodded again. "And you have been staying at his castle ever since? Does he still have that housekeeper with red hair? I think she was very shocked the first time she saw me; she had never seen anyone with black skin before. And, tell me," she added, "are you Aruendiel's mistress?"

Startled, Nora shook her head as vigorously she could.

"I am sorry, I do not mean to offend you. Well, too bad for him!" Hirizjahkinis chuckled.

Nora shook her head again, smiling very deliberately in such a way as to say never in a million years.

"I only ask because in times past, he would have expected, as a matter of course—well, I must tell you, Aruendiel saved my life, too. Oh, yes. This was long ago, back in my home country, when I was very young. I was a nun, a priestess of the Holy Sister Night, but I broke my vows of purity. So they were going to stone me to death, until Aruendiel happened by, saw me tied up in front of the temple, and decided to spirit me away. It was not easy—the witch priestesses are powerful—but he managed it. We escaped into the mountains, we found a cave to spend the night in, and then!" She went into a brief gale of laughter.

"Well, I was very grateful for my rescue, but not *that* grateful. It took me some time to make him understand the situation. Aruendiel had assumed that I'd broken my vows with a man. Lady moon, he was furious!"

With slight consternation, Nora telegraphed another question with her eyebrows.

"Oh, no, Aruendiel did not force me, nothing like that. But he was very disappointed! He was used to a different reception from women he wished to bed." Hirizjahkinis laughed again, then looked suddenly troubled. "I would be happier if you were his mistress. It would be a sign that he takes some joy in living. Do you think he does?"

Nora looked blank, then made an equivocating gesture with her hand: I guess so. I don't really know.

"I do not think he does, myself. He takes pleasure in magic, of course—how can one not? But to hole up in that backwoods castle of his for so many years, and this obsession with Ilissa! She is a bad one, but she is not worth so much attention. She is the sort of creature who, if she cannot be loved, is very pleased to be hated. It would be much worse for her to simply be forgotten."

Hirizjahkinis sighed. "Well, I am rambling on. Let us see about taking off this spell." She studied Nora from several different angles, peered down her throat, rubbed a finger along her neck, touched her own neck, muttered to herself, and then sat back to regard Nora once again.

"These Faitoren spells, there's no logic to them," she said, more to herself than to Nora. "I can't even find where this one begins. Well, we must try something."

Her first attempt only made Nora's ears ring. The second did nothing. The third produced a violent coughing fit. After the fourth try, Nora found that she could sing but not speak, and in fact could only sing snatches of an aria that she thought might be Puccini. "Very pretty," said the magician. "But I suppose you want to be able to talk, too." Slightly to Nora's regret, she undid the singing spell and made a few more tries until Nora's throat began to feel as though she were in the first stages of a cold.

"By the sweet night, Aruendiel! What sort of task have you set me?

Now we must really hope Ilissa does not kill him again, because I am running out of ideas."

Nora wondered if she had heard Hirizjahkinis correctly. "Did you say kill him *again?*" she tried to ask, forgetting that she had lost her voice.

Hirizjahkinis had no difficulty understanding. "Oh, yes, Ilissa killed him," she said composedly. "That is another reason for him to hate her."

"Killed? Dead?" Nora mouthed, but Hirizjahkinis only laughed a deep, rumbling chuckle, as though she enjoyed keeping Nora in suspense.

"I can see you are very impatient to retrieve your voice," she said. "I have one more idea. I confess that I cannot neatly unpeel this spell and take it off in one piece, as Aruendiel might be able to do, but I know another way. A little cruder and not as pleasant for you, but you will have your voice back. Would you like me to try it?"

Apprehensively, Nora nodded.

Hirizjahkinis pulled off one of her golden bracelets. In her hands it reshaped itself into a pair of long tweezers. "Open your mouth," she said, leaning closer. "Wide, wider. Take a deep breath. Now—"

Nora choked, her throat clogged with something solid that had not been there a moment before. Worse, the thing was alive. She could feel it moving just below her larynx. She would have shrieked if she could, but all she could do was gag.

"Careful, careful!" Standing up, Hirizjahkinis forced Nora's head back and reached carefully into her mouth with the tweezers. Another sickening throb in her throat, and then the blockage loosened. Hirizjahkinis pulled out a pale, wet, writhing ribbon and dropped it on the table. Nora went into a prolonged coughing fit.

"What is it?" she asked hoarsely, when she could get her breath.

Hirizjahkinis poked disdainfully at the white thing with the tweezers. It was fat, segmented, and many-legged, much like a large millipede. Its armored body had a silvery, mother-of-pearl opalescence.

"It is Ilissa's spell. Lovely, isn't it? I simply gave it a physical form, something I could get a grip on."

"Ugh!" Nora cleared her throat passionately again, and then again.

There was a knock on the door, and a young man in a long blue coat came in. His brown hair was scraped back in a braid from a doughy face; Nora recognized him as the magician who had been talking to Hirizjahkinis earlier. "Lady Hirizjahkinis," he said, ducking his head slightly, "I wondered whether you might need some assistance with the silencing spell."

"If you had come sooner, I might have used your help, Dorneng. The spell was very stubborn. But I have prevailed, as you can see." She indicated the pale curling thing on the table.

"Oh, how interesting," he said, coming closer. "I have never seen a Faitoren spell—it's still very much alive, isn't it?"

"Yes, although it will probably die soon. If it doesn't, I will kill it, the horrid thing."

"Oh!" He seemed mildly shocked. "Would you mind if I took it away with me? There is so much to learn about the Faitoren magic, and so few opportunities."

"Please," said Hirizjahkinis with a wave of her hand. Dorneng produced a blue glass jar from a pocket of his coat, and, using a napkin, he carefully nudged the insectile form into the jar and inserted a plug. He thanked Hirizjahkinis with more warmth than Nora felt the disgusting thing in the jar justified, then left the room.

Nora thanked Hirizjahkinis, too, and was about to ask whether all Ilissa's spells were similarly repulsive, when she remembered the questions she'd wanted to ask: "What you said before—that Ilissa killed Aruendiel—what did you mean by that?"

"I meant that she killed him."

Chilled, Nora objected: "But he's not dead."

"Not anymore." Hirizjahkinis gave a knowing smile.

"Do you mean magicians don't die?"

"Magicians die, as any human does. But sometimes they have friends who are other magicians."

After a moment, Nora said: "You raised him from the dead."

"I helped. There were several of us."

"You can do that?"

"Sometimes."

It was easier to believe that magicians could control the weather or turn people into stone. But if you could bring back the dead—Nora felt a kind of greedy, astonished hope, then reflected that Hirizjahkinis might simply mean something like the kind of miracle that paramedics accomplished every day in her own world for victims of heart attacks or drownings. "How did he die?" she asked.

"He fell," Hirizjahkinis said, still smiling, but with a trace of sadness. "It was in the war, during a skirmish in the mountains. He was riding an Avaguri's mount—it's a flying device—and Ilissa managed to unseat him. He fell a long way down onto a mountain. And then an avalanche took him away. We didn't find his body for weeks."

"Oh. How awful." It felt odd to be expressing condolences for someone who was no longer dead. Another thought struck her. "An Avaguri's mount, is it made out of wood and feathers?"

"It can be. Why do you ask?"

"We flew here to Semr on one."

"He flew here on an Avaguri's mount?" Hirizjahkinis said. "That is surprising. He does not like to fly now—at least not when it's not his own wings."

"When he fell, is that how he broke all of his b—" Nora began to say, when the door opened and Aruendiel walked into the room. She couldn't help uttering a small gasp when she saw him. It was almost like seeing a ghost.

Aruendiel looked severe as he caught Nora's strangled exclamation. "Have you not been able to remove the spell, Hiriz?"

"No, Mistress Nora can speak quite well again—or she could if I were not talking so much myself," said Hirizjahkinis.

"I'm fine now," Nora said. She stared at Aruendiel, looking hard for some sign that he had once been dead. His face and voice seemed tired, his body hunched beneath his long traveling cloak, but he was apparently quite alive.

"Are you sure? I can barely hear her," he said crossly to Hirizjahkinis. "So how did you undo the spell? There are always at least two or three major, undefended flaws in every piece of Faitoren magic, no matter how strong it is."

"If there were any in this spell, I did not find them!" Hirizjahkinis said. "I used an embodiment spell and then pulled it out of her throat. I have made quite a study of embodiment magic in recent years, you know. It's very useful for exorcisms."

Aruendiel gave her a look that registered both disbelief and disapproval. He pulled open Nora's mouth, and surveyed her throat critically. She felt an irresistible tickle, so that when he let go of her jaw, she went into another coughing fit. At last she hacked up a translucent filament, recognizable as one of the legs from the millipede creature.

"Not up to your usual standard, Hirizjahkinis," Aruendiel said.

"Who knew the thing would have so many legs!" Hirizjahkinis said.

He turned back to Nora. "The palace chamberlain, when I encountered him just now, went to some pains to tell me what a treasure you broke today. One of the few artifacts to escape the destruction of Old Semr."

"I didn't do anything," Nora said. "I wasn't even close to it when it broke. I'm not sure, but—well, it looked almost as though it jumped."

"Unusual behavior for a clay figure," Aruendiel said. He dropped his gaze downward. "Your fingernails are dirty."

She noticed, to her chagrin, that he was right. "So what? I was working in your garden," she said, curling her fingers to hide the dark crescents under her nails. "I didn't have time to clean my hands before we left your castle."

"Or any time since we arrived, apparently. You're hardly in a state to be presented to the king. He has specifically commanded that you attend him tonight."

"Do I have to?"

"Unfortunately, not only are you required to go, but Hirizjahkinis and I must go, too. But you are the main object of the king's interest. He is eager to meet the woman who has been the center of so much controversy today, especially since he has learned that you come from another world. Let us make haste."

"Don't be absurd, Aruendiel," Hirizjahkinis said sharply. "We certainly have time to make ourselves more presentable. I for one am feeling quite dingy after such a long day." To Nora's eye, she looked as fresh as she had that morning, every pleat of her linen robe still crisp. "And what of Ilissa? Where is she now?"

"I followed her to the place where I left Raclin turned to stone. When I left, she was engaged in the task of transporting him home so that she can undo my spell there."

"Oh?" asked Hirizjahkinis with interest. "He must be very heavy."

Aruendiel laughed aloud. "She is nothing if not resourceful. She is also determined to punish that unfortunate Faitoren who was posing as Bouragonr. Gaibon, his name is. I could overhear her abusing him savagely for being stupid enough to be unmasked."

"So—"

"So she is forcing him to *carry* that massive piece of stone all the way back to the Faitoren lands. They're stronger than humans, the Faitoren, but still, I could tell it was a strain. She kept telling him to go faster, too."

Gaibon was the Faitoren who threw Moscelle over, Nora remembered. Odd that Ilissa hadn't taken Vulpin along for such an important assignment; perhaps he was still out of favor for letting Nora escape.

She pictured Gaibon's richly dressed figure staggering through the dark woods under the weight of a multi-ton gargoyle while Ilissa scolded him from behind. It was hard not to feel sorry for him—but equally hard not to laugh.

Nora coughed a little instead. Her throat still felt scratchy.

# Chapter 17

Whatever the king had anticipated, Nora evidently did not live up to his expectations. His broad face wore a faint, dull frown of puzzlement as she answered his questions.

He showed a stirring of interest when she mentioned that her world had no magicians in it. "But how can that be?" he asked.

"Machinery," said Nora in a clear, confident tone that, she hoped, implied that the exact functioning of such devices was self-evident. She was still mindful of having once tried and failed to explain electricity to Mrs. Toristel. "We have complex mechanisms that do the work that magicians do in this world. Machines that can fly or travel at great speeds—all kinds of things."

The king seemed struck by this idea. "These mechanisms, can they make war?"

"No," Nora lied firmly. It had taken him no time to make that particular connection. Rulers must be much the same in all worlds, she thought. She lost his attention for good when she mentioned that there were also very few kings in her world. He dismissed her with a nod.

Nora curtsied and backed away, glancing behind just in time to avoid falling off the dais. She descended to the main level of the banquet hall, into the throng of courtiers. In the press of silk, velvet, and brocade, she was uncomfortably aware of the plainness of her dress; Hirizjahkinis had pressed a palace maid into finding Nora something more suitable for court than Mrs. Toristel's hand-me-down, but even Nora could tell that the severe blue-and-black gown she'd borrowed was unquestionably out of style. At least her fingernails were clean now.

This was different from Ilissa's court, she thought, struggling through the crowd. The candles were smokier, dimmer, hotter, making the room unpleasantly warm. The people in it were lavishly dressed but not all of them were young, slender, and lovely. They moved less gracefully than the Faitoren did, with more vigor. They were at work, she thought as she watched one man waylay two more richly dressed courtiers, ignoring their attempt to ignore him. A young man addressed a middle-aged woman, his eyes sliding to the teenage girl behind her. There was more at stake here than at a Faitoren ball, Nora guessed: matches to be made, patrons to be flattered, alliances to be forged, enemies to be humiliated. Not that all those things didn't happen among the Faitoren, too, but it was more of a game for them, to keep from dying of boredom in their tiny prison kingdom. Or maybe, she thought, the energy in this room had something to do with the fact that the people before her were human beings, not Faitoren, with only a human lifetime to accomplish all of the things that they wanted to do.

Of course, some people in the room had already had more than a human lifetime. Her eyes sought out Aruendiel, his dark head visible above the crowd. What was it like to die and return to life? No wonder there was something spooky about him. But he had saved her life today, she reminded herself. Again. Even if only to get back at Ilissa.

The music coming from the gallery suddenly grew louder. A bard was singing, and the crowd moved toward the walls, opening a space in the center of the room. Nora found a perch on steps leading to a side door. A pair of dwarfs cartwheeled through the crowd and began juggling glass balls. Then a third dwarf, a woman, joined them for an acrobatics exhibition that was bawdy, borderline sadistic, and extremely funny if you liked fart jokes. Most of the court apparently did. The dwarfs were followed by another bard, who sang for a long time in what sounded like a very old-fashioned form of Ors about a battle, a river, and a boat with black sails. As he sang, the room filled with the cheerful buzz of conversation again. The queen yawned.

When the bard finally finished, a new figure came forward, the young magician whom Hirizjahkinis had addressed as Dorneng. Bowing, he plucked a silver apple from the fruits embroidered on the draperies of the king's throne, and cut slices for the king and queen. Then he dropped the apple core into a goblet and made it grow into a full-size tree. At his nod, it exploded into bloom.

Nora had seen something like this before, performed by the ordinary, sleight-of-hand magicians of her world. It was even more impressive when you knew actual magic was involved. If only Dorneng had kept it simple. Instead, the apple tree began to sing. A chorus of sugary voices rose from the blossoms, singing an anthem in honor of the king and queen. It was not as long as the bard's song, but long enough.

Finally the song was over. The tree grew heavy with silver fruit. Ceremoniously, Dorneng picked an apple and placed it back on the drapery.

"I'll take care of the tree, Dorneng." Hirizjahkinis had joined him in front of the dais. Was every magician present expected to perform? Nora wondered. She glanced apprehensively at where Aruendiel stood.

Hirizjahkinis put one hand on her breast, touching the leopard skin she wore, and smiled at the crowd. Nora began to feel a throb of physical anxiety in her own body. Either part of her dinner disagreed with her, or there was strong magic going on nearby.

At first it was hard to say exactly how the room was different. But the candle flames in the silver chandeliers flickered. The same draft ruffled the leaves of the apple tree.

Nora turned and saw that the door and wall behind her had vanished, replaced by heavy, aromatic darkness. A pale green moth fluttered toward the candles. Looking up through leaves and branches, Nora could see the moon and a spill of stars. This night had a humid, tropical feel, alive with the trilling of insects.

She turned back to the assembly, still lit by chandeliers suspended from God knows what, since the ceiling was gone. The king's and queen's thrones looked faintly absurd, their carved legs sunk in green grass. The courtiers murmured uneasily.

The king cleared his throat. "Lady Hirizjahkinis, this is indeed a marvel. May we ask what you have done with our palace?"

"Your palace is perfectly fine, Your Majesty," Hirizjahkinis said politely. "I have taken you and your court out of it for a few minutes, that is all. We are in the land of my birth, in the forest just outside the temple precincts of Gahz. It is only a short walk to the temple itself, a very beautiful sight by moonlight. The hunting here is also very good." An animal's scream cut through the darkness, not far away.

The king looked hard in the direction from which the scream had come. "Thank you," he said. "Very interesting indeed. We prefer to return to Semr now."

"Of course," Hirizjahkinis said. The paneled walls of the banquet hall took shape, blocking out the night sky and the shadowy foliage. The smell of candle smoke, perfume, and overheated, overdressed bodies returned to Nora's nostrils. Everyone seemed to start talking at once, their voices loud with relief. The apple tree was gone.

The door behind her opened, and someone slipped in beside her. "Have I missed dinner?" he asked.

Nora turned to look at him: A man about her own age, ginger-haired, with lively eyes and a face that comfortably occupied the middle ground between ordinary and good-looking. Wearing a blue tunic and a short gray cloak, he was more plainly dressed than most of the courtiers in attendance.

"I just rode in from Luerwisiac, and I'm completely famished. Is it too late for me to get a morsel of food?"

"I'm afraid so," she said. "They finished dinner some time ago."

"Ah, the only thing keeping me going those last dozen miles was the thought of a nice slab of roast beef."

Nora smiled back at him. "It was roast goose, oysters, and venison tonight."

"Please don't make it harder for me. Where else can I find some food?"

"You can try the palace kitchen."

"I'll do that. And what is happening here? They don't seem to have started the dancing."

"No, some of the magicians have been performing magic."

"Oh, Bouragonr?" the man asked carelessly. "Did he do the fire maiden again?"

"Not Bouragonr," Nora said, emphatically enough that the ginger-haired man looked curious. Then she felt obliged to tell him of Bouragonr's capture and rescue, although she left out her own part in the events because it seemed too complicated to explain. The man listened with deepening interest.

"Now I'm even sorrier that I was late. I've never seen a Faitoren. Is the Faitoren queen as beautiful as they say?"

"She's all right," Nora said. "Oh, I don't mean to sound sour. If you like them beautiful and deadly, she's the woman for you."

After an instant, the man laughed. "Thank you for the warning. Well, she must be as old as a rock by now, if what I've heard about her is true. And you say it was the wizard Lord Aruendiel who freed Bouragonr?"

"Partly, yes." She wished now that she had mentioned her own role. She would have liked to impress this young man a little.

"Is he here tonight?"

"Yes, right over there. The tall man with dark hair—the black woman is talking to him." Hirizjahkinis was nodding for emphasis. Aruendiel's crooked back looked especially stiff and unyielding, as though he were annoyed at what she was saying.

On the dais, the king turned his broad face toward the two magicians. "Lord Aruendiel," he called out. "We have admired the wonders these other magic-workers have conjured. Now we would be pleased by a demonstration of your art, as well."

Aruendiel hesitated, then stepped forward—propelled in part, Nora saw, by Hirizjahkinis's hand on the back of his arm. As he made his way into the center of the gathering, the room grew quieter.

"Your Highness, I fear that I would make only a poor showing after the remarkable and intricate spells worked by my colleagues. They have done magic with an artistry few could match. I beg Your Majesty to be content with the magic that I have performed earlier today in your service, as well as the delightful enchantments that the magicians Hirizjahkinis and Dorneng have so brilliantly wrought."

It was a surprisingly graceful speech for Aruendiel, Nora thought, but it lost some of its effectiveness by being delivered in a tone of rapid-fire contempt. The king leaned forward.

"Lord Aruendiel, you are too modest. We will judge for ourselves the artistry of your magic. Please commence."

With a wooden bow, Aruendiel replied: "Then I will do my best to please. What sort of magic does Your Highness wish to see?"

The queen spoke up quickly. "Lord Aruendiel, I have a great curiosity to speak with the dead. I have always wondered what life is like for the dead."

At the back of the room, someone tittered. Aruendiel's face was immobile. "Many others have wondered the same thing," he said simply.

"Then let us find out the answer!" There was a bright, challenging smile on the queen's young face. "Bring back one of the dead, and let us ask what lies after death. Do the dead eat? Do they sleep? Do they marry? How do they amuse themselves?"

"Your Highness, each of us will find out the answers to these questions in good time."

"I would like to know now," said the queen. Aruendiel was shaking his head, but she went on: "I would like to speak with my aunt, the Lady Mirigian of Akl. We were always very close. I am sure she would be very happy to speak with me. I am also curious to hear how she came to fall down the staircase, because she was not a clumsy woman, and no one saw her fall, not even my uncle, who was in the next room. So I want you to summon her.

"Except—" The queen paused. "Well, if she is very frightful-looking now, perhaps her voice would be enough. It would be a great pleasure for me to hear even her voice again. You can do this, can you not?"

"Your Highness, I will not. I am sorry. I will not raise your aunt, nor any of the dead."

"You are afraid to do this," the queen said. "Or you cannot." The king made a move as though to intervene, but Aruendiel spoke first.

"It is a perilous thing to raise the dead. They may not wish to be raised. But you have given me an idea. I will not revive the dead, but I will revive a sort of shadow of the dead."

The queen looked suspicious and not at all pleased by this promise. Aruendiel walked a few paces, his gaze lifted. Nora realized that he was looking at the portraits that hung on the walls. He stopped near a full-length painting of a young woman in a blue dress more high-waisted and full-sleeved than the current fashion. She stood outdoors in a space framed by green leaves, one hand resting on a gate, the other holding a wide-brimmed straw hat.

"Queen Tulivie," Aruendiel said. "She was your grandmother, I believe, Your Highness?"

He had addressed King Abele, who nodded. "Yes, my father's mother. But I never knew her." After a moment, the king added, "The same artist painted her in her coronation robes—that portrait hangs in the long gallery—but my father preferred this one."

"It is a good likeness," Aruendiel agreed. "It captures not just her beauty, but something of her gentleness." The words hung in the air for a moment. "Well, she is dead and gone, and we will not disturb her. But this portrait can show us a little of what she was, on that summer day when it was painted."

"Of course it can," the queen broke in. "But that has nothing to do with magic."

"Your Highness!" Aruendiel said, raising his voice. "Your Highness!" But he had turned away from the king and queen to face the painting.

The woman in the portrait moved her head, a movement so quick that Nora almost missed it. The painted eyes now gazed toward Aruendiel. A whisper went around the room.

"Your Highness!" Aruendiel called again.

This time there was no mistake. The figure in the painting leaned forward, lifting her hand to shade her eyes. "Who is calling me?" she asked.

"It is the magician Aruendiel, ma'am."

"Oh, it's you!" she said, smiling. "Can't you see that I am having my portrait painted?"

"I apologize for disturbing you."

"No matter, I am getting horribly stiff." She gave a quick, unregal shrug of her shoulders. "But what are you doing here? I thought that you and my husband were closeted with the Orvetian ambassador. Is the king finally finished? I've barely seen him all day."

"I imagine he is still occupied, Your Highness." There was something constrained in Aruendiel's voice, as though he were searching hard for the right words and the right tone.

"A pity. Nurse is bringing the baby into the garden after his nap, and we're going to see the new plantings around the oval basin. Will you tell the king, when you go back? He might want to join us." The portrait of Tulivie gave a frown. "It is too bad that he will probably have to leave again on campaign so soon. The prince has barely had a chance to know his papa."

"It will be a short campaign, ma'am."

"You sound so sure! Does your magic tell you this?"

Gathering up her skirts, the image of Tulivie started forward as if to hear more, stepping lightly onto the floor of the banquet hall. She bore herself confidently, apparently unaware that she had left her canvas garden behind or that a roomful of people were staring at her.

It was impossible not to stare. She was so obviously not flesh and blood—Nora could see the brushstrokes on her skirt—and yet she was not a paper doll. Her body was solid-seeming; she moved through space like any living creature. She also looked brighter, more vivid than any of the people around her. Like a cartoon, Nora thought. Everything a little simplified or exaggerated, closer to the ideal than we ever see in real life.

Aruendiel took a step forward, too, moving into the shadow of the column beside him. "I am no fortune-teller," he said. "But I know this to be true. The Orvetians are ill-prepared for war, and your husband will beat them soundly. So you must put your mind at ease, Your Highness."

"Thank you, I will try." She added, a little wistfully: "Are you sure you cannot tell what is to come? There are a few things that I would like to know."

"Such as?" he asked warily.

"Such as—will it rain soon? I am worried about my new plantings. It has been so dry lately. If the king were not so occupied with these stubborn Orvetians, I would ask him to lend me his chief magician to ensure that we have some favorable weather."

"Your Highness, I am always happy to be of service to you."

"Then perhaps you could arrange a little rain sometime after midnight, after my dinner guests have gone home? Enough to give the ground a good soaking. And then, of course, another clear day tomorrow."

Up until this point, she and Aruendiel had been conversing as though it were only the two of them, both standing in the garden where she was posing for her portrait. (Presumably the painter was waiting at a respectful distance nearby.) The watching court was absolutely silent.

But now there came a minor commotion in the crowd, the sound of sobbing. At the edge of the crowd, Nora glimpsed a bent white head. An old woman crying, racked with untidy grief.

The painted queen turned with concern on her smooth, uncanny face. For the first time she seemed to notice someone else in the room besides the magician. "Oh, the poor thing," she said. "What is the matter? My dear old grandma'am, what's the matter?"

The old woman held out a skinny hand toward the queen. It took her a minute to restrain her sobs. "Dear lady, it is so good to see you," she said, gulping. "It has been so many years. You are just the way I remembered you."

"Am I? That's good. Now, we must get you looked after." She glanced over at Aruendiel. "She's confused, poor thing. Someone must have left her here; I don't think she could have wandered far by herself. What is your name, grandma'am?"

"I'm Lady Marisiek Uliveran," the old woman said with a hint of pride.

"Oh," the portrait said, puzzled. "One of the ladies of my bedchamber is Lady Marisiek. Are you one of her relations? I will summon her at once."

"No, that's me, Your Highness. Surely you know me. I was one of your ladies before I married. I used to help you dress the little princes. You gave me a pendant, a gold peacock with emeralds. Look, I am still wearing it," she said, fumbling in her dress. "I remember that day so clearly, clearer than yesterday. Well, I am old, you know, but you are just the same. I don't quite understand it. I thought you were gone, how many years ago? It rained at the funeral; they could hardly get the pyre to burn. Oh, that was a sad day. How is it that you are here again, as beautiful as ever?"

As Marisiek spoke, Tulivie's image stared at the tiny gold bird that the old woman had pulled from under her shawl, and then looked hard at her gnarled face. "Marisiek?" she said finally. "Marisiek? Merciful gods, what has happened to you? Impossible!" She looked to Aruendiel again, her hand gripping Marisiek's shoulder protectively. "This is some wicked enchantment. Lord Aruendiel, you must do something."

Aruendiel said nothing. After a moment, he shook his head gently.

"What do you mean? Someone has put a spell on this girl and turned her into an old woman. I command you to undo this evil magic."

"It is not magic. It is only time." His voice was slow, as though the words were heavy.

"Time? What do you mean? I saw Marisiek only this morning. Of course this is magic, and we must find the magician who has cast such a terrible spell."

"Madame!" It was the king who had spoken. "Madame, there is no need to fear," he called from the dais. "We would like to welcome you to the court of Semr—welcome you back, that is. We are greatly honored by your presence."

"Who is this man?" Tulivie's portrait asked with open bewilderment. "Welcome me back to the court of Semr, when I am already here? What is he talking about?"

"I am privileged to follow your husband on the throne of Semr." When she still looked blank—and a little angry—the king added, "I am Abele the Fourth, King of Greater Semr. My father was your son, Abele the Third. I am your grandson."

"My grandson!" Now she looked as though she would like to laugh. "My boy Abele is a baby. He is just learning to walk. This is absurd."

"Nonetheless, I am your grandson," the king said with a trace of starchiness. He rose and bowed. "Grandmother, this is a rare and remarkable meeting. I used to hear my father speak of you. I have admired your beauty in your portraits here in the palace. I never thought that I would one day greet you face-to-face."

"How could you be my grandson? You are a man of middle age. You are at least twenty years older than I am!"

("At least," Nora murmured. The man in the gray cloak caught her eye and smiled.)

"This is strange to me, too, Grandmother. Lord Aruendiel has brought you out of the past to visit us tonight, that much I understand."

"Lord Aruendiel, what is he talking about?" The portrait of Tulivie turned back to the magician. "What kind of magic have you done? Who is this man—and who are all these people?" She glanced around with an air of disquiet; she had just noticed that she was surrounded by strangers. "What have you done?"

"He is right. There is no need to fear—" Aruendiel began.

"But what have you done?"

"I have opened up a window, in a manner of speaking, between one day and another," he said carefully, and then paused as though to observe her reaction.

"You are speaking in riddles."

"It is not a real window," he continued. "But it allows you, Your Majesty, to look forward at these people, as it allows them to look back at you." When she shook her head in incomprehension, he added: "Forward in time. Into future years."

"I am looking forward in time?" Her gaze fell upon the aged woman with horrified understanding. "You mean, this is Marisiek, and she is old because—she is old?"

"Yes," Aruendiel said, bowing his head a fraction.

"And this man here?" she asked, gesturing at the king.

"He spoke the truth. He is your grandson."

"My grandson. And he sits on the throne of Semr?"

Her confusion and distress were painful to watch; the painted face registered emotions with a heightened intensity. One could almost read the thoughts cascading behind it like falling dominoes: "If this man is king of Semr, then my husband is dead, and if this king is my grandson, then my son is dead, too. And as for me—" The image from the portrait glanced around the room, as though dreading to find a superannuated version of herself.

But not to see yourself, Nora thought, that would be worse.

"No!" the portrait said, shuddering.

"Grandmother, are you not pleased to see that your line continues and that your descendants still rule Semr?" the king asked. "I wish that my second daughter were here tonight. She resembles you closely, although her hair is darker."

"Why would you do such a terrible spell?" the portrait said to Aruendiel.

"Tulivie—" He made a gesture as though to calm her, but he did not leave the shadow where he stood.

"Why would you show me such wicked lies? My son is a baby, asleep in his nursery. My husband is king. I am queen. Marisiek is a girl of seventeen. I know these things are true."

After a long moment, Aruendiel said quietly, "Yes, they are true."

"Of course they are true!" She drew herself up. "I do not understand what sort of magic you employed to trick me just now, Lord Aruendiel, but I do not appreciate it."

"I apologize, Your Majesty."

"You have played a very bad joke on me."

"I could not agree more."

"The king would be displeased if he learned of how you have been tormenting me today," she said.

"Yes, he would."

She smiled suddenly. "I will forgive you, though, and not tell him, if you promise not to frighten me again like that."

"I promise." Meeting her gaze, he added, "You know I wish nothing but Your Majesty's continued happiness." There was something rough and raw in Aruendiel's voice, under the polite formula.

"Thank you, that is very kind of you! And now I must let the painter finish for the day. Although he can come back tomorrow—if it doesn't rain."

"It will not rain," he said. "I promise."

She laughed. "I will hold you to that promise, too." With a rustle of painted skirts, she walked swiftly back to the tenantless painting. Stepping into the frame, she took up her pose again, one hand on the gate, the other holding her hat. "Tell my husband not to dally too long with the Orvetians," she called out. "I will declare war on them myself if they keep him much longer."

The ribbon on her hat rippled gently in an unseen breeze and then stopped moving. The surface of the canvas darkened slightly, as her face and body took on a hard, flat sheen. She smiled out at the room, blindly young and happy.

There was no sound in the room, except for the soft, querulous voice of the old woman muttering something that no one could make out.

# *Chapter 18*

Oh, if I ever had a doubt, now I know the rumors were true—you bedded Tulivie," Hirizjahkinis said.

"Of course," Aruendiel replied matter-of-factly. "But not until many years later. She was older then. She had had many disappointments. Tonight it was strange to see her so—so untouched."

Nora, coming up behind them, stopped in her tracks. She slipped behind a statue of a bare-chested man with a bull's head and fixed her eyes innocently on the dancing. Fortunately, with two dozen male courtiers stamping and leaping in the middle of the room, the magicians seemed to feel no need to lower their voices.

"Yes, she seemed very young, a baby herself. But what on earth were you thinking of, raking up that old scandal?" Hirizjahkinis asked. "You could have performed that spell on any of the portraits in this room— although I am grateful that you did not pick the king's grandfather, that old scorpion," she said, looking at the painting nearest them. "Why throw it in the king's face that his grandmother might have been your mistress?"

Aruendiel gave this a few moments' consideration. "Do you think he believes that he might be my grandson?" he asked gravely. "Does he expect me to acknowledge him?"

Hirizjahkinis waved his answer away with a flip of her hand. "Be serious. What possessed you? It was an impressive spell, I grant you that."

"It's from a manuscript of Duisi Tortor's. I reworked it slightly." He glanced at the other side of the hall, where Tulivie's portrait hung, but the painting was hidden by the angle of the wall. "Of course, that wasn't really her," he added.

"She seemed real enough. Obviously not a living creature, but the voice, the mannerisms—I recognized them."

"It was only a sort of echo. Why did I do the spell? I don't know. I was out of temper, I saw her portrait, and I thought, Why not? She was infinitely more pleasant company than her grandson. It was a fool thing to do," he added with a grimace.

"I'm surprised to hear you admit that."

"Oh, not because it gives idiots something to gossip about. No, it was cruel to bring her back, even her shadow." He frowned at the floor.

"Well, it is quite dangerous to raise old ghosts, Aruendiel, especially when a person has lived as long as you or I. You are no better than that silly queen over there who wants to find out what happened to her dead aunt. Although that is not such a silly idea, now that I think about it. Perhaps I will try to find an answer for her, while I am here. And you? What are you going to do now? I hope you will not head back to your drafty castle right away. Abele will want your advice as he chooses his new chief magician."

With a shake of his head, Aruendiel said, "I leave tomorrow morning, following Ilissa, to make sure that she and Raclin cause no further trouble on the way home. Dorneng will accompany me."

"Dorneng? Really? He could become the king's new chief magician, if he wants to be. But not if he leaves the capital right now."

"He says he is interested in the Faitoren," Aruendiel said, shrugging.

"I am surprised," said Hirizjahkinis, with an arch of her eyebrows. "He seemed to me tonight to be in zealous pursuit of the court position. That singing tree! I believe even Abele was embarrassed."

Aruendiel's mouth curled into an arid smile. "Do you expect anything better of such performances? Dorneng at least understands that he will learn more magic dealing with the Faitoren than conjuring singing trees at court. I have a mind to get Lukl to hire him. There should be a magician up there, keeping watch on Ilissa."

"Lukl? Oh, yes, the one-eyed knight who lives next to Ilissa. What a terrible idea! His castle is even more isolated than yours. You would convince poor Dorneng to give up a chance at being chief royal magician to help a backwoods peer keep track of his sheep!"

"Dorneng asked to go with me. And he was Micher Samle's apprentice; he had to live in a cave for ten years. Lukl's castle could only be an improvement."

Hirizjahkinis laughed and then gave Aruendiel an appraising look. "Well, if someone must keep an eye on Ilissa, better Dorneng than you or me. Especially you."

"What do you mean?" His voice was suspicious.

"I mean that you enjoy hating her too much. She is not worth half the trouble you take over her."

"You can say that after today?" he asked, incredulous. "After she kidnapped Bouragonr, bamboozled the king, and came within a fingernail of making Semr hers?"

"Well, we stopped her, Aruendiel! Let me be clear. You have good reason to hate her. But you should not let that hatred govern you. It will hollow you out; it will devour your heart."

"My heart?" He gave a quick, contemptuous bark of laughter.

"Or whatever serves you for that purpose." When he did not answer, she added, "Well, perhaps it is too late for you anyway. Look at you tonight, conjuring up poor Tulivie's shade. Do you have nothing better to do than moon over a dead woman?"

"Tulivie? I was not mooning over her."

"No? I saw the way you kept to the shadows, so modestly, so she could not see you clearly. You were afraid she would find you changed."

"Well, she would have found me changed," he said angrily. "Greatly changed. I tell you, Hiriz, I was not mooning after her, as you put it, but would it be such a bad match, for me to take up with a dead woman? Under the circumstances."

Hirizjahkinis sighed and shook her head with a dramatic sweep, the way a parent might do when reprimanding a small child. "Ah, Aruendiel, be sensible. What can I say? Is it so hard to enjoy the life that you've been given?"

Aruendiel wheeled and looked away, toward the center of the hall, where the dancers were now swinging at one another with painted wooden swords. He noticed that the girl Nora was also watching the dancing, half-hidden behind a statue of the god Reob, and wondered irritably whether she had overheard anything of the conversation. She turned as though she sensed his eyes on her, and flushed slightly.

"How did you do that spell?" Nora asked him. "It was remarkable. It was—um—powerful."

Heartbreaking, Nora meant, but she'd decided not to use that word, not after listening to Aruendiel just now. There was something terrible about Tulivie's innocence, the innocence of the unknowing past; no wonder the magician sounded pained as he spoke to Hirizjahkinis.

As though the girl could possibly understand any kind of magic, Aruendiel thought—let alone a spell as complex as this. Nevertheless, he was pleased that she could at least recognize good magic when she saw it. "Thank you," he said, more graciously than he usually spoke to her. "But I could not begin to explain it to you."

She was not satisfied. "Would it work with any kind of painting, even a portrait that was not so realistic?"

Nora was thinking of Picasso, but was not sure how to explain, say, *Les Demoiselles d'Avignon*.

Intrigued, Aruendiel tilted his head reflectively. He had not considered the question before. "Like the pictures they make in Tfara, where they like to show their emperor with wings and the claws of a lion? It should work, as long as the painting was done from life."

"And their empress with six breasts, to show how fecund she is—decidedly, Aruendiel, you must take this spell to Tfara one day," Hirizjahkinis interjected. "But I am wondering: When do you return to Semr, after you leave tomorrow?"

"Not until next year, if I can help it—and I can," Aruendiel said, with feeling.

"So we're leaving tomorrow?" Nora asked.

Aruendiel frowned suddenly. In planning the pursuit of Ilissa, he had not thought to account for the girl.

"No," he said. "I can't take any extra burdens with me."

"So what will I do?" Nora asked.

He stalled. "If I follow Ilissa all the way to her domain, it will be easier to return to my own lands than to come back to Semr."

"You mean, you would just leave me here?" the girl demanded, some fear in her voice.

"Don't be so rude and unkind, Aruendiel," Hirizjahkinis cut in. "Of course he is coming back to Semr," she said to Nora. She smiled broadly, but her head was cocked at a watchful angle, as though daring the other magician to contradict her. "He will return to see me again and to report that Ilissa is safely bound to her own domain and that we can all go about our business. You can stay here at the palace, as my guest, until he returns. Does that not sound like a good idea, Aruendiel?"

"It is out of my way, coming back to Semr," he objected.

"Now I am insulted. I have traveled thousands of miles from my own land to come to Semr, and you, my old friend, cannot make a slight detour, a day's journey or less, to spend a little more time with me."

Aruendiel glowered; Hirizjahkinis met his gaze with equanimity. "It is more than a day's journey," he said grudgingly. "But yes, I will stop at Semr on the way back."

"Very good," Hirizjahkinis said. "So, Mistress Nora, you can leave with him then. And meanwhile, you have a few days to enjoy yourself in Semr."

"All right," Aruendiel said. He added to Nora: "Although perhaps when the time comes, you won't want to leave. You might find some other situation here in Semr. Did you not tell me that you could cook? Or maybe you will find another protector."

Nora's lips tightened slightly as she considered the implication of his last words, but she only nodded and said that she would see what came along.

As Aruendiel regarded her, though, he thought ruefully that both options were equally improbable. It was troubling to consider how out of place, how vulnerable the girl was. She was too plain, too poorly dressed to attract attention from the men of the court; the slashes on her cheek were healing well, but they had not vanished completely. And even though one might easily take her for a servant at first glance, in that unflattering dress, on a closer look there was something about the way she carried herself that made him doubt that anyone would give her a position.

She was bold when she should be silent and ill at ease when she should be assured, and she stared too intently into his face when she spoke to him, the way a good servant would never dream of doing. Was she happy? he wondered suddenly. A strange question. Sometimes she brightened—as she had just now, asking about the spell—and you could see a warm and lively wit in her face that almost made you forget about her scars. More often she looked discontented, a little bewildered. She did not seem to appreciate completely the kindness he had shown in taking her in.

And something in her manner a few minutes ago had made him uncomfortable, as though she were trying to be kind to *him*. He disliked kindness from some quarters. It was presumptuous. It felt too much like pity.

He was glad to take his leave of both women.

Another situation? Another protector? Aruendiel's words kept returning to Nora over the next few days.

She found herself taken up by a group of court ladies that included her roommate, Lady Inristian. Nora's recent adventures—her role in the freeing of Bouragonr; her near kidnapping by the beautiful, dangerous Faitoren queen; her presentation to the king—all had made her the object of some curiosity, and Inristian was obviously delighted to find that her accidental association with Nora had become a social asset. She made a point of pulling Nora into her group's after-dinner gossips, their pickup *ben* matches on the palace lawn, and their promenades to Semr's more select shopping district, an intersection near the palace where an array of tiny shops sold cloth, ribbon, jewelry, perfume, tapestries, rugs, and gold and silver tableware.

Hers was not the most fashionable circle in the court—Nora could tell that almost at once, instinctively—but that hardly mattered. It was pleasant to be lionized, even by the B list. People seemed to be endlessly interested in hearing about Nora's own world or about Ilissa and the Faitoren, although Nora was deliberately vague about her exact situation in the Faitoren court. It was not something she cared to discuss.

Find a protector? Even if she were inclined to, there was far too much competition. A protector was exactly what all the other young women were seeking, in the form of a husband. That was why they had left their country estates and come to Semr with their mothers, fathers, brothers, or married sisters to run interference for them. (At court, Nora discovered, a marriageable young woman could not speak to a man who was not a near relation unless chaperoned by a family member.) Inristian's parents were dead, a handicap for her marriage chances; she had only an elderly uncle with a passion for gambling to help her find a husband.

"Once an evening, if I'm lucky, he introduces me to an acquaintance for a few minutes," Inristian complained to Nora. "Then just when I'm at my most charming, he goes back to his game, so what can I do but go back to my seat? And then he tells me it's a disgrace that I'm not married yet." Her tone was light, but there was something forced about it. She was almost twenty-three, she had those pockmarks, and from little hints she dropped— and the darns in her skirts—Nora had the idea that her estate in the Valley of the River of the White Boar, wherever that was, was not very prosperous. Once, in a corridor, they passed a young woman wearing an elaborate red head-covering, and Nora saw Inristian frown and look away. Someone told Nora later that the red headdress was a betrothal veil.

Tearing through *Pride and Prejudice* in her spare moments, Nora found that the scene where Mrs. Bennet upbraids Lizzy for turning down Mr. Collins had a slightly different resonance now. "If you take it into your head to go on refusing every offer of marriage in this way, you will never get a husband at all," cried Mrs. Bennet, "and I am sure I do not know who is to maintain you when your father is dead." Mrs. Bennet had a point, although it pained Nora to admit it.

Of course, Inristian already had an estate of her own, however poor. "Maybe you shouldn't feel so much pressure to get married," Nora said to Inristian one day, as they were coming back from a visit to the shops. Behind them trudged the palace footman who had to escort them every time they went outside the palace walls. "You could take more time and find someone who's really right for you."

Inristian didn't understand what she meant. "Oh, all the young men that I've met are right!" she said. "Some men at court do have very bad reputations, it's true, but my uncle would never introduce me to them. He is careful about that, I will say. It's only that he's so lazy, he won't do

anything more than introducing me. It's as though he expects me to nego-
tiate my own marriage!"

"Well, couldn't you arrange the marriage yourself, if you had to? That's
what we do in my country."

Inristian looked both amused and nonplussed by Nora's naïveté. "Oh,
you know," she said finally, "a marriage is not just between a man and a
woman; any prospective husband of mine will want to know, well, how my
family and friends can help him."

"A dowry, you mean?"

"More than that. Politics, you know."

Nora had opened her mouth to reply when it suddenly struck her that
for all the evident shortcomings in Lady Inristian's method of finding a
husband, it was better than Nora's. After all, hers had also been a political
marriage of sorts. Even with only an apathetic uncle to oversee the process,
the countess was unlikely to find herself married to someone who turned
into a flying reptile during the day. "I hope you find a good husband,"
Nora said. "I'm sure you will."

"Well, you know," Inristian said with a giggle, "this is quite shocking,
but I am almost certain that Lord Morasiv tried to catch my eye last night.
He has a very nice estate in the south, smallish, but warm enough for a
vineyard, is that not interesting? Of course wine can be quite lucrative. I
think his chin is rather handsome. And I do like yellow hair. Have you
seen him?"

Nora shook her head with a smile. But she remembered Lady Inristian's
description, and that evening, as she was passing through a crowded room
in the palace, she saw a man who matched it: blond, a stalwart chin. His
eyes looked a bit like grapes themselves, green and bulgy. He was talking
to someone else that Nora recognized: the young man who had arrived too
late for dinner a few nights before.

Nora had seen Inristian just a few minutes ago. She retraced her steps,
meaning to alert Inristian. Perhaps the uncle could be torn away from his
game to make an introduction.

Starting down a staircase, Nora recognized the hard, high tones of one
of Lady Inristian's friends, Baroness Fulvishin, coming from below. Then
she heard her own name.

"So how did this thing Nora get the scars on her face?"

Nora's first thought was that her command of Ors was getting to be quite good. Effortlessly, she had registered the grammatical mistake in the baroness's question. It was an error in word choice: using a demonstrative pronoun meant for inanimate objects or animals to designate a person. That is, Nora.

But the baroness had not made a mistake, Nora reflected. She had heard courtiers use that construction a few times in the past few days, to refer to servants or peasants. She hesitated, wondering: Do I really want to hear this?

"—an accident," Inristian said.

Another person said something else that Nora couldn't quite catch, but that provoked a small storm of giggles.

"Honestly, Soristia!" said a fourth voice, laughing. "Aren't you being a little—"

"Well, he murdered his wife, everyone knows that. This poor Nora thing, she must not have pleased him enough."

"Or maybe that's how she pleases him."

More laughter, agreeably shocked.

"No, but to be serious." Inristian's voice. "At first I assumed she was, but she has shared my bedroom every night. And she has said nothing to indicate that she is his whore."

"Oh, don't be naive, sweet! Besides, I know what a sound sleeper you are."

"Isn't it obvious? He sent her off to separate lodgings so that he can sleep with other women while he's here!"

"But he is so ugly. What woman would ever—?"

"Wizards can make anyone fall in love with them. And my grandfather says there used to be all kinds of stories about him. Even the queen—remember the portrait the other night, the one that came alive?"

"Oh, that was so boring. I wanted the dwarfs to come back—I've never laughed so hard in my life."

"You know the old saying 'Never trust a wizard'? My grandfather says that it's because of Lord Aruendiel."

"Did he really murder his wife?"

"Yes. And her lover."

"Then she was a slut, what did she expect?"

"Well, I feel sorry for Nora, having to—you know—with a man like that."

"I feel sorry for *him*. She's nothing to look at, even if you don't count the scar. And her clothes!"

Nora had heard enough. Gathering her skirts, she moved back up the staircase as quietly as she could. She tried to summon a smile at the lurid spectacle of herself and Aruendiel playing out some kind of sadomasochistic sex game. It would be easy enough to go downstairs and tell them how wrong they were. But why? She was a thing, not a person to them, no matter how often she'd gone ribbon-shopping or played *ben* with them.

She wandered into an adjoining gallery and sat down on a bench, attempting to give her full attention to the musicians piping nearby.

It didn't matter if they thought she was sleeping with Aruendiel, Nora thought angrily. First, because she wasn't. And second, why should it matter? At home—the real world, Nora thought—having sex out of wedlock didn't make you a whore. That was something she'd never liked about nineteenth-century novels: All those fallen women—Hester, Tess, Maggie, Hetty—one slip and they were ruined. Lydia, too, if not for Mr. Darcy. It was one thing to read about a society obsessed with female purity—quite another to find yourself living in one. Inristian and her friends, they were the real whores, strategizing about how to make their fortunes by luring vineyard-owning noblemen into matrimony.

The music ended, and Nora stood up, so suddenly that the person passing in front of her had to step back. She turned to apologize and found herself facing the ginger-haired man she had spoken to a few evenings ago, the one she'd seen earlier with the presumed Lord Morasiv.

He seemed almost embarrassed to see her. His eyes darted away, and he mumbled something about begging the lady's pardon.

"For what? I'm the one who got in your way just now."

More signs of distress, then he spoke crisply: "I apologize for my regrettable forwardness the other night. I am very sorry if I caused any offense—it was entirely unintentional."

"What do you mean? You didn't offend me," Nora said, surprised.

"I'm afraid I did not realize to whom I was speaking. I hope there was no misunderstanding."

"Misunderstanding?" Nora considered him for a moment, then looked down at the unfashionable blue-and-black dress. "Oh, you thought I was a servant, didn't you? Someone's maid. That's why you asked me about getting some dinner."

He bowed very low, the tips of his ears reddening. "I am terribly sorry. It was a completely absurd mistake."

"And now you're concerned you're not supposed to talk to a well-behaved young lady without a chaperone, right? Well, don't worry, I'm not a well-behaved young lady."

Her admission did not seem to reduce his confusion.

"By the way, my name is Nora," she added.

"I know who you are. And I apologize again. I hope I do not offend the Lord Aruendiel by speaking to you."

"Offend—? I see." So he was another one. Nora felt her temper rise. "You and everyone else here assume that I'm screwing Lord Aruendiel, is that right?"

He recoiled slightly at her choice of words. "Listen, I hate to disappoint you," Nora went on, "but you're wrong. It's not like that at all. I'm not Lord Aruendiel's mistress, and I don't have any desire to be. And my guess is that he's quite happy that I'm not. Is that clear?"

The young man bit his lip. "Yes, that's clear. I—"

"Please don't apologize again."

For the first time, he smiled. "Then I will not." For a moment, she saw the affable young man she had met the other night, and then his face grew serious again. "But I should explain myself. Lord Aruendiel is a notorious rakehell. He has an extremely bad reputation where women are concerned."

"I've heard something on that subject since I came to Semr," Nora said. "A little more than I wanted to know. Although, frankly, these stories surprise me. I have lived in his household for months, and it's as quiet as, well, as a tomb."

"Well, if he hasn't made you his mistress, you're fortunate."

The young man's sober tone struck her. "Because of what happened to his wife?"

"What do you know of that?"

"I've heard talk." She frowned, trying to follow a silky wisp of memory from the Faitoren court. "Is it true? Did he kill her?"

The young man returned her gaze steadily. "He stabbed her. She was pregnant."

It was Nora's turn to flinch. "Ugh." She was silent for a moment, picturing the scene. "And what happened to him? Was he tried for murder?"

"Technically, Lord Aruendiel was within his marital rights," said the young man. "So he wasn't subject to the king's justice."

"Ugh," Nora said again. So this was how Mrs. Toristel's story about the errant wife ended. "Because she was unfaithful?"

He gave a brief, stilted nod. "But very few men would have been as brutal as Lord Aruendiel was. I'm saying this not to slander him, but because you should know these things, if you are living in his household— even if not quite in the manner that everyone thinks."

"Well, yes, I will be careful," she said. "Though the thing is," Nora added, with a sudden, harsh laugh, "as bad as Lord Aruendiel was to his wife, *my* husband was worse."

## Chapter 19

Nora pulled the door of the palace kitchen shut. The greasy hubbub behind her diminished slightly, but she could still hear the noise through a solid inch of oak. She sighed. "Now I remember why I left restaurant work," she said aloud as she mounted the staircase, back to the upper regions of the palace.

Nora had gone to the kitchen with the intention of asking for a job. She'd lasted about an hour. The chaos, the heat, the noise, were all familiar to her from her earlier life as a cook. But here it was trebled. Rats scrabbled in the corners over scraps of spoiled food, the chickens destined for tonight's dinner ran around clucking underfoot, and a quarrel between two of the cooks exploded into a sudden knife fight. A flurry of spectacular jabs, and then the loser exited cursing, a reddening napkin held to his face, while the rest of the staff jeered. Nora finished chopping her onions, took off her apron, and made her escape.

It might be safer to live with one murderer than to work with a whole staff of likely ones, she thought.

Passing by a window, she saw that Lady Inristian and her friends were playing *ben* on the lawn, but she felt no interest in joining them.

She heard quick, purposeful steps behind her. Nora turned. It was Hirizjahkinis. Nora had seen little of her since the banquet. "Mistress Nora! Good day to you. I am glad to have the chance to say good-bye."

"Good-bye? Are you leaving?"

"No, but I believe you are. Have you not seen Aruendiel yet?"

So he *had* returned as he had promised, even if he had not bothered to inform Nora. "He came back last night, and is leaving today," Hirizjahkinis said. "I have tried to persuade him to stay longer, but he is implacable. I suspect he worries that the king will ask him to be the new chief magician. Me, I will stay in Semr a little while longer. I am getting plenty of work." She laughed, shaking her head, and the gold beads at the ends of her braids clicked together. "Ilissa has been very good for my reputation. I must thank her the next time I see her."

"And after Semr?"

"Oh, I will return home, certainly before the winter comes. I have no wish to experience another northern winter, ever. And I mean to attend the autumn sacrifices at Gahz. I used to care nothing for such things, but"— she shrugged—"I am becoming sentimental as the years pass."

Nora asked her about the autumn sacrifices, and decided from Hirizjahkinis's description that they sounded more like a large-scale barbecue than anything else. Then Hirizjahkinis began to question Nora about her own world: how people traveled, what they ate, what gods they worshipped, what demons they feared, and most of all, how they got along without magic.

Answering Hirizjahkinis's queries made Nora feel homesick. "Do you know anything about traveling between worlds?"

Hirizjahkinis shook her head. "I have never studied that kind of magic, myself. This world is wide enough for me."

"You'd like my world," Nora said impulsively. "I think you'd fit right in. Maybe even better than you do here."

"Better?" Hirizjahkinis raised her eyebrows.

"Well." Nora stalled for an instant. "There are more educated, self-sufficient women, like you. And people of all different skin colors and"—Nora

Fee is $2.00.

# H.W. WILSON

## Indexes That Will Guid
## & Help Your Patrons F

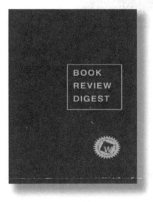

**Book Review Digest** is an esse
wide range of genres from adu
academic sources. This valuab
essential for readers' advisory
citations to, and descriptive su

Virtually every book has at lea
two additional reviews cited fr

---

**Short Story Index** unlocks the contents of thousands of
genres that would otherwise be invisible to the library p
to the individual story level for each short story collecti
discover short stories about the topics that are of interes

This unique reference aid is a guide to important conten
literary researchers and other library users. It provides t
coverage of short stories written in or translated into En

paused, unable to translate "sexual preferences" into Ors—"women who take women as lovers, or men who take men as lovers, can do so openly. Most of the time."

Hirizjahkinis blew air out of her cheeks, a puff of pure incredulity. "I make no pretenses about whom I invite into my bed. And in my country, let me tell you, there are no white people. I fit in very well." She shrugged her shoulders under the Kavareen's pelt. "Furthermore, I am a magician. Of course I am self-sufficient. It goes without saying."

"I'm sorry," Nora said. "I hope I haven't offended you."

"No, no. It is true, there is no one *exactly* like me here. Plenty of women practicing a little ignorant country magic, but very few who are trained magicians."

"How did you become a magician?" Nora asked curiously.

"I started out as a witch—a nun of the order of the witch priestesses of Kirajahn Alanafar Muris, the Holy Sister Night. My parents dedicated me before I was even born, as a thanks offering for a prayer that was granted. So I learned the chants and the rituals, and worshipped the goddess, and grew to be quite a strong witch, in my way. Of course, all that was almost useless, after I had to leave the order and the goddess withdrew her blessing. I did not learn to wield real magic until I studied with Aruendiel."

Hirizjakinis's account raised more questions than it answered. "How did you get Aruendiel to teach you magic?"

"Oh, it was a kind of trade. He was interested in some of the spells that I had learned in the order." She added, after a moment's reflection, "There is always this kind of exchange going on among magicians. There is always something to learn, even from bad magicians. At least you can learn what not to do."

An idea bloomed rapidly in Nora's mind as Hirizjahkinis was speaking. She thought: I bet Hirizjahkinis would teach me magic. And I'm sure she never stabbed anyone to death. How hard is it to learn magic? How long before you get to be really good? Nora pictured herself, grave and puissant, lifting a hand with lazy grace to summon a thunderstorm or—better yet—making Ilissa cower.

But Hirizjahkinis didn't know the magic to send Nora home again. And as for becoming a magician—how much do I want to believe in this stuff, Nora thought rebelliously. There was *something* there, you couldn't deny that. But was it really magic? Whatever magic was.

She wanted to take up a number of questions with Hirizjahkinis, not the least of which was the little matter of Aruendiel's wife. But just then, a servant came up to them to say that Lord Aruendiel had requested that the ladies meet him at the south gate, and Nora had to go to her room to gather up her things. She changed, with some regret, out of her borrowed dress back into Mrs. Toristel's brown one, and wrapped *Pride and Prejudice* inside her gray smock for discretion and safekeeping.

Making her way to the gate, she found Aruendiel looking rather tired but obviously in good spirits as he talked to Hirizjahkinis. The reason, she gathered, was that he had just been paid. It was compensation for the job he had done for the merchant cursed by the sea god. One of his client's ships had arrived in Semr with a full cargo the day before; Aruendiel had collected a purseful of gold for the share promised to him.

"You see," said Hirizjahkinis, "it was a very good idea to come back to Semr. Otherwise you would have missed the ship and, I am sure, forgotten all about collecting your reward."

"He would not dare to let the debt go unpaid," Aruendiel said with a crooked smile. "The consequences would be regrettable."

"Only if you remembered that he owed you the money. So you will not stay here longer? It is late to be setting out; it is almost midday."

"No, there is a banquet tonight, and I have no desire to be pressed into service to amuse a roomful of tipsy fools a second time. Although that ridiculous episode has had an interesting sequel," he added. "Both Savo and Tirinist asked me to work the portrait spell for them. Savo wishes to see his first wife again, after thirty years. And Tirinist possesses an antique portrait of an unknown woman, with whom he wishes to become better acquainted."

"You would have many more such commissions, you know, if you occasionally took the trouble to remind people of what a powerful magician you are."

"Commissions? I said no to both."

"No! Tell me you didn't. Tirinist, at least, is a very rich man."

"I will not work that spell again."

"Then you must teach me the spell, and I'll do it," Hirizjahkinis said. To his raised eyebrow, she added, "I came to Semr to work. One travels lighter with a full purse. Would you have refused Savo and Tirinist if your purse were not so full?"

"Yes," he said shortly. "But if you wish, I will tell you how to do the spell. It comes from Duisi Tortor's *Concerning Necromancy and Other Reversals of Fate* (although there is almost no true necromancy in the entire book). It's an elaboration of an ordinary testimony spell, the kind of charm you'd use to get any stone to speak. So you work the summons on the painting itself. The trick is to push it hard, and perhaps help it along with an awakening charm or a manifestation sequence. But the paint is fragile, so you need a fat wick. Tortor used to sacrifice a baby."

"That's a great deal of power."

"More than really necessary," Aruendiel agreed. "Fire or water work just as well."

The spell he'd described almost made sense in a general way, Nora thought. But then Hirizjahkinis asked a string of questions that were too technical for her to follow. Aruendiel answered them in equally obscure terms.

"Did you resolve the little problem of the queen's aunt—her unexpected death?" Aruendiel asked, lifting his travel bag and easing it onto the shoulder that stood slightly higher than the other.

"With great success. And no, I did not raise the dead, you will be pleased to hear," Hirizjahkinis said. "Although the queen's uncle *thinks* that I did. Fear loosened his tongue amazingly."

Aruendiel looked at her for a moment. "Good for you, Hiriz. You always find a way."

"Peace be your friend, Aruendiel."

"And yours." He turned away.

Nora said swiftly to Hirizjahkinis, "Thank you for everything. I hope that I'll see you again."

"Well, I do not come north very often these days—but I would like that, too. Be safe, little one." She raised her hands briefly to lay them against Nora's hands, a formal dab of leave-taking, and then Nora ran to catch up with Aruendiel.

The magician's gray gaze slid toward her as, out of breath, she fell into step beside him. "So you do not wish to remain in Semr?"

"No."

"Why not? It will be dull for you, back at the castle, with no one to talk to except Mrs. Toristel."

"That's true enough," Nora said stolidly. "But I've had enough of court life."

The answer seemed to please him; at least, his mouth curled for an instant and he stopped questioning her. He led the way downhill through the tangle of streets until they entered another marketplace, bigger and shabbier than the one that Nora had visited with Inristian, with a greater variety of goods. The narrow shop fronts and the open stalls were piled with ceramic pots and plates; copper kettles and pans; harnesses and saddles; iron tools, some recognizable, some not; bolts of cloth; animal hides; wheels of cheese; crates of live chickens, frogs, and doves; casks of beer and wine; glass beads; glass bottles; spices; salt; knives, swords, and shields.

Aruendiel picked his way through the maze of stalls and then ducked into a small, dark storefront that, unlike the other shops, had a lettered sign above the door. Nora remained outside for a moment, carefully sounding out the letters, then followed Aruendiel inside. He was talking to an immensely fat man whose girth had been poured into an equally massive leather-sided chair. Behind the fat man shelves and boxes overflowed with books, scrolls, and maps in various stages of dogearedness.

"... *The Augur's Companion* just came in, but I don't think it's to your lordship's taste, is it?" the fat man was saying. "You've never bought a single book of divination from me."

"That's because they're all claptrap," Aruendiel said.

"Not everyone's of your mind, thank the gods. Most popular magical books I carry. What else? I have Ostr the Younger on strategy. No? Let's see, there's your own book on transformations—you wouldn't be wanting a copy of that, I suppose."

Aruendiel frowned briefly. "Burn it," he said. "I knew nothing when I wrote it."

The fat man shook his head. "You should do an updated edition. It still sells quickly enough, when I get hold of a copy. What else can I tempt you with? Well, I have some of Ierbe Norinun's notebooks, that's something you don't see every day."

Aruendiel inclined his head, and the fat man pulled himself upright to rummage on one of the bookshelves. His chair, Nora noticed, shrank to more normal dimensions as soon as he was out of it. After a minute, the shopkeeper turned back to Aruendiel with a half-dozen books bound in green cloth.

"How did you get your hands on them?" Aruendiel asked, opening a volume. "I thought that—what's that wizard's name?—Ruenc, Kelerus Ruenc had bought them all up years ago."

"Oh, he did. But now—" The fat man clutched an imaginary glass and tilted the imaginary contents toward his mouth, then gave a sagacious nod.

"Ah," said Aruendiel, still leafing through the notebooks. "Well, he's not parting with the best stuff yet. This is very early, pure juvenilia."

"Oh, your lordship should look more closely," the fat man protested smoothly. "I'm no wizard—or magician—but there was another magician in the shop last week, could hardly tear himself away. Ice demons, he was interested in. And some unusual weather magic."

"Who was it?" Aruendiel asked, sounding bored.

The fat man's laughter took a few seconds to ripple through his huge body. "Your lordship knows I have to be discreet about my customers."

"Obviously he didn't buy them. You must be asking far more than they're worth."

"Ten gold beetles for the lot. Yes, it's steep, but it's a fair price for such a treasure, your lordship. I had to pay almost that much to the wizard Ruenc."

"How much to have them copied?"

The fat man laughed again, even more heartily this time. "I never have original manuscripts copied, as your lordship well knows. If you buy them, you can be assured that no other magic-worker will have access to their secrets."

"Unless they've already pawed through the notebooks themselves and set a copy imp to transcribe them."

"I have a half-dozen protection spells on this shop to guard against it, all from different magicians. No offense, your lordship, but I'd challenge even you to steal words from my shop."

"Be careful with your challenges, Gorinth," said Aruendiel. "I might take you up on that boast. But assuming I want to pay for the goods I take, like an honest man—what if I work you another protection spell? That's worth at least five gold beetles."

"That would be kind of you, your lordship. But as I said, I already have six spells, so it's hard to see how another protection spell would be worth so much to me."

They went back and forth, with many throat-clearings on Aruendiel's part and more laughter from the fat man, until finally it was agreed that the magician would pay eight gold beetles and work a protection spell in exchange for the notebooks and a three-volume history of the doomed republic of the Endueruvan wizards.

It took Aruendiel only a minute to do the spell. Nora could tell from the throb in her gut that he had not stinted on the magic, either. He was paying the shopkeeper the gold when the fat man said, "So is that the girl?"

"The girl?" Aruendiel said, frowning.

"The one that found the king's chief magician locked away in a book."

"Yes, that was me," Nora said quickly.

"What were you doing looking in a book, miss?"

Nora shrugged. "I thought I might read it."

The fat man laughed again, so hard that he had to sit down in his chair (which promptly extended its arms to embrace him). "That's a good joke. I must say, it didn't do me any good when that story got out. People got very nervous for a few days, wondering what might jump out at them if they opened a book."

"I've actually read it once before," Nora said.

The fat man was still chuckling as she and Aruendiel walked out of the shop.

"So you are famous," Aruendiel said as they made their way through the marketplace. There was something waspish in his tone, as though he felt that she were stealing some of his glory for liberating Bouragonr.

*You have no idea,* she thought, remembering the gossip she'd overhead at the palace. Aloud she said, "Why did he think it was so funny that I might read the book? Because I'm a woman?"

Aruendiel's only response was to make a disapproving sound at the back of his throat and to walk a little faster. When they came to a store that sold dry goods, he stopped and pulled a slip of paper from inside his tunic. "One more errand. For Mrs. Toristel."

The interior of the shop was a cave made of bolts of cloth stacked, standing upright, or leaning aslant against the walls. Two thin, dark-haired women sat talking in the middle of the store, one knitting, one nursing a baby, their voices cushioned by the soft jumble around them.

"Four yards of black worsted, best quality," Aruendiel read from the paper. "Five yards of gray, second-best quality. Six copper buttons." The knitter put down her needles and slid off her stool to bring out the rolls of black and gray cloth.

As she was measuring, Aruendiel turned to Nora. "Pick out two lengths for yourself. You'll need something heavier for winter." Startled, she stared at him. He waved her toward the nearest pile of fabric. "I can't have you taking any more of my housekeeper's dresses," he said.

Remarkable how a shop looked more inviting once you knew that you could actually buy something there. Nora prowled back and forth in front of the somber rainbow of fabric, trying to make out colors in the dim light, and finally picked out some thick, smooth-napped woolen cloth, one bolt rust red, one bolt sky blue.

The knitter measured out five yards of each color. "Six dozen and four silver beads for everything."

Seventy-six, Nora thought, idly working the arithmetic in her head, as Aruendiel opened his money pouch and produced three gold pieces. They looked like thinner, cruder versions of Egyptian scarabs. As with scarabs, there was writing stamped onto the flat side.

The knitter dug through a box full of tiny, hollow silver cylinders with lettering on the sides, the same as the beads that Nora had seen Mrs. Toristel use in the village market.

"How many silver beads in a beetle?" Nora asked. Aruendiel looked at her with the sort of frown that implied she might be an idiot. "I just want to know how the money works here," she said.

"Three dozen," he said.

The knitter counted out twenty beads. Aruendiel pocketed them and motioned to Nora to pick up the bundle of cloth. Nora hesitated, running through some quick mental calculations. "She didn't give you enough change," she said.

Aruendiel frowned again, as though his earlier suspicion had been confirmed, and moved toward the door.

"Wait, she still owes you, um, a dozen beads."

"Let us go, Mistress Nora." He flung the words over his shoulder.

The knitter was scowling, too, beginning to bridle. "I'm sorry," Nora said to her. "I think you just miscounted. You said it was six dozen and four silver beads?"

"Yes."

"And he gave you three gold beetles. So that's, let's see"—one hundred and eight, she calculated—"nine dozen beads. You should have given him, um, two dozen beads plus eight."

Before the knitter could respond, the other woman broke in. "She's right, sister," she said placidly, shifting the baby to her other breast. "Give them another dozen silver beads."

Slowly, as though she were not entirely convinced, the knitter counted out the dozen beads into Nora's hand. Nora thanked her. Then, looking up, she saw that Aruendiel had already left the shop.

Going outside, at first she did not see him at all. She had a moment of panic, and then she spotted his dark head moving through the crowd, twenty yards down the street. Nora followed him as quickly as she could, edging her way between stalls and jostling the other pedestrians. She was relieved to see that he had stopped to wait for her in front of a tavern, just before the street forked.

Something about the rigidity of his posture told her how furious he was. As soon as he saw her approaching, he turned and began to walk rapidly down the right-hand street.

Catching up, she told him, "I have the rest of your money."

"You may keep it, if it means so much to you." At the next intersection, he veered left without appearing to pay any attention to whether Nora was following him or not.

"She gave you the wrong change," Nora said. "It was a simple mistake. I just pointed it out, that's all."

"You would have done better to have left well enough alone. In the future, perhaps you will let me conduct my financial affairs myself."

"Don't worry, I will!" Nora snapped, suddenly furious, too. "Is that why you're angry, because I dared to intervene in your finances?"

"No," Aruendiel said. They turned down another street before he spoke again. "What you did was very unseemly."

"Unseemly?"

"To challenge those shopkeepers."

"Challenge? She made the wrong change, and I corrected her. That happens all the time in a store. I wasn't accusing her of cheating you."

"A gentleman does not quibble with a shopkeeper over money."

"Not even if he's being shortchanged? I don't believe that. Besides, you were haggling with the man in the bookstore."

"That is entirely different. Gorinth is a learned man, an old acquaintance—"

"I see! He's closer to an equal, not that anyone's ever quite equal to you. So it's fine to engage in a little gentlemanly bargaining with him. But not with a couple of women selling fabric in a little shop—even if one of them, at least, is better at math than you are."

"You have only the crudest grasp of social niceties," Aruendiel observed.

"Well, in my world people can ask politely for correct change without committing a social crime. By the way," she added, "you do agree that she shortchanged you, right?"

He shrugged, his pale eyes elsewhere. "The exact tally of a few silver beads is of no concern to me."

"I thought so," Nora said. "You still aren't sure about the math."

They walked along in silence, single file because of the crowds. The rank, salty smell of the river became more pronounced. At last they came to a gate in the city wall. When Aruendiel gave his name, the guards waved them through, with a curious glance at Nora. She wondered what exactly she was famous for this time—rescuing Bouragonr, or being the mistress of a prominent magician and murderer?

Ahead was a long quay lined with a thicket of tall-masted ships, dark-timbered, weather-beaten, burlier and more disreputable-looking than the gleaming white sailboats she remembered from the shore back home. The wind off the water whipped through her hair.

"Are we taking a boat back?"

"To the other side of the river." Aruendiel dropped his bag and walked down the quay, looking for the ferry.

I could still turn back, Nora thought. She glanced down at the bundles she carried. All her possessions in the world—this world—consisted of a change of clothes, a paperback book, and twelve silver beads. Would that be enough to pay for even one night's lodging somewhere? She had no idea. There was also the fabric that Aruendiel had just bought her. That could be sold. Another dozen or two dozen silver beads. She worked her hand through the wrappings of the bundle from the dry goods store and fingered the blue worsted. It was good material, thick and felty. Warm for winter.

Mrs. Toristel might have asked him to buy it. But lately Mrs. Toristel had been talking about making over one of her daughter's old winter dresses for Nora. Would she even dare to ask the magician to buy Nora material for new clothes? The cloth was bound to be more expensive in Semr.

Aruendiel was looking over the water, arms folded. Nora suddenly thought—why?—of the day they'd flown to Semr, after Raclin chased them, and how Aruendiel had stood alone, checking his hand for tremors. Did he find any? She could not get the image out of her head. Then she remembered the calm weight of his hand—the same hand—on her shoulder when she faced Ilissa. He would not let go, even when Ilissa's magic fought him through Nora's body.

An undefined emotion nagged at her. I want to know more, she thought—about magic and how magicians are made. About this magician. If I leave now, I believe I'll regret it.

She hesitated, then picked up the bundles and walked along the quay until she reached the spot where Aruendiel stood. Across the water, a skiff was making its way toward them.

"I haven't thanked you for buying me that fabric. It was very—" She wanted to find exactly the right word, one that would not annoy him all over again. "Very decent of you."

"There's no reason to thank me," he said, not looking at her. "It's my duty to see that those living under my roof are fed and clothed."

"Well, I thank you anyway, because I'm pleased to have something comfortable to wear when the weather gets cold."

Aruendiel nodded, then turned to regard her. "I should remember to make allowances for you. You are a foreigner. It is not your fault that you do not always know what is appropriate and what is not."

It was not much of an apology. But Nora could not bring herself to apologize for asking the shopkeeper for correct change, either. The ferryman rowed another ten strokes closer before she answered. "I did not think that you were so concerned with social niceties."

"And why not?"

"Because you're a magician. Because, from what I've observed, you usually do what you want to do without worrying about the opinions of other people or their notions of propriety."

"That may be true. But here we are talking about *my* notions of propriety."

"Then maybe you should reexamine them."

The skiff bumped against the quay, and the sunburned young ferryman helped Nora into the boat. She sat in the bow and watched the walls and roofs of Semr recede across the water, the gray bulk of the palace crouching at the top of the city. Aruendiel sat crookedly in the stern, looking out to sea.

Whistling, the ferryman steered them against the dock. "Fastest crossing I've had all day," he remarked, sounding pleased. "Tide's running hard right now, but we hardly felt it. That'll be four silver beads for the both of you."

Aruendiel gave him two beads. "The lady can pay for herself," he said. Nora did so, wondering if this was some gesture of respect, but thinking it was more likely that Aruendiel was simply being cheap.

## Chapter 20

Aruendiel jerked his horse's head around and circled back to where the girl was plodding along on the bay mare that he had just paid too much money for. "Is your mount lame, that it cannot go any faster?" he inquired.

"No. *I* can't go any faster." Nora was clinging to both the reins and the saddle pommel with white-knuckled concentration, in the untested but powerful conviction that if she loosened her grip, she would instantly tumble to the ground. She shifted her weight in the sidesaddle, searching for a comfortable point of balance, not finding it.

"Ridiculous," he said. "Your mare is about to take root, she's moving so slowly. Have you never ridden a horse before?"

"I used to ride all the time. At Ilissa's."

He snorted disdainfully. "Do you think that was really a horse?"

"What else would it have been?"

"A sheep, a goat—even a Faitoren that Ilissa felt like punishing."

"Whatever I was riding, it didn't seem as tall, and it was a lot steadier. How far to your castle?"

"Normally, it's three days' ride. At this rate—" Aruendiel leaned over, twitched the reins out of Nora's hands, and slapped the horse with them. The mare broke into a slow trot. Feeling as though she were perched at the top of a swaying ladder, Nora restrained a shriek. "At this rate, perhaps we will get home in five days," he said. "It's a waste of horseflesh, putting you on that mare. You would have done just as well on a donkey, and it would have cost half the beetles."

"I thought gentlemen didn't quibble about money."

"We are traveling by horseback for your benefit, Mistress Nora," he said. "If I were to travel as I prefer, I would be home by tomorrow morning."

"And how is that?" she asked. He urged his horse forward without bothering to reply.

They were riding through a landscape of thorny scrub and tidal marsh, strewn with a rubble of stone blocks. The place felt oddly desolate, for all that it was so close to the city across the river. A row of columns lay prone and half-covered by mud and sea grass, but still perfectly parallel. The remains of a paved road surfaced under their horses' hooves, then disappeared into the soil. Nora tried to piece together in her mind's eye the buildings and streets that had once been here.

Bracing herself, she gave the reins a shake as she had seen Aruendiel do and caught up with him. "What is this ruin?" she asked.

"Old Semr."

"What happened to it?"

He looked faintly annoyed at her question, but answered: "The city was taken by a hostile army, the Taurnii. It fell, literally. The walls and roofs came down, and the sea rushed in. The besiegers slaughtered those who managed to escape."

Another of those explanations that only raised more questions. "Do you mean there was an earthquake?"

"No, it was poor magic. Or rather, powerful magic that was poorly used."

"I don't understand."

"Of course not. You know nothing of magic, or of history."

"But I'm interested," Nora said swiftly. "Please, tell me what happened."

"Well," he said, after a moment's consideration, "in truth it is not such a long story, if one leaves out the history of King Perlo's War.

"Old Semr was built with magic, most of it—its walls and gates and towers and palaces and hanging gardens. The wizard Mererish Agor laid it out for King Corbos Bullface centuries ago. They say it was a magnificent city. New Semr, where we just came from, is an overgrown trading village by comparison.

"That ceramic lion you broke," he added, "it came from Old Semr."

Before Nora could correct him about breaking the lion, he went on: "The risk of using magic to build something, whether it's a building or an entire city, is that the edifice is only as strong as the magic itself. If something happens to the magic, the structure simply collapses. The Taurnii wizards removed the spells that had built Old Semr, and the stones and timbers flung themselves apart like mad things. So said the few survivors."

"Why was the city never rebuilt?" Nora asked.

"That is the more complicated part of the story. The simplest reason is that people began to consider this site unlucky."

That would explain why the place was so quiet, Nora thought. Nothing moved among the rocks and marshes except for a few shorebirds and a distant boy clamming on a muddy inlet. The silence felt as big and clean as the sky after the clamor of New Semr.

After half an hour, they rode through a pair of broken pillars, and Aruendiel said that they had just gone through one of Old Semr's twelve gates. The countryside took on a more domestic, bucolic feel, as they began passing fenced plots and whitewashed houses. Chickens and the occasional pig wandered across their path. Nora kept reining in the mare to avoid a collision until Aruendiel told her sharply that her horse could find its way around the other animals without her interference.

After a while she said, with some resentment: "I didn't break that lion."

"The lion?"

"The ceramic lion in the palace. I didn't break it. I told you that at the time."

"It's an interesting question, how that figure came to be broken." He gave her a searching glance. "I don't know the answer yet."

"Frankly, it looked to me as though the lion jumped," Nora said. "Could it have been, well, some kind of magical figure?" Listen to me, she thought irritably, I sound as crazy as the rest of them.

"It was an ordinary clay figure," Aruendiel said. "Nothing unusual, except for being extremely valuable."

Nora looked down at her left hand, holding the reins. The ring gleamed on her finger. "Do you still think that I'm Ilissa's spy?"

Aruendiel turned to regard her again. "No."

"Why not?" she asked.

"I could tell how much magic Ilissa was using, when she tried to kidnap you," he said. "She obviously encountered a great deal of resistance. I still don't trust that ring of yours, but—" He shrugged. "She was not using it to control you."

Nora felt a hidden knot of tension loosen. But she was not entirely free. "I have to be honest," she said haltingly. "Part of me wanted to go with her. I was so afraid, and it seemed that if I only let go and gave in to her, everything would be all right."

"And you did give in," Aruendiel said.

"I thought I would be stronger, the second time I met Ilissa. I wasn't."

"What makes Ilissa's magic so dangerous," he said, "is that, usually, she does not force you to do anything truly against your will. She only makes you do what you wish to do." The wind blew strands of hair across his face, making it hard to read his expression.

"I did try to fight—" Nora began.

"Her kind of magic is very difficult to resist. Because it speaks to the secret wishes of the heart, the fears and desires that we may not even recognize ourselves. I do not imagine, Mistress Nora, that you had any great wish to follow Ilissa back to her domain and become enslaved to her again. But even a slight inclination, a divided mind, would be enough for her. She offered you something you wanted, in some measure. It would be strange if you did not take it."

Quickly Nora looked away, to study with blurred vision the bent backs of laborers in the adjacent barley field. She did not know exactly why the tears had sprung up, whether it was because she was ashamed or relieved to hear what Aruendiel had said.

"I am not telling you this to discomfit you, Mistress Nora," he said. "Whatever hidden thoughts that Ilissa found in your heart and turned to her own uses—you might never have acted on them otherwise. I do not pretend to read them; they are your private concern."

Nora nodded, unwilling to trust her voice to hold steady. They had ridden well past the barley field before she ventured to speak again.

"But how can anyone resist her, then?"

"Knowing your own secrets before Ilissa can steal them, that is one protection," he said. "Easier in theory than in practice. Otherwise, some shielding spells are effective. But she has entrapped many people, including some skilled in magic, who should have known better."

"You said that before," Nora said. "Are you one of those people?"

She could tell just from the way his gloved hands shifted their grip on the reins that the question made him angry, and she knew what his answer would be. "Yes," he said.

"What happened?"

"What happened? I was a fool."

Nora said cautiously: "You had a love affair with her."

"At one time, yes."

"Because of her magic?"

"No," he said with a dry laugh. "She didn't need to use magic, at least at first. I was idiotic enough on my own to take her as my mistress. The magic she worked came later."

"What kind of magic?"

"Oh, there were various spells, very subtle, layer upon layer," he said, grimacing. "Gods, I kept finding them and pulling them away, like cobwebs, for weeks afterward. Spells to rule my thoughts, to cloud my judgment—but everything was done very carefully, nothing so obvious that it might give me alarm. A more accomplished version of what she did to you.

"It was pleasant while it lasted, I will give her that. I remember feeling extremely fit and alert, although in reality I was blind and deaf to what was happening to me. Ilissa's magic, her presence itself, seemed to hone and amplify my own. I began to think of all kinds of interesting possibilities that I had never brought myself to consider before.

"Ilissa had certain ambitions—still has them now, no doubt. She wanted to rule over more than just the Faitoren. She thought that I would be the perfect partner—or instrument—for her purposes. Well, I began to agree with her. Emperor over the five kingdoms? Why not? With my magic and Ilissa's combined, no one could stand against us."

Fascinated, Nora felt a faint consternation that Aruendiel had been so easily seduced by Ilissa's grandiose plots. "And what happened?"

"You know how it is with the Faitoren, do you not? Always another ball, another hunt. We talked grand strategy, and meanwhile the days seemed to slip away."

"Yes," Nora said thoughtfully, "it was like that for me, too. Without the plans for world conquest, of course."

"From time to time, I was fleetingly aware of odd thoughts, as though there were a voice muttering in my head, questioning things that I accepted to be true. I was far too beguiled with Ilissa and her plans and the Faitoren's endless, mindless merrymaking to pay attention.

"Then one evening I was passing time with Raclin and his companions, as had become my custom, I regret to say. They were casting lots and drinking, until fisticuffs broke out between Raclin and another Faitoren. The one called Gaibon, in fact—the Faitoren who took Bouragonr's place. Raclin knocked Gaibon down, and Gaibon swore that he would be revenged, and Raclin swore that he would knock Gaibon down as many times as it took to teach him not to cheat. And the rest of us all laughed, and I thought to myself what good, high-spirited fellows they both were, Raclin and Gaibon, and how fortunate I was to have them as comrades.

"And the voice in my head said very clearly, 'Raclin and Gaibon, they're a pair of treacherous louts, both equally worthless, except that Raclin is the more vicious of the two.'

"I felt a great sense of release to hear this. It was my voice, I realized—my own mind speaking to me.

"After that, I began to notice all kinds of occasions when my thoughts seemed to diverge in completely opposite directions. I would spend the day hunting with great pleasure, and yet recall how much hunting bored me. There was a human girl there, too, a peasant girl that they'd married to Raclin, same as you, and something about the way they treated her bothered me. But I did nothing.

"Eventually—after far too long—it occurred to me that I'd been enchanted."

"I heard a voice, too," Nora said. "But I didn't listen to it, most of the time."

"A mistake on your part," he said. "But it was unpardonable carelessness for me, an experienced magician, to miss so many obvious signs of enchantment." He smiled, but there was no good humor in his expression.

"I went to Ilissa and taxed her with my discovery. Of course she did not deny it. She could not. Instead she tried to soothe me, first with caresses and sweet words, then—incredibly—with more magic. The arrogance of that woman! As though I had not already learned to recognize the touch of her spells, like poison lullabies.

"But it was fortunate that she overstepped in that fashion. It goaded me. I fought back, undoing every piece of her magic that I could find. I didn't know as much then about Faitoren magic as I do now, but I knew enough. I found more spells that Ilissa had cast on me, and destroyed them, and then I began to unfasten the spells around me, the ones that are woven into the fabric of her domain. By the time I paused, the place where we stood looked very different—you would never recognize Ilissa's palace without her magic—and for the first time I could see that Ilissa was frightened. She was afraid that I would strip it all away, no doubt, all the pretty things around her, even her own face.

"She rained down abuse on me, both verbal and magical. For a while, it was rather entertaining, and then I grew tired of hearing what a vain, deceitful, barbaric, clod-headed, puny-loined cad I was. I came away knowing that I had a new enemy, although not realizing quite how much Ilissa hated me or to what lengths she would go for revenge. That was only the first engagement in what has been a very long war.

"And it makes a long story. It is not a tale that I have broken in by frequent telling, so it tends to run away at a gallop when given the chance. At any rate, you see that you are not the only one who has been Ilissa's dupe."

"What happened to the girl? The peasant girl? You didn't try to save her?"

"No." He sounded grim. After a moment, he added, "It was only later that we realized how many young women had disappeared in the vicinity of the Faitoren, and discerned what was happening to them."

"How many—?"

"I could not tell you."

They rode on for a while in silence, and then Aruendiel asked brusquely, "How did you know that Ilissa had been my mistress?"

Nora tried to untangle the threads of her intuition. "Because you two hate each other so much! And you talk about her as though you knew her well. Also, something she said to you in Semr made me wonder."

"Indeed." He did not seem pleased by her deduction. "I thought that Ilissa might have told you. Or that you had heard some old gossip floating around in Semr."

"No, I didn't hear *that* in Semr," Nora said, and then regretted it.

"Ah, what did you hear?" he inquired. When she did not reply at once, he laughed sardonically. "I suppose they told you all kinds of interesting things. People love to gossip about magicians."

"They said you killed your wife," Nora said, surprising herself, the words slipping out of her mouth as swiftly as an arrow.

Aruendiel's face hardened. "Well, I did. So the fools have a good story to pass along to other fools."

There was nothing graceful to say at this juncture, so again Nora said the first thing that rose to her lips. "Why?" Even if she knew the answer already, she did not understand it. No matter how awful Adam had been, Nora had never thought about killing him.

"Did they not tell you in Semr?" he asked.

She dropped her eyes to the back of her horse's head. "I'm sorry," she said. "I don't mean to pry."

"But you are prying," he said. "We have wasted enough time today discussing my biography."

He spurred his horse ahead and vanished around a bend in the road. Did he mean to abandon her? Nora cautiously urged her horse to a faster gait, but for the rest of the afternoon, he was in sight only occasionally, when the road straightened for a stretch.

They spent the night with one of Aruendiel's friends, a magician named Nansis Abora, who lived in a tidy cottage surrounded by vegetable plots. He had disheveled gray hair and a faint stutter. That night she lay in bed in a slant-ceilinged loft over the kitchen and listened to the two magicians talk late into the night, mostly about Nansis Abora's recent work on various problems in time-travel magic. It sounded like a fairly abstruse branch of magic because of the complicated astronomical calculations involved; she wondered sourly if Aruendiel was really following the other magician's explanation. In the morning she was so sore from the ride of the day before that she could hardly climb down the ladder from the loft, let alone mount her horse. Nansis Abora insisted on doing a spell to relieve the pain, for which she was very grateful. Aruendiel had not offered to help.

He was in a better mood, though, as they set out. At least, he stayed within view. From time to time, he pointed out a castle that he had once helped capture or made an acid observation about the condition of a farmer's livestock. By the end of the day she had learned nothing more about magic, but had picked up a few tips about siegecraft and animal husbandry that, she supposed, might prove useful someday.

On the second evening, Aruendiel arranged lodgings at a farmhouse, paying the young farmer with a silver bead and magic: spells to keep the rain out of the thatch, cure a toothache, and sweeten the well water. Nora awoke once during the night and saw, in the moonlight, that the space in front of the hearth where Aruendiel had been sleeping was vacant. She lay awake on her pallet for some time, wondering what she would do now that he had abandoned her after all. But in the morning he was lying there as though he had never stirred, his long limbs looking somehow askew even under the folds of his cloak.

As they were preparing to leave, she asked Aruendiel how much farther they had to go. About a dozen *karistises*, he said. She pressed him to put it in terms that she could understand. "We could be home by late tonight," he said, "if the roads are not too bad, and if you are not as slow as you were the first day."

"I could go faster if I didn't have to ride sidesaddle," Nora said. "It's ridiculous to make women balance sideways." As though horses weren't huge and terrifying enough already.

She expected a caustic remark on her ignorance of social niceties, but to her surprise, Aruendiel smiled fractionally. "I agree with you. Women had a little more sense when I was younger. My mother never rode sidesaddle in her life."

"Really?" Nora said, taken aback. Of course Aruendiel had had a mother, but it was odd to contemplate. "When did they start riding sidesaddle?"

"It was one of those crazes that start in the cities. It came in with the modern fashion for long skirts."

Intrigued, Nora almost asked him for more details about this piece of fashion history, but thought better of it. "If I had the right kind of saddle," she pointed out, "I could ride astride, and we could make better time." Without answering, he heaved his own saddle onto his horse's back and tightened the cinch under the horse's belly. "Or would it be too unseemly for me to ride astride?" she asked sharply.

With a grunt, Aruendiel lifted her saddle from the fence. "There is nothing seemly about a bad rider," he said. "You sit on the horse as though you're made of wood. I once turned the Forest of Nevreng into cavalry for the count of Middle Duxirent. They rode much as you do."

"Well, they didn't have to ride sidesaddle, did—oh!" She had just noticed the saddle's transformation. "Thank you! I don't suppose you could shorten my skirt, too?"

"I am no tailor," he said, frowning. "Rip the side seams out if you must."

Riding astride on the transformed saddle, Nora did not exactly feel as though she and the horse were one, but at least they seemed to be more or less on the same team. It was easier to keep pace with Aruendiel. "There's something I don't understand," she said to him. "Why can't you just use your magic to wish us home? Hirizjahkinis moved the whole court to her country the other night and back again. Why can't you do the same?"

"That was a temporary dislocation spell—and the Kavareen had much to do with it, if I'm not mistaken," he said in a disapproving tone. "She is becoming far too dependent on that creature."

"All right, but why can't you do, um, a permanent dislocation spell, without the Kavareen?"

"Would you like me to summon up the winds to blow you to my castle, the way they took you from Ilissa's castle?"

"No," Nora said definitely. "That was enough excitement for one lifetime. But here's the real question. Why don't you use magic more often? Last night you could have changed, oh, a spoon or something into a bed for yourself, instead of sleeping on the floor. Or why even pay the farmer for a night's lodging? You could have made him believe that you paid him, I'm sure."

"Ah!" The question seemed to stir up a mixture of disdain and interest in Aruendiel. "The wizard Po Luin, when he traveled, used to construct a new city every night and then dismantle it in the morning. He used pebbles and twigs for the buildings, ants or field mice for the people. He disliked the country intensely; he found it dull."

Nora wondered how interesting a city of former ants could be. But she said: "Why not do something like that? Everyday life is hard here, much harder than in my world. Why not use magic to make things easier?"

"Ilissa asked me a similar question once."

Nora ignored the implied reproach. "What did you tell her?"

"I told her that magic was not a plaything. She found that very amusing." He rode along for a few moments before speaking again. "I have been in worlds where people use almost no magic, like your own, and worlds where they use magic for almost everything. The Faitoren must have come from a place like the latter, originally. They cosset themselves with magic, and well, you see the result. It's a pretty life, but none of it is real.

"Also," Aruendiel added, his voice quickening with irritation, "it would be dishonorable to use magic to cheat a peasant."

"I wasn't seriously suggesting that."

"I hope not."

Another few minutes of silence, until Nora said: "Hirizjahkinis said that you taught her how to be a magician."

"Yes. She was an excellent pupil."

Before she could lose her nerve, Nora asked: "Will you teach me? I'd like to learn how—how to be a magician."

The question amused him more than she would have liked. "A doubtful prospect. Very few are suited to become magicians."

"What does it take?"

"Years of study and practice. But first one must know what magic is."

The road dipped, and they splashed across a stream. "Well, what is magic? Do you command spirits, like Prospero? Did you sell your soul to the devil, like Faustus?"

Aruendiel wanted to know who Prospero and Faustus were. She tried to explain: "Magicians from stories in my world. Written, oh, some four hundred years ago." She had never thought about it before, but surely the Elizabethans were almost the last to use magic as a plot device in serious literature. After Cervantes, the enchanters were living on borrowed time. "Prospero has a couple of magical servants," she went on, "the most powerful being a spirit, Ariel, who can do things like raise storms and tread the ooze of the salt deep. Faustus makes a deal with the devil to acquire magical powers, but in the end he goes to hell, if you know what that is."

"I do not command spirits," Aruendiel said, with asperity. "It's true, there is magic that is based on enslaving demons and spirits of various kinds, and I have studied it, but it is not the kind of magic that I practice now."

"Well, then, what is magic? The kind that you practice now?"

He gave her a penetrating look. "Once you have worked magic, then you start to understand it."

"That seems a bit circular," Nora objected. Aruendiel's only response was an impatient tilt of the head. "All right, I see," she said. "If you have to ask, you'll never know."

He seemed struck by the sentiment. "That is well put."

"Thanks, but I didn't think of it myself," Nora said.

# Chapter 21

The countryside took on a different character when they left the lowlands around Semr. The road dwindled to a muddy track that snaked around wooded hills scabbed with bare black rock. Aruendiel said that once they crossed the Trollsblade Hills, they would enter the basin of the river Uel, which would bring them into his own lands. Nora asked, as a joke, whether there were any trolls in the area, and Aruendiel said no, not for at least two hundred years. She registered the stippling of yellow in the leaves of the trees, and was just wondering if the winters here would be as bad as Hirizjahkinis had warned, when they came into yet another tiny village.

This one seemed unusually lively. A crowd of at least fifty people were gathered around a wooden framework in the village square. As Nora and Aruendiel rode closer, Nora figured out what the frame was for. A rope dangled from the top beam. The prisoner crouched at the foot of the gibbet, bound with ropes.

"They are having some sport," Aruendiel said, spurring his horse forward. When Nora caught up, he was already talking to a man in brown with a small, tight-featured face like a pebble. The village headman, Nora gathered as she listened.

He gave short, reluctant answers to Aruendiel's questions. The prisoner had been condemned to death for murder. A little girl, missing three days. No, they hadn't waited for the magistrate.

"This village is the possession of Lord Olven Obardies, is it not?" Aruendiel asked. "Lord Olven is my vassal; I am Lord Aruendiel of the Uland.

He would not be pleased to have one of his peasants put to death without proper authority."

"The bastard confessed already, your lordship. And it's good riddance. No kids are safe around him."

"Yes," said Aruendiel, glancing at the prisoner huddled beside the gibbet. "I see he lost a hand. The left hand, so it was not theft."

"We caught him pawing a boy, two years since. We should have hung him then."

"Remarkable that he managed to kill a child with only one hand," Aruendiel observed. "How did he kill her, by the way?"

"We can't say," said the headman, a note of exasperation entering his voice. "We can't find her body, and the maggot won't tell us."

"You have not loosened his tongue enough."

"We've tried, your lordship. The stones and irons both. But she wasn't either of the places he said. We thought we'd have another go with the irons before we hang him."

"Leave him to me," said Aruendiel. "It's my right and obligation to examine him, and he will not lie to me."

The man in brown looked thoughtfully at the prisoner, then back to Aruendiel. "They say you're a wizard, as well as a lord. You have spells to make him talk?"

"A magician. I have spells that will pluck the truth from him as fast as the ravens pluck the flesh from a hanged man's carcass."

The man in brown seemed pleased by the simile. He nodded at the two men who stood guard over the bound man. They yanked the prisoner to his feet, his face brocaded with blood and dirt, as Aruendiel slid off his horse. He studied the man for an instant, then touched his forehead.

The prisoner jerked back as though he had been burned. He screamed once and fell to his knees, heaving for air, pawing uselessly at his throat with the stump of his unbound arm. Interested, the crowd pressed closer. Nora looked away, then back again in time to see a new, bright stream of blood trickling from the prisoner's nose.

Enough, Nora said to herself. Over the heads of the crowd, she called out to Aruendiel to stop, then realized that she was speaking English. Even when she switched to Ors, Aruendiel gave no sign of hearing her. The people around her did, though; she was collecting unfriendly looks.

Suddenly the prisoner broke into speech. "No," he howled. "No. I didn't." Another scream, and then, more clearly: "No, I didn't kill her. I went to the house because I was hungry. I thought Massy would give me something to eat. The little girl wasn't even there."

"He's lying, the bastard," someone else said. Angry cries of assent rose from the crowd.

"He's gone back on his story," said the man in brown, in deep frustration. "I thought you said you'd get the truth out of him."

"He's telling the truth," Aruendiel said. "He lied to you before, when he said that he killed her. He did not kill her, and he does not know who did. You can let him go."

The two men on either side of the prisoner looked from Aruendiel to the headman and back again.

"I said—" Aruendiel began.

The man in brown evidently came to the end of a quick calculation. "Let him go, boys," he said. "You heard his lordship. Let the sheepfucker go. He didn't kill the little girl, his lordship says. His lordship's magic says."

The guards began to untie the prisoner's bonds. Discontent buzzed through the crowd.

"We don't know who did kill the little girl, your lordship," the headman said. "Now that you've told us who didn't kill her."

"Where did she live?" Aruendiel asked.

The house was smaller than most of the others in the village, a one-room wooden hut in a yard of brown dust. An ancient apple tree grew by the front door, bare and dead except for one last green limb. As they approached the house, a middle-aged man stood up uncertainly from where he had been lying in the meager shade of the tree, and called out something unintelligible.

"Too drunk to go see his own daughter's killer hanged," said the headman disgustedly.

The girl's mother led them into the house. She had been standing next to the gibbet, Nora recalled, a slight woman in a black shawl. The headman called her Massy. Along one wall was a fieldstone hearth; on the other side of the room, a rough bedstead and a pile of straw, covered by a blanket. A trio of low stools stood in the middle of the dirt floor.

Aruendiel prowled around the room, peering into earthenware crocks, sifting the hearth ashes through his long fingers, while a group of children straggled into the hut. The missing child's siblings, evidently: a boy around six, two smaller girls, and a half-naked toddler. The children milled about with a shy restlessness. Massy wrapped her arms protectively around the boy's shoulders until Aruendiel told her to sit down. "When did you last see the child?" he asked.

There was a hesitant, almost grudging tone in Massy's voice as she answered, but slowly the story emerged. The girl, Irseln, had been feeling poorly that day. A stomachache. She had stayed inside the house while the other children went out to play. Massy had been doing the wash. Coming back from the well with a load of water, she had seen Short Bernl behind the hut, near the shed. She didn't like seeing him there. Everyone knew Short Bernl was filth. She asked him to leave. After he left, she did the wash in the yard. Only then did she go inside and see that Irseln was missing. At first she thought that the girl must have felt better and gone out to play. But when the other children came home, Irseln was not with them. Massy gave them supper and went out to find the child. There was no answer to her shouts.

"Where was your husband during all this?"

He got home late that night and went right to sleep, Massy said. "Fat Tod and Pirix say he was with them all day," interjected the headman. "Helped them take some goats to market and then drink up the proceeds."

The next day, presumably more sober, Irseln's father had found blood-stains inside the shed.

"I see," said Aruendiel. He looked at the children clustered around their mother. "Mistress Nora," he said sharply, "take the children out of here."

"Me?" said Nora, disappointed. She had been following Massy's story with close attention. "Take them where?"

"Anywhere—but well away from here."

Massy looked as though she would like to protest, but said nothing. With some difficulty, Nora managed to herd the children out of the house, carrying the toddler in her arms. The older boy stood defiantly beside his mother until she told him in a low voice to go look after his sisters.

Behind the hut was a small clearing with the remains of a vegetable garden, a tangle of thirsty, yellowing leaves and vines. To one side was the shed that she had already heard so much about, a small, fragile structure of weather-roughened boards.

"Irseln got killed there," said the older girl, pointing at it. "Want to see the blood?"

"No," said Nora untruthfully. "Also, I don't think we should disturb your father." He was slumped against the side of the shed, snoring gently. Man and building seemed to be propping each other up.

"He's not my father," said the boy contemptuously, tossing his hair out of his eyes.

"That Irseln pa," said the smaller girl.

Nora looked at the children more closely. It was true that none of them bore much resemblance to the heavy-framed sleeping man; they were all fine-boned and slender, like their mother. Painfully thin, in fact, like a family of young sparrows. "Where's your father, then?" Nora asked.

"Our father's dead," said the boy. "We used to have a bigger house, and chickens. Then Ma married Rorpin," he said, looking at the sleeping man with distaste. "He drinks all the time. He's been drunk ever since Irseln got killed."

"Maybe he misses her," Nora said.

"Maybe," the boy allowed. "No one else misses her."

"Why not?" Nora asked.

The boy shrugged. "She cried and complained all the time. She didn't like us. We didn't like her."

"She hit me," said the older girl. "She hit me a lot. And Gissy, too."

"Irseln hit me," said the smaller girl, rather proudly.

"Ma said her pa spoiled her. Irseln wouldn't do what my ma said, ever," said the older girl self-righteously. "Is that man in there really a wizard?"

"Yes," said Nora.

"Is he going to do magic?"

"Probably."

"Can we watch?"

"No."

"Why not?"

"He doesn't want to be disturbed," Nora said. "Where were you playing the day Irseln was killed?"

"Down in the meadow." The girl indicated a path leading through the trees.

"Will you show me?"

"I guess so. Have you seen him do magic before?"

"Yes. A couple of times."

"Like what? Can he turn things into gold?"

"Can he talk to animals?"

"Can he fly?"

Keeping small children entertained becomes much easier if one has spent some time in the company of a practicing magician, Nora discovered. Even a spare, relatively unemotional account of how Aruendiel had arranged her escape from the Faitoren held the children's attention on the way to the meadow. Along the way she learned that the boy was named Horl, the two girls were Sova and Gissy, the wooden spoon that Sova clutched was actually a doll named Princess Butter, and no one seemed to call the toddler anything but the baby.

The children began a rambling, unstructured game of tag, all of them chasing one another around the meadow, except for the baby, who functioned as home base. It was a good game for unsupervised kids, Nora thought, because it meant that someone was always running after the toddler. She could not quite rid herself of the faint apprehension that Irseln's killer might be lurking nearby, but the only other visitor to the meadow was a skinny dog that raced around with the children, barking.

His name was Browncoat, Sova informed Nora; sometimes he belonged to her family, sometimes he belonged to the family in the next hut. "Right now he belongs to them," she said, flopping down on the grass and hugging the dog, "because Ma says we can't feed him. Except sometimes. I miss Irseln," she added suddenly.

"I thought you and Irseln didn't get along."

"No, but she could run fast. She was good at this game." Sova twisted a lock of hair. "I wish she could have run away from the killer. Then she would still be alive."

"We don't know what happened yet," Nora said carefully, but Sova shook her head.

"Gissy saw her ghost. Felt it."

"Her ghost?" Nora said dubiously. Maybe Irseln *was* alive and Gissy had seen her.

"She pinched Gissy, like she always did. But there was no one there."

The game was slackening. Gissy came trotting up slowly, tired, wisps of dry grass in her hair. "Tell Nora how Irseln pinched you last night," Sova urged.

Gissy shook her head rebelliously. "Hungry," she said. "I want stew."

"Irseln pinched you, remember? Say yes, or I'll pinch you."

"Hold on, Sova. No pinching," Nora said hastily. "Why don't we go back to the house now?" Would there be anything to eat there? She hoisted the baby onto her hip and took Gissy by the hand. As she and the girls walked through the grass, Sova scolded her doll: "Did you pinch Gissy? Bad girl, do you want a whipping? There, how do you like that? Stop crying, you bad girl! I've never known a brat as bad as you."

"She's crying because you're slapping her," Nora said.

"If she won't stop crying, I will hit her with a stick. She has to mind her ma. She's a bad girl, as bad as Irseln."

Horl ran over to them. "Are we going back?" he asked.

"Gissy's hungry, so we're going back to the house," Nora said.

"There's nothing to eat there," Horl said flatly.

"I want more stew," said Gissy, her face crinkling. "The stew Ma made."

"It's all gone now, Gissy," Sova said.

"You be quiet, Sova," said Horl. "You don't know what you're talking about."

"I do, too!" Sova said with indignation. "My ma found a hurt goat, it was going to die," she explained to Nora. "So we had stew."

Horl sighed dramatically. "We weren't supposed to say anything about that, remember? The goat might belong to someone."

"It wasn't Nora's goat. Was it, Nora?"

"No, not mine," Nora said lightly. "Was the stew good?"

"Yes. I wish we had more. Could the wizard turn a rock into stew?"

Nora had entertained similar questions. "I think so," she hazarded. "But what if it turned back into a rock inside your stomach?"

They debated the potential side effects of transformed foodstuffs all the way back. Shadows were lengthening; the sun was low on the horizon. The dog accompanied them, running in and out of the woods with muddy paws. He carried a light-colored, knob-ended stick in his mouth; Nora found something about its shape disturbing.

When they came in sight of the house, Aruendiel and the headman were standing near the shed, talking. Horl broke into a run. "Where's my mother?" he demanded.

"She's inside," Aruendiel said curtly, then watched as the boy ran into the house, slamming the back door behind him. Sova and Gissy followed more slowly, pulling the toddler between them.

Nora walked over to the magician. Aruendiel was having a discussion with the man in brown that was obviously growing heated, but had not quite risen to the level of argument. After a moment, Aruendiel broke off and looked down at her. She was struck by how somber he looked, the lines around his mouth as stark as cracks in ice.

"Aruendiel," she said, "I have to talk to you. I think something absolutely terrible has happened."

"Ah," he said, seizing Nora's arm and leading her a few steps away, "what did the children say?" He spoke more warmly than she expected; it crossed her mind that he was pleased to have an ally.

"There's no proof," she said, trying to marshal her thoughts and impressions, feeling dismayed because they made such a motley array. "But I have a bad, bad feeling. Irseln misbehaved, she wouldn't mind her mother—who's her stepmother, did you know that?" Aruendiel nodded, and Nora went on: "The little girl, Sova, she talked about hitting her doll with a stick because it was a bad girl, like Irseln. And they're all so thin— practically starving—but they had a big meal recently. Some kind of meat, a stew. The boy didn't want to talk about it. And then I saw the dog with a bone in its mouth, like a femur—oh, this sounds ridiculous."

Aruendiel clenched his mouth. "No, this is an ugly business. Mistress Massy is lying about something, you don't need magic to see that— although that's what my magic says, too. But the headman doesn't want me to force the truth out of her. It's all right for that pathetic woodlicker, but not for the stepmother of the missing girl. His first cousin, too. We must find the girl's body. Where is the dog?"

"The dog?" Nora blinked. Aruendiel repeated his question with some impatience. She looked around but Browncoat had already wandered away. After some inquiry, and curious looks from those they asked, they tracked the dog to a neighboring hut. The dog lay outside the door, contentedly grinding a round stub of bone.

"That's not the same bone," said Nora with disappointment.

"Where's the bone you had before?" Aruendiel demanded. He spoke with a rough familiarity, as though he and the dog were old acquaintances.

The dog raised its head and looked hard at Aruendiel, mildly surprised. It thumped its tail in the dust.

"Fetch it for us, please."

The dog stood up slowly, stretching, and then trotted away toward Massy's hut. About halfway there, he left the path, scratched in the earth under a bush, and then emerged with a longer, more slender bone in his mouth.

"Good, very good, thank you." Aruendiel bent down to rough the dog's fur behind the ears. He took the bone in his hand. "Yes, human. A child's thighbone. Where did you find this? Can you show me?"

The dog uttered a short whine.

"I don't have any here."

Another whine, with an emphatic tilt of the muzzle.

"Very well. But first, you take me to the place where you got the bones. Mistress Nora," he added abruptly, "there's some ham in my saddlebag. For our friend."

"We're all mad here," Nora said to herself, going in search of the ham. "I must be, too, or I wouldn't have come."

When she came back, the hut's yard was empty, but she could follow the sound of voices through the deepening twilight. Off the path to the meadow, she found a sizable group gathered: the magician, the headman, and the men from the village. She could hear the scrape of spades against soil and pebbles. The villagers on the outskirts of the crowd were muttering to one another, something about how clever wizards thought they were.

After a few minutes, a spade hit something hard. Aruendiel said something to the diggers. They knelt and began using their hands to remove the dirt. There was a sudden pale wash of light; Nora recognized the illumination spell that Aruendiel had used in the library in Semr. Low murmurs traveled through the small crowd.

"Something's gnawed those bones. Curse these dogs."

"Looky how that one's cut, straight as a rule. No dog did that."

"Something funny about the color. Those bones, they aren't raw."

"Horsecock, you're right, they're cooked. Somebody cooked her."

The diggers piled the remains onto a piece of cloth, Aruendiel directing them not to miss anything. When he was finally satisfied, they wrapped up the bones and handed them to the magician. He and the headman turned back to the hut. The crowd, now curiously silent, trailed after them.

Nora was about to go, too, when she felt something brush against her knee. She looked down. Browncoat gazed back expectantly, his nose aimed at the greasy package she held.

Nora waited outside Massy's hut with most of the village. Aruendiel was inside, with Massy and the headman and a few others. The children had been extracted forcibly from the hut by a couple of men and taken to their aunt's on the other side of the village. Their wails dissolved slowly in the night air. In her mind, Nora ran over the clues that seemed to point to a horrific crime—the missing child, the hints of abuse, the bones that had been split and gnawed—and wondered how to make them add up to a different result.

At last the door of the hut opened again. The headman stepped out. He looked around at the villagers outside the hut, their faces tired and rapt, and said, "The girl's murderer has confessed. Time for you folk to go home."

"Was it Massy?"

"Massy killed the girl?"

The headman said nothing; confirmation enough for the crowd.

"Did she cook the kid?"

"Did she eat her?"

"Go home," said the headman again. Two more men came out of the hut, the same men who had been guarding Short Bernl in the afternoon, but now they were holding Massy, her arms bound behind her. The crowd began to shout at her. Massy looked away, head held proudly on her slender neck, as her captors pulled her toward the village, along the same path her children had taken.

A light still burned inside the hut. As the yard emptied, Nora went inside. Aruendiel stood alone in the center of the room, rubbing the back of his neck. There was a slow, mechanical quality to his movements. Turning, he saw Nora.

"What do you want?" he demanded. Then he seemed to recollect himself. "Well, you were right," he said in a more civil tone. "It was much as you reckoned."

"What did she say?"

"She killed the girl. Not deliberately. The child would not stop crying. After some chiding, she began to scream—and kick—and bite. The woman, Massy, had chores to do. She hit the child again. The girl fell and bruised her head. On that iron pot." He nodded at a black shape near the fireplace. "Mistress Massy says Irseln sat up and seemed well enough. She put the child back to bed. But the girl did not answer her when she returned. A little later, she was dead."

Aruendiel paused and seemed disinclined to continue.

"And then?" Nora asked.

"And then Mistress Massy had four hungry children to feed, and a drunken worthless lout of a husband who was drinking up whatever wages he'd managed to earn that day."

"That's no excuse!"

"It was also a way to eliminate all traces of her crime. When the unfortunate Short Bernl came to the house that day, she even found a culprit for the child's disappearance."

Nora reached for one of the stools, which lay overturned on the floor, and set it upright. "He said he thought that Massy would give him something to eat."

"Don't sit there," Aruendiel advised sharply. He went on: "Yes, he must have smelled cooking. But there's almost nothing in Mistress Massy's stores."

"What do you mean, don't sit there?" Nora asked. "On this stool?"

As if to answer her, the stool reared onto two legs, then toppled over. "Some of your magic?" she asked.

"Not at all. It's the little girl. Irseln."

"You're joking!" Nora said. But there was Sova's story. Nora looked at the stool dubiously. "Um, the little girl Gissy said Irseln pinched her, and there was no one there," she added, in a more subdued voice.

"Irseln is still very angry about being killed and eaten by her family," Aruendiel said drily. After a moment, he added: "Mistress Massy was resourceful enough to find her way around a truth-telling spell, which is to say nothing at all. But she found the stool's continuing movement unsettling. That is what finally drove her to confess."

"Oh, so you didn't have to torture her?" Nora said, with an edge in her voice.

"Torture? Oh, you are thinking of Short Bernl. I only subjected him to some additional unpleasantness because no one in the village would have believed him otherwise."

Nora frowned. "You didn't have to do that."

"They accepted his first confession, even though it was obviously false, simply because they had tortured him. That's the problem with torture," he added irritably. "It is practically useless unless it's combined with a truth spell. Most people will say anything under torture, even before the irons are fully hot."

"There are other reasons why torture is bad, but at least we can agree on that one," Nora said. She was silent for a moment. "Did the other children know what Massy did? They told me their mother found an injured goat and made it into stew."

Aruendiel shrugged. "The taste of goat and the taste of human flesh are quite different."

"How would you know that?"

He gave her a sideways look. "There are some old spells that call for the magic-worker to consume the recently dead. A small portion."

"That's such a foul idea I don't even want to know where the dead bodies come from," Nora said. Her idea of practicing magic someday suddenly seemed slightly less attractive.

"It's a very obsolete branch of magic," Aruendiel said. "Well, the children might not have known the taste of goat, either. The only time peasants like these eat meat is the Black Offering at New Year's." He added: "The father might have noticed something amiss—if he hadn't been in his cups. Massy told how much he had enjoyed the stew."

"Horrible. Poor Irseln! I don't blame her for being angry."

Aruendiel made a vague noise of assent and passed a hand over his face. "I will judge Mistress Massy's case tomorrow, before we leave." His gaze was locked on the bones, still wrapped in cloth and lying on the hearth. Suddenly the story that Hirizjahkinis had told came back to Nora, and a mad, shimmering, impossible notion took shape in her mind.

"Can you bring her back?" she asked.

The stool lying on its side righted itself suddenly, then fell over with a thud.

Aruendiel rubbed the back of his neck again. He spoke as though he were talking to himself: "Can I? The child's spirit is here and willing; there is no need to summon it."

"Oh, if you can, of course you must!" Nora said passionately. "Yes, bring her back! You can do it?"

"It is perilous to wake the dead," he said, much as he had told the queen in Semr.

"But she's already awake." The stool rocked and shuddered as though to underscore her words. "And Irseln was only a little girl," Nora added. "All those years ahead, stolen from her. She deserves to come back, to live her life."

Aruendiel met her eyes with a long, pensive look. He spoke more kindly than before: "Many, many children die. They cannot all be returned to the living world."

"I don't know, maybe they should be," Nora said. She dropped her gaze, annoyed at the quaver in her own voice. "But here we're talking about just one child. Irseln."

Aruendiel looked away, as if in search of another thought, and his crooked shoulders seemed to tighten under an invisible load. "Very well," he said. "Fetch some wood for the fire, Mistress Nora."

Aruendiel laid the fragile bones out carefully on a quilt taken from the bed, reassembling Irseln's skeleton as best he could. With the kindling that Nora had brought, he filled in the missing parts of the skeleton, then scooped up the bones and twigs and dropped them into the iron pot. He emptied one of Massy's pitchers into the vessel. Then, with a heave, he hoisted it to hang on a hook above the fire. Using his pocketknife, he scraped up some dirt from the packed earth floor and threw it into the pot.

Without a word, he went out of the hut. Nora waited, listening to the restless movements of the fire and the faint hooting of owls outside. Irseln's stool creaked from time to time.

Aruendiel returned half an hour later, carrying a saddlebag over his shoulder and a small, stunned-looking brown rabbit pressed against his chest. The animal roused itself to a last spasm of hopeless kicking before Aruendiel killed it with a casual wrench of the neck. Like unscrewing a jar of pickles. Nora hoped he had not seen her wince.

Aruendiel put the rabbit into the pot and poked the fire. Obediently, the flames surged around the base of the pot. He watched for several minutes with an appraising eye, and then turned away. "You gave all of the ham to the dog?" he asked.

"Yes." She added, a trifle defensively, "There wasn't much."

They dined on the rest of their provisions—bread, a sliver of cheese each, and Nansis Abora's peach preserves—while the iron pot simmered beside them. After a while the meaty smell of broth filled the hut. Nora, not quite full, tried to ignore it. She was dying to find out more about what was happening inside the pot, but Aruendiel seemed disinclined to talk. The only time he responded with more than a monosyllable was when she asked how long the spell would take.

"As long as need be," he said irritably. "Are you an idiot? How long does it ever take to die or be born?"

After that, he pushed his stool back and settled himself stiffly with his back against the wall, arms resting on his knees, his eyes half-closed. Nora waited where she was, not wanting to miss anything in case the spell took a dramatic turn, until Aruendiel frowned at her and directed her to find a sleeping place. It seemed indecorous to take Massy's bed. Nora opted for the pile of straw, feeling somber.

It had been a long, fatiguing day, but her sleep was uneasy. She woke up several times, thinking that the spell must be over by now, that she would now find out what had taken shape inside the darkness of the closed pot, but each time she opened her eyes to see the fire still burning and Aruendiel still crouched spiderlike in the shadows across the room.

Toward dawn Nora fell into a deeper sleep and dreamed that she was about to fail a high school French exam.

# Chapter 22

The magician was gone and the fire was out when Nora awoke. Milky morning light streamed through the windows of the hut. The iron pot still hung in the fireplace, the lid firmly in place.

In the quiet of the new day, she felt faintly embarrassed to recollect how seriously she had urged Aruendiel to bring the dead child back to life. She had gotten carried away: Irseln's death was a crime right out of one of the more gruesome Grimm's fairy tales, and she had imagined a fairy-tale ending. If she looked inside the pot now, Nora thought, there would be only a few bones and sticks floating in a gritty broth.

The flimsy door opened and Aruendiel entered. His eyes were shadowed with lack of sleep, but he moved more easily than Nora would have expected, the way a younger man would carry himself. He grunted by way of greeting, then went over to the fireplace. Wrapping his hand inside a fold of his cloak, he uncovered the pot, but replaced the lid before Nora could see inside.

"Is she alive?" Nora asked.

"Still dead."

"Oh." Despite herself, Nora felt deflated. "That's too bad."

Aruendiel snorted and tore a piece from the loaf of bread he had brought into the hut. "They'll bring up Mistress Massy soon to be judged. We can leave after that."

After a moment Nora ventured to ask: "Will she be executed?"

"It's the penalty for murder," Aruendiel said with a twitch of his shoulder, the expression on his face so black that Nora felt disinclined to pursue the conversation.

They were finishing the bread when footsteps and voices sounded outside. It was a large crowd, judging from the noise, but only the headman, Massy and her guards, and a few others came inside. Massy's face was drawn, her eyes reddened but dry.

As she entered the hut, the stool in the middle of the floor creaked loudly.

One of the other men was Rorpin, Massy's husband, shaky and pale under an unkempt beard. He had obviously sobered up enough to learn exactly what had been happening in his family over the past few days. He stood a small distance from his wife, as though he could not bear to be too near her, but there was something painfully protective in how he watched her.

The headman greeted Aruendiel with more friendliness than he had shown the day before. "Here she is, your lordship," he said. "All that's left is for you to pronounce sentence, and then we'll take her down and hang her. You'll be wanting to resume your journey, I'm sure."

"Thank you, Pelgo," said Aruendiel, with a faint curl of his lip. "There is, however, another matter to attend to first." He directed two of the villagers to remove the pot from the fireplace. It was only barely cool enough to handle; they let it down suddenly with a thud. "Open it," said Aruendiel to the headman.

Lifting the lid carefuly, Pelgo stared down in puzzlement. "What's this?" Then he gasped.

"It is the child Irseln's body," said Aruendiel, just as Nora recognized that the dark tangle of hair inside the pot was the top of a head.

"What do you mean?" Pelgo said. "She was just bones. They *ate* her."

"What was consumed has been restored," Aruendiel said.

Gingerly, Pelgo prodded the head with a finger. "More of your magic," he said grudgingly. "It's a marvel, your lordship, but I can't see the use of it. She's still dead, isn't she? And you'll never get her out of that pot, not in one piece." Nora had to agree: It was a large pot, but Irseln's body was wedged into it as tightly as an orange into its peel.

Grasping the girl by the nape of the neck, Aruendiel somehow—Nora did not quite see how—pulled her free. The child's body dangled from his hand. Massy gave a cry and jerked against the restraining hands of the guards. Aruendiel laid the small, naked corpse on the dirt floor. It was perfectly formed, pale as pearl, the face relaxed and empty. Irseln's father inched forward, knelt, and took the body in his arms. "Irseln?" he said. She did not look as though she were either dead or asleep, Nora thought—more like an extraordinarily realistic doll.

"You see where her skull cracked," said Aruendiel in a conversational tone. He indicated the wide, curving dent that began at the girl's temple. Skin flowed smoothly over the break, as though the injury had healed years ago.

Irseln's father touched the scar as though to wipe it away, then ran his hands over the child's limbs. It was as though seeing his daughter's body whole again, almost unblemished, made him realize for the first time that she was really dead. He looked up at his wife. "Massy?" he said, his voice raw and puzzled. "You did this? You killed her?"

Aruendiel cleared his throat. "Put her down," he said. "There, by that stool." He squatted to carve a circle in the dirt floor around Irseln with his pocketknife, then set the stool upright inside the circle, next to the body. The wooden stool shuddered, and then began to burn, although Aruendiel had not touched a flame to it. There was almost no smoke. The fire gnawed at the stool for a few minutes until nothing was left except a fine gray powdering of ash.

It was hard to say what was different about Irseln's body. A faint flush in the white skin, perhaps. A subtle tension or readiness in the small limbs, as though they were once again bound to a governing will.

"Ah," Aruendiel said, exhaling satisfaction. He lifted Irseln's wrist, feeling for a pulse. "Her heart begins to beat. She is nearly ready."

"She is not breathing," Rorpin said after a minute.

Aruendiel reached inside his left sleeve and withdrew a long gray feather. He inserted the plumed end into one of the child's nostrils and twisted it briskly.

Irseln sneezed.

It seemed to Nora that almost everyone in the room sucked in their breath at the same moment—Irseln included. Her body pinkened as her chest rose and fell, again and again and again, stronger each time.

"Irseln? Irseln?" After a second's hesitation, her father picked her up again. She opened her eyes and looked blankly at him, then at the other adults. "Irseln, little one, are you all right?"

A look of wondering surprise crossed Irseln's face. "Pa?" she said. Then the child's eyes fell upon Massy.

Massy smiled nervously. "Irseln, chick—"

Irseln screamed, her small face contorting. "Ma killed me! She threw me down, she hurt my head!"

"Hush, hush," Massy said, her smile fixed. "You're all right now, sweet, everything's fine. You were asleep, you see, and now—"

"No, not asleep, I died! My head hurt, I was scared!" Irseln clung to her father's neck, glaring at Massy. "I hate you!" Her wails gained strength. There was nothing wrong with her breathing now.

"What happened, Irseln? Tell me," Rorpin said, with a glance at his wife.

"She hurt my head," Irseln said, putting a hand on her temple. "I laid down. Then I couldn't get up. I tried to say help me, but she didn't hear me. No one heard me."

"Then what happened, sweet?" her father asked.

For a moment Irseln screwed up her face in concentration; then she closed her eyes and shook her head, looking frightened. "She killed me!" she said with an air of explaining the obvious. "I hate her! I hate her!"

That was all they could get out of her, no matter how her father pressed her to tell what she had experienced after she lay down and died. "It's useless to ask her," Aruendiel said at last. "She remembers nothing more—they never do." He was standing a little apart, his arms folded. "Now," he added, "we have other business. Let us go outside."

"Yes," said the headman, with a slight look of confusion, glancing at the child in Rorpin's arms. "It's time for the sentencing."

As the assemblage regrouped under the decrepit apple tree, Nora was conscious of a low rumble of dissatisfaction in the crowd. Rorpin was holding Irseln, now dressed and calmer, by the hand. People stared at her and muttered. Nora assumed at first that they were questioning the justice of sentencing a murderer when the murderer's victim was now alive and well and trying to pat a friendly dog—the same dog, Nora noticed, who had been chewing one of Irseln's leg bones the day before. Listening more closely, however, Nora discovered that the villagers were more concerned that Irseln's resurrection meant that there would be no hanging.

The headman recited the charges in round, official tones. Whatever doubts he might have about the propriety of condemning Massy now, he showed no signs of them. Massy had not only committed murder and cannibalism and lied about it, but she was also guilty of wifely disobedience and an offense called child theft, depriving her husband of the fruit of his loins. They had thrown the book at her.

Massy herself seemed to pay little attention. With a peevish expression, she turned her head slightly from side to side, her eyes flicking indifferently over the faces of the spectators.

"Massy Rorpinan, you have been shown culpable of these crimes by your own confession and by signs and proofs indisputable and clear to the minds of men," Aruendiel said rapidly, as though running through a formula that he had recited many times before. "You have violated most grievously the laws established and upheld by your liege lord and by His Majesty the Most Glorious Abele the Fourth. It is the will of these princes that lawbreakers suffer commensurate punishment so that injustices are avenged and the peace of the land is restored. Before I pronounce sentence upon you, Massy Rorpinan, what do you have to say on your own behalf?"

"Why I should be punished, I don't see," she said bitterly. "I don't know what it was you done to her, but she's fine now."

"True," said Aruendiel with what Nora thought might have been a trace of amusement. "But she was dead—not to mention cooked and eaten—by your hand, and the law is strict about such matters. Do you have anything else to say for yourself?"

There was an agitation in the crowd, the sound of running feet, high-pitched cries. Massy turned her head, eyes alight.

The boy Horl erupted from the crowd, ducking away from a man who tried to hold him back, and threw his arms around his mother. An instant later, his sister Sova followed, bawling.

A red-faced woman, tendrils of hair plastered damply to her neck and forehead, pushed through the crowd. "I had them shut up," she said to Pelgo, panting a little, "but they slipped out when I was seeing to the goat. They been like wildcats ever since they heard what's happening to their ma."

"Pig's blood, get them out of here, will you? They'll have another chance to see Massy before—that is, later."

The children were less than comforted. Sova's sobbing redoubled. Massy tried to embrace them as much as her ropes allowed. Then suddenly, with a fierce movement of her hand, she shushed the children and raised wet, angry eyes to Aruendiel. "You asked me what I have to say for myself, your lordship? These kids are what I have to say for myself.

"I didn't mean to push Irseln that hard. Then before I knew it, she was dead. She's a handful—you saw what she's like—but I never meant to kill her, I swear.

"What I did next—well, your lordship, I looked at her lying there, and it just came to me. Do you know what it's like to hear your children crying because they don't have enough to eat? Night after night? I do. At least my kids got one good meal. They didn't know where it came from. They were just glad to have their bellies full, for once.

"Rorpin knew. He didn't say anything, but he knew, for all that he's acting so sweet to the kid now. He was hungry, too." Massy took a deep breath. "When I think of it, how my kids' faces looked after they'd eaten their fill, how they fell asleep like kittens, I'd do it all over again.

"But now—" She began to cry again. "I don't know what's going to happen to them. Rorpin's no father to them. If I'm gone, who'll look after my children? What does one dead kid matter—who's not even dead anymore—compared to four living kids?"

The crowd grumbled its disapproval. "I got hungry kids, too, and I never chopped up one to feed the others," muttered a woman standing near Nora.

"Well, I tell you, if Massy gets off, she won't have any trouble getting her kids to behave," said a man. "Especially right before dinnertime."

Aruendiel's voice cut harshly through the commentary. "What of the innocent man who was almost executed for the crime you committed?"

"It wasn't I who said he should die!" she said, flaring up. "And what if they did kill him? He was lucky to get off with losing a hand when they found him with the boy!"

Aruendiel looked at her for a long time before he spoke again. "Massy Rorpinan, you took a human life, and you have shown little or no remorse," he said. "Under the law and custom of this land, you deserve to be put to death."

Both Horl and Sova were crying now.

"You have pleaded that your children will suffer if they are deprived of their mother. Yet it hardly seems a kindness to let them be raised by a mother who has already killed a child."

Massy groaned and drew her son and daughter so close that it seemed she would smother them against her body. She cried, "It's death for my kids, too!"

"No, only for you," Aruendiel said. "But there is another way. As you say, the child Irseln has been restored to life. The unfortunate Bernl was not actually executed. The harm you have done has been remedied. I can offer you an alternative to the rope. Imprisonment, of sorts."

An audible wave of disappointment moved through the crowd. The headman narrowed his eyes. "We don't have a place to lock her up, your lordship."

"You could stay here, Massy Rorpinan, with your children. You could live in their midst as they grow up. It would not be life as you live it now, but it would be life. Your punishment would be that you could not see them or hold them or speak to them." Aruendiel paused, and his mouth twisted sardonically. "You would, however, be able to feed them."

Massy looked frantically at Aruendiel. "What do you mean?"

"I mean exactly what I say. You have heard my offer."

"Not see my children?"

"No."

"Never!"

"Very well," said Aruendiel, with a slight nod, as though to courteously acknowledge her choice. "As suzerain of these lands by blood and sword, taking into account the crimes of which you stand guilty, I hereby condemn you, Massy Rorpinan, to die by—"

"Wait!" Massy shrieked. She was trembling. "You say—the other way—I would live?"

He nodded.

"Then I choose that way!"

"You are sure?" he said, folding his arms.

"Yes," she said, sounding not sure at all.

With the rest of the crowd, Nora waited for Aruendiel to reply, to pronounce the legal formula that he had begun to recite before.

Instead Massy uttered a gurgling, half-strangled cry. Nora had the impression that she was getting to her feet—no, Massy was actually growing taller, her body elongating to impossible proportions, losing its human shape. She loomed swaying over the crowd, like a bent and twisted column. Eight feet above the ground, her thin face looked down, distorted with surprise, and she opened her mouth to say something. But the words were never heard as her features thickened and disappeared under the dark tide of a coarse, encroaching carapace devouring her skin. Massy spread her arms as if in entreaty, stretching them and bending them, snakelike, until they stiffened, grew hard and still, while dozens of twigs bearing leaves like green flags sprouted triumphantly from what had been soft flesh a few moments before.

The new apple tree growing next to the old one trembled in the morning light, its thousands of leaves whispering urgently of fear, remorse, love, or only the movement of air.

The crowd of onlookers stepped backward almost as one. The two children, stunned into quiet, stared up into the canopy of leaves above them, looking at the spot where Massy's face had been. After a moment, an apple fell from a branch and thudded into the dust near Horl's feet.

He picked it up and looked at it as though he had never seen an apple before. Then he wiped it off and tucked it carefully inside his shirt.

Even after the horses were saddled, the headman seemed reluctant to let them go. "Twenty years, you say, twenty years she has to stay inside that tree? Why twenty years?"

Nora could see that Aruendiel was irked to hear Pelgo say—as people already had many times that morning—that Massy was *inside* the tree. As the magician had informed Nora snappishly when she made the same mistake, Massy was not inside the tree; she *was* the tree. At this point, though, Aruendiel seemed to have abandoned hope of correcting the general misapprehension.

"So the child Irseln will have time to grow up," he said, shrugging.

"And does it hurt her, being inside there?"

"She'll suffer the way trees suffer, if there's no rain. Or if the winter's bad," Aruendiel said drily.

"It doesn't seem like much of a punishment, then, does it? I would have hanged her, myself, but then I'm not a wizard."

"No," said Aruendiel, with a cold smile. "Oh, you might tell your villagers that there's a curse on anyone who takes an axe to that apple tree before the twenty years is up. Just in case someone decides that Mistress Massy hasn't suffered enough."

"A curse? No need to do that, your lordship. No one will touch the thing. I wouldn't even eat the apples, myself." He spat, painting a dark mark in the dust.

"Just as well," Aruendiel said. "They're not for you."

The village seemed almost deserted as Aruendiel and Nora rode through it. The brief holiday excitement of crime and punishment was over, and the villagers were back at work, in their fields or huts. Or, Nora thought, intercepting a few glances from behind chinked shutters, they had decided to make themselves scarce until the magician had left town. When she and Aruendiel stopped at the baker's hut to buy bread for the journey, it took a long time for the door to open, as though the baker had to gather his courage to answer Nora's knock.

Coming out of the hut with two loaves under her arm, Nora saw Horl and Sova watching from behind the corner of the building. "Hello," she said hesitantly.

The children looked at her, their eyes serious, until Sova broke the silence. "That wizard turned my ma into a tree." Sova sounded almost proud of this fact, but Nora heard something accusatory in her words, too.

"I know," she said guiltily. "You must be sad about that."

"Irseln pulled my hair because I wouldn't give her Princess Butter."

"Well, you should share," Nora said, feeling a faint sense of déjà vu.

She'd said the same thing, in English, about a thousand times to her own sisters when they were around Sova's age.

"Princess Butter doesn't like her," Sova said haughtily.

Horl made a sudden movement as though to silence his sister, exactly the same gesture Massy had made that morning. "That man, that wizard—what he did to Ma—I'd like to—"

"You'd like to do what?" Aruendiel came up behind Nora.

"I'd like to kill you!" Horl exploded.

A faint smile coiled its way along Aruendiel's mouth, as though the threat rather pleased him. "You're welcome to try," he said. "But I am bigger than you and a powerful magician to boot, so I would probably kill you instead, and then who would look after your sisters?"

A look of chagrin crossed Horl's face, but he refused to back down entirely. "You shouldn't have done that to my ma. Irseln isn't even dead."

"Irseln lives because of my magic, as does your mother. Would you rather have your mother hanged?"

"She's not alive. You made her a tree. A tree! She can't even move."

"No," said Aruendiel seriously, "you are right, she can't move, but she lives the way trees live. And one day, twenty years from this morning, she will be restored to you as a human woman again."

Horl scowled, but Sova seemed interested. "Does she know it's us?" she asked.

"In some fashion. Trees are perceptive when they wish to be."

Sova nodded. "I told you so," she said to Horl.

Aruendiel twitched an eyebrow, then bowed toward Horl and Sova. "Good fortune to you both, Massy Rorpinan's most excellent children," he said, using the most ceremonial kind of Orsian address.

"Good fortune to you, your most excellent lordship," Sova responded correctly, bowing in return. After a moment, Horl bowed, too, a little awkwardly, and muttered the same formula.

Enveloped in his black cloak, Aruendiel looked down at the children, then bent again and gave something to Horl. A small gray feather. The boy looked up, puzzled. "In case you have great need," Aruendiel said, before turning on his heel and disappearing around the corner of the hut.

"Take it. Keep it," Nora said. "It's magic. That's how I got away from the Faitoren—remember, I told you?"

"I remember," said Sova, delighted. "Can I see it?" she asked her brother.

Horl was looking both uncertain and a little angry, as though he would like to throw away the feather, but his sister's request prompted him to clutch it more tightly. "He gave it to me, Sova," he said.

"Well, I must go now, too," said Nora, regarding the children critically. She noticed again how thin they were, and remembered the bare larder in Massy's hut. The children couldn't live on apples alone. It might have been more practical for Aruendiel to turn Massy into a nanny goat or a cow. "Here," she said, reaching into her own pocket and pulling out the twist of rag in which she had wrapped the silver beads from Semr. Counting out four quickly, then a fifth before she could reconsider, she held them out to the children.

There was an avid look on Horl's face, but he said: "We don't need your money."

"That's fine, take it anyway," Nora said, pouring the beads into Sova's palm and closing the girl's fingers over them. "For Gissy and the baby."

She hurried around the side of the baker's hut, back to the horses, leaving the children bent over the money. She was hoping that Aruendiel had not overheard her last exchange with them. But as they rode on, he asked how much she had given them. He raised his eyebrows when she told him.

"Five silver beads is a small fortune in a village like that. They could live for months on that sum."

"Oh?" Nora said airily, feeling a twinge of dismay. She had not meant to be *that* generous. "But it cost two silver beads just to cross the river at Semr."

"Everything is expensive in Semr. These peasants are lucky to see a dozen silver beads in a year. Why did you give them the money? Trying to make up for the loss of their mother?"

"No, just to help them survive. What of it? *You* offered to help them in great need. I don't have any magic, and I do have some silver. They have nothing—except for those apples."

"There are many children with worse fates. You already talked me into bringing one unlucky imp back from the dead. One cannot provide for them all."

Nora remembered the flush of blood and breath in Irseln's waxen body, and felt an odd, disproportionate surge of happiness, as though part of herself had been restored to life, too. "What you did was amazing! How did you do it? It was one of the most wonderful things I've ever seen."

For a moment Aruendiel looked rather gratified, an unexpected light coming into his gray eyes. He frowned to compose himself: "It went very well. The hardest part was restoring her body. It required a complex of interwoven spells—transformation, enhancement, some time manipulation."

"Yes, but then, the way she just woke up, as though she'd been asleep—that was incredible."

"That was the least of it. If a dead soul comes across a body that is, so to speak, empty but perfectly usable, it will often take possession of it. Especially its own body. There is likely to be recognition. Curiosity." He spoke the last word with a hard edge in his voice. "And Irseln was eager, very eager, to return to her body," he went on. "So that part, bringing Irseln's soul and body together, was easy. It's much chancier, of course, to bring back the dead when the soul has truly departed. The dead may not wish to return."

Nora thought about this for a moment. "Why wouldn't they?"

He gave her a slicing, sideways glance. "If you cannot imagine, Mistress Nora, then you have led a fortunate life indeed."

"Oh, I can think of dozens of reasons to wish to be dead," she said. " 'And by a sleep to say we end the heartache and the thousand natural shocks that flesh is heir to.' " The lines translated rather well into Ors. "But once dead, would one want to stay dead? I don't know. What happens after death?" She looked at him expectantly.

"I don't know."

"Not with all your magic?" Or from having died yourself, she wanted to ask—but something in his expression held her back.

"No," he said at last.

"But this isn't the first time that anyone has raised the dead?" Nora pressed.

"Resurrection of the dead is a well-established branch of magic. There is always a demand for it. Although good resurrection spells are difficult even for the most skilled magicians. If they're bungled, the results can be unpleasant, not to mention dangerous."

That meant zombies, Nora guessed. "Irseln—will she be all right? She'll have a normal, healthy life?"

"More or less." After a moment, he added: "She will not have children, of course. That's one thing magic cannot give back to the formerly dead—the power to bring forth life."

"Too bad," Nora said. "Still, better than being dead."

"Oh, she'll live all the longer. These peasant women wear themselves out in childbearing; half of them are dead by thirty. There are always plenty of widowers with motherless children in these villages. If Irseln wants a brood of brats," he added carelessly, "she can follow her stepmother's example and marry one of them."

"Yes, and look how well that turned out in Massy's case. Those poor kids," Nora said sadly.

"No doubt you think I should have spared their mother, and left her to take care of the ragamuffins."

"No, I don't," Nora burst out. "In fact, I think you let Massy off easy. She killed that little girl and lied about it and fed the dead child to her own children. It's like the violent fairy tales in my world that had to be sanitized for children. What I mean is, when something like this happens, people tell horror stories about it for generations. I don't like the idea of executing anyone. But if anyone deserved it, it's Massy."

"You don't know what it's like to have a cottage full of hungry children," Aruendiel said shortly.

"No, I don't," she said, slightly abashed. "Why, do you, Lord Aruendiel?"

He scowled. "I've lived around poor peasants all my life. They may be stupid and brutal as beasts, some of them, but they're not beasts. Children with empty stomachs, an empty larder—I cannot pass the harshest of judgments on Mistress Massy."

They rode along in silence for a minute, and then Aruendiel said: "*You* had no liking for the idea of being transformed into a geranium, even for a few days."

"No, but I hadn't killed anyone, either."

"True. Have you never killed anyone, Mistress Nora?"

No one except for EJ. Did that count? It was only a matter of turning off a machine. A family decision, everyone had to be heard. And she'd said: We have to, he's already gone.

"Not recently, no," Nora said.

"Ah," Aruendiel said, looking at her curiously, as though struck by the seriousness in her tone. "Well, neither have I—recently."

"Are you glad or sorry about that?" she could not resist asking.

"Oh, very glad. Killing someone usually turns out to be an enormously complicated solution to what was a much simpler problem."

There were any number of questions that Nora would have liked to ask him at that point. She chose carefully. "But if you killed someone, and things became . . . too complicated, couldn't you bring the person back to life again?"

Aruendiel drew his dark eyebrows together. "Did you not hear me say just now how difficult it is to cast a successful resurrection spell? And it's a rare ghost who returns willingly at his murderer's summons.

"Of course," he added reflectively, "there is the famous case of the wizard Spornil Fivesheep, who killed his brother in a quarrel over land, and then, stricken with remorse, brought him back to life again. Some commentators, though, think that it was really an inferior Eoluthian substitution. His brother, newly revived, promptly killed *him*, which tends to support that theory."

"What's an Eoluthian substitution?"

"One life in exchange for another." Aruendiel spoke sharply, as though annoyed at her ignorance, but his lined face was becoming more animated. "The sacrifice must be willing, or the revival is only temporary. In that case, to stay alive, the person brought back from the dead must keep sacrificing more and more people. It becomes very messy very quickly, but that never stops people from trying it. Now, a timestone—"

Nora nodded, listening hard, trying to make sense of it all. She still had no clear understanding of the nature of magic, or why it worked, but perhaps if she picked up enough of these enticing details—timestones, Eoluthian substitutions—some greater meaning would slowly unfold for her.

"—the longer one waits, the more unpredictable the results. Portat Nolu recommended that no more than an hour should elapse—"

Aruendiel was well launched. There was a long day's ride ahead, but as far as she could tell, they would not have any difficulty filling up the hours to come.

# Chapter 23

Nora pushed a stray lock of hair back from her face and grimaced, catching the smell of apples on her fingers. She had always liked the sweet, mild odor of apple flesh, but that was before she had to peel and slice a dozen bushels of apples for drying in the autumn sun, press more bushels for cider, and load still more apples into the castle cellars. Not to mention having to pick the fruit in the first place. At first their smell reminded her of Massy and her children, but now she was only sick of it.

The trip to Semr seemed to have happened a long time ago. Since then Nora's life had been nothing but trying to wrest and preserve every last nutrient and calorie from the autumnal fields and forests around the castle. Before the apples, it was mushrooms. Before that, chestnuts and cabbages. She fell into bed exhausted every night, only to get up at first light to start working again. She had not had time to dip into *Pride and Prejudice* or to work ahead in the Orsian grammar or even to visit the bathhouse more than once or twice, another reason for the faint aroma of apples that clung to her skin and hair.

She had seen little of the magician since their return. He seemed to be spending most of his time in his tower workshop or in the forest. A few times he had swept past while Nora was working, slowing his pace not to greet her so much as to cast an approving eye over the foodstuffs that she was handling. It was a good harvest this year, everyone was saying.

"What did you expect?" Nora asked herself, picking up the knife again and reaching for another apple. The pile of fruit in the basket before her seemed to be getting no smaller. "That he would be your best friend? That there would be lots more little chats about magic and what have you?"

*The problem is, Maggie—*

She had begun writing letters to Maggie in her head again, although she was so busy that she rarely got a chance to finish them to her own satisfaction.

*The problem is—I have to be honest—I have a strange sort of a crush on him.*

*You wouldn't believe it to look at him. I suppose it has something to do with the fact that he saved my life a couple of times. And then we had these conversations on the ride back from Semr, mostly about magic, but other things as well, and I did enjoy talking to him.*

*But now I'm the invisible castle drudge again. Hard physical labor all day, no time to read or think. And this could be my life for years.*

*Everyone in Semr assumed I was his mistress. I'm not. And I'm not saying I'd want to be. He killed his wife—he told me so.*

*But I keep thinking about him, and wondering about all those stories that I heard in Semr that I can't quite bring myself to ask him about, and wondering what it's like to be able to do magic. He intrigues me. That's always dangerous, you know.*

*It's been years since I had a serious hopeless crush on anyone, unless you count my Donne thing. (Truly hopeless, that.) As I recall, if you wait long enough, it flames out, eventually, and you wonder what you ever found attractive in that particular person and you thank your lucky stars nothing actually happened.*

Mrs. Toristel came into the kitchen from the courtyard, looking distracted, pushing the door open with her shoulder. She held a basin full of something slick, convoluted, and streaked with blood.

"Brains?" asked Nora, looking up. "Where did those come from?"

"The white calf. Broke its leg. Toristel is butchering it."

Nice to have some meat for a change, Nora thought. "Why didn't you ask him to fix it, though?" She jutted her chin upward, toward the tower.

"It's the bull calf, we were going to kill it anyway," Mrs. Toristel said distractedly. "And he hates to be disturbed for such things. Nora, you're slicing the apples too thick."

Nora put down her knife tiredly. "Sorry."

"You'll have to do those over." Mrs. Toristel glanced at the water clock and suddenly looked distressed. "Sun and moon, here it is two hours past noon already, and I have to put these brains to soak and then help Toristel finish the butchering. The flies are something awful. Take up some lunch for *him*, Nora, will you? Some bread and herring. An apple or two. He won't want much."

With a faint flutter of excitement, Nora stood up. "How will I get in? The wall—"

"You just go through it. Now what have I done with the good knife? Not the one with the nick in the blade. Nora, have you seen it?"

After locating the knife, Nora put bread and herring and apple onto a tray, and then went to the place in the great hall where she thought the entrance to the tower was located, more or less. She tested the stone wall with her fingertips. Solid to her touch. She stood there for a moment, considering what to do.

The cat, which had followed her and the herring from the kitchen, regarded her haughtily, its tail twitching. Then it walked through the wall.

"All right then," Nora said, taking a deep breath. She closed her eyes and stepped forward, raising an arm to shield her face.

It was a curtain of sand that she encountered, a rain of fine, cool particles sifting against her skin. Then she was on the other side, trying to make out her surroundings in the half-light of an oil lamp hanging from the wall. A staircase wound upward along the curving wall of the tower, its treads coated with dust except for a narrow path wiped clean by footsteps in the middle. The cat ran lightly upstairs.

Nora followed. Shadows flickered at the corners of her vision, but when she turned to look, there was nothing there. She climbed faster, and felt some relief to emerge into a large, round room where she could glimpse sunlight threading through narrow windows.

"Oh, it's you," the magician said. He leaned over the scroll open before him. "Where is Mrs. Toristel?"

"She's helping Mr. Toristel butcher a calf. It broke its leg."

"Oh? How did it come to break its leg?" He glanced balefully at Nora as though she might have had something to do with it.

"I don't know." Nora's attention was elsewhere. She had not seen so many books since the royal library at Semr. Their dark spines encircled the room; there were even rows of books lining the ceiling, held up by some magical means, she assumed—a neat space-saving trick, if you were tall enough to reach that high. Aside from the shelves of books, the room held only the table at which Aruendiel sat and another, longer table that was half-covered with papers and still more books. A spiral staircase led upward.

"You have a wonderful library here," she said.

"Thank you," he said briskly. "No, don't put that here—on the other table."

She took so long that after a minute Aruendiel put down his brush and lifted his head to see what was keeping her. She was bending over a book that he had left open.

"That can't be very interesting to you," he said, "since you can't read it."

Nora turned quickly. "Oh, but I can. Not very well, but I'm trying to learn," she said.

"I see. What is it you're reading?" he said, freighting the last word with a small load of irony.

"A book of spells, I think."

"A magician's library is bound to have many books of spells."

"I'm not guessing." She pointed to the page. "This is an invisibility spell. 'For invisibility,' it says."

"A brave start. What does the rest of the spell say?"

Nora opened her mouth to read the spell aloud, then caught herself. "What if it works—and makes me invisible?" she asked, some challenge in her voice.

Aruendiel raised an eyebrow. "If you can work the spell, no doubt you will be able to perform the counterspell, too."

Nora smiled quickly, with an air of pleased excitement, and glanced down at herself as though taking one last look before she disappeared. " 'Contemptuous needle—' " She halted, scanning the line again. "It doesn't quite make sense." No explanation or encouragement from Aruendiel. " 'Contemptuous needle something my ways—cloak my ways from, um, something eyes—tracking eyes.' And this other word has to be 'unsound,' even though the sentence sounds strange.

" 'Contemptuous needle unsound, cloak my ways from tracking eyes.' " She repeated it, more confidently. "Well? How did I do?"

If she were truly invisible, though, Aruendiel's cool eyes would not meet her own gaze so precisely.

"You read it correctly. It's an old, rather elementary invisibility spell—from the *Compendium* by Morkin the Asymmetrical. Well, I see you can read a little. Not fluently, but you can navigate simple sentences. I congratulate you on your progress."

He spoke the last words dismissively. Hunching his shoulders, he picked up his brush again to make a note on the parchment in front of him.

Nora made no movement toward the stairs. She cleared her throat. "The spell didn't work."

"No," he said, not looking up.

"Did I do something wrong?"

Before answering, Aruendiel dipped his brush in the ink and wrote a couple of lines. "In general, with spells of this sort, it helps to cut the throat of a small animal, or to burn hanks of your own hair with dried fox dung and blood mint, as an offering. But even so, you would never be able to work the spell."

"Why not?"

"Because you are female."

"Are you serious? What do you mean?"

He shrugged. "You could recite that charm a thousand times, and nothing would happen. The same for every spell in that book. The spirits to whom those spells are addressed would simply disregard the puny, trivial pleadings of a female voice. And now, Mistress Nora, if you will excuse me, I have work to do."

Nora walked sedately, furiously down the tower stairs. She checked herself just short of actually stomping. It was a dignified withdrawal she was making, she told herself, not a humiliated retreat.

*Dear Maggie,* she thought as she exited the tower through the wall, *now that I think about it, there's another way to end a hopeless crush: When the object of said crush behaves like such a jerk that you instantly lose all interest in him and realize what an idiot you were for entertaining any such feelings in the first place.*

She went back to the kitchen, spread the sliced apples to dry in the back courtyard, fed the parings to the pig, brought in a load of wood for the stove, and decided to wait until after the butchering was completed before cleaning the kitchen floor.

*I'm overreacting,* she told herself sensibly, heading out to help the Toristels with the calf. *He was just stating facts.*

It was the way he said it. Something really nasty in his voice. As though he were angry at the whole idea of a woman doing magic.

Hirizjahkinis—it didn't bother him that she did magic. And obviously there were some spells women could do. But which ones? Perhaps Hirizjahkinis was a special case. A former witch priestess—that must help. A lesbian.

He didn't have to be so damned superior about it, she thought irritably, swatting at the whining black cloud of flies around her head while

Mr. Toristel cut into the calf's haunch. He didn't have to brush me off like a servant. Except that he treats his actual servants with more respect than he treats me.

The next day Morinen came up from the village to help with digging turnips. As she and Nora went down the rows, squatting on the chilly soil, their hands gloved in mud, Nora took a perverse pleasure in telling her about the visit to the court at Semr. Morinen, she could tell, was picturing the palace at Semr as a version of Aruendiel's ramshackle castle, so Nora went to some lengths to emphasize how much bigger and grander it was. With a slight edge in her voice, she described the lavish banquets, the ornate dress of the courtiers, the days of busy idleness in which noble ladies like Inristian had nothing to do except fret about getting married.

It would be no bad thing, Nora began to feel as she talked, if Morinen and others like her could be brought to recognize that they worked and slaved and starved (sometimes) to support an essentially parasitic class, qualified to rule only by hereditary privilege.

Morinen was not a ready subject for revolutionary conscious-raising, however. She listened without saying much, and seemed to be as impressed to learn that the streets of Semr had cobblestone paving as by any detail of court life. She did look a little puzzled, though, by what Nora told her about Inristian.

"A great, rich lady like that, and she can't find a husband?"

"She's not as rich as some of her rivals," explained Nora, but the answer did not seem to satisfy Morinen. Looking up the social scale from a turnip patch, Nora thought, it was difficult to discern degrees of wealth. "She also has smallpox scars."

Morinen sighed. "Poor lady. I feel sorry for her, not able to be married."

"Inristian? I suppose." Nora looked at Morinen more closely and considered the faint droop of her mouth, the fact that she was quieter than usual. Mrs. Toristel had mentioned that the blacksmith's wedding to the miller's daughter would take place next month. "You're right," Nora said. "I think she's lonely."

Morinen ducked her head lower, running her hands carefully through the soil, although she had already searched that particular spot. "I don't know if you heard about Dorviv."

Dorviv was the miller's daughter. "I heard she's getting married, yes."

"You know who she's marrying?"

Nora nodded. "You liked him, didn't you?"

Morinen gave a noncommittal shrug without raising her eyes. Nora abused the blacksmith for a few minutes.

"It's all right," Morinen said finally. "He's not a fool. She's pretty, Dorviv is. Not as big as me. Her father's giving them a field—freehold, not just leased from his lordship. I was all upset at first, but Ma gave me a talking-to. She said I had no right getting my hopes up. It's not as though we have any land."

"Well, you're pretty, too, Morinen," Nora said staunchly. "And you know—I'm not sure if this is what your mother meant, but honestly, if all this man wants in a wife is land, you're better off not marrying him."

Morinen gave Nora a bemused look. "But who'll ever marry me, when I don't have any land? Ma says men always like to have a wife with a strong back, but they don't like it if she's bigger than they are. Gravin's like an ox, he didn't mind how tall I was. I wish I hadn't been so free with him now," she said sadly.

"Free? Oh. Well, you really liked him, didn't you?"

"I did like him, and I thought he'd surely marry me," Morinen said, her face suddenly crumpling.

"Oh, Morinen," Nora said, wiping her hand on her apron and putting her arm on the girl's shoulders. A thought struck her. "Are you pregnant?"

"No," said Morinen, with a shake of her head. "I wish I were! Then my brothers would make him marry me."

Nora almost laughed, but Morinen was in earnest.

"Listen, Morinen," she said. "You're better off without him. You have to realize that men—they really only care about themselves." Nora jerked at a turnip so roughly that the green top tore off in her hand. "They don't think about whether they might be hurting someone else. They're just wrapped up in themselves and what they want. It's true in my world—and it's even truer here.

"You know, sometimes, very innocently, you can develop a sort of fascination with a man, and then you see all these little signs that actually don't mean anything, but it's too late because you're reading in them exactly what you want to read. Be careful, is all I'm saying. It's easy to get fooled."

Nora stopped, hoping that Morinen would not wonder whom, exactly,

Nora was really addressing. "Well," she said, with an apologetic smile. "I didn't mean to get carried away."

Morinen uttered a short, grudging laugh. "You sound just like my ma," she said.

With only a little care, Nora found, it was possible to avoid almost all encounters with the magician. He had no real fixed routine, which made it hard to predict his comings and goings, but Nora contrived to spend more time in those places where he was less likely to go—avoiding in particular the great hall, where he might unexpectedly pop out of the wall.

It was absurd, she knew, to go to such lengths to keep from running into Aruendiel. It was also easier. She could still hear those contemptuous words on his lips: "the puny, trivial pleadings of a female voice." They burned in her memory, dosed with some venom that she guessed had something to do with her own dashed hopes for—whatever it was she'd been hoping for. Better to keep a safe distance.

When Mrs. Toristel directed her to carry a message to Aruendiel one afternoon—the first afternoon in weeks when Nora had found some time to settle down with the Ors grammar—Nora could barely conceal her annoyance.

"He's not in the tower?"

"No, he went out a while ago, down the path to the river."

"To the forest?" When Mrs. Toristel nodded, Nora said: "The last time I went down there, he almost bit my head off. Accused me of trespassing."

"Oh, he won't mind," Mrs. Toristel said, although she looked concerned. "Just go and come back quickly. He wanted to know how young Dandelion was doing, and I just got back from the village and they're saying the leg will have to come off."

"Ugh," said Nora, rousing herself.

She took the path through the orchard, where the gnarled trees were now stripped of both fruit and leaves. The grass was wet and slippery from rain earlier. Ahead, the hills on the other side of the river had tarnished to a dirty bronze, except where the black stands of fir trees held their ground. Autumn was subdued here, Nora thought, just rain and gathering chill, no wild scarlets or golds to cheer the heart.

There was no sign of Aruendiel near the river. Nora made her way across to where the path continued on the other side. "Hello?" she called. Her voice struck her own ears as being unnaturally loud, yet it could hardly press past the heavy branches of the firs.

Just go and come quickly, Mrs. Toristel had said. Nora walked as fast as she could up the sloping path, a narrow corridor between the trees. The sound of the rushing water faded behind her. After ten minutes or so, the track grew steeper and less gloomy, as the fir trees gave way to rusty-leafed oaks. The path forked just ahead, in front of an oblong boulder. A goat-hide sack with a drawstring top rested on top of the rock.

Aruendiel must have left it there. But it was impossible to tell which way he had gone. Fallen leaves covered both trails, holding no trace of a passing boot.

Seizing the chance to catch her breath, Nora sat down on a dry patch on the rock. She decided to wait for a few minutes, and then if—when—Aruendiel failed to appear, she would go back and tell Mrs. Toristel that she couldn't find him.

One of the paths continued straight up the hillside; the other angled west along an old stone wall. Hadn't Aruendiel said that once sheep had been grazed here? Hard to imagine now. The tree trunks were burly with age; they must be more than a hundred years old. Some sunlight made its way between clouds and thinning leaves to warm Nora's face. It was pleasant to have a chance to sit at leisure, alone, away from the castle—although the castle was not so far. She could see one of the towers through the trees, perhaps a half mile away.

Nora closed her eyes and listened to the breeze stirring the dying leaves and the occasional drops of water falling from the trees around her.

There was another noise, too, one that she could not quite make out. She found she could follow the tenuous thread of sound best by letting her mind wander slightly. It had a shape, like music, like a long, meandering conversation, overheard from some distance away, between people who know each other so well that they do not always need to finish their sentences to be understood. At the same time, it was so delicate, so weightless in her ears, that she began to wonder whether it came from within her own body, the way the roar of the ocean in a seashell was supposed to be the sound of blood in the arteries. This was even more fragile, though. It was like the noise that a school of fish makes as it swims; it was the rustle of air in a bird's wing as it flies; it was the silence in the center of the thunderstorm.

Someone coughed impatiently.

"Bestir yourself, Mistress Nora." Aruendiel was standing in front of her, a tall shadow against the sunlight. "What are you doing here?"

She blinked. It took her a moment to remember. "Mrs. Toristel sent me to find you."

"Is there something wrong?"

"Someone in the village—Dandelion—is worse. She said you'd want to know." Nora got to her feet slowly, feeling queasy, her body agitated, trembling. She took a deep breath, hoping that she was not about to faint.

Aruendiel was surveying her with narrowed eyes. "Are you ill?"

"I was dozing."

"This is not the proper place in which to—"

"I know," Nora said. "I can tell. There's something going on here, something to do with your magic. You told me that before, but now I've seen—heard—for myself. Some background noise that isn't really there. And I've got that weird feeling I get when you do magic."

Aruendiel raised his eyebrows. "You did not tell me that. An uneasiness in the gut, is that it?" He tilted his head to one side, still studying her. "There is nothing here that would hurt you seriously." He sounded almost apologetic. "But, well, I am surprised that you could discern anything out of the ordinary."

"I'm not as slow as you think I am, even if I am a woman." She turned and started down the path. After a moment, she heard him follow.

"What of the boy's leg?" he asked, as they neared the river.

"Mrs. Toristel said it might have to come off," Nora said, not looking back.

"Good," Aruendiel said. "There is a new spell I mean to try for regrowing severed limbs."

"And what if the spell doesn't work?" Nora shot an irate glance over her shoulder. "Why not just try to save the boy's leg in the first place? If you can raise the dead, I'm sure healing a gangrenous limb would be no trouble at all."

She stepped carefully from stone to stone across the water, remembering how she had fallen the last time. Behind her, she had the vague impression of sudden movement, a flurry in the air. Looking back from the other side of the river, she was not entirely surprised to see that Aruendiel had vanished.

Back at the castle, the cow and goats had to be milked, the milk strained, firewood and water lugged into the kitchen, the bread dough set to rise. The copper pots could have used a good scrubbing, too, but by the time she had finished kneading the dough, Nora had had enough.

It was dark outside. Her shoulders ached. Mrs. Toristel had gone back to her quarters some time ago. The magician might not return for hours. The castle was quiet, aside from the faint rustling of mice in the wall.

Nora helped herself to a bowl of soup from the pot on the back of the stove—some of the white calf's bones had gone to make it—and took her dinner into the great hall. She lit an oil lamp, fetched the Ors primer, and began to read laboriously about the vengeance that the wrathful Lord Devris Bearcrusher took on his ungrateful comrades. It reminded her of the first book of the *Iliad*, except that Devris was in a funk because he had been deprived not of a girl, but of three dozen horses, a golden necklace, and a shield made of magical cowhide.

Turning the pages of a book at the long table in the dim hall was oddly comforting. After a while, she recognized why. It was like being back at school, studying under the vaulted ceiling of the reference library or in the cafeteria during the quiet hours between meals.

Devris had just decapitated his chief rival, Udidin the Fair; reclaimed his magical shield; and was in the middle of an unpleasant ritual involving the dead man's liver and testicles—was this book really for children?—when the door to the courtyard opened and Nora heard Aruendiel's limping footsteps. She nodded briefly as he appeared in the feeble circle of light cast by the oil lamp.

"Is there more of that?" Aruendiel asked, indicating her soup.

"In the kitchen." After a fractional pause, she added, "Shall I get some for you?"

With a shake of his head, he sat down at the table, not in the high-backed chair at the end but on the bench opposite Nora, near the lamp.

"The boy Dandelion is improving," he announced. "The report was wrong. The leg will not have to come off."

"Too bad. You'll have to wait to try your new spell."

"There will be other opportunities," he said as a bowl of soup appeared before him, followed by a mug of water.

She could not resist commenting on the soup he had conjured: "Isn't that a fairly trivial use of magic?"

"Yes," he agreed, more readily than she expected, "but I am weary tonight, and I did not come to rouse you from your dinner—"

"Thanks, I'm almost done."

"—or your book."

Then why did you sit down? Nora thought, but he seemed to be in no particular hurry to begin a conversation. After a moment, she bent over the book and began to read again. It was harder to concentrate now, with Aruendiel drinking broth from his bowl, not silently—they did have spoons here, so why did no one think of using them for eating soup?—but she did her best to lose herself in the cascade of Ors brushstrokes.

The action picked up again, which helped. Just as Devris was enjoying his victory meal, Udidin's younger brother, Udesdiel the Hasty, launched a surprise attack seeking revenge. Devris, protected by his magical shield and fortified by all the fresh liver and mountain oysters he had just consumed, slew half a dozen of Udesdiel's men and was closing in on Udesdiel, but Udesdiel had a spear that would always find its target—

Nora turned the page to find out how this would play out—her money was still on Devris, despite Udesdiel's nifty spear—but the next page was almost completely unreadable. She gave a low, frustrated sigh. Long ago, someone had spilled a thick puddle of ink in the middle of the paper, and then, evidently reluctant to let so much fine, wet ink go to waste, had dipped a brush into it and sketched a series of energetic caricatures across the page.

She made as if to close the book, but her sigh had attracted Aruendiel's attention. He reached across the table and took the book from her, then flipped through a few pages.

"Why are you not reading the book that you took from the palace library?" he asked suddenly, putting the book down. "That one is written in your own language, is it not?"

"I didn't—" Automatically Nora began to deny her theft, and then thought better of it. The evidence was upstairs in her room. "How did you know? Is there some sort of magical antitheft device attached to the book? Or have you been using magic to spy on me?"

"Neither. I saw you hide the book in your bag once during the ride home."

"It was my book originally, you know." Although she was trying not to sound defensive, she felt a certain shiftiness creep into her tone.

"So you said."

"The king has no use for a book written in English."

"He has no use for books written in his native tongue, from what I can tell," Aruendiel said. "But you have not answered my question. Why are you reading this child's primer? It is an account of the Thelbron War. An important passage in history, but not very relevant to your concerns."

"How would you even know what my concerns are?" Nora said—civilly enough, she thought. "I told you before. I've been teaching myself to read Ors. Mrs. Toristel said that she had learned out of this book, and I've been trying to do the same."

"Why do you wish to read Ors?" Aruendiel speared a chunk of meat from his bowl. "What use will it be to you?"

"I don't know," Nora said tiredly. "I don't like being illiterate. I need something to keep my mind occupied." The defaced page stared up at her. "There's no real reason."

There was a silence. "I can remove this ink stain, if you like," Aruendiel said. "So that you can continue reading."

Nora shrugged. "I suppose. It's just some child's scribbles."

Aruendield picked up the book again. "My sister's," he said. "I recognize her hand. These figures are perhaps intended to represent my brothers and myself."

"Really?" Intrigued in spite of herself, Nora leaned forward for another look. "This was her book? Which one are you?"

"We all used this book for lessons. The smallest is me, I would think. The one who is drawn with an open mouth."

"Huh," said Nora, not seeing much resemblance. "You were the youngest?"

"Oh, yes," Aruendiel said, with a trace of asperity, as if surprised at her ignorance. "That is why I am called Aruendiel—Aruen's third son. You have not reached the section in the book that treats the grammar of familial naming, I take it."

"No. I can't wait." She saw what she had not suspected, that there must be a thread of genealogical information coiled inside Ors names. Udesdiel was another third son, obviously. Another code to break, another rule to learn—and for what? So she could survive, so she could peel apples and grub turnips in this alien world for another decade, or more.

Aruendiel was turning the pages of the book. "There are one or two other grammatical topics that I particularly recommend to you for study."

"I thought that I speak fairly good Ors at this point."

"Better than you once did," he allowed. "Certainly you have nearly lost that vile Faitoren accent. But you have difficulties with the future potentive, for instance. It is more correct to say, 'I will not be able to wait' instead of 'I can't wait.' "

"I was being ironic." By some small blessing, Ors had a word for "irony," or something close enough.

"And you are careless with the verb genders, too. Very frequently you use the masculine form instead of the feminine."

"What do you mean?" It was news to Nora that the Ors verbs had genders. With a lift of his eyebrows, Aruendiel began to explain the language's feminine verb prefixes. As she listened, it dawned on Nora that what she had assumed to be brief syllables of hesitancy—the equivalent of the English "um" or "ah"—in Mrs. Toristel's or Morinen's or Inristian's speech was actually a construction intended to assure the world that the speaker was a woman.

"So you ought to have said, 'I was being ironic,' " Aruendiel finished. He used the feminine form. The sentence sounded strangely tentative, coming out of his mouth.

"That doesn't sound right," Nora objected. "The extra syllables make the sentence seem weaker."

"It's the way women speak."

More codes to master, Nora thought. In fact, she had consciously tried not to mimic Mrs. Toristel in this particular linguistic habit, taking the filler sounds as a sign of lazy, uneducated speech. A bit of snobbery that had backfired.

"I was trying to copy you," she said. "I thought that was the correct way to speak."

"It is correct for me," he said.

"Well, yes! Everything is basically correct for you." Nora's hands made fists in her lap. "You can do what you please, because you're a magician and a lord—but most important, a man. You can travel, you can talk to anyone you please, you can read a book without being laughed at. Tell me any woman could do the same."

Aruendiel did not contradict her. "You are unused to the ways of this world," he said.

"Listen, I'm not trying to change the world—*your* world. I'm just passing through. But then I think about that bookseller in Semr, how he thought I was joking when I said I could read, and it makes me want to scream. Can you even imagine how that feels? Of course you can't. The Lord Magician Aruendiel is not accustomed to having his intellect or status questioned.

"And now it turns out that women can't even talk like men. Which is a clever way to invalidate women's discourse, isn't it? No wonder women can't do magic; no wonder spirits won't listen to their puny, trivial voices. It's all woven into the basic structure of the language." She stopped, looking at Aruendiel's impassive face, thinking that none of what she had just said made sense to him, but feeling a certain relief that she had said it.

Aruendiel skewered the last piece of meat from his bowl and chewed it thoughtfully. He tilted the bowl toward his mouth, drained it, and put the empty bowl on the table. "I never said that women cannot do magic."

"You said that the spirits would not listen to women."

"Do you think that is all there is to magic, begging favors of spirits?"

"I don't know. I have no idea. You've never explained to me what magic is."

"And what do you think it is that Hirizjahkinis does, if not magic?"

"I don't know. I suppose she has some special dispensation."

"No, she is only a very fine magician, and yet she is a woman, or so I understand." He made a noise deep in his throat that could have been a very dry chuckle, then closed the book. "I will give you no more suggestions for your grammatical studies. You must decide for yourself what is worthy of your attention."

"As you like." Nora shrugged. She was thinking that it was time to bring the conversation to a close and make her escape to bed. Something new had engaged Aruendiel's fancy, however. He reached for Nora's bowl and brought it closer to the light.

"This is an old one," he said.

"What, the bowl?" she said, taken aback. "Well, I suppose. It's not like the others."

"The other ones in the set must be long since broken. We used these bowls when I was young." He rubbed a finger over the rim, tracing the pattern of interlocking spirals under the brown glaze. "We had a potter in the village then, who made these for my mother. Oxleg, they called him. This red-and-white stuff," he added, looking at his own bowl, "is newer."

"It's from the potter in Barsy, Mrs. Toristel said." Nora pushed the bench back and stood up. The sight of the book and now the bowl had obviously stirred up some odd nostalgic current in the magician, but she was in no mood to give him a sympathetic ear. She held out her hand to take the bowl from him, intending to take it back into the kitchen.

He made no move to return it. "Why did you choose this odd one, instead of one from the set?"

"It's a good size and shape. I use it a lot." Although she did not wish to say so, she had come to think of the bowl as her own. She usually ate alone; it wasn't as though her dish had to match the rest of a table setting.

"Do you?" he asked, cocking an eyebrow. "You like it, then?"

"Well, yes."

With a fluid motion, Aruendiel lifted the bowl and flung it onto the floor.

Nora flinched as the bowl smashed on the flagstones. She looked at Aruendiel round-eyed. "What? Why did you do that?"

"Fix it," he said calmly.

"Fix it?" she sputtered. "How?" Confusedly she thought of the little white Elmer's Glue bottle with the pointed orange top. Was there anything like that in this world?

"That's the same bowl you broke some time ago, if you don't remember. I repaired it then. Now you fix it yourself. Make it as perfect as it was a minute ago. You want to know what magic is, Mistress Nora? Now you have an opportunity to find out."

## Chapter 24

This is hopeless," Nora told herself for the twentieth time. She picked up two of the shards that lay on the kitchen hearth and touched the broken edges together. An exact fit—but she knew that already. The shattered bowl was a jigsaw puzzle that she had learned by heart over the past two days. Yet the jagged pieces refused to adhere to each other, falling inexorably apart as soon as she took her hands away.

The crack in the teacup opens a lane to the land of the dead. Of course, where else would it lead? There was no reversing time or entropy. Mechanically, she moved her hands over the broken pieces, keeping an ear cocked toward the great hall. She wondered if the coast was clear yet, if she could make her way upstairs now. No, she could still make out the low hum of voices through the door.

She was not keen to see Aruendiel, with no mended bowl to show him. Nor was she especially eager to encounter his visitor.

Two days before, she had been crossing the courtyard around midday, still a little groggy from sitting up the night before to fit pottery fragments together, when Aruendiel came around the corner of the house, his cool eyes meeting hers, and she knew that he was going to ask her about the broken bowl. She was saved when the dogs in the courtyard began to bark. Aruendiel walked to the gate and looked out. An instant later, he turned back, his brows knotted, and called out to Nora to find Mrs. Toristel, a guest would be arriving shortly.

It was Aruendiel's niece—Lady Pusieuv Negin, of Forel—Mrs. Toristel informed Nora, as they watched him help a woman in a long blue traveling cloak out of a glossy black carriage. Her fair hair was carefully arranged into a style that Nora had seen among the court ladies in Semr, known as "eels and baskets" or "whips and shields," neither term quite conveying how complex or unflattering it was. She was on the small side; as she embraced Aruendiel, he had to stoop to kiss her on the cheek.

Forel was in Pelagnia, the housekeeper added with a touch of pride.

"I didn't know he had a niece," Nora said.

"Grand-niece," Mrs. Toristel corrected herself. "From his sister's line, that married the duke of Forel. Oh, what will we do for dinner now?

Trouteye in the village killed his pigs early—we might could get a fresh ham." She sighed. "*He'll* be angry if we don't show her the best hospitality."

Lady Pusieuv Negin was sweeping toward them across the courtyard, accompanied by Aruendiel. Mrs. Toristel dropped a stately curtsy, and Nora did her best to imitate her.

"My housekeeper, Mrs. Toristel, will see to your—" Aruendiel began, but his niece interrupted him.

"Of course I remember Ulunip—it is Ulunip, is it not?" she said, with a wide smile.

"Yes, ma'am." Mrs. Toristel colored slightly, pleased.

"It is always a pleasure to hear a good Pelagnian voice in these harsh northlands. You come from the Four Rivers district, isn't that right?" Mrs. Toristel said no, ma'am, the Purny Basin. "The Purny! One of my favorite places. The hunting there is excellent." Lady Pusieuv discoursed briefly on the amenities of the Purny Basin, while Mrs. Toristel gave short, respectful assents. Then, abruptly, Lady Pusieuv broke off and looked directly at Nora.

"And this is—?" she asked quizzically.

"Mistress Nora Fechr," Aruendiel said. "She is a guest here."

"Fischer," said Nora.

"I am delighted to make your acquaintance!" Lady Pusieuv said. Her round brown eyes bored into Nora's. "I heard so much about you when I was in Semr."

"Oh, you've come from Semr?" Nora asked politely.

"Yes, I arrived there just a day after you and my uncle left. Everyone was still buzzing about Uncle—and his companion. So clever of you to have found that poor wizard! I was terribly disappointed to have missed the two of you. So I decided to come pay Uncle a visit."

Nora expressed regrets that their paths had not crossed in Semr and hoped that Lady Pusieuv's journey had been an easy one.

"Oh, upriver was fine, but the roads past Noler have not gotten any better since I was here last, Uncle!" Lady Pusieuv launched into a rapid-fire account of a flooded ford and a broken axle. The trip, Nora thought, had obviously required a great deal of determination on her part.

Nora joined Mrs. Toristel in the kitchen a few minutes later. A dusty wine bottle stood open on the table, next to two blackened goblets. Mrs.

Toristel was slicing hastily into a rather sticky-looking brown loaf. "One bottle left of the tawny Sprenen, can you believe it?" she said. "Here, you polish the goblets. He doesn't even know we have them. He sold all the silver settings years ago, but I held back a few pieces."

Nora fetched vinegar and salt from the pantry and began to polish the goblets with a rag. "Isn't that the honey cake you made for Mr. Toristel?"

"Yes, and he won't be pleased to see it go, but we don't have anything else fit for her ladyship. You know he doesn't care for sweets, as a rule."

"Mmm," said Nora, sorting out, with a little thought, the two different parties that Mrs. Toristel meant by *he*. "Is she really worth all this trouble?"

Mrs. Toristel sniffed. "She's his only family left, she and her line. Lady Pusieuv used to visit at Lusul, she and her parents, when she was just a little thing," she added, her voice softening. "Lady Lusarniev doted on her. I can see her now, letting the little girl play with her necklace."

"So Lady Pusieuv must be well over fifty now," Nora said meanly.

"Tsk, it doesn't seem possible." The housekeeper sighed again. "What a darling little girl she was." Mrs. Toristel disappeared into the pantry and returned with a crock of the sweet-pickled blackberries. She added a generous purple dollop to the plate that held the sliced cake. "I wonder," she said, in a crisper tone, "what brings Lady Pusieuv all this way?"

"What do you mean?"

"I mean it's been more than a dozen years at least since she visited here last. And you heard what she said about the roads. Mark my words, she has some reason for coming here now."

"I can tell you why," Nora said. "It's because of me."

Mrs. Toristel gave her a look that, by its very neutrality, expressed deep skepticism.

"She came because of what she heard in Semr. You know, when I was there, they all assumed I was his mistress. Aruendiel's mistress," Nora added, to be perfectly clear. "Absurd, of course, but that's how people there think." She was conscious of trying a little too hard to keep her voice casual. She had never told Mrs. Toristel about the stories, true and untrue, that she had heard circulating in Semr about Aruendiel, or what he had told her himself. "So I'm sure Lady Pusieuv wanted to get a look at me. See what sort of baggage her uncle has picked up." If she tries to pull a Lady Catherine de Bourgh and break up our impending nuptials, Nora thought, I will be pleased to set her straight.

"I've never known his lordship to take any interest in women since Lady Lusarniev," Mrs. Toristel said with a sniff.

"All the more reason for Lady Pusieuv to see what all the fuss is about. She came a long way for nothing, obviously."

"She'll figure out which way the river flows soon enough. One look at you, she should know."

Nora laughed, a little bitterly. "Once upon a time, before I got clawed by a monster and when I could wear decent clothes, I wasn't considered that bad-looking."

Mrs. Toristel looked at her critically. "Your face isn't so bad. Those scars have faded a bit. But to think that a great lord, especially one that was married to Lady Lusarniev, would take you as his mistress—well, the folk in Semr must be as idiotic as he always says."

"I wouldn't dispute that," Nora said, suppressing an urge to mention that the great lord in question had, by his own account, murdered the beautiful Lady Lusarniev. Mrs. Toristel didn't know that. Well, she knew it, Nora thought, but she wouldn't admit it.

That was two days ago. To Nora's relief, she had had only the briefest of encounters with Lady Pusieuv since then. Yesterday, Aruendiel had taken his niece riding downriver—"Lady Pusieuv is an excellent horsewoman," Mrs. Toristel murmured approvingly—and in the castle, Lady Pusieuv was little in evidence. Except for mealtimes, she spent most of her time in one of the drawing rooms on the first floor, because—Mrs. Toristel had heard her tell Aruendiel—the great hall was drafty and old-fashioned.

"But those other rooms are a mess!" Nora exclaimed to the housekeeper. "There's no furniture! They're a ruin!"

Mrs. Toristel laughed unexpectedly. "Not today," she said. "For once, they're as fine as they should be. With all the proper chairs and tables and tapestries and such."

"How—?"

"He did it. Well, he couldn't put her in an empty room, could he?" She laughed again, drily. "He does it every time she visits. It's the only time he bothers."

"Too bad he couldn't have done the same for her bedchamber," Nora said. The day of Lady Pusieuv's arrival, she and Morinen had spent a hurried hour upstairs dusting, sweeping, scrubbing, and changing the linens for her ladyship.

But Mrs. Toristel, Nora suspected, would not trust magic, even Aruendiel's magic, to provide clean sheets.

Tonight Aruendiel and his niece were dining in the great hall, as Nora waited in the kitchen, her hands sorting the broken shards of pottery. They felt cool and hard and intractable under her fingers. If Lady Pusieuv had not been here—if Nora had not been working harder than ever since their guest's arrival—there might have been more time to steal away to a quiet place where she could be undisturbed and could focus, focus, until the magic words came into her mind, or whatever it was that would make the shattered pieces snap together.

Or maybe, she thought, they never would.

The door to the great hall opened, and she saw Aruendiel's lean figure in the doorway.

"Where's Mrs. Toristel?" he asked.

"She's gone back to her quarters," Nora said. "Do you need her?"

He made a gesture of annoyance, as though snatching at a fly. "What in the name of Nagaris did she leave for a sweet course?"

"Do you mean the pie? It's on the table already."

"There's something resembling a tart, yes. It appears to be full of pebbles."

"Walnuts. It's a walnut pie."

"Your handiwork?"

Nora nodded yes.

"I see," Aruendiel said, packing an extraordinary amount of skepticism into a few syllables. Then he noticed the shards of crockery on the hearth. "You have not mended the dish yet?"

"No," she said shortly. "Still broken."

"Ah," he said, with a shrug. Nora could almost hear the unspoken thought: I expected no better. "Leave that and come help me amuse my niece."

"I wouldn't want to intrude on a family dinner," she demurred. Strange to hear the magician ask for help, even of the social sort.

"It is no intrusion. We have reached that stage in conversation when another party begins to be most welcome."

At the sight of Nora, Lady Pusieuv looked surprised, then smiled graciously. She expressed equal wonder to learn that the pie was made with walnuts, that Nora had made it, and that Nora had come from another world.

Come on, Nora thought, walnuts in a pie, it's not such an earthshaking idea. She'd simply made a pecan pie using neither pecans nor corn syrup. She tried a bite. Not bad. It would have been better with cinnamon.

"I heard," Lady Pusieuv said, "that you actually used to live among the Faitoren." She glanced at her uncle, but Aruendiel, who was taking a cautious bite of pie, said nothing. "And what was *that* like?"

What exactly was she getting at? Nora wondered, but she answered: "I enjoyed it at the time. I would not care to repeat it."

"I saw a Faitoren once, ages ago. They're very attractive, aren't they? The men and women both."

Nora gave a noncommittal shrug. "They put on a good show."

"Of course, they are not to be trusted, I know. They've caused a great deal of trouble, over the years. Shocking." Lady Pusieuv took a sip from her goblet, and Nora noticed how flushed her cheeks appeared in the candlelight. The bottle of wine that stood on the table was empty. "A great deal of trouble," she repeated.

Nora nodded in agreement, wondering how Aruendiel was reacting to this line of conversation, but it was impossible to read his expression. Even the black eyebrows were decorously still.

"What I hear is that you had the unfortunate experience of being married to one of them," Lady Pusieuv burst out.

Ah, so that's it, Nora thought with a half-smile. The other woman's tipsy curiosity filled her with unexpected cheer, as though she had just downed a glass of strong drink herself.

"It's absolutely true," she said. "I married the son of the Faitoren queen."

"Indeed! That must have been, oh, dreadful."

"It was not a good idea," Nora allowed. She turned to the magician. "Aruendiel tried to talk me out of it, but I wouldn't listen."

"Oh?" Lady Pusieuv was alert, her eyes flitting back and forth between Nora and Aruendiel.

After a moment's hesitation, Aruendiel took his cue. "Luklren's men picked her up on the border, so we interrogated her, then sent her back. It was clear she was enchanted, but there was nothing we could do then."

"Aruendiel helped me escape later on, though," Nora said, letting a trace of huskiness creep into her voice.

"Mistress Nora called for help, and I responded. Any unfortunate in the power of the Faitoren deserves no less."

"I owe him my life," Nora said, with a confiding smile to Lady Pusieuv. She sighed, as though overcome with emotion. "I can never fully repay him."

Aruendiel gave Nora a sharp look. She herself was interested to discover, after two days of resenting Lady Pusieuv for assuming that she was Aruendiel's mistress, how wickedly pleasurable it was to encourage the misperception—or at least to allow the falsehood to flourish unchecked. It felt strangely liberating.

Aruendiel, though, had evidently had enough of Nora's rescue. He changed the subject, remarking that he expected to make fewer journeys to the Faitoren borderlands from now on, since he had finally persuaded Luklren to retain a magician of his own. Had Lady Pusieuv seen Luklren at court? She had not, but she had seen his cousin Lord Oslewen, who had just married the second daughter of Baron Marn.

They moved into a discussion of recent dynastic alliances in the kingdom, including the pedigrees of each party—Aruendiel seemed to have known most of their immediate ancestors going back two or three generations—and then moved inevitably into politics. Lady Pusieuv had a range of sharp observations to make on the players at the Semrian court; Nora had no way of judging how accurate her analysis might be, but it sounded trenchant enough, and Aruendiel seemed to be listening carefully.

The interest he showed was surprising, Nora thought. She would have bet money that this sort of talk would have bored him senseless, and from time to time, as Lady Pusieuv held forth, she thought she saw a shade of weariness in his eyes. But when he responded to his niece, he spoke with a practiced, easy courtesy, a smooth attentiveness, which was far removed from his usual manner. For the first time, Nora thought, she could credit the stories about the women that he had seduced long ago.

Or perhaps, as a landholder and peer of the realm, even as a magician who played some role in the affairs of government from time to time, he was more concerned with the political landscape in the kingdom than she had imagined.

Nora, unfortunately, did not share the same interest. She was thinking longingly of her bed upstairs, and wondering whether her candle stub was long enough to let her read for a few minutes about Devris and Udesdiel before going to sleep, when a sudden change in Aruendiel's tone caught her attention.

"No," he said, shaking his head, "it is out of the question."

"But poor old Lord Tirigan died without near heirs; now it could go to some distant cousin who's half Orvetian and doesn't have nearly as good a claim as you do. Really, it's a scandal to let a rich estate like that, in the heart of the kingdom, fall into the hands of foreigners."

"I have no claim at all," he said coldly.

"That's not true, Uncle. You've always had a good claim, and to be frank, I think it's mad not to assert it, especially now. Unfaithfulness cancels all dower rights, you know. Lusul should be yours."

"The estate passed to my wife's cousin, her nearest legitimate relation, as was just."

"Well, he's dead now. And the rumor in Semr is that the Pirekennys will raise a claim, too. I saw the grandson at court."

"That is no concern of mine."

"Well, I think it's very shocking. The nerve of those people! They should be ashamed." Aruendiel was silent, so she went on. "I apologize for bringing up this old unpleasantness, but—well, think of the good of the family, Uncle. We still have four girls to marry off. It would be such a blessing to be able to offer them with part of the Lusul patrimony in their dowry."

"Surely the Forel is enough to provide for your family?"

"It's no Lusul!" she said vehemently. "For your own sake, too, Uncle, please consider it. It's a shame that you have to live here, in this poor little castle, in this miserable northland, when you could be so much more comfortable." Her glance moved across the table and fell upon Nora. "I'm sure that Nora would prefer living in a modern palace, on a great estate like Lusul. Wouldn't you, Nora?"

Nora was taken aback, and now a little regretful about the impression that she had fostered about her relationship with Aruendiel. "I'm actually not very particular," she said awkwardly.

"My dear Pusieuv, we have spent enough time on this subject. There is nothing more to discuss. Would you care for more wine?" Aruendiel reached for the wine bottle and discovered that it was empty. He rose from his chair. "Excuse me, ladies, I will bring out a new bottle."

"Would you like me to get it?" Nora asked, but he waved away her offer and limped toward the kitchen.

"Uncle is stubborn," said Lady Pusieuv into the silence that fell after the kitchen door swung shut.

"I've noticed," Nora said.

Another pause. Lady Pusieuv took a last bite of pie and chewed it delicately. "You know, my dear," she went on, "I think it falls upon me to remind you of something. My uncle is known as Lord Aruendiel. No matter what you call him in private, it is very important that, at least in company, you refer to him by that title. Or as his lordship. It is the proper address for one of his station."

"He has never asked me to refer to him that way," Nora said. "And certainly he does not hesitate to correct me or anyone else, when he believes it necessary."

"My uncle tolerates—to some degree encourages—many lapses of decorum. He would be pleased, though, if you were to stop addressing him in such a familiar manner. It would show that you know your place."

"My place!" Nora looked incredulously at Lady Pusieuv. The other woman seemed to be completely serious.

"Yes, your place. You are not of the same rank, you know, so you must see that it is quite impossible for you to address him as an equal."

For a moment, Nora was speechless, or rather the only words that would fluently express her feelings were English words. She made a random gesture of frustration, and the ring on her finger flashed in the candlelight. It gave her an idea.

"Of course Aruendiel's not my equal," Nora said, with stony hauteur. "I prefer more informality myself—it's how we do things where I come from—but it's quite true that he and I don't occupy the same rank. As you know, I am separated from my husband," she went on, "but until my domestic situation is sorted out, I am still married to a Faitoren prince, and therefore, I hold the rank of princess.

"By rights Aruendiel—and everyone else of a lower rank—should address me as 'Your Royal Highness,' but I do not insist upon it. Like him, I can tolerate some lapses of decorum."

Lady Pusieuv pursed her thin lips and appeared thoughtful.

"More wine, my dear niece?"

Aruendiel had appeared with the bottle in his hand. He filled her goblet without waiting for her reply. "And would you like some?" he said to Nora. He spoke to her with a degree more politeness than he normally did, and there was a curl of amusement at the corner of his mouth. She noted that he had refrained from addressing her by either name or title.

"Yes, please," she said.

The wine was surprisingly good. There was little in the castle wine cellar except for a scattering of very old, vinegary bottles and a barrel of raw red wine, like liquid sandpaper, that Mrs. Toristel had bought from a trader in Barsy last year and still hoped would age into something drinkable. Nora wondered whether Aruendiel had resorted to mellowing the red with a quick spell. He seemed not to be drinking any more wine. Lady Pusieuv, though, enjoyed it. After finishing a goblet, she had a second piece of the pie.

She seemed to have decided on a more conciliatory tack toward Nora. "So you simply invented this dish? And it turned out as well as this?" Lady Pusieuv shook her head as if in disbelief. "I do enjoy fussing in the kitchen, when I have a chance—my mother insisted all we girls learn to cook—but I would be terrified to try something really new, unless my cook was standing right there to help me."

"Well, I had a basic recipe in mind, and the ingredients—the honey, the walnuts," Nora said. "I knew what they could do, how they could fit together. That's what good cooking is."

"Not only cooking," Aruendiel said suddenly. His eyes caught hers, pale as smoke. "It is always essential to know one's ingredients, how they fit together."

What was he getting at? Nora felt a prickle of anticipation. "I suppose so," she said slowly. "For making something. Or remaking something— something that was broken."

He gave her a brief smile, unusually cordial. "It starts with a certain basic understanding of the materials. A kind of sympathy."

"Did you see the wonderful marquetry work that is all the rage in Semr just now?" Lady Pusieuv asked. "Like a painting, but all made of different-colored pieces of wood fitting together. The cabinetmaker must know all the various sorts of wood, and how their colors change as they age, and how to carve them just so. It is truly an art. I've ordered a table with a double portrait of myself and Negio, in profile."

"It sounds most impressive," Aruendiel said.

## *Chapter 25*

T he sky was gray, stuffed as full of snow as a quilt is of down, but not a single flake had fallen. Nor would any fall for some time to come. Aruendiel had no intention of allowing his niece's departure to be delayed.

He rode alongside the coach as far as the Barsy road, to see Pusieuv safely on her way. Privately, he wagered with himself that she would bring up Lusul one more time. With a touch of sardonic enjoyment, he found himself proven right as they approached the turnoff for Barsy. "Uncle," she said, leaning out the carriage window, "have you come to your senses yet, about making your claim for Lusul? There is no one with a better right to it."

"No, my dear," he said, speaking as lightly as he could, "I wish to have nothing to do with the place again." Pusieuv looked baleful for an instant, but then she smiled and began to talk enthusiastically about the avenue of oaks that her husband had been planting at Forel in her absence, how she was looking forward to seeing it when she returned home.

That was one of the things that Aruendiel appreciated about his grand-niece, how quickly she could recover from a setback with grace and apparent good humor, when she chose to. It was not something that he had ever developed a knack for. Nor had his sister, come to think of it—Pusieuv must have gotten it from some other branch of the family.

Long ago he had given up looking for any trace of his sister in Pusieuv's face. The eyes, perhaps, and a tendency to plumpness in middle age. But then many people in Pelagnia—the Uland, for that matter—had brown eyes. He did not like to think about how many generations lay between his sister and her descendant. It was commendable of Pusieuv to keep up the connection. Sometimes tiresome, when she made unexpected visits like this one, but commendable. He had enjoyed having a woman around the castle for a few days, and he was even more pleased that she was leaving.

At the Barsy road, she gave him her hand to kiss. "Well, Uncle, I'll see you at the assembly next year in Semr. Unless—if we happen to marry off one of the girls before then, you'll come to the wedding feast, of course?"

The "of course" was a nice touch. Aruendiel had not attended the wedding feasts of the three children who were already married. "I will send my blessing," he said.

Aruendiel occupied himself on the ride home thinking about various spells to keep unwanted visitors away. With natural magic, you could easily lay spells that would instantly neutralize anyone who came to attack or enchant you. It was more difficult to design a spell that made more subtle distinctions—that would repel a charming, well-intentioned, but officious grand-niece, for instance. Micher Samle had been interested in that sort of magical problem, getting spells to think for themselves, grant wishes, and so forth—was probably still working on it, wherever he was. In the girl Nora's world, presumably.

Thinking of Nora, Aruendiel scowled. Mrs. Toristel had complained to him twice already about Nora's efforts to mend the bowl. Reluctantly, Aruendiel had to agree: It was a waste of the girl's time. She might have some sort of receptivity to magic—the incident with the lion in Semr, for instance—but that was hardly enough to make smashed crockery new again. He regretted having given her the task. Why had he bothered? Across the table the other night, he'd recognized something familiar in her tired, angry face. She was exiled, dispossessed, and weary of it. The girl was inquisitive, she had a good brain—intriguing if she could be taught to do something with it—but now she would only be more sullen after failing with the bowl.

He let the snow begin falling as he neared the castle. Pusieuv must be well past Barsy by now. Fine powder sifted down, dappling the ground with uneven patches of white. The first snow of winter, but the earth was still warm enough to keep it from sticking. That would change soon enough.

Back at the castle, he was heading to the tower to look up an old spell for confusing unwelcome visitors—it steered them away from your dwelling, unless they turned and walked in the opposite direction—when Mrs.

Toristel accosted him in the great hall. His attention was needed for the estate accounts.

"Can this not wait until later, Mrs. Toristel?"

"That's what you said last week, sir. And tribute is due at the end of the month."

Aruendiel groaned and settled himself at the table. Mrs. Toristel began to recite the tally of the year's harvest and what it had brought at market.

". . . Six dozen *wiar* of wheat, two beetles three beads the *wiar*—"

"That's all that we got for wheat this year?"

"The harvest was a good one. Prices were low."

He shook his head. "I can never understand why an excellent harvest should leave me poorer than ever. Next year, though, I will turn the villagers into grasshoppers and I will personally curse with rust every wheat field within three days' ride, and perhaps I will get a better price for my wheat."

Mrs. Toristel cleared her throat. "Also, the river was low, so that knocked ten beads off the price. Extra transport costs."

"Why didn't you let me know? I would have filled the river to the top of its banks."

"You were in Semr at the time, sir."

Aruendiel swore briefly under his breath. "An expensive journey that turned out to be. And I bought horses there, too—how much did Toristel get for them?"

"He sold the gray but not the bay. It brought"—she thought a moment—"a dozen and three beetles."

"I paid almost twice that in Semr," he said gloomily. "Why didn't he sell the bay?"

"He thought you might want an extra mount. For Nora. If she was to travel again."

"What? The horse deserves better on its back, someone who can actually ride. Tell Toristel to sell it at the next horse fair."

Mrs. Toristel coughed and looked past Aruendiel's head. He chose to ignore the signal. If Mistress Nora was in earshot, she had already heard his views on her riding. After a pause, the housekeeper began again: "Six dozen *wiar* of wheat, two beetles three beads the *wiar*, one dozen dozen six beetles in all. Three dozen *wiar* of rye . . ."

When she came to the end, the earnings from the harvest totaled two dozen dozen seven beetles and two dozen four beads. Aruendiel drummed his fingers on the table and tried to work out whether it would be enough to pay the king's tribute and cover the household expenses until next spring's shearing. He still had some cash from the work done for the merchant last summer. Thinking it over, Aruendiel decided that they would make it into the next year, but it would be close. He exhaled loudly. "Thank you, Mrs. Toristel."

"You're welcome, sir. Would you like to go over the internal stores, as well?"

"Later, please. I have had enough ill news for one day."

She nodded and went into the kitchen. As Aruendiel rose, he turned to find himself face-to-face with Nora.

"Good afternoon," he said, making a step to brush past her.

"Good afternoon," she said, moving with him. "You know, I didn't want to correct Mrs. Toristel, but I think she might have made a small mistake when she was adding up those numbers. It's actually two dozen dozen six beetles and eleven beads."

"How would you know?"

"I couldn't help listening, and I added the numbers up in my head. I believe I've gotten the hang of your number system." The girl looked ridiculously pleased with herself.

"I believe I asked you, once before, to allow me to conduct my own financial affairs."

"That's true. I apologize," she said. She did not look sorry. She was still smiling. "There's just one other thing—" she went on, pulling out a dark object that had been hidden in the folds of her skirt. "I wanted to show you this."

"Ah." He took the bowl from her and ran his fingers over the glazed surface, smooth, annealed. "It is the same bowl, the one that was broken?"

"Yes."

"You mended it yourself?"

"Yes."

"How?"

"I don't know, precisely."

Aruendiel raised an eyebrow.

"This morning I was shuffling the broken pieces around and they all came together. It happened in a second."

Aruendiel turned the bowl over in his hands, considering. A fine accomplishment for a beginner. But what did it signify? The result was too random, more likely the product of lucky inspiration than intelligent technique. She did not understand yet what she had done.

He hurled the dish against the floor.

"No!" Nora cried, throwing out her arm, too late. She knelt and fingered the broken pieces, then looked up at him. "Why on earth did you do that?"

"You fixed it once. Do so again, and this time have the wit to tell me exactly how."

She said something in her own language, but he had no trouble understanding her.

"Bring it to me when you are finished," he directed. "I will be in the tower for the rest of the day."

I should have known he would do that, Nora told herself as she put the shards of the dish into her apron. It's just the sort of thing he would do— and oh, merry hell, how on earth did I do it before? They don't want to fit together at all now, do they? It was so simple this morning, it was like magic. Well, it was magic, she thought with a small flare of pride.

It had something to do with what Aruendiel had said the other night about sympathy, understanding the materials. That was a big hint; she had been mulling over his words ever since, as she played with the fragments of the bowl, wondering how to develop sympathy with a clay pot. Evidently she had succeeded. But how? She tried to recall exactly what she had been thinking just before the bowl sprang back to life, as it were, under her fingers.

Mrs. Toristel came into the great hall and reminded her that the chamber that Lady Pusieuv had occupied needed tidying.

If the magician had truly expected that she would return with the mended bowl that afternoon, he was mistaken. It was not until the evening of the second day, as she sat up in bed, playing with the pieces of pottery, her hands half-remembering the shape and heft of the old, unbroken dish, that she felt the fragments somehow organize themselves, take hold of one another, and choose to be a bowl again.

Nora exclaimed aloud. Only connect. She laughed.

She looked out the window of her room, up at the tower, where a light still burned, then shook her head. She knew what his response would be. She looked at the bowl for a few minutes, admiring its completeness, the way the candlelight melted and swam in the glossy, unmarred glaze. She got out of bed, took the bowl over to the hearth, and gave it a good, swift blow with the poker.

Aruendiel was eating breakfast in the great hall when Nora put the bowl on the table, next to his mug of ale. There were dark smudges under her eyes and mad wisps of hair escaping from her braid, but her mouth was set in a calm, decisive curve.

"Here it is," she said.

Aruendiel looked up from his oatmeal. "Yes?" he said, sounding bored. He hardly glanced at the bowl she had deposited. "Is that all you have to say for yourself?"

Nora was still not sure how to explain what she had done. "I know how to mend it now." That was not quite right. "The bowl can mend itself." Still not right. "The fragments remember the shape of the bowl. I touched them, and they knew me, and I asked them to remember, to reconfigure, and they were willing. That's all. They were waiting, and I asked, and they were willing."

Aruendiel watched her closely with his wintry eyes. Then he raised his eyebrows and took a swallow of ale. "I see," he said, but his voice was no longer bored. It held a rumble of what might have been approval.

He reached for the mended bowl, but Nora was too quick. She snatched it away and smashed it against the floor. The pieces had hardly stopped shivering on the flagstones before she was on her knees, gathering them, fitting them back together. She clambered to her feet and put the bowl on the table again, whole and entire.

A smile flickered at the corner of Aruendiel's mouth. He spooned up the last mouthful of oatmeal in his own bowl, one of the red-and-white set from Barsy, and then handed the dish to Nora. Hesitating for only a second, she broke it against the flagstones.

At first she thought she was not going to be able to mend this one. It felt utterly different, the fragments alien to her touch. For a few long minutes she scrabbled helplessly with the myriad pieces. Then suddenly it was all right, they were at ease with her, she had only to drop a mild hint, and the red-and-white bowl had reconstituted itself in her grasp. She handed it back to Aruendiel and then pointed to his mug.

"May I?" she asked.

He lifted the mug and poured the ale inside carefully into the air. The liquid hung above the table in an amber bubble, foaming slightly, as Nora smashed the mug and put it back together again. Aruendiel let the ale drain into it again, then took a thoughtful sip.

"What else?" Nora said, smiling, challenge in her voice. "I'll break all the dishes in the kitchen and then mend them, if you want."

"No," Aruendiel said, "it would upset Mrs. Toristel, and I myself have heard enough crockery shatter for one morning. So, Mistress Nora, you wanted to know what magic is. And now you have done some yourself. Are you satisfied, now?"

"No," she said, without hesitation.

"Good," he said. "Come to my study this afternoon. I have another task for you."

There seemed to be a hundred interminable chores that day, from cleaning the kitchen to sweeping the great hall to polishing the pots and pans to helping Mrs. Toristel sort the laundry to turning the ripening wheels of cheese in the buttery. The light was fading outside when Nora finally stepped through the wall and went up the winding stairs in the tower.

The magician's study was as she remembered it, a room virtually encased in books. The rows of dark volumes along the wall and ceiling gave the room a cavelike feel, and yet it seemed almost cozy as she mounted the last steps. There was a flickering yellow glow from what seemed to be dozens of candles burning along the walls—surprisingly extravagant for Aruendiel, until Nora saw that the small lights were not attached to candlesticks. It was the pale flame that he had conjured in the library at Semr, now dispersed into luminescent droplets. Aruendiel himself was hunched over a table by the fire, two books open before him while he wrote rapidly on a sheaf of papers.

"You said you had a job for me?" Nora inquired. She had an instant's fear that he might have forgotten.

Aruendiel raised his pale eyes for a moment as he dipped his brush into the inkwell. "Over there," he said, nodding to the other table.

She followed his gesture and saw, among more unshelved books and scrolls, a sizable heap of broken crockery. It looked as though someone had smashed an entire set of dishes.

Nora seated herself at the table and began to pick through the fragments. A few pieces were as big as her palm, but most of the shards were tiny. She tried and failed to picture the original form of the thing she was trying to reconstruct. The broad curves of the larger fragments and the few lines of red and yellow glaze that decorated them offered no obvious clues.

"What is this?" she asked after a few minutes.

"Can you not tell?" His tone did not invite further questions.

By sheer chance Nora found two pieces that fit together. Holding them next to each other—combined, they were no larger than a quarter—she saw they bore some sort of raised pattern. She began hunting through the fragments for similar pieces. There were many, although none of them seemed to fit the ones she already had. The jigsaw puzzle from hell, she thought. Not even a picture to go by. The last time she worked on a jigsaw puzzle had been at the age of twelve, during a rainy vacation at the shore. It was a view of St. Giorgio Maggiore; she and her brother had never finished it, defeated by the luminous, identical waves of the Venetian lagoon. In the intervening years she had not once had the urge to do another.

Yet now, sorting through the broken crockery, she felt a sense of slow recognition. Her fingers had touched this clay before. It even seemed to her that she had some sort of claim on it. Is this something I made? Nora asked herself. No, it was too old for that, it had spent a long time in the form that it was in. But this clay knew her and seemed pleased to feel her touch again.

Two fragments grew together in her hand, and then without even thinking about it, she laid her fingers on a third piece that fit with them, melding seamlessly into place. She let this odd, intuitive intimacy with the clay guide her hands—the trick was not to concentrate too much—and gradually, as she added fragment after fragment, a form began to emerge from the broken pile.

An animal with a rather human, playful expression, and a mass of curls, like a great wig. "I should have known it was you," she said, fitting part of a round ear into place. Her old friend the lion from the palace in Semr.

Footsteps sounded overhead. Nora looked up with a start as Aruendiel came down the spiral staircase. She had been too absorbed in her work to hear him go upstairs.

"You recognize that now, of course?" he said.

"It's the statuette that Ilissa broke."

"No, the statuette that you broke. Or, rather, that threw itself off the mantelpiece at your request."

Nora frowned, remembering the tawny blur of movement and a secret thrill of pleasure that had seemed out of place in the middle of her fear. "Did I really do that?"

"No one else did."

"But I certainly didn't intend to. How could I have done it?"

"The same way that you are mending it now," he said, with the twitch of an eyebrow. "You reached an understanding with the elements from which it is made, and they responded to your will. Of course, what you willed them to do was not very powerful or sophisticated magic," he added, "but you have achieved the first, most basic step in working true magic, upon which everything else is built."

Nora wanted to protest, feeling that inspiring a clay figure to animate itself and then to dash itself to pieces was magic of quite a sophisticated order, but he had not answered the question to her satisfaction. "Nothing like that ever happened to me before. Why me, now?"

"That, I cannot answer," Aruendiel said, a shade of displeasure passing over his angular face. "You remarked at the time that you had been working in the garden. I wondered whether you had awakened some natural sympathy in the clay. If digging could produce a capacity for magic, though, there would be many more magicians and fewer farmers.

"Perhaps the Faitoren spells to which you were subjected made you more sensitive to the currents of natural magic. I know of one case in which a man developed an aptitude for magic after undergoing a powerful enchantment. Or it may be that this world remains strange to your senses in some deep way, and therefore you perceive things differently from those born here."

It would be nice to think that being an alien here brought with it an unusual talent—some compensation for feeling like an idiot so much of the time. Privately she was not quite sure that the explanation was so easy. "How do magicians—people who want to become magicians—how do they discover that they can do magic?"

"Usually boys are sent off to school or to apprentice with a magician, and some of them discover that they can work magic and some discover that they cannot. Those who can work magic become magicians."

"Is that what you did?"

"I went to school, yes. I had teachers."

"And is that where you discovered you could do mag—"

"Once a person acquires some understanding of magic, the more interesting question is—what do you do with that understanding?"

"Well, I'd like to learn more," Nora said quickly. "Become a magician."

"Developing real skill in magic requires a great deal of work," Aruendiel said harshly. "It is not like fitting together a few broken pieces of pottery."

"I understand."

"It is no trivial pastime, to be dropped whenever it becomes dull or discouraging."

"Of course not."

"Years of painstaking, often tedious study are needed, for true proficiency."

"I'm used to that."

"It is sometimes dangerous."

Nora nodded. "I know."

"Knowing about the risks is not the same as experiencing them."

"It seems to me that I've already run into quite a lot of danger in this world by *not* knowing anything about magic."

"Hmm. Even great skill in magic is no substitute for good sense," Aruendiel said. "That is not something that I can teach you."

"But you can teach me to be a magician?"

"I can teach you to work magic, yes. Whether you can learn enough to call yourself a true magician, that is still unknown."

"All right. Well, there's only one way to find out."

Aruendiel gave a cursory nod.

"What happens to the boys who go to school and then discover they can't be magicians?" she asked.

"They find another occupation. Some memorize a few spells and set themselves up as wizards. There is always some demand for basic spell-working in the villages."

"I hate to admit this," Nora confessed, "but I have never quite understood the exact difference between wizards and magicians. Although I gather," she said, seeing Aruendiel's frown, "that it's better to be a magician."

"You are even more ignorant that I expected. Must I define the most elementary terms for you? Very well, let the first lesson commence. Wizardry is the branch of magic that depends upon commanding various magical creatures to do one's bidding. The wizard does not work magic directly, but relies upon the power of spirits or demons—or more commonly, upon spells that bind spirits or demons to perform certain specific tasks. That invisibility spell that you read some time ago, that was a spell addressed to a particular demon, Contemptuous Needle Unsound."

"That's its name?"

"Demon names are difficult to pronounce, at least for humans. Most demons choose a name in Ors that are rough translations of their own names, or that they fancy will be intimidating. They do not always grasp the nuances of the language. At any rate, that invisibility spell is a rather poorly drafted command, addressed to Contemptuous Needle Unsound, to hide the speaker from those who might be following him."

"Why is it poorly drafted?"

"Because it is vague. There are a number of omissions—most important, the invocation does not say how long the invisibility must last. There is no provision to stop the demon from making the wizard visible again whenever he likes, or never. A good spell of this sort will include a very specific list of directions to the magical servant, so that the wizard does not have to rely on a demon's goodwill in interpreting any small ambiguity in the wording.

"You see, this sort of spell is really a compact between a demon and a wizard, one that is invoked each time the spell is recited. Which is why it would not work for you."

"You said it was because I was a woman," Nora said, unable to keep the resentment out of her voice.

"Yes, because a demon will not consider itself bound to honor the agreement if the spell is spoken by a woman."

"Why not? Demons consider women inferior?"

"They consider all humans inferior," he said coldly. "The restriction on women originates with the language of the spell's underlying contract, which is almost always defined as a pact between Fiend and Man.

"Wizards, then," he went on, "practice magic only through indirect agency. It is possible for a man with no magical ability at all to become a wizard, simply by acquiring a book of spells."

"So wizardry is really rote learning," Nora said. "Whereas magicians are more creative, more powerful——?"

"Wizards can be quite powerful," Aruendiel corrected her. "Wizardry should not be underestimated—it was the magic that I learned when I was young, the only accepted form of magic at the time, and we used it to great effect. Wizardry is still a good entry point into the study of magic. But natural magic, real magic, is more powerful still, and you do not have to rely on a demon to wield it. I don't see you writing any of this down," he added. "You must have an excellent memory."

"Oh," Nora said, looking around quickly, "do you have a notebook that I could use, and something to write with?"

"A notebook? Paper is too dear for a pupil. There are some wax tablets on the table. You should take down each day's lesson; when you have learned it, melt the tablet clean and use it again."

"All right," Nora said, when she had located a stylus and made a few notes, "so real magic—or natural magic, you called it—is what mended the bowl?"

"Correct." Aruendiel had crossed the room to hunt along the shelves. He brought two volumes back to the table and leafed through them. "Here, this is one of the classic spells for repairing broken pottery, from Hom Marn the Silent. And this is another, very different approach to the same problem, from an anonymous Vinovian wizard. Once you have learned them both by heart, you will identify for me the essential elements of these spells and explain why each wizard organized his spell as he did."

The Hom Marn spell took up most of two pages of an oversize book. The Vinovian spell was shorter, but written in a crabbed hand that Nora could barely decipher. "But this is wizardry, isn't it?" she said, disappointed. "Why do I have to memorize these spells, especially since they probably won't even work for me?"

"They will not," agreed Aruendiel. "But you must still learn these spells, their parts, how they are structured, until they are second nature to you."

"I already know how to mend broken pottery."

"Could you mend a pot that has been ground into dust? Or rebuild a pot from a single fragment? Or mend a pot that you have never seen, whose pieces are scattered to the far corners of the earth?"

"No," said Nora, trying to estimate how often a magician might have to take on the more complicated sort of pot-mending project. "But is it really neces—"

"You must learn how spells are constructed, and this is how to begin. Once you have a basic understanding of the forms, we will discuss how to cast these spells with true magic." Turning back to the other table, Aruendiel sat down and picked up his brush again. "The sooner you begin, the more rapid your progress."

Nora began to read through the Hom Marn spell, fighting down a feeling of faint unease. What had she gotten herself into? But then Aruendiel had warned her of the obstacles ahead. This is a test, she thought. He's trying to scare me to see how serious I am. The reflection steeled her as she tried to understand the purpose behind each of the nine variant openings to Hom Marn's spell.

PART

# THREE

# Chapter 26

The days settled into a new pattern. Nora awoke each morning in the chilly, predawn gloom and spent some time convincing herself to get out of bed. Then she dressed quickly, her arms pebbled with gooseflesh: linen shift, a layer of knitted woolens, one of her new winter dresses, long stockings, a pair of Mrs. Toristel's old boots. And still the cold gnawed at her until she had been up on her feet for a time—feeding the animals, bringing in firewood, hauling water.

The entire morning was taken up with chores. In addition to the usual cleaning, Mrs. Toristel had enlisted her to organize the attic storerooms, a treasury of dented armor, rusty weapons, faded tapestries, and chests of mildewed clothes. The thought had crossed Nora's mind that perhaps Mrs. Toristel had assigned her this task to try to minimize the time spent in the magician's tower. The housekeeper seemed deaf or distracted whenever Nora mentioned her new studies, and after a while Nora stopped making any reference to them.

Around noon each day Nora climbed the stairs to Aruendiel's study with the same tickle of apprehension that she'd felt before certain graduate seminars. Sometimes she would arrive to find that he was absent, or she would hear his footsteps in one of the upper rooms; sometimes he was so buried in his books that he paid no attention as she took her seat at the other table. Then the afternoon would pass quietly, with Nora working slowly through the spells that he had set for her to learn or reading over the notes she had made on a growing pile of wax tablets. Other days, glancing up as soon as she came in, he would challenge her to recite a spell and then to explain how it was put together and exactly when one might use it; why the wizard who wrote it had chosen this particular form; why he had included various commands and contingencies; what he had left out, and why; and—with a lift of the eyebrow—what he could have done better.

She could usually tell when she had made a mistake by the immediate spark of irritation in Aruendiel's face. When she finished, there would be some pointed questions—had she not noticed the obvious such-and-such? Then he would deliver a detailed, waspish accounting of everything she had missed or misunderstood. She had found, though, that the harshest sarcasm came at the beginning of his critiques. Once he had progressed into a discussion of the underlying magic, explaining general rules and the interesting exceptions, citing past authorities and the history of certain famous spells, his tone would mellow, his asperity would shift toward enthusiasm, and he would be more or less civil until her next blunder.

Sometimes, halfway through the afternoon, Aruendiel would tell her to get her cloak and they would set off for the forest across the river. The first time, Nora made the error of asking a question about a spell she had been studying. "We are not here to converse," he said severely, striding ahead. What they had come for, he did not say, but it had something to do with the half-heard murmur, the almost-tangible presence that she could sense intermittently in the woods. She was not so sure that they had not come to converse. The shadows of the bare trees lay long and black on the earth as the sun sank westward, and sometimes it seemed as though nothing moved there except for her and the magician. Yet the forest seemed flagrantly, almost dangerously alive. At the end of these walks, no matter how tired her legs were from climbing hills, Nora often found herself ablaze with nervous energy, as though she had been at a long and stimulating party.

Some days—not frequently enough, in Nora's view—Aruendiel would set her to work an actual spell. Gradually, she learned how to mend a broken plate without touching it, without looking at it, and then without being in the same room with it; and then how to reconstitute two separate smashed dishes whose pieces lay jumbled together in the kitchen while she stood in the tower. There was a trick to it, she found: You had to work through the spell in your mind, while keeping the same kind of connection to the clay fragments that she had first felt while manipulating them with her fingers. How this insight would apply to other kinds of spells, she could see only dimly, but even Aruendiel seemed grudgingly impressed by the progress she had made in crockery repair.

She did not know why he was taking such pains with her. Boredom or loneliness, perhaps. More likely, she thought, he could not resist anything to do with magic, even if it involved spending hours teaching the rudiments to a rank beginner.

Following her afternoon lessons, she made dinner from whatever Mrs. Toristel had left for her to cook. Then there was a little time for more study: translating a few pages of *Pride and Prejudice* into Ors. That was another assignment from the magician. Nora had been rather proud of keeping her notes in Ors instead of English, but when Aruendiel saw them, he was appalled at her handwriting and said that her spelling was even worse. After some debate about the best way to improve both—Aruendiel's preferred solution was to have her copy out a hundred lines of the *Nagaron Voy* every day—Nora suggested that she would translate passages from *Pride and Prejudice*, and Aruendiel would correct them. To her surprise, he agreed. He was curious about the book that had been used to imprison Bouragonr, he said.

At first, it seemed that the famous first sentence would be a fatal stumbling block. After reading Nora's translation, Aruendiel was puzzled, a little contemptuous. He took issue with the basic premise. "Why would possession of a large fortune mean that an unmarried man needs a wife?"

Nora launched into the freshman English explanation of irony. There was a certain satisfaction in being the teacher again.

"Yes, yes, I do not need tutoring in the basics of rhetoric," Aruendiel said impatiently. "But no young girl of good birth would marry a man only because he is rich."

"Are you joking?" Nora said. "When I was in Semr, that was all the young women talked about, marrying a wealthy man."

"Did they?" A flash of amusement passed across his rough face. "But money is only part of it. If not, they might as well marry a tradesman."

"A tradesman? Oh, I see what you're saying. To be eligible, he'd have to be part of your crowd, an aristocrat."

"My crowd? We cannot all be royalty, Mistress Nora. No, it is not just a matter of birth. A suitable bridegroom would have land, family alliances, some skill in battle—"

"Hmm. I suppose the best translation would be 'A single gentleman in possession of a great estate must be in want of a wife.' Does that make more sense?"

"That is better. Write it down. No, that is not how one spells 'estate,' not when it follows the adjective."

The rest of the first chapter went better. Something about Mr. Bennet's drily embittered sense of humor appealed to Aruendiel. He read her translations with more interest than she would have expected. In some ways he was more familiar with Austen's stratified, preindustrial world than Nora was, and he was also particularly adept at helping her find Ors equivalents for the formal, faintly antique diction of the novel.

They usually went over her translations at night in the great hall, where, with the coming of the cold weather, wooden panels had been set up around the huge fireplace to block the drafts. Aruendiel took a more detached tone in correcting Nora's translations than he did in critiquing her magical work, expressing only a sarcastic wonderment at her grammatical and orthographical mistakes. Afterward, in the reddish firelight, over the remnants of dinner, he was more approachable than he had been during the day, more willing to entertain Nora's questions about things other than magic, or sometimes to question her.

"The society, the countryside, in your book are different from what I remember of your world," he objected once, after they had penetrated several chapters into the novel. "Is this the sort of life that you led there?"

Nora explained that the novel was more than two hundred years old. A present-day Elizabeth Bennet would be in college at age twenty, probably thinking more about the job market than marriage. "Tell me more about your travels in my world," she said after a pause. "Why is it that this world is full of magicians, but there are none in mine?" Not so long ago, Nora thought, she would have asked the question as a joke. Now she wanted to know.

"Some of the stones and mountains in your world had known magicians before me. But no, I never found another active magician there. A pity, for there were some rare opportunities to practice magic. There was great power in those cities—Chigago, and then the city across the ocean whose name sounds like 'Dead Fish.' "

"London" was the closest English synonym. "What do you mean, there was great power in those cities?"

"I mean that the cities themselves generated power, from the crowds, from the action of the iron machinery in those enormous workshops. It was a new kind of magic. I spent a year working there, in a peasant's job, in order to study it. Quite powerful, but unpredictable."

"What sort of peasant's job?"

He would not say, but from another comment he made later, Nora deduced that he had been shoveling coal. He had traveled to London via ship, she gathered, to reach the gateway to his world that would allow him to go home. But in London he discovered that a great war was raging in precisely the area where he wished to go.

World War II, Nora hazarded. "What did you do?"

"I am a magician," he said, with a sliver of a smile. "And I did not need any particularly complex protection spells—they only had to be very strong, given the kind of artillery that I had to make my way through." His face darkened. "I had never seen anything like the kind of warfare you practice in your world. Thousands upon thousands of men being torn to pieces by bits of flying iron. It was butchery."

Nora agreed, but she felt obliged to observe: "Carving people up with swords isn't so wonderful, either."

Aruendiel remarked that it was more honorable to meet an enemy face-to-face in fair combat than to blow holes in him from two *polists* away. "And more enjoyable, too. But I admit that I myself have lost much of my taste for making war since—" He broke off, his eyes fixed on the fire.

"Since you were injured?" Nora asked delicately.

"Yes, since I was injured. And I am older than I was. War is for the young men." Offhandedly, still looking into the flames, he added: "We must start you on fire magic soon."

"Good, that sounds more exciting than mending pots," Nora said rashly.

Aruendiel pointed out, with some severity, that she still had more work to do in that area. "You have not learned to induce a ceramic vessel to change its form, or to break a dish so that only you can mend it, or—"

"All right, yes, I saw there's a whole treatise by Setisonior the Left-handed on that. Aruendiel, will this magic I'm learning help me defend myself if I meet Ilissa again?"

He turned his head to look at her. "Not unless she decides to attack you by breaking all the dishes."

"When will I learn something that will actually let me defend myself?"

"I can teach you a basic shielding spell, once you have some expertise with fire magic. It would hold Ilissa off for a few minutes. To truly protect yourself, though, you cannot let Ilissa know your heart better than you yourself do. It's the only sure way. I've told you that before."

In a milder tone, he added: "There is no reason to think that you will encounter her again. She is confined to her lands, and before the next king is fool enough to let her out, you will likely have returned to your world already."

"Yes," Nora said, unsatisfied, twisting the ring on her finger. "But sometimes I can't help worrying."

"Then you have learned some wisdom, I see," he said with severe approval.

Later that night, as she lay in bed, her feet curled against a warm brick, she listened to Aruendiel's tread up the stairs and down the corridor, one long step and then a shorter one, and she thought about what he had said. A daunting task, to take careful inventory of one's own heart. Which, of all the secrets that were hidden there, would be most useful to Ilissa?

There was her low-grade obsession with Aruendiel. Nora had given up calling it a crush; it had lost some of its urgency, and it seemed indecorous now that he was officially her teacher. (Even across the worlds, she felt the invisible contraints of the sexual harassment policy of the Graduate College of Arts and Sciences.) Perhaps that was why her fixation had moderated: She had wanted Aruendiel's time and attention, and now she had it, in some measure—in the lessons, in their oddly companionable evening talks. But she still felt something that might be termed an unhealthy interest. It was not really romantic in nature, she told herself sternly. More of a morbid curiosity. There were too many questions that she had not dared to ask or that he had refused to answer. His murdered wife was only one of them.

And she was ever mindful of his lank, battered, precariously balanced body. His face was not always so hideous, when he took the trouble to smile. Once or twice, when they leaned over a book together, she was troubled to think that she might feel the accidental warmth of his shoulder against hers, or even that his hand might suddenly take hold of her own.

Nothing like that ever happened, fortunately.

Ilissa would make hay with all of these repressed and tangled wishes. (Nora imagined her delighted laugh.) "The problem," Nora reflected clinically, "is that I'm lonely and horny and starved for companionship—not to mention that my sex life has probably been permanently scarred because I was married to Grendel's uglier brother—so naturally I feel hot and bothered when I get close to an eligible man, any man, no matter what he looks like."

It had been almost six months since she had fled from Ilissa's palace. Had things turned out differently, she would be a new mother by now. (Or dead, according to Aruendiel.) The happy mother of a baby pterodactyl. Would she still have loved it, her own flesh and blood made monstrous?

Of course she would have, under Ilissa's smiling, adamantine enchantments—but in truth, the enchantment might not have been necessary, because whatever the child looked like, it would have at least earned her pity by being tiny and helpless, and by then there would have been nothing else for her to love.

It was all so wrong. So unfair. Although she could not be sure of the real object of her outrage: Ilissa or Raclin or her own gullibility. She'd been an easy mark, so greedy for love that she had given the best of her own heart without stopping to consider what she received in exchange. Just as with Adam. If she could not learn to be more discerning, the only safe course was to avoid love altogether. Leave me, O Love, which reachest but to dust.

How old did you have to be before you learned the difference between the simulacrum of love and the reality? Listening to an owl calling outside, she tried to sleep.

The lessons in fire magic began a week later. Aruendiel refused to let Nora try any fire spells near his books; she had to practice with a pile of wood shavings in the great hall, with a bucket of water nearby. A wise precaution, Nora had to admit, after charring a hole in her apron.

Aruendiel was not amused. "It is the kindling that is meant to burn, not you."

"Either nothing happens"—which was most of the time—"or pop, suddenly I'm on fire."

"You must be firm with it. Fire wants to please, which is one of the things that makes it so useful, but sometimes its enthusiasm becomes dangerous. It will come straight to you if you do not direct it elsewhere. Keep it in check."

Nora looked over at the fireplace, at the fire she had built there in the ordinary way, stacking the logs and then applying a hot coal from the kitchen. Somehow she was supposed to draw on its power to set the shavings alight. "This fire doesn't look very enthusiastic. Maybe I should start again."

"The wood is damp," Aruendiel said disapprovingly. "But that should not affect the spell."

She kept trying. Aruendiel, obviously bored, returned to the tower, after putting a spell on the water in the bucket so that it would dowse the flames if Nora caught fire again. "If you do not wish to be drenched, you had best master this spell," he warned. By the end of the day, Nora had singed the end of her braid, causing the water in the bucket to slosh about alarmingly before she managed to extinguish the spark. The smell of burnt hair lingered.

Coming into the hall from the kitchen, Mrs. Toristel paused to sniff, then looked hard at the almost-untouched pile of shavings. "You haven't started the fire yet," she observed.

"No, not yet."

"You've been at it all afternoon. I would think it frustrating to keep trying, with no luck."

"Yes, but I'm close, I can feel it. I can feel the fire, sometimes. It's an amazing feeling."

"There's nothing remarkable about feeling the fire, if you're close enough to it."

"I feel it inside." Nora smiled, elated enough to disregard her self-imposed rule about not talking to Mrs. Toristel about her magic studies. "I feel flashes of something that's—it's not exactly happy—it's excited, very excited, and hopeful. Hungry. I know it's there. Now I just have to make it do what I want."

Mrs. Toristel looked unimpressed. "You don't have to be a magician to make a fire. How long before you learn to do the kinds of things that he can do?"

"I don't know. Someday."

"Someday. Well, if you have the patience for it. And if he has the patience. Why is he trying to teach you this, do you know?"

Nora had to say again that she did not know. "I assume it interests him, somehow."

"He takes these fancies, sometimes, about teaching people what he thinks they should know. He tried to have me read one of those great long poems once, when he taught me my letters. I didn't know half the words. I had to tell him, I wasn't cut out to be educated." Mrs. Toristel frowned, her features growing pinched. "Well, maybe it will be a help to him to have someone around who knows a little magic," she added grudgingly. "At least you can mend the broken plates now, that's useful. I never liked to ask him before."

Once Nora could reliably set the shavings, and not herself, on fire, the next lesson involved precision: lighting every other candle in a twelve-branched bronze candelabra. It was surprisingly hard, after she had gotten the hang of lighting a fire magically, to learn to hold back and *not* light some of the candles. The fire that she wielded seemed all too willing, and the magic did not seem to understand that some of the candles should remain unlit. Every time she wound up with the whole candelabra enthusiastically blazing.

She knew exactly what Aruendiel would say when he came down to check on her progress: that skillful magic was as much about control as about power, and would she have the grace to remember that candles are expensive? When Aruendiel finally appeared, she almost told him to spare his breath.

Then she saw his face. Hollowed out with rage, his eyes cold and wild.

## *Chapter 27*

What's wrong?" Nora stood up. Her eyes went to the scroll Aruendiel held.

He took a deep breath. "I have just heard from Dorneng Hul. Concerning Hirizjahkinis."

"Dorneng Hul?" It took Nora a half second to place the name: the magician from Semr who'd gone north with Aruendiel, trailing Ilissa back to her domain. She had the vague impression that he was up there still, working for one of Aruendiel's friends, keeping a watchful eye on Ilissa. "What—"

Aruendiel brandished the scroll as though it were a weapon. "He writes that it has been three days and two nights since Hirizjahkinis and Hirgus Ext drove into Ilissa's kingdom, and that he is growing concerned, since he understood that they meant to spend only one night there. Spend the night? Paying a call upon the Faitoren? Has Hirizjahkinis gone mad?"

"Jesus," Nora said, and Aruendiel fixed her with a stare.

"Did she say anything about this in Semr?" he demanded. "Any hint that she was considering such a thing?"

"No, not at all. She said—she told me she didn't even think about Ilissa that much—that Ilissa wasn't worth bothering about."

Aruendiel swore a few hot syllables. "She will know differently by now.

Three days! And Dorneng only now thinks to inform me. What possessed her? Why did she say nothing to me?"

"Who is Hirgus Ext?" Nora asked.

"That's another mystery. He is a wizard of no great skill from Mirne Klep. As tedious as his tongue is long. I have no idea why Hirizjahkinis would spend an hour in his company—let alone travel to Ilissa's domain with him. Yet Dorneng says they arrived together at Luklren's castle and went on together." Aruendiel glanced suddenly at Nora as though he had just been reminded of something. "I do not think—"

"No, nothing like that. He doesn't sound like her type," Nora said at once. "Are you sure they're actually in Ilissa's kingdom? Dorneng isn't mistaken?"

Aruendiel shook his head. "There is no reason to doubt him. I can find a few traces of Hirizjahkinis's magic northeast of here, near the Faitoren. They are at least a day old, nothing more recent. She has my token. But she has not used it to call for help."

"That's a good thing, isn't it?" Nora saw, as soon as the words were out of her mouth, how stupid her question was. "Unless, of course, it means she can't use it," she finished lamely. "Because the Faitoren have enchanted her."

"Or worse." Aruendiel turned away, back to the tower. "I will leave shortly to find Hirizjahkinis. Tell Mrs. Toristel to pack a bag for me."

Take me with you, Nora was about to say, but at the same time she remembered Ilissa smiling at her in Semr, the kind of silken smile that could bind your soul in an instant and never let you go. Nora flushed and stopped in her tracks as Aruendiel went through the wall.

"At nightfall, at this time of year? In this rain, he's leaving?" Mrs. Toristel put down the onion she was holding and wiped her hands on her apron with a kind of studied vehemence. Nora had finally located her in one of the storerooms. "Dear gods, and where is he going?"

Nora began to explain again about Hirizjahkinis having fallen into the hands of the Faitoren.

"Well, she was fool enough to put herself in danger, wasn't she?" Mrs. Toristel demanded. "And now *he* has to get her out of it?"

"Yes, of course!" The words came charging out louder than Nora had anticipated. She found that it was a relief to shout, although Mrs. Toristel only looked sour. "Of course he has to. Look what the Faitoren did to me. And they'll treat her worse."

Nora had had time, as she searched for Mrs. Toristel, to consider exactly how Ilissa might deal with a captive and defenseless Hirizjahkinis. "Hirizjahkinis is their enemy, she fought them before. They'll torture her, humiliate her. Raclin will—" Nora spread her hands frantically, helplessly.

"Will do what?" Mrs. Toristel asked.

"If she's lucky, he'll just eat her," Nora said. She went flying out of the room, headed for the tower, propelled by an incoherent conviction that somehow, with the right argument, with the right amount of insistence, she could persuade Aruendiel to take her with him.

Nora was disconcerted to find him sitting quietly at his usual table, a piece of paper in front of him. "Aruendiel, before you go—"

"I'm not going." His voice was sharp with frost. "Not yet."

She stared at him blankly. "Not going!"

"There is another letter," he said venomously. "From Luklren. Ilissa holds them hostage. She is trying to tie my hands."

"Oh." Nora waited, but there was no other explanation forthcoming. "May I see it?"

The parchment was covered with large, rather childish brushstrokes. She skipped over the long greeting, studded with Lord Luklren's various titles and Aruendiel's, and read:

*The Faitoren queen sent an emissary today to inform me that she has taken prisoner the two magic-workers who entered her kingdom three days ago. I said that had nothing to do with me. The emissary said that his queen understood that perfectly and then asked that I pass this message along to you.*

*For the lives and safe return of the wizard Hirgus Ext and the witch Herezjawkenus*—judging from the smeared ink, Luklren had made several attempts at the name—*the Faitoren queen wants you to dissolve the imprisonment spells around the Faitoren kingdom. She asks that you then swear to abandon the practice of magic and that you surrender to the Faitoren. She also wants ten thousand additional* silmas *of land and two thousand head of cattle.*

*As immediate proof of your good faith, she asks that you return her son's wife, the princess Nora, by dawn tomorrow. If not, one of the captives will be killed. If you come near or attempt to enter the Faitoren domain before the dissolution of the imprisonment spell and your surrender, both of the captives will be killed.*

Lord Luklren evidently felt himself ill-used by all sides. His handwriting grew still larger and more agitated as she read further. *I told you the last time I saw you not to stir up trouble with the Faitoren. If that imprisonment spell goes, they'll steal everything on my lands that they can carry away. What were those two magic-workers up to? I warned them not to go in. I've already told the Faitoren that I'm neutral in this dispute, and I do not intend to be a party to any hostilities. . . .*

Her eyes raced through the remaining lines of the letter; then she handed it back to Aruendiel. "He thinks you should send me back," she said.

"Yes. I must apologize for his language there. He has an imperfect grasp of the situation." Aruendiel stood up abruptly, as though he were tensed for some great exertion, but he only turned and began to pace fitfully in front of the fire.

"*Are* you going to send me back?" Nora asked.

"No." He made it sound like a reprimand.

With a sense that she was stepping over a precipice, Nora said: "But otherwise Hirizjahkinis might—"

"I said no," Aruendiel sliced through her words. "I do not intend to present Ilissa with any proof of my good faith. She knows exactly whom she is dealing with."

"It's outrageous, what she demands." Briefly Nora wondered how large a *silma* of land was, but filed the question away for later. "The only good thing—we know that Hirizjahkinis and Hirgus Ext are still alive."

"No, I don't think we do." He spoke with more weariness than before. "Ilissa is not negotiating in earnest, I fear. Her demands are too outsized. And she offers no evidence that her prisoners still live.

"That makes my course more difficult to plot just now. If they are alive, I must proceed more cautiously. If they are dead—if Hirizjahkinis is dead—I will have a free hand to attack." Arundiel gave a quick, hard smile, and Nora had the icy thought that perhaps he almost welcomed the idea of Hirizjahkinis's death, if it meant that he had an unshakable reason to destroy Ilissa.

"You sent a wind for me," Nora said. "It carried me away, right in front of Ilissa, and she couldn't do anything to stop it."

Aruendiel was already shaking his head. "It was almost the first thing I tried, this time. Ilissa is better prepared now. My winds cannot cross into her domain."

"Well, what then? Why not—" Nora balled her fists, thinking in fury of how little she still knew of magic. "Why not just attack Ilissa herself? Make her drop dead? Raclin, too."

"This calls for more subtlety. I will tell Ilissa that I must have proof that Hirizjahkinis and Hirgus are alive. And in the meantime, I will start to dissolve the spells that hold the Faitoren captive."

"Let Ilissa go free?"

"Those spells are walls that keep the Faitoren in—but they also bar or blunt many other kinds of magic. For example, a spell to make Ilissa drop dead." A gleam of anticipation in the pale eyes. "Or to extract a captive. Ilissa has her own defenses, of course. I must think of how best to take them apart."

He threw himself down at the table and began to write rapidly on a sheet of parchment. Nora, after hovering for a moment, went downstairs to tell Mrs. Toristel that Aruendiel would not be leaving at present. When she returned, Aruendiel sent her down again to ask Mr. Toristel to bring out the chains from the dungeon and all the nails he could gather. "And the spikes from the old mercy bed."

Mr. Toristel's arthritis had been bad lately. Nora had to help carry up the biggest chains, the links as thick as her index finger. It took four trips to get it all moved into the courtyard. The spikes from the mercy bed were heavily rusted, as though they had not been cleaned after their last use.

In the kitchen, Mrs. Toristel was assembling a tray of bread and mutton for the magician. "I suppose he'll be up all night. Make him eat something, will you?" Nora said she would, although she herself felt no desire for food. Mrs. Toristel sawed at the meat with irritating slowness.

"When I was a little girl in Pelagnia, there were elves in the forest that had black skin," the housekeeper said suddenly. "My granny told me about them. They liked to steal little children and eat their tongues. You had to be quiet and not speak, going through the forest, so they wouldn't know you were there."

Nora saw where this was headed. "Hirizjahkinis isn't a black elf."

"No, but I always think of them when I see her." Mrs. Toristel was silent for a moment, tearing the bread. "Those Faitoren, they put spells on *you* to make you look different—prettier." She gave a sideways glance at Nora, gauging her reaction. "Will they do the same to that Hirizjahkinis? Make her skin white, maybe?"

Astounded, Nora opened her mouth to retort—*she looks fine the way she is*—and then closed it. If you looked past all the ways in which Mrs. Toristel's inquiry was depressingly narrow-minded and offensive, there was a good question buried in it. What were Hirizjahkinis's secret wishes, and how would Ilissa twist them to torture her? Nora could not say. She was fairly sure, though, that they did not include being white.

"No, Mrs. Toristel," she said finally. "I don't think so."

Nora took the tray upstairs. Both tables in the library were now piled with a jumble of books, most of them lying open, and Aruendiel's eyes were locked to the page of the folio in front of him.

"What has taken you so long?" he demanded, not looking up. "The second volume of Vros—find it, will you? I need the section on inanimate-to-animate transformations. And then Seethros on reversals. And my notebooks on Faitoren illusionwork."

She had only begun to master Aruendiel's library cataloging system— which grouped books by subject, by date, and also by how skilled a magic-worker Aruendiel judged the author to have been—but she found the books as quickly as she could. By then he had a new list of volumes to be fetched.

"Do you have a plan yet?" she asked him, when books covered the floor around his chair.

"Yes. Do you not see it? Are you paying no attention?" But he was too much occupied to direct any more abuse at Nora's lapse. He jerked up from his chair after a few minutes and went upstairs to his workroom without a word. Nora, bent over a treatise by Trankias Mins on augmenting spells over distance, felt her stomach clench and roll and was thankful that she had not touched the mutton that Mrs. Toristel had prepared. Only rarely since she started practicing magic herself had Nora felt queasy in the presence of magic; whatever Aruendiel was doing up there, it was stronger magic than she had experienced before.

Sooner than she expected, Aruendiel clattered down the stairs, pausing in the library only long enough to tell Nora to follow him down to the courtyard. Outside, the day's heavy rain had eased to a freezing drizzle. Nora shivered and hugged her elbows, but Aruendiel seemed not to notice the cold. A single torch burned in a niche, showing a rumpled mass on the ground, where Mr. Toristel had bundled the chains and nails under an oiled tarpaulin to keep them dry. Aruendiel snatched away the cover.

"I need more," he said after a moment's inspection.

"That's all we could find," Nora said.

"It's not enough. Iron—that's what I want. Anything made of iron or steel."

"The old armor in the attic?" She had been sorting it all week; Mrs. Toristel was after her to polish it.

Aruendiel made an impatient gesture, as though flabbergasted why Nora was dawdling. "Bring it here."

She came back with helmets stacked in her arms like bowls. Now Aruendiel was in the center of the courtyard, looking upward. He held something in his left hand—a fistful of iron nails, Nora saw as she came closer. Methodically, he selected a few at a time to toss upward into the air. They disappeared into the darkness. Nora found herself waiting for the ping of nails falling onto cobblestones, but there was no sound at all. Or was that a faint clanking above?

Something black flapped past Aruendiel's head—a bat, Nora thought, recoiling instinctively. Aruendiel did not move. Not a bat, she decided after getting another glimpse of it. Not exactly.

With mounting excitement, she watched him work until she was sure. When he had finished all the nails, he began to break the smaller chains into separate links—some cleaving spell, she thought—and then he threw each piece of iron into the air.

"You're making iron birds," Nora said. Aruendiel nodded tersely, his eyes on the air. "That's how you're going to attack the Faitoren," she said.

"It's how I will break down the walls of the Faitoren kingdom," he corrected. "All the spells that Ilissa has wrapped around her lands to keep me out."

Nora clapped her hands softly. "Your birds will fly there—and iron is poisonous to the Faitoren—"

"And each one carries a reversal spell that can take apart the Faitoren magic. Then I can send a wind—or some other emissary." Suddenly the largest chain, still lying at Aruendiel's feet, uncoiled itself with a creak and streaked toward the gate, looking less chainlike and more serpentlike with every instant. The other big chain, studded with manacles, gathered itself, then rose on four legs and hurled itself out of the courtyard, following the serpent. "The wolf is for Raclin, the snake is for Ilissa," Aruendiel added. "Although it does not matter if they switch."

"Will they be there by dawn?" Nora asked. She had not checked the water clock in the kitchen for some time, but the night was advancing. The Toristels had retired some time ago.

"Oh, yes. They will attack two hours before dawn, all of them together. The timing is very delicate." He hefted a broken link in his hand, as though weighing it, and then threw it into the air. "The Faitoren defenses must come down at once, before Ilissa realizes what is happening, and then I will have to pull Hirizjahkinis out immediately—"

"And Hirgus Ext."

"I will save Hirgus if I can. At any rate, the hostages will have to come out quickly—"

"Before Ilissa can kill them," Nora finished, her momentary elation draining away.

"If they are even alive now," Aruendiel said. "Give me those helmets, and bring me more iron."

Nora brought down the rest of the old weapons from the attic—Aruendiel reserved only a broken sword, he did not say why—and then went hunting cautiously in the kitchen and storerooms for ironware. She had a strong feeling that Mrs. Toristel would not be pleased to see her best kitchen implements given wings and sent flying away, and was grateful to find an iron cauldron with the bottom rusted out nestling in a stack of old barrel hoops.

Sometime after midnight Aruendiel let the last of the iron creatures flap away into the night. "There is no use in sending any more," he said. "They will not arrive in time."

Nora watched the departing bird. It looked small and clumsy as it clambered upward into the cloudy air. "Do we have a Plan B?"

"I beg your pardon?"

"A second plan, in case this one fails."

Aruendiel shrugged. "Then I will attack again. In person this time."

Nora could not keep herself from saying: "You said once it would be suicidal to take on Ilissa in her own territory."

"Did I?"

Without any more words, they went inside. The fire that Nora had lit in the great hall that afternoon had burned out, and the room was black and almost as chilly as the courtyard. Aruendiel told her that she must go to bed. When she protested, he said seriously: "It is important to sleep before battle. You don't know when you might next have the chance to sleep, in a war."

Nora had not thought of what they were doing as war, exactly, but then reflected: What else would it be? "I don't want to sleep through the attack," she said.

"I will rouse you beforehand," he said, frowning, and she decided it would be better to believe him.

Nora went upstairs and stretched out on top of her bed without changing out of her dress. About a quarter of the night left before the sun rose, Aruendiel had said. Not so long ago she had lain here sleeplessly, worrying about Ilissa, and yet now that moment in the past seemed to be one of almost infinite security and comfort. She pictured the great snake and the wolf racing to the northeast, under the cloud of birds that Aruendiel had made, and wondered how much farther they had to travel. The creatures might be made of metal, but they didn't move like machinery. But not exactly like living animals, either. She watched them reach the top of a ridge and plunge down the other side, starlight gleaming dully on their sleek backs—

Nora's eyes popped open. She sat up and looked toward the window, which was noticeably brighter, the panes catching a reddish glow. Dawn, she thought.

Damnit. Aruendiel let me sleep through the whole thing.

She ran downstairs as fast as she could, a hand against the wall to keep from stumbling in the dark. The silence in the house was ominous. The assault failed, she thought. He's left already to fight Ilissa. He never woke me up, he never said good-bye.

But as she crossed the great hall, she heard noises in the courtyard. The stamping of horses. Voices. The orange light that came through the windows flickered and danced.

She yanked open the door. Aruendiel was standing with his back to her, arms folded, a few yards away. In front of him was what Nora took to be an enormous bonfire.

Two figures stepped composedly out of the flames. The smaller one she recognized as Hirizjahkinis.

# Chapter 28

"Greetings, Aruendiel!" Hirizjahkinis stepped forward, pulling the Kavareen's hide more tightly around her shoulders, and then held out her hands to Aruendiel.

Aruendiel unfolded his arms and stepped forward. Nora could not see his face, but there was tension in the angle of his shoulders. He ignored Hirizjahkinis's proffered hands and looked hard into her face. Then, with one hand on her shoulder—he seemed to be bearing down hard—he grasped her chin and moved her head so he could stare into each of her ears, and finally her nostrils.

Hirizjahkinis submitted, a half smile on her lips. "It is very good to see you, too!"

"What on earth, Hirizjahkinis?" Aruendiel said finally, taking her by both shoulders. Nora had the distinct impression he would like to shake her. Hirizjahkinis perhaps had the same idea, because she gave a discreet wiggle to set herself free.

"No enchantments?" she asked briskly. "Good. We spent the whole drive picking them off each other, Hirgus and I. Ilissa's palace is no better than the inns in this country—you must be careful what you take away with you. You know Hirgus Ext the Shorn, of course?"

The two men bowed. Hirgus Ext—stout, swathed in furs—began to say something about being a keen admirer of the magician Aruendiel and how pleased he was to renew his acquaintance. Nora could stand it no longer. She pushed past Aruendiel and threw her arms around Hirizjahkinis. It was obviously not the correct greeting—Nora could sense the surprise in Hirizjahkinis's small, straight-backed body—but after an instant Hirizjahkinis returned the embrace warmly. "*Now* I begin to feel welcome," she said to Nora.

"We were so worried," Nora said. "What happened? Are you all right?"

"I am perfectly fine. Hirgus's conflagration carriage is marvelously warm. I felt no cold at all—until we got here." She adjusted the Kavareen's hide again and gave an exaggerated shiver. Nora looked back at the bonfire. Now she could make out the black outlines of a carriage under the fire's brilliance. The flames, she noticed, had an oddly stylized quality, curling with rococo flair. Grinning faces in the fire winked and thrust out long tongues. Harnessed to the coach were a pair of black horses, larger than any horses Nora had ever seen.

"But the Faitoren?" Nora asked. "Are you sure you're all right?"

"Yes, except that Hirgus and I are famished!" She smiled up at Aruendiel, who had turned again to her, relief and irritation visibly struggling in his face. "Faitoren food is not as filling as you think it is when you are eating it."

Aruendiel's face tightened again. "Mistress Nora, let Mrs. Toristel know that we have guests for breakfast," he said brusquely.

Nora found the Toristels already up. They had seen the glow of the coach in the courtyard, and first had thought the house was on fire.

"So she didn't need him to help her after all," Mrs. Toristel said, putting a shawl over her shoulders. "All that worry, for nothing." She sniffed and looked balefully at Nora, as though to reproach her for rousing needless fears. "And what are we supposed to give that Hirizjahkinis for breakfast? She won't eat oatmeal. Oh, no! Last time she was here, she wouldn't touch it."

"Because black elves eat children's tongues, not oatmeal?" Relief made Nora giddy.

"None of your silliness," Mrs. Toristel said, amicably enough. "See if she'll have some of that mutton."

As Nora hurried back through the courtyard, Hirgus Ext was directing Mr. Toristel as he unhitched the black horses from the fire coach. The great hall was empty. Aruendiel and Hirizjahkinis were in the tower, she guessed. She piled logs in the fireplace, then urged them into flame. It took only two tries, although the wood was damp from yesterday's rain.

"Very nice! You are a magician yourself now." Hirizjahkinis came forward from the entrance to the tower, smiling.

"Not exactly," Nora said, pleased and abashed. "But Aruendiel's been teaching me."

"He did not tell me. How do you like him as a teacher? Very strict, is he not? Show me what you have learned." Nora was dying to ask Hirizjahkinis about her escape from the Faitoren, but Hirizjahkinis looked at her with a calm expectancy that brooked no refusal. She watched gravely as Nora ran through her small repertoire of spells, and provided some useful guidance on the vexing candelabra problem. ("Why are you lighting each candle one by one? Try lighting them all at once—only the ones you want to burn—and leave the rest of them out.")

She doesn't really want to talk about the Faitoren, Nora thought suddenly. It seemed to her that, even in the soft light of the candles, Hirizjahkinis's face looked grooved and tired, sadness tucked into the corners of her mouth. Should I say something? Nora wondered. Tell her I know what it's like to be the Faitoren's prisoner, to have Ilissa use your dreams and fears to make you her plaything? And then the kitchen door swung open: Mrs. Toristel with a pair of mutton chops on a plate, catching Nora's eye in a way that meant there was something to be done in the kitchen.

By the time Nora came back, bringing ale and bread and a fierce solicitude for whatever Hirizjahkinis had endured, she found Aruendiel, Hirgus Ext, and Hirizjahkinis already seated. The sound of Hirizjahkinis's laughter greeted her.

"—I think you are disappointed to see us alive, Aruendiel. We have ruined your plans for a war with Ilissa."

Aruendiel did not smile. "I have stayed my attack," he said, brows knotted, "as you asked. But not willingly. The Faitoren have repeatedly taken prisoners and broken treaty terms. They will continue to do so until they are punished for it."

"You are probably right." Hirizjahkinis leaned forward. With her arms stretched before her on the table, she looked like a small, proud lioness. "But you cannot wage war against Ilissa alone. Even you, Aruendiel! Your king in Semr is a little wiser than he was—he will not trust her so easily again—but he has no stomach to take up arms against the Faitoren. Not without good reason." She smiled broadly. "And as you say, there is no reason now. The prisoners have freed themselves."

Hirgus Ext the Shorn gave a rumble of assent. "While I objected very strongly to being deprived of liberty, I can't say that the Faitoren mistreated us. No, they were quite civilized." Aruendiel grunted malevolently, but Hirgus Ext continued to smile with imperturbable bonhomie. He was stout and, as his name indicated, completely bald, but he was evidently a man who elected to grow as much hair as possible on his chin if he could not grow it on his head. Gold and silver threads and a few jewels were woven into the graying strands of his long, pointed beard. He wore one earring shaped like the sun, another like the moon, and his blue velvet robe was embroidered in silver with a text in a language that was foreign to Nora, although it used the Ors alphabet. He was the first person that Nora had met in this world whom she would have identified unhesitatingly as a wizard even before she knew such beings really existed.

Nora put the ale and bread on the table and sat down next to Hirizjahkinis as inconspicuously as possible.

"I fail to understand," Aruendiel said, "exactly why two experienced magic-workers would put themselves in the power of the Faitoren. Why they would abandon all good sense and visit the Faitoren realm in the first place." His eyes rested on Hirizjahkinis.

"There were promises made, guarantees of safe conduct—" Hirgus began.

"And you believed them."

"Oh, no. Give me credit for that much good sense, as you put it, Aruendiel," Hirizjahkinis said with some passion. "I have heard you say it often enough—that the Faitoren cannot be trusted! And that is exactly what I told Hirgus when I met him at the inn in Foluks Port."

Aruendiel raised his eyebrows. He looked genuinely shocked. "What were you doing in Foluks Port?"

"A dreadful place," agreed Hirizjahkinis. "But I was not there by chance. I went there as a favor, let us call it, to your king."

She glanced around the table as though challenging any of the others to turn their attention away, and seemed pleased by what she saw. "You remember that portrait spell you taught me, Aruendiel? I must thank you for it again—it made my time in Semr very profitable. Everyone wanted their pictures to speak! I was hired many, many times. One of the king's ministers—ah, it doesn't matter who!—summoned me to work the spell for him. And then he asked me afterward if I would undertake a different sort of job on behalf of the king."

"Was it Falfn?" Aruendiel asked.

"It was a lord who had some heated words with the portrait of his mother," Hirizjahkinis said. "But that is not important. He told me they had it on good authority that the emperor in Mirne Klep had been exchanging messages with the Faitoren for some months now."

"Only one emissary every three years, they are allowed under the treaty," Aruendiel said.

"Yes, well, we ought to have known that Ilissa would not stop at trying to charm only your Semran king. She wants to get out of her little prison very badly. But I am going ahead of my story.

"In Semr they knew the emperor and Ilissa were in communication, but they did not know exactly what sort of messages were going back and forth. Your king needs better spies in Mirne Klep, Aruendiel. They did know that the wizard Hirgus Ext had left Mirne Klep for a tour of the northern countries in the middle of autumn, an odd time to be heading north.

"The minister asked me to find out what I could about Hirgus's mission."

Hirgus held up a plump hand with an air of deprecating protest. "My dear friends, I hope there is no misunderstanding. I travel for pleasure and research only—and of course my conflagration coach is perfectly adapted for cold weather."

"Hirgus, there is no misunderstanding at all," Hirizjahkinis said, smiling at him fondly. "You were off to visit Ilissa about a silly toy that she had. And whether you were acting on a hint of the emperor's or his command, it is the same thing.

"I found Hirgus at the Green Head in Foluks Port—that carriage is very easy to track, you know," she went on before Aruendiel could say anything. "We had a long talk, Hirgus and I, and I told him very frankly that he was mad to go alone to the Faitoren kingdom. It was not so difficult to persuade him that I should go with him. He had heard about Bouragonr already."

"I am always pleased to have your company, Madame Hirizjahkinis," Hirgus said.

"But why would you go at all?" Nora asked urgently. Hirizjahkinis turned to her at once, her dark eyes dancing.

"I wanted to see what was afoot! Hirgus was very cagey. I did not find out until we arrived at Ilissa's that he was seeking Voen's Chalice. Yes—" She looked significantly at Aruendiel. "Voen's Chalice."

Aruendiel uttered a snort that sounded suspiciously like laughter.

Hirgus flushed slightly. He said: "The Chalice has a range of significant magical properties, all worthy of study. Poisoning one's enemies, conveying invulnerability—"

"I'm quite aware of the legends surrounding the Chalice," Aruendiel interrupted. "And it is part of the empire's official coronation paraphernalia, is it not? Only the rightful emperor can drink from it, the day he's crowned, and live. But it disappeared some years ago."

Nora was beginning to catch on. "And the emperor would like to have it back? To prove that he's the legitimate emperor?"

"Or to keep someone else from proving that he's the emperor," Hirizjahkinis said, shrugging a little under the Kavareen's hide. "The Chalice was not always very selective."

"In fact, the Chalice was a sham," Aruendiel said, resting his chin on his hand. "There was almost nothing magical about it at all." He sounded so certain that Nora almost asked how he knew, but Hirgus spoke first.

"I must beg to differ with you, sir," he said. "There is a long record, going back centuries, of the powers of the Chalice. When I heard that it had come into the hands of the Faitoren queen, and that she was willing to discuss parting with it, quite frankly I was beside myself with anticipation. The opportunity to study a unique magical artifact like the Chalice—" He shook his head as though overcome with emotion, and the sun-shaped earring flashed in the candlelight.

"So Ilissa tried to use the Chalice to bargain with the emperor," Aruendiel said thoughtfully. "What did she want?"

"Her freedom," Hirizjahkinis said at once. "She wanted Hirgus to lift the barriers around her kingdom. That was why the emperor sent a magic-worker."

Aruendiel gave Hirgus a long look and the corners of his mouth twitched once, but he said only: "I see."

"Of course," Hirizjahkinis said slyly, "Ilissa's Chalice was a fake. I mean, it was an imitation of the real fake, the original Chalice. She was not pleased when I told Hirgus so, in her presence. And neither was Hirgus, I believe."

"Disappointed, dear lady! Disappointed beyond all measure. But I am grateful. The Faitoren magic can be quite convincing—up to a point, I mean."

"You should be grateful to Hirizjahkinis," Aruendiel said. "The emperor would have been even more disappointed with a false Chalice. I suppose it was really an old shoe or something of the sort, once you got the spell off, Hiriz?" He raised an eyebrow expectantly.

For the first time, Hirizjahkinis seemed chagrined, a ripple of hesitation flexing her wide mouth. Then she laughed. "Most of it came off, Aruendiel. Enough that we could all see that the Chalice wasn't a chalice."

Aruendiel began to look stormy again, and Nora remembered his scorn back in Semr, when Hirizjahkinis had turned Ilissa's silencing spell into a large, gelatinous insect because she could find no other way to remove it from Nora's throat. Well, Hirizjahkinis did get the damn thing out, Nora thought loyally; not everyone had spent years studying Faitoren magic. But she could tell exactly what Aruendiel was thinking now, because she was thinking the same thing: To go into Ilissa's domain recklessly unprepared— knowing almost nothing about Faitoren magic—it was utter madness—

"So what precisely happened, when you got there?" Nora asked. "Ilissa wasn't expecting *you*, was she?"

"No, but she was very gracious." Hirizjahkinis seemed amused at the recollection. "She kept saying how happy she was to have the chance to get to know me better, after all this time. There was a splendid reception, and then we had a smaller dinner party—Ilissa, Raclin, Hirgus, and I. That was when she brought out the Chalice."

"What possessed you to eat her food?" Aruendiel demanded. "It's the easiest way for her to enchant you."

"Oh, the whole place was awash in enchantments. There was no avoiding them. I thought, Well, I might as well enjoy it! We were hungry, and the food was delicious—although it is true, after we left I was starving."

Aruendiel's long, crooked nose had a pinched look, as though he had smelled something foul. Before he could say anything, Nora said swiftly: "Did Ilissa say anything about me?"

"Yes, indeed!" To her surprise, it was Hirgus who spoke. "Several of the Faitoren mentioned your spectacular departure. They regard it as very unsporting." He chuckled a little.

"Ilissa called you a dear daughter-in-law," Hirizjahkinis said, "and asked is there any chance you could be persuaded to return home. I said she is doing quite well where she is. And then Ilissa said that if any harm comes to you, she will take revenge on that criminal Aruendiel to the last drop of his black blood."

"Thank you for bringing that message, Hiriz," Aruendiel said. "Were there any others for me?"

"They were all in that vein. But truly, we did not spend *that* much time talking about you." She laughed.

"What did you talk about?" Nora asked.

"The evening became a little awkward, once I pointed out that the chalice was not the Chalice. But Ilissa made things smooth again. She has very good manners—yes, she does, Aruendiel! She asked me to tell her something of my history, and she is a good listener. And then—" Hirizjahkinis cast a heavy-lidded, amused glance around the table. "I was back at home—my first home, before I went away to the temple, eating my mother's *guanish* pudding, listening to my grandfather tell stories about sailing on the ocean when he was young. I mean, I was really there. Sister Moon, I haven't had *guanish* pudding so good in years and years."

"Illusions." Aruendiel raised his hands as though he could wrestle some relief out of the air. "Fraud. She was tricking you."

"Yes, of course, Aruendiel. I do know *something* about magic—I was quite aware I was being enchanted. But there was nothing to do but try to take some pleasure in it. After a while I was at the temple of the Holy Sister Night again, keeping vigil in the moonlight with my dear friend Janixiya. You know, you are not supposed to talk all night long. So we had to find other ways of passing the time." A small, private smile played over Hirizjahkinis's lips and then vanished. "It was a surprise to me—that Ilissa could do such good work."

Aruendiel exploded: "Good work?"

Nora suddenly had a very clear recollection of the time, sophomore year of college, when Petra from her dorm told her about trying heroin with a new boyfriend: "And, Nora, it was heaven, it really was amazing." Petra was doing fine, out of rehab for a couple of years now, Nora reminded herself.

"Then Janixiya disappeared, and I was back in Ilissa's dining room," Hirizjahkinis said, her tone still wry, controlled. "She and Hirgus were gone. I was alone with Raclin. He had not said much at dinner. He let Ilissa talk and talk. Now I asked him, 'Where are the others?' "

" 'My mother is at work on your fat friend,' Raclin said—I am sorry, Hirgus, but that is what he said. 'And you're at work on me?' I asked him. He laughed and poured more wine for himself. 'Not yet,' he said.

" 'I didn't have the pleasure of seeing you when your mother was in Semr this year,' I said.

"That set him off, mentioning Semr. He ranted about you for a while, Aruendiel—I think he was not happy to be a statue, not happy at all—but mostly he wanted to complain about his mother. Yes, his mother! The mission to Semr was a waste of time, he said, just like her scheme to fool the emperor with the fake Chalice.

" 'She keeps coming up with these ridiculous plans that never work,' he said. 'And she pulls me into them, and she won't listen when I tell her how stupid they are. Look at all those awful human women I had to marry—so that she could have an heir.'

" 'My sympathies are with those women,' I told him.

" 'I know you met the last one, Nima, in Semr. Ilissa was so proud of finding her and fixing her up. When I saw her afterward, with the cripple, I couldn't believe how ugly she was, her natural face.' "

Nora's mouth fell open. "It's not as though the Faitoren are so good-looking, under all that magic! *Nima?* He couldn't remember my name?"

"Raclin's observations are as degraded as he is," Aruendiel said. He had been sitting absolutely still, withdrawn into a state of icy, looming disapproval. "Must we hear them all in such detail?"

"Nora, I hope it does not pain you too much?" Hirizjahkinis said.

"No, I'm glad Raclin has obviously—moved on." She wasn't sure if the idiom would translate, but Hirizjahkinis, at least, seemed to understand it.

"That's what I thought, too," Hirizjahkinis said, her eyes narrowing, "but when I said to Raclin, Oh, then you are done with her—and her name is *Nora,* by the way—he said no, not at all. Again, he started to rant. It was very tedious. I will spare you the details, but he is still angry at what he calls your insolence, the dishonor you have brought to him, and so forth." She blew air out of her cheeks. "Like a little boy when someone takes away the kitten he was torturing."

"Right," Nora said, not entirely at ease with Hirizjahkinis's simile. She thought she merited a full-grown cat, at least. "Well, I guess I'll have to live with that."

"What I saw very clearly"—Hirizjahkinis was addressing Aruendiel now, and her tone had crispened—"there is division between Ilissa and Raclin. They both want to escape—he told me how bored he is!—but he is impatient with her plots. He wants to act, to make war."

Aruendiel stirred. "Ilissa has always kept him on a short leash."

"He wants to break it."

"Perhaps I should not have called off my attack."

"It would be wiser to bring others into the fight first." Her sudden laugh sounded forced. "Raclin will give you your provocation, if you wait. He is not subtle. Not subtle at all."

Aruendiel said: "What did he do to you, Hiriz?"

She folded her arms on the table. "You remember that day at Nazling Putarj?" When he nodded, she looked from Nora to Hirgus. Her eyes were old. "That was the first time I met Aruendiel," she told them. "It was after I had been thrown out of the temple. I was to be stoned, then fed to the lions. Punishment for my disobedience."

"Raclin made you go back there," Aruendiel said. His tone was neutral but each word seemed to be weighted with his full concentration.

"Yes," said Hirizjakinis, smiling fiercely. "I could feel the ropes again. I could smell the lions in their pit. I was parched—the guards were supposed to give me water, but they forgot, or the high witch priestess wanted me to die of thirst as well as blows and bites.

"That day, I saw you in the crowd, Aruendiel, your strange white face in the middle of all the angry ones. Do you remember, you winked at me?"

Aruendiel cocked his head meditatively, as though to examine the past more closely. "I suppose I did."

"I did not know what it meant, that wink, but I kept looking at you. I remember you came up to the very edge of the scaffold, as they started to throw the stones, and one of the guards tried to shove you back.

"And then all the stones turned into butterflies, and the lions were out of their pit and on top of the guards, and my ropes were gone, and the white-skinned demon who had winked at me was dragging me through the shrieking crowd." She chuckled. "I did not realize at first that we were invisible."

"It seemed prudent," Aruendiel said.

"This time, though"—Hirizjahkinis almost spat out the words, and Nora understood she was no longer talking about the old memory—"there was no wink. You looked at me and you turned away."

"Ah." Aruendiel's eyes were hard.

"You disappeared in the crowd, and then the stones hit me." Hirizjahkinis shook her head, emitting a small hiss of vexation. "On and on. All parts of my body. The lions smelled the blood, they began to roar. It was just—just as I had feared. Raclin enjoyed it very much, I am sure.

"And all the time he whispered in my ear that I could free myself if I untied the ropes—they were magic ropes, do you remember, Aruendiel? Only a magician could untie them.

"Raclin's voice never stopped. 'Save yourself, lift the spell. You know how. Lift the spell.' " She mimicked Raclin's caressing bass with eerie accuracy, and involuntarily Nora hunched her shoulders.

"And if you had lifted the spell—" Nora said hesitantly.

"You would have lifted the barriers around the Faitoren realm," Aruendiel finished.

"I think so." Hirizjahkinis nodded.

"But you didn't," Nora said.

"No. I decided, enough of the Faitoren and their silly games!" There was a golden note of triumph in Hirizjahkinis's voice now. Deliberately she stroked the leopard skin where it covered her upper arm. "I called my servant the Kavareen from where I had left him, outside Ilissa's realm. He came at once—he gave Raclin a great scare—" Hirizjahkinis clawed the air with her fingers, bared her teeth, laughed. "And there was no more silliness about untying magical ropes.

"Then," she added cheerfully, "I went to find Hirgus, who was engaged in a *very* private discussion with Ilissa—"

"She was still negotiating for the removal of the magical barriers around her kingdom," Hirgus said, blinking, his mouth pursed inside the tapestry of his beard. "Of course I could do nothing for her—"

"Of course," said Aruendiel.

"And I am appalled to learn now how badly Madame Hirizjahkinis was treated in my absence. All of us may not always have the same interests," Hirgus said, with a vague gesture, "but I like to think there is such a thing as professional courtesy among magic-workers. There is no question of dealing with the Faitoren in good faith after that."

"Thank you, Hirgus. I am pleased that you and I feel the same way." To Aruendiel, Hirizjahkinis said: "Well, we came away, and here we are."

There was a pause. Aruendiel looked down at his bowl of oatmeal, almost untouched, but it seemed to Nora that he did not really see it. He raised his head again to address Hirizjahkinis. "And if you had not had the Kavareen, or if it had disobeyed you?"

"But I had the Kavareen," Hirizjahkinis said, with the air of stating the obvious. "And it always obeys me."

"All demons in the thrall of a human are ready to turn against their master," Aruendiel said, looking at the Kavareen's yellow eyes with dislike. "Even the ghost of a demon."

"Then I would have to let my friend Aruendiel rescue me—again!—and I would hope you would not make me wait long," Hirizjahkinis said with some severity. After a moment, she laughed and touched Aruendiel's hand lightly. "Peace, I gave you some cause for fear, and I am sorry for it. But you see, I was not completely unprepared.

"And now—I saw Hirgus yawn just now, and I am fatigued myself. We must demand more of your hospitality, Aruendiel."

Nora glanced at the window. The sun was up, finally.

Aruendiel obviously would have preferred to continue the discussion, but he could not ignore the reminder of his duties as a host. Hirizjahkinis was canny, Nora thought. He managed to assume a blander, more pacific demeanor and said something conventional about his roof, bread, and sword being at the service of his guests, then directed Nora to tell Mrs. Toristel to prepare their rooms.

Nora came back to catch the tail end of what Hirizjahkinis was saying. "—No, I do not think it was wasted effort, not at all. I have passed an interesting night, sometimes pleasant, sometimes not—and now we know more about Ilissa's plans." Hirizjahkinis gave an emphatic nod.

"What do you mean, a night?" Aruendiel asked roughly. His newfound courtesy had evaporated again. "The letter I got from Lukl said you had been three days in Faitoren territory."

"You are joking. Three days!" Hirizjahkinis drew back, and for a moment, panic looked out of her eyes. Then she recovered. "Ah, no wonder I was hungry! The Faitoren enchantments confounded my wits more than I knew." She laughed.

"They do that," said Nora, almost to herself, as she came up behind them. She doubted that anyone heard her. But Aruendiel glanced back, frowning, watchful behind the battered walls of his face.

As Aruendiel came up the stairs from his study, Hirizjahkinis looked up from the tarnished silver cup that she had been studying—Voen's Chalice, in fact—and put it back on the shelf. "It is gracious of you to give Hirgus free rein with your library," she said. "I do not recall your being so generous in the past. You have books that you never let *me* read—that second volume of Firginon Sior's memoirs, for instance."

Aruendiel gave a quick, determined shudder, like a cat shedding water from its fur. "It is better than having to converse with him myself. And you need not feel slighted. Hirgus can read as much as he likes of certain books. There are others that he will never be able to open, and if he should succeed, one glance at the page would blind him forever."

Hirizjahkinis laughed. "You are a considerate host!"

"He would do the same to me," Aruendiel said. He seemed to take a certain amount of pleasure in the observation.

"I hope he would not be so rude to a guest. There are a few books in Hirgus's collection that I am looking forward to reading myself when I am in Mirne Klep this winter."

"Is that why you accepted his invitation to visit? I am still flabbergasted that you would willingly spend more than a few hours with that pompous fathead."

"I have always liked Hirgus. It is not his fault that Ilissa's magic almost swallowed him up. I think he is a very good-natured man. He says nothing of great interest, that is true, but nothing that is very disagreeable, either. And then I am so fond of his wife."

"Oh, he has a wife." Aruendiel's tone indicated that no further explanation was needed.

"A lovely girl! Do not sound so disapproving. You also have enjoyed the company of pretty wives not your own. Hirgus is pleased that she will have a companion this winter. They have no children, and she is much younger than he—he fears that she suffers from boredom. Really, he is very lucky that I am available to distract her, so that she will not form a more perilous attachment."

"Indeed." Aruendiel picked up a green glass jar from the workbench, shook it gently, and guardedly uncorked it. A low moaning filled the room. Frowning, he recorked the bottle and returned it to its place, then turned to Hirizjahkinis. "You should be in that library, not Hirgus," he said brusquely. "I want you to go through my notebooks on Faitoren magic while you're here, and you must get the unmasking spell right. You bungled it with the Chalice, obviously."

"Yes, yes, but it is not so easy to practice when there are no Faitoren around! And frankly, I have had enough of them for now."

"I, too," he said, lifting an eyebrow. He pulled a scroll from the shelf.

"But you should not have to rely on the Kavareen to protect you from Faitoren magic."

They had already had this discussion twice since the morning of her arrival, and neither had derived any particular satisfaction from the exercise. With a grimace, Hirizjahkinis turned back to the window. In the courtyard below, two small, cloaked figures were visible, Nora and Mrs. Toristel. The two seemed to be discussing Hirgus's coach, which burned with a low flame near the castle wall.

Hirizjahkinis looked back at Aruendiel, bending over the scroll. "This little one Nora, she is very interested in magic," she said casually.

Aruendiel grunted as he made a note on the parchment.

Hirizjahkinis pursued, in the same nonchalant tone: "So you have made her your pupil rather than your mistress?"

Aruendiel's head jerked up, the Faitoren and the Kavareen forgotten. "What? You are impertinent, Hiriz. Do not speak to me of absurdities."

"The nights are growing long and cold, this time of year." Hirizjahkinis laughed as though inviting Aruendiel to join in. "When I met Nora in Semr, she told me she was not your mistress, but by now, I thought—"

"What? Well, she spoke truly, although it was no concern of yours. Nor it is now."

"You are my old, dear friend. I am always concerned with matters of your happiness. What is holding you back? Each time I see Nora, I think she is very engaging. And prettier than when I saw her last. Her scars are less obvious than they were. She is a good age, too, not too green—ripe to be a merry bedmate."

"What, are you the girl's pander?" He spat out the words.

"Peace, I am teasing you," she said, "but you puzzle me. I saw your face when you summoned Queen Tulivie's shadow. You looked at her with sadness and hunger, even though I do not think you were so much in love with her when she lived. And yet when you have the chance for a real, living, flesh-and-blood love affair, you scowl and do nothing."

Aruendiel put his brush down and moved his hand above the scroll, making a faint breeze spiral over the wet ink. The parchment rustled on the table. "He who hunts the stag does not chase squirrels."

"Hmmph. It depends on how hungry the hunter is. In *my* country we say a starving man needs no salt or oil for his termites."

"Even with salt and oil, termites are no delicacy," he said, with a harsh laugh. "I have traveled enough in your country—with a good appetite, too—to know that."

"We are speaking of Nora."

It was past time to curtail this discussion, Aruendiel felt. He chose his words carefully for greatest effect. "What of her? She is lowborn and no great beauty and the soiled former chattel of a lecherous Faitoren half-breed, but I would not have thought to compare her to a termite." He added coolly: "It is unkind of you, Hiriz."

Hirizjahkinis looked at him, her gaze the only live thing in a face that might have been carved from wood. "Ah, is that what you think of her?" she said finally. "I miscalculated. I was thinking of your welfare, but I must consider Nora's, too. Perhaps she is better off not being your mistress."

"Now you are talking more sensibly."

"So why are you teaching her?"

"She has an interest and some aptitude," he said, twitching a crooked shoulder. "We will see where it leads."

"Didn't Holo Nev come to you once, asking you to be his teacher? He had interest and aptitude, and gold, too. And you sent him away."

"It would have taken a dozen years for him to unlearn all the bad habits he had already picked up."

"And that young man from Reskorinia?"

Hirizjahkinis would not give up, Aruendiel thought. "A dilettante. He had no true understanding of magic."

"At least some of them had the discernment to seek you out, Aruendiel, and you always turned them down. I do not know of anyone but myself who can truly call themselves your protégé."

"There were a few others, years ago. Norsn, Micher, Nansis, Turl. They were wizards of middling ability before I taught them to be magicians."

"I did not realize that Turl had studied with you!"

"Yes, although he will never admit it. Well, I do not care to own him, either. He taught me a lesson, to be careful about whom I choose to teach my craft.

"Well, it is a good choice to teach Mistress Nora, for whatever reason you are doing it. You are right. There is talent there."

Hirizjahkinis was still probing; he was still on his guard. "Some talent, yes," Aruendiel said with a tilt of his head, "but who knows what it will amount to? Novice magicians are notoriously lazy. They learn a few spells and then have no interest in learning more."

"I do not think you need to worry on that score. Yesterday she lit candles for me with as much joy as if each flame were a new star. I had to beg her to stop, and to promise that I would help her again today."

"It is all new to her. Her mind is eager. I confess, it is refreshing to observe so much enthusiasm, even for the most elementary forms of magic." Aruendiel's voice warmed, and the hard knots in the corners of his mouth loosened. When Nora lit the candles, she was like a flame herself, he thought. "She is a hopeful presence," he could not help adding.

Then, before Hirizjahkinis could try to make something of his admission, he went on quickly: "There is another thing, Hiriz. It is time that I think of my legacy, to pass on the knowledge that I've accumulated. Mistress Nora is not, perhaps, the heir I would have chosen, but when you, who studied with me longest, have learned so little as to venture unprepared into the Faitoren—"

"What is this talk of a legacy?" Hirizjahkinis demanded, showing no interest in further talk of the Faitoren. "Are you dying, that you are so morbid?"

"No, not dying. You forget," he said, a dark smile carving deeper lines into his face, "I am already dead."

"Now *you* are speaking of absurdities." She waited for him to respond, but he said nothing. Hirizjahkinis pulled herself even straighter than she had been standing. Although she did not reach Aruendiel's shoulder, she gave a fair impression of looking him directly in the eye.

"I see. You are still sulking, just as you were in Semr," she said severely. "And I am tired of being blamed for the kindness of giving you back your life. If I had known you would be so ungrateful, I would have left your corpse frozen on that mountaintop. What is so terrible? You have your health, your work—"

"My health! I have not had a day without pain for four dozen years."

"I am sorry for that. But you are not crippled, you can walk, you can ride, you are not bedridden as you were. And you will not use magic to salve the pain, will you? No, you are too stubborn for that."

Hirizjahkinis was relishing the chance to lecture him now, he thought sourly. "It is bad enough to know that it is only magic that keeps my heart beating and my lungs breathing and my body from turning into a withered husk."

"But that is different, I had nothing to do with that. It is the same for me and everyone who practices true magic. I would be a dried-up old lady by now"—Hirizjahkinis's mouth suddenly curved into a broad smile—"or dead myself, if you had not taught me to be a magician."

Aruendiel passed a hand over his face, avoiding the roughest places by habit. "I don't blame you, Hiriz, for what you did," he said slowly. "On the road back from Semr, I brought a child back who had been dead three days. It is a tempting thing, to bring someone out of the dark into the light. And that sort of magic—you can feel the tendrils of power growing through your very soul."

"Three days? That is not so hard. *You* had been dead for weeks."

"She had been eaten down to the bones."

"Ah, that is a little more difficult. You should do more spells like that, and you would feel better."

He made a disgusted noise deep in his throat. "Gods forbid! I still do not know whether I did that child good or ill."

"Good, of course. There can be nothing ill in giving someone so young another chance at life."

"That is what Nora said." Mistress Nora, he should have said, but fortunately Hirizjahkinis did not notice the slip. Carefully, he rolled up the parchment on which he had been taking notes and passed a thin black ribbon around it. The ends of the ribbon lifted lazily, like a pair of drowsy snakes, and tied themselves amorously into a complicated knot. "Well, perhaps it is better with a child. A child is resilient, she will not remember the darkness."

Hirizjahkinis regarded him watchfully. "You told us that you remembered nothing of death."

"Nothing. But I know, now, that it is always there."

"Oh, enough of your mewling, Aruendiel! Every living creature is under sentence of death. All the more reason to savor the life you have—especially if it has been taken away once and then returned to you. So, the pain," she added briskly. "It is still your back?"

"Only when it is not my head or half a dozen other parts of my body that never healed properly."

"Let me take a look."

"Never mind my back," he snapped. "It is no better nor worse than ever."

"Corverist of Vaev gave me a new spell for stiffness in the joints."

Aruendiel hunched his shoulders. "I will not use magic as a drug. Not again. Well, is Corverist still going in for animal magic?"

"Oh, yes! Corverist told me that he learned it from a snake. A very old snake. It claimed to have known Nagaris the Fat."

"I have never known snakes to be very truthful," Aruendiel said.

## *Chapter 29*

The candle flames burned skittishly for a second, and then made a sudden leap upward. Nora blinked, even though she had been expecting it. She was standing in the great hall with Hirizjahkinis, who was showing her how to make a candle flare even when there was not the slightest current of air stirring.

"I cannot teach you anything more about lighting fires," Hirizjahkinis had said firmly, when they started. "Aruendiel has done a good job of that already, and he will be irked if I teach you something that he disagrees with. So I will teach you something that he will not think is so important— but can be very useful, in the right circumstances. A few little tricks with a candle flame once persuaded a very suspicious prince in Haiah that the local lion god did not wish for me to have my head chopped off. Here, let me show you—it is only a matter of giving the flame a little love."

When it came to explaining magic, Hirizjahkinis's directions were not quite as clear or detailed as Aruendiel's—he never talked of love—but after a few attempts Nora got the idea. Her candles flared vigorously, although compared with Hirizjahkinis's neat row of squibs they had a slightly ragged appearance. Afterward, Hirizjahkinis tried to teach her how to make the candles burn in all the colors of the spectrum. Nora got from yellow to blue.

"Not bad for a first attempt," Hirizjahkinis pronounced. "I will tell Aruendiel that you have done credit to him today."

Feeling a little dizzy from her efforts, as though she would turn blue instead of the candle flame, Nora thanked Hirizjahkinis for the lesson. "I think Aruendiel is still working in the tower, if you would like to rejoin him," she added.

"Oh, there is no hurry," Hirizjahkinis said. "I made him a little angry this morning. It is better for him to have some time to cool his temper."

"Is he still angry about your going to Ilissa's?"

"Of course he is—but now the problem is that I gave him some good advice, too."

"That is the worst kind to give," Nora said drily. Whatever Hirizjahkinis's counsel, Nora had no doubt that it had been eminently sensible, unsparingly delivered, and soundly rejected. She also had the faint, haunting, ridiculous fear that somehow it involved her, Nora. Why she felt this way, she could not say—something in Hirizjahkinis's tone or gaze. At least this time Hirizjahkinis had not asked her whether she was Aruendiel's mistress. Changing the subject, she said: "I found something in the storeroom this morning that he might want to see." She went to the end of the table and brought back a small wooden box. Opening it, she began to leaf through the papers inside.

"There are notes here on various spells—maps—a few letters—but this is what caught my eye. It's from my world." She was trying to sound casual.

Hirizjahkinis took the yellowed square of paper from her and glanced politely at the image printed upon it. Then she looked more closely. "Ah, that is Aruendiel! As he used to be. I almost did not know him."

"I thought it was him. I wasn't sure."

"Oh, yes, that is him. He was very handsome, was he not?"

It was hard to tell definitely from the small, pale oval behind the stiff collar, under the brim of the dark hat. But, as Nora looked at the picture, almost intuitively she agreed with Hirizjahkinis. The figure in the picture was smiling boldly and held itself straight as the Ionic column beside it, unthinkingly confident in the way that comes from an abundance of good health and good looks.

"What sort of image is this?" Hirizjahkinis asked. "It is not a painting. Very shadowy and gray."

"It's what we call a photograph," Nora said, giving the English word. "We can make pictures with a box, a kind of mechanical eye, and print them on paper."

"Oh, yes," Hirizjahkinis said, nodding. "Like a scroll of Soiveron. Whatever the magician sees is recorded on the parchment. A very useful spell, although I sometimes have difficulty with the perspective."

"Ours has to do with, um, light rays." Nora went on quickly before Hirizjahkinis could ask her for a more precise explanation: "So this picture must have been made while Aruendiel visited my world, I guess."

"Is that writing at the bottom?"

"Yes, the photographer's name and address. Schroeder & Kubon, in Chicago. And there's a date—more than ninety years ago." It was 1915: the First World War—not the Second—raging in Europe. Horses in the streets along with motorcars. Telephones but no radio. Three of Nora's grandparents not yet born—Grandpa Hank a round-eyed toddler in a wicker pram.

"Ninety?" Hirizjahkinis repeated carelessly.

"Hirizjahkinis, how old is Aruendiel?"

"How old?" The magician shook her head, smiling, the beads in her hair chattering. "It is likely that time flows differently in your world."

"Yes, but still, ninety years over there must count for a lot of years here."

"He is older than I am. How old would you say I am?"

"I believe you are older than you look—" Nora began cautiously.

"I am older than I was yesterday, and younger than I will be tomorrow, and that is all I will tell you." Hirizjahkinis laughed. "But no, I do not show all my years. Magicians age slowly, more slowly than nonmagicians. Magic is very good for the health, you know. How do you feel after lighting those candles? Good, yes? It feels even better to raise a storm or find a necklace that was lost a hundred years ago or make a blind man see—or capture the Kavareen," she said, touching the leopard pelt on her shoulder. "If you keep lighting candles, Mistress Nora—and doing other, more complicated spells—you may find yourself living longer than you expected."

"That would be nice."

"I think so, too! There is nothing wrong with a long life, nothing at all." Hirizjahkinis spoke with a shade more vehemence than Nora would have anticipated.

"So Aruendiel could be more than ninety years old."

"Oh, certainly. Why don't you ask him? Or—I know! We could ask *him* when he was born," Hirizjahkinis said, taking the photograph into her hand again.

"What? Oh, the spell that brings paintings to life—?"

"Yes." Hirizjahkinis grinned wickedly. "Let us ask Aruendiel, *this* Aruendiel, right now. I have a wish to see my old friend as I first knew him. He was not as gloomy then as he is now. And he will be delighted to see me, I am sure, since as far as he knows he is in your world—Sheecaga, you say? So he will not be expecting me at all."

Nora was tempted. A younger, unscarred, more genial Aruendiel. She was curious to see just how good-looking he'd been. The man who'd been Ilissa's lover, Queen Tulivie's. But then Nora remembered the bewildered fear on the painted figure's face. "Will he mind?" she asked.

Hirizjahkinis assumed she meant the present-day Aruendiel. "He will not know," she said confidently. "Not until the spell is already over. It will only take a minute."

But after she worked the spell, the image on the paper was still mute and unmoving. Hirizjahkinis frowned. "Did Aruendiel put a counterspell on this picture, to prevent anyone from speaking to it? That would be extreme vigilance, even for him."

"Maybe the spell doesn't work on photos," Nora said, slightly relieved.

"Bah!" Hirizjahkinis threw the photograph down. She began to turn over the other papers in the box. "What is all this? A spell to make iron float . . . a letter—no name, just an initial M, a woman's writing . . . hmm, obviously on very good terms with Aruendiel . . . Holy Sister, I see why she did not sign it."

"I read that, too," Nora confessed. "Is she talking about an actual spell that he did, or does she have a very vivid erotic imagination?"

"Well, you could achieve the same results without magic, perhaps. It would take more time. . . . I think I know who M is. I treated her for gout, years later. She had burned three husbands by then. The only client I've ever had who said she liked a female magician better than a man." Hirizjahkinis laughed a deep, rumbling chuckle. "Maybe Aruendiel could tell us why."

"*You* can ask him that."

"Wait, I may not need to. Here is another letter from M, even longer. . . . She is not very happy with him now . . . terrible, terrible, Aruendiel, if that's true! But she is so vicious, I am sorry for him, too. . . . What else? . . . A spell for being in two places at once. I know this one, it gives me a headache. . . . Who is this? Another crazy mistress?"

Hirizjahkinis had fished out another portrait, this one a painting, a miniature the size of her hand. The head of a woman, not young, not yet into middle age. Her dark hair was coiled beneath a crimson headdress, and she wore a necklace of small silvery pearls. Straight, prominent, rather bony features: the sort of face that could have had an avian, exotic beauty if it had not looked so strained, even fearful. Her gray eyes looked out warily beyond the borders of the painting, not meeting the eyes of the spectator, as though she hoped to escape notice.

"I thought at first it might be his wife—" Nora began.

"Oh, no! She was a blonde with a face like a bowl of milk."

"—but then I realized that this woman looks a bit like a picture of Aruendiel's sister that I saw once. It's got to be someone in his family—the coloring, the eyes."

"Yes, I think you are right. I never met his sister, so I cannot say if this is she. His mother? An aunt? One thing I can tell you, this is an old hairstyle—when I first came to Semr, there were only a few old ladies still wearing it." Hirizjahkinis touched the painted headdress gently. "Or," she added suddenly, "it is his daughter!"

"He has a daughter?"

"He has never mentioned one, but it stands to reason!" Hirizjahkinis said with a laugh. "She would have been born on the wrong side of the blanket—so he hid her picture away with these old papers. Yes, look how she is dressed like a noblewoman, but with no emblem on her necklace, anywhere, to indicate who she is. I have looked at many, many pictures now, and I can tell you, when peers sit for their portrait, they do not wish to be anonymous. They always have a crest or a signet ring, or they pose with a falcon on their hand, because the symbol of their house is a falcon, or some such thing."

"Whoever she is, she doesn't look very happy, does she?" Nora said. "She looks as though she's had a hard life."

"Why don't you ask her about it?" said Hirizjahkinis. Holding the portrait at arm's length, she addressed it directly, her tone half-commanding, half-cajoling. "Madame? Madame? I beg a few minutes of your attention. Madame! I call you!"

"It is better if you know the name of the person," she added to Nora, in an undertone. "But the spell works without it, too. They cannot ignore you for very long."

"This might be a shock for her," Nora murmured. It occurred to her that Hirizjahkinis's casual remark about the crazy mistress might have been at least partly on target: There was something about the woman's face that made you wonder if she was wholly sane.

"No, no, I have done this spell a dozen dozen times now. I know how to handle her." More loudly, Hirizjahkinis spoke to the picture again: "Madame, we wish to speak with you. Just for a few minutes, and then you will go back to having your picture made. We are standing right here, Madame, my friend and I."

The face in the frame turned slightly, toward Hirizjahkinis's voice. "Good afternoon," she said, in a formal tone.

"Good afternoon, my name is Hirizjahkinis, and this is my friend Nora. And you, Madame, you are—"

She frowned slightly, as though the question discomfited her. "You would like to know my name?"

"Yes, Madame."

"I am called Wurga."

"We are pleased to make your acquaintance, Wurga. We have been admiring your portrait. For whom are you having it painted?"

"No one," Wurga's image said dully. "It was Lady Aruendian Fornesan's idea. She is having her portrait painted, too, and her children's."

Nora looked questioningly at Hirizjahkinis, who nodded confidently. "His sister," she mouthed. To the portrait she asked: "Lady Aruendian?"

"Yes, my kinswoman. I am visiting her here at Forel, from my home in Sar Lith."

"Sar Lith! That is a long way to come to visit kin."

"It was a long journey," the portrait agreed, without any sign of interest.

"I am acquainted with one of Lady Aruendian's brothers. I wonder whether you know him?"

Wurga's face was suddenly alert. "Her brother? Which one?"

"It is Lord Ar—"

"What is this?" Aruendiel's voice said, beside Nora. He looked over Hirizjahkinis's head and saw the live portrait. A pained, startled expression came over his face.

"You!" The portrait of Wurga had seen Aruendiel, too. Its small features contorted and its voice rose to a shriek. "Is that you? Yes, you are changed, but I know you! What are you doing here? It's you who—you have—" She broke off with a moan, panting, then tried again: "I—you—what you did to—?"

"Did what?" Hirizjahkinis said sharply.

"Oh, I cannot bear it, oh no. You destroyed—you stole—no, no, no—"

"Enough of this," Aruendiel said, his fingers closing on the portrait. Wurga's wailing stopped immediately. When he took his hand away, she was back in her original position, staring slightly to one side, her mouth tightly closed, the same as before, except that Nora thought she looked crazier than ever.

Aruendiel's eyes were freezing, but Nora forced herself to meet them. "Who is she?" she asked in a small voice. "She recognized you."

"What did you do to the poor woman, Aruendiel?" Hirizjahkinis asked.

"Nothing, nothing at all," he said curtly.

"But you know who she is."

"An old family connection. She mistook me for an enemy."

"Why would she do that?"

He gave a crooked shrug. "She was a poor, distracted thing, who had had troubles in a distant land. My sister gave her refuge for a time."

"What sort of troubles?"

"I do not remember."

"What happened to her?"

"She left my sister's house and disappeared. That was a very long time ago." He said to Hirizjahkinis: "I am sorry now for teaching you that spell, if you can do nothing better with it than torment the shade of a long-dead madwoman."

Hirizjahkinis's mouth twitched with what appeared to be a mixture of abashment and impatience. "She was perfectly calm until you appeared!"

"Let the dead stay dead, Hirizjahkinis."

"Yes, yes, I understand. They will never forgive you, otherwise," she said, biting the words off. "They are very ungrateful, the dead."

"Your impertinence grows tiresome."

"So does your rudeness, Aruendiel. I am sorry now for ever thinking your life was worth saving." Hirizjahkinis flung the miniature into the wooden box. Immediately the nest of papers exploded into flame.

The fire rose quickly, cheerfully from the box. No one moved. It devoured the parchment, then chewed through the portrait of Wurga. Her face charred and crumbled.

Not until the box itself began to burn did Aruendiel rouse himself to pick it up and deposit the remains in the fireplace. He gave it a series of blows with the poker, then turned stiffly, as though his back ached.

"I should start working on dinner," Nora muttered, rising. Hirizjahkinis announced that she would rest before dinner. Aruendiel said something about not leaving Hirgus alone.

The kitchen was quiet and dim. The fire in the stove had burned low and drowsy. Adding a new log, Nora wondered which of the two magicians had set the papers on fire. They were Aruendiel's; he might have felt entitled to burn them. But maybe Hirizjahkinis was angry enough to burn them simply because they belonged to Aruendiel. What would have happened, Nora thought, if the box *hadn't* caught fire—and what were they fighting about?

She found a knife, sat down, and began to peel turnips in the half-darkness. The knife was a shadow in her hand, and she could barely distinguish the white skin of the turnips from their white flesh.

Without thinking, she turned her eyes to the candlestick on the table beside her and watched as it flared into light.

Dinner that evening was not as awkward as Nora had feared, at least at first. By some unspoken agreement, the Faitoren were not mentioned. Hirgus was bubbling with pleasure over the books and manuscripts he had encountered. Aruendiel, initially cantankerous, was gradually flattered into a reasonable simulacrum of cordiality.

"... and you have an unredacted edition of Piris's *Fruits of Hell!* It makes all the difference to have the proper dosages, with poisons. And then, Torgin's commentary on the *Metamorphoses*! I've heard about it all my life, but I'd begun to think that it was just a hoax, like that Rgonnish manuscript you were telling us about."

"My Torgin is quite genuine."

"Of course, I could see that at once, but how did you manage to get hold of it?"

"A present from an old teacher—one of Torgin's students," Aruendiel said. Hirgus beamed at him insinuatingly until he added: "Lord Burs of Klevis."

"Lord Burs! Chief wizard to Tern the Sixth! Well, that goes back a bit. They won the Battle of the Chalk Hills together, didn't they?"

"Not just that battle," Aruendiel said, in a tone that was familiar to Nora from her own lessons, "but the whole southern campaign."

"Marvelous! You were there? There was a famous engagement—the Rout of the Dogs, they call it."

"I was Lord Burs's aide-de-camp." Aruendiel's black eyebrows knitted together. "Yes, the Rout of the Dogs is famous, but almost no one understands the real significance—" Apparently, Nora gathered, Lord Burs had turned an opposing battalion into a pack of dogs and then introduced a bitch in heat onto the battlefield. "—more important, the Orvetian battle order was completely disrupted, and their morale—"

Hirizjahkinis caught Nora's eye across the table and smiled. "In the end they must rely on a female, even in war," she whispered. She was eating with a good appetite; there was no obvious sign that any recent disagreements with Aruendiel had dampened her spirits.

"There's one thing I've been meaning to ask you, my dear sir," said Hirgus, when Aruendiel had finished his analysis. "Your Lord Burs was a wizard, was he not? Like myself."

"Everyone was, in those days."

"So how did you train as a magician, eh? When did you acquire your expertise in simple magic?"

"Real magic," Aruendiel said snappishly.

"Real magic, true magic, simple magic—the point is, how did you learn to practice it? I've taken a special interest in the history of real magic—you might not think it of me, but it's true. One of my great disappointments was finding that I have absolutely no aptitude for real magic, so at one time, I delved deep into the study of its origins, thinking that I might find some way for even a talentless dullard like myself to practice it. Alas, I had to content myself with being an ordinary wizard." Here Hirgus smiled, ivory teeth showing through the curls of his beard. "But what surprised me was how suddenly real magic appeared on the scene, and how quickly it became the dominant method of working magic. And from what I can tell, you, sir, were the first of the magicians."

"There were several of us," Aruendiel corrected him. "Micher Samle, Nansis Abora, Norsn—and we were not the first magicians, far from it. The most ancient magic-workers you can name—the Frogskinner,

Nagaris, Rgonnish, the Master of Hons—all practiced true magic. It was only later, as men discovered that they could entrap or entice spirits to do their magical work for them, that they began to practice wizardry. It was easier—in some ways more powerful. Eventually wizardry supplanted true magic entirely; for centuries it was almost forgotten. We did not invent true magic, my friends and I, we rediscovered it."

Hirgus leaned back in his chair and placed the ends of his fingertips together. "Very interesting indeed! Of course, those ancient magic-workers left very little in the way of written records. It is hard to say exactly what they practiced."

"It is clear enough, if you are intelligent enough to know what to look for."

"It is not so clear to me, but then I am a mere wizard! All right, assuming your theory is true, sir, how did you and your friends develop a working, practical knowledge of real magic?"

By the look on Aruendiel's face, Nora thought that he might be considering whether to end the discussion by turning Hirgus into something small and voiceless. "We built upon the writings of the early magicians," he said finally.

"But there is so little! Only fragments! Unless—" Hirgus held up a finger, half-teasing, half-admonitory. "Unless they left some writings that remain unknown, or *mostly* unknown? Perhaps some of those books in your library that I was unable to open today?"

Aruendiel raised an eyebrow and smiled very briefly. "That may be so."

"Ah! Well, we all have our trade secrets. I hope someday I may persuade you to share a few more with me. I must confess my real motive: I have a book in mind, a history of magic—there has been nothing authoritative written since Kerenonna's *Annals*. So there is a real need for a history that covers the appearance—or revival—of real magic and takes us up to the present moment, and I think that your recollections, dear sir, and perhaps your papers would be at the heart of such a history. I am not asking anything, not now"—Aruendiel was already shaking his head—"I am simply mentioning this project of mine. We will talk some other time about how I can best record your contributions to the development of modern magic."

"By the sweet night, Aruendiel, I had no idea that this was in Hirgus's mind," Hirizjahkinis said, laughing. "And now I see why he so generously invited me to Mirne Klep this winter."

"Any help that you can provide me with, my dear lady, would be much appreciated," Hirgus said, the metallic threads in his beard glistening as he nodded. "I must say," he added to Aruendiel, "that I am delighted to hear you acknowledge that wizardry has some advantages over simple magic. That is a theme that I hope to explore in my book, in a balanced way, of course. Wizardry, for instance, gives you far more control, in some situations, than simple magic. My new carriage"—Hirgus lifted his goblet and waved it vaguely toward the courtyard—"would have been impossible to construct with real magic."

"There was a magician from Ou, years ago," Aruendiel observed, "who made a carriage out of fire, and one out of water, too. He used no wizardry."

"Ah, but we are speaking of my carriage, which is not simply a utilitarian vehicle, but a thing of beauty, too. You must have observed how it is decorated, the wonderful little faces, their clever expressions—all wrought in living fire. It's the work of an artist. The best magician would be hard-pressed to duplicate it."

"I see." Aruendiel's face was almost expressionless. "You have either found a very unusual fire demon or—"

"I do have a fire demon, but it is a different spirit who does the decoration. One of the palace sculptors in Mirne Klep, a young fellow, very talented. He was sentenced to die for knifing a man, so I bought the execution rights. Not cheap, but the result is well worth it, don't you think?"

There was a pause. "I don't understand." Nora's query sounded, to her own ears, as loud as a stone dropped into water.

"In some places," Hirizjahkinis said quietly to Nora, "condemned prisoners are sold to people who wish to make special offerings to the gods—"

"—or sold to wizards who are too lazy or too incompetent to treat with demons or the other spirits that already exist," Aruendiel said. "Who have to make their own ghosts to do their will."

"Make a ghost? You mean, they kill someone, and then put his ghost in a spell?" Nora asked.

"Precisely," Aruendiel said. "In this case, this ghost is probably bound to the carriage itself, to create that rather vulgar ornamentation."

"My dear young lady," Hirgus said, a dark wrinkle of annoyance appearing on the gleaming expanse of his forehead, "this was a matter of carrying out the emperor's justice. The boy would have died in any event. And this way, his work lives after him."

Nora frowned, weighing what to say next, reluctant to be overtly rude to a guest, although Aruendiel had set the bar high on that score. "Where I come from," she said finally, "we have legends about vehicles that have ghosts attached to them. And it's always very bad luck for the people who happen to ride in those vehicles."

"This sort of spell is perfectly safe when done correctly. As I am sure you can attest, Lord Aruendiel—you must have killed often enough for the sake of a spell, when you were a wizard, before you discovered simple magic."

"Often enough to find that unwilling spirits make for poor magic."

"My carriage is sound enough, as the Lady Hirizjahkinis will tell you."

"Hirgus, I can say that your fire demon is very well trained and does a fine job of keeping us warm, even in this abominable season. To be quite honest, I do not care a pinprick about these decorations you are so proud of. As though a fiery carriage does not attract enough attention!

"But as for ghosts—pff! If they can be useful, let them be useful." She fingered the Kavareen's vacant head and smiled.

# Chapter 30

The next day, Mr. Toristel was cautiously harnessing the giant black horses to the fiery carriage by the time Nora found another opportunity to speak to Hirizjahkinis alone. She found Hirizjahkinis finishing her breakfast in the great hall, dipping a piece of bread into broth in a desultory way.

"I wanted to tell you," Nora said, "I'm sorry that things have gone badly between you and Aruendiel this visit."

Hirizjahkinis waved a nonchalant hand in the air, although the corners of her mouth flexed with irritation. "Oh, Aruendiel has such a bad temper, sometimes he makes me lose mine, as well. But it will all be forgotten by both of us, eventually.

"It is ridiculous of him to be so angry at me for my visit to Ilissa," she added, with a faintly malicious grin. "I am not more reckless than *he* was, once upon a time."

"I know—he had an affair with Ilissa," Nora said.

"How do you know about that?" Hirizjahkinis's eyes were wide, prepared to be amused.

"Well, he told me. That is," Nora corrected herself, "I guessed that, ah, something had happened between them, and he said that was right."

"Yes, exactly," Hirizjahkinis said, erupting with laughter. "They burned up the sheets together, he and Ilissa. He does not like to think of it now. He might have married her—but then he married that poor, foolish Lady Lusarniev instead."

Nora shifted on her stool. "Hirizjahkinis," she said, after trying to think of a polite way to say what she wanted to say, and not finding it, "he also said he killed his wife."

Hirizjahkinis gave a quick, definite nod. "Yes, he did."

"Well, what do *you* think about that? I mean, we've been talking about how dangerous Ilissa is, but sometimes I wonder—"

Hirizjahkinis's eyes met Nora's, quick and shrewd. "Ah! You think, 'Aruendiel murdered his wife, perhaps he will murder me, and I am not quite as accomplished a magician as Hirizjahkinis—not yet—so I would be helpless to defend myself.' "

"I know it sounds silly."

"Not so silly. Aruendiel is a very powerful magician with a bad temper, as we have seen. Are you afraid of him?"

"No," Nora said immediately. "Not at all. I mean, I've gotten used to his temper now, and it's not always pleasant, but I never feel threatened. Then I think perhaps I'm just naive. Maybe I *should* be afraid of him."

Hirizjahkinis thought for a moment, the lines around her mouth deepening, and then she shook her head. "I do not think you should fear him. He would never harm you, a woman living in his household—his pupil, yet. In fact, he would go to some trouble to protect you from harm, as he has done already."

"Yes, but what about his wife? He didn't protect her, quite the opposite."

"Ah, that was a mistake, a series of mistakes. Poor Lady Lusarniev, she was not worth killing! He should have been happy that another man took her off his hands. But he was angry—at her, at the friend who had betrayed him. He does not like to be made a fool of."

"Why do you say she was not worth killing?"

"Oh!" Hirizjahkinis smiled. "Well, there was nothing wrong with her. She was pretty, kind, very rich—and not stupid, either. But magicians should not marry, in my view. I told Aruendiel that, at the time, but he did not listen."

"Tell me what happened." When Hirizjahkinis hesitated, Nora added quickly: "It would make me feel better, to know the facts."

"Well, to allay your fears, then! There is no sign of Hirgus yet, is there? And Aruendiel is still upstairs. I will try to make sure that he does not overhear us.

"Let me see, where to begin? This happened years ago, as you know. I was in Semr then, an exile—at home I was still sentenced to death—and I made my living by doing magic for whoever would hire me.

"Aruendiel had been away, on a long journey, exploring other worlds. And then he came back. He had gone away because of some unpleasantness at court—Queen Tulivie, I think you remember her?—but she was dead by then, and so was the king her husband, so it was safe for Aruendiel to return. He caused a great stir. People had assumed he was dead or lost. And he came back with a thousand wonderful tales from the worlds he had visited, some odd magical things—and gold, quite a bit of gold. He wanted to get married, you see.

"I remember how we sat up, one night after he returned, and Aruendiel told me all about the places that he had visited. But after he finished his stories, he said he was weary of travel and loneliness. 'I've been roaming for more than a lifetime,' he said. 'It is time to root myself. I want to take a wife from among my own people, I want to go back to my ancestral lands and live the way my fathers lived.'

"The idea sounded absurd to me, and I said so. 'You're a magician,' I said. 'You would not be happy in the simple life of a country lord. The magic always comes first. You taught me that.'

"That made him a little angry. 'I'm not going to give up magic,' he said. 'But there's no reason why I can't be a magician and still have the life that any other man would want to live.' He was very serious, so I nodded and tried to imagine which of the pretty little girls who had come up to court to get married that year might become Aruendiel's wife. It was not easy."

"Ilissa was a distraction from this marriage plan of his. She and the Faitoren were new arrivals in the north country. They had come from no one knew where—a few at first, and then dozens of them. They settled then where they live now, far to the north, but in those days there were no restrictions on their travel, and Ilissa and the other Faitoren came quite often to Semr. I remember the sensation Ilissa caused at court. So beautiful, so charming—and so powerfully magical, even if she was not a trained magician. We did not know quite what to make of her. All the men in court fell in love with her, and the women were so busy trying to copy her, they did not seem to mind.

"After Aruendiel met Ilissa, I did not hear anything more from him about getting married." Hirizjahkinis smiled broadly. "Ilissa set out to charm him, and she succeeded, of course! For several months, they were always in each other's company. Part of the appeal, I am sure, was her skill in magic. She was his equal or better.

"Frankly, I was relieved. Another love affair—it seemed more suitable than those marriage plans of his. Although perhaps he intended to marry Ilissa. Or she intended to marry him. It would have been a brilliant match—magic, riches, beauty on both sides. He was still handsome in those days! Aruendiel would have been king over the Faitoren and perhaps more, given Ilissa's ambitions. But then one day he returned from Ilissa's castle alone, and it was clear that he wanted nothing more to do with her. He would not tell me what had happened."

"He said she had enchanted him," Nora interjected.

"He told you that?" Hirizjahkinis eyed Nora for a moment, raising her eyebrows slightly. "Well, a year or so later, he did marry, the heiress to Lusul. She was better for him than most of the young ladies at court, I thought—she had some education and it seemed to me that she took time to think before she opened her mouth. Aruendiel settled down to be a country lord who practiced a little magic, just as he had predicted.

"I visited once or twice. He gave me the impression of a man who wants everyone to know how happy he is. He and his wife, they talked about nothing but the estate and court matters—the things she was interested in.

I thought Aruendiel was bored but would not admit it, even to himself. I expected that after a few years he would find other ways to amuse himself, magical or otherwise.

"Meanwhile Ilissa had started her famous war. Some of the Semran lords supported her and the Stoian king; some of them supported the Pernish. A huge mess, like most of the history of this dreadful country. I was very busy advising one of the Semran nobles opposing Ilissa, Lord Kersan, and then one day I heard that Lady Lusarniev had gone away with another man. The capital was buzzing like flies on meat! Most people said it was a judgment on Aruendiel, for seducing the wives of other men—but you know, he never actually stole another man's wife, it was more a matter of borrowing them.

"Some time later," she added with a roll of her eyes, "I heard that he had tracked down his wife and her lover and killed them both."

"And then?" Nora asked. "He wasn't tried or punished?"

"Oh, no! People thought it was in very bad taste, very old-fashioned, to kill a runaway wife, but they saw he was within his rights. And then he came into the war and fought against Ilissa and the Stoians—and then he was killed, too—at least for a little while. So—" Hirizjahkinis's hands opened, palms up, as though to indicate there was nothing more to say.

Nora was not satisfied. "But what did he tell you about all this? Was he sorry, did he regret what he'd done?"

"Regret?" Hirizjahkinis closed her eyes for a moment, as though she were trying to summon up a recalcitrant memory. "When I first saw him after she died, he looked darker than I had ever seen him. But then it was wartime. I gave him condolences for the death of his wife—in these situations, you know, you are supposed to pretend that she died of something like pneumonia—and at first I thought he was not even listening. Then he looked at me and said, 'You advised me not to marry, Hirizjahkinis. You were right.'

" 'I am sorry that it has ended so sadly,' I said.

" 'I am, too,' he said, and that was all he would say. I could tell he was angry, but at whom I could not say. Perhaps at me, for being right all along! But what did he expect, marrying a girl young enough to be his granddaughter—at least—with no interest in magic?" Hirizjahkinis made a clucking noise with her tongue.

"You are safe enough with him, Mistress Nora!" she went on. "Better than being under the tender protection of Ilissa, no? But, listen, if it will ease your mind, I will give you a present. Here——" One of Hirizjahkinis's bracelets became a small pair of golden scissors. With one snip she cut off the end of one of her slim cornrow braids. She slipped the gold bead from the end of the cut piece, then handed the braided locks to Nora.

"That is my token," she said. "You can use it to call me, if you are in desperate need——if Aruendiel tries to murder you, for example."

"He gave me something like this, when I was with the Faitoren," Nora said, watching Hirizjahkinis rethread the bead into her hair. The shorn braid had already regrown to its full length.

"Ah, his feather? Then you know how to use it. Listen, is that Hirgus coming downstairs, finally? If I had known how long he would lie abed, I would not have gotten up so early myself. But then we would not have had a chance to talk, you and I. Well, remember my token——and remember that Aruendiel also gave you his token. Certainly he was willing to help you escape *your* dangerous husband!"

"I see your point," Nora said, as Hirgus came smiling across the great hall, rubbing his hands and calling out a greeting. "Although it's not quite the same situation."

"What on earth were you talking about with Mistress Nora this morning, that you needed a silencing spell?" Aruendiel asked Hirizjahkinis as they walked out of the house and into the courtyard.

Hirizjahkinis smiled unconcernedly. "She had some inquiries of an intimate nature, things she could only ask another woman."

"As though I would be interested in overhearing any such exchange. A silencing spell was certainly an excess of caution."

"Servants gossip, even your wonderful Mrs. Toristel! And Mistress Nora was really worried, poor girl. You know," she added, with vague suggestiveness, "a forced Faitoren marriage is not something that one gets over quickly."

Aruendiel narrowed his pale eyes, surprised and a little irritated at the continued interest that Hirizjahkinis seemed to take in the amatory life of the girl Nora. The ghost of a question rose in his own mind. He usually preferred not to think about Hirizjahkinis's own tastes in love. This attention to the girl—he could not tell for sure whether it was friendship, the confidences that women share, or something else. Odd, definitely odd, on top of the insufferable suggestions Hirizjahkinis had made yesterday.

And what exactly was worrying the girl anyway? Aruendiel was debating whether to demand more details when a cry from behind halted his ruminations. Hirgus, following Hirizjahkinis and Aruendiel across the courtyard, had just gotten a good look at his carriage.

"My coach!" he shrieked. "My coach! Oh, you filthy blackguard!"

"Hirgus? What's wrong?" Hirizjahkinis turned quickly.

"What's wrong? Can't you see? It is ruined! Ruined!" He pointed at Aruendiel. "You thieving, lying, broken-backed son of a pig! You child of vipers! You did this!"

"Hirgus, I pray you, do not insult my parents," Aruendiel said, well pleased.

"You cheat! Barbarian! Vandal!"

Nora, who had been walking behind Hirgus, looked at the burning carriage more closely. The flames were pale, almost watery in the daylight, but they had looked that way yesterday. Something else was different. "The faces are gone," she said. "The little curls along the roof, the decorations."

"Yes! He stripped it bare!" Hirgus roared. "He took off the spell!"

"You did not, Aruendiel!" Hirizjahkinis frowned, making herself look very stern.

"You have offended against all the laws of hospitality, sir! You have willfully destroyed the valuable property of a guest beneath your roof."

"Not destroyed, Hirgus. Your carriage is still perfectly functional."

"But defaced now. Ruined! This was not the act of a gentleman. No civilized host treats a guest thus—"

"But your slave ghost, the one powering your spell, he was a guest in my house, too. And I have treated him as a considerate host should—by releasing him from an irksome bondage."

"You had no right to do so. This is an outrage. Your rudeness last night was inexcusable in itself—and now this. You did this as a deliberate insult."

"If you take it so, Hirgus, I do not see how I can persuade you otherwise."

"You were jealous of my work, you mad, old, vulture-faced cripple." Hirgus took a deep breath and clutched the tresses of his beard with curled fingers, as though his hands itched to wring Aruendiel's neck instead. "You could never create such a thing of beauty in a hundred years with the crudities of simple magic, so you took your pathetic revenge on a practitioner of a nobler art. I am a fair-minded man, I have not listened to all the tittle-tattle about you—how you hide away in your rotting castle, nursing old grudges, crazy with fear of the demons from whom you stole the secrets of your wretched magic. I came here, ignoring those tales, thinking that I would be honorably received—instead, you treat me with the utmost disrespect!"

"Are they still telling that tale about the demons?" Aruendiel asked with interest. "I thought that old story would have been forgotten by now. Are you going to put it in your book?"

Hirgus gathered his cloak around himself with a furious shudder. He muttered something under his breath, while sketching a complicated, looping gesture in the air with one hand.

"Oh, Aruendiel," Hirizjahkinis said, with a sigh. "Dear Sister Night, did you have to provoke him quite so much?"

"On the contrary, I have been more tolerant than he deserves, Hiriz. I have not called *him* insulting names like an angry schoolboy."

"But I am the one who will have to listen to his complaints all the way to—"

The fire covering the carriage grew brighter, a brilliant jack-o'-lantern orange, and then suddenly exploded outward. Nora felt its heat rise like a shining wall around her. Blinded by the glare, she shut her eyes and cringed, not knowing where to turn, as her throat filled with smoke.

Then she could breathe again, cold air salving her skin. She opened her eyes to the gray courtyard, half-shadowed in the angled morning sunlight. Hirgus stood trembling beside his carriage, his velvet cap askew, his face flushed. His carriage itself was a blackened shell, a few flames feebly licking the charred roof. The horses whinnied and shifted uneasily in their traces.

Aruendiel looked up. Following his gaze, Nora saw that one of the house's eaves was ablaze. But as she watched, the flames disappeared and the smoke petered away.

"I am afraid your fire demon may be testy for the rest of the day, Hirgus." Aruendiel turned back to his guest. "They never enjoy being quenched."

Hirgus's reply was unintelligible. With a jerk of his head, he climbed into what remained of his carriage.

"Perhaps I should have informed you before letting your captive ghost go free," Aruendiel allowed. "But it was rude of you to try to burn up my house. Shall we call it a draw?"

"I am leaving now," Hirgus called to Hirizjahkinis. "If you wish to leave this lunatic's company, please come with me now. I will not wait any longer."

"You can wait another minute, Hirgus," Hirizjahkinis said crisply. She looked back at Aruendiel. "You are incorrigible! I do not understand what drives you to find quarrels with everyone around you, including your oldest friends. If that is what makes you happy, then you must be very content right now."

"Content enough," he said, a shadow passing over his face. "I wish you a good journey, Hiriz. And I thank you for your visit. We may not always agree, you and I, but your company is always one of my greatest pleasures."

"Hmmph, you do not always make that obvious!" Hirizjahkinis said. "At least, it is never dull when I see you. Peace be your friend. And yours, too, Mistress Nora. You will need it, living under his roof," she added, with a glance at Aruendiel.

She waved once as the carriage went through the gate, Hirgus a stiff and outraged profile beside her. "This is soot on your forehead," Aruendiel said to Nora, who was waving back.

"I'm not surprised," she said, rubbing her forehead. "I almost burned to death just now."

He gave her a long look. "You must learn how to quench fire, now that you know how to light it. I will not have you setting any more of my private papers on fire."

So her inchoate, guilty suspicion was right: Neither Aruendiel nor Hirizjahkinis had ignited the box of papers. "That was an accident," she said.

"All the more reason for you to learn to put fires out. Between you and Hirgus, I am lucky the whole house has not gone up in flames. I would have thought him more subtle than to loose a fire demon on me, but I may have overestimated his capacities. And for him to say that I was jealous of him. The vanity of that imbecile!"

"You have a smudge on your cheek, too," Nora informed him.

Running a hand over the rough terrain of his face, Aruendiel laughed unexpectedly. "What did Hirgus call me? A vulture-faced cripple?"

"Something like that."

"At least the fool is observant," he said as they went inside.

## Chapter 31

ruendiel went north for a few days to visit Lord Luklren and to discern whether the magician Dorneng Hul was maintaining the magical barriers against the Faitoren to the standard that Aruendiel expected. He was almost—but not entirely—satisfied in this, Nora gathered when he returned. She felt some sympathy for Dorneng, who had had to refortify the barriers under Aruendiel's supervision. It was decided that the flock of iron birds, currently roosting in trees and stony hills just outside the Faitoren realm, would remain as an additional safeguard. Back in his own castle, Aruendiel had the blacksmith in Red Gate send over two dozen horseshoes and a keg of nails, and spent an afternoon turning them into more birds, which took clattering flight and disappeared into the gray autumn sky.

She noticed a change in Aruendiel's manner. The lessons resumed, but at a more erratic pace. Some days Nora did not see him at all. He spent more time in his workroom at the top of the tower, where she had never gone, and he stopped taking his dinner when she did in front of the fire in the great hall. Her translation of chapter fifteen of *Pride and Prejudice* remained uncorrected. His instructions to her were more curt and perfunctory than before.

She was having trouble with the next stage of fire magic: extinguishing fire. No matter how hard she concentrated, willing them to go out, the candles burned serenely on. She wondered distractedly whether this failure was the result or the cause of Aruendiel's loss of interest in her magical studies.

Mrs. Toristel noticed a difference. "He's not giving you a lesson today?" she asked one day in the kitchen as Nora scoured a pot with sand.

They had been making sausages. The air was still rich with the smells of herbs and meat, and the loops of fresh sausages hung above their heads like celebratory bunting.

Nora had been wondering if there was a spell to clean dishes, and then reflected that at this rate, she might never get a chance to learn it. "No, not today."

"Nor yesterday, either."

"No."

Mrs. Toristel sniffed. "Well, he changes his mind about things, you know. He gets a notion into his head, and then he drops it, and no one can say why."

If her words were meant to be consoling, she had miscalculated. "Is he all right?" Nora asked after a moment. "He seems more irritated than usual."

"He's been in a foul mood since that black woman was here," Mrs. Toristel said.

"I think he was more annoyed by the man, Hirgus."

"That carriage! I wouldn't ride in something like that for anything. The man himself was pleasant enough. But you never know when *he* will take a dislike to someone."

"Yes," Nora said, thinking that the someone might be herself. She cast about for a new subject. "Mrs. Toristel, I'm sorry to say this, but I don't think these boots are going to last me through the winter." It was too cold for clogs now. Even the poorest peasant women wore boots in the winter— surprisingly elegant boots, some of them: thick-soled, no heels, but expertly cut to show off the curve of the legs and ankles. Nora fantasized sometimes about taking a few dozen pairs back to her own world and selling them through some Madison Avenue boutique to pay for a year or two of school. The old boots that Mrs. Toristel had given her, though, were too small and almost worn out, the leather uppers eroded, the soles slick and spongy.

Mrs. Toristel set her mouth and looked at Nora's feet. "I thought Toristel stitched them up for you."

"He did, twice, but they're still leaking, and he says the leather's too rotten for him to put on another new sole."

"Can't you make them do a little longer?"

"They're pretty hopeless." Nora had finally given up on them the day before, as the pigs were being slaughtered. Averting her gaze from a struggling pig, she had stepped in a puddle in her leaky boots and had to go around the rest of the day with her feet soaked and stinking with blood. The clotted mess in her stockings—indescribable.

Mrs. Toristel sighed. "Well, ask *him* about having a new pair made. I can't afford it, out of the housekeeping money. And you should talk to him soon. He's off to Stone Top tomorrow for the assizes, and there are a couple of horse thieves to be hanged. He's likely to be away for most of a week."

"Oh," said Nora. Aruendiel had not mentioned the trip to her. But then he had said almost nothing to her for the past several days.

She broached the subject of new boots as he was eating breakfast the next day. For the assizes, he was dressed with unusual formality, a fur-trimmed tunic over a shirt of finely crimped linen. His riding boots were beautifully polished.

Aruendiel interrupted her before she had finished. "What about the boots you are wearing?"

"They won't last much longer," she said, trying to be both firm and polite. "I wouldn't ask if it weren't important."

"Don't you have some money of your own?" he said, turning back to his oatmeal. "I cannot afford to pay the wardrobe bills for a lady of fashion."

"All I want," Nora said, her jaw tight, "is to have dry feet while I'm helping to get your pigs slaughtered."

He glanced down at her old boots, the toes still stiff and dark with blood. "You should be more careful where you step," he said, rising from the table.

After he had gone, Nora went upstairs to her room, opened the drawer of the table beside her bed, and untwisted the square of cloth where she kept the silver beads she had brought back from Semr. Two beads left, out of the original dozen. Two for the river crossing, five beads to Massy's children, two for her lodging at the inn at Stone Top on the journey back from Semr. (Foolishly, she had insisted on paying her own way, after the fuss that Aruendiel had made at the ferry in Semr.) Another bead for reshoeing her horse, when it cast a shoe on the road. The animal had later been sold; "Aruendiel should pay me back," she muttered, twisting up the two beads again. Surely two beads would be enough for a new pair of boots. It was ridiculously stingy of Aruendiel to insist that she buy her own boots, but the money had come from him in the first place, so she could not complain too much. Perhaps there would be some money left over.

She was disabused of this comforting thought at the cobbler's hut later that morning. "Four silver beads! That can't be right."

"Well, you're from the castle, aren't you?" the cobbler said.

"Yes. What does that have to do with it?"

"That's what the gentry pays," he said shortly. "And his lordship still owes me for his last pair of boots. I can't work for nothing, you know. I have to eat. So does my wife." The cobbler screwed up his face and shook his head.

"What if you make me the boots for two silver beads, and I'll make sure his lordship pays you what he owes you?" Nora asked boldly, although she was not sure that she could persuade Aruendiel to settle his bill.

The cobbler evidently entertained the same doubts. "No'm. Four silver beads. I can't charge less than what the boots are worth, just to please a lady."

"I didn't ask you to do that," Nora said, "and besides, you as good as said you were overcharging me anyway."

She went away fuming, stopping at Morinen's hut to report. Morinen and her mother, carding wool in front of their fire, were gratifyingly shocked, and gave her a mug of cider as a restorative. "Four silver beads!" Morinen said. "He must think you're rich."

"Yes, he probably thinks I won't pay because I'm as tightfisted as Lord Aruendiel," Nora said bitterly. (Morinen's mother laughed, showing all seven of her teeth.) "But all I have are two beads. Aruendiel wouldn't give me anything to buy my boots with."

"Most people don't even pay Cobbler in cash. What did we trade him last time for my boots, Ma? Was it some goat hides?"

"Goat hides, yes." Morinen's mother nodded. "And a cheese."

"I don't have any goat hides," Nora said. "Or cheese. He wants to be paid in advance, too. I don't know what I'm going to do. My boots are all right when it's dry, like today, but when it's wet, they're a disaster."

"Snow tomorrow," Morinen's mother said.

"I won't go outside this winter. That's all I can do." She put down her mug after a last swig of cider. Standing up—a little unsteadily, the cider was stronger than she'd realized—she accidently kicked her empty mug into one of the hearthstones. It broke into several pieces. Nora began to apologize before she recollected herself. Stooping, she picked up the fragments and handed the mug to Morinen, whole again.

"What!" Morinen stared at the restored mug, then laughed. "That's some of the magic you've learned from his lordship, eh?"

"That, and lighting fires."

Morinen's mother was interested. "Where's the candlestick you broke yesterday, Morinen?" Her shawled head nodded at Nora. "She can fix it."

"It's on the rubbish heap, Ma. She doesn't want to bother with that."

"No, I'd like to," Nora said. "Lead me to it."

She and Morinen pulled on their cloaks and went outside. Behind the hut, the rubbish heap was a pile of old barrel staves, worn-out harnesses, and broken glass and crockery. They assembled as many of the pieces of the broken earthware candlestick as they could find, and then Nora patched them together, adding a little extra to substitute for the missing fragments.

Morinen turned the candlestick over in her hand admiringly. "Ma'll be pleased. She gave me a tongue-lashing that you never heard the like of. You should come around more often—I'm always breaking things. As a matter of fact—" she said hesitantly.

"Tell me."

"Fori next door, she dropped a platter last week that belonged to her ma, that died last winter. She was all upset about it. I think she saved the pieces. Would you mind—?"

"Of course not!" It was gratifying to be able to exercise her new skill.

Fori was the woman whose pregnancy Nora had noticed the summer before. Now she was nursing the baby, her eyes vague with tiredness. Besides the baby, there were four other small children in the hut, wrestling with an excited puppy. In the tumult, it took some time for Morinen to explain why they had come. Fori looked doubtful, but she nodded toward the corner of the hut. "In the chest there. I couldn't bear to throw it out just yet," she said, almost apologetically.

Opening the chest, Nora lifted out the pieces of the dish. This was easy, they wanted to become one again, she could feel it. She let them coalesce under her hands.

Fori took the restored platter wonderingly. "That's magic, isn't it?"

She seemed about to say something else, but one of the children jerked the puppy's tail, provoking a frenzy of yelping. Morinen and Nora turned to leave. They were a few paces outside the hut when Fori called after them. Nora's first thought was that the platter had already been broken again. But Fori was waving two pale strips of cloth in the air.

"Stockings," she said, pressing them into Nora's hands. "Thank you."

"You don't have to—"

Fori had already disappeared inside, drawn by a fresh wail from one of the children.

"That was nice of her," Nora said, examining the stockings. "Lambs' wool."

"Just good manners to pay you back for the favor." Morinen paused, then said meaningfully: "You know, I believe everyone in the village has got some kind of broken dish they'd like to have fixed."

Nora looked at Morinen. "You really think so?"

"I could ask around."

"And they might express their gratitude with more stockings?" Nora laughed. "Or goatskins?"

"Goatskins." Morinen nodded, smiling back at Nora. "Cheese."

"Well, that's very interesting." Nora considered for a moment. "I could come back tomorrow morning and see if anyone needs any pots mended."

"Oh, they will," Morinen said. "People always drop things. I wish I had a pair of stockings for every dish I've broken."

The next morning, after finishing her chores as quickly as she could, Nora went back to the village, a little reluctantly. She was feeling a kind of stage fright—terror that she would forget how to do the spell. But that wouldn't really matter, she reasoned, because Morinen was probably wrong and no one would be interested in having her mend their broken dishes.

"People always want to see magic!" scoffed some brash interior carny that, until then, Nora had not known she carried with her. Strangely enough, it sounded a bit like Aruendiel.

When she entered Morinen's hut, pushing aside the sheepskin that hung inside the door, she saw that Morinen was not there. But Morinen's mother and two of her brothers—one sharpening a scythe, the other fitting a new wooden handle to a mallet—looked up as though they had been expecting her.

"Mori said for you to meet her at Caddo's," said Resk, the one with the mallet.

"All right," Nora said, trying to remember which house was Caddo's. "That's on the other side of the village, right? Next to the river?"

"I'll take you," the other brother, Posin, said. "Mori said I wouldn't want to miss this."

When they reached Caddo's hut, Morinen was waiting inside with Caddo—Big Faris's wife, Nora remembered now, who kept bees—and almost a dozen other women. There was a large basket of broken crockery by Morinen's feet.

"Morinen, did you tell everyone in the village about this?" Nora asked in an undertone.

"Oh, yes," Morinen said. "It's not as though you could keep it secret, anyhow. Here's Caddo's pots—we dug them out of her rubbish heap this morning. I reckon there must be five years' worth of broken dishes here."

"You're not kidding," Nora said, nudging the basket with her toe. She felt the leather of her boot pulling away from the sole, and the sensation steeled her resolve. She knelt beside the basket and rummaged through the contents, looking for pieces that might have come from the same dish. Caddo came forward to help her. By the end of ten minutes, they had what appeared to be the pieces of four separate dishes and a pile of unidentified shards.

With her hands on the broken pottery, Nora began to feel more confident. She picked up two curved fragments from the largest pile, both with the same reddish-brown glaze, and touched them together experimentally. The shards grated roughly against each other. Wait, she corrected herself, reaching into the pile again, *this* one goes with *that* one. Two pieces flowed together, then a third. Finding the right piece got easier as you went along—the pot practically showed you how to put it back together.

It turned out to be a pitcher with an old man's face molded into its round belly. "Here you go," Nora said, handing it to Caddo, who looked both gratified and suspicious. She turned the pitcher over and over, looking for flaws. "Go ahead, fill it with water if you want," Nora urged. She turned her attention to the other piles of broken crockery. A bowl. Another bowl. A platter, painted with an intricate design of radishes and carrots. She was conscious, as she fit the fragments together, that the finished dishes were being passed around the room with whispers.

Then the pile of miscellaneous fragments. It was much harder to reconstitute an entire pot from a single shard. You had to summon the missing pieces from wherever they were, if they were even still in existence, or re-create them if they were not. You really needed the clay's cooperation here, and some fragments were more apathetic than others. If it had been a very long time since the original pot was broken, the piece might have almost forgotten that it was once part of a shaped and greater whole. Aruendiel could reliably bring back an old pot from a fragment as small as a fingernail, but Nora's success rate was perhaps one in three.

So this was good practice. By the time she had gone through the entire pile, she estimated that she had raised her rate to almost one in two, and Caddo was back in possession of another bowl, some roughly formed mugs, and a chamber pot with a sententious motto painted around the rim. ("Foul are my contents but sweeter than filth from the mouth.")

"All right," Nora said finally. "I think I've done all that I can do." She stood up and looked questioningly at Morinen: What now?

Morinen had evidently prepped Caddo, who glanced shrewdly one more time at the newly mended dishes and then produced a small flagon of honey wine and three beeswax candles. After a second's hesitation, she also handed Nora one of the reconstituted pitchers. "I thank you, most excellent lady, for this favor you have shown me," Caddo said, with a curtsy, "and I beg you to accept an unworthy gift in return."

"Your gifts far outshine my humble offering, Faris's most excellent wife, and I thank you for your generosity," Nora said, returning the curtsy. She was fairly sure that she had gotten the formula right—she had heard Mrs. Toristel go through the same ritual exchange when bartering with one of the villagers. Even so, the others in the room, even the little boys who had crowded in, seemed to be amused.

She got the same reaction—someone even tittered—at the next hut, when Morinen's aunt Narl gave her a skein of crimson yarn for mending a couple of plates and an oil lamp. "Did I say something wrong?" she murmered to Morinen as they left.

"No, no, what do you mean? You're doing fine," Morinen said. "Aunt Narl was a little cheap, though. She could have done better than that yarn."

"I don't mind giving your family a discount."

"Not so loud—the whole village is family. Now, Pelinen's next. She'll probably have some cheese for you. We should start doing a little trading, or you'll never be able to carry all this stuff."

"Trading?" Nora asked. "What should I—"

"Leave it to me."

Pelinen was a square-faced widow of forty who owned the village's two best dairy cows. After Nora mended a cracked pickle crock, a chamber pot, and—a new challenge—a small square of looking glass, Morinen drew Pelinen into a muttered side consultation. Nora could not hear the details of the discussion, but she got the sense that both parties were volleying back and forth with practiced ease. A few minutes later she and Morinen left without the beeswax candles and yarn, but with half a wheel of cheese that they had to trundle between the two of them, since even Morinen was not strong enough to carry it by herself.

At the tanner's, the cheese and the honey wine and a half-dozen mended dishes turned into two goatskins. At Trouteye's, the rubbish heap had been excavated down to bare earth in Nora's honor; she spent more than an hour mending pots for him and his wife and left with a side of bacon. Lus had only a few items to be repaired, but he took the bacon in exchange for a cask of ale. At their next stop, as Nora mended dishes, the ale and one of the goatskins became a woolen blanket; at the hut belonging to Morinen's cousin Porlus, the other goatskin became an iron skillet.

There was an unusual amount of joviality accompanying each of these transactions, it seemed to Nora. Sometimes people would glance at her worn boots and laugh. It took her a while to realize, from snippets of overheard conversations, that they were not laughing at her, but Aruendiel. Morinen had evidently told all—how Aruendiel had refused to buy new boots for her and how the cobbler was charging her at least double the usual price.

Further, Nora gleaned, one of the accused on trial before his lordship in Stone Top at this moment was a boy of nineteen from the village, known as Ferret—Morinen's second cousin. Ferret was probably destined for the gallows anyway, everyone said, but most believed him innocent of the crime that he was accused of, beating and robbing an elderly peasant of his horse. The judges were likely to sentence him to hang.

"So everyone's helping me because they're angry at Aruendiel?" Nora asked Morinen, as they went from one hut to another.

"No, I wouldn't say angry, not at all." Morinen glanced around with a trace of uneasiness. "They just think it's funny, you having to buy your own boots. And they do like having their dishes fixed."

By this time, the light was fading. Nora had mended at least three dozen dishes and cooking vessels, two mirrors, four glass bottles, and two small clay figures of a rabbit-headed gnome with an oversized phallus. ("That's Gingornl," Morinen said matter-of-factly. "He brings children. Folks keep him in the bed with them, so he's always getting broken.") Nora was not tired at all—the opposite, in fact—but she was beginning to think that her brain would explode into tiny shards from working an unceasing succession of three-dimensional jigsaw puzzles.

"So what have we collected?" Nora asked Morinen.

"A skillet, three sheepskins, a goatskin, a kerchief, a flask of blackberry cordial, a dozen sausages, three skeins of yarn, and a bag of dried peas," Morinen said with satisfaction.

"And the stockings that Fori gave me. Do you think that's enough for my boots?"

"I think so. Let's go over to Bitar's now; he might give us some cash for this lot."

Bitar's small, cluttered hut was the village's closest equivalent to a general store. He bartered for goods in the markets in Red Gate and Stone Top, then traded them to the villagers for a premium, and was rumored to have a box of gold beetles buried under his hearth. Mrs. Toristel said that she would never eat anything that came out of Bitar's hut, but she sometimes went to him for small oddments like needles or string if she had no time to go to Red Gate on market day.

Bitar greeted them by complaining that they had ruined his business in dishes for the next six months. "No one wants to buy your bowls anyway, they're much too expensive," Morinen retorted. "But this is your lucky day, Bitar. Look at all the lovely things that Mistress Nora and I have to sell to you. Didn't Porsn do a nice job of tanning these hides? We have some of Blue Dove's blackberry wine, and this skillet, very clean, no rust on it anywhere, not like that iron pot you sold my ma last year."

"She got a good price on that pot, I don't know what you're complaining about." Bitar pointed out the dent in the skillet and the stain on one of the sheepskins. He and Morinen haggled for a few minutes until he finally agreed to pay them three silver beads for the lot, except for the sausages and the yarn. "I couldn't give those away," he said, scratching his chin. "Not this time of year, with everyone killing pigs. And I've got bags of yarn already. What would I be wanting more for, especially this coarse stuff?"

"You don't know good wool when you see it," Morinen grumbled, watching as Bitar fished a leather purse from somewhere in the region of his crotch and then slowly counted out three beads. They were black with tarnish. Morinen polished them on her apron until she was satisfied that they were real silver.

"He robbed us—we could have gotten twice that in Red Gate," she said to Nora as they went outside. "'Course, it would have taken us all day to get there and back."

"And it's snowing now, too," Nora said, turning her face away from the wind. "You did a fantastic job, Morinen, not just with Bitar but with all those people. Three silver beads is better than I expected. I couldn't have done it alone—I wouldn't have known what all those things were worth, let alone how to bargain for them."

Morinen smiled, her eyes squeezed tight against the blowing snow. "I used to go to Red Gate with my pa to sell kids and lambs when I was little—now, that's some hard bargaining. This was easy. And living in the village, you know who needs what and what they'll give for it."

"Well, here, you take the extra bead—you earned it. Take the sausages, too, and the yarn. No, I insist," Nora said, as Morinen began to demur. "We have plenty of sausages, and if I take the wool back to the castle, Mrs. Toristel will just make me knit it into something." Nora was thinking, too, that if she returned with sausages or yarn, Mrs. Toristel would want some explanation. Not that the day's activities would remain secret for long—one of the villagers would be sure to spill the beans—but she wanted time to prepare her story.

On the way home, she stopped by the cobbler's hut to order her new boots. He laughed when he saw her. "If I'd known you were so handy at fixing dishes," he said, "I would have asked you to fix the bowl I threw at my wife the other night."

"I'm done for the day," Nora said.

## Chapter 32

Snow fell all night, a shadowy curtain blowing restlessly around the house, and continued into the next day. "Is it like this all winter?" Nora asked, staring out the window.

"This isn't so bad," Mrs. Toristel said, with a short, rueful laugh. "After the Null Days is the worst. We never had winters like this in Pelagnia, never, with the snow deep enough to bury a man. Although *he* goes out in the worst weather."

The following day was clearer. Nora was trying to decide whether to chance walking to the cobbler's in her old boots when Morinen's brother Posin struggled up the hill with the new ones. Nora thanked him and brought him into the kitchen to warm up, where he filled Mrs. Toristel in on the latest news from the village.

The new boots fit perfectly—better, in fact, than any shoes that Nora had ever owned in her life. In her own world, she reflected, it would have taken a lot longer than a single day to earn enough money for a pair of custom-made shoes. After Posin's departure, she hiked up her skirt to show them to Mrs. Toristel. The calfskin boots came up to her knee, high enough even for the snow that covered the ground now, and—pleasing her just as much—they had an interesting clunky, sexy look. She would have liked to wear them with tights and a miniskirt, although she did not mention this to the housekeeper.

"Cobbler does good work," Mrs. Toristel allowed. "Mind, you polish them with tallow now, to keep the damp out."

Nora went out late that afternoon to feed the animals, fearless of wet and cold. The leather boots gleamed in the lantern light; she enjoyed glimpsing her well-shod feet among the bustle of chickens demanding their dinner. At the kitchen door, she stopped and carefully wiped a crumb of dung off the top of her right boot.

"—two hours retrieving a fool who tried to make the pass at Witch-needle the night of the first storm."

Aruendiel was back, still wearing his traveling cloak, a looming black pillar in the middle of the kitchen. His pale eyes flicked toward Nora and then back to Mrs. Toristel. "And then it was slow going to Red Gate," he went on, "so I spent last night there."

Mrs. Toristel reached for his cloak. "Any news from the inn, sir?"

"A lot of idiotic talk about the assizes. One of the drunkards presumed to tell me I should have hanged the lot. A shame that I cannot hang a man for stupidity." Aruendiel glanced in Nora's direction again, without acknowledging her. "Clousit from the village was there, too, with a most amusing story. I could hardly avoid it, since he shared it with the rest of the taproom. He said that he had encountered our own Mistress Nora in the village, casting spells to mend the peasants' broken dishes."

Mrs. Toristel, catching a sarcastic lilt in Aruendiel's tone, folded the cloak over her arm and turned to look at Nora. "Yes, she mentioned that."

"Did she mention that she went house to house, through the whole village, taking payment for repairing chamber pots and Gingornls' cocks? She needed the money—so said Clousit—because his lordship refused to give her money for new boots. They had a good laugh over that at the Two Rams—at least, those who were too drunk to know I was in the room."

Abruptly he turned to Nora. "Those are your famous new boots?"

"Yes," she said, with a sinking feeling.

"You will take them off, and Mrs. Toristel will have them burned."

"No!"

"Nora, is this all true?" Mrs. Toristel said, her thin face tightening.

After a moment, Nora nodded.

"Oh, dear, Nora." Mrs. Toristel closed her eyes and looked faintly ill.

Nora tried to stay calm. "Yes, but I mended all kinds of dishes, not just chamber pots and whatsits. And yes, people paid me with cheeses and bacon and various things, and then I bartered them for cash, which I used to buy these boots. I'm sorry I let it slip that you wouldn't pay for them—"

"I am not accustomed to hearing my financial matters being discussed in the public room of the Red Gate tavern."

"I'm very sorry, I shouldn't have said anything about that. But otherwise I don't see what the problem is."

"The problem?" Aruendiel smiled unpleasantly. "You have only made a public spectacle of yourself. You took the magic that I taught you and used it to cheat ignorant peasants."

"I didn't cheat them! I mended their pots, and they were happy to pay me. It was a fair trade."

"Nevertheless, it was unseemly for you to charge them, and unseemly to put yourself on public display, to make yourself—and me—the object of village gossip."

"As if you're not already, come on," Nora said, feeling the growing temblors of her own anger. "People in the village gossip about you, they gossip about me, they gossip about each other, they have nothing else to do. And I wouldn't have had to earn that money in the first place if you had paid your own bills at the cobbler's. He charged me extra—four silver beads—because he said I was gentry—"

"He was mistaken there."

"—and because you hadn't paid him for your last pair of boots." What happened to his statement that a gentleman doesn't quibble with shopkeepers, she wondered.

"That is a matter between him and me," Aruendiel said icily. "If he tried to overcharge you, you should have informed me."

"You weren't here."

"Or Mrs. Toristel."

"She would have said to wait until you got back, and in the meantime, my old boots were falling apart," Nora shot back. "You should be pleased that I put the magic that you taught me to good use. So what if I repaired some chamber pots? They're useful, and I saved the villagers the cost of replacing them.

"What you're really angry about," she added, "is that a lot of peasants laughed at you in a tavern. Well, I'm sorry about that. But that doesn't mean I should give up my boots."

She made a point of returning Aruendiel's stare. When finally he spoke, the edge of sarcasm was gone from his voice, replaced by something meaner, blunter. His face was blank with rage. Whenever she had seen Aruendiel angry before, she realized now, there had always been a sense that he was savoring the chance to frame exactly the right insult or give voice to his feelings with precisely the degree of force required. The black irony, the barbs, were a sign that he was in control. All that was gone now. "You do not even understand how you have disgraced yourself," he said flatly. "Remove your boots and give them to Mrs. Toristel."

Nora shook her head. "No," she said, not as loudly as she wanted to.

"Then you will not remain under my roof."

Her immediate response was relief. There was an escape. She was not going to be transformed into some small, crawling thing or run through with a sword. "All right," she said.

"Sir!" Mrs. Toristel's voice had regained some strength. "Nora has certainly behaved badly, and I'm very sorry for it. I would have stopped it at once if I'd known."

"I know you would have, Mrs. Toristel," Aruendiel said in clipped tones.

"But is it necessary to turn her out of doors in winter? She has nowhere to go."

"She cannot live in my household, if she will not obey my wishes."

"Nora," said Mrs. Toristel, "you must do as he asks. Come, give me the boots."

"He's not asking," Nora said, "and no."

"Don't be silly, girl. You've been protected here, fed, clothed. If you leave here—in this weather—a lone woman—what do you think will happen to you?"

"I'd rather go anywhere else than be treated like this."

"If you leave, Nora, there's nothing I can do to help you," Mrs. Toristel said sadly.

"I know," Nora said, working hard to keep her voice steady. "I'll be all right. I have a skill now," she added stubbornly. "I can earn my own living, that's one thing I've learned from this stupid mess. People will pay me to mend pots. I can go from village to village and earn food and shelter and silver. I'll be fine."

"You can hardly expect to travel from village to village unmolested," Aruendiel remarked.

She jerked her head up to look at him. "Well, I expect you to make sure that I can pass safely through your lands. After that, what happens to me is of no concern to you."

Mrs. Toristel shook her head. "Mending pots, Nora? You'll make a poor living."

"I made three silver beads yesterday, and I could make a lot of money in Semr, mending fine porcelain for the nobility. And I'll pick up other spells, like bringing rain—" Seeing the contemptuous expression on Aruendiel's face, she faltered for a second. "Or curing warts or whatever. There's all kinds of useful magic that people will pay for."

"At least think it over," Mrs. Toristel said, with a sigh. "Don't be foolish."

"She has made her choice," Aruendiel said shortly, his eyes sliding away from Nora as though he found the sight of her distasteful.

"I'll leave tomorrow morning," she said. Shouldering past him, she went out of the kitchen and upstairs, her heart thudding.

The whole dispute was trivial, absurd, she thought, sitting in her small chamber—not hers anymore, after tomorrow—and yet now the conflict seemed inevitable. If Aruendiel was going to play lord of the manor—which of course was exactly what he was—then something, anything would have been bound to set him off eventually. No reasonable person could predict when she might unintentionally break one of their repressive, ridiculous, medieval codes. In her own world, what she and Morinen had done would be admired as plucky, smart, entrepreneurial. Sheer bad luck that the one time she had ever discovered a way to make some money, it had to be in a place where her initiative would only land her in disgrace.

Of course, Mrs. Toristel was right, she reflected more soberly. She, Nora, might be raped, robbed, murdered, frozen to death, reenchanted by Ilissa, as soon as she moved beyond the protective radius of the magician's power. But then his power was the problem. That was why she couldn't stay here to be ordered around like a slave. Better to die a free woman. If any woman in this wretched world could be said to be free.

Hirizjahkinis. She had given Nora her token. Nora felt relief flood her. If she got into real trouble, she could call on Hirizjahkinis. Maybe it would work, after all, this plan of going out to make her living by fixing pots. Nora already knew how to set things on fire. Hirizjahkinis could teach her other spells to protect herself.

She recalled, with some chagrin, how easily she'd told Hirizjahkinis she did not fear Aruendiel. Well, it was true then. Hirizjahkinis said he would not hurt her. Maybe Hirizjahkinis had never seen him as he had been today, rage freezing every trace of reason or compassion. He had been irritated with Nora for weeks, and now this. She had no idea what might have first turned him against her. It didn't matter now.

Mrs. Toristel called her downstairs to the kitchen and tried to get her to eat something. Nora forced down a few mouthfuls of stewed lentils, aware that this might be her last warm dinner for a while, but she felt too anxious to eat much. Seeing Nora's agitation, Mrs. Toristel began to plead again that she reconsider, apologize, surrender her boots, and stay at the castle. Aruendiel was nowhere to be seen, but Mrs. Toristel spoke in an urgent whisper, as though she were afraid he might overhear. Her eyes were wet. On the verge of tears herself, Nora tore herself away and went back upstairs.

She had little to pack. Her few clothes, *Pride and Prejudice*, Hirizjahkinis's lock of hair. When she had made up her bundle, Nora sat on the bed and tried to map out a plan. Her first stop should be Red Gate, she decided. If everyone there was gossiping about her pot-repairing exploits, she might as well take advantage of the free publicity. With luck and a good pace, she could be there by tomorrow night. Probably she could work out some barter arrangement for shelter at the inn. Any establishment for eating or drinking would have plenty of broken dishes.

She thought she would not sleep at all. But she awoke, startled, from fractured dreams. Ilissa had featured in them, in some disturbing cameo. Well, Ilissa had been right about Aruendiel, what a bastard he could be— you had to give her that. Nora dressed herself as warmly as she could. It was still dark, and Mrs. Toristel wasn't up yet. That made her exit easier. She would have liked to say good-bye, though. She wrote a note instead, on a leaf torn from the endpapers of *Pride and Prejudice*: "Thank you. You have been a kind friend to me, and I am sorry to leave." The words sounded curt and insufficient as she read them over, yet she was afraid that if she wrote something longer and more eloquent, Mrs. Toristel might have trouble reading it.

She wrapped up a loaf of bread and a sausage for the day's provisions. Mrs. Toristel would not begrudge her a little food, even if the magician might. Then, swinging her cloak over her shoulders with a sudden flourish, as though waving defiance at the world, she stepped outside, crossed the still-shadowy courtyard, and shoved at the castle gate, stuck in the snow, until it let her through.

The sun had risen over a world of clean and seamless white. Two or three inches of fresh snow had fallen during the night, softly blurring the double line of tracks that Posin's feet and Aruendiel's horse had left the day before. Thank God, she thought, I have good boots.

Wrapping her cloak tight against the cold, Nora started down the hill to the village, stepping in Posin's trail. It was slower going than she had expected. Once she wandered off the road and stumbled in the deep snow.

Perhaps she could stay with Morinen until a few days' use cleared the roads. The idea cheered her, until it occurred to her that the magician might take some revenge against Morinen and her family.

She looked up, after some minutes, and saw that she was not alone after all. Someone else was struggling up the road from the village. It was laundry day, when Losi came up to help Mrs. Toristel.

This was early for Losi, though. And the figure was taller and thinner than Losi. Something about the ungainly way it pushed through the snowdrifts was very familiar. Aruendiel.

There was no way to avoid him. If she stepped off the road, she would not be able to make her way through the snow. And it would look as though she were afraid. He did not give any sign that he had seen Nora, although he was heading directly toward her. Nora kept going, part of her mind preoccupied with trying to work out how he had gotten to the village. No other fresh tracks but hers led from the castle. Some magical means of transportation that he had never bothered to tell her about, probably.

Finally, they were close enough that she could see his features clearly, reddened with the cold. Nora halted first, waiting to see what Aruendiel would do. He stopped an arm's length from her, slightly out of breath.

Nora looked at him coolly. Oddly, she was not afraid of him anymore. Something about his face, mobile, imperfect—it looked alive again, not like the frozen, furious mask that she had seen yesterday.

"I have something for you," he said without preamble. His gloved hand reached under his cloak and pulled out a small leather pouch. He handed it to her.

Puzzled, Nora slipped her right hand out of its mitten and upended the pouch into her left palm. Two silver beads slid out. "What is this?"

"I am returning what is rightfully yours. The cobbler charged you too much."

She frowned at the silver beads, then at Aruendiel. "Did you—?"

"I have settled my account with the cobbler. He has agreed to return your money."

Nora searched for something to say, then settled for the obvious. "Thank you." She added: "I didn't expect this."

"You should not have to pay what was my debt," Aruendiel said.

"Right," she said, with a brief nod. "Well, these beads will be useful, I'm sure. Thank you for straightening all this out." Clumsily, her fingers stiff with cold, she put the beads back into the pouch and then looked point-edly past him. "I'll be on my way now."

He did not move out of her way. "You need not leave," he said abruptly.

"I'm sorry?"

"I said you need not leave." Aruendiel gave a small sigh of exaspera-tion. "You may keep—that is, I do not ask you to give up the boots that you have gone to some trouble to acquire. And you are free to continue living in my household."

Nora stared. "You changed your mind?"

"Yes," he said, after a long moment.

"What about my unseemly behavior and making a public spectacle of myself?"

Aruendiel seemed to be gritting his teeth. After a moment, he said: "It has occurred to me that Clousit might have exaggerated some particulars, in telling his story to a crowded barroom."

"I'm sure he did. But the basic story was true," Nora said defiantly.

"Well, you suggested to me once that I reexamine my notions of pro-priety."

"And have you?"

"I have," he said. "On the whole, I am satisfied with them. But as you also observed, I do not always follow other people's idea of correct behav-ior myself. So perhaps I should not insist that you follow mine. I think—I hope we are in agreement on some basic standards of propriety," he said, with a lifted eyebrow. "But there are areas, obviously, where we must dis-agree."

Nora nodded slowly, frowning a little. Perhaps it was only because he stood downslope from her, so she did not have to look up at him, but she had the novel sensation that he was addressing her as an equal. She noticed for the first time that in the open air, against a luminous blue sky, his pale eyes took on a surprising blue cast, faint but clear.

"I still have to leave here," she said.

"Why? I have said you do not have to."

"Last night you lost your temper and told me to get out. I can't stay here, knowing that could happen again."

"I see," he said, his mouth tightening.

"I was afraid," Nora said seriously. "I am tired of being afraid."

He sighed again. "I have a bad temper, and I often govern it poorly."

"I've noticed."

"But I govern it somewhat better than I once did. You must believe that I would not harm you. I am sorry that I made you fear me."

He did sound regretful. "Well, thank you for saying that," Nora said. "But you know, it takes more than words to counteract fear."

"If it comes to fear—" Aruendiel said, with a grim laugh. "Listen, Mistress Nora, here is the meat of the nut. I do not wish to see a blameless and—and good-hearted young woman, who is also a student of mine who may show some promise if she applies herself, become subject to the dangers of the open road because of my own folly and bad temper. I don't think you would starve," he said quickly, as Nora opened her mouth to make an interjection. "You are right—you could probably make a living mending dishes. You did sound work in the village the other day, evidently. But there are many other risks, which you are intelligent enough to be aware of.

"I knew a woman, years ago," he went on, his face darkening, "who tried to make her way in the world knowing one or two spells. She had a wretched time of it. I recommend—I ask you not to put yourself in that position. If you are determined to leave my household, at least wait until I can teach you enough magic so that you can protect yourself properly, not to mention support yourself by doing something more interesting than mending pots."

"It wasn't bad," she protested. "Maybe a little tedious—after a few hours."

"You are likely capable of better. It would be a waste to stop your studies now. My advice," he added, "is to stay here, conquer your fear of me, and learn some serious magic before you try to set yourself up as a magic-worker. That way, you will do more credit to yourself, and to your teacher."

For the first time that day, Nora laughed. "I see what this is all about. Your reputation! You are afraid of how it would look to have a student of the magician Aruendiel traveling around the countryside fixing pots."

"I have had students turn out worse." Aruendiel studied her for a moment. "I do not think that you are as frightened of me as you say you are."

"Not so much, now," she admitted.

"Then, would you be so kind as to accompany me back to the castle? It is as cold as a dead man's—it is viciously cold out here."

She hesitated, glancing at the buried road before her and then back at his face, broken and alert. He waited. "Yes, it's cold," she said. "Let's go."

A faint smile moved across his lips; it seemed to Nora for a moment that he looked as relieved as she felt. Neither said anything on the way back to the castle. Once, after Aruendiel had struggled through a snowdrift that reached halfway up his thighs, he gave Nora a quizzical stare, as if to convey that she must have taken leave of her senses to set out in such a snowfall.

Mrs. Toristel turned around quickly when Aruendiel came into the kitchen. Her eyes went immediately to Nora, just behind him.

"Good morning, Mrs. Toristel, I encountered Mistress Nora as she was departing," Aruendiel said loudly. "We have come to an agreement, she and I. She is to remain here and apply herself with diligence to the study of magic and behave with as much propriety as she sees fit, and in return I will endeavor not to frighten her. Is that your understanding?" he asked Nora.

"And I can keep my boots," she said.

"That is correct. You need not burn her boots, Mrs. Toristel. I will be at work upstairs this morning, not to be disturbed. Mistress Nora, I will expect you in the library this afternoon. You have missed several lessons of late. There is much work to be done."

After the kitchen door had shut behind Aruendiel, Mrs. Toristel pursed her mouth. "Well, I'm thankful you've seen reason," she said.

"It wasn't me who had to see reason, it was him," Nora said. "And he did. It was—surprising."

"Oh, yes, taking off on foot in the middle of winter, that's very sensible. When I saw your note this morning, I thought, Well, I'll never see that one again."

"It would have been a better plan in summer," Nora admitted. "Did you say anything to him? To make him change his mind?"

"Do I look as though I can make him change his mind? Him, in a rage like that? I wouldn't know where to begin. Oh, you don't know how lucky you are. You could be out there lying dead in a snowdrift somewhere. I wouldn't let Toristel go past the village today, not with the roads in the state they're in."

"I'm sure I'd survive for at least a few hours," Nora objected, smiling. "But it's good to be here. Did you want me to make the bread today?"

In the magician's study that afternoon, she found a pile of books waiting for her, with almost a dozen spells marked for her to learn. Duminisl on how to conjure smoke without fire; Vlonicl on how to set fire to your enemies' bowstrings in the pouring rain; Morkin on how to build a fire underwater, among other things. She felt it was unlikely that she might need to burn up a bowstring, no matter what the weather, but Aruendiel was a great admirer of Vlonicl. Very few wizards or magicians, he said, wrote with such absolute concision and confidence, paring spells down to the bare minimum, yet always achieving a result that was more powerful than you would expect. Nora set to work, taking notes on her wax tablet, savoring the peace of the book-lined room. The fire sputtered companionably. The heavy parchment rustled gently under her fingers as she turned the pages. She tried not to think, as she read, of how nearly this small haven had been lost to her.

She could hear Aruendiel's footsteps faintly overhead. Once he came down in search of a book. He gave an absent nod when he saw Nora seated at the table.

She did not speak to him again until the evening. After finishing her last kitchen chores and her dinner, she went to sit by the fire in the great hall to practice the spell that she had not yet been able to cast successfully: Concentrating on the candle that burned on the table, she willed it to extinguish itself. Over and over again, it refused.

She began to wonder if she would ever be able to do the spell. That made it worse. The flame shone with a dreamy intensity, like a child too absorbed in a game to hear his mother calling.

Odd noises overhead distracted her attention, too. From time to time, a deep-pitched throbbing came from the tower. Once she thought she heard a groan. She got up to investigate, but she discovered that she could not enter the tower through the wall. Aruendiel had sealed it off, presumably because he was working some sort of complex and risky magic up there. She returned to her own, more elementary spell, keeping her ear cocked, but she heard nothing more.

Some time later, the door to the courtyard opened unexpectedly, letting in Aruendiel, his boots powdery with snow, and a wave of freezing air. The candle's flame faltered for the first time that evening.

"I thought you were up in the tower," Nora said, confused. "What's going on up there?" Aruendiel's leather tunic had been ripped at the shoulder. As he came closer, she saw that the knuckles of his right hand were dappled with fresh blood. With some concern she said: "You look as though you've been in a fight."

"Only a new project that has proven to be more unpredictable than I expected." There was also a raw-looking bruise on one cheekbone. Yet he moved more lightly than usual, and looked fresher, less worn than when she had seen him in the afternoon. Candlelight is flattering, she thought, and she also remembered what Hirizjahkinis had told her about how strong magic kept magicians young.

"What kind of project?"

"I will tell you about it later. And what is occupying you this evening?"

She had to confess that she had been practicing the spell to extinguish fire, with no success. Aruendiel frowned. He began to say something, then checked himself. "Show me," he said.

She tried again. The flame did not even waver.

"I can feel the fire," she said. "And it can feel me. I know it can understand me. But I tell it to die—and it won't. It just ignores me. And the whole thing gets harder as I go on. I start thinking, Who am I to kill this fire? It wants to live. After a while, I'm not even sure I could blow out the candle in good conscience."

Aruendiel shook his head slowly. "You are letting the element control you—which is very dangerous."

"I know. But I just can't bring myself to kill it."

He was quiet for a moment. "You don't need to kill it. You only need to master it. Let us try again." The candle went out at his silent command, leaving them in near darkness. "Light it."

Nora did so, watching his angular features reappear, grave and intent, in the glow of the candle. The new flame flared slightly and then steadied.

"Now," he said, "take it lower." At her asking, the flame diminished slightly. "Lower, lower." She dimmed the flame again, until it was a bright bead clinging to the candlewick. "Now, you put it to sleep. Push it down. You're not killing it. Fire does not die, it is eternal." The flame brightened again momentarily. "No, bring it lower. Good. There is always fire somewhere, hungry for your attention. But when you have no need of it, you must be able to dismiss it, make it sleep, put it away from you, because you are its master, Nora. Do you see what I mean?"

The tiny bead of light dissolved, filling the air with the smell of burnt wick. "I think so," she said into the blackness.

"Good," he said. "Well then, good night."

"Good night," she said, and listened to the lopsided rhythm of his steps move away across the hall and up the stairs. She did not relight the candle until he was gone.

## Chapter 33

Aruendiel lived up to his promise to keep Nora busy. There seemed to be an endless number of fire spells to learn. It also became tantalizingly clear that, once you had a real command of fire magic, you could use that understanding to power other spells that had nothing to do with fire: spells to make objects float in air, to make wild animals docile, to breathe underwater, to read unknown languages, to render an army invisible.

"But you would never use fire for a spell to build a wall, for example," Aruendiel instructed. "Unless you only needed the wall for a short time, to hold off an enemy for a single day, say. Fire is eager, but it grows bored easily. It does not lend itself to spells in which the effect is intended to be permanent."

"But what if you need to build a wall?" Nora asked.

"You would draw on the stones directly, or you could impose a spell on them with wood. Wood is very strong and it will last a long time, and there is also a kind of intelligence to wood that is useful. It can outfox stone, persuade it to do things that it might not otherwise do. Stone is very stubborn and resists suggestion, although if you can master stone, the spells that you cast with it will last forever. Which is why," he added severely, "you must never use stone for any spells that might need to be reversed. Most transformations. Some curses. Love spells."

"*Love* spells?"

"Love spells should always be reversible and preferably temporary. In almost every case, the party who casts the spell, or for whom it was cast, falls out of love first. Then the enchanted party becomes desperate, sometimes vengeful. It can be very ugly," Aruendiel said reflectively. Nora had a strong suspicion that he was speaking from personal experience. "If you ever cast a love spell, do it with fire, so that the attachment will be fierce and short-lived—but I advise you not to cast any love spells at all."

"No fear," Nora said. "I've been on the other end, you know."

It was fascinating to hear about all the spells that, theoretically, she would be able to work using fire, but in fact, she could as yet work only a few of them. The most successful was the light-conjuring spell that Aruendiel had employed in the royal library at Semr. Nora stood in the courtyard at dusk, shivering, trying to coax some illumination from the kitchen fire. After several evenings of effort, she achieved a vague, flickering glow that might have allowed her to read the headlines on a newspaper, if any had been handy. Aruendiel could pull light from the village fires or from as far away as Red Gate. From what he said, Nora gleaned, he had a sort of constant, low-grade awareness of the nearest sources of magical power—fire, stone, forest, things that she had not yet learned about. He registered them automatically as he went about his business, the way a driver might note potential parking spots on a crowded city street.

"You must be more alert, you must be able to sense the presence of useful elements," he said. "You do not want to be the sort of magician who must build a fire every time he wants to work a spell."

"Or *she* wants to work a spell." Campaigning for nonsexist phrasing was a losing battle in Ors, where gender governed even the choice of preposition, but sometimes Nora could not resist. Usually Aruendiel tolerated these corrections with a minimum of sarcasm.

"I speak of mediocre practitioners only," he pointed out now. "I have encountered few female magicians, but they have all been good ones. I hope that you will not prove an exception."

"Really?" Nora asked with interest. "What other female magicians have you known, besides Hirizjahkinis? Do you mean Ilissa?"

His expression shifted, like a door yanked shut. "Ilissa is hardly what I would term a magician. I was thinking primarily of Hirizjahkinis."

Interesting, though. He had certainly used the plural. Aruendiel's past life was much on Nora's mind these days, in part because of the new project with which she was assisting him. Hirgus's visit had apparently inspired Aruendiel to free the ghosts that he himself had bound into spells at the beginning of his career, when he still called himself a wizard. So far the process had been quieter than she had feared: no more nocturnal explosions or unexplained bruises. Instead he had asked her to search through some of his old books and papers for a few specific spells.

Here Nora found lists of demons and their attributes, recipes for potions, incantations—the sort of magic that she had never seen him practice. His handwriting was rounder and looser than the spiky hand he wrote now. In his younger days, Aruendiel also seemed to have been considerably less organized. Some spells were scribbled on the back of bills (twenty-two gold beetles for an inlaid dagger sheath, eight beetles six beads for scented gloves); others filled the margins of a manual on cavalry tactics, *The Cunning Horseman in Battle*.

She read with curiosity, looking for hints of the life that Aruendiel had led as a young man. Much of the magic had some military function, direct or indirect. There were spells to keep sword blades sharp; to embolden cowards; to redraw an opponent's maps; or to revive a man who has been cut in half. She lost count of the number of spells for panicking an enemy's horses. He had scrawled notes alongside many of the spells. *Best under a quarter moon. More sulfur*. A thicket of calculations, not always accurate. *Whoever said this would cure the clap should be fucked backward*. There were several such spells for curing venereal diseases—always useful in an army camp, no doubt. She found no love spells, although she noted a disturbing spell for making a woman as drunk on one glass of wine as if she had drunk three.

"Did you compose all of these spells yourself?" she asked Aruendiel one day, as he came into the library.

"Some of them," he said indifferently. "Most I swapped with other wizards, or found in books. How are you progressing? Have you found the spells I asked for?"

"Two of them so far," she said, consulting the list on her wax tablet. "The spell for making men grunt like pigs, and the one for making it rain poisonous toads. There are half a dozen spells for wrapping an army in fog—which one did you want?"

"The one I require starts with roasting the heart and feathers of a black rooster over a fire of dung—gods, the smell!" Aruendiel grimaced. "Is there a black rooster in the flock now?"

"No, he's speckled. Glory be to God for dappled things—all things original, counter, spare, strange," she added in English. Aruendiel fixed her with a questioning eye. "Sorry," she said, switching back to Ors, "something that just came to mind."

"Was that a spell in your language?" he asked with a trace of suspicion.

"Poetry. There's a black rooster in the village, in Porlus's flock."

"It'll be expensive, three weeks before the Null Days," Aruendiel said, clicking his tongue with annoyance. He went back to his workroom upstairs, hunching slightly as he climbed the spiral staircase.

Three weeks, two days, Nora thought as she went back to her scroll. The Null Days were looming large in her life. Currently, she and Mrs. Toristel were engaged in a general housecleaning for the holidays, to be followed by a kitchen round of roasting and baking. Mrs. Toristel worked with an unusual air of animation; her daughter and a grandson were coming to visit from Barsy.

The Null Days, Nora had learned from Mrs. Toristel and an old almanac in Aruendiel's study, were the five, sometimes six days that were not counted in the official calendar of 360 days. They fell when the nights were at their longest, after the old year had ended, before the new year began. No legal business could be transacted then, no new enterprises undertaken. It was considered unlucky even to light a fire during the Null Days, so the same fire was kept burning continuously throughout the holiday—not that anyone let their fire go out at this time of year anyway—along with special, fat candles designed to burn for days. While the Null Days lasted, Nora gathered, one did as little as possible. No cooking, no cleaning, and only the most necessary chores involving the livestock—all fine with her—but also no reading, writing, or practicing magic. Then came New Year's Day, when a new fire was kindled and a yearling animal, all black, was killed with a stone blade. Mr. Toristel had set aside a young black ram some months ago for this purpose.

In other words, the Null Days were a solstice holiday, a lighted pause in midwinter darkness, celebrated with food, fire, conviviality, idleness, this world's equivalent of Christmas without the religious backstory. Nora was looking forward to it with cautious interest. "So what do people do to pass the time?" Nora asked Mrs. Toristel one morning as they rubbed beeswax into the railing of the gallery in the great hall.

"Well." Mrs. Toristel sighed. "Back home in Pelagnia, we always took care to observe the Null Days properly. None of this feasting or merrymaking. We fasted every day, all of us, and some folks would flog themselves at nightfall."

"That doesn't sound like much fun."

"We know what's owed to the sun lord. You have to show him proper respect. Here, they don't take it as seriously. All this eating and visiting they do. And the drinking! My father never took a drop during the Null Days until the New Year. Toristel's gotten as bad as the rest of them. He has his ale the same as ever and a little extra. He says winter's worse up here, and a man has to do something to keep the chill off.

"Oh, heavens," she added, with another sigh. "So much left to do. Nora, can you sweep the hall, or are you going up to see *him* now?"

With some reluctance, Nora thrust the broom under the long table and began fishing out a quantity of grit, wood ash, and dog hair. A small object among the sweepings caught her eye. She noticed it only because she had seen something like it in the courtyard recently. A small, whitish object, roughly oval. It had a smooth, organic look, like the chrysalis of a large insect. Experimentally, she stamped on it with her boot. Inside, a bundle of bones, delicate as needles. The remains of a mouse, perhaps.

Nora looked around thoughtfully, up toward the crossing beams that supported the roof of the hall, then back at the litter of bones on the floor.

"I'd like to know more about transformations," she announced to Aruendiel when she arrived in his library that afternoon.

Craning his neck, Aruendiel stood studying the books lined up across the ceiling, searching for a title. With his head thrown back, his long, dark hair falling away from his face, his lanky form looked more skewed and off-kilter than ever, like a marionette hanging from twisted strings. "Transformations?" he said after a minute. "That's far too advanced for you. You cannot even work a levitation spell reliably yet."

"I'll have to practice some more today, with that nice light gray feather that you gave me," Nora said cheerfully. "I wonder where it came from, by the way. We don't have any chickens that color. But going back to transformations, I'm just interested in the general theory. Why a magician might want to turn himself into—oh—an owl, for instance.

"Would it be because of a curse, or because for some reason he enjoyed being an owl? Could he turn himself into other things, too? What is it like to be an owl? Would he know how to fly? Would he be friendly with real owls? Would he remember being a man? Would he mind eating small animals raw and then throwing up their bones later on? I'm just curious as to how all this might work."

Aruendiel turned and looked piercingly at Nora. She cocked an eyebrow at him and waited.

"Those are excellent questions," he said finally. His harsh voice was mellowed with amusement. "You have touched on one of the more important concerns for any magician working a transformation—how thorough the change should be. The simple answer is that it depends on the spell. But to answer your particular questions, a magician of any skill whatsoever transforms himself only at his own will, not because of any curse. Yes, he would know that he was really a man, but he would also be an owl for the length of the spell, so yes, he would be able to fly and he would find the owl's diet and habits, ah, perfectly acceptable."

"And why wouldn't he mention this practice of his to other people?"

"I doubt he would go to great pains to keep it secret. But he might feel that it was his own business. And he might be aware that some people find such transformations frightening."

"Well, disconcerting. All the more reason to give someone fair warning."

Aruendiel inclined his head to suggest that she had a point. There was only the suggestion of a smile on his lips, but he had the air of enjoying himself. "And why this sudden interest in owls?"

"I should have figured it out sooner," Nora said, with some frustration. "I couldn't understand how you made it to the village ahead of me that time without leaving tracks in the snow. And I've heard owls outside at night I don't know how often. And the little feather you gave me when I first met you. But I didn't put it all together until I found an owl pellet inside the house. That's a little disgusting, you know," she added severely.

"Owls are messy birds. But I shall have to take more care in the future."

"Do the Toristels know? The villagers? Am I the only one who didn't know?"

"Mrs. Toristel no doubt drew her own conclusions long ago from the number of times she has found my bedroom window open. She is always careful not to close it. The villagers—they probably scare their children with some garbled tale."

"Probably," said Nora, remembering how Morinen had glanced around nervously in the twilight at the suggestion that the villagers might be angry at Aruendiel. "Why an owl, anyway? Is that the only thing that you can change yourself into?"

"Of course not," he said quickly. "But I almost always change shape at night, so it is logical to take the form of an owl."

"Why at night?" Nora asked doubtfully, reminded of Raclin.

"My back is often stiff and sore, it is hard to sleep." He rubbed one crooked shoulder ruefully. "I find it a relief to slip into another body and use those muscles without pain."

"Oh," she said, slightly nonplussed. "I'm sorry. You never mention that."

"It is also true that some shapes feel more natural than others. I have always had a fondness for birds of prey. When I was younger, I often chose the form of a hawk or perhaps a raven. Hirizjahkinis has a preference for songbirds. My friend Micher Samle usually turns himself into a mouse."

Nora considered this information for a moment. "What if you forgot that you were really a man, or forgot the spell? Would you remain an owl forever?"

"Again, that depends on the spell, but that risk is one reason why transformation spells are a relatively advanced form of magic. Even some very good magicians have made serious mistakes in that area."

"So when can I—"

"You are a long way from the point where you might attempt a simple transformation," Aruendiel said, with a frown. "You had better work on your levitation spell first. You should be able to keep that feather in the air for longer than half a minute by now."

Aruendiel seemed more at ease with her now, for some reason, Nora thought, watching the feather that lay before her. It moved upward in little jerks, then sidestepped her attention and floated gently down to the table-top again. The change in his manner had something to do with their clash over the boots and how they had made peace. The understanding that they had reached then was more complicated than the one he had outlined to Mrs. Toristel, but she could not quite explain it even to herself. Some sort of treaty had been drawn up, establishing secure, well-defined borders and allowing safe commerce over them.

She picked up the feather and brushed it lightly against her nose, then set it carefully in the air. Two minutes, she estimated, when it finally drifted down, but Aruendiel had already left the room.

# Chapter 34

Is lordship's got a visitor," said Morinen's brother Resk with a faint air of importance, ducking through the door and coming into the hut.

Nora looked up from the floor, where Morinen had been showing her how to grind acorns for a Null Days pudding. "He's not expecting anyone. But Mrs. Toristel's daughter is coming from Barsy for the holiday."

Resk shook his head, evidently enjoying the chance to display superior knowledge. "I know Lolo—this wasn't her," he said. "Besides, Lolo can't fly." He jerked his head upward. "This one was flapping on something like a big bird."

Intrigued, Nora thought for a moment, trying to decide which of the few magicians whom Aruendiel considered his friends might pay a visit with no notice. "Was it a woman? With black skin?"

"A man, for sure. Coming from the northeast."

"The northeast?" The Faitoren were somewhere to the northeast. Instantly Nora was on her feet, brushing crumbs of acorn meal off her skirt. "It wasn't a *scaly* kind of big bird, was it? Like the dragon that was here last summer?"

"Never saw the dragon—I was in Red Gate that day," Resk said with some wistfulness. "No, this one looked like a big bird to me."

"I think I'd better get back," Nora said to Morinen. "Mrs. Toristel will be wondering where I am, anyway. I told her I'd be home right after market."

Morinen rubbed her shoulder—she had been doing most of the grinding—and grinned at Nora. "Maybe it's someone to see you," she said.

"That would not necessarily be a good thing," Nora said, thinking of the Faitoren.

She ran most of the way to the castle, the cold air raking her lungs, her mind busy with a convincing premonition of catastrophe. If the flying visitor was not an enemy—Resk might be wrong, the wings could belong to something like a dragon, to Raclin himself—then it was all too likely he was a friend with bad news. Had something happened to Hirizjahkinis again?

She pushed open the castle gate cautiously. In the muddy snow of the courtyard was an apparatus that she recognized: gigantic wings growing from a wooden stem. An Avaguri's mount. So it wasn't Raclin who had come, some comfort there. She raced into the house. The great hall was empty, but there were a few traces of snow on the floor, slowly melting. Without taking off her cloak, she ran into the tower. There were voices above, but she couldn't make out what they were saying as she clattered up the steps.

When she reached the top of the stairs—breathing hard now—both Aruendiel and his visitor turned to stare at her. They were sitting near the fire, each with a goblet of ale. Aruendiel was leaning on his elbow on the table beside him; the other man had crossed his legs and was comfortably clasping one knee with his arms. Neither of their attitudes indicated great tension, but Nora took in the visitor's fleshy features and knew she had seen him before.

"What's wrong?" she blurted out.

"There is nothing wrong, Mistress Nora," Aruendiel said sharply. The initial look of inquiry on his face was replaced with impatience. "For once, we have a visitor who brings us no ill news. This is the magician Dorneng Hul, whom you may remember from Semr."

"I do." Nora said something polite about meeting Dorneng again, too rattled to remember the correct Ors form, but it was close enough. "But you've been guarding the Faitoren, right? What are you doing here?"

A slightly anxious smile twitched Dorneng Hul's thick lips. "Oh, I wouldn't presume to 'guard the Faitoren.' That's beyond the power of most magicians, present company excepted." He gave a quick nod in Aruendiel's direction. "But I do keep an eye on them in case they try to cause any trouble."

"That's what I meant," Nora said. "So why are you here?"

"I'm traveling to visit my mother. For the Null Days. She's almost seventy, and I haven't seen her for a year. Lord Luklren has given me leave to be away for a fortnight." He seemed, belatedly, to understand what Nora was really asking. "I have been giving Lord Aruendiel a report on the Faitoren. They have been very quiet. No problems to report. Not even a sheep missing."

"Oh. Well, that's a relief." Nora looked down at the cloak she had not paused to remove, the snowy boots that were beginning to leave wet spots on the floor of Aruendiel's study. "I'm sorry to disturb you," she added, speaking mostly to Aruendiel. "I thought there might be some trouble with the Faitoren."

"A pretty lady like yourself should not distress herself about such things," Dorneng said gallantly.

Nora blinked at him, making a point of not smiling. Aruendiel looked as though he found Dorneng's comment almost as annoying as she did. "Mistress Nora has more reason than most to be concerned about Faitoren malfeasance," he said.

"Oh, yes, I know about that," Dorneng said. "So unfortunate." He frowned a little.

Nora waited for the inevitable: Dorneng would now stare discreetly at the ring on her left hand. He had no doubt heard about the ring from Aruendiel or Hirizjahkinis, and everyone did stare at it, eventually, when the subject of the Faitoren arose—herself included, although in her case it was more of a lingering case of denial, the mad hope that someday she would look and find the ring gone. She had noticed Aruendiel looking at it askance just the other day, after she'd asked a question about Faitoren candles during a lesson on fire illusions.

Dorneng's large light-brown eyes remained innocently fixed on Nora's. "What a blessing your ordeal is over," he said.

Dorneng paid no particular attention to the ring that evening, either, even though the Faitoren provided the main topic of conversation. He was curious about what exactly had transpired during Hirgus Ext and Hirizjahkinis's time in the Faitoren kingdom; the letter he'd received from Hirgus afterward was lengthy but not particularly informative.

Briefly, in a clinical tone, Aruendiel recounted the enchantments to which Ilissa had subjected her visitors. Perhaps out of loyalty to Hirizjahkinis, he restrained himself to calling the mission a foolhardy venture and a breathtaking example of how even an experienced magician could fall prey to Faitoren beguilement.

Dorneng listened closely, his round shoulders slightly hunched. When Aruendiel finally paused, he fiddled with his goblet for a moment. "I did think, when they set out from Lord Luklren's castle on the way to the Faitoren lands, that they were taking a great risk. But Lady Hirizjahkinis seemed very confident—"

"She is always confident," Aruendiel said. "Sometimes with good reason."

"I am sorry that I didn't go with them," Dorneng said.

"It would have done them no good. Ilissa would have enchanted you as well."

For a fraction of a second, Dorneng looked inclined to disagree. Then he seemed to recollect himself, and his heavy-lipped mouth tied itself into a rather shy smile. "But it would have been an opportunity to observe Faitoren magic at close hand. That's what I regret missing. To be honest," he added, "I was hoping to see more of the Faitoren when I took this position with Lord Luklren. To learn more about their magic, which is unique, as you know, and not well understood. But I've only encountered them on a handful of occasions."

"You would not have learned much about Faitoren magic while you were enslaved by it," Aruendiel told him.

Dorneng reached into the collar slit of his large, rather baggy tunic. He had brought out his Semr court finery for this dinner with Aruendiel, Nora thought, watching him fumble under the port-colored brocade, embroidered with black beads that winked in the candlelight. He brought forth a small glass bottle, half-filled with what looked to Nora like crumpled plastic wrap. When he shook it, a few rainbow flecks glittered in the dry folds inside.

"This is the only piece of Faitoren magic I've been able to study closely," Dorneng said, with the same hesitant smile.

Aruendiel took the bottle from him, holding it with the tips of his fingers. "Where did this come from?"

Unexpectedly, Dorneng nodded at Nora. "From her. It was the Faitoren queen's silencing spell. Lady Hirizjahkinis gave it to me, after she embodied the spell and removed it."

Interested, Nora leaned forward to scrutinize the bottle's contents. "It was alive then. Something like an insect."

"It lived three weeks and five days," Dorneng said with a touch of pride. "That was with no sustenance. I did try to reintroduce it to another subject, but it would not attach itself. One of Lord Luklren's servants—it was in lieu of a flogging." Nora frowned, and Dorneng looked slightly flustered. He went on, addressing Aruendiel: "I've been trying to re-create the spell—the effects of the spell—with the creature's remains. So far I've had no success—"

"Nor will you," Aruendiel said, putting the bottle down disdainfully. "You might as well expect a dead horse to carry you. A Faitoren spell has a kind of life because it is part of the Faitoren who created it. Eventually, the link grows weak and the spell dies. But that can take a very long time. If that silencing spell had remained in place, attached to its intended victim, Mistress Nora would have been mute far longer than three weeks and five days."

Dorneng nodded, his brow furrowed. "Who *are* the Faitoren?" he asked suddenly. "Their ultimate origins, I mean. Where do they come from?"

"They came from my world," Nora said, although the question had clearly been intended for Aruendiel. "Through the same gateway that I used. But after they came here, they couldn't go back, because in my world an iron fence had been built around the gateway. They were trapped."

Dorneng looked to Aruendiel as though for confirmation. "That is true," Aruendiel said. "Although I don't believe the Faitoren originated in Mistress Nora's world. They are a mongrel race, as anyone who has seen a Faitoren in its natural condition can attest. They show traces of parentage from half a dozen different worlds.

"I have heard them talk—in the days when we still had dealings with them—" Aruendiel seemed to be measuring his words carefully; Nora had the clear sense that he was recalling, reluctantly, some long-ago pillow talk with Ilissa. "They used to talk sometimes of a homeland that they had left, or were driven from. You could never get a clear story out of them, exactly what happened.

"And what the Faitoren looked like then, I don't know. But they were magical creatures from the beginning. Then, in the course of their travels, they intermarried with other races to increase their numbers—as they have tried to do here, so many times, with human women." Aruendiel's gaze veered toward Nora but went past her, fixing itself on the chimney instead.

"Can the Faitoren breed among themselves?" Dorneng asked.

"I doubt it. Not now. Otherwise, they would not go to such lengths to acquire brides for their princeling." Aruendiel's eyes narrowed as he contemplated the chimney stones.

"So they're actually dying off, as a people?" Nora asked uncertainly. She had not considered the Faitoren in this light. "Or can they die?"

"They are very long-lived, but not immortal."

"So that's why they want to escape so badly," Nora said. "They want children." Like the child Raclin tried to have with me, she thought, and for the first time, she considered the lost baby with neither regret nor anger. They used me, but not because Raclin and Ilissa either liked or hated me. It was just a survival strategy for them.

With a twist of his torso, Dorneng shifted in his chair. "I wonder— would it be so dangerous to allow some freedom to the Faitoren? To allow them *some* intercourse with the outside world—if only so that they could be studied more thoroughly?"

"The best reason to study Faitoren magic," Aruendiel said, and here he glared briefly at Dorneng, "is to defend against it."

The subject of the ring did not arise until the following morning, and then it was Nora who brought it up.

Breakfast was over, but a gusty north wind had delayed Dorneng's departure. Aruendiel went up to his workroom to moderate the weather. He invited Dorneng to accompany him, but Dorneng said—with a wide smile showing crooked teeth, another reminder that this world contained no orthodontists—that it would be inexcusable to leave a lady alone and that he would be pleased to remain downstairs to keep Mistress Nora company.

The half hour that followed was painful. They soon exhausted the weather as a topic of conversation. Nora tried to segue into a discussion of weather magic, but Dorneng answered her questions with the blandest of generalities. Either he had no interest in the subject or he did not take hers seriously, or both. What he really wanted to discuss, it gradually became clear, was Nora's experiences with the Faitoren.

That wouldn't be so bad, Nora thought, except that Dorneng wouldn't come out and ask his questions directly. He kept circling around the subject with ponderous tact, which Nora first found funny and then annoying. When he said, "I have heard that the Faitoren lure young women with jewelry," and looked at her in a searching way, Nora finally sighed with exasperation.

"Look," she said, spreading the fingers of her left hand, "if you're so interested in Faitoren jewelry—this is a Faitoren ring."

Dorneng stared at her hand as though he had never seen a ring before. "Why are you still wearing it?"

"Because I can't get it off! Aruendiel can't get it off, Hirizjahkinis can't—no one can." Even Hirgus Ext had had a try. "It's enchanted to my finger. You want some Faitoren magic to study—go right ahead."

Dorneng looked sincerely happy. "Thank you," he said warmly, and grabbing Nora's hand, he bent over it until his eyes were only inches from the ring.

Several minutes passed. Nora stared down at the meandering white part in Dorneng's rather sticky-looking brown hair. Was it really necessary to hold her hand that tightly? His palm felt so damp she thought the ring might just slide off her finger when he released her.

Dorneng looked up, biting his lip. "Would you like me to try to remove it?"

"Please," Nora said, with a shrug that she hoped did not convey too eloquently her total lack of any expectation of success.

Dorneng reached into his tunic and pulled out a small, oblong silver object, looking much like the pen that a man in Nora's world might take from inside his jacket. He rolled the cylinder between his palms with some care, then held it in front of his face. The top portion slowly lengthened, thinning in the process, and bent itself into a hook.

"What is that?" Nora asked.

"It's called an Eafroinios key," Dorneng said with some pride. "It's for removing spells."

Dorneng got some points for originality: This would be a new way of failing to remove the ring. "Well, no one has tried one of those before."

"They're very rare."

Dorneng leaned forward and tried to hook the ring with the key, with the evident aim of pulling it off Nora's finger. Immediately it was clear that the hooked end was too narrow. With a little scowl, Dorneng drew the key back and squinted at the bent tip for half a minute, until the metal widened into a shallower curve. Then he went back to the ring. This time, the mouth of the hook slid loosely around the gold band. Dorneng looked up at Nora and smiled hopefully. She gave him a mechanical smile in return, as the tip of the Eafroinios key dug painfully into her skin.

Dorneng tugged on the key, trying to guide the ring over the first joint of Nora's finger. The ring did not budge. He pulled harder.

"Well," Nora said. "Nice try."

"I'm sure this will work, though," Dorneng said quickly. "This is a—a very powerful tool. Let me try here." He inserted the hook at another spot on the ring's curved edge and yanked again, but with no better results. Changing the angle at which he held the key did not help, either. When Dorneng resorted to using the hook as a sort of lever, jamming it through the ring and twisting it as though he could snap the gold band, Nora finally protested.

"That *hurts*. Look, this isn't working."

"It has to work, though," Dorneng said, looking flushed, with an edge of troubled excitement in his voice. For a moment, she was afraid he might burst into tears.

"I told you, no one has been able to get this damned ring off." Pulling her hand away, Nora was relieved to see, over Dorneng's shoulder, Aruendiel's dark-clad figure slice though the tower wall. "Don't worry about it."

"Let me try again," Dorneng said, snatching for Nora's hand. She tucked it behind her back.

"Aruendiel," Nora said loudly, "Dorneng has, very kindly, tried to remove the Faitoren ring for me."

Aruendiel's footsteps quickened by a fraction. When he reached them, he looked down at Dorneng for a moment, and then at the hand that Nora was replacing in her lap. The pause before he spoke was just a beat too long to be absolutely polite. "I don't recall giving you permission to practice magic on Mistress Nora," he said to Dorneng.

Dorneng began to say something about wishing to be of service to the lady and hoping to repay Lord Aruendiel's hospitality. A perfectly fine sentiment but Dorneng could not seem to find a way to express it succinctly. "I told him he could," Nora said abruptly, interrupting. "He has something called an Eafroinios key. He was trying it out."

Aruendiel's dark eyebrows angled sharply. To Dorneng, he said: "And where did you get an Eafroinios key?"

Dorneng at first seemed inclined to equivocate, but then said: "From the wizard Kelerus Ruenc. He is selling off his collection."

"I never heard he had an Eafroinios key."

"He kept it quiet, mostly. I found out about it by a lucky chance." An element of boastfulness came back into Dorneng's voice.

"Anyway, it didn't work on the ring," Nora said.

Aruendiel seemed both unsurprised and—Nora thought—somewhat amused at the news of Dorneng's failure. He sat down with an unhurried air and extended his hand to Dorneng. "Let me see it." After a second's hesitation, Dorneng handed him the key. Aruendiel weighed the small silver tool in his hand for a moment, then held it up to inspect the hook that Dorneng had fashioned. He turned it back and forth, looking at it from different angles, and ran an exploratory finger over the curved metal. His face brightened slightly with an expression of pleased concentration.

"It is the real thing," Aruendiel said. "I congratulate you on your acquisition, Dorneng. There have been many, many false Eafroinios keys circulated. The magician Eafroinios the Fearful finished fewer than a dozen," he said, glancing at Nora. "Silver has some limited antimagical properties to begin with, and then he literally trained the metal, day and night for years, to intensify those qualities." Delicately, Aruendiel continued to stroke the hooked end, pausing every so often as though to admire the instrument. "Eafroinios was almost certainly mad. No one else has ever had the patience to replicate his effort. But the amulets he made can counter a wide range of spells. They require some skill to use properly, of course.

"Mistress Nora, your hand, please. The one with the ring."

Feeling mild curiosity, Nora laid her left hand on the tabletop, fingers fanned, and leaned her chin on her right hand to watch what developed.

Deftly, as easily as he might skewer a piece of meat at dinner, Aruendiel hooked the tip of the Eafroinios key around the ring. The curved tip fit perfectly, pinching the gold band so tightly that hook and ring almost seemed welded together. He gave the key a long, steady pull.

Something was different this time—Nora could tell before the ring slid over the first joint of her finger. Whatever had been holding the ring in place had suddenly, finally let go. Still, she watched the ring bump along the length of her finger with a sense of unreality. It looked like any ordinary gold ring as it came off her fingertip, still held in the grip of the Eafroinios key.

"It's gone," she said wonderingly. "It's *gone*."

Aruendiel put key and ring carefully on the table and then looked at Nora, his smile lifting like a kite tossed by the wind. He looked happier than solving a difficult magical problem—even succeeding where Dorneng had failed—could account for. "Yes, it's gone," he repeated.

Dorneng uttered an uncertain sound, but when she glanced at him, he was beaming. "Good work, my lord!" he said. "Beautiful work!" He clapped Nora awkwardly on the shoulder.

"After all this time," Nora said. She clenched her hand into a fist, then spread her fingers again, admiring their splendid nakedness. "Thank you—*thank you,*" she said to Aruendiel, who looked a shade more gratified. He bowed slightly in acknowledgment. "And thank you for bringing the Eafroinios key," she added politely, for Dorneng's benefit. "It was your idea to try it."

"Well, I'll have to practice more with it," Dorneng said, with some ruefulness. "His lordship got it to work on the first try."

"That's the only way it will work," Aruendiel said. "You can never force it."

"What will you do with the ring now?" Dorneng asked.

"Destroy it," Aruendiel said, and Nora felt no inclination to argue.

Her finger felt strange without the gold band. She had gotten so used to the minor irritation of its presence, its subtle weight—now that the ring was gone, her hand felt oddly numb, sensationless.

Nora raised her hand for closer examination, a faint question in her mind. The flesh didn't look healthy, she thought. It didn't look right. Skin and nails had turned the same slightly yellowish white. She tried to flex her fingers, but they were frozen in place.

"My hand—" she started to say, and then discovered that she could not move her arm, either.

Panicked, she jumped up from the bench. On the other side of the table, Aruendiel leaped up, too. He lunged toward her. "Something's wr—" Nora started to say.

She couldn't finish the sentence. Aruendiel's fingers were wrapped around her throat, digging into her windpipe. She goggled at him, unable to breathe. Why was he trying to kill her? She twisted away, trying to free herself, but her body felt stiff and unresponsive. Aruendiel grabbed her right arm, as though to restrain her, and hauled her across the table toward him. Her hip banged the wood. Crockery shattered. But then his grip on her throat loosened slightly, and she found her breath again.

"What the hell are you doing?" Nora screamed. Aruendiel, breathing hard, did not seem to hear her. He held her facing him, his fingers tightening again on her throat, his other hand still squeezing her arm.

"Can you move your legs, Nora?" Aruendiel asked levelly.

The big muscles of her thighs tensed. But they did not move at her command. She could not sense the floor under her feet.

"No," she said. "It's like I'm buried in cement. Let me go!" Nora made as if to pull away from him, and discovered that her hips, waist, torso, were all immobile. She could not even shift her weight.

She lifted her eyes and stared into Aruendiel's eyes. "You broke my neck. I'm paralyzed."

"Your hands, Nora. Look at your hands."

She looked down. Past the edge of her sleeve, her left hand was no longer recognizably hers. That is, it was a copy of her hand in cream-colored stone. Marble, maybe.

The right hand was, blessedly, its normal light tan, faded a bit for the winter, the nails pale and a little ragged. This living hand, now warm and capable. She tried to move her fingers. They wiggled at her in a friendly fashion. Her eyes went up the arm to where Aruendiel gripped it so maniacally just above the elbow.

"Stone?" It was all she could bring herself to say.

"Stone," he said.

"And you're holding it back. Otherwise, my arm—my head. My whole body."

"I am slowing it as much as I can." He spoke with a precise, deliberate calm that was itself a kind of urgency. "What feeling do you have in your body, below the neck?"

"It feels tight. All over." Yes, she could breathe, but pressure corseted her ribs; she tried to take a deep breath and found herself gasping. The import of Aruendiel's words sank in. "You're only slowing it? You can't stop it?"

"The stone is only skin-deep, so far. Dorneng!" Aruendiel's voice suddenly rose to gale force. "Do you perform a counterhex, *now,* or I will spill the curdled filth you call your brains."

Behind Nora, out of her sight, Dorneng began to babble, something about Manathux petrifaction. "This is not the Manathux curse," Aruendiel snarled. "This is Faitoren."

"My hand hurts," Nora said. Was it her imagination, or was it getting heavier, too? "It hurts *a lot.*" As though she were wearing a too-tight glove that was getting smaller still, surrounding and binding each finger with meticulous, implacable force. She wanted very badly to wring her hands.

"But the stone is crushing the flesh, as it grows," Dorneng said. "That's Mana—"

"The ring, wormsnatch," Aruendiel thundered. "Destroy the ring."

"Oh." Dorneng sounded apologetic. "Where is it? It's not on the table. She must have knocked it to the floor."

"*Find* it," Aruendiel said. Nora started to moan, long, wavering notes that were wholly inadequate to the discomfort she was feeling. She needed to howl, but there was not enough air in her lungs. The small bones in her fingers were splintering, giving way. She could hear them crackle and shatter, even through her rapidly thickening skin of marble.

So that was how it worked—the stone spread from the outside in, and it pulped all the tender, living flesh within. You would think that turning to stone would be a painless process, but you would be mistaken. Was this what Raclin had felt, what Massy felt when she became an apple tree?

The big joint at the base of Nora's thumb popped, and this time she did howl, very briefly. Now the long, delicate bones that ran through the hand were collapsing, one by one. Nothing left of her hand but pain. That would be her whole body in a few minutes, Nora saw. Her rib cage would implode, her pelvis would crack, her skull would crumple—

Aruendiel was speaking to her, she realized. After a moment she understood that he was asking if she wanted an anodyne, a spell for numbness.

"No," she said despairingly, because the sickening pain in her hand was already gone. She could feel nothing at all, and she could guess what that meant. Stone had conquered flesh, all the last remnants of it. Now the marble was already starting to compress her forearm—her wrist caught in a vise. But at least she could feel something. Her body would be numb and dead, solid stone, soon enough.

Dorneng was scrabbling around on the floor, giving running commentary on his efforts to find the ring, as though to document how hard he was trying to help. Aruendiel's mouth was set, and his eyes seemed to be looking at something very far away. She was suddenly aware of the magic he had unleashed, roaring and tearing at her marble skin, but it was—quite literally—like listening to a hurricane from inside thick stone walls.

"If it's Faitoren magic, is all this an illusion?" she asked him in a whisper. Almost a joke. Aruendiel scowled, twisting his mouth as though determined not to let the words escape, but she knew what he meant anyway: Illusions can kill.

"Found it!" Dorneng said, just as Nora noticed that her right hand was whiter than it had been. Aruendiel saw it, too, and swore. She willed her fingers to move, to play an arpeggio in the air, but only her index finger responded, and then it too froze, pointing upward as though in admonition. Reluctantly, Aruendiel took his hand away from her arm; she could not even feel his touch lifting.

A blue flash, a thunderclap, so close it seemed to swallow her up. The concussion left even her marble hand vibrating. Lesser crashes followed, like tiles falling off a roof. Nora opened her eyes, not remembering when she had closed them. Off to the side, Dorneng looked stupidly at the floor, then stooped to pick something up.

He must have tried to do something to the ring. Still gripping Nora's neck, Aruendiel held out his free hand, calling Dorneng a fool, demanding the ring. Running feet, fear in Mrs. Toristel's voice: "What in the name of all the gods, your lordship?"

They can't destroy it, Nora thought. Maybe the ring can never be destroyed. Inside its marble sleeve, her left arm was being ground to powder. The stone methodically crushed her elbow, then the shoulder joint. The nerves shrieked as they died.

"Aruendiel," she said, her voice less than a whisper. Her panicked lungs were locked inside a shrinking box. "Aruendiel." Finally he heard, and turned back toward her, stooping slightly to put his ear next to her mouth, so close her lips almost brushed his hair.

"Put it back," she breathed. "The ring. Put it back."

He jerked his head around to glare at her, black eyebrows diving with rage and astonishment.

"Now. Please," she managed just before her lips grew hard and her tongue froze. Light turned to darkness as stone filled her eyes.

It's over, Nora thought with disbelief. All of it. I'll be a statue, forever, unless Aruendiel finds a way to change me back. Or, if he does, wouldn't I just be a messy little puddle of crushed bone and blood? Her lungs struggled hopelessly for one more thin breath. Her head was heavier than before; she could not hold it upright if her neck were not already turning to stone. It was not death, for I stood up, and all the dead lie down, she thought, but there was no comfort there.

Her knees gave way. She collapsed.

Someone grabbed at her, but she landed on the side of her hip, hard, the same spot she'd barked on the table before. Her hands smacked the chilly stone floor, too late to break her fall.

In a rush she understood that the flagstones under her stinging palms were cold because her hands were warm and alive. Her lungs gulped air gratefully. She raised her left hand for inspection: healthy skin over living muscles, nerves, blood, and bone. And Raclin's ring encircling the third finger.

It was what she had wanted, sort of, but Nora began to cry anyway. Her sight blurred, the ring mockingly brilliant as it dissolved into golden light. She covered her face and curled into a ball and sobbed passionately with all the grief and fear and heartbreak that marble statues can never feel. Someone took hold of her shoulders with kind, strong hands. She turned to Aruendiel gratefully.

But it was Mrs. Toristel pulling her close, patting her gently on the back, calling her a poor little mouse. Nora leaned her head against Mrs. Toristel's thin shoulder and cried harder than ever.

After a while Mrs. Toristel helped her to her feet. Nora stood up shakily. On the other side of the great hall, near the outside door, Aruendiel was talking to Dorneng, evidently showing him out. Dorneng, she thought, looked wilted. As he went out the door, he sneaked a glance back at Nora, but he looked away quickly when he saw her looking at him.

Aruendiel followed Dorneng's glance. As soon as the door was shut, he came over with long, limping strides. Mrs. Toristel was steering Nora upstairs, to be dosed with hot applejack and honey and then to spend the rest of the day in bed; Nora could not think of a reason to oppose the plan. The housekeeper gave the magician a reproachful look—daring for her, Nora thought—and asked him if it was really necessary to scare the poor child so. She seemed to be under the impression that all the mischief stemmed from the explosion that Dorneng had used to destroy the ring.

Aruendiel hesitated for a moment, then said: "I regret any anxiety I may have caused you, Mistress Nora. How are you feeling now?"

Nora was about to say that it wasn't his fault. But then it came to her that *he* was the famous magician, after all—perhaps he should have known that removing the ring would make something terrible happen. "I'm all right." She lifted her hand with a rueful smile, showing him the ring. "At least this worked."

His pale eyes flicked over the ring. "It is not much of a cure," he said venomously.

"You could try cutting off my finger." She wasn't sure whether she was joking or not. Maybe, she thought angrily, that was the only way to get rid of the ring. It might be worth trading a finger to avoid the risk of ever becoming a marble statue again.

Aruendiel's face contorted. For a moment he looked stricken, then wrathful. Mrs. Toristel uttered a cry.

"What a terrible idea, Nora," she said, pursing her lips. "There's no reason to do that, even if you can't get it off. If you must have it gone, I'm sure his lordship will find a way eventually, but *I* think it's a handsome ring, after all, nothing to be ashamed of, and it never caused any trouble before."

Not exactly, Nora thought, but she let herself be led off to bed. The applejack took away some of the lurking dread that still oppressed her spirits, but she found she did not want to drink the entire enormous draft that Mrs. Toristel had pressed on her. Anything that threatened her control of her own body seemed anathema. What she did drink sent her to sleep for a few hours. Nora dreamed not of marble statues, thankfully, but of a disjointed conversation with EJ—something about not forgetting their mother's birthday—that ended when she remembered that he was dead.

She awoke in a contemplative mood and spent some time regarding the ring on her finger, wiggling her toes at intervals just because she could. There was some solace in Mrs. Toristel's observation, Nora thought wryly: At least she wasn't stuck with something ugly on her finger. How fortunate that Raclin had decent taste in jewelry. After screwing up her courage, she gave the ring a tentative tug to see if it would come off. To her secret relief, it did not.

At last she arose and went in search of Aruendiel. She found him, as she expected, in the library, where he was bent over a large volume whose pages were completely black, except for a painted border of twining vines bearing fat bunches of skulls.

"What is that?" she asked, pointing at the book.

"*Recipes for Silence.*" Raising his head, Aruendiel closed the book. "Come here." He took hold of Nora's chin and did a rapid check for enchantment in her ears and nostrils.

"I'm fine," Nora said. "Except that my neck's still a little sore where you grabbed me. I suppose you're trying to decide on the best way to kill Raclin?"

"Yes," Aruendiel said without visible emotion. "It is time to finish this matter. I have let it fester far too long."

"I don't want you to," Nora said.

"I beg your pardon?"

She took a deep breath. "That turning-to-stone spell—I don't ever want to go through it again. And we"—she meant *you*—"don't know what might set it off. If you attacked Raclin, who knows how he might retaliate. Or, killing him could trigger the spell again—or something worse." Seeing the expression on Aruendiel's face, Nora raised her hands as though to protect herself or placate him. "I know this is not the honorable thing to do— maybe I'm a coward—but I almost died today, and you couldn't help me."

"If I had destroyed the ring, the enchantment would likely have been broken entirely."

"Maybe. Or maybe I'd be solid marble now. You don't know. And Hirizjahkinis is right. You shouldn't take on the Faitoren all by yourself. Just leave them alone."

The rough white scars stood out on Aruendiel's flushed cheeks. "Do you retain some tender feelings for your estranged husband, that you argue for his life?"

"That's not fair. You know that's wrong. Whatever feelings I ever had for Raclin, they were fake to begin with. But if you kill him—who knows what the ring will do to me?"

"I will force him to break the enchantment. He does not have to die quickly."

"But it's still risky." Nora clenched her fists. "I don't want any more bad things to happen. Not right now. Not—for a while."

Aruendiel looked as though he wanted to take her by the throat again. "Do you know how much danger you're in, as long as that Faitoren viper lives?"

"Yes," she said evenly. Silence, during which they both heard her unspoken words: Because you can't protect me. Nora cleared her throat. "I mean, what sort of spell was that, this morning? Do you even know how to reverse it?"

"Any spell can be reversed," he snapped, "given study. That petrifaction spell was Faitoren magic of unusual power and intensity."

"Well, exactly," Nora said. She looked at the floor and sighed. "How long would I have been a statue before you reversed the spell?"

"Too long," Aruendiel said, his voice thick with fury. He rose with a jerk from his chair and carried *Recipes for Silence* across the room, then fitted it into an empty space in the bookshelves. An instant later, it vanished. "As you wish," he said, turning to glower again at Nora. "I will not seek vengeance, not yet."

"All right, thank you," Nora said awkwardly.

He returned his attention to the bookshelves. There seemed to be nothing more to say.

## *Chapter 35*

The Null Days began. At first Nora was in no mood at all for the holiday. Her nerves were still frayed, the castle seemed less secure than before, Aruendiel had not had a cordial word for her ever since she had asked him not to kill Raclin, and unsettlingly, Nora found herself being equally brusque with him. There was no logic to it, she knew. She should be angry at Raclin, but it was Aruendiel who had taken the ring off her finger—to show that he could do what Dorneng couldn't, really—and then failed to save her from the consequences. What if he had refused, at the last minute, to put the ring back on her finger? He had certainly hesitated.

She had more time to brood about this because her lessons were suspended, and suddenly there was nothing in particular to do, after the rush of last-minute cooking: smoked fish dumplings, pickled eggs and vegetables, meat cakes, lard buns, beet pudding, barley soup to stay warm on the back of the stove. Far too much food for the castle household to finish in five days, but much of it, Nora quickly saw, was intended for the visitors who arrived in a small but steady trickle. It was evidently the custom during the Null Days to present one's host with branches cut from fir trees.

The sight of the evergreens displayed in the great hall like trophies, the hum of mingled voices, the platters of food—they were familiar cues; it was more like Christmas at home than she would have imagined. Despite herself, her spirits began to rise.

Oen Lun, one of Aruendiel's vassals, rode over from Broken Keep, wearing a rusty breastplate. He looked very much the way Nora had always imagined Don Quixote. Some of the farmers who worked Aruendiel's more distant holdings came, including Peusienith, the young widower whom Aruendiel had once suggested that she marry. He was pleasant-mannered, with a solid, successful air, but Nora could not bring herself to be very friendly. She made a point of introducing him to Morinen, who came calling with her mother and her brothers, and they discovered that they were third cousins twice removed.

Nora was more interested to meet another of Morinen's cousins: Ferret, the boy who had gone up before Aruendiel for assault and horse theft at the last assizes. Contrary to expectations, Ferret had not been hanged. He seemed to regard his near execution as a good joke. "His lordship said I'd lied about some things, and the other bastards, he said they lied about everything," Ferret recounted. "He wasn't going to hang me on their say-so. He gave me the lash instead. Said it was because I'd been fool enough to steal horses with worthless scum who sold me out the first chance they got."

"He also said this was your first offense," Morinen added warningly. "And that next time it'll be your hand."

"There won't be a next time," Ferret said confidently. "Either I won't steal horses again, or I won't get caught, because I'll steal them with boys that I can trust, you see?"

"His lordship is right, Ferret, you're an idiot," Morinen said.

The Toristels' daughter and one of her teenage sons were staying in the Toristels' quarters. It was cramped over there; Aruendiel had said that the guests could stay in the manor house, but Mrs. Toristel thought that it wouldn't be fitting and said that she didn't want to impose on the master. Which was ridiculous, Nora thought, because Aruendiel was clearly pleased to see Lolona and her son. A plumper version of her mother, Lolona had spent her childhood in the castle, and she was one of the few people— Hirizjahkinis being another—who seemed to have absolutely no fear of either the magician or Mrs. Toristel. Aruendiel listened to news of her children and her brewery with courteous attention, and promised a charm to rid one of her vats of a rope infestation.

Nora liked Lolona's cheerful, no-nonsense air, although she was slightly alarmed by the way Lolona kept remarking that her mother's housekeeping had declined with age and that, if not for the Null Days, she and Nora would have a grand old time cleaning the castle from top to bottom. There, Nora found it hard to respond. She thought she and Mrs. Toristel had done exactly that.

But by the afternoon of the third day, the Null Days were living up to their name. A new snowstorm had discouraged visitors. The woolly gray light outside hardly penetrated the windows; inside, the big Null Days candles, made for endurance, not luminosity, barely interrupted the gloom. Nora took a seat by the fire in the great hall and wondered morbidly where Aruendiel would have put her statue if he had not been able to remove the Faitoren spell. When he came in, she said peevishly: "You know, I don't worship the sun. I don't see how he could be offended if I did some magic or some reading—or *something*—during the Null Days."

Aruendiel, warming his hands in front of the fire, looked at her thoughtfully, as though measuring the bile in her tone. "You have been talking to Mrs. Toristel," he said. "She is very much attached to her sun god. In this part of the world, it is the Lady Ewe whom we honor during the Null Days. And in Stone Top, they will tell you that the holiday is for Erkin Sheafbearer."

"Right, the god of beer." Nora had learned this fact only yesterday. Lolona had a shrine to him next to her vats. "Do you believe in this religious—stuff?"

"Me? I prefer to have as little truck with gods as possible. I have never found them to be very reliable allies."

She snickered, but he seemed to be quite serious. "You're talking about actual gods," she said. "You believe in them?"

He shrugged. "They exist, whether I believe in them or not."

Nora pondered this for a moment. In a different tone, she asked: "Is that where your magic comes from? Some kind of gift from the gods?"

Aruendiel rounded on her. "Have you learned nothing at all, that you could ask such a ridiculous question? Do you have no understanding of the nature of magic at all?"

"Well, I'm still learning," she said defensively.

"Painfully slowly, I see," he said. "You should know from your own experience that real magic comes out of what is around you, it is born from the long conversation, negotiation, fellowship that human beings have with the things of the world. A god would never give us such a valuable gift. Humans had to learn it for themselves." He flung himself into the chair opposite Nora and frowned at her again, but there was an expectancy in the cool gray eyes that she had not seen for some days.

"Well, then, how did *you* learn magic?" Nora's question hung in the air for a moment. "I'd like to hear that story."

"Hmm." Aruendiel looked away, into the fire. "Your time would be better spent learning actual magic than in listening to that tale."

"I can't do magic now, because of the holiday," she said. "And I'd like to know, because it might help me understand some things better. Why *I* can do magic, for instance."

"I don't know the answer to that question," he said, twisting his mouth dismissively. "But it is less important than the fact that you *do* work magic."

"You mentioned a couple of possible reasons once. I thought of another one. This," she said, holding up her finger with the gold ring.

"Absurd."

"It might somehow have influenced me—or *tainted* me—I don't know." She could not put her inchoate anxieties into words.

Aruendiel was shaking his head. "No, that cursed ring, no matter what evil it contains, has nothing to do with your ability to practice magic."

"But how can you—?"

"Nora, I am sure of it," he said with some intensity. "If I thought there was any chance at all, I would not have taught you a single spell, nothing." She knew that was so. Of course, he still might be mistaken about the ring's influence, but she felt a little better.

"It's far more likely," Aruendiel went on, "that your capability for magic comes about because you are an observant, intelligent woman, a scholar—"

Nora was strangely moved by the compliment, but she could not quite bring herself to show it. "Hirgus Ext is a scholar," she observed.

"Hirgus!" Aruendiel snorted and sank back in his chair, a little stiffly. His back appeared to be more painful than usual, Nora thought. Had he not even worked the owl transformation since the Null Days began? When she asked him, he admitted snappishly that it was true.

"Are you worried about offending Lady Ewe?"

He snorted again. "No! I mind my own business, and I expect the gods to mind theirs in return. The Null Days, though, can be an unlucky time of year," he added in a more thoughtful tone. "Magic is more likely to go awry at this season than any other. I used to pay no mind to the Null Days, and sometimes that led me into difficulties."

He had even abandoned his usual careful shaving, Nora thought. There was a silver stripe in the stubble in his chin. "What kind of difficulties?" she asked, although she had a feeling he would not tell her. She was right.

"What of your own gods?" he asked her, flicking aside her question with an impatient gesture. "What about your own Null Days?"

"Christmas?" She had mentioned it to him the day before.

"Yes, your Gresmus. How do you celebrate it, at home in your own world?"

Nora felt a sudden tug of longing. "Well, we put up a fir tree in the living room and cover it with decorations, lights—" She did her best to explain what the holiday was supposed to be about and how it was actually celebrated. It was difficult. She found herself digressing to describe shopping malls and credit cards. She was not sure that Aruendiel would understand what the frenetic exchange of expensive gifts had to do with the birth of a divinity in Bethlehem two thousand years ago, but then a lot of people wondered about that.

"My mother and stepfather live out in the country, and they go out and chop down a tree on their land. They always have white lights on their tree—my mother thinks colored lights are a little tawdry," she said. "And they *always* go to church—they're very religious. My father and Kathy, his wife—they might go on Christmas Eve, if things aren't too crazy. My sisters go nuts at Christmas. Well, Leigh's getting past that—she's thirteen now—but Ramona's only ten." Nora became aware, as she went on, that she was talking more for her own benefit than for Aruendiel's. She was also aware of how much she missed them all.

After she had finished, Aruendiel stirred and took his gaze away from the fire. "Your parents, they are not married to each other?"

"Well, they were, once!" Nora said quickly. Her status in this world was complicated enough without the suspicion of bastardy. "They were divorced, oh, fifteen years ago. They're friendly enough now," she added, anticipating the next question. "Not friends, but friendly."

"You have no brothers?" Aruendiel inquired. When she shook her head, he said: "Your father, I suppose, married again to try to beget a male heir."

"Oh, no," Nora said, shaking her head. But she could not say that he was completely wrong. "Well, yes and no," she amended. "In fact, I did have a brother. He died. And my parents got divorced, and they each re-married, and then my sisters came along. But my father was happy enough with daughters." She added: "It's not as though he has any ancestral estates to pass down."

"How did your brother die?"

"He was killed in a car accident."

Aruendiel's pale gaze was steady. She took that as an indication to continue. It still pained her that someone as smart as EJ had died in such a stupid, trite, unnecessary way. Kevin, who was driving, had had six beers. Blood alcohol, 0.14. EJ had only two beers, and he was a big guy, so if *he'd* been driving, they probably would have been okay. But it was Kevin's car, and EJ was too nice to take the keys away from him. If only—once in his life—EJ had been a jerk.

Nora paused to collect her breath, aware that she had been speaking a mixture of Ors and English, and that Aruendiel could not know what blood alcohol meant, among other things, but he was nodding slowly.

She talked about EJ for some time. It was always that way. She almost never mentioned him anymore, but once she started, she couldn't stop. Nora had a vague but powerful sense that it was unfair to her brother to sum him up only by the circumstances of his death. Yet even when she tried to talk about his life, she always returned to that unchangeable fact. "He was kind of a nerd, you know. Very smart, but a little overweight, and shy around girls. A girl from his class came up to me at the funeral. She'd had a crush on EJ, but she never told him. It broke my heart, that he could have had a girlfriend, he could have been out with her that night instead of Kevin and Nick. She was a nice person—Valerie Chin. I kept up with her for a while. She went to medical school. Maybe that was a little weird, keeping in touch. I don't know."

Sometimes people remarked that it must be a comfort to have her two little sisters in EJ's place—a remark that left Nora slightly stunned every time, because as much as she loved Leigh and Ramona, it was not because they could ever replace EJ. If you faced facts, after all, if EJ were still alive, her parents might not have divorced, her sisters would never have been born.

Aruendiel did not strain to find the silver lining. Instead, he said: "It is hard to lose a brother or sister. I had several siblings, and while I was not equally fond of all of them, I was surprised to find how much I missed them—even my brother Aruendic—when they were dead."

"I'm sorry," Nora said, wondering how to express condolences in Ors. "Losing one brother was bad enough."

"It was a long time ago," he said. "When did your brother die?"

"I was thirteen—so sixteen years ago at least, depending on how much time has passed back home."

Aruendiel pondered this for a moment. "You are older than I thought."

Startled, Nora gave a small snort of laughter. "Well, I'm almost thirty! I probably *am* thirty by now. Why are you surprised?"

"You said that, in your own world, you were still a student. How long does your course of study last?"

The duration of graduate school, always a sore subject. "Oh, two or three more years, at least." Or four or five. Nora sighed. "How old are you, Aruendiel?"

He seemed entertained rather than offended at the bluntness of her question. "Old enough so that thirty seems—well, I can barely recognize the arrogant fool I was at thirty."

"Some forty-year-olds would say the same thing."

"Old enough that even I have trouble figuring my age."

"Hmm," Nora said, unimpressed. She did not have high confidence in Aruendiel's mathematical skills. "That's an obvious evasion."

"Old enough," he said finally, "that the granddaughter of my grand-daughter is an old woman."

"Really!" Nora sat up straight. "Who is she? I didn't know that you had children or grandchildren—or great-great-grandchildren. I never heard Mrs. Toristel mention any."

"Mrs. Toristel does not know every branch of my family tree," Aruendiel said sharply.

"That must be at least—" She began to calculate. Say twenty-five or thirty years for a generation. "One hundred fifty years? One sixty?" She watched Aruendiel's face closely, but he gave nothing away. "Two hundred!"

"I am not *that* old," he corrected her. "The last time I bothered to count, some birthdays ago, it was close to one hundred and eighty."

"Goodness." After a moment, she added: "That's not as old as I thought you might be."

"Oh?" He arched his black brows.

"You made it a bit of a mystery—I thought you might be five hundred, or a thousand."

"Gods forbid!" he said, an unexpected raw edge in his voice.

"As long as you don't actually look or feel that old—" Aruendiel's chilly look interrupted her thought. "Hirizjahkinis said that working magic keeps you young," she added, a little lamely.

"To most appearances." His tone did not encourage a response. They sat in silence for a few minutes, and then he stood up, grimacing as he straightened his back. "My spine feels even older than the rest of me," he said, with a shade of bitterness. "It is turning to iron as I sit here by the fire like an old woman. Come, it is still light enough for a walk to the forest."

"It's snowing," Nora said, twisting to look at the hall's windows.

"Are you so frail, a sprig of thirty?"

The air outside, alive with lightly falling snow, was bright enough for them to see all the way to the river, although it was almost nightfall. They walked a little way into the woods, past the frozen river.

The elusive background murmur of the forest was not so elusive today. It washed into her ears and then out again, but not before she could sense a shape to it, a current of meaning, even if she could not understand what it meant. She could tell that Aruendiel had joined in the long, meandering song, a small, distinctly human voice among the wild, slow voices of the trees. Wood was his favorite among the elements that he commonly used in working magic. He lost patience with stone; air and fire were fast and showy but lacked staying power—whereas, he said lovingly, you could do almost anything with wood.

And all these trees, with their fat trunks and interlocking branches, were younger than he was. Sheep had grazed here, he'd said, within his lifetime. One hundred eighty years, when some people lived only sixteen.

"Have you any more passages of your book to be corrected?" Aruendiel asked, coming into the great hall toward the end of the fourth day. He must be very bored, she thought. Reading her last translation, before the holidays, Aruendiel had complained sharply about Mr. Collins. He was not a reader who suspended judgment easily, or who took pleasure in meeting characters in the pages of a book whom he would not want to meet in real life.

"As a matter of fact, yes," Nora said, after a moment's consideration. She had done some surreptitious translation that morning while keeping an eye on the fires.

"Bring it out," he directed. "I might as well correct it now as later."

"It's not unlucky to go over homework during the Null Days?" she asked slyly.

"Let us consider it more in the nature of storytelling. That is something that people always do at this season, when there is nothing else to pass the time."

"The Toristels were telling stories last night," she remarked, rising to fetch her book and wax tablets.

"Mrs. Toristel talked about the black elves, I suppose?"

"Yes, she did." The black elves, Nora had learned, sometimes lured their victims with haunting music played on flutes made from human bones. Or they called out in the voices of the recently dead. Even when they knew better, many people couldn't help calling back when they heard those lost, familiar tones—only to be chased down by the black elves with their small, powerful hands and their needle teeth. "Do black elves really exist?" Nora asked Aruendiel.

"I have never seen one," he said with a snort, reaching for the wax tablets.

As usual, it took him some time to read through her translation, as he kept stopping to point out the deficiencies in her handwriting, spelling, and grammar. She was curious what he would make of the ball at Netherfield, but his only response was some skepticism that polite society would allow men and women to dance together in public. "I myself would not care one way or the other, who dances with whom," he said, "but it does not seem very realistic."

Something about Lydia had caught his fancy—he seemed to enjoy her brash waywardness—and Mr. Bennet had appealed to him from the beginning. But Aruendiel seemed to dislike Mr. Darcy as much as Elizabeth Bennet did at first. Mr. Darcy's famous pride, Aruendiel noted once, was excessive for a man who seemed to have little to occupy his time and was not even a real peer. Nora was taken aback by his reaction until remembering something Freud had said about how the people who annoy us most are those who remind us of ourselves.

"Even if you prefer not to use the feminine verb forms yourself, you should make sure that Mistress Bennet uses them correctly," Aruendiel said as he put down the tablets.

"Must I?" Nora frowned. "It takes something away, to have those little ladylike hems and haws when she's sparring with Darcy. She's supposed to be impertinent, not demure. That's the problem with translations," she added sadly. "You can never quite reproduce the flavor of the original."

"Then let Mistress Bennet speak as you think she should," Aruendiel said unexpectedly. "No one would take her for a well-bred Semran young lady, anyway."

He seemed lost in thought for some moments, tapping his fingers slowly on the arm of his chair. Nora had the strong sense that he had been talking about her as much as Elizabeth Bennet. Was it a veiled criticism? His tone had been mild enough.

"How are you recovering?" he asked suddenly. He gestured toward her hand.

It was the first time Aruendiel had alluded to the ring episode since before the Null Days began. "Very well, thank you," Nora said.

But he seemed disinclined to let the matter drop. "An unwilling transformation is difficult. Galling for the spirit. And what you endured was particularly vicious."

"So, transformations aren't always that painful?" When Aruendiel shook his head, Nora asked: "What about Massy, the woman you turned into an apple tree?" She had been thinking about Massy lately, trying to remember the exact expression on her face as flesh became wood.

"No, she felt nothing except surprise. And as I recall," he added with a lift of his eyebrows, "you said that I had been too gentle with her."

"I've since changed my mind," Nora said. She grinned at Aruendiel, and fleetingly he smiled back. She seized the moment. "Aruendiel, will you tell me how you learned magic? It *is* the season for storytelling." He was about to demur, she could tell, so she went on: "I want to know everything there is to know about magic. Everything. So that I can use it well, so that I can protect myself and other people against the Faitoren or whatever they need protecting against. So that I don't misuse it."

"Ah, and you think there are some lessons in my biography about the misuse of magic?"

"I wouldn't know," Nora said. "You tell me."

He snapped an eyebrow at her, then fell into another reverie, shadows from the firelight picking out the broken places in his face. She waited.

"It is a long story," Aruendiel said warningly. Nora began to say that she didn't mind, she liked long stories. Then she saw that she did not need to say anything. He grinned crookedly at her. "But first it is time for dinner."

## *Chapter 36*

Aruendiel was silent at first, as they spooned up their barley soup and sipped the wine he himself had brought up from the cellar. (Some of the empty bottles in the far corner were not actually empty, if you knew how to examine them in the right way.) He was thinking back more than a century and half, sorting through his private stores of lost time and deciding what to bring into the light. The far past, that was the safest place to begin.

"In your world," he suddenly said to Nora, "how did you decide on your course of studies—the stories and poems?"

"Because I was good at that sort of thing—some of it," she said. "Because I was tired of being a cook. Because the life of a"—she searched for an Ors translation of *professor*—"a teacher was appealing to me."

"What do you mean—you were good at some of it?" Aruendiel asked.

"Oh, I didn't have any big ideas," Nora said ruefully, thinking of that last conversation with Naomi. "I was good at reading and understanding individual poems, for instance, but I had trouble working them into some bigger framework." She noticed that she was talking about grad school in the past tense.

Aruendiel did not seem displeased by her answer. "That may help explain your capacity for magic. One cannot practice real magic without an understanding of the individual things—*this* stone, *this* stand of trees— from which the magic comes."

Ha, Naomi, did you hear that, Nora thought, but she did not allow this intriguing theory of Aruendiel's to divert her from the main purpose of the conversation. "Did you always know that you had a capacity for real magic?" she asked. "Is that why you became a magician?"

"I trained as a wizard first," Aruendiel said, parrying. "That was my parents' decision—at least in the beginning." He glanced at Nora and then went on before she could speak again: "Perhaps it would be best to begin with an account of my upbringing, my education.

"This castle, of course, is where I grew up. It had been the seat of my mother's people for some six or seven centuries before I was born. My great-grandfather rebuilt the fortifications and the house in their present form, including this hall. He fought well in the Five Battles War, and was awarded lands as far south as the Old Ram River. You can see him hanging on the wall over there"—Aruendiel nodded toward the far end of the hall—"in the fur robe, wearing the gold that the king gave him.

"By the time my mother was of marriageable age, though, the line had dwindled. Her father had been killed in the Salt War, and she was the only heir. The estate was not as rich as it had been. Our wool did not fetch the price it once had, because of cheap wool from the new grazing lands in the far north. The lands my great-grandfather had won were in dispute— the lords of Lusul had laid claim to them, and my mother had no one to protect her rights.

"I am telling you this history, not just because it was drummed into my head when I was a boy," Aruendiel added, "but because it does have some bearing on how I became a wizard.

"My mother was a perfectly handsome-looking woman, in my view, but she was not considered a great beauty. So she could not hope for a great match."

"What did she look like?" Nora asked.

"She was like most people in her line, dark-haired, dark-eyed, more sturdiness than stature. There are half a dozen women in the village now who could be taken for her at a little distance."

"But you're tall," Nora pointed out.

"In that, I resemble my father. He was a very tall man, lean, with light hair and eyes, not like the people of the Uland. He was from Sar Lith, the youngest of five sons of a middling peer with mediocre holdings."

"Where is Sar Lith?"

"South and west of here, two or three weeks' ride. There was a distant connection—one of my mother's great-aunts had married into his family.

At any rate, although this small, poor estate in the northern hills could not have been very attractive to my father, by marrying my mother, he could at least secure a very old and honorable title of his own. So he came here and took the name Lord Aruen.

"My father had grown up in a family that was vassal to several different powerful and disputatious lords, and he had learned something about diplomacy and forging alliances, which my mother's family never much bothered with. He set about building better ties to other peers and to the court in Semr, in order to enforce our land rights. My father was a clever man," Aruendiel said thoughtfully. "He had a knack for a sort of patient, intelligent prudence that I have never quite mastered.

"Because of these alliances, he was often away on campaign when I was a small child. My mother ran the estate and oversaw the upbringing of me and my siblings."

"You were the youngest," Nora prompted, when he paused for a moment.

"Well, the youngest who survived. There was actually an earlier Aruendiel, who died so soon after his naming day that my parents decided it made no sense to let the name go to waste and gave it to me when I was born. My sister used to tease me by telling me how much superior the first Aruendiel had been to me, although I am sure she was too young to remember him at all.

"There were four of us who lived to grow up: Atl Aruendies, then Aruendic, then my sister, then me. Dies was eight years my senior. We all looked up to him, not only because he was the eldest—he was strong, fair-minded, an excellent warrior. My second brother, Aruendic, was very different. He had a short temper that was even worse than mine is. I cannot tell you how many times I felt his fists before I grew big enough to defend myself. I learned to be a very fast runner, as a child."

Nora made a sympathetic noise, but Aruendiel shook his head. "I cannot say that I would have treated him differently, if our positions had been reversed," he added. "We never got on well, Aruendic and I. Although it is not true," he added, "that I was responsible for his death."

"What?"

Aruendiel was a shade startled by his own words, and regretful. If he was not careful, he thought, he would find himself telling this odd, clever girl with the luminous brown gaze the entire history of his life. "That is a different story. Where was I? My brothers. In fact, though, I spent more time with my sister when we were small. She was only a year older than I.

"We had an irregular series of tutors. One, I remember, was a sailor who could barely read, but he could teach sums and geography—he drew chalk maps from memory on the floor. Another was a wizard—although he taught us no magic," Aruendiel added, seeing the question in Nora's face. "We learned some astronomy and the *Nagaron Voy* and the *Ride of Brougnisr* from him. He would doze off during our recitations, but he had some sort of spell or spirit—probably a very clever copy imp—that would tell him how many lines we missed. It was a switch for every line—two switches if you missed the same line twice. Usually we had lessons in the deep winter. The rest of the year we spent on the usual childish things."

"Such as?"

He thought for a moment. "It seems to me now that I spent entire weeks on the back of a horse when I was young. At planting and harvest, we helped in the fields. When I was ten, my father came home for good—he had lost an arm at Glous—and after that, he coached Aruendic and me in swordplay. At any rate, by the time I was twelve or thirteen, I had probably spent a total of two years at my schoolbooks."

Nora could not resist observing that his early education was spotty by the standards of her world.

"If my father's estate had been larger, he might have hired a full-time tutor," Aruendiel said, frowning. "Still, when I went away to school, I was not far behind the other boys. And they knew nothing of the higher branches of mathematics, such as the multiplication tables, which I had learned from Izl Whitehead, the sailor," he added with some pride.

Nora gave a wicked grin. "I learned the multiplication tables by the age of seven."

"Through twelve times twelve?" he asked.

"Yes. My brother taught me—he liked to do stuff like that. All children in my country learn multiplication. Of course, they learn nothing of magic," Nora added quickly, as Aruendiel's face darkened.

"Are you sure that you wish to hear this tale?"

"Yes! Please continue. I won't interrupt again."

Aruendiel raised a skeptical eyebrow, but he continued: "Where was I? Well, my brother Dies had gone into training to become a knight. My parents sent him to the court of Lord Boena. It was not inexpensive to send him there, but Boena was one of the great lords of the kingdom, and it was a great opportunity for Dies, whom my parents considered, quite rightly, to be the most promising of their sons.

"My brother Aruendic hoped to join Dies at Lord Boena's court, but my parents could not afford to maintain two sons there. Instead, Aruendic went to Lord Inos, who had a midsized estate on the White Boar River. Inos was a good fighter, a friend of my father's, but his court was a stagnant backwater compared to Boena's. My brother was quite bitter about it.

"I found Aruendic's disappointment very funny. Without thinking much about it, I was confident that, when it came time for the next stage of my education, my parents would send me to someone more like Lord Boena.

"But my father's means were straitened, and my sister was approaching marriageable age, which meant that he had to gather the funds for a dowry. You remember her portrait?"

"The one that I broke?"

"It was painted around that time. My parents had it made so that they could send it to prospective bridegrooms. And indeed, the eldest son of Lord Forsne was very taken with that same portrait. She was married on her fourteenth birthday."

"Fourteen!" Nora could not stop herself. "And how old was he?"

"Twenty-seven or twenty-eight, something like that."

She shook her head, disgusted. "Fourteen is too young to be married, especially to a twenty-seven-year-old."

"I agree," Aruendiel said, surprisingly. "But the youngest brides are often the most desirable. Perhaps if my parents had waited, she would not have made such a brilliant match."

"Were they happy together?"

"Not particularly." His mouth hardened for a moment. "But I am digressing again. My sister had just been married when I learned that I would not be going away to Lord Boena or even Lord Inos. My father had determined that he could not afford to send me anywhere at all.

"He felt I should stay home and manage the estate. I was smaller than my brothers had been at that age—they used to call me the piece of string, because I was so thin. It would be a waste, my father said, to train me as a knight.

"My mother did not disagree outright. But she said, 'Aruendiel has a good mind. He has always been quicker than his brothers. He would benefit, I think, from further study.' She was thinking of wizardry school. There were quite a few, in those days. A wizard in need of funds would board pupils in his house and undertake to beat some spells into their heads in exchange for a dozen beetles or so. 'It is always useful to have a wizard in the family,' my mother said. One of her great-uncles had been a wizard, although rather an indifferent one.

"My father was not convinced, at first. Wizardry was not altogether respectable. Anyone could be a wizard, if he was clever enough. I myself thought it was a terrible idea. My own thought was that I could go to sea as a cabin boy on a warship.

"My mother prevailed, however. The only thing that made it palatable in the smallest way was knowing that I was to be prepared to do something my brothers could not do. So I went away to wizardry school at Norus-on-the-Lok, three days' ride from here. It was run by a wizard named Odl Naxt out of his house—not a large house, either. Only one of the boys came from any kind of noble family—the youngest son of Lord Evarnou. The other pupils were the sons of merchants or manor-farm tenants, and one was just a peasant boy whose father brought over some vegetables every week for his tuition. I was pained to think that I would be trained for the same calling as these clods.

"The first weeks of school we did nothing but memorize and recite. Odl Naxt used to mumble, and coming from his mouth, even the geography of hell sounded as dull as the cow pasture outside. I had just about decided that I had had enough of this experiment when our teacher finally felt that that we might work one small spell.

"It was an elementary levitation spell—"

"Which one?" Nora asked.

Aruendiel gave a quick half nod, as though the question pleased him. "One of Morkin's. The invocation was to a spirit called Blood-Streaked Appalling Vermiform Putrescence. An apt description, according to my friend Abuka Lier, who once saw it materialize.

"At any rate, I tried the spell four times and failed, and then, the fifth time, a stone that I would have had trouble shifting with my own hands rose into the air and rested there as solidly as though it were still lying on the ground. I felt a sort of joy at this new power, and I thought then that perhaps the study of magic might be worth my time and attention after all."

"*Five* tries?" Nora asked, all innocence.

"In the practice of wizardry—which you are spared," Aruendiel said, with a lift of his eyebrows, "it is not just the words that matter, it is how you say them. The tone, the pronunciation, the rhythm. There is a whole series of spells that must be sung to be effective—I had a terrible time with them at school, until my boy's voice had finished turning into a man's."

"Was this one of those spells?"

"It was not. Have you heard enough of this story, then?"

"No! Go on. You decided to stay at the school—" she prompted.

"Yes, I stayed. As it turned out, Naxt was not as great a hack as some of the wizards who go into teaching. He had worked for Baron Brodre, so he knew something of how magic is practiced at a great lord's court. We learned our share of the kind of simple, utilitarian spells that even a village wizard would know—how to keep milk from souring and the like—but also we also learned more complex magic as well. Some military spells, illusions, basic transformations, spells of influence and dissimulation. Naxt had a library of a dozen books or so, which was not bad for a school like that, and he corresponded with one or two wizards around the kingdom, so he had some knowledge of the latest developments in the practice of magic.

"Naxt was the sort of wizard who, without being very successful himself, had known many wizards who were, and he had some little story to tell about each of the prominent wizards of the time—how Firga Bearsnout had a charm against poisoning tattooed over his liver or how he, Naxt, had watched Jhonin the Drunk turn back a flooding river with his handkerchief. So we green boys learning spells to cure gout could think ourselves connected to that community of great wizards who shaped the destiny of kingdoms or did magic that no one had ever done before.

"I stayed there for almost four years. At that point, I could have set myself up as a fairly competent general wizard in some town like Stone Top, as most of Naxt's other pupils planned to do. That prospect chilled me. My brother Dies was by now a seasoned warrior who had helped capture Quouth the year before and won a commendation from the king. Even more galling, Aruendic had been in battle twice and acquitted himself well. I had no interest in living in ignoble obscurity while my brothers went on to win honor and renown.

"But something had happened that changed my family's situation dramatically. My father's last living brother died of a fever, leaving only a daughter, my cousin Yirnosila, a child of ten, who was quickly betrothed to my brother Dies."

"That's worse than what they did to your sister," Nora said.

"Dies and Yirnosila were not married until some years later," Aruendiel said, a little stiffly. "But what I am getting at is that my family's fortunes were suddenly much improved. My brother Dies would now have the estate in Sar Lith, which would leave my mother's estate, the Uland, for my brother Aruendic. My own expectations were not changed, but now there was more money to pay for my education.

"I was wild to become a knight. My father could now afford to send me to Lord Boena's court—and I was no longer the undersized boy that I had been at thirteen. I was as tall as my father. But he was skeptical. 'Do you mean to abandon your magical training?' he asked. I think he was aggrieved to think that the gold he had spent at Naxt's school might have been wasted.

"Then Odl Naxt came to my father with a proposition. He told my father that he had taken the liberty of writing to another wizard on my behalf. From time to time, Naxt said, his correspondent would take on a young wizard for a sort of advanced apprenticeship—choosing only candidates of exceptional magical talent and excellent birth. I was certainly Naxt's star pupil, except perhaps for the peasant boy, who was obviously unfitted for a position close to a high-ranking nobleman. Naxt had described my rank and my abilities and the fact that I had trained under him, Odl Naxt, and the other wizard was willing to grant me an audience.

"My father was not entirely pleased to hear that Naxt had taken it upon himself to tout my capabilities to an unknown wizard. 'Who is this man?' he asked.

"Naxt was clearly very proud of himself. 'It is my old colleague Lord Burs,' he said. Of all the wizards that Naxt could have mentioned, Lord Burs was perhaps the only one whose name would carry weight with my father. He came from an old family—not quite as old as ours, but old enough—and was one of the king's best-trusted advisers. Yet he was also independent-minded enough so that when King Tern launched an idiotic feud with the duke of Cliem, Burs refused to enter the hostilities. After the king's defeat, Burs brokered the peace and returned to royal favor. My father respected him, even if Burs was a wizard, because he was neither a lackey nor a bearer of grudges. Burs was also considered one of the three most powerful men in the kingdom, including the king—and some put Burs ahead of *him*.

"So my father consented for me to travel to Blesn, Burs's seat, for an audience. When I arrived at his castle, Lord Burs quizzed me for a few minutes—how would I counter the Deesk silencing curse; how would I compose a spell to appeal to a spirit of the Scabrous house; how would I move an army across a river in the shortest possible time? And then when I had answered his questions, which were simple enough, he said, 'Let us see how you sit on a horse.' He ordered me a fresh mount, and we set off and did not stop until we pulled up in front of the king's tent the next morning, just before the battle of Raitornikan."

"How do you counter the Deesk silencing curse?" Nora asked.

"You write the counterspell on a piece of paper and burn it," Aruendiel said. "And there are a hundred ways of moving an army across a river—I think I told him I would raise the river out of its bed and let the army march under it. In practice," he added, "I found later that the mud on the river bottom can slow the men down considerably."

"What about the Scabrous spirit?"

"Fornication," Aruendiel said detachedly. "Scabrous demons are attracted by the sight and sounds of fornication. I was still very young. I told Lord Burs I would use a couple of cats."

He took a sip of wine and cleared his throat. "I was extremely fortunate to become Lord Burs's assistant. There was no better education in wizardry. During campaigning season we traveled with the king's army, so I had a matchless opportunity to see Lord Burs in action. He was a master at tactical magic. I learned from him the overlooked value of subtlety in war."

Seeing that Nora looked blank, he went on, "Commanders often assume that a magic-worker can win the battle for them. They tell their magician or wizard, 'Turn the enemy into frogs,' or some such thing, and then they are disappointed and angry when the spell does not work—because the wizard or magician on the other side has already put into place a counterhex to ward off the transformation spell. This is one reason why generals have a strong distrust of wizards and magicians. In fact, most military magic is essentially defensive in nature—a good practitioner will anticipate the big magical attacks that the other side launches, and will defend against them, allowing his soldiers to fight without interference.

"Lord Burs was very good at that sort of thing, but his real genius was in casting smaller, less predictable spells that threw the enemy off balance or otherwise gave our side an advantage. At that first battle I saw, Raitornikan, he rendered some—not all—of the enemy's runners deaf and mute so that they could not deliver orders to the front lines. The wizard on the other side did not even realize what had happened until after the battle was lost. At the battle of Barrel Hill, Lord Burs moved the tower that Lord Diven was trying to take—moved it to the enemy's rear, so that Diven's troops, after breaking through our lines, had to turn around and fight back through them.

"When we were not on campaign, we were at Blesn, which was another sort of education. Lord Burs kept a rather grand court, second only to Semr. I learned something of the polish that one normally picks up as a knight in training. Swordplay, dancing, how to speak in company—how to speak to women," he added. Then, more briskly: "I never went in for poetry, although it was all the rage, or for playing the *gensling*—I had neither talent nor interest. I did learn how to drink and gamble like a gentleman, and then, more slowly, how to do neither to excess.

"The other thing that I learned from Lord Burs—he was one of the few wizards who still composed some of his own spells. Most spells had been written generations before. Good wizards made it their business to collect as many as possible. But from Lord Burs I also learned how to conjure up spirits and bind them to do my will in spells of my own writing. Demons, mostly. Sometimes human ghosts.

"I stayed with Lord Burs for almost five years. By the time I was twenty-two I had come into my full powers as a wizard, and I was ready to make my own way in the world. I began by working for one of my old master's allies as house wizard, and then I moved to Semr and set myself up as an independent practitioner. I worked mostly for a small group of noblemen close to the king, going to war at their side or handling other assignments." He laughed suddenly. "Curing their gout, if need be.

"Occasionally I worked for the king. Usually he relied on Lord Burs, his old friend—but I could see the day was coming when Lord Burs, who was over sixty, would be less interested in riding all night to fight a battle the next day, and then it would be me going to war under the royal standard. Wizards do not live any longer than ordinary men, you know," he added.

"Unlike magicians," Nora said.

"Unlike magicians," Aruendiel echoed moodily. After a moment, with a twitch of his shoulders, he continued: "I came to know all the other wizards of the kingdom, those of my generation and those older, and none of them was any better than I was. The most powerful men in the kingdom sought me out—I had my pick of interesting magical problems. My purse was heavy. I bought horses and books and fine armor. One day, I thought, the king would award me a great estate, or I would marry an heiress, but for the moment I was content enough. There were plenty—well, you would not know it now," he said, a little awkwardly, "but I was considered a handsome man then. Women found me pleasing. I fell in love and out of love and made sport with them as often as I could."

Aruendiel coughed, bemused to find himself saying these things to her.

Nora was nodding. "Mmm, I can imagine," she said in so knowing a tone that Aruendiel looked at her in mild surprise. She flushed. "Well, I found a letter of yours in one of those notebooks. I don't think it was ever sent. You were going to send some money to a friend of yours to pay a gambling debt, and there was also a discussion of some ladies named Lark and Frishi. It was very—candid."

"You read one of my private letters?" Aruendiel said.

"I read everything in those notebooks," she said virtuously, "looking for the spells you wanted."

He grunted. After a moment he shook his head. "Lark and Frishi—I cannot recall them. Whom was the letter addressed to?"

"Someone named Goffil. You talked about a battle near the Pir River, and you said that you would be back in Semr as soon as you finished off the old ox."

"The old ox?" Aruendiel repeated, sitting upright. Nora looked at him: There was something wary in his gray eyes, a startled animal dodging away into cold mist. "The letter was never sent?"

"I don't think so. Why, what happened? Did the old ox win the battle?"

"He lost it."

"Oh. And he was—?"

"Lord Els of Haarevl—his family crest was a crowned ox." With Nora looking at him expectantly, Aruendiel frowned and made himself go on, stacking up facts like bricks: "He had allied himself with the Pernish pretender. I was advising Prince Totl and his allies. We pursued Els along the Pir for some days, and yes, he lost the battle."

"But you never sent the letter," Nora said.

"It's possible," he offered, "that I realized I would return to Semr before the letter would arrive there."

Nora nodded. "Go on," she urged. "I interrupted again. Anyway, it sounds as though you were having a wonderful time back then." She could not quite rinse a shade of sarcasm from her voice.

"Those were heady days," he agreed. It was pleasant to recall them, even while reflecting what a blind and cocksure fool he had been. "The only thing that clouded those years was the death of my father. My brothers divided his titles and estates. There was nothing for me, but I had already achieved a greater position than either of them." He added: "I would see Dies and Aruendic at Semr when they came to sit in the Assembly. Normally they would take precedence over me, a landless younger brother—I had no seat myself—but I was usually up on the dais with the king and the highest lords of the kingdom."

"How did they like that, your brothers?"

"Dies and I were always on the best of terms. Aruendic—well, if he ever tried to hide his resentment, he did a poor job of it. I did not help, particularly." Aruendiel laughed quietly. "I was brash, I baited him when I could, and he did likewise. We brawled on the quay in Semr in broad daylight once, after Aruendic made a gibe about the cowardice of wizards.

"There is always this idea among the knights," he added with some warmth, "that wizards and magicians are not real warriors, because they rely on magic, because they do not fight with steel. But I carried a sword into battle, and most of the time, I had occasion to use it."

"Mmm. What about your sister? What was she doing?"

"My sister? Busy with her children. I visited her at Forel a few times."

He was quiet for a moment, curling his fingers around the empty goblet, tilting it back and forth against the table. "Gradually, though, I became aware that something was not quite right."

Another pause. "Something not quite right with your sister?" Nora prompted.

"Oh, that—but no, I was thinking about magic. It had become a sort of open secret among magic-workers that wizardry was in decline. No one was writing spells as complicated or powerful as those from the distant past. Some famous spells had stopped working altogether. You remember passing through Old Semr?"

"The ruined city."

"That was a city built with magic. When I was young, people were still talking about rebuilding Old Semr. It was one of those perennial topics at court—what would the rebuilt city look like, how would the king pay for it, what sort of defenses should it have? The real question, though, was *how* the city would be rebuilt, and that was discussed only among wizards. No one was powerful enough to re-create the charms that had held Old Semr's stones together.

"We had lost some essential knowledge of how to deal with the spirits that powered our spells. The wizards of my day could not command spirits the way the wizards of the distant past had. The more powerful demons had stopped responding to our calls at all. They broke their old covenants, and we could not punish them, and so our spells—some of them—became worthless.

"It was not something that I thought about very often. I was too busy, too happy, and most of the time, my powers were more than ample for the tasks I set them to. But occasionally I was aware that—for all the victories that I won, the ingenious and powerful spells that I worked, the fame that I earned—I had become preeminent in an art that might be dying."

Again, Aruendiel asked himself why he had just told Nora this. Well, she'd expressed some curiosity about Old Semr, the day they rode through it. Still, if he wasn't careful, he would lead her right back to the Pir River. Somehow, as he talked with her, the distant past seemed less distant; he almost forgot how much he had lost there.

Aruendiel stood up abruptly, flinching as his back straightened. He was suddenly aware that he would like very much to stay and keep talking—in fact, he realized with some alarm, he wanted nothing so much as to tell the whole long tale, to share it piece by piece with Nora and watch her turn it over in that lively, attentive, compassionate mind of hers. But that temptation was also why he could not tell her.

"What? It's not late."

"Late enough. I am growing tired—it is no small thing for a man as old as I am to recall the details of his earliest youth."

Nora looked up at him, her clean young face pleasant and watchful. "There's a lot you haven't told, though. How you discovered real magic . . . what was going on with your sister that wasn't quite right . . . what happened to your brother Aruendic . . . or the peasant boy?"

"The peasant boy?"

"The one who was at school with you. Odl Naxt's other star pupil."

"Oh, him," Aruendiel said, a splash of relief in his voice. "You've met him, as a matter of fact. That was my old friend Nansis Abora."

"The magician we stayed with on the way back from Semr? The one doing time-travel work—who gave us those preserves!"

"After we left school, he went back to his village, but our paths crossed again, much later. Nansis was one of the first to practice real magic with me. He has a very disciplined, patient intellect, and a good head for numbers. There are not many magicians who could even attempt the kind of astronomical magic that he is pursuing. He worked in Semr for a while—he had a spell as the king's chief magician—but he retired to the country as soon as he could. It sometimes seems to me that Nansis gleans more satisfaction from digging in that garden of his than from practicing magic.

"Aside from that," Aruendiel added, "he is not quite as great a clod as I first thought him."

## Chapter 37

Nora came downstairs the next morning to find that Aruendiel had ridden away at daybreak to pay a Null Days call. He was visiting someone named Lernsiep in the next valley—an old friend in ill health, Mrs. Toristel said.

He was away the next day, too. As afternoon turned into evening with no sign of him, Nora grew uneasy. It was the last of the Null Days. Tomorrow was New Year's Day. If he returned too late, would he pick up the thread of his story again? She had a half-superstitious fear that he was telling her as much as he had about his past only because it was the holidays, because he was bored, because officially this slow, dark stretch of time did not exist. If he did not finish the tale tonight, he would never finish it for her.

Well, she thought, at least I know most of the story. But what was that about being blamed for his brother's death? Nora ladled out some warm soup for herself, saving the rest for Aruendiel, then took up *Pride and Prejudice* and began translating. Elizabeth was reading a letter from her sister Jane, absent in London and now undeceived about the hypocritical Miss Bingley. Nora could not help thinking of her own sisters, never very dependable correspondents, but now completely out of reach. Would she ever see them again, she wondered, not for the first time.

The water clock in the kitchen had been stopped for the Null Days, but surely it was not so late yet. Nora laid another log on the fire, put on a second shawl, and went back to the book and her tablet. After a while, she put down her stylus and did the translation in her head, not bothering to write it down. Then she put her head down on the table for a moment's rest.

The touch on her shoulder was so light, almost shy, that it hardly roused her. Then she realized that she was very cold, with an evil crick in her neck, and she opened her eyes.

"Mistress Nora, is anything amiss?" Aruendiel asked sharply. "Why are you sitting here so late?"

"I was waiting for you," Nora said. Her voice was slow with sleep. She tried to sound more alert: "I was just sitting up for a little while."

Aruendiel's face was shadowed. "It will be dawn in a few hours. You should go to bed, or you will risk a chill."

Nora nodded, feeling suddenly foolish. Aruendiel was still in his traveling cloak, a trace of snow caked to his shoulders. He might have been riding all night. She stood up, flexing her neck carefully, and turned to go upstairs. Aruendiel walked beside her, his gait more labored than usual. "How is your friend, the one you were visiting?" she asked, to be polite.

"He is dying," Aruendiel said.

An awkward pause, which she tried to fill with some sympathetic words. Aruendiel did not respond. After a moment, she asked: "What is he dying of?"

"The wasting disease. There are unnatural growths throughout his body—they are draining his strength. He is as thin as a winter branch."

"Oh," she said, understanding. "That. It is common in my world."

"How do your doctors treat it?" he asked with a gleam of interest.

"Surgery, or drugs to kill the growths. Can you treat it with magic?"

He shook his head. "I have tried, but the growths returned. Lernsiep helped save my life once, years ago. And now I cannot save his. He says he does not mind so much. He has lived long enough, he says." Aruendiel gave a sour chuckle.

"Well—" Nora looked down. You couldn't force someone to stay alive, if the person was already dead, or as good as dead. She had surrendered to that unyielding logic after watching the vacant face in the hospital bed, the blinks and twitches that had no meaning. "But you'll miss him," she said.

"Certainly." They were upstairs now, in front of Nora's door. "I suppose that is why Lernsiep went to the trouble of saving *my* life."

"I would think so. You don't sound very grateful."

"No?" Aruendiel limped down the corridor without saying good night.

In the morning, the sky was so thickly bandaged with clouds that it was hard to tell the exact moment the sun rose. Standing in the courtyard, Nora watched the gray air brighten slowly, the other figures around her accumulating color and detail. Mrs. Toristel whispering to her daughter; her grandson yawning; the young black ram twisting suspiciously at the end of the rope held by Mr. Toristel; Aruendiel standing silent, holding a knife with a short, triangular blade.

At some point Aruendiel decided that it was dawn—either through some magical means or simply because he was tired of waiting. He nodded to Mr. Toristel, and the other man yanked the ram toward the magician so quickly the animal's hooves skidded on the icy cobbles. Aruendiel bent over the animal; it struggled as he tilted its head back. Nora looked away. When she looked back, the basin that Mrs. Toristel held under the sheep's throat was already half-full of blood, and Aruendiel was walking rapidly back toward the house as though he wished to speak to no one.

For most of the day, Nora worked in the kitchen, as the dead ram became roast mutton. She wondered if Aruendiel would summon her for a lesson, now that the Null Days were over, but she heard nothing from him. He spent some hours in the tower—Mrs. Toristel carried up a plate of mutton to him—and then he went out on horseback.

In the afternoon there was a bonfire in the courtyard, all the evergreen branches that visitors had brought during the Null Days. Nora watched as they burned with a slow angry crackle. People from the village came and went, laughing, drinking the hot ale that Mr. Toristel ladled out for them. There was a sheen of satiety and contentment on their faces. It was the one day in the year when everyone ate meat, everyone was alike, whether you could afford to sacrifice a black calf for the New Year or only a scrawny black rabbit.

As the bonfire died down, Nora turned to go inside, only to find Aruendiel behind her, a long shadow in his dark cloak. With a moment's confusion, she wondered how long he had been there.

"I was about to walk in the woods," he said. "Would you care to accompany me?"

They took the usual route down to the river, but once there, Aruendiel chose not to take the path into the wooded hills. Instead, he turned to follow the frozen gray track of the river, partly covered with snow. Watching him scramble down the bank, moving more nimbly than he had the night before, Nora deduced that he must have taken prompt advantage of the end of the Null Days to work some magic. He had shaved, too.

Uncharacteristically, he waited for Nora to catch up before moving forward.

"The ice is thick enough to hold us?" she asked.

"Oh, yes. It is frozen to the length of a man's forearm now, and it will not melt until spring." After a moment he added, "When I was a boy, this river often froze solid. Winters are milder than they used to be."

Aruendiel generally eschewed conversation on their walks; this was unusually loquacious for him. Nora took advantage of the opening.

"Aruendiel," she said, "I still want to hear the rest of your story—how you became not just a wizard, but a magician."

He glanced at her. "That is why you were waiting for me last night?" She nodded. Aruendiel's mouth curled, whether with amusement or annoyance she could not tell. "It is not as interesting a tale as you imagine," he said.

"I *need* to know more about real magic if I'm going to be a magician," Nora said. "You told Hirgus Ext that you rediscovered it. How?"

"As I told him—from the works of the earliest magicians."

"Well, but how did you find their works?"

"The same way that one comes across any book from an earlier time."

Aruendiel stared down at the ice, stepping carefully. "Some of the old writings came from the libraries of wizards who did not understand their importance. Some had been cached and forgotten, or had decayed to fragments. Some had been buried in the tombs of the dead. It was the work of years to discover them and then to understand their significance."

His voice sounded duller than usual, Nora thought. "Will you show those books to me?" she asked.

"You are too inexperienced. You would not understand them."

"But you could explain them. And after all, I know something about real magic already, more than you did when you first read the works of the old magicians."

"No." He shook his head. "It's impossible."

"I'm not like Hirgus Ext—I'm not planning to write a book," she pointed out.

Aruendiel laughed aloud. The face he turned to her was brighter, oddly quizzical. "No, you are not like Hirgus."

They came to a place where a dead tree had fallen across the river, blocking their path. "Have you done any magic today?" Aruendiel asked.

"Mended a broken cup, is all."

He jutted his chin at the tree. "Try lifting that."

Concentrating hard, Nora got the tree to shift a little. It swayed from side to side like a large, clumsy animal. Aruendiel watched critically. "You have very poor control," he said. "There is no need to fling it about the way you are doing."

"I've never tried to levitate anything so large," Nora said, feeling lightheaded. "It's an entire tree, it's enormous."

"All the more reason to make sure it does exactly what you wish it to, and no more."

They climbed over the tree, ducking through its limbs. Aruendiel remarked that she would have to remove it by spring or navigation would be impeded.

He was trying to change the subject, Nora saw. "So you won't tell me any more about the discovery of true magic," she said, aware that she sounded like a disappointed child. He did not trust her, for some reason. The thought was painful.

They walked in silence for what seemed like a long time. Finally

Aruendiel said: "No, I cannot tell you. Not now." He shook his head, but it seemed to Nora that the movement was more like a shudder. That, and the unease in his voice, reminded her suddenly of how he had looked—when was it? Not so long ago. Something that had happened when Hirizjahkinis was visiting.

"Will you tell me more someday?" Nora asked, suddenly oppressed with a sense of apprehension.

Aruendiel moved his shoulders stiffly under his cloak. "Perhaps."

They were coming to the place where the river curved to the north, leading deeper into the forest, away from the cultivated lands. Aruendiel turned and climbed the riverbank with a long step and a grunt. Nora scrambled up after him. Together they emerged from the trees that fringed the river, and began to walk across the snowy pastureland toward the red-and-purple sunset. For some reason Nora thought of a woman's painted face disappearing into flame.

"Your discovery of true magic—does it have anything to do with that woman Wurga?" she asked.

"Wurga?" Aruendiel said, too quickly. An extra jolt in his uneven stride.

So she had her answer, but she said: "The woman in the portrait I burned. The one who was afraid of you."

Aruendiel uttered a rough-edged syllable that took her a moment to recognize as laughter; it was not entirely mirthful. "Mistress Nora, you are as keen on the scent as a blind hound. Will I have no secrets from you?"

"Was she your lover?" Nora hazarded, remembering her other lucky guess, the one about Ilissa.

"Certainly not," Aruendiel said, frowning. He hesitated, then said: "She was a magician, of sorts."

"A magician!" It was more than Nora had expected to get out of him. "And what became of her?"

"As I told you before: She disappeared, after leaving my sister's house."

"How did you know her? Did you teach her?"

"Enough," Aruendiel said in a tone of finality. "It is a pitiful subject."

A suicide, Nora speculated, remembering the woman's crazed expression. She felt chastened. But she made one last venture: "Hirizjahkinis thought she was your daughter."

Aruendiel seemed surprised. "No, she was not my daughter."

They walked for a while in silence. The sun had set, but the snow on the ground cast a cold radiance in the air.

"You did have a daughter, though," Nora said, picking up on something in his tone.

Aruendiel acknowledged this with a nod. "From an old liaison, far from here. Her mother was a whore," he added matter-of-factly. "I saw that the child was provided for, although naturally I could not publicly recognize her as my own."

The "naturally" irked Nora, but she decided not to call his attention to it. "You told me that your granddaughter's granddaughter is an old woman now."

"Did I say that?" He brooded for a moment. "Well, it is true."

"Who is she?"

Aruendiel gave Nora a long, appraising look. "It is Mrs. Toristel."

"Mrs. Toristel!"

"You must never tell her this," he said with some sternness. "She does not know of her relation to me. Not precisely."

"Why not?" Nora was indignant. "She has worked for you all her life, and you never told her that you're her however-many-greats-grandfather? She deserves to know!"

"She knows there is an old family connection. Mrs. Toristel was a poor peasant girl when she came to work for me. It would not have been appropriate to make the relationship known."

Nora shook her head. "This is one of those times, Aruendiel, when we are not going to agree on appropriate behavior."

"But you will not tell her?"

"No, I won't," Nora said reluctantly. "She should hear it from you. And you *should* tell her. She would be so happy to hear it, you know."

"It is difficult," he said with some heaviness. "I brought her and Toristel here because they had lost their livelihood through no fault of their own—because of their loyalty to me, in fact. Because of that and the ties of blood, I felt some responsibility. There were complexities I should have foreseen, perhaps—but it does not matter, they have served me well."

"They certainly have. Mrs. Toristel works incredibly hard, and she's not young anymore. I hope you're paying her well."

"Well enough," he said. "They have never complained to me."

"They wouldn't," Nora said.

She and Aruendiel were in sight of the castle now. Aruendiel began walking faster, perhaps eager to escape further interrogation. Nora saw, with some chagrin, that he had managed to distract her, with his revelation about Mrs. Toristel, from the origin of real magic and Wurga's identity.

"You told me once that all of the female magicians you'd known were good magicians," Nora said. "But Wurga was only a magician 'of sorts,' you said."

"Her training was haphazard," Aruendiel said dismissively. "She would have improved with more practice."

That seemed to be all he would say on the subject. But when they were almost at the castle gate, he checked himself, wheeling to face Nora.

"It is hard to become a good magician, Mistress Nora, but it is not any more difficult to become a good female magician. At least, that has been my experience. Do you understand?"

Nora nodded, shivering a little in the cold air. "Yes, I do."

"I fear I have been remiss as a teacher today," he went on. "I have not told you what you asked to know about my first researches into real magic. And in truth, it is a story that I would rather entrust to you than to anyone. Not least because you may have special use for it."

Nora considered this, not seeing exactly what he meant. "So why can't you tell me?"

Aruendiel sighed. "I have kept this story to myself all these years, not wishing it to be known, and yet I do not want it to be entirely lost, either. I would cut out my tongue before I told the history of my life to such a fool as Hirgus Ext, but he was right to ask me about the origins of true magic. I must ask your forgiveness, Nora, and your patience. I will tell you this story—someday. I promise you this."

She wanted to argue—why not now, she could keep any secret he asked—but the seriousness of his expression dissuaded her. She tried to ignore the sudden dread that rose inside her, the fear of what he was not telling her. Could it be worse than killing your wife? "All right," she said. "I understand."

When they reached the castle, Nora saw that the bonfire had been doused, but there was a dark, upright, spiky shape in the courtyard, a little taller than a man. As they came closer, she recognized it as a fir tree.

"What is that tree doing here?" she asked.

"The tree is for you," Aruendiel said. "So that you may get in some practice in light-conjuring. I had Toristel set it up." When Nora did not respond, he added, with some impatience, "Did you not say that it is the custom in your world to garland a tree with lights at the time of the New Year?"

For some reason, something that Nora had told him about her own winter holiday had stuck with him. Perhaps he had seen similar trees in Chicago. She found she was smiling. "Oh, yes," she assured him. "It's called a Christmas tree."

Aruendiel flung up one hand as though to show that he had no interest in whatever the tree was called. "Very well, then. Begin."

As a homework assignment, it was a challenging one. She had conjured light before, but she had never tried to make dozens of smaller lights at once. And the tiny, ghostly flames refused to stay in place, slipping off the tree's needles to hover like winter fireflies. Aruendiel pointed out that she had left out the spell's locative step, and she had to start again. Then, as she was getting the hang of it, daubing light along the branches, he added another twist, making her pull illumination from two different sources, the Toristels' fire as well as the kitchen grate.

When Nora was done, she stepped back to look critically at her handi-work. She had not managed to make all the lights the same size—some were like sparks, some were the size of apricots—but she decided she was pleased with the effect. The lights borrowed from the kitchen burned slow and reddish, like coals; the others flared and flickered. Probably Mrs. To-ristel was poking her fire. Recognizably, it was a Christmas tree, although it was a wilder, less cozy, more restive creature than anything you could as-semble by plugging in a string of electric lights and throwing them over a tree in your living room.

"What do you think?" she asked.

Aruendiel frowned, staring at the tree, and she could tell that he was tallying up her errors: the false start, the various-size flames ("poor con-trol"), the time it had taken her to finish, and the other mistakes of which she was not even aware.

"It's very pretty," he said.

On an impulse, Nora groped for Aruendiel's hand and squeezed it. "Merry Christmas, Aruendiel," she said in English. "Happy New Year," in Ors.

Faster than thought, his fingers slid around hers. He looked down quickly, meeting her gaze, and in his startlement she saw a soft flash of hope, of wanting.

She saw with sudden emotion that she could follow the path her eyes had made and put her face near his, her lips on his lips. He was so close. It would not be difficult at all. In the glow of the tree, his gray eyes watched, gentle, restless oceans waiting to engulf her.

Nora froze, looked away. She gave his hand another, more abrupt squeeze and dropped it, rocking back on her heels, away from him.

"A prosperous New Year to you, Mistress Nora," Aruendiel said crisply.

They stood there for another few minutes, looking at the tree, talking— Nora could not for the life of her remember afterward what they talked about—until Aruendiel stamped his feet in the snow and turned to go inside. At the door of the manor house, he paused.

"Ask the Toristels to come over, will you?" he said. "I will have a New Year's toast with them."

He spent a good two hours that night drinking hot wine with the Toristels in the great hall. Aruendiel warmed the wine himself, not on the fire. Probably the Calanian protocol for generating heat, Nora thought. She did not ask him. She drank a goblet, but it did not shake the chill she felt.

PART

# FOUR

# Chapter 38

The kiss that Nora had not given Aruendiel on New Year's Day proved to be more durable than she would have imagined. It remained with her, invisible, inert, not gaining power but not losing it either. In those winter months she felt as though she were wearing it like a locket on a chain that would not break, and she was thankful that Aruendiel never noticed it.

Or seemed not to. Lessons had resumed. She spent half of every day in Aruendiel's company, but there was a reserve between them, an empty place that neither tried to traverse, although Nora found herself watching him across it. He no longer asked her to accompany him on walks into the woods, although he did not refuse if she asked to come. He did not talk about his past life again except in the most impersonal way—explaining how he had come to use a certain spell for the first time, for instance. The translation of *Pride and Prejudice* stopped, at his request.

"We're only halfway through, there's much more to come," Nora said, feeling the weight of the lost kiss. Elizabeth had just rejected Darcy. (Was it Nora's imagination, or had Aruendiel's face set into harsher, stoic lines as Elizabeth declared: "You could not have made me the offer of your hand in any possible way that would have tempted me to accept it"?)

"More of the same trivialities of courtship, you mean," Aruendiel said dismissively. "It is a wonder that anyone took the trouble to write down anything so negligible." Nora's grammar and orthography still needed polishing, he added, but she would make faster progress if she focused on the exercises in her grammar book.

Faster, faster. Aruendiel had a new preoccupation with how quickly she was advancing. He had started her on water magic while they were still deep in fire magic. It was hard to switch back and forth between the two, since water required an entirely different mind-set, but Aruendiel was unsympathetic. A good magician should be able to draw on multiple sources of power at the same time. Water was not as responsive as fire, it was secretive and mutable and aloof, you had to wait for it to heed you.

She had less time for household chores, for which she was secretly grateful, and yet she felt torn because it meant more work for Mrs. Toristel, for whom she felt a new sense of responsibility. It seemed unfair that Mrs. Toristel would never know how closely she and *he* were related. With a few words, Nora thought, she could reveal the truth. But Aruendiel would be furious. Or somehow wounded by her betrayal.

The dead kiss pulled on its unseen chain, knocking against her heart. It was as persistent and troublesome as that damned ring of Raclin's that she still could not remove from her finger, either. The kiss was worse. *Coward*, it said to her. *What were you afraid of?*

Perversely, she had started to dream about him. Very ordinary dreams, mostly—once she dreamed they were driving in a car together in Washington, D.C., of all places—but sometimes (too often? not often enough?) the dreams were blatantly erotic. Then she was amazed at how warm and solid his long body felt as she wrapped her arms around him and he kissed her with a mouth that was fervent and sure. One night the kiss went on and on, Aruendiel's hand cupping her breast—Nora arching herself against him, wanting to devour him, yet knowing that Mrs. Toristel could walk into the room any minute—Aruendiel pulling up her skirt—pressing deliberately into the aching secret heat between her legs—

Nora woke up. She found she was panting slightly. Raclin was sitting on the edge of her bed, smirking. He looked very handsome in the moonlight.

"Are you that desperate, that you'd screw *him*?" he asked. "I thought my wife was used to better than that."

"At least he's not a monster," Nora said.

Raclin laughed again. Ilissa's voice, from somewhere Nora couldn't see, called: "Raclin? What are you doing?"

"It was only a dream, Mother," Raclin said, glancing over his shoulder. Ilissa giggled. "Oh, then leave poor Nora alone," she said.

Nora woke up for real that time, in the freezing dark of her bedroom. She lay for a long time without moving, listening with dread for Ilissa's and Raclin's voices to return, also wishing she could take a long, hot shower and scrub away a lingering sense of befoulment. She thought about calling out to Aruendiel, a few rooms away—Raclin had seemed so real—but another kind of anxiety stopped her.

In the daylight, the dream itself looked much more like psychological dramatizing than Faitoren magic. Meeting Aruendiel unexpectedly that morning, she was flustered enough to drop a jug of water. She did a spell to collect the spilled water and flubbed it—twice. She was almost grateful for his caustic critique of her performance, because it meant she didn't have to say anything.

Otherwise, the winter days blended almost seamlessly together like snow falling on snow. Mrs. Toristel knitted dozens of socks. Mr. Toristel's arthritis flared up, got better. When the snow was too deep for walking or riding, Aruendiel practiced his swordplay in the great hall against an opponent jerry-rigged into life from old rope, a broomstick, and a powerful animation spell. There was no grace in the way that he moved—the old broken places in his frame were more obvious than ever—but he wielded the sword against the puppet with grim precision. Nora developed an exasperating tic in her spellcraft, a light rain—sometimes sleet—that fell as she worked through particularly challenging spells. At first she was rather pleased with herself—she had not even gotten to weather magic!—but after the second wetting it was only a nuisance. Aruendiel lectured her once again on control and banished her to the great hall to practice spells, safely away from his library.

Then, one afternoon in the second month of the year, Aruendiel received a letter from the magician Nansis Abora. Something white bumped against the glass of Aruendiel's study window. When he brought it inside, Nora saw that it was parchment that had been folded into an angular bird-like shape, like an origami crane. It quivered in Aruendiel's hand and then was quiet.

After reading the letter, Aruendiel snorted. "Nansis thinks he's reconstructed Mernil Blueskin's observation spell. The right one, this time."

"What do you mean, this time?"

"Oh, some years ago a magician named Klexin Ornasorn claimed to have rediscovered the Blueskin observation spell hidden in the binding of an old book on weather forecasting. Of course he wouldn't let any other magician read the spell, let alone try it." His mouth twitched. "Hirizjahki-nis and I went to some trouble to obtain it. It was an obvious fake. *Some-one's* observation spell, but not Blueskin's."

"What is Blueskin's observation spell?"

"An observation spell," he said, "lets a magician see what's happening elsewhere. Mernil Blueskin devised the first true observation spell back in the days of the Thaw. It was lost centuries ago, but it was supposed to be the best of its kind, with almost limitless range. As far as the other side of the world—even other worlds."

"*Other* worlds?" Nora repeated. "Really."

"At least, so the story goes," Aruendiel said thoughtfully, nodding. "It would be intriguing if—" He drummed his fingers on the tabletop. Scanning the shelves, he took down a couple of books and disappeared up the stairs to his workroom, still holding Nansis's letter.

Nora was in the great hall, attempting a basic transformation—changing the color of a bowl from red to blue, and trying to ignore the delicate drizzle that swirled intermittently around her head—when Aruendiel reappeared, some hours later.

There was new energy in his uneven step. "It's a good spell," he said. "Better than I expected. I've been looking around, at various things all over the world. Semr. Skililand—the western continent. The range is excellent. It *could* be Blueskin's spell."

Nora set the bowl, which had achieved a rich eggplant tint, carefully aside. "Did you try looking outside this world?" she asked.

"Not yet. Come," he said, with a lift of his chin. "I require your assistance."

She followed him into the tower, up the stairs. At the top, his workroom was dark. Aruendiel lit a candle, and Nora saw a circle drawn on the floor in charcoal, about eight feet in diameter.

"Take this," Aruendiel said, handing her the candle. He lit another for himself. "Now, we are almost ready. We are going to have a look at your world."

"All right," said Nora, taking a deep breath. "Any particular part of my world?"

"Anywhere you like," he said carelessly. "But choose something. The spell works better, I find, the more specific your intentions."

Nora had a momentary impulse to show Aruendiel her apartment and some of her regular campus haunts, then dismissed the idea as faintly embarrassing. There were all the places she'd always wanted to visit: Angkor Wat, the Lake District, Tokyo. Aruendiel would probably be impressed by Tokyo. But that wasn't what she really wanted to see.

"Have you chosen a place?" Aruendiel asked impatiently.

"Yes. What do I do now?"

"Think of it as you would any destination, as you set out on a journey—with some purpose, some intention. Keep tight hold of your candle. And then step into the circle."

That was all? She felt distinctly skeptical as she stepped across the charcoal line. But she felt the internal shudder that signaled strong magic—and the light from her candle hit vague clutter on the ground that she had not noticed before. A stone floor—no, cement. Something caught the light and threw it back to her: chrome, spokes, glittery pink and purple streamers. A little girl's bike. Next to it, a lawn mower. Over there, a blurry glistening bulk that she knew, even without being able to see it clearly, was a silver Toyota Camry.

The light of a second candle appeared, over her shoulder. Aruendiel looked around curiously. "What is this place?" he asked.

"It's my parents' garage," Nora said. They were standing where Kathy's car, the minivan, was usually parked. She must be out somewhere.

He repeated the English word inquiringly.

"Garage? It's an outer room, like a barn," she said. "Where vehicles are kept." She gestured at the Camry, not sure whether he would know what it was.

"So the house of your parents is nearby?"

"In here," she said, moving automatically toward the kitchen door. "Actually, it's my father and stepmother's house. He bought my mother out, when they got divorced."

Nora reached for the door handle. It felt dull and distant, but the knob turned. She opened the door and went up the three steps to the kitchen.

She fumbled for the light switch and then realized that the lights were already on. A sluggish pale streak spilled down from the light fixture over the sink.

"Why is it so dark?" she asked Aruendiel, just behind her.

"Use your candle," he instructed.

She began to understand how the spell worked. Inside the two circles of flickering candlelight, hers and Aruendiel's, objects had color, definition, solidity. She could see clearly her booted feet on the creamy vinyl tiles. The white plastic coffee maker, shockingly clean and bright after the smoke-blackened wood and stone of Mrs. Toristel's kitchen. The squat green numbers on the microwave clock: 11:13 PM.

Beyond the reach of her candle, the world was grayish, elastic, unformed. The edges of the room heaved slowly. Nora strained to see them more clearly, then looked back at her candle when she started to feel seasick.

"It's nighttime," she said to Aruendiel. "Late. I think everyone might have gone to bed by now." There were still dirty supper dishes in the sink. She went cautiously forward. The slippery dimness resolved itself into the far end of the kitchen, then the den.

She was wrong; her father was still up. Barely. He slumped on the couch, soaking in the glow of the television screen.

"Dad!" Nora said softly, not wanting to startle him. "It's me, Nora."

He did not respond, so she called again, louder. His eyes did not move, even when she went over to stand directly in front of him, blocking the television.

"What's wrong with him?" she demanded.

"He can't see you," Aruendiel said, coming into the den.

"What do you mean, he can't see me?" She held her candle closer to her father's face.

"It's an observation spell, Nora. We are not really here. We can see him, but he cannot see us."

Her father moved suddenly. He reached for something on the floor—a can of Bud—and took a long swallow. A small collection of empties nested beside the couch.

"This is your father?" Aruendiel inquired.

"Yes," Nora said. Even if Aruendiel had never seen a beer can before, he probably could figure out what it was from the avidity with which her father was tilting out the last of its contents. "He doesn't usually drink this much."

Aruendiel seemed more interested in the television, holding his candle up to see it more clearly. "I remember this from Chigago," he said, with an air of satisfaction. "Moving pictures, it is called."

"Television," Nora corrected him absently. "It's similar." She looked worriedly at her father, the shadows under his eyes, the puffiness along his jaw. He had gained weight. Then, because he and Aruendiel were both gazing fixedly at the TV screen, she did so, too. The Weather Channel. It was snowing in Minneapolis.

From the other side of the house came the faint sound of the front door opening. "Who's there?" her father called out, raising his head, suddenly alert.

"Leigh." Her sister's voice sounded tinny.

Her father did not relax. "What were you doing out? I thought you were upstairs. Come in here."

After a minute, Leigh appeared, a shadow that gained substance as she advanced into the light from Nora's candle. Since Nora had seen her last, her sister had grown an inch or two. She was wearing her jeans tighter now, her sweaters clingier. "I was at Marissa's," she said. "Doing homework."

"I don't want you staying out so late. What time is it?"

"I dunno, not that late."

"It's too late to be walking home alone."

"Her brother drove me."

"Her brother? How old is he?"

"He's nineteen. He can drive at night."

"You need a ride, you call me."

Leigh chortled, rolled her eyes. "Like you could even drive right now, Dad."

Her father's slurred voice rose. "I don't like that tone, Leigh, and I don't like you driving around with nineteen-year-old boys I haven't met. You're grounded. Two weeks."

An exasperated sigh. "That is so unfair. I wasn't doing *any*thing."

"Then whatever you weren't doing, you can not do it at home."

"Who cares, you won't even remember this tomorrow."

"Enough of your crap, Leigh. Go to bed."

"I was about to, before you hauled me in here."

"I said, that's enough. Shut up and go to bed."

Of Nora's two sisters, Leigh seemed more determined to grow up fast, and the last few times Nora had seen her, she'd been toying with an exciting new air of adolescent disgruntlement. But this kind of mutual contempt between Leigh and their father was new. "Was I that bad when I was her age?" Nora asked herself. Worse, maybe, but her father had never told her to shut up. And she'd never seen him so drunk then, except after EJ—she did not finish the thought.

"My father is scolding my sister for being out too late," she said to Aruendiel.

"That is your sister?" Aruendiel was surprised. He was about to say something else when his attention was captured by the TV again.

Leigh stomped away, losing shape as she moved into the queasy darkness outside the candleglow. Nora heard her footsteps echoing up the stairs. Then Leigh shouted something, a parting shot. Nora caught her own name: "—like Nora."

"Leigh?" Nora moved after her sister. "What did you say?" This was maddening, to see and hear and not to be seen or heard.

Leigh's door was closed when Nora reached the top of the stairs. The knob resisted her. "Leigh! Leigh! Can you hear me at all? It's Nora." The only response was the beat of a pop song vibrating through the door; her sister had barricaded herself with sound.

"Nora?" A fluting question, slightly hoarse, from behind. Nora turned. The door to Ramona's room was open. Nora entered cautiously, holding up the candle. Dimly she made out her youngest sister sitting up in bed. "Nora, is that you?"

"Ramona! You can see me?"

Ramona's dark eyes looked at her with the stillness of wet stones. "I can see you. Not very well."

"Is this better?" Nora moved to Ramona's bedside, her candle spilling its light on the child.

"Yes, that's better," Ramona said, with a small exhalation. She sat hunched against her pillows, her arms drawn protectively around her knees. "Why were you calling Leigh?"

"I wanted to ask her something," Nora said. She hesitated. "I don't think she can hear me, though, and I couldn't open the door."

"She locks it. Mom and Dad don't like it, but it makes her feel safer, and the counselor said to let her."

"Oh," Nora said, digesting this information. "Leigh's seeing a counselor? Is she having a tough time at school or something?"

"I guess." Ramona looked away, then back at Nora. "Nora, what are you doing here? Do you want something?"

"Do I want something?" Nora laughed, a little puzzled. "I wanted to see how everyone's doing."

"We're doing okay," Ramona said tightly. She added: "I miss you."

"I miss you, too, honey," Nora said, settling herself on the edge of the bed and reaching out for Ramona. She could barely feel her sister's shoulder. Ramona flinched.

"I'm sorry, I shouldn't have done that," Nora said, stricken. "You know, I'm not really here—it's hard to explain."

"That's okay," Ramona said stoically. "Your hand just felt weird. And you don't have to explain. I know what happened."

"You do?" Nora looked hard at her sister and saw the fear in her face. She gasped. "Ramona, I am *not* dead."

From Ramona's expression, she was plainly unconvinced. "You don't feel real," Ramona objected. "How do you know you're not dead?"

"I know it." Nora thought for a second, then held up one of her braids. "Look, see how long my hair has grown. That wouldn't happen if I were dead."

"This boy at school, Zach, said your hair and fingernails keep growing after you're dead."

"Not this long. Ramona, I promise, I'm not dead."

"Then what happened?" Ramona asked, her voice wavering. "It's been *six months* since you disappeared. Mom and Dad won't say anything, but I know they think you're dead. Dad talks to the police—"

Nora remembered the yellow crime scene tape in the mountain graveyard. She wanted to give Ramona a hug, then decided against it. "Listen to me, Ramona, I'm not dead, I just got lost. Really lost. This is hard to believe, I know, but I'm actually in a totally different world. I'm just visiting though, um—through magic."

Ramona stared at her for a long minute. "Oh," she said finally.

"So I'm not dead, okay? Do you believe me?"

"I guess," Ramona said. "What kind of magic?"

There was a gleam of light from the hallway. The second candle advanced into the room, Aruendiel's dark figure behind it. He looked quizzically at Nora.

Ramona sucked in her breath. "Snape!"

"What are you talking about?" Nora asked. "This is Aruendiel—the magician Aruendiel." She cleared her throat. "He's the one who did the magic that I was telling you about."

"You mean it, Nora?" Ramona asked, sounding almost angry. "He's a *magician?*"

"Yes—I know it sounds unbelievable," Nora said, half-apologetic. She looked up at Aruendiel. "This is my little sister Ramona. She can see us, Aruendiel," she said in Ors.

"Very curious," Aruendiel said, leaning closer. He and Ramona stared at each other. In the bright, cozy clutter of the child's bedroom, next to the pink-shaded lamp and the poster of the palomino, he looked especially dry, gaunt, imposing. All at once Nora felt oddly protective, and not just of her sister.

"Don't be frightened, he's really very nice," she said to Ramona quietly.

"What did you say to him? What language were you speaking?" Ramona demanded.

"It's called Ors—it's the language of his world," Nora said. "I was telling him that you can see us. Leigh and Dad couldn't."

"Really?" Ramona seemed pleased by the information. She did not resist when Aruendiel took hold of her chin and tilted her head up so that he could look into her nostrils, then turned it to the side so that he could examine her ears.

"How old is she?" he asked.

"Ten—no, wait, eleven," Nora said. "I've been away for six months, apparently."

"Now what are you saying?" Ramona said.

"He wants to know how old you are." In Ors: "Does her age matter?"

"A child, a girl who has not reached the age of womanhood, might be more receptive to sensing something otherworldly," Aruendiel said reflectively. "She also is feverish. Perhaps she sees us because she is delirious."

"Feverish!" In English, Nora asked her: "Ramona, are you sick?"

"I have a sore throat," Ramona allowed.

Nora put her hand to Ramona's forehead, but could not judge the temperature of her sister's skin. "Where's your mom?"

"She has an overnight shift at the hospital."

"Did you tell Dad you're not feeling well?" Nora asked. Ramona shook her head. "Well, you need to tell him and ask him to give you some children's Tylenol."

"No, he's—Mom says to leave him alone at night."

"When he's drunk, you mean?" Nora gave a sigh of frustration. "When did that start? He never used to drink more than one or two beers a night."

The glance that Ramona shot at her was half-contemptuous, half-pitying. "Well, what do you think, Nora? We thought you were dead."

"Oh, balls," said Nora. She clutched her forehead.

"Well, not everyone. *Your* mom thinks you've been kidnapped by pagan cultists. She keeps calling Dad about it." No wonder he was hitting the bottle, Nora thought. Ramona went on: "She had a vision of you worshipping fire."

"Fire, really?" Nora forgot her sense of guilty unease. "You know, my mom is a little creepy sometimes. I *have* been doing some fire magic—Aruendiel is teaching me. Not worship."

"You're learning magic! That is so cool! Can you do some magic now?"

Nora hesitated. In her own world, the idea of inducing fire or water to do her will suddenly struck her as unlikely. "I can do it in the other world, but here, I'm not sure," she confessed. "I'm still pretty new at this."

"Could the magician, Aruendiel—" Ramona pronounced the name carefully. "Can he do some magic now?"

Aruendiel had been moving around the room, solemnly inspecting Ramona's menagerie of stuffed animals, her books, the map of Narnia, her soccer trophies. He had paused in front of a shelf that held two large framed photographs. One was of Nora, smiling, squinting a little, in graduation robes. Now he turned.

"Your sister is not satisfied with having visitors from another world?" he said, his brows swooping together. "She would like to see still greater magic? Kings have been grateful for far less."

"Aruendiel! You understand English?" Nora asked, shocked, pleased.

"It comes back to me," he said, with a nonchalant tilt of his head. "Not everything, but some of it."

Ramona looked entreatingly at Aruendiel. "Please?" she said. "Ask him—ask him to make Friday talk." She pointed to the foot of the bed. For the first time Nora noticed the cat drowsing there.

"Oh, Ramona, I don't know if that's even possible." To Aruendiel, in Ors: "Did you get that? She wants the cat to talk. Shall I tell her no?"

"Tell her to be patient for a little while." He bent over the cat, holding the candle so close it seemed that he might set the animal's fur alight. Affronted, the cat uncoiled its head, and gazed haughtily up at Aruendiel. There was something eerily similar in their respective stares.

Aruendiel straightened and nodded at Ramona. She flung herself forward and pulled the cat onto her lap. "Friday! Friday! Can you understand me?" she asked solicitously. "Can you say something?"

The cat squirmed out of her arms and leaped from the bed. "I was *trying* to sleep," it said as it stalked out of the room. "Stupid bitch."

"Oh, my gosh!" Ramona's mouth worked like a goldfish's.

"There are a number of good spells for making an animal speak," Aruendiel said to Nora. "It is far more difficult to make them say anything worth listening to."

"That was amazing!" Ramona said, although she looked a little shaken. "Nora, are you going to learn to do that? What else can he do?"

"What do you say, Ramona?" Nora asked warningly.

"I was going to say it! Thank you." She bobbed her head.

Aruendiel replied with a formal bow. "Tell your sister I am pleased to be of service to her."

Nora translated, then broke off with an exclamation. A drop of hot wax had scorched her finger. Gingerly, she adjusted her grip on the candle. It had burned down to a stub so small it was hard to hold on to.

"What happens when the candle burns out?" she asked Aruendiel.

"What do you think? The spell is over."

"I was afraid you would say that." In English, to Ramona: "Honey, we don't have much time left. The spell lasts only as long as the candle."

"Then get another candle," Ramona said promptly. "I want to know about the other world. How did you get there? Are there lots of magicians there? Can I come visit you? Are you going to stay there forever?"

"No! I'm going to come home as soon as I can. It might take some time. Aruendiel will help me."

Ramona dropped her voice slightly. "Are you *married* to him, Nora?"

"No, certainly not." Nora shook her head, coloring slightly. "Whatever gave you that idea?"

"You're wearing a wedding ring," Ramona said, pointing at Nora's hand.

"That's—well, it was a mistake," Nora said. The candlewax nipped at her fingers again. Her light was shaky, dwindling.

"Are you married to anyone?"

"Listen, Ramona, please tell everyone I'm okay, will you?" She paused. "You probably shouldn't mention the magic. It might worry them. I'll be home—"

The last thing Nora saw as her candle's flame dissolved into blackness was Ramona's face, interested, alarmed. Then Ramona was gone.

Nora stood quietly for a moment, regaining her bearings. A floorboard creaked under her foot. The room was chilly, dark, scented with candle smoke. This, she could sense intuitively, was a real place, where things had weight and substance, unlike where she had just been. But it was not the real world, not at all.

# *Chapter 39*

They won't believe her, of course. They'll think she's fantasizing, that she's crazy." Nora paused. "You're sure she's the only one there who can understand the cat?" Aruendiel nodded. She groaned and went on: "And the real reason they won't believe Ramona saw us is because they think I'm dead.

"Ramona thought I was a ghost, you know. You saw that picture of me on the shelf?" Aruendiel nodded again. "The other picture was my brother, EJ. At first I thought, how weird that she had his picture up. She never even knew him. But then I realized, it's a shrine to her dead siblings." Nora shuddered. "Was she upset when I evaporated in front of her?"

"She was agitated for a moment, yes," Aruendiel said. "But she seems to be a child of some resolve and self-control," he added, with a note of approval. "She asked me a question in your language. I believe she wanted to know whether you had returned to this world. I said yes. And then I extinguished my own candle."

Nora spooned up some broth, then let it fall back into her bowl. They were eating dinner, an hour after a journey that, strictly speaking, had never happened at all.

"I must point out," Aruendiel said, "that although it's true that my spell made the cat intelligible only to those present at the time, it was a remarkable feat of magic. There are *perhaps* two other magicians now practicing who could cast a spell from one world into another with any hope of success."

"Nifty," Nora said in English. "Well, then," she said in Ors, "can't you do a spell that will let my family know that I'm alive and well? Is there a way to send messages between worlds? A letter in my handwriting—would they believe *that*?" She was asking herself as much as Aruendiel.

"A letter?" He frowned, as though still piqued at Nora's failure to appreciate the power and artistry of the magic he'd performed on the cat, but then the notion of sending a letter to her world seduced his attention. He drummed his fingers slowly on the table. "You could do it with a twinning spell, what Morkin calls a correspondence spell. It puts the same object in two different places. A wax tablet, say—so that if you wrote on it, being in this world, the same words would appear on the tablet in the other world."

"Really? Let's do that!"

"The difficulty," Aruendiel added, "is that the enchanted tablet would have to be physically introduced into your world." He looked at her to make sure that she understood. "We would have to send it there the same way that you came here—through a gateway between worlds. So—"

"So in that case I could go back myself," Nora finished in leaden tones. "All right, so when can I go back?"

"I have told you, I do not know."

"There's no sign of a gateway?" she demanded. "How often do you check?"

After a beat, Aruendiel said: "Frequently." He added with a trace of waspishness: "I do not wish to detain you in this world any longer than need be."

Nora bit back a sarcastic thanks, then tried to explain: "You saw them—they're mourning me. They're grieving. And I can't do anything about it. Do you understand how awful that makes me feel? My father getting drunk, fighting with my sister—that's because of me. He lost one child—"

"What did you think they were doing all this time, your people?"

"I don't know! I thought they were basically fine. I was hoping not too much time had gone by over there. A couple of weeks, maybe." Nora was aware as she spoke of how ridiculous this sounded.

"To be honest," she added, "I didn't think they would miss me so much. But—to see them like that, and not to be able to do anything. I feel like crap. I've been—" Nora shook her head, angry at herself, angrier at Aruendiel for providing the sly distraction of learning magic, making her forget what she owed to her family, her own world. "What was I thinking? And meanwhile they think I'm *dead*."

"And what if they do?" Aruendiel asked. He pushed his empty bowl away. "Do you have some obligation to their grief?"

"Well, of course! They're grieving for me."

"What does that have to do with you? Their grief belongs to them alone."

"But I don't want them to grieve!"

"If you *were* dead, as they believe, you would owe them nothing."

"What are you talking about?"

Aruendiel shrugged, one shoulder mounting higher than the other. "The dead should not have to answer to the claims of the living, even the sharpest grief."

Nora sat in rebellious silence, considering what he had said. "Do you really believe that?" she asked. She was not sure exactly what he was getting at, but it had a flavor of callousness, or arrogance, that repelled her. "And I'm not dead, in any case. I do owe my family something, some reassurance. You said it could be years before I get back."

Her tone was accusing. She could not soften it much, even as she made her request—it came out as more of a command—to do the observation spell again that night. She had the conviction that if she could just return to her father's house, in whatever form, she could find some way to communicate with him or her stepmother.

Aruendiel refused. There was no guarantee, he pointed out, that they would reach her father's house on the same night. Days or weeks could have passed already. And if her sister's fever had gone, she might not be able to see them.

Furthermore, he added, Nora was distraught—a poor frame of mind for doing strong magic.

He was regretting, it was clear, that he had ever performed the observation spell in the first place.

"So I should just let my family think I'm dead?" she demanded at last. "Do you think that's right?"

"For now, Nora, you do not have a choice," he said wearily.

She sat in silence, thinking again of the twin photographs in her sister's room, wondering why Ramona had chosen those two. The Nora in the photograph was grinning a bit too broadly, trying to cover up her disquiet at the prospect of figuring out what to do with the degree she had just earned. In EJ's case, it was his school photo from tenth grade. The camera had caught him with his mouth slightly open, revealing the glint of braces, giving him an undeserved appearance of dullness. It was an awful picture, really. Maybe those two photos were the only ones that Ramona could find to fit the frames.

"So I'm dead to them," Nora said resentfully. The phrase did not have the same resonance in Ors that it did in English. "I suppose there's no chance that I'm really dead, is there? You said no once—but I did give Ramona a scare."

"Of course not," Aruendiel said, his expression softening. "You are very much alive."

His assurance relieved but did not mollify her. Nora cast about for a new direction in which to loose her roiling guilt and anger. "*You* were dead once," she said, with a sense that her words would burn. "Really dead. Isn't that right?"

The gray gaze might have slipped sideways for an instant—impossible to say for sure. "Where did you hear that? More tittle-tattle from Semr?"

"Hirizjahkinis told me."

"Ah, Hirizjahkinis," he said brusquely. "She should scratch her own fleabites and leave my affairs in peace."

"She helped bring you back to life."

"She's proud of that."

"Why shouldn't she be?" Nora said, pressing for something more, not sure what.

"It was Euren the Wolf's magic, more than hers. And as a piece of magic, it was—well, only adequate. It took years for me to recover from my injuries." With a grimace, he added: "Even now, I am not healed completely."

"Well, you're alive," Nora said, irked on Hirizjahkinis's behalf by his lack of evident gratitude.

"They should have spared themselves their trouble. There was no good reason to resurrect me," Aruendiel said in the tone of one stating an unvarnished fact. "They would have won the war without me, eventually. I'd lived a long time. I had no close ties. My children were gone by then, even my grandchildren. My wife was dead. I had killed her not long before."

He added the last piece of information deliberately, as though Nora might have forgotten it.

"Yes, you'd mentioned that," she said coolly. Then, her voice rising slightly, she added: "That's something I can't figure out, by the way. I just don't understand. That you would kill someone weaker than yourself." The thought of Aruendiel stabbing his wife had become more terrible over time, not less. "It seems"—she chose her words carefully—"dishonorable."

Aruendiel's eyes narrowed. "She was the one who'd behaved with dishonor."

"So it was all right to kill her?"

"I was very angry," he said flatly.

"Is that an excuse?"

"Of course not. You asked for an explanation. She cried and clung to his body. What did she expect?" Aruendiel's voice was taut. "That I would spare him, the one who stole my wife from me? It was my right to challenge him. I used no magic. It was a fair fight. I won. And then she wept, she screamed. She was holding him, her belly swollen with *his* child. It was as though she did not even see me. I put the blade between her ribs and walked out of that cursed room."

Nora thought of Aruendiel's swordplay with the rope-and-broomstick puppet in this very hall: snick snick snick thrust. She looked straight at him, taking in every line of the harsh, graven face; unable to think of what to say, she fell back on Shakespeare. "Yet she must die, else she'll betray more men?"

"More men? She betrayed *me.*" He added abruptly: "She loved him."

"Well, presumably—"

Aruendiel fixed her with a pale glare. "You fail to understand. She loved him. I meant to free her from enchantment—but there was no enchantment. No spells of any kind infecting her heart. She'd gone with him of her own free will. It was the cleverest and cruelest part of Ilissa's revenge."

"Ilissa?" Nora asked.

"Of course. It was all her doing."

"*You* stabbed your wife."

"Ilissa set the trap," Aruendiel said. "It was her trickery. She hated me. She had been my mistress," he added, his voice hard.

"You told me that once. So you think," Nora said, not bothering to keep the disbelief out of her tone, "Ilissa arranged for your wife to fall in love with someone else?"

"Exactly." He was silent, then spoke with a kind of grim eagerness, as though he had made up his mind to advance through hostile territory no matter what the cost: "From the moment my marriage was announced, I feared Ilissa would strike at my wife. I took precautions. I guarded Lusarniev with the most powerful protection spells I could devise. I watched to ensure that she was under no kind of enchantment.

"When Lusarniev gave birth to a stillborn boy, I thought instantly of Ilissa. But to all signs the child had died of natural causes. It was the same when Lusarniev miscarried again, and then again. The third time, I even called in another magician, my friend Nansis Abora. He waited upon my wife and then told me privately that he could find no enchantment, and he confirmed what the doctors had said, that she should regain her strength before she became pregnant again.

"Lusarniev herself was terribly fearful of bearing another dead child. So I absented myself from the marriage bed until she could grow stronger. It was not strictly necessary. There are magical means to keep babies from coming. But it made Lusarniev calmer in her mind.

"And then one day I came home to find my wife gone. She had left with Melinderic, a knight attached to my household.

"He was not much older than my wife. His grandfather had been one of my comrades in the Pernish wars. I had made Melinderic my principal deputy for the sake of the old connection and because he was intelligent, forthright, reliable. I trusted him completely.

"For all the care that I took to make sure that Ilissa had not enchanted my Lusarniev, I never thought to examine Melinderic."

"You're saying that Ilissa put a love spell on *him*?" Nora asked.

"Yes, of course," Aruendiel said impatiently. "You should know something about Faitoren love spells. It was quite powerful."

"And your wife—" Against her will, Nora found herself believing him. Ignorant of magic, Lady Lusarniev would have known only that the young man was in love with her. And knowledge might pity win, and pity grace obtain.

"So he seduced her," Aruendiel said. "And then there was a child on the way." He laughed starkly. "All my concern for my wife's health went to good account, did it not? She only wished to avoid bearing a child to *me*." More quietly, he added: "I would have staked my life on her honor. I had never known her to do anything before that was not correct and graceful."

At these last words, Nora felt sudden dislike for the dead woman. She tried to ignore it in the cause of female solidarity. "But your life *wasn't* at stake, was it?" she said. Aruendiel did not answer. "I feel even sorrier for her now," Nora said staunchly. "She died because of a love affair that wasn't even real. He only loved her because of magic."

"Her feeling for him was real enough," Aruendiel said acidly. "She made me a laughingstock. People said I should have known better, after all the times that I'd cuckolded other men. But—" He shook his head. "That was exactly why I never imagined she'd be unfaithful. The wives I'd seduced were discontented. Their husbands neglected them. Lusarniev— we'd been married only three years. I would have sworn she was completely happy to be my wife. I paid her every attention, and she ranked among the greatest ladies of the kingdom."

"Why did you marry her?"

"Why?" He seemed surprised by the question. "She was precisely the kind of woman I intended to marry. An excellent lineage. A lovely face. She was only eighteen when I met her, but she had a composure and bearing that I admired, that came from being carefully brought up. She knew how to behave at court, how to run an estate. I understood the sort of people that she came from. She was perfectly suited to be my wife."

"It sounds as though you were hiring her for a job," Nora said tartly. "What did she think about your being a magician?"

He opened his hand in a dismissive gesture. "That was not her concern. She was pleased to be the wife of a famed magician, of course, but it mattered less to her than other things."

"Well, it doesn't seem like a great marriage to me," Nora said, "not that that was any excuse for killing her. You chose her because she was safe and predictable, she wasn't interested in what you're most interested in—and we haven't even touched on the age difference. She was eighteen, and you were what, a hundred and thirty?"

"It was a fine marriage," Aruendiel said. "If not for Ilissa's meddling." He brooded for a moment. "Yes, I was far older than Lusarniev, but it meant only that I knew what I needed in a wife. Lusarniev was all that, and I cherished her for it."

Nora felt another uncomfortable twinge of irritation toward the deceased Lady Lusarniev. "Too bad you killed her, then." Honorably, she added: "And maybe you shouldn't blame her so much for falling in love with another man. Ilissa probably put some extra glamour into that love spell to make Melinderic more attractive."

"He was handsome enough already," Aruendiel said, with distaste.

"Your wife was what, twenty-one? That's very young."

Aruendiel glanced at her with a flicker of what might have been amusement, but it faded. "Yes, she was very young," he said heavily. "You know, I cannot even recall exactly what she looked like, except for that last wild look before she died. I remember that she was beautiful, but I cannot picture her beauty.

"Then I went after Ilissa. She'd stirred up her own war by then. I did not especially care what the war was about. I only wanted to kill Ilissa.

"Instead, she killed me.

"In battle, those last weeks, I was strangely distracted, clumsy. I thought that anger would sharpen my powers, as it always had in the past, but not this time. I could not seem to judge the strength of my own magic— my spells were either far too strong or not strong enough. Did Hirizjahkinis tell you how I died?"

"She said you fell from one of those flying contraptions."

"An Avaguri's mount," Aruendiel said. "There had been other near misses in combat, but I was lucky the other times, or my allies covered for me. That day, in the Tamicr Mountains, I was chasing Ilissa, putting all my energies into the curse I was sending after her, and suddenly I felt myself falling. One of her illusions, I knew, and yet I reflexively leaned hard to the right, trying to correct my balance. And then I really did fall, right off my mount."

"You could have saved yourself," Nora said crossly, feeling a perverse satisfaction in pointing out the missed opportunity. "You could have raised a wind—transformed yourself into a bird—summoned the Avaguri's mount back to you."

"For some reason, I did none of those things," he said. "I remember the sunlight on the snow below me was so dazzling that I had to close my eyes. And then I remember hitting the mountainside and not being able to move. Then I fell again. This time the ground fell with me. That was the avalanche, from what they told me later. I don't remember anything else. Evidently I died very quickly."

"And then what?" she demanded.

"Then they found my body and revived it, Euren, Hirizjahkinis, and the others, sometime later."

"But what happened in the meantime?"

"In the meantime? I was dead."

"What do you remember? You must remember something." When Aruendiel said nothing, Nora pursued: "You—your soul must have been somewhere. Or they wouldn't have been able to bring you back."

"Those who come back from death have nothing to tell. Were you paying no attention when I resurrected the child Irseln?"

Nora remembered the puzzled shadow on Irseln's face, the way she had ducked her father's greedy questioning. Was she fearful because of what she remembered, or fearful because she could not remember? "She was a little girl. You're a grown man and a magician," Nora said. "You must have some recollection."

Slowly Aruendiel's gaze pulled away from Nora's and roamed across the darkened hall. "I remember a sense of—engagement," he said. "I was occupied with something that required my full attention. I can remember this only because I was conscious of being interrupted when they called me. I had no great interest in answering their call, but they persisted. So then I went to see what it was all about."

"What do you mean, 'went to see'? Was it an actual journey?"

He shook his head. "It was not a matter of physical distance. I found the four of them: Euren, Meko Listl, Hirizjahkinis, Lernsiep. I do not think I could have named them, then, but I knew who they were, and I knew they were there because of me. Their concern for me seemed absurd, misguided. I watched them, bemused that they were going to such trouble.

"Then—I do remember this quite clearly—I recognized my corpse, lying in the middle of their small circle. I could not see it exactly as the living see, but I could perceive that it was wrecked, empty. Whatever utility that body had once served was ended. And that should have been enough for me.

"The corpse was familiar, though. That was what drew me. I was curious"—he spoke the word with contempt—"the way one might have a whim to visit a place that one knew long ago.

"So, I lingered. I could see the corpse more clearly now, probably through the eyes of the others. I felt no particular emotion when I saw that half of my face was a smashed ruin. But my hands—" He lifted them from the table and turned them back and forth, inspecting them thoughtfully. "In some ways, we know our hands better than our faces. In life, I had never seen them so still and helpless. I felt pity that they would never move at my will again. And then—more curiosity," Aruendiel said. "I wondered what it would be like to enter into the flesh again.

"That was all it took. I was caught.

"In an instant, I knew what it was to be alive again. Suddenly I needed air; I had no choice but to fill my lungs. I remembered cold, and then I remembered—well, I discovered what it is like to be broken in a dozen dozen places.

"As I said," he added, with a sour rictus, "there was no good reason to resurrect me."

He stopped speaking. Nora ran a fingertip over the table, tracing a figure eight. "You didn't encounter your wife while you were dead, by any chance?" she asked suddenly.

"I don't know."

"You don't remember anything, except at the very end, when you came back."

"This is correct."

Aruendiel's calm assertion of seamless ignorance—so uncharacteristic—was profoundly unsatisfying. She wondered if he was lying. But if he was not lying, what then? To know that there was something after death but not to know what it was, the undiscovered country still undiscovered, whether it was torture, hellfire, bliss, boredom, nothingness—what was the comfort of that?

"How did they bring you back? What spell?" she demanded.

For once, Aruendiel seemed oddly reluctant to talk about the particulars of a piece of magic. "Some of Euren's wolf magic, to try to heal the corpse's wounds and make it fit for life again," he said dismissively. "A binding spell, to help bring spirit and body together. And to summon the spirit, that was more wolf magic. They simply sat together, the four of them, and called for me for a long time."

"What do you mean, called for you?"

"By name, by thought." He shrugged irritably. "It's how the wolves call back their dead, according to Euren. Very loose, subjective, like all animal magic."

Nora shook her head violently, as though she could dispel the sudden wave of fearful recognition that had washed over her. "I don't believe you," she said.

Aruendiel glanced at her, surprised.

"You know, after my brother's accident, when he was in the hospital," she said, finding her voice shifting, unsettled, "that's exactly what we did, my parents and I. We spent *days* in his room, talking to him, looking for any sign that he heard us. And there was nothing. He wasn't even dead yet.

"If he had been somewhere, if he could have heard us, he would have come. If it had been possible to bring him back, we would have done it. Even without magic, we would have done it."

Aruendiel answered slowly: "I cannot say whether your brother heard your call or not, Nora, or whether he could have answered it. Perhaps it was better for him not to."

"Better? Better?" Nora stood up. Finally her surging discontent had found a suitable outlet. "Is that what you meant when you said the dead owed nothing to the living? That we shouldn't disturb the dead with our grief? The way your friends disturbed you? Listen, you were lucky that they did that! You were lucky to have friends who loved you enough to sit around your dead body and grieve and call and try to drag you back into the world. Because I can tell you, it's painful to do that, it's horrible, to call and call and not know if anyone will answer.

"But you don't appreciate that. You're still angry at Hirizjahkinis for raising you from the dead. It seems like selfishness to me."

"You know nothing about it," Aruendiel said, with a furious wrench of his mouth.

"*You* can't even remember being dead; how do you know it was so wonderful?"

"That doesn't matter. It was what had befallen me. It was my fate."

"They gave you a gift, bringing you back to life."

"Which I never asked for."

"If that's your attitude, life was wasted on you."

Aruendiel leaned back in his chair and folded his arms. He smiled slightly, unpleasantly. "I fear that you are right."

## Chapter 40

On winter mornings, the barn was dark but milder than outside, full of the animals' warm breath and the funk of their manure. Nora fed the chickens first, then the sow, finally the goats and the two cows. She hauled water for them, then took a pitchfork and spread a fresh layer of bedding.

This morning she took extra pains, spreading the straw deeper and more evenly than usual. Some levitation magic would have made the work go faster, but today she found a certain comfort in having to exert herself. The physical effort made remembering the evening before slightly less painful.

What had put her into such a foul humor? That small, tantalizing glimpse of home had started it. And then Aruendiel's dark mood, his death wish—all laced with self-pity, but naturally he wouldn't see that. She wished that he had not told her so much about murdering his wife. She wished he had not told her anything about his wife. And yet she wanted to know everything about his wife. How humiliating to feel this species of jealousy toward a dead woman. Perverse, too, considering how she had died. Nora stabbed the pitchfork into a pile of manure, then held out a handful of straw to one of the cows. Its big tongue brushed Nora's hand. Running a hand down its warm, shaggy face, she still felt raw, exposed, regretful. Not so much because of what she had said but because of what she had made him say.

As Nora came into the kitchen, stamping the snow from her boots, Mrs. Toristel looked up from her mixing bowl. "He's got visitors already," she announced, nodding toward the great hall.

"So early?" Mingled frustration and relief that she would not encounter Aruendiel alone. "Who is it? I thought the roads were still bad."

"She didn't need a road this time," Mrs. Toristel said, the disdain in her voice unmistakable. "They flew here. Two of those flying mounts in the courtyard."

"She?" Nora asked with a tinge of alarm. Her first thought, after last night, was *Ilissa*. Then a more encouraging notion struck her. "Do you mean Hirizjahkinis? With Hirgus Ext?"

Mrs. Toristel nodded. "No, the other one who was here. Dorneng, his name is. You didn't see them? *He* looked serious."

"He always looks serious."

Mrs. Toristel clicked her tongue. "I'm sure it's nothing to joke about, whatever it is that brought them."

As soon as Nora opened the door to the great hall, she could hear Aruendiel swearing, and she knew instantly that yes, this was something about Ilissa. Dorneng stood directly in front of him, a woeful look on his fleshy face. Hirizjahkinis, standing to one side, watched the other two magicians with a slightly fixed smile; she had the attitude of someone who is just barely containing herself from tapping her foot with impatience.

Nora caught her eye, and instantly Hirizjahkinis's smile became more natural. She came forward.

"What's going on?" Nora asked in a low voice. "Is it Ilissa?"

Distractedly, Hirizjahkinis put her hands on Nora's shoulders by way of greeting. "Of course it is Ilissa!" She laughed, but her laugh sounded tired. "Why else would I have to fly all night in a snowstorm? It is very inconsiderate of her to cause all this fuss in the middle of winter."

"What has she done now?"

"She has broken out of her prison. So now we must go to the trouble of finding her."

No wonder Aruendiel was cursing. "How did she get out? Aruendiel put in all those new defenses—"

"Dorneng let her out."

"What? That seems pretty stupid, even for him."

Hirizjahkinis rolled her eyes. "It was very stupid of him—but then he had no Kavareen to call on, when Ilissa enchanted him.

"He was afraid to tell Aruendiel what he had done—he came to Mirne Klep to fetch me first. As though I did not want to bite him into tiny pieces myself when he told me."

"Well, Dorneng wanted to know more about Faitoren magic," Nora said. "I guess he knows now." Aruendiel brushed past them into the kitchen, giving no sign that he had noticed her. "Where is Ilissa now? Does anyone know?"

"Dorneng thinks she is going east," Hirizjahkinis said. "He thinks."

At the sound of his name, Dorneng lumbered dejectedly toward them. "Yes, east, toward the Ice," he said. He sounded as though he had a cold.

"Terrible, she has no consideration," Hirizjahkinis said with a shudder. "I think we should simply let her freeze there, but of course that's not enough for Aruendiel. We must hunt her down and lock her up again."

"Well, that doesn't seem like a bad idea," Nora said cautiously. She gave Dorneng a polite greeting, for which he seemed to be effusively grateful. He said it was wonderful to see her in good health—which Nora took to mean not a marble statue—and then he began to apologize to Hirizjahkinis for putting her to so much trouble. From the look on Hirizjahkinis's face, Nora could tell that this was not the first apology she had heard from him. Something about Lord Luklren's lost sheep—"I never even asked myself, why are they on the wrong side of the barrier? I just let them through, thinking Lord Luklren would be relieved to have them back—"

"The thing about Faitoren magic is they can make you believe what you want to believe," Nora said, meaning to offer a word of understanding, but Dorneng did not look any more at ease.

"Ilissa made a great fool of Dorneng, right enough, but this is hardly the first time that she has tricked a clever magician," Aruendiel said, coming toward them, a worried-looking Mrs. Toristel on his heels. "As you well know, Hirizjahkinis." He frowned, but there was grim excitement in his face. Nora saw that, ironically, the current state of emergency, the opportunity to punish Ilissa, had improved his mood. "Now, Dorneng—"

Mrs. Toristel was plucking at Nora's sleeve. "I must pack his clothes," she said in a lowered voice. "You go into the kitchen and get their provisions ready. Sausages, dried apples, whatever bread we have left—if only I'd known sooner, we could have made more. Hurry!" She gave Nora a small push toward the kitchen.

"They're leaving now?" Nora asked, but Mrs. Toristel was already heading for the stairs. Aruendiel was still giving directions to Dorneng while Hirizjahkinis listened. Nora went into the kitchen. Hastily she packed two bags with food, then carried them into the great hall. Hirizjahkinis and Dorneng were bent over a map on the table. There was no sign of Aruendiel. On an impulse, Nora tried the entrance to the tower. It was open. Half-running, she went up the stairs to Aruendiel's study.

He stood by the window, running a whetstone over the blade of his sword. The same sword that had killed his wife? Probably. When Nora mounted the last stairs, he looked up, surprised, as though he had forgotten all about her.

"You're leaving now?" Nora asked.

"Yes, of course." It was the familiar clipped tone, skeptical that anyone could be so dense. "I hope you have not come to beg clemency for the Faitoren," he added.

"I want to go, too," she said.

"No."

"I know enough magic now to be useful."

"No, you don't." He sighted along the blade, focusing on something outside the window. "And you will be safer here."

"I'd be safe enough with you and Hirizjahkinis."

"We will have more to keep us busy than protecting you. This is war, not an excursion to Semr."

"I know that! I want to help."

"It will take more than mending pots to recapture Ilissa."

"You know I can do much more than that! You taught me. Besides," she added hesitantly, "I'd have tactical value beyond my magic skills."

"Indeed?" He eased the sword into its sheath and then buckled it around his waist.

"Yes, you saw how Ilissa went for me in Semr—and what happened with the ring," Nora said, sounding almost as confident as she wanted to. "Ilissa hates me. You might need a decoy. I could distract her while you counterattacked."

Aruendiel's chilly eyes widened slightly. "Absolutely not," he said shortly. He regarded Nora for a moment, frowning. "You are not coming with us, and what's more, you will not leave this castle while we are gone, do you understand?"

She stared back at him, feeling mutinous. He went on: "Your proposal is absurd, but you're right about one thing—to her, you're prey. I've deprived her of her prey thrice already, and she would like nothing better than another chance at you. You know that."

Reluctantly, Nora nodded.

"So you are not to stir outside the castle gates," he said. "Not one step. Is that clear?"

"Clear enough," she said, her voice flinty.

"Good. Now"—he looked around the room—"I have what I need, so let us go down. I will seal up the tower until I return."

That was something she had not considered. "Wait! May I take a book to study?"

"One book," he said. "No, not Morkin," he added irritably as she selected a volume. "Vlonicl."

Hastily she put down the Morkin, picked up the other book, then started down the stairs. Aruendiel followed her more slowly. From what she could tell, he was setting various magical traps. She waited for him at the bottom of the stairs.

"I hope you'll be careful," she said awkwardly.

In the dim light of the oil lamp that burned there, his scarred face looked faintly, sardonically amused, but otherwise, he went through the wall as though he had not heard her.

"Honey's getting low. This woman, Ilissa, she's the one you escaped from, isn't she?" Mrs. Toristel asked out of the gloom.

It was the afternoon of the second endless day since the magicians had left. She and Nora were in the store cellars, taking an inventory of the household's food stocks. Before his departure, Aruendiel had repeated to Mrs. Toristel the injunction that Nora was not to leave the castle. To Nora's frustration, the housekeeper had interpreted this instruction more strictly than even Aruendiel, surely, would have thought necessary, and had forbidden Nora to go out of doors at all.

After two days of virtual confinement in the house, even visiting the cellar was a welcome expedition.

"That's right," Nora said in answer to Mrs. Toristel, holding her candle close to one of the bins where the root vegetables were stacked, layered under soil and straw. But something had been after the carrots; they were strewn half-gnawed around the dirt.

"And now this. She never gave him so much trouble until you came along."

"No, that's not true," Nora said. A dubious silence from Mrs. Toristel, so Nora added the thing that she could not stop thinking about: "Ilissa's the one who made him fall, all those years ago."

Mrs. Toristel sniffed. "I knew he'd had a fall. I never liked to ask how. Not my place." Nor Nora's place, either, her tone suggested. She added briskly, "Well, he has a lot to pay her back for, then. You don't know how bad it was for him at first, after that accident. He was like a bundle of cracked sticks. He was lucky to be alive."

"Yes," said Nora. Her hands worked mechanically, picking out the lengths of carrot that had been chewed by small teeth. "Mrs. Toristel," she said, "what if he doesn't come back?"

"What?" Mrs. Toristel half-turned in indignation, her candle sending long shadows scuttling across the cellar walls. "Of course he'll be back. You don't think this Ilissa, whoever she thinks she is, could defeat a magician like his lordship?"

Only if he let her. Only if Aruendiel wanted Ilissa to finish the job that she had tried to do fifty years ago. Nora held the thought up for quick scrutiny, and then thrust it back into the darkness from which it had come.

"You know what a great magician he is," Mrs. Toristel went on. "Or you should know, anyway, all the time you spend studying with him."

"I know. It's just—" Nora hesitated. "This all happened so suddenly, it's unnerving."

She was thinking that Hirizjahkinis had the Kavareen to protect her. Why could she not press the battle while Aruendiel directed the campaign behind the lines, preferably from the safety of his own castle? It had occurred to Nora, too late, that she could have given him the New Year's kiss before he left. She would have unburdened herself, and the kiss would have been only a little worse for wear. But perhaps he no longer wanted it.

"I wish we knew what was going on," she said in frustration. "Whether they've caught up with Ilissa—if anything has happened yet."

"Don't expect to hear anything until it's all over," Mrs. Toristel advised. "Whenever he goes away, it's as though he vanished from the earth. Unless, of course, there's something he wants done," she added broodingly. "Then he's quick enough to send word."

"How?" Nora asked, wanting to be prepared for even an unlikely communication from Aruendiel, and also curious about the spell he used.

"There'll be a letter appearing somewhere, and then I'll have a job puzzling it out. Well, I suppose you could read it to me now, that's a blessing. *If* he writes."

Wind magic and demi-transformations, Nora thought, remembering the letter from Nansis Abora that had flown to Aruendiel's study on its own paper wings. Or perhaps he simply caused the letter to be written at his own desk and then moved it to where Mrs. Toristel could find it. Either way, she felt slightly cheered, knowing that a message from Aruendiel could materialize at any time, even if it was only a directive to Mrs. Toristel to sell the yearling heifer.

Instead, the next day there was Hirizjahkinis, alone, knocking imperiously on the castle gates.

Nora was ready to run outside to greet her, but Mrs. Toristel grabbed her arm. "Remember what the master said."

"But it's Hirizjahkinis." Mrs. Toristel did not let go. Impatiently, Nora watched from the window as Mr. Toristel led Hirizjahkinis across the courtyard. Once inside, Hirizjahkinis shook the snow from a pair of brilliant red boots, gave Nora a lavish smile, and let herself be embraced.

"Why did you come back? Where is Aruendiel? Did you find Ilissa?"

"Aruendiel is still searching for Ilissa," Hirizjahkinis said. She cast a speculative eye around the room, then nodded graciously at Mrs. Toristel, emerging from the kitchen. "He has tracked her quite a long way, but he has not caught up with her yet."

"Then what are you doing here?" Nora demanded.

"I am here for you," Hirizjahkinis said, with another wide smile. "I am to take you back with me."

"Me?" Nora glanced at Mrs. Toristel. "Aruendiel told me specifically that I could not go. That I'd be in the way. That it was too dangerous."

"Of course you won't be in the way." Hirizjahkinis pulled a small scroll from under the Kavareen's hide and handed it to her. "What foolishness!"

"Well, I agree, but he told me not to leave the castle at all," Nora said as she unfurled the scroll. A few curt lines in Aruendiel's crabbed script directed her to accompany Hirizjahkinis.

What seized her attention, however, was the last sentence: "We have need of your talents here." The acknowledgment of her magical abilities, however terse, made her feel a small surge of pride and hope.

"He said that Nora shouldn't go anywhere," Mrs. Toristel said firmly. "Not even outside."

"Well, but he does ask me to come," Nora said, showing her the note. "He says they need me."

Mrs. Toristel glanced at the letter, then waved it away. "It takes me too long to make out his scratch," she said. "It says for you to leave with *her*?"

"Yes, that's what it says."

"Well—" Mrs. Toristel looked hard at Hirizjahkinis. "How is she supposed to travel?"

"We can fly. I have a lovely mount, just outside. But we should leave as soon as we can, so that we don't have to travel in the dark." Hirizjahkinis's voice was suddenly serious.

"All right, I'll get my things." Nora ran upstairs to put an extra shawl and some knitted undergarments into a small bundle. When she came down again, tying her cloak, Hirizjahkinis was sitting in Aruendiel's chair at the long table in the great hall. Mrs. Toristel hovered nearby, broadcasting silent disapproval.

"How quick you are, Nora," Hirizjahkinis said, rising gracefully. "That is very good. Are you sure you have everything? Yes? Then let us be off."

Nora turned to Mrs. Toristel, who was frowning ferociously. "Please don't worry about me. I'll be fine. I'll ask Aruendiel to send a message when I get there."

Before Mrs. Toristel could reply, Hirizjahkinis said: "I will make him do it!" She laughed and moved toward the door. "Come, we must hasten, so that he does not have to face that wicked Queen Ilissa all alone."

"Right," Nora said. She smiled at Mrs. Toristel. "Yes, it's better if Hirizjahkinis gets back quickly."

"He said for you not to leave the castle," Mrs. Toristel said stubbornly. She trailed them outside.

"But this is Hirizjahkinis. I'll be safer with her—and with Aruendiel—than I am here. And Aruendiel says that they need me." Again, Nora savored his words: They had need of her talents.

Hirizjahkinis's red boots were moving through the snow with swift determination.

"Why didn't you land in the courtyard?" Nora asked her.

"Oh, Aruendiel's protection spells are ridiculously strong!" Hirizjahkinis said. "It is almost a sign of timidity, don't you think?"

"Well, I wouldn't say that," Nora said, although, as always, she could not help but relish the élan of Hirizjahkinis's pronouncements on Aruendiel. At the gate she thought again of Aruendiel's injunction not to leave the castle. Not one step, he had said. But now he had authorized her leaving, had ordered her to leave.

Sure enough, nothing terrible happened as she went through the gate. An Avaguri's mount was tethered just outside the wall. Nora was reassured to see that Hirizjahkinis's mount, unlike the one that Aruendiel had made, had a broad saddle with stirrup-like supports for the feet. Hirizjahkinis indicated that she should seat herself. Nora turned to Mrs. Toristel for a good-bye hug.

"*He* wouldn't send for you, not this way," Mrs. Toristel hissed in Nora's ear. "He'd come to fetch you himself. He wouldn't trust even *her*—not with you."

Nora hugged Mrs. Toristel a little tighter and thought of black elves and how Mrs. Toristel had never liked Hirizjahkinis; what a shame she couldn't be more tolerant of female magicians and people with darker skin. And yet what Mrs. Toristel had said about Aruendiel—that he would come himself—felt like the truth. She heard again the cold, angry seriousness in his voice when he had called Nora Ilissa's prey and forbade her to leave the castle.

Was there some mistake? That was definitely Aruendiel's handwriting in the note, Nora thought, as she turned away from Mrs. Toristel and toward Hirizjahkinis. But Mrs. Toristel must have seen the confusion in her face.

"I should send some supplies with you," the housekeeper said loudly, catching Nora's arm. "Some bacon, in case his lordship gets tired of the sausage." She bobbed a slight curtsy toward Hirizjahkinis. "It won't take but a few minutes, if you come back to the kitchen to help me, Nora."

"We are leaving now," Hirizjahkinis said. She stepped toward them and took hold of Nora's free wrist. All playfulness was gone from her voice. "We can't waste any more time."

"What?" Instinctively, Nora tried to pull her wrist out of Hirizjahkinis's grasp.

Mrs. Toristel screamed. Loosing Nora's arm, she sank down on her knees, her face like crumpled paper. Nora bent down to help her, but Hirizjahkinis jerked her away.

"Hirizjahkinis? What the hell? Let me go!"

"Please don't struggle," Hirizjahkinis said, grabbing Nora's other wrist. "You'll just tire yourself out, with nothing to show for it." Her hands were like iron clamps. Nora kicked at her, hard, but the red boots feinted neatly. "Don't be tiresome, Nora."

"This is Faitoren enchantment," Nora said, kicking again—this time she connected with one of the red boots, and Hirizjahkinis grimaced. "Hirizjahkinis, listen to me. Ilissa has gotten to you—she's tricked you. You don't want to do this—not really."

"Oh, yes, I do," Hirizjahkinis said, pulling Nora by the wrists toward the Avaguri's mount. Nora scanned her dark face for signs of enchantment, submission to a foreign will, but she looked as wise, kind, and tough as ever. "Come on, sweet," Hirizjahkinis added. "I don't want to make things any harder for your friend than I have to."

"Mrs. Toristel? What have you done to her?" From the corner of her eye, Nora could see the housekeeper thrashing about in the snow. The sight energized her; with a mad twist, Nora pulled one wrist free.

"Darling, I think I need a little help here," Hirizjahkinis called.

The Avaguri's mount moved. It was not an Avaguri's mount any longer. Its wings lifted—webbed and leathery, not feathered. It raised a long, toothy grin as friendly as a chain saw. Nora forgot to breathe, although her mouth was open.

"Raclin, why don't you take her now?" Hirizjahkinis said. "And—oh, what *is* this?"

Blue fire had suddenly erupted underfoot, clutching at the red boots and the fur trim of Hirizjahkinis's cloak. She clucked in annoyance, stamping her foot. The flames skirted Nora, but swarmed around Raclin's clawed feet. He growled, raising one forelimb and shaking it. A spray of blue fire flew through the air and landed hissing in the snow, but it was not quenched; the flames streamed determinedly back toward Raclin.

Aruendiel had not left his domain undefended. There was a new tension in the atmosphere, the throb of deep magic. From the direction of the forest came a savage howling.

"Take her, I said," Hirizjahkinis shouted, except that—it was all too clear now—she was not Hirizjahkinis. For a moment Nora wondered crazily if there had *ever* been a Hirizjahkinis. Then there was a blur of dark wings and blue fire, and she felt Raclin's claws seize her from behind, digging into her arm and rib cage. He's going to try to claw me to death again, she thought, and then her feet left the ground.

"No!" Nora swung her legs, trying to wrench herself out of Raclin's grasp, and for a glorious instant she felt his claws slip on her heavy cloak, but almost immediately he found a better grip under her armpit. She looked down. Mrs. Toristel was sitting up in the snow, her hand pressed to her chest—already too far away for Nora to make out her expression clearly. Nora leveled her gaze and found herself rising past the window of Aruendiel's tower workshop, some four stories above the ground, and after that she could not bring herself to struggle anymore. With horrified fascination, she watched the castle roof and the snow-covered fields spin and dwindle beneath her dangling feet.

She became aware that some sort of conversation was going on behind her—Raclin shrieking like broken machinery; a cool, sweet voice saying something musical and interminable in what Nora recognized, with heaviness in her heart, as the Faitoren tongue. She-who-had-pretended-to-be-Hirizjahkinis must be riding on Raclin's back. She was trying to soothe Raclin, Nora decided after listening for a little while—perhaps something to do with the blue flames that were still licking around the edges of his wings, although unfortunately they seemed to be causing little real damage.

"Ilissa!" Nora called over her shoulder.

A delighted laugh. "Nora, dearest! You *did* know it was me, after all."

Too late, though. "Where are you taking me?" Now they were flying over forests—heading northeast, Nora guessed from the sun.

"It's going to be a lovely surpri—oh!" The air darkened around them; something whizzed past. A sound like rain hitting a metal roof. Raclin bellowed. The feathered shaft of an arrow was caught in the edge of his wing. Ilissa began speaking very fast in Faitoren, sounding angry.

A flock of birds—they looked like starlings—wheeled innocently nearby. Then suddenly each bird slung itself again at Raclin, lean, sharp, faster than any starling could fly. The cloud of arrows hissed through the air, glinting in the sunlight. Steel tips, Nora thought—thank you, Aruendiel! She remembered how his sword had once bounced harmlessly off Raclin's reptile hide, just as most of the arrows were doing now. But the creature's skin must be thinner on the wings. A couple of hits in the right place could bring him down.

A mixed blessing for me, Nora reflected, as another arrow punctured Raclin's right wing, near the tip. They were at least a hundred feet in the air.

The starlings were gathering again. Ilissa said something urgently to Raclin, who did a half twist in the air. He thrust Nora forward, holding her body between himself and the birds, and dived toward them. The arrows flashed, coming straight on, aiming so true that Nora saw them only as a sort of vibration in the air. Raclin, you coward, hiding behind me, she thought disjointedly, then closed her eyes.

Something brushed her cheek, a feather's kiss. She opened her eyes to find that the air was full of birds, flapping and swooping in a rather aimless fashion. Behind her, Ilissa laughed—a little shakily, Nora thought. "Ah, you see? I thought so. Aruendiel's ready to spill Faitoren blood, but not yours, Nora darling. So lucky we brought you with us today!"

# Chapter 41

They flew for several hours. Nora had a faint hope that Raclin would burn up in a blue blaze—he kept screeching as though he might be in pain—but Ilissa kept crooning in Faitoren, and eventually the blue flames died away. By then, the light was fading. Below them, Raclin's shadow stretched out huge and ominous against the reddening snow.

But he'll be human again as soon as the sun sets, Nora thought. I mean, Faitoren. And what happens to us then? Will we just fall out of the sky? It might be an opportunity to escape. But where would I go? The landscape below seemed to be empty of everything but an occasional bare tree.

Suddenly, Raclin changed course slightly. After a minute, she saw that what she had taken for a tree's long shadow was actually a framework of some kind. An Avaguri's mount. Raclin landed next to it with a jolt. Nora staggered a little, her legs twitchy and numb after dangling unsupported for so long. A stout figure in a long fur cloak came toward them, stamping through the snow. There was just enough light left for Nora to see his face.

She looked hard to make sure she was not mistaken. "Dorneng?" she said, disbelief tipping into anger.

Dorneng gave a nervous laugh and stepped past Nora, evidently with the aim of helping Ilissa off Raclin's back. But Ilissa was already picking her way past Raclin's outstretched wing, her slender hands emerging from a froth of white fur to seize Nora's.

"Nora, you did wonderfully well," she said warmly. "Dorneng, she came just like a lamb, almost no trouble at all, and on the way here, she saved us from one of Aruendiel's spiteful little tricks." Nora basked in a sudden glow of pride; then, horrified, she tried to slide her hand out of Ilissa's clasp. Ilissa smiled beautifully at her and tightened her grip.

Dorneng was looking worried. "So some of his defenses were still active? I thought I'd found ways to block all of them."

"Some of them, darling. Poor Raclin bore the brunt." Ilissa cast sorrowful eyes at Raclin, who gave an explosive hiss, like the door of a subway train releasing. "But Dorneng, you did very well. I'm so grateful."

Ilissa's smile was luminous in the twilight. Releasing Nora, she kissed Dorneng lightly on the lips, then shifted backward as he reached for her. If it was an evasive maneuver, she made it appear to be part of the lovely, continual dance of being Ilissa.

"I must talk to you—privately," Dorneng said to Ilissa, jerking his head toward Nora. "I have news."

"Good news?" Ilissa said invitingly.

"It might be." He took Ilissa by the arm. After what looked to Nora like a fractional second's hesitation, she let him lead her away into the dimness, until all Nora could make out was the blue-white sheen of Ilissa's fur robe and the low, somewhat urgent murmur of their voices.

"Eeew," Nora said aloud. Dorneng and Ilissa, that was a pairing she had never contemplated. And that Ilissa did not quite like to contemplate either, judging from appearances. Poor Ilissa, she thought with some glee, quite a comedown after Aruendiel.

At her side, a man laughed. Nora spun around. "My mother's paramour, you mean? It's no worse than what I had to put up with in *my* bed, darling," Raclin said. "All for the good of the Faitoren people."

It was too dark to see him clearly, and Nora was rather thankful for that. Because his voice, even when he was insulting her, was rich, confident, caressing, and she remembered now how much she used to love listening to it. "Sorry about that," Nora said through clenched teeth. "Terrible misunderstanding on both sides. So why go to all this trouble to bring me back? I mean, look, you got rid of me once. You're free."

"Oh, that's not the point," he said. "The point is, you shouldn't have done what you did."

"You mean, run away because you tried to kill me?"

"I didn't try to kill you," he said reasonably. "It was an accident, and you made it worse by panicking and falling down those stairs. So that was stupid, but what you did afterward—leaving, taking up with that man—that was unforgivable. Ilissa was beside herself." Raclin laughed again, a little bitterly. "It would have been all right if you'd died," he added, with the air of trying to find something agreeable to say. "My mother loves planning funerals almost as much as weddings."

"Is that why you kidnapped me?" Nora hated the way her voice shook. "So you can have my funeral?"

Raclin made a tut-tutting sound, elaborately soothing. "I'm not going to hurt you. Unlike some men, I don't murder my wives."

"Turning me into a marble statue—that wouldn't count as murder?"

"Ah, well, it was very wrong of you to try to take off my ring. It's a symbol of your fidelity, your purity." He went on, ignoring the rude noise that Nora had just made. "And the cripple—he should have known better than to turn *me* into stone."

"I liked you better that way," Nora said, as Dorneng came crunching through the snow. He held a coil of rope in his gloved hand.

"Your mother wants to talk to you," he said shortly.

"It's a great pleasure to see you again, my dear," Raclin said to Nora. He leaned down casually and put his lips on her mouth. For a moment, she had a maddening sense of déjà vu, a vivid recovery of those deep, endless kisses of Raclin's that used to make her feel as though she might melt away down to her bones. She could taste the old sweetness. Pulling back, he laughed and said something in Faitoren—a joke, from the tone—and crunched away through the snow. Too late, Nora spat after him, trying to get the tang of something burned out of her mouth.

Dorneng came closer, pushed her down into the snow. He began to wrap rope around her ankles. "I'm cold," Nora said, but he did not answer. He conjured a silvery light—starlight, Nora guessed—and laboriously tied a knot. His bulldog jaw was clenched, giving him an obstinate, dissatisfied look. "Why are you helping her?" she whispered. "She's only using you."

He gave a contemptuous grunt and went to work on binding her arms. He could have perfectly well tied the rope with magic—but then, Nora reflected, he would not have been able to grope her breasts. Sucking in her breath, she felt his fingers map her chest. "Has Ilissa actually slept with you?" she asked softly, "or is she just stringing you along?"

"Shut your mouth," Dorneng said. His free hand slapped her face, just hard enough to remind her who was the prisoner.

"I thought so," Nora said. "Get your hands off me, sheepfucker." She twisted in his grip as he raised his hand again.

"Enough of that, Dorneng." Ilissa's voice, silvery hard, from behind him.

"I'm just tying her up, as you said."

"Thank you, darling." She smiled at him. "I'll look after her now. And now I think you'd better hurry, don't you? So that no one's alarmed by your absence."

"They don't suspect anything," Dorneng said, but he began to move toward the Avaguri's mount. He gave Ilissa a sidelong, greedy look as he went. She blew him a kiss.

The Avaguri's wings started their slow cadence. Nora shivered in the gust of ice air as Dorneng took flight. "Well, thank you for making him stop," she said to Ilissa.

"You are still my daughter-in-law," Ilissa said. "I cannot allow a wretch like that to manhandle my son's wife. Now, do I need to tie up your hands, darling? Or can I trust you not to run away?"

"Where would I go?" Nora asked.

"I just don't want you to do anything foolish. But you won't, will you? You're always so sweet, so reliable—at least when no one is filling your head with silly falsehoods. Of course I can trust you, isn't that right, darling?"

Nora nodded, felt a giddy rush of pleasure at the thought that Ilissa still trusted her, and then the prick of shame to have ever doubted someone so beautiful and gentle. How wonderful—but how typical!—of Ilissa to forgive such monstrous ingratitude. Nora let emotion flood through her. Then, from another part of herself, high and free, she watched it slowly ebb and dry.

*Know your own secrets before Ilissa can steal them*, Aruendiel had said. I miss Ilissa, she thought calmly, I miss how she made me feel: cherished, complete. That doesn't mean I should trust her or believe anything she says, even if she can't tell a lie.

Nora pulled herself as straight as she could and shrugged off the rope. Then she reached inside her cloak to adjust the clothes that Dorneng had disarranged. It took her a little while. When she was finished, she wrapped the cloak around herself more tightly and finally looked up at Ilissa, her fists clenched in her lap.

Help, Nora thought. Help. I'm Ilissa's prisoner and I need help *now*.

"I guess Aruendiel was wrong about one thing," she said. "You can read and write. Like the note that you forged from him."

"Those little markings on paper?" Ilissa laughed incredulously. "Oh, darling, I don't even know what it said. But you did, and that was all that mattered."

"Why did you kidnap me, Ilissa?" Nora asked. "Just so you can get back at Aruendiel?"

"Do you really think Aruendiel cares anything about you, my dear?" Ilissa asked. She asked the question as though it were worthy of some consideration. "He hasn't shown many signs of it, has he? In all this time, he's never slept with you."

"My private life is none of your business," Nora said. Had her months of uneasy celibacy left so obvious a mark? Or did Ilissa's creepy intuition, the way she could so deftly find and manipulate one's private fears and hopes, extend to literal mind reading?

"Did he not even try to seduce you once?" Ilissa asked sympathetically. "Strange. He's a man of strong passions, as I have reason to know. But perhaps you don't appeal to him. You are no great beauty, after all. Not now."

No, not since Raclin had scarred Nora's face. Not since Aruendiel removed the glamour that Ilissa had bestowed.

Nora thought frantically: If I hadn't asked Aruendiel to take off that spell, if I'd kept the face Ilissa gave me, maybe he wouldn't have found me so repulsive. Because Ilissa's right, Aruendiel never showed any sign— only that one time. He'd rather be alone than sleep with me, she thought despairingly. If I were lovelier, like Ilissa—

Careful, Nora told herself. *Know your own secrets.* All right, she thought sternly, I'm insecure about my looks. And yes, I'm jealous of Ilissa because Aruendiel was in love with her once. And maybe he still is, Nora thought, her heart wrung. Oh, hell, is it me or Ilissa thinking that?

"I know you had an affair with him, years ago," Nora said. "And then he dumped you to marry someone else. Quite humiliating."

"Oh, there are always two sides to these stories," Ilissa said quickly. "Perhaps I was tiring of him. You know, he was a fine, passionate lover— well, *you* wouldn't know. But I have had even better ones. Yes, far better.

And in the end he showed his true colors. He broke off with me in the most crude and abusive way imaginable."

"Then you must be glad to be rid of him."

"Of course. He would not leave me alone, though. The trouble that man has caused me! All these years later, and he still hates me, still won't leave me and my people in peace."

"Well, you also destroyed his marriage and killed him," Nora pointed out.

"I see he has told you all sorts of hateful things about me," Ilissa said. "Yes, he was foolish enough to face me in combat, and he had the worst of it. I only defended myself. As for his wife—well, no one, least of all me, forced him to murder her."

There was something bracing about this conversation with Ilissa. Nora had never heard her speak so directly. "Dorneng must be a nice change for you. You don't seem to have any trouble ordering him around."

"Dorneng. A sweet boy, really. So clever. He has been invaluable."

"He helped you escape, I see. And now what? Are you trying to start another war? Bring down Aruendiel for good?"

"I wouldn't mind that at all," Ilissa said, smiling. "If the opportunity arises, I will take it. But what I really seek is peace and freedom for my brave, suffering people. We have been prisoners for too long! All we truly want is a place where we can live undisturbed, without walls, without hatred."

Another scheme for world domination, Nora was willing to bet. "And why do you need me?"

"That is the best part, my dear. We are going to send you home again! Back to your own world. You'll like that, won't you? Poor thing, you've had such a hard time in this one."

"Mostly because of y—" Nora began to say, but broke off in a sudden yawn. All at once she was so exhausted she felt drunk. It was impossible to channel her thoughts properly; they flowed in every direction and disappeared.

Her head dropped forward. After a moment, she sank down onto the ground, grateful to lie down and close her eyes. The deep snow cradled her body comfortingly in its strong grip, even as the chill sent a warning to her drowsing brain.

I'll freeze to death, she thought with some effort; I have to get up again.

"Don't worry, my dear, I'll see that you're warm. We want to keep you safe for now." Ilissa's silken voice waved above her like a bright banner. It was not entirely reassuring, but Nora could not stay awake long enough to remember why.

Nora opened her eyes to find herself in a small room with stone walls. Light trickled reluctantly through a high, wooden-barred window. It was very cold, although Nora was lying under a couple of blankets. Sloughing them off, she tried the wooden door, but was unsurprised to find it locked.

A thought struck her, and quickly she searched through the folds of her skirt, the blankets she had slept in, and finally the straw on the floor of the cell, without finding what she sought. Discouraged, she wrapped a blanket around herself and tried to think of a plan. She tried working some magic, but she could neither break down the walls nor open the door. Perhaps because the walls were not real walls, the door was not actually a door, she thought, remembering what Aruendiel had said about Faitoren magic.

She did manage to levitate herself enough to peer out the window, but all she could see was a snow-covered flatland. Here and there the skeletal trunks of stunted trees rose in clusters. She lowered herself to the floor and waited, shivering.

Some hours later she heard movement outside. Then suddenly she was blinking in the explosive brilliance of unclouded sun on snow. The stone walls of her cell had disappeared, but now a silver chain led from Nora's neck to Ilissa's slim hand. Ilissa held it lightly but firmly, the way one holds the leash of a favorite small dog.

Sunglasses, Nora thought, squinting painfully into the fierce white glare, what I wouldn't do for a pair of sunglasses.

"Here, darling." Ilissa held out a pair of Ray-Bans. "You always have such good ideas," she said approvingly.

Nora took the glasses numbly and put them on. Ilissa slipped on a pair of her own, with big smoky lenses that emphasized the delicate planes of her face. She *can* read my mind, Nora thought. Did she do something to me while I was asleep? She found—

"That nasty little braid of hair you were clutching—was it Aruendiel's?"

"Hirizjahkinis's," Nora said reluctantly. "Her token."

"I should have known. Such coarse hair. You had it hidden in your clothes, didn't you? All the time we were talking last night, you were calling her. I'm disappointed, Nora. It was not very trusting of you."

"No, not really," Nora agreed.

"And you really believe that woman will answer your summons." Ilissa looked at her with mocking pity.

Nora shrugged. "I wouldn't be surprised."

"If she manages to rescue Aruendiel, perhaps she will spare some time for you."

Nora felt her breath dwindle. "Where is he?"

"Don't worry, my sweet! He was still alive, at least when Dorneng left him."

"Where?"

Ilissa only laughed. "You must be hungry." She indicated a small lacquered table that had just appeared in the snow. A pair of roasted partridges roosted in a silver dish, mantled in a thick brown sauce.

Until a minute ago, Nora had been famished. She had no interest in food now.

"Just a bite?" Ilissa coaxed. "Perhaps something sweet?" The partridges were replaced by a satiny disk of dark chocolate cake, studded with fresh raspberries.

Nora shook her head. "Where is Aruendiel?" she asked again.

"You should eat *something*, my dear," Ilissa said as a shadow passed overhead. Nora cringed, thinking of Raclin, but it was just the Avaguri's mount. Dorneng landed, then stomped through the snow toward the two women.

"We can leave now," he said to Ilissa.

"Already? Good." Cake and table disappeared. "Come, Nora." Ilissa tugged gently on the silver chain, smiling.

Nora braced to resist, but once again she was dragged onto the Avaguri's mount while her arms and legs were bound. Dorneng and Ilissa moved away to confer just out of earshot. Dorneng looked tense; Ilissa, assured and radiant, pressing some point that he seemed reluctant to accept. After a few minutes, they evidently reached some sort of resolution, and walked back to where Nora waited.

Ilissa smiled at her as Dorneng took his seat on the Avaguri's mount.

"You're going back to your world now, darling! I'll see you again soon." She leaned close to remove the chain from Nora's throat and to adjust Nora's wool cap, pulling it securely over her ears. Her warm fingers brushed Nora's cheek, smelling of roses and cinnamon.

For a moment, Nora wished fiercely that Ilissa was as good and kind as she made herself appear. She forced herself to look away. As the Avaguri's mount rose, she watched Ilissa waving gracefully, and felt a crushing sense of loss and sorrow.

Nora reminded herself that she was in deadly peril, and the burden lightened.

Dorneng steered the Avaguri's mount at a low altitude as though he were anxious to avoid scrutiny from afar. They were heading toward a thread of smoke in the bright western sky.

"How long have you been working with Ilissa?" Nora asked. When Dorneng did not reply, she prompted him: "I'm assuming since sometime before you came to visit and almost turned me into a marble statue."

He shifted in his saddle. "That was a—she was giving me a proof of her good faith. She told me that I would be able to remove the ring that no one else could."

"For that, I almost wound up a statue?"

"She didn't say what would happen."

"Oh, she didn't even hint?"

Under his furs, Dorneng hunched his shoulders. "The transformation was supposed to be fast," he said. "Painless. But Lord Aruendiel insisted on trying to slow it down, to stop it. Otherwise you wouldn't even have known it was happening."

"I doubt that very strongly," Nora said.

Finally, they landed beside a small fire, burning sluggishly, surrounded by trampled snow—and then, a vastness of untrampled snow. Nora could see nothing else.

But Dorneng was alert. He scrambled off the Avaguri's mount and paced a wide circle around the fire. Occasionally he stopped and seemed to paw the air with a gloved hand. When he returned to the Avaguri's mount, he looked excited, anxious. "Everything's ready," he announced, as though Nora would know what he was talking about. "They should be here shortly."

*They* were Ilissa and Raclin, presumably. "Ready for what?" she asked sharply, but Dorneng paid no attention. He scanned the empty sky, frowning, looking for Ilissa.

Nora hazarded a guess: "Is there a door here to my world?"

"Yes," he said, with a suspicious look.

"How do you go through it?"

Another question that Dorneng refused to answer. He kept glancing at the sky as though willing Ilissa to appear. He made another circuit, now with the air of someone trying to distract himself.

"Maybe they ran into trouble," Nora said when he drifted close to her again.

Dorneng bit his lip and eyed Nora speculatively. "She wants to kill you herself," he said suddenly.

"Kill me?" Nora repeated.

"You married her son, right? She says she's the only one entitled to kill a member of the Faitoren royal house. The problem is," he added, with a harried expression, "we don't have much time."

"What do you mean, kill me?" Nora tried to rinse the panic from her voice. "What does that have to do with the door to my world?"

"I need you to hold it open. It could close at any time, unless I set a guard on it. So your blood needs to be spilled now." He declared, as though to himself: "I don't think I can wait."

"Oh, but I think you'd better," Nora said quickly. "Ilissa will be very angry if you go against her wishes. You know what she's like."

"She'll be angrier if I let the door close," he said. "It's best to have a guardian."

Something stirred in Nora's memory. *I must wait, condemned for centuries long to guard this gate.* The words engraved on a tombstone in a mountain graveyard. A spell, Aruendiel had speculated. Emmeline Anne, that was the name on the stone.

"So this is one of those spells that's powered by a dead person?" Nora asked incredulously. "You're going to try to put me, my ghost, into a spell so that I can hold some stupid door open for you and Ilissa?" And the rest of the Faitoren, she realized. That was what Ilissa meant by a place where they could live undisturbed. Nora wondered if this meant her unsuspecting, unmagical world was in danger. Only if Ilissa didn't get a TV show or a movie deal within a couple of weeks.

Dorneng sighed. "I can't wait for her," he said, as though he had come to a decision. "She won't mind that much. It's not as though you were born royal."

Nora was dragged from her seat by invisible power. Inexorably she was hauled, pushed, rolled, pummeled through the snow. As she struggled in vain, Dorneng paced beside her, looking more relaxed now that he had made up his mind.

"It will be quick. Not like the petrifaction spell. And when your blood is spilled in this world, and then your corpse is returned to your world, your ghost will haunt what's in between," he explained helpfully. "So the gate stays open."

"I won't let you through!"

He chortled. "You'll do exactly as the spell commands you."

Oh, hell, Nora thought. Not how I'd planned to spend my afterlife. *Aruendiel, where are you?*

"Aruendiel will be furious when he finds out what you and Ilissa have done," she said aloud. "He'll find you and kill you."

"I don't think so," Dorneng said. He chuckled again.

In fact, she reflected, Aruendiel would also be furious with her, Nora, for being tricked by Dorneng, for not escaping, for not using the magic he had taught her. Think, she admonished herself. Think. There's a fire right over there. I can borrow some of its power. I could burn these ropes right off, she thought. And damn, probably my clothes and most of my skin, too.

They had stopped. This was the place where she would die. No more time left. Nora wriggled helplessly inside her bonds. Dorneng was fumbling under his furs. She heard the clank of glass as he produced a small stoppered bottle.

"I want to save a little of your blood," he explained.

"Oh? What for?" Nora asked, buying time. "A souvenir?"

"There may be some ancillary spells that I can use it for." He reached under his fur cloak again. This time he drew out a dagger. He handled it with some pride, Nora thought. It had a silver handle inlaid with gold. Very pretty.

He looked up at the sky one more time. "I don't see her," he said.

"Probably because she's too busy begging for mercy from Hirizjahkinis," Nora said.

"I doubt that very much," Dorneng said, but he waited another minute. Then he leaned down and rolled Nora over onto her stomach. Standing astride her torso, he grasped a handful of her hair and yanked her head up from behind, much the way Aruendiel had held the ram at New Year's. Dorneng's grip was surprisingly strong.

She saw the gleam of the blade from the corner of her eye. Then Dorneng paused as though to consider something.

"These are new gloves," he said thoughtfully. "They'll be ruined." Putting down the dagger, he pulled off his right glove with his teeth, then picked up the dagger again with his bare hand. The blade scratched her throat as he searched for the artery.

She had never actually tried the spell before. But in her mind's eye she could see it on the page of Vlonicl's *Magical Tactics*, just past the beginning of the second chapter. "How to Roast Your Enemy Inside His Armor." Here the enemy was wearing no armor, but the principle was the same. She hoped.

The blade sketched a line of fire against her neck. She jerked back with a cry, thinking: It's too late. He cut my throat.

But Dorneng was screaming. He thrust his hand wildly into the air, as though to fling the dagger away, yet his fingers remained curled stubbornly around the handle. The air smelled like burned meat.

Nora looked down. No blood on her cloak. A burn, not a cut. He'll slash my throat anyway, she thought, if he keeps waving that blade around. She threw herself backward against Dorneng, and heard the muffled sound of breaking glass, then rolled off his body to one side.

Dorneng sank hand and dagger into a rapidly melting snowdrift. His eyes were closed and he was swearing.

Nora struggled against her ropes. She hadn't realized how strong the spell was. She hadn't expected it to cook his fingers—at least, not so quickly. Dorneng was now holding his blackened hand to his chest, and she could see the wondering rage in his face, the shock and fury that she had not only wounded him but tricked him, too.

Grasping the dagger with his gloved hand, he wrenched it away from his injured one, then got to his feet. He had shredded her spell. The dagger was cool enough to touch now, cool enough to kill her with.

Nora pushed herself backward, her eyes fixed on the blade. Dorneng took a step and stood over her. He was swaying, about to lunge. She braced herself.

He shouted something. It took her a second to realize that he was shouting for help.

Something round and white, like a balloon, hovered beside Dorneng's head. No, not a balloon. She had the confused impression that he was clinging to a marble bust. Or it was clinging to him. The white thing touched his face, obscuring it.

Dorneng's cries halted. Then, with a spastic effort, he shoved the white thing away from his face with his good hand. The dagger dropped into the snow.

"Help me!" he roared.

"Why?" Nora dived for the dagger and managed to grab it with her bound hands. "You're trying to kill me."

"Ice demon! You broke the bottle!"

She began sawing at the ropes around her wrists, a complicated process that required her to hold the dagger as though she were about to stab herself. "Where's Aruendiel, then?"

"Help me!"

"Where's Aruendiel?"

"Aruendiel? He's—" Dorneng was craning his neck, trying to pull away from the white thing—the ice demon, apparently—but it was still holding him as close as a lover. Its head practically rested on his shoulder. "Maarikok—the keep—Ivory Marshes."

"Where's that?" Nora demanded, but he only kept calling for help. "I can't do anything right now," she hissed. "You tied me up! Where's Maarikok?"

The blade frayed the last strand of rope, broke it. Nora's hands were free. She went to work on the ropes on her ankles. As she hacked away, she registered from the corner of her eye that Dorneng was still struggling, the white head of the ice demon now pressed tightly against his face.

When the rope finally gave, Nora stood up painfully and looked around. Dorneng had fallen to his knees. The ice demon had wound him into a tight embrace. He was quiet now. What does it do, kiss you to death? she wondered. There was something terrible about how limp and unresponsive his body seemed in the ice demon's grasp.

Then the white head swiveled toward her. Its face was as blank as a sheet of paper except for a mouth that bloomed bloodred. The mouth smiled at Nora.

"Oh, good," it said. Its voice was pure and high, like a child's. "Another one."

She backed away, near Dorneng's small fire, and picked up a piece of burning wood for protection. But the ice demon had turned back to Dorneng, who now slumped sideways, his eyes dull. The thing pawed at his chest, trying to reach inside his furs. Now, with a better view, Nora saw why she had first mistaken it for a marble bust. The demon's form was oddly truncated: a head, shoulders, a single arm.

Is that all? Nora wondered. If not, where was the rest of its body?

The answer came to her all at once. She ran straight toward Dorneng and the demon, the burning brand leveled like a sword. "Get away from him!" she yelled.

Disdainfully the ice demon smacked its red lips at Nora and continued to scrabble at Dorneng's clothes. She swatted at it with the burning wood. The flame sputtered and went out. Behind her, the fire choked in a cloud of white smoke.

"Oh, hell," Nora said. The ice demon's magic could evidently extinguish fire.

Throwing down the wood, she took the demon by its shoulders and yanked it away from Dorneng with all her strength. The single arm snatched at her face, but she flung the flailing thing as far as she could. It landed ten feet away, facedown, and went into a spasm of activity, trying to right itself.

Nora bent over Dorneng, pulling open his fur cloak.

It was as she had expected. There were five small glass bottles secreted inside the pockets of his tunic. Three were full of what looked like water; one looked empty; and the fifth was broken, although there was still a tablespoon or so of clear liquid inside the intact bottom half. In a second she had mended the broken bottle, then gathered up all five. She held them carefully against her chest as she looked back at the ice demon.

It was crawling through the snow with short, jerky strokes of its arm. "Give those to me!" it snarled. "They belong to me."

"Sorry, but no," Nora said. "It's the rest of your body, isn't it?"

"He trapped me," the demon said. "He locked me up in those horrible bottles."

"I see. And then one of them broke and part of you escaped. What did you do to Dorneng?"

"I ate him," said the demon. With some distaste it added: "A poor meal. Very dry and sour. I'm still hungry."

"Is that so?" Nora glanced at Dorneng. Aside from the vacancy of his gaze, he looked perfectly normal. She called his name once, twice. He seemed not to hear.

The demon kept squirming in her direction. Nora stepped back. "You mean you ate him as in—his mind? His soul?"

"The living part, the tasty part. Not the foul meat. You, now," the demon said, "I can tell that you are delicious."

"You won't have the chance to find out." Nora turned and began to walk rapidly, not sure exactly where she was heading. All directions looked very much the same, anyway—snow stretching out to a dim horizon. It was beginning to grow dark.

"Where are you going with my body?" the demon called after her. "Come back here!"

"Sorry, I don't want you eating me."

"It doesn't hurt!" the demon said. Nora kept walking. "And you don't even know where you're going!"

"I'll figure it out," Nora said, but she slowed her pace and then stopped.

"I know how it is with you humans," the demon continued. "You're weak. You can't survive long even in this mild climate. You'll wander around for a while and then you'll die. And then you'll be no good to me at all."

"Bad luck for you, then." Her hands were already growing numb as she held Dorneng's bottles. What if she dropped one? She looked back, trying to locate the ice demon, a blur of white on white.

"Is it Maarikok you want?" the demon called suddenly. "You're going in the wrong direction."

"You know where Maarikok is?" Nora asked suspiciously.

"I used to catch humans there all the time."

"How far away is it?"

"I could be there in a few hours—if I had my legs."

"I'm not going to give you your legs," Nora said. Was there any reason to think that the ice demon was telling the truth about Maarikok? In the twilight, she could not see the thing clearly, but she could hear it rolling in the snow some distance away, like a grotesque baby.

Giving it a wide berth, she ran back to the Avaguri's mount and climbed into the saddle, but she could not make it rise. When she tried a levitation spell, it only shuddered and shed some feathers.

The demon was still talking—whining, really. "It will take me months to regrow my legs and my other arm," it said. "And the nights are growing shorter. I won't be able to walk before the brutal spring heat arrives."

"Will you melt?" Nora called, curious in spite of her fear.

"I'll melt and soak into the ground and wait for the cold again, with nothing to eat, nothing. It will be agony."

"What direction is Maarikok?" Nora asked unsympathetically.

"I'll take you there," the demon said promptly, "if you give me my body back."

"No, thanks."

"I'll promise not to eat you," the demon wheedled.

"Why should I believe you? You just said you were still hungry."

"I never break my word."

Nora let out a disbelieving snicker, then scanned the barren landscape around her. She was hoping to see some speck, some eminence on the horizon that could, conceivably, be the keep at Maarikok. Nothing.

She could try to find Maarikok on her own—and probably die of exposure, as the demon predicted. She could wait here for someone to find her—it might be Hirizjahkinis, it might be Ilissa—and die of exposure anyway. Somewhere around here was, or had been, a gateway to her own world, but she did not have the slightest idea of how to identify it. Meanwhile, Aruendiel was a prisoner.

Nora gritted her teeth. She must have heard Aruendiel say a dozen times that demons were not to be trusted, but now she had no choice. Wizards had made plenty of pacts with demons before, she reminded herself. "If you take me to Maarikok—and don't eat me—then I'll give you your legs and the rest of your body back," she said. "*After* we get there."

"Give it to me now!" the demon countered.

"Absolutely not."

"Can I have just a little of you, to keep my strength up?"

"No! You just ate Dorneng. That should last you a while, no matter what he tasted like. If you try to eat me, even the slightest attempt—if you even tell me how delicious I would taste—the deal is off."

There was silence for a moment. "All right, then," said the demon. "I agree. I hope there is something to eat at Maarikok, though."

## Chapter 42

I t took them more than a day to reach the edge of the Ivory Marshes. Either the ice demon was a poor judge of distance or—more likely—it was a faster walker than two cold and tired human beings, one of which it had recently consumed.

As Nora trudged across the frozen marshland, past curtains of brittle reeds as tall as herself, from time to time she could glimpse the higher land ahead, rocky islands hidden in the middle of the wetlands. Maarikok was the largest of these islands, with a ruined fortress on its highest point, according to the ice demon. Its own depredations, Nora gathered, had led to the castle's abandonment. She was elated the first time she saw the keep's tiny silhouette against the sky, but, as they kept walking, it did not seem to grow any larger.

Dorneng shuffled beside her, head lowered, mute. Evidently, being eaten by an ice demon didn't kill you—at least, not at once. Instead, Dorneng seemed to be drowned in a vast apathy. He could walk, if Nora took his arm and pointed him in the right direction; he would eat, slowly and mechanically, if food was placed in his hand; but he did nothing to express or fulfill any volition of his own. "I told you it doesn't hurt," the ice demon said carelessly. This was after Nora had noticed, with a sick feeling, the white gleam of bone showing through the peeling flesh of Dorneng's burned hand. Dorneng had not complained; he did not even seem to favor the injured hand. "They don't care about anything, afterward," the demon said.

She would have made better time without Dorneng—more than once she thought of leaving him sitting in the snow—but frustratingly, she also felt a certain painful obligation for him. He was pitiful in a way that was too familiar, even though she knew perfectly well that saving Dorneng would do nothing, nothing at all to make up for EJ. And at least Dorneng could carry the ice demon. It rode on his slumping shoulders, its arm crooked jauntily around his neck.

So far the thing had abided strictly by their agreement—it had not actually *tried* to eat her—but that did not prevent it from asking several times a day if it could do so, and complaining of hunger pangs when she refused. When Nora protested, the demon pointed out that it was only inquiring about renegotiating the contract, something either party could do at any time. She began to see exactly why Aruendiel disliked demons so much.

The first night, she hardly slept at all, afraid that the demon would attack her. How she would get to Maarikok without dying of fatigue, she was not sure at all until, thankfully, the next morning she made a chance discovery: The ice demon liked poetry.

*One must have a mind of winter,* she was thinking as she plodded along, lost in the white tedium of the landscape. *And have been cold a long time.* Being warm, so comfortable that you didn't even think about where your skin stopped and the air began, had begun to seem distant and abstract, a happy condition she had only heard about. To distract herself, she said the whole poem aloud. There were relatively few great English poems about winter, she reflected, compared with the huge number of poems about autumn—the approach of cold and death being perhaps more poignant than their actual presence.

As she recited, she was conscious of a sense of longing, of powerful appetite. It was not hers, but so near to her that she felt the pang of frustrated desire almost as though it were her own. It belonged to a creature—she could sense this now—whose origins lay in silence, stasis, and cold. To move, to live, it needed Nora's life, the thin filament of her consciousness. In return it promised an end to hope and pain alike.

"—'nothing that is not there and the nothing that is.' " Nora pulled back, just barely. The vast hunger retreated. She was safe, she still belonged to herself. She looked up to see the empty face of the ice demon turned fixedly to hers as it clung to Dorneng's neck. Its round mouth, which had faded to pink since it fed on Dorneng, had reddened again.

"That was very good," the demon said. "Not as filling as it could be, but still delicious. You see, it doesn't hurt just to give me a taste, does it?"

Still shaken, Nora said: "What? A taste? That's just a poem."

"Whatever it is, it's a nice morsel," the demon said, stretching its mouth greedily. "Do you have any more?"

"More poems?" Nora stared at the ice demon. Was there was a way to keep it fed without sharing Dorneng's fate? "I know quite a few. But you don't speak English, right? How can you understand what I just said?"

"I don't need to understand it," the demon scoffed. "I just savor it."

Interesting. She thought for a moment. "Try this: 'Whose woods these are I think I know'—" The demon listened intently as she pulled the poem, line by line, from her memory. This time, somehow, she was better able to keep some distance from the demon's insistent desire, like watching a shark's grin through the aquarium glass.

"That was even better," the creature said in its flat, piping voice. "There is some lovely despair there. I have eaten many men full of the same dark juice. More!"

"Later," said Nora, quickening her step.

The ice demon had catholic tastes. It lapped up almost anything she could recite, and turned up its nose only at one of Ashbery's mandarin lyrics. She did not always need to recite an entire poem to satisfy the demon, but it demanded constant novelty, never a poem repeated. Her memory was good but not perfect. As she walked, she excavated fragments from her mind, trying to restore them into something whole. After a while, her thoughts skipped in iambic pentameter. She estimated she knew enough poems to keep the ice demon fed for a few days, not more than a week. After that—if worst came to worst, Nora told herself, she would write her own damn poems.

By the end of the third day, Maarikok's tower was bigger and more distinct than it had been that morning. Less than one more day of walking, Nora guessed. That night, for the first time, she was able to light a fire with magic instead of the flint and steel from Dorneng's pack. Where she had pulled the fire from, she was not sure, but she took it as a good sign. She made sure that Dorneng was well wrapped in his fur cloak—he did not sleep now, as far as she could tell, but at night his torpor increased so much that he might as well have been asleep—and then she recited Donne's "Elegy XIX" to the ice demon, which lay in the snow with its head propped on its elbow, a safe distance from the fire.

" 'Full nakedness! All joys are due to thee' "—the idea of taking off one's clothes had never seemed less appealing than in weather like this. Yet the poem still warmed her, as it always did. Aruendiel would like it, she thought, more than he liked Jane Austen. Its frank lust, its humor. All those women he had seduced, years ago—no, better not to think of that.

Afterward, trying to sleep, curled up between the fire and a bank of snow piled up against the wind, she could still hear little icy rustles from where the demon lay.

"What is it?" she said finally, trying to sound stern.

"There's another human nearby," the demon said.

Nora sat up. "Who is it? Can you tell?"

"Very tasty, tender. A young one."

Not Aruendiel, then. "Is it definitely human?" she asked, thinking of Ilissa.

"Of course, those are the best to eat!" The ice demon was scornful of her ignorance.

Nora stood and conjured a dim, reddish illumination from the embers of the fire. Cupping the light in her hand, she stared into the darkness. A shadow moved—no, it was a clump of reeds.

Suddenly, the ice demon launched itself toward something at her left, scuttling through the snow like a drunken crab.

She heard footsteps crunching, then the flat, dull bite of steel into ice. Someone grunted. Holding her light aloft, Nora ran over to where the noise came from.

She saw the ice demon first—glassy in the darkness, oddly contorted. Then she realized that it had wrapped itself around a man's leg and was trying to shimmy up his body. The man was trying to push the demon back with his sword, but the tip kept slipping. The two strained at each other until finally the man managed to hook the demon in the armpit. With a thrust, he propelled the demon into the air and several yards away.

The ice demon rolled over twice and immediately began to struggle back toward the man.

"Watch out," Nora called to the man. All she could see of him was that he was wearing a helmet and a long cloak. "Don't let it near your mouth."

"What in the blood of the sun is it?" the man asked. The demon was right: He had a young voice.

"An ice demon—it wants to eat you." To the ice demon, she said severely: "Stop! Stop right there!"

"I'm hungry," the demon groaned, but as Nora stared at it, it slowed. "Can't you see I'm *starving*?"

"I'll feed you again, in a minute. Just stop, hold it right there!"

Reluctantly, the demon paused, muttering. The man kept his sword poised as if to strike it again.

"I didn't know ice demons were so small," he said.

"It's only part of an ice demon. But wait, let me just feed it quickly."

Clearing her throat, she tried some Whitman. Halfway through she realized that she had mixed up part of "Out of the Cradle Endlessly Rocking" with "When Lilacs Last in the Dooryard Bloomed," but, tangled in the long, rich lines, the demon seemed not to notice.

"All right?" she asked it when she was done.

"That was good," the demon allowed. "May I eat him now?"

"No, you may *not*," Nora said. She took the man by the arm and pulled him toward the fire. To her relief, the ice demon did not follow. "It will leave you alone now—I hope," she said. "It always says it's starving, but given how much poetry it's been sucking down, it can't be that hungry."

The man looked back toward where they had left the demon. "I have never met an ice demon before, but I understand that they are nothing to trifle with."

"No, not at all," Nora agreed fervently. "We have an agreement—the demon is guiding me to Maarikok, and then I will give it the rest of its body back. But if it didn't like poetry so much, I think it would have eaten me already. It already ate Dorneng." She gestured at Dorneng, hunched by the fire.

The young man was suddenly interested. "Dorneng? Dorneng Hul, the magician?"

Nora nodded. "But he's not much of a magician now." The man shook Dorneng's shoulder and spoke to him, but got no answer. "He's been like that ever since the ice demon attacked him," she said.

"They say ice demons kill everything but the body," the stranger said. "And the body doesn't survive long." Straightening, he looked more closely at Nora in the firelight. "We've met before, haven't we? I thought I recognized your voice."

Nora was at a loss. "We have?"

"Yes—although I'm confused. What is the woman who is *not* the mistress of Lord Aruendiel doing in the middle of the Ivory Marshes with this poor addled-brained fellow and an ice demon?"

Nora felt herself flush. "What—?"

"Forgive me, I am too familiar," the man said. "But you should know that I am still smarting from the scolding you gave me, when we last spoke in Semr, for my incautious assumption about the nature of your relations with Lord Aruendiel."

"Oh, that!" Nora said. That evening at the palace came back to her. The young man with the reddish hair. "You warned me about Aruendiel."

"I did," the young man said.

"Well, actually, I'm here to rescue Aruendiel," Nora said, a defiant note in her voice. "Or whatever I can do. He's a prisoner at Maarikok. Dorneng and Ilissa somehow captured him. I don't know if you know that she escaped and——"

"I know about the Faitoren rebellion," he interrupted. "That's why I'm here. But, wait, you say Dorneng *and* Ilissa?"

"Yes, Dorneng was working with Ilissa." The young man whistled under his breath as she went on: "And before the ice demon made a meal of Dorneng, Dorneng told me that they had captured Aruendiel and were keeping him at Maarikok. So I'm going there."

"Wait, tell me all that slowly," he said.

Nora went through the story again, starting with how Hirizjahkinis and Dorneng had come to Aruendiel's castle to give the alarm. After she had finished, the young man was silent for a minute.

"Lord Aruendiel a prisoner, imagine that," he said finally. "And how do you plan to free him, once you get to Maarikok?"

Nora hesitated. "I'll have to figure that out. And you? You're here because of the Faitoren rebellion?" An unpleasant thought struck her. "Which side—"

"I'm here to fight against the Faitoren, not with them," he said. "I rode north with my cousin Ourvelren, but we were separated in a skirmish with the Faitoren, and my horse was killed. Now I am trying to rejoin the king's forces. So we are on the same side, you and I—and perhaps we should introduce ourselves properly. I am Perin Pirekenies. I am ashamed that I don't remember your name, Lady—"

"Nora."

"Lady Nora, good," he said, with brisk approbation—for what, Nora was not quite sure, but there was something so reassuring in his manner that she felt her spirits rise. "When I set out," Perin continued, "I did not envision myself rescuing Lord Aruendiel—but he is too valuable an ally to leave in the enemy's hands, so I offer you my services." She felt him studying her again. "You must be fond of him to travel to his aid in deep winter in the company of an ice demon."

"Yes, well, Aruendiel is my teacher, and he has been very good to me," Nora said. She thought of saying that he was her friend as well as her teacher, but—remembering her last conversation with Perin—was afraid of being misinterpreted. "He has treated me with nothing but respect," she added meaningfully.

"I am glad of it," Perin said.

Nora had to promise the ice demon double rations before it would agree not to eat Perin in the night. She was running rapidly through her stock of poems, not to mention Dorneng's small supply of food. It was fortunate that they were so close to Maarikok.

Perin, though, was not so sanguine about their route. The next morning, as they ate a rough gruel made from melted snow and dried-out bread, he suggested that they circle north to avoid Faitoren patrols. He sketched a rough map in the snow.

"So we're not far from Faitoren territory, then," Nora said, studying it.

"Frankly, I think you are lucky not to have met them already." The new route, he said, would add perhaps another day to their journey.

"All right." She sighed. "But I warn you, Dorneng doesn't travel very fast. It will be more like two days."

Perin frowned and glanced over at the former magician. Dorneng's mouth hung open, a trickle of gruel staining his unshaven chin. He had barely eaten this morning. With each passing day he seemed more shrunken, less responsive.

Perin was no doubt ready to suggest that they leave Dorneng behind. Nora steeled herself to resist, while wondering if she was being incredibly stupid to give a damn about Dorneng's welfare. Instead, Perin said, rising: "We can make better time than you think. There's an ice-bull skeleton nearby—I almost broke my ankle tripping over it last night."

"A what?" Nora asked, but he had already disappeared into the reeds.

He reappeared dragging two enormous curved things that Nora at first took for staves of weather-bleached wood. Then she saw that they were bones—the ribs of a very large animal. After another trip, he brought back two more. "The skull must be frozen under this ice," he said. "The tusks would be worth a pretty penny in Semr—if you want to come back after the spring thaw." He grinned at her.

"This is an ice bull?" A dinosaur seemed more likely, from the size of the bones.

"Why do you think they call it the Ivory Marshes?" Perin said.

With leather ties from his pack, he made a crude sled from the bones. They set Dorneng on it and let the ice demon—still sulky, still muttering about how delicious Perin would taste—ride in his lap. Perin pulled the sled while Nora contributed a mild levitation spell to keep the runners from sticking. They could travel twice as fast as she and Dorneng alone, she found.

At last, she thought, something is going right.

In daylight it was easy enough to recognize Perin as the young man she had met in Semr, even though that encounter felt as though it had happened years ago. Now she remembered not just the red hair, but the ease and openness of his manner. He bore himself as though he were inclined to be pleased with whatever or whomever he encountered. And yet there was nothing naive about him: His shrewd brown eyes, already edged by a few wrinkles, seemed to miss very little. The overall effect, Nora found, was to make you feel determined to live up to the warm opinion that he had already formed of you.

She learned he was a captain in the King's Guard. He was twenty-seven years old, the oldest of nine children. His father had an estate in eastern Muergen, wherever that was. He was unmarried, although his parents had started telling him it was high time to secure a suitable bride. His father also wanted him to obtain a position at court, but Perin was still weighing the idea.

"The king has plenty of flatterers already," he said. "Not that I am so opposed to flattery, but I've had relatively little practice in it, and the competition in Semr is terrible."

There were no awkward pauses in conversation with Perin, Nora found. After a little while, it was as though she had known him a long time, and in a way she had—he reminded her of certain young men she'd known in her own world, cheerful, responsible sorts launching themselves in medicine or law or business with energy and optimism. She often found them attractive—they had frank and fearless smiles and well-tended, athletic bodies—but regrettably they were always engaged to longtime girlfriends they'd met in college. She almost forgot her fears for Aruendiel as they went along, it was so refreshing to talk to someone of her own age who talked un-self-consciously about himself but who was even more interested in finding out about Nora. He seemed surprised to learn that some of the rumors he had heard about her in Semr were true.

"You are really from another world?" Nora assured him that she was. But he was not entirely convinced. "You are not very different from someone born here. You speak the same language—you have the right number of eyes, ears, limbs—"

Nora laughed. "Thank you! Although in fact we speak a different language in my world—you heard me recite those poems. I've been told that I speak Ors rather poorly."

"With a strange accent, but no stranger than other accents I have heard." Perin smiled and shook his head. "Well, which world do you prefer?"

No one had asked her that before. "Oh, I miss my own world a lot," she started. "My family, my friends." He wanted to hear more about them, so she talked about her parents and her sisters until she began to be afraid that she was boring him. "On the other hand," she said, seeking to change the subject, "there's no magic in my world." People always seemed to be startled by that notion. Perin was, too, but not quite in the way she had anticipated.

"By the day-blade, you're lucky! This world would be a better place without magic, to my mind. Sorcerers have too much power, nothing happens in this kingdom without their say-so—and yet so much of their magic is useless."

"I wouldn't say that."

"Look at why we're here. Wizards at war with other wizards, but in the end it will be decided by swords and men. That's always the way, in all the battles I've ever been in, no matter which wizard we had on our side."

"Hmm. Aruendiel would say that a good magician—or wizard—can turn a battle, but not just with magic—it takes brains and strategy." She added: "And of course he'd say that you need good soldiers, too."

After a moment, Perin said: "For all the ill things I've heard of Lord

Aruendiel, I never heard that he was a stupid man or a bad wizard. How was he taken captive?"

"I don't know," she said unhappily. What had Ilissa found, rummaging through Nora's mind? Nora remembered again that awful last night at the castle, how she and Aruendiel had quarreled over his poisonous regret at being alive. Ilissa traps you with what you want. And if what you want is to die—

She wrenched her attention back to Perin. "I don't know. He's been in worse fixes than this."

Without hesitation, Perin said: "Then he will certainly get out of this one, too."

## Chapter 43

The route that Perin had chosen took them along the northern side of a chain of narrow islands that rose from the icy marsh. The high ground provided some shelter from the wind, and also helped screen them from observation from the south and west. There was a deepening smudge of smoke on the southwest horizon—army campfires, Perin said. Twice, late in the afternoon, the wind blew the faint sound of a military horn to them.

The problem was that they could not tell which army was closest. Perin climbed a hill on one island for a better look, but could not make out any standards.

He looked thoughtful, though, as he came down the slope. "It's a sizable force," he said. "In this climate, an army—at least, a human army—has no reason to put off fighting any longer than it has to. Our forces will attack as soon as they have sufficient strength."

Nora heard some regret in his voice. "Do you want to join them?" she asked.

"I'll try to make up for my absence by delivering Lord Aruendiel."

He was always careful to use Aruendiel's title, although Nora never did. It seemed uncharacteristic of Perin to be such a stickler for correctness, like Lady Pusieuv, but perhaps if you were in line to have Lord in front of your name someday—as Perin evidently was—you paid more attention to things like titles.

It might also be, Nora thought, that Perin was the sort of person who found formality more useful in dealing with those he did not consider friends. His pleasant face always looked slightly harder whenever the magician's name came up. She remembered the warning he'd given her in Semr.

His antipathy to the magician was odd, though, since he could be affable even to the ice demon. Gradually, he managed to coax the demon to tell them what it could about its former hunting ground of Maarikok. The castle, they learned, occupied a rocky promontory on one side of the island, and its gates opened to a narrow track, easily defended, carved into the side of a ridge. There was no other entrance.

Nora groaned inwardly at this. If the Faitoren mounted any kind of defense at all, she did not see how she and Perin could get into the castle. She wished that she had learned even one invisibility spell, or a transformation spell advanced enough to work on a human being.

"How did you get into the castle?" Perin asked the ice demon.

It preened slightly. "I went around to the back. They thought they were safe, but when they saw me—oh, they were so afraid, it was a feast."

"But exactly how did you get in?" he pursued.

"I went up the cliffs. And through the wall."

"How? Is there another entrance?"

"I made one. I made my hand into water and slipped it into the crack." The ice demon's single hand swerved back and forth to illustrate. "And then I made my hand hard, and the stones broke apart."

Perin looked puzzled, but Nora nodded, thinking of how a glass filled with water will crack in the freezer. The ice demon had used some basic kitchen science combined with its own brand of magic. "You can melt yourself at will?" she asked.

"If I wish to. But why should I wish to? People will only lock you up in little glass bottles." The demon's pink mouth worked savagely.

"I haven't forgotten our bargain," Nora said soothingly, although she was dreading the moment when she would have to fulfill her promise. It seemed suicidal to give the demon its body back, and she kept wondering if she should renege and refuse to open the glass bottles she carried. And yet the ice demon, so far, had lived up to its side of the agreement—and more, since it had left Perin untouched.

Later, she thought, I'll sort this out later. Let me get into Maarikok first.

They camped that evening on an islet, Maarikok no more than two hours away. Perin at first opposed lighting a campfire so close to the enemy, until Nora showed him that she could build a fire with jet-black flames and smoke that trickled away inconspicuously along the ground. The smoke spell came from Vlonicl; the black flames were her own idea, a variation on one of the spells that Hirizjahkinis had taught her. She was pleased to see that Perin was impressed.

"I was not sure what to think when you told me that you had been learning magic," he said, watching a tendril of smoke flow across his foot.

"You thought that a woman could not be a magician," Nora said.

"That's right. But I was more surprised that a person like you—honest and good-hearted—would want to practice magic."

"I enjoy it," she said, smiling. "Why don't you like magicians?"

"We don't have much use for wizards in my family. There's more glory to be gained with a good brain and a good sword."

"But you see magic can be useful," she said, indicating the fire.

"I don't dispute that. Why do you enjoy practicing magic?"

"Oh." Nora stared into the fire's shadowy flicker, only a shade lighter than the gathering twilight. Because magic was interesting and because she seemed to be good at it. But that was not the whole answer. She glanced at Perin, and the steady current of his interest emboldened her to try to explain. "Practicing magic takes a kind of awareness that you don't feel ordinarily," she said haltingly. "You have to really *know* the things around you and make them know you. And when you manage that connection, it's as though the world belongs to you. You feel more at home in it. As though you could do anything."

More drily she added: "That's when everything goes well, of course. There are a lot of details that you have to get right. That's what I spend most of my time working on."

"And Lord Aruendiel is your tutor." It was not a question, but there was a faint note of incredulity in Perin's voice.

"Yes, a very good one." She told him about working in Aruendiel's study in the afternoons, how he assigned her spells to learn, then watched and critiqued the way she performed them.

"And the rest of the time, what do you do?" Perin asked. She told him. Now he was openly shocked. "You cook and clean and take care of the livestock? Doesn't Lord Aruendiel keep enough servants to spare you such work?"

Nora smiled: Had Perin forgotten how he had taken her for a servant once? "Just the housekeeper and her husband."

"You surprise me. The great Lord Aruendiel, with only two servants?" With a knowing grin, he added: "I suppose the peasants are afraid to work for him."

"Possibly," Nora said. There was truth in Perin's observation, but she was unwilling to say anything that would turn him more strongly against Aruendiel.

"And how large is his garrison?"

"He doesn't have one. I don't think he needs one, being a magician."

"Perhaps not." He questioned Nora more about the size of Aruendiel's holdings. Nora regretted that she had brought up Aruendiel's finances—guiltily she remembered the near fiasco of her new boots—but it was difficult to be guarded with Perin. Finally he said, sounding faintly amused: "I didn't know that Lord Aruendiel had such a modest estate. It sounds much smaller than my own father's estate, which—I will be honest with you—is not grand at all. But the rumor in Semr is," he added, with a shrewd look, "that Lord Aruendiel will soon be much richer."

"What do you mean?" Nora asked, flabbergasted.

"I've heard that he intends to lay claim to another, much larger estate—Lusul."

"Oh, I've heard of Lusul. It used to be his."

"It was his wife's estate. He held it through his marriage."

"Aruendiel has never said anything about claiming it," Nora said. Then she frowned. "Wait, his niece, Lady Pusieuv—she mentioned Lusul. She wanted him to claim it. As a dowry for her daughters." The details came back to her now. "There's an inheritance dispute, right? Lady Pusieuv said that Aruendiel should have kept Lusul all along because—well, his wife was unfaithful."

"It's a very rich prize, Lusul," Perin said. "It's no surprise that Lord Aruendiel would want to recover it, especially given his reduced circumstances."

"But he doesn't want it. He told Lady Pusieuv so."

"That's hard to believe."

"It's true." She shook her head. "If there are rumors going around Semr that Aruendiel plans to claim Lusul, it's because of Lady Pusieuv. She's probably telling people he wants it in hopes he'll change his mind. Although he won't."

"Why not?"

He would want nothing to do with anything that reminded him of his wife. "Aruendiel's very stubborn," Nora said. "Once he has said no, he will not shift." She stood up, uncomfortable—why should she feel so disloyal, talking about Aruendiel with Perin?—and pulled her cloak more tightly around her shoulders. "I should go feed the ice demon."

By now, she had already fed the monster almost all of the poems she knew. She had a moment's panic when it turned its mouth up to her, a deep well waiting to be filled.

Then a verse came into her head. It was from a long poem, and she didn't know all the lines, but she knew enough. " 'That's my last duchess painted on the wall'—"

When she returned to the fire, she and Perin divided the last of the dried beef from his kit. Chewing the rank, salty strips of meat made her jaws ache. Nora felt disinclined to speak of Aruendiel again—it seemed uncertain ground—so she asked, after finally swallowing a particularly stringy morsel: "If you don't want to take a court position in Semr, what would you rather do?"

Perin laughed, a little ruefully. "I'm happy enough serving in the King's Guard, but my father is right. I can't stay there forever. There's not much chance for promotion or spoils these days, unless this Faitoren rebellion turns into a greater war. All the more reason, my father says, to make a good match."

"You mean, to marry an heiress."

Perin said nothing, but in the dimness, Nora made out a half nod. Then he said: "You said in Semr that you had had a cruel husband."

"Yes." Nora found that she did not much wish to discuss Raclin with Perin, either. "It was not a real marriage," she added awkwardly. "I mean, he deceived me—I didn't know what he was really like."

"This was the Faitoren prince?" So Perin had heard that story in Semr, too. Was he going to press for details? No, he only said: "You deserve a far better husband." He spoke with surprising warmth.

"I hope so!" Nora said. She laughed, and after a moment Perin laughed with her.

"So you think one ought to know what a husband—or a wife—is like before marriage?" he asked. Nora said yes, very firmly. "It's not so easy, you know," Perin said. "My family recently began marriage negotiations for me with Lord Denisk of Kaniskl, for his oldest daughter. I have met her just once. If the negotiations are successful and the marriage takes place, I would probably see her four or five more times before the wedding."

Nora was surprised to register a pang of disappointment. But her instinct had been right: Men like Perin were always engaged. She said: "I think you should get to know her better. How did you like her when you met her?"

"Pretty, very shy. She wouldn't talk at all at first, but I played with her puppy and I think she liked me a little better then. She is thirteen years old."

"You can't marry a thirteen-year-old!"

"She'd be fourteen or fifteen by the time of the wedding." Perin sighed, an uncharacteristically gloomy sound. "To be honest, I'd much rather have a wife who is ready to cuddle her own babies, not just a puppy."

"Then don't marry a child! I think you should find someone closer to your own age to marry, to have children with. If that's what you really want, a family," Nora added, fumbling a little. "It sounds like it."

"Oh, yes." Perin's tone was definite. "Not just to honor my ancestors, either. I like children—preferably a houseful of children, like the one I grew up in."

Nora had a sudden, vivid mental picture of Perin with his yet-unborn family—roughhousing with the boys, carrying a little girl on his shoulders, holding a wiggling baby with gentle awkwardness. He seemed to cast a circle of light in which everyone was happy and safe; all of them were laughing, including the shadowy woman by the cradle. "You'll be a good father, whoever you marry," Nora said.

"The negotiations with Lord Denisk were not going well, the last I heard," Perin said cheerfully.

The next morning they broke camp well before dawn. Nora groped her way over to Dorneng, hoping that it would be easier to rouse him this morning. Yesterday he'd been almost completely inert.

Today, though, as soon as she put her hand on his shoulder, she could feel that Dorneng was gone. His body was rigid, ungiving. She felt both relieved and somber. *Every man's death diminishes me.*

"He had already departed," Perin said gently when she showed him.

Nora remembered saying almost the same thing herself, the other time. "It was probably a stupid idea to drag him all this way," she said. "But I couldn't just leave him."

"No, I see that," Perin said. "You are not easily discouraged when you want to help someone."

"Oh, no, it's not that—" He was giving her too much credit, but his words made her glow. In silence together they weighted Dorneng's corpse with stones, so that he would be buried in the marsh with the first thaw of spring.

By the time the stone towers of Maarikok turned pinkish gold in the first light, Nora and Perin were looking up at the castle from the eastern tip of the island. "Hmm," said Perin. He was no doubt thinking the same thing that Nora was: *Higher than we thought.* On the island's northern side, the hill on which the fortress was built reared almost straight out of the marsh.

Perin turned his gaze to the south and took off his helmet. The wind coming across the marshland ruffled his short-cropped hair. Nora admitted to herself that he was better-looking than she'd first thought: well-knit features, a level glance. *Watch it*, she told herself, recognizing the symptoms: not a crush yet, but a distinct tingle.

Perin held up his hand. "Listen," he said. "The battle has begun." She could make out only phantom shouts, a distant clatter. No gunfire, as there would be in her world. "It's good for us," he said reassuringly. "It's a distraction."

"Right," she said, nodding. "Well, let's take a better look."

They made their way along the northern side of the island, under the cliff. From time to time, Perin glanced back at the ice demon on the sled. "Here?" he asked.

"Not here. Keep going." The demon's face was impassive as always, but there was poorly suppressed excitement in the way it shifted its position on the sled. It was looking forward to freedom and, Nora feared, a really satisfying meal after days of nothing but poetry.

Looking up, Nora could see how the demon had been able to climb the

cliff on its earlier raids. The stone had split and eroded into jagged protu-
berances, where an exceptionally enterprising mountain goat—or an ice
demon—might be able to find a path.

"Here," the demon announced suddenly. "This is the way."

"You're sure?" Perin asked.

"I forget nothing," the demon said.

Perin looked at Nora, a trace of skepticism in his glance. "Well, what
do you think? Can you manage it?"

"I think so," she said. Now that they were finally here, the rough wall
of stone waiting to be attempted, she felt more sure of herself.

"Then—" He raised an open hand, an invitation that was mixed with
faint bemusement. "Would you like to go first?"

Nora examined the rock in front of her and decided to aim for a ledge
about eight feet off the ground. She took a moment to gather her thoughts.
Then, putting a foot and a hand on the rock face, she worked as powerful a
levitation spell as she could manage.

An instant later, she was scrambling up the cliff, moving easily, almost
bouncing against the stone. The slightest purchase on the rock was enough
to propel her higher. She went past the ledge she had been aiming for and
pulled herself onto one above it.

She looked down at Perin's upturned face and laughed. "It worked!"

He grinned up at her. "You can do the same with me?"

"Of course!"

As Perin swung himself upward, she did the spell again, keeping her
eyes fixed on him. He moved rapidly up the cliff face and landed next to
Nora.

"That's a fine trick," he said.

"Thank you," she said with a small thrill of pride. She looked upward,
trying to spot the next ledge.

"Wait!" It was the ice demon below, clambering down from the sled.
"You are not going to leave me!"

Nora exchanged a look with Perin. "We can't carry you up," she called
down. "Wait for us."

"I want my body back!" the demon said. "I have fulfilled my side of the
bargain. I have guided you to Maarikok. I have shown you the way that I
took into the castle."

"Well, we're not in the castle yet," she said. "I'll give you the rest of your body when we come back."

"*If* you come back," the demon said suspiciously. "I am coming, too." It scuttled to the bottom of the cliff, then reached up the rock face and began to climb. After a moment, Nora saw how: The demon could grip the rock by freezing to it, then pulling itself upward.

"Let's keep going," Perin said in her ear. She nodded. They went up the cliff by turns as the ice demon doggedly inched up the rock face below them. Nora decided it was better not to look down, to focus on nothing but working the levitation spell correctly and finding secure places to plant her hands and feet.

But during the brief intervals when she and Perin were side by side on the same ledge, she was embarrassingly conscious of the feel of his body against hers. She found herself looking forward to the moments when he would put his hand protectively against her back as she clung to the rock wall. Incredible that she could even think of sex in the middle of scaling a cliff, but there you have it, she thought. It had been a very long time.

Above, the castle wall rose smoothly from the rock, but when they were close to the top of the cliff, Perin pointed out the small dark gap at the base of the wall. One of the stone blocks was missing.

There were only a few yards to go—Nora had just pulled herself onto a ledge directly below the gap—when she heard the flapping of wings. Something bright flashed in the corner of her vision. She looked around carefully. A small bird whose feathers shone like mirrors had found a perch on a jutting piece of rock nearby. It fluffed its feathers against the cold and turned its head to look at her.

Nora frowned, then said hesitantly: "Hirizjahkinis?" The bird trilled, a faintly admonitory sound, and then took flight.

"What did you say?" Perin asked.

"The silver bird, did you see it? I think it belongs to a magician I know, Hirizjahkinis. You saw her at court." Hirizjahkinis close by—perhaps Aruendiel was rescued already. Or could Ilissa mimic the flight of birds as well? Nora helped Perin onto the ledge, wondering how hopeful she dared to be.

"Let me go ahead," Perin said, looking up at the hole in the wall. When he had gone past her, she looked down cautiously. The ice demon was still making its way up the rock face, perhaps a hundred feet below. Another disquieting thought struck her—could the bird be Hirizjahkinis's own call for help? Once before, she had used it to summon Aruendiel to Semr.

Apprehension mounting, Nora scrambled through the wall opening into musty darkness. "Perin?" she whispered.

"Here." His voice came from a few feet away. She caught the gleam of his helmet.

"Do we risk a light?"

"I think so. I don't hear anything."

Standing up, Nora conjured a weak light. They were in a low-ceilinged room about twenty feet square, the single doorway half-blocked with a rubble of stone and wood. Gritty icicles hung from the ceiling. Perin stooped and picked up a rotted barrel stave from the floor. "We're in one of the old storage cellars," he said. "We'll need to find our way to the dunge—"

"So you did escape Ilissa!" A new voice, speaking louder than either of them.

Perin stepped forward, his sword already in his hand. Nora hastily summoned a brighter light and peered at where the voice at come from. "Hirizjahkinis?"

A column of air thickened, grew viscous and murky, then resolved itself into the shape of a woman, almost invisible except for her pale dress and the watery gleam of her jewelry.

"Hirizjahkinis?" Nora said uncertainly. "Is that really you?"

"Don't be alarmed—it is only a fetch!" It was Hirizjahkinis's voice, strong and confident. "I am some little distance away—and there is a Faitoren army between us, in fact—so I have come to see you without my body, so to speak."

Nora badly wanted it to be Hirizjahkinis—but her own avidity was a warning sign, she reminded herself. "I don't mean to be rude, but how do I know that you aren't one of Ilissa's illusions?"

Laughter, slightly strained. "You are cautious, little one."

"That's the sort of thing Ilissa would say to distract me." Although Ilissa would have called me "darling," Nora reflected.

"I am Hirizjahkinis herself, the only one, and if I were a Faitoren counterfeit of me, I could not say that. And are *you* a Faitoren illusion yourself?"

"No, I'm Nora, not a Faitoren. I'm sorry to be skeptical, but that's how Ilissa kidnapped me, pretending to be you."

"I would have liked to see that! She is a tricky one—cleverer than I thought, I must admit. It would be much easier—" Hirizjahkinis hesitated, uncharacteristically. "You know that we do not have Aruendiel now."

"Ilissa said he had been captured. How—?"

"He lost his temper!" Hirizjahkinis laughed, a little bitterly. "I have never seen him so angry. He would not hold back, he would not wait for the rest of us—he *would* go after Ilissa and that lying scorpion Dorneng by himself—and by some means they took him."

"Angry?" Nora was startled. She had been so sure that whatever had weakened Aruendiel must have come from his own blackest wishes, that Ilissa had tempted him by promising to do a second time what she had done once before. "What was he angry about?"

Hirizjahkinis stared straight at Nora. "You."

"Me?"

"He was enraged that Ilissa had taken you. We were awaiting two other magicians, Euren the Wolf and Fargenis Gouv, when I heard your call, that you were with Ilissa and you needed help. I told Aruendiel—and then there was no stopping him.

"And now I see that you are free and well, remarkably enough. Unlike Aruendiel!" There was no mistaking the rancor in Hirizjahkinis's tone now.

Nora put her hand to her face. "I never thought—"

"Never thought what? That Aruendiel would be such an idiot? You have done well enough without him or me, it seems. And now you are sneaking into a Faitoren stronghold. Or are they expecting you?"

Nora shook her head, her throat tight.

"Forgive my sharp tongue," Hirizjahkinis said fiercely, "but I need to know the truth. Did you summon me at Ilissa's bidding?"

"No, of course not. She didn't even know I had your token—at least, not then."

"But she let you go unharmed, I see."

"It wasn't like that at all," Nora said, her voice rising. "I got away by pure luck, an accident. Dorneng was about to kill me—"

"Dorneng? Where is *he* now? We have lost track of him for some days now."

"Dorneng is dead." Perin spoke up matter-of-factly. "He died last night."

The ghostly Hirizjahkinis looked at him for the first time. "Dead? How?"

"An ice demon killed him."

"An ice demon? One of your vile northern monsters. Well, it served him right, but I am surprised. Dorneng was a good magician. He should have been able to fend it off."

"He was too slow." The ice demon's piping voice came from behind Nora. She turned to see it clamber through the opening in the wall. "I took him before he could use his horrible magic. A very poor meal, though. I'm so hungry."

"That's how I got away, when the ice demon went for Dorneng," Nora said. Edging closer to Perin for safety's sake, she recounted the events of the past few days as quickly as she could. She could not tell from the apparition's filmy countenance whether Hirizjahkinis believed her.

When she had finished, Perin added: "You must know, we would not have risked our necks climbing that cliff if we were to be guests of the Faitoren." He spoke courteously but with nothing yielding in his tone.

"But why are you here?" Hirizjahkinis demanded. "Do you plan to take on that Faitoren garrison upstairs by yourselves?"

"No, we're here to rescue Aruendiel," Nora said.

"What?"

Nora could not decide whether Hirizjahkinis sounded more incredulous, affronted, or amused. "Dorneng said Aruendiel was here at Maarikok," she said.

"He is not here." Hirizjahkinis's voice was definite.

"What do you mean, he's not here?"

"I would know. I would know his magic anywhere, and he is not here. I can tell that there is only one magician in this castle right now, and that magician is much, much weaker and clumsier than Aruendiel." Hirizjahkinis laughed, and her laughter sounded colder than usual. "I do not mean me. I am not really here."

Dorneng lied, Nora thought. Or they moved Aruendiel somewhere else. Or—

"Well," she said, at a loss for words.

"Lady Nora's magic got us up that cliff," Perin said quickly. "She might not be as expert as some, but it's the results that matter."

"And who are you," Hirizjahkinis said, "who risked his neck to escort Nora up that cliff?"

"My name is Perin Pirekenies."

"That name is familiar. You are—ah, Holy Sister, I know who you are! And you came along with Nora—"

"To help her rescue Lord Aruendiel, yes. I did not like to see a lady take on such a dangerous task alone."

Hirizjahkinis shook her head. "Lady Moon, what Aruendiel would say! Perhaps it is as well that he—I knew your grandparents, Perin Pirekenies." Perin gave a brief nod of acknowledgment. "Perhaps they were not very sensible, but they were brave, they did the best they could with bad luck—I respect them both. And here you are, coming to Aruendiel's aid! Well, I am sorry that I do not have better news for you."

"Hirizjahkinis," said Nora, "if he is not here, where is he?"

Hirizjahkinis looked very steadily at Nora, and her image seemed to grow a shade more defined, as though she were concentrating hard. "I am sorry, little one, I was too harsh with you earlier. I did not know what to think, seeing you alive and Aruendiel gone."

"Gone where?"

"Aruendiel was my teacher and my friend," Hirizjahkinis said soberly. "I knew his work almost as well as I knew my own, and if I listened carefully, I could always hear the echo of his magic, even from the other side of the world. Those echoes are quiet now."

"No," Nora said.

"He is not here, he is not anywhere, Nora. I cannot tell you any more." Hirizjahkinis paused, as though she were waiting for Nora to say something, and then she went on: "Perhaps he even welcomed it. He complained to me so often—he was so bitter about being alive."

Nora looked down, scrutinizing a scrap of wood near her foot as though she would memorize every detail. She did not trust her voice. Aruendiel was bitter, yes, but there were things that he loved. Magic, his books, the forest, oatmeal and ale in the morning, his castle, his lands, even Mrs. Toristel, although he would never tell her so or why. Maybe even me, she thought numbly.

She felt as though she had been sitting in a warm house and suddenly the door was gone and cold air was hitting her face—but this was nothing, this was just the beginning, it would take time before the whole house chilled to freezing and she understood what true cold was.

"Nora, we can grieve later," Hirizjahkinis was saying. "I must go back to this absurd battle. Imagine how annoyed Aruendiel would be if we lost."

Nora nodded, made herself smile.

"Will you come join the fight? Perin, we could use you, I am sure."

Perin bowed. "I will be there as soon as I can escort Lady Nora to safety."

"Hmmf. Not too long, though. Nora is not so helpless." The pale figure of Hirizjahkinis grew paler, and then it was gone.

There was a long silence in the room. It seemed darker than before. Nora realized that she had forgotten about the light she had conjured; the spell was running down. Dutifully she strengthened it, holding the flame away so that her face would be in shadow.

Perin cleared his throat. "Lady Nora, I honor your gri—"

"That's enough talk," said the ice demon. It had kept a wary distance during Hirizjahkinis's appearance, but now it came scrabbling across the floor toward Nora. The round mouth was almost as white as the rest of its empty face. It must be very hungry. She had not fed it since early that morning. "Give me my limbs, the rest of my body, now. You promised."

"Yes, I did," Nora said vaguely, after a moment. She should have asked Hirizjahkinis about how to defend against ice demons. She glanced at Perin, half-apologetically. "I did promise."

He looked at her with a question in his raised eyebrows, his sword at the ready.

"No, I have an idea," she said. "I think it will be all right. Do you want to leave now?"

"Of course not," Perin said, although his smile was doubtful.

"Now!" the demon said, its mouth contorting.

"All right," Nora said. She had to pull herself together, shake off the dull heaviness that was dragging at her thoughts. Otherwise there was no chance this would work. She pulled out Dorneng's small glass bottles from inside her cloak. They hardly seemed large enough to hold the rest of the ice demon's body, but presumably there was some magic involved to make the liquid fit inside. Uncorking the first bottle, she poured the contents over the ice demon.

She knew it would be fast—she had seen how quickly the ice demon had reconstituted itself when it attacked Dorneng—but it was still startling to see how rapidly the ice demon's new arm lengthened and solidified. The bottle was hardly empty before the demon was chortling and doing a sort of push-up on its newly matched limbs.

Biting her lip, Nora emptied the other bottles. The ice demon's torso grew back, then its legs, and then—she was surprised to see—its tail. The full-sized demon was also bigger than she had expected, taller than Perin.

"Much better, much better than in those cramped bottles!" the demon said, flexing its arms.

"Good," Nora said, stepping back. "So we're all even. Right?"

"But I'm still so hungry," said the demon, its tail lashing. "I'm starving. Oh, it's terrible! I have my body back, but look how thin I am!"

"There's a Faitoren garrison upstairs. How about eating them?" Perin suggested.

"Faitoren—faugh! They're no good. Horrible, chewy things. No," said the demon decisively, "give me a good, tasty human. Like you."

Perin grasped Nora's arm. She could sense him measuring the distance to the doorway. "You know, if you eat me, I won't be able to give you any more poems," Nora said.

The demon paused, as though it were thinking it over. "That's true," it said. "I could still eat him *and* the other one. I'm so hungry, though. I don't think that will be enough."

"I'll give you another poem now if you want," Nora said, racking her brains for verses. "Um, had we but world enough and time—"

"You did that one already."

"I did, that's right. Let's see, just a moment—"

"Which other one?" Perin asked suddenly.

Another poem, Nora thought, but the demon said: "The other human, so close. I can almost taste it from here. A good one."

"Another human? Here in the castle?"

"That's what I said," the demon retorted. "Now, come here, I'm hungry." It made a grab for Perin.

"No, I don't think so," Nora said with sudden decisiveness. The ice demon suddenly toppled over, its arm still extended. It fell like a dislodged statue, petrified, static.

A few flakes of snow whirled around the room as they stared down at the unmoving form of the ice demon. Nora smiled, and in her own heart—so much coveted by the ice demon, but still free and unconsumed—she thanked Aruendiel for insisting that she begin the study of water magic, the art of making the most fickle and yet stubborn of the elements do her bidding.

# *Chapter 44*

I only thought of it yesterday," Nora confessed to Perin as they hurried down the corridor. "I'd been carrying around those little bottles of demon-water, and suddenly it dawned on me—hello, it's water, and I can make water do what I want. Sometimes, anyway.

"I can't hold it forever," she added. "Sooner or later it will be able to move again."

"Oh, with luck we'll be far away by then, or maybe the weather will warm up," Perin said. "Bring your light—here's another door."

They checked the rooms along the narrow corridor and found nothing but dust and rodent droppings. At the end of the hallway stone stairs spiraled upward; Perin put his ear to the door at the top before pushing it open. They picked their way carefully across a large room filled with debris, trying to make as little noise as possible, but Nora could not help gasping when she saw that the round stone next to her foot was a skull.

"The ice demon's handiwork," Perin whispered. Nora nodded. The skull and the vertebrae scattered nearby were dry, discolored. This was no new death.

"We don't know for sure that the ice demon was talking about Aruendiel," she whispered to Perin, for her own benefit as much as his. "That other human, I mean."

"No, but if there's any human in this fortress besides us, I'd like to try to save him."

They went through an archway into another corridor. Here there were signs of more recent traffic, a muddle of footprints on the dusty floor. Perin moved cautiously down the hallway, his body tensed. Nora followed a few steps behind, trying to marshal in her mind the spells from Vronicl that seemed most relevant: How to Confuse Your Enemy's Sight; How to Blunt His Sword; How to Make Him Drop His Arms. The corridor turned, then turned again. They passed more empty rooms, then rooms streaked with daylight because the roof had fallen in. The last chamber showed evidence of occupancy and a taste for comfort: embroidered rugs and tapestries; fresh flowers in lacquered vases; a stout, opulent sofa; and a bank of candles left burning although no one was in the room.

"The Faitoren," Nora mouthed to Perin as they tiptoed past.

A minute later, as the corridor turned again, Perin suddenly pulled Nora against the wall, then put his finger to his lips. "There's a guard ahead," he breathed in her ear. "You stay here, and I'll take him."

"Wait." Hastily she ran through the spell to confuse the enemy's sight—although, never having actually performed it before, she was not sure that it would work. "Good luck."

Perin slung himself around the corner. She could hear his running footsteps, a cry, and then a sustained metallic clatter.

Flattening herself against the wall, she peered around the corner. Perin and a Faitoren in gold-tinted armor were swinging swords at each other with great concentration. She thought she recognized the Faitoren. Sarcom, his name was. He was bigger than Perin but Perin appeared to be more agile. Whether that was because of the sight-confusing spell, she did not know.

As she watched, the Faitoren suddenly wheeled and ran in the opposite direction. Perin pounded after him. Nora began to follow, but halted where the Faitoren had been standing. He had been guarding something. A smaller corridor led off at an angle. She took it at a run, then pelted down the stairs at the end of it.

This was the place. She knew that, even before she could get her bearings in the new room, which was large and shadowy and seemed to be filled with many small, dark alcoves. The air was dense, tight with powerful magic. A single torch burned at the far end of the room. Starting toward the light, she bumped into something, a wooden bench. It fell over with a noise that made Nora catch her breath in apprehension, but nothing, no one moved in response.

The torch showed her a mess of old clothes bundled into the last alcove. She came closer. It took her a moment to see the fragile outline of the curled body under the folds of cloth, the long, wasted legs tucked into boots far too heavy for them. A hand like a dried leaf, the long black hair gone white. He lay half-collapsed on his side, his head drooping toward the ground, as though he no longer had strength to turn himself. She knelt and bent her head sideways to try to look directly into his face, searching for his familiar features in the mask of crumpled silk that hung loosely from his skull.

She hoped he hadn't heard her gasp. "Aruendiel?" Nora said, willing her voice to be steady and gentle. "Aruendiel, it's Nora. I'm here."

A white-lashed eyelid lifted on a stare as worn as an old coin, then closed with weary suddenness. That was all. She reached out to touch his shoulder.

And then she was sprawled on her back, shaking convulsively, sucking down great gulps of oxygen as though she had been underwater for a long time. She had the feeling that more than a few minutes had passed. There was a pulsing pain on one side of her brain and an unpleasant twitching sensation up and down her spine. She raised her head and saw that she was lying about a dozen feet from where she had been.

Nora got up slowly and went back to the huddled figure in the alcove. She kept a warier distance than before.

"Aruendiel?" No reaction at all this time. Nora was braced for the worst, but to her relief, the black cloth of his tunic rose and fell in a slow but regular motion. He was alive, but it seemed to her that at any sudden movement he might tear like old newspaper.

"What is this?" she asked wildly. "What did they do to you?" An aging spell. No, a spell that made Aruendiel look and feel his real age. No one lived to be that old naturally. He could die of old age at any minute.

"Aruendiel?" she tried again. "Can you hear me? It's Nora—Nora." He might be senile. He might not even know her now.

It was too hard to look at his wasted face. Ashamed, she let her eyes slide away.

Hirizjahkinis was right to blame me, she thought. If I hadn't been stupid enough to be tricked by Dorneng, if Aruendiel hadn't tried to save me, this would never have happened.

She made herself look back, and she noticed that Aruendiel appeared to be suspended just above the floor—not on it—as though he rested on some invisible support. Under him, there was a circle drawn on the stone flagstones, a yard or more across, its circumference completely girdling Aruendiel's folded body.

She raised her eyes. There were circles on two walls of the alcove—again, each framing Aruendiel. *Weave a circle round him thrice and cross yourself in holy dread.* Together, the three circles defined a rough sphere, a bubble, a prison. That was the force that confined him, that had flung her across the room. She had seen Aruendiel use similar barriers in spell-making, although she had never seen him use more than one circle at a time.

"All right, I see what's holding you," Nora said aloud. "Now, how do I get through it?"

She tried spells for knocking down walls, for breaking pottery, for opening locked doors, for snapping your opponent's spear like a toothpick, for splitting an object into two smaller, equal-sized versions of itself—any spell that seemed remotely relevant, and some that weren't. Her rainmaking tic was back. Snow filled the air and then covered the floor with a dusting of white.

Yet after she finished every spell Aruendiel was still locked away like a mummy in a museum case.

Was he still breathing? She kept stopping to check. Sometimes it was hard to tell. She was watching him, hardly breathing herself, when she heard footsteps. The white figure of the ice demon, somewhat grimier than before, emerged from the darkness.

"Oh, it's you," Nora said tiredly. The demon had thrown off her spell, and no doubt it had come to eat her now. The prospect did not seem as terrible as it once had.

The ice demon clumped toward her, then stopped a few feet away. Aruendiel's still form had caught its attention. "That's no good," the demon said. "I can't eat that one. I can't get to him."

"I know," Nora said.

The demon's round mouth curled in frustration. "He's dying. Soon he will be no good to anyone."

"I know." Nora clenched her teeth. She added, a little nastily: "But you're a demon. You can't get through a little magical barrier like that?"

"He's locked up the same way I was in the glass bottles," the demon said. "That is terrible, terrible magic.

"And it wasn't fair, what you did," it added sulkily. "You made me fall, and I couldn't get up. And the weather is growing dangerously hot. I could have melted."

"Wait." Nora looked up, her eyes sharp with dawning comprehension. "You mean this spell here—the one that's keeping him trapped—is the same spell Dorneng used to put you in those bottles?" She remembered how Dorneng had slipped that gelatinous insect-creature into a similar bottle, back in Semr. It must be some kind of impermeability spell that he'd used to store magical specimens, she thought—something that blocks all magic.

"It's terrible to use magic that way. It's a good thing I ate that magician."

"Well, except that, now that he's dead, he can't undo this spell." Nora glanced hopelessly at Aruendiel, and then looked away, frowning. "Dorneng didn't need to put an aging spell on Aruendiel," she said suddenly. "Dorneng just had to somehow catch him in this impermeability spell, and then he was cut off from any source of magic—fire, wood, water, whatever." Trapped, Aruendiel was helpless, and then he began to grow old. Or, rather, without magic, his true age consumed him.

Another piece clicked into place: "That's why Hirizjahkinis didn't know Aruendiel was here! She couldn't sense his magic."

"If you could undo that bad magic and let him out, I could eat him," the ice demon pointed out.

"If I could undo the bad magic, you certainly could not eat him," Nora retorted. *If* she could undo the magic. Her elation at figuring out Dorneng's stratagem faded. She knew nothing about impermeability spells; she was no closer to freeing Aruendiel.

"I'm hungry," the demon said.

"Oh," she said, finally realizing what the demon was getting at. "You want more poetry."

There was not much left on memory's shelves to feed the demon. The only verses that came floating out of the darkness were the lines that some kid in her section always insisted were not a real poem, they weren't about anything.

" 'So much depends'—" she began.

When she finished, the ice demon had not moved. Nora watched it with some apprehension, waiting for it to demand more. But the demon sat down heavily, leaning against the wall with the calm deliberation of someone who is occupied entirely with internal matters of digestion and happy to have it that way. "Oh," it said, and for the first time Nora thought she could hear something like contentment in its voice.

So it took William Carlos Williams to satiate an ice demon's ravenous appetite for human feeling. That fact would be an interesting addition to a classroom discussion—but looking back at Aruendiel, Nora felt black and empty, almost as though her soul had indeed been consumed. The thing that everyone remembered about that poem was that Williams had written it while watching at the bedside of a sick child. What Nora could not re-call now—if she had ever known—was whether the patient had ever recovered.

Aruendiel's bony hand twitched spasmodically. A sign of returning vi-tality? She watched closely for a time, she called his name, but the hand did not move again.

"I'm sorry, Aruendiel," Nora said helplessly. "I just don't know what to do." She worked another few spells at random, trying anything. Nothing changed. Aruendiel's lank, white-haired body still hung motionless in its invisible prison. The curved lines that bound him still marked the floor and walls, roughly outlined in black charcoal.

Those circles. She had not really considered them before. The burned stick that Dorneng must have used to draw them still lay on the floor.

Maybe the answer was very simple. "What happens if I just erase the circles?" Nora asked aloud, her hand already reaching toward the circle on the floor. But she pulled back, warned by a fiery prickling in her fingertips. If she wasn't careful, she'd be blasted across the room again.

Perhaps the circle could be magically persuaded to erase itself. She tried a spell to command the streak of charcoal on the floor, and found the mate-rial impervious to her suggestion. She stared at the three circles, unwilling to admit defeat. They reminded her of something. For some reason, she was thinking of her parents' driveway in New Jersey. The smooth, gray cement right in front of the garage.

If you could make the circles invisible—no, that wouldn't work.

Now it came to her why she was thinking of her parents' driveway. EJ drawing a circle in yellow chalk on the cement, tracing the bottom of a garbage can.

What on earth had he been doing? He wanted her to calculate pi, that was it. He was supposed to be helping her with a couple of geometry problems, and instead he made her calculate pi from scratch. Typical. It didn't help her grade. That was just a week before he died.

Nora forced her thoughts back to the situation at hand. What about just blasting the floor into bits? Again, a solution beyond her powers. She glanced up to make sure that Aruendiel was breathing.

In her mind's eye, EJ was still bending over, chalk in hand, to write on the driveway. He was writing formulas, including some that she hadn't had yet in school. He liked to do that sort of thing. He was showing off, but he also thought she'd get something out of the advanced stuff.

"This is what you need to know about circles and spheres, Nora," he'd said.

*What I need to know.* She sat very still, as though by listening hard she could remember what he had said next.

$$x^2 + y^2 + z^2 = r^2$$

The alien symbols swam lazily out of the depths. Dimly she recognized them: It was the Cartesian formula for a sphere. You plug in the coordinates from the x-axis, the y-axis, and the z-axis. Add up the squares, and the number on the other side of the equals sign, the $r^2$, is the square of the sphere's radius.

What if, instead of trying to break into Aruendiel's cage, you just made it much, much bigger?

The charred stick was already in her hand, the same stick that had drawn the circles. She rolled it back and forth between her palms, then rubbed a space on the stone floor clean. She wrote EJ's formula down slowly, making each letter perfectly clear. She set the volume of the sphere equal to 1.

This was the bubble that imprisoned Aruendiel. She stared at the formula until she knew in her bones that the formula she had written and the sphere that Dorneng had conjured were essentially the same.

Just as carefully Nora began writing a series of zeroes after the 1: 1,000—1,000,000—1,000,000,000—bigger. Make the round walls of Aruendiel's prison grow larger than the world. If he was dying in isolation— if he could not find and draw on the elemental sympathy of a flame, a forest, a mountain—then bring them to him. Cram them all within the confines of Dorneng's spell. Maybe Dorneng's magic would hold, maybe not.

Mathematics commanded, and with slow, reluctant inevitability, magic obeyed. Nora was still writing zeroes, somewhere north of a trillion, when Dorneng's spell was forced explosively outward. It ballooned with supernova suddenness. The shock was a brick wall falling on her.

Someone was touching her shoulder. Someone was calling her name. The back of her head hurt.

Aruendiel—she'd been trying to free Aruendiel.

She opened her eyes eagerly. In the torchlight, it took her a moment to recognize Perin. He leaned over her, his face keen with concern.

"Lady Nora? Are you all right?"

"I think so." She shifted her arms and legs experimentally. Cautiously she sat up, then winced as a wave of pain and dizziness washed through her skull. Perin steadied her and inspected the back of her head.

"There is some blood," he said. "I have seen worse, but that must have been a hard knock, for a woman. What happened?"

"The spell knocked me down."

"What spell?"

"The spell that was holding Aruendiel. I didn't realize it would expand so quickly." She paused, collecting her shaken thoughts. "Aruendiel! Is he all right?"

Perin looked uncomprehending. She craned her neck to look past him, ignoring the pain from the sudden movement. Aruendiel lay much as she had last seen him, except that his limp body was now sprawled on the floor. He must have collapsed there once Dorneng's spell was gone. She should have thought of a way to cushion his fall. Old bones were so brittle.

"Aruendiel?" she said, moving to his side. She reached out to touch him—nothing in her way now. His arm was broomstick-thin. His bony shoulder felt as hard and delicate as porcelain.

His eyes opened, bright gleams in a mass of wrinkles. She couldn't tell where they focused, if he saw her. His dry lips trembled, and a bubble appeared at one corner of his mouth.

"You're free, Aruendiel," Nora said, then repeated herself more loudly. He might have become deaf. "You can do magic again. Can't you feel it? Just reach out." She turned to Perin. "He looks a little better, I think."

"*That* is Lord Aruendiel?" Perin said with frank amazement. "He is much older than the man I saw in Semr."

"It's what happens if he can't do magic," Nora said in an undertone.

"But he is just——" Perin broke off, staring at Aruendiel as though looking for something he could not find. He hesitated for a moment, as though tempted to suggest an unpalatable course of action, and then said: "Can we carry him without injuring him?"

"Oh, I don't think we should move him. Why do we have to leave?"

"Well, I dealt with that Faitoren guard, but met another, who got away. I don't think there's more than a handful of soldiers in the castle, but all of them will be looking for me."

"Aruendiel could take care of them—if he gets a little stronger," Nora said.

"He can't take care of himself or much of anything right now," Perin said.

"True." How were they going to manage this? Nora stood up, wondering if they could improvise a litter for Aruendiel. She noticed something. "Where's the ice demon?"

"The ice demon?"

"Yes, he followed me here. I fed it and it sat down over there. Is *that* it?"

There was a pile of something white on the floor where the ice demon had been sitting. Perin prodded it with his toe. "Looks like broken ice."

"Good lord," Nora said. "What happened? Did it get pulverized by the same spell that knocked me out? I got off easy."

"It must be quite a spell."

Nora was still thinking. "Yes, the spell broke the demon to pieces because the demon was full of magic. Me, I'm an apprentice magician with only a little magic in me, so it just threw me down.

"You know," she added hopefully, "the Faitoren are magical beings. Maybe it destroyed them, too."

Perin considered this, then shook his head. "We can't count on that."

Nora felt like protesting, but she saw that Perin would not be easily persuaded by any line of reasoning involving magic. She turned back to Aruendiel and knelt beside him.

"Aruendiel, we need to leave—the Faitoren are coming. Perin and I will help you—and my levitation spellwork is getting pretty decent—so I think we can get you out of here. Do you think you could walk if we held you up?"

She was heartened to see that Aruendiel lifted his head a fraction. His lips moved again. He was mumbling something. She bent down to hear.

"I'm hungry."

The words did not come from Aruendiel's mouth. Nora looked up. Perin whirled around. The ice demon was standing just behind them.

Of course the demon could put itself back together as neatly as one of the pots she'd mended. She knew that. Stupid to assume that Dorneng's spell had smashed it to pieces for good.

"I'm hungry," it said. "That magic went right through me. It hurt very much. I'm hungry."

"Um." Nora stood up. Squaring her shoulders, she stepped forward to stand beside Perin. "What about that poem I just gave you?"

"It's gone. I'm hungry *now*."

"All right, I'll give you another poem." She looked down, stalling. Her mind seemed to be as clean and blank as the ice demon's gleaming white body. Performance anxiety. Maybe she had a concussion. Perin was looking at her expectantly.

" 'That time of year'—" She waited for the rest of the lines to come. " 'That time of year thou mayst'—" She stumbled. Another line came to mind, but it was from later in the poem; she could not find the path of words that led to it. *Bare ruined choirs where late the sweet birds sang.* The single verse echoed solitary in her mind. Her head ached. It was hopeless. One of her favorite poems, silent, gone.

"I don't know," she said awkwardly. "I can't think of any more poems right now."

"Then I will eat all three of you," the ice demon declared.

Perin reached for his sword, but the ice demon was faster, grabbing his wrist. Without missing a beat, Perin swung his other fist at the demon's head. The creature took the blow without seeming to notice it.

Its other hand caught Nora by the nape of the neck. She tried to twist away, but its iron fingers seemed to freeze to her neck. Her mind felt paralyzed, unable to summon either poetry or magic."

"You first," the demon said to her. "I have been waiting so long to eat you."

Still struggling, Nora gazed up at the ice demon's looming, empty countenance. "No, please! Just give me time. I'll think of another poem."

Perin landed another useless blow. She shut her eyes and turned her head, trying to keep her face as far away from the monster as possible. She could already feel the chill flowing from its body like the promise of death.

The demon's hard mouth touched her cheek, seeking her lips. She had never been so cold in her life.

But the kiss of the ice demon was soft and scorching. She gasped. Unexpectedly, she found herself staggering backward because there was nothing to stop her. The demon's grip on the back of her neck was gone.

Opening her eyes, she felt even more disoriented. She could see nothing but white—a swirling cloud of hot mist.

"Lady Nora?" Perin's gloved hand materialized out of the fog and clasped her hand. "Are you all right?"

Nora's reply was drowned out by the wind—a sudden, howling gust that swirled up around them with a concentrated fury, dissolving the mist, ripping it to shreds, banishing it.

And then the wind was gone, the air quiet again. Nora and Perin stared at each other. Perin wore the slightly harried expression of a man who has been pressed to the limits of his patience by too many unnatural oddities for one day.

"Are you all right?" he said again. "What happened?"

Nora turned. "Aruendiel!"

Slowly, shakily, one hand on the wall, Aruendiel was getting to his feet. Nora slipped her hand out of Perin's and went over to help him, but he waved her off with thin peremptoriness. She waited beside him, ready to catch him if need be.

Aruendiel moved with even more than his usual stiffness, and there was an uncertainty in his efforts that tore at her heart. He must be afraid of falling, even if he would not admit it. But there were black streaks in the white mane now, and when she got a good look at his face, it was recognizably Aruendiel's, even if it was still harshly worn and wrinkled. His skin had lost that look of parchment transparency.

He could pass for a well-preserved seventy now—eighty, tops.

Still holding the wall for support, Aruendiel peered down at her, his gray eyes sharp.

"What did that viper of an ice demon do to you, Nora?" His voice was brittle but full of its old authority.

"Nothing," Nora said, unable to stop smiling. "Nothing at all. You vaporized him before he could eat me."

Aruendiel was not satisfied. With his free hand, he took hold of her chin and tilted her head upward, looking up her nostrils, then to the side so that he could examine her ear.

"It's all right," she protested. "I'm fine. My soul—my heart is as good as it ever was."

Letting go of her chin, Aruendiel frowned, gray eyebrows knitting together. "You should have been able to stop the demon yourself," he said. "It was a relatively simple application of fire magic—an intensified form of the Calanian heat protocol."

"Well, yes," Nora said, "but the ice demon can put out fires, so I wasn't sure where to get the fire for the heat spell."

"Ice-demon magic has a limited—" Aruendiel broke off with a sharp intake of breath. He stared over Nora's shoulder. Under its rough white stubble, his face went still, then sagged as though he had rapidly aged again.

She glanced back, confused. There was only Perin, who stepped forward and bowed with formal courtesy, his hand on his sword hilt.

"My name is Perin Pirekenies," he said. "Of course, I have heard much of the famous Lord Aruendiel. It is a great occasion to make your acquaintance."

"Perin Pirekenies," Aruendiel repeated slowly. The look of shock was replaced by a kind of resignation. He nodded as if to himself. "Pirekenies. Of course. You resemble your grandfather closely."

"So I've been told," Perin said, his eyes fixed on Aruendiel's face. "I never knew him, obviously."

Aruendiel paused as though he were bracing himself. His cracked voice spoke with a mixture of resolution and irony: "Have you come to kill me, then?"

"What!" Nora exploded. She looked from Aruendiel to Perin. Neither was smiling.

"No, the opposite," Perin said after a long moment, although it seemed to Nora that there was a shade of reluctance in his voice. "I'm here because, on my way to fight the Faitoren, I met Lady Nora, who told me that she was trying to rescue you." He nodded toward Nora. "She was accompanied only by an ice demon and a dying man, the wizard Dorneng. I could not leave a lady alone in such danger. And I knew it would help our cause to deliver you from the enemy.

"My father swore an oath to kill you," he added easily. "But he still lives, so it's not my obligation yet."

"What are you talking about?" Nora demanded. "You never mentioned this."

"He swore that oath a long time ago," Aruendiel said acidly. "I have wondered whether he had forgotten about fulfilling it."

"Not at all," Perin said.

"I am happy to hear it. I look forward to crossing swords with him one day." There was a new stoop in Aruendiel's crooked shoulders as he tried to straighten to his full height. He grimaced. "Let us leave this place," he said suddenly. "I am very tired of looking at these walls, and I perceive there is a magical engagement of no mean size being fought nearby." Letting go of the wall, he took an unsteady step forward.

"I've gotten to be pretty good at levitation," Nora said hesitantly. "Perhaps I could support you—" She stopped at the flash of anger in his pale eyes.

"I don't need to be carried," he snapped. After another faltering step, he appeared to reconsider somewhat. "But if you would be kind enough to let me steady myself—"

"Of course," Nora said. Perin made a slight movement, as though to help Aruendiel himself, but she shook her head no. Aruendiel grasped her shoulder, and together they followed Perin across the room, Aruendiel's thin fingers digging into her flesh. As they approached the door, Aruendiel pointed with his free hand.

"My sword," he said, breathless.

It was lying near the wall. Neither Nora nor Perin had noticed it before. She had the feeling that they were both thinking the same thing, that Aruendiel would be better served by a cane than a sword. Silently, Perin picked up the sword and handed it to Aruendiel, who staggered slightly as he took it, then with frayed deftness maneuvered it into its sheath.

"Did I hear correctly that you were traveling with an ice demon?" Aruendiel hissed in her ear as they began to mount the stairs. "The same one that I just boiled away?"

"The same one," Nora said, waiting while his foot groped for the next step.

"Do you know how dangerous that was—how foolhardy?"

"I didn't have a choice. I kept reciting poetry—it liked poetry. That worked for a while."

Aruendiel grunted, with effort or contempt. A few steps higher, he said: "And Dorneng is dead?"

"Yes. The ice demon killed him."

"Pity. I hoped to kill him myself." A moment later, in a low voice he said: "Filthy coward. He tricked me into drawing that circle against him. And then I could not get out."

"It was a magical impermeability spell," Nora volunteered. "You were cut off—"

"Yes, of course, I knew that," Aruendiel said with a flicker of his old impatient energy. "It was a spell that Dorneng modified. It came from, from—oh, what's the fellow's name. Part of that group from Yrsl. Named after a plant."

"Parsley Micr?" Nora guessed.

Aruendiel sighed, suddenly deflated. "No. Why can I not think of it? Well, it was an old spell. I knew just how to undo it. But I could not quite summon—there was not enough magic to do my will."

One more step, and they were on level ground again, in the passageway leading to the main corridor. Motioning them to be silent, Perin edged forward to reconnoiter.

"Filthy coward," Aruendiel repeated querulously. "He was afraid to face me—he had to steal my power." Glancing back, Perin put his finger to his lips again. Aruendiel snorted, an exertion that made his lean frame tremble slightly. "Tell your friend," he said to Nora, "that we are wrapped in a silencing spell that even the subtlest Faitoren could not penetrate."

He went forward with a shade more vigor. But his grip on Nora's shoulder did not lighten.

"Was it you who freed me?" he asked in a low, harsh tone. "Or him?"

"It was me," Nora said. "He's not a magician."

"No, of course not, he's a simple knight. But you, Mistress Nora—I would have thought it was beyond your powers to undo Dorneng's spell."

"I didn't—I just sort of stretched it." She sighed suddenly. "And how I did it, I'm not really sure now."

"What spell did you use?"

"I used algebra."

Aruendiel repeated the word inquiringly. "What is that?"

"Algebra is, um—a form of arithmetic. So unlikely that I would even think of using it." Nora shook her head with mild bafflement. The formula had been so clear, so insistent. She had known exactly what to do, as though someone were showing her the way, step by step. Now that calm certainty was gone. "I used algebra to make the bubble bigger, that's all."

"It would be useful to know this sort of arithmetic," Aruendiel said musingly. "Can you teach me algebra?" There was unusual respect in his tone.

Nora almost laughed. "It would be the boar teaching the bull to dance," she said, using an expression of Mrs. Toristel's. "If you want, though, sure, I'll teach you what I can."

Her words were almost drowned out by a sudden din echoing down the corridor. The stomp of many booted feet, the clank of weapons, a wild chorus of shouting.

Ahead, Perin had his sword out. The Faitoren poured around a bend in the corridor, dozens of them—tall, broad-shouldered warriors in golden armor, swords and spears gleaming, the dewy, cinematic perfection of their Faitoren faces contorted with battle fury.

Aruendiel stopped and pulled himself as straight as he could, letting go of Nora's shoulder. "Ah, excellent!" he said with satisfaction.

Perin was already surrounded, trying to fend off two Faitoren at once. The magician watched him coolly for a moment, as though appraising the younger man's swordplay. Another Faitoren dodged past Perin and made a swing at Aruendiel.

Aruendiel lifted his chin slightly. The Faitoren vanished.

So did both of the Faitoren dueling with Perin. The ranks of Faitoren seemed to evaporate. All at once the corridor was quieter and mostly empty again, except for a flurry of movement on the floor. Nora looked down to see long naked tails and frantic rodent haste.

Only one of the Faitoren soldiers remained standing. He seemed taller but thinner, his armor loose. Perin ran at him. The Faitoren swung his sword clumsily, then dropped it.

Probably, Nora guessed after a second look at the Faitoren's furry arm, because the Faitoren now lacked an opposable thumb.

"Bind him with iron," Aruendiel directed.

The Faitoren prisoner in tow, they walked along the corridor, faster now. The encounter with the Faitoren had done Aruendiel good. His hair was darker, the old man's timidity gone from his movements. As they went along, he discoursed on Faitoren fighting tactics. The kind of attack they had just witnessed, he said, was typical. The Faitoren always made a show of overwhelming force, but if you peeled back the spells, there would likely be nothing but a few outnumbered Faitoren and a pack of confused rats.

"That's fine for magicians," Perin said politely. "What can a simple knight do against the Faitoren?"

Aruendiel gave Perin a level stare. "One good steel blade could take down that whole company," he said. "A direct thrust would dissipate one of their puppet soldiers—or kill an actual Faitoren. The difficulty is in surviving long enough to deliver a blow to every soldier. Their bronze swords can inflict real wounds—or make you think that you have suffered real wounds."

The corridor led into the fortress's main courtyard. Although it was drizzling lightly, the air seemed very bright after the confines of the castle. Aruendiel looked thoughtfully up at the overcast sky. "I must make my own way to the battle now," he said, and glanced at Nora, his expression unreadable. "You will need protection on the way to camp."

"I'll look after her," Perin said, but Aruendiel ignored him. "Would you prefer the Dinthiak or the Pasnvos Nen spell?" he asked Nora.

"The Nen," Nora said, after thinking for a moment. There was always a trade-off with protection spells, strength versus duration.

Aruendiel nodded. "You will have to hurry, then." She felt the faint, internal quiver of strong magic, and something shifted in her vision, so that everything around her looked slightly farther away. Then, with an easy, practiced movement—perhaps the most graceful thing she had ever seen him do—Aruendiel swung himself upward and was gone. A gray owl flapped silently to the top of the castle wall.

Nora was as startled as Perin. Although she and Aruendiel had talked about transformations, she had never actually seen him perform one. It was unnerving to see how neatly a man's long body could be folded up into a bird's. Even a large bird's.

Together they watched the owl float away, until the castle wall blocked their view and they could not see it anymore.

# Chapter 45

"Why didn't you tell me who your grandparents were?" Nora said to Perin. She was surprised by how wounded she felt at his omission. Perin had always seemed so forthright, so splendidly frank, she had never imagined he might not be telling the whole truth. Much like Wickham, she thought suddenly. Hopefully not as bad.

They were making their way along the road that twisted from the entrance of the Maarikok castle down to the marsh's edge. The ridge flanking their left blocked their view of the frozen marsh, but the noise of battle was growing louder, like hidden machinery.

After a moment Perin said: "I should have. I didn't know how much you knew of my family's history—or Lord Aruendiel's."

"You and Aruendiel both told me that he stabbed his pregnant wife because she'd been unfaithful," she said. "*You* forgot to mention that she was your grandmother. So the baby survived?"

"That was my father. Lord Aruendiel *told* you how he killed my grandmother?" The notion seemed to distress Perin.

"He wasn't boasting about it. I asked him to explain why he'd done such a thing."

"Did he explain it to your satisfaction?"

"He told me what he had done." She added: "He regrets it very much, I think."

"It is late for regrets," Perin said.

"Is your father really going to try to avenge his parents' death?"

"One of these days! He's no coward, my father." Perin glanced at her as though he were anxious that she should understand that point. "He swore that oath when he was young and unattached—and then he married and had a family to raise. But he hasn't forgotten. We all grew up hearing the story of how he was orphaned before he was even born."

Nora thought that Perin's father sounded rather self-pitying, even if justice was on his side. "And if they did fight, Aruendiel and your father, and Aruendiel won, what would happen? Would you have to try to kill him, too?"

"*If* Lord Aruendiel won. I wouldn't put high odds on that, after seeing him today. He's not what I expected. He's a feeble old man."

"He's not always like that!" Nora protested. "He was like that only because he'd been imprisoned. You saw what he did to the Faitoren—and he turned himself into an owl—"

"But those are all magician's tricks. And yes, he did seem stronger as we went along, but that was a magician's trick, too." Perin shook his head decisively. "My father will be furious to hear that I had Lord Aruendiel at my mercy and did *not* kill him, but blood of the sun! I couldn't attack a defenseless old doddard like that. It would be almost like killing my own grandfather."

Nora looked curiously at Perin and wondered if there were any chance at all that—but no, Aruendiel had recognized in Perin's face the features of the man who had stolen his wife. "So tell me the truth, Perin," she said resolutely, "when you said you'd help me find Aruendiel, what were you really thinking? Were you planning to kill him? Because I would hate to think that I almost betrayed him, leading you there."

"You know I never pretended to be a friend of Lord Aruendiel's," Perin said. "But I said that I would help you, and I did."

She nodded, not entirely satisfied, but wanting to give him the benefit of the doubt. "How did your father survive, when his mother died?" she asked.

"My grandfather had hired a wizard. Otherwise Lord Aruendiel would have found them much earlier. The wizard saved the baby and brought him to one of my grandfather's cousins, who adopted him."

Aruendiel stabbed his wife in the chest, Nora thought. Between the ribs, he said. He could have killed both mother and baby, but he didn't. She thought of pointing this out to Perin, but had a feeling that it wouldn't appreciably change his opinion of Aruendiel.

They were almost at the marsh's edge before the road abruptly snaked to the left and gave them a view of the battlefield. "Oh," said Nora.

"Look at that," said Perin. He sounded almost appreciative.

The Faitoren were everywhere, wave after wave, stretching to the edge of sight. They blotted out the white marshes, moving with steady, inhumane precision. Even under a slate sky, their bronze swords and helms glittered. Like wasps swarming, Nora thought.

She looked around frantically for their own side, and found it. The human soldiers mustered in ragged bands against the encroaching sea of bronze. Their armor was pewter in this light. Not everyone had armor.

In the distance, a cloud of something like smoke suddenly descended on one section of the Faitoren army—a flock of birds, she realized—and it seemed to her those Faitoren ranks thinned slightly. Aruendiel's iron birds.

"It's not real, that army," Nora reminded herself and Perin. "Not all of it. They're just mice. A lot of mice."

"Right," Perin said. "Do our men know that?" He studied the scene before them for a minute, then pointed out what appeared to be the tents of the human army, about a mile to the west. The frozen marshland that lay between them and the camp was mostly empty, Nora was relieved to see. "We'll be at the camp in a quarter of an hour," Perin said. "You'll be safe there." He was eager to join the battle, she could tell.

They reached the stone quay at the foot of the hill and started across the marsh. Rain had mashed the snow into a heavy, slippery sludge, and it was slower going than Perin had predicted. Nora slipped once, but was up again in an instant. The main fighting was going on several hundred yards to the left. Massed shouts were punctuated by the crunch of metal on metal, over and over again. It was odd to be walking past a battle in progress; Nora was reminded of the peculiar isolation she used to feel when she went past the stadium on Saturday afternoons in football season on her way to the library.

Something made her look up. Pure instinct—there was no shadow to alert her.

"Run!" she screamed at Perin. Absurdly, she flung up her hands and waved them around her head as she ran, the way you might try to shoo away flies. Perin, running beside her, said something about a dragon; he sounded both worried and excited. "Worse than that," Nora panted.

She splashed through a patch of red slush, and almost stumbled over something soft. A man cried out. "Oh, I'm so sorry," she said, wincing. Running, she was finding it a little hard to navigate, her sight skewed by Aruendiel's protection spell. The ground looked very far away. She dodged past another red spot with a dark, huddled mass in the center.

The protection spell. Nora stopped in her tracks. She didn't have to run from Raclin, not this time. Of course, Perin didn't have a protection spell, but he did have a sword. Nora turned and scanned the sky with a sense of righteous indignation, as though she might well summon Raclin down and finally have it out with him.

But Raclin was just a pair of distant wings against the clouds. Like a tea tray in the sky, and just as harmless-seeming. Vaguely annoyed, Nora lowered her gaze, just in time to see the looming bulk of a galloping horse and the golden flash of a Faitoren sword—missing her, not by much. The protection spell cuts it close, she thought, and then saw where she was. Human and Faitoren soldiers were on all sides of her.

A Faitoren knight swung his blade at the belly of a young soldier with curly black hair, and it came back trailing pink and red ribbons, as the black-haired boy crumpled. Another pair of soldiers, better matched, were trading sword blows—Nora had to scramble out of their way—until the human pinked the Faitoren on the shoulder. Looking greenish, the Faitoren dropped his weapon and staggered backward; his opponent stepped forward confidently and hacked through the Faitoren's windpipe. Another horse ran past, this one riderless. A couple of human soldiers bore down on a Faitoren—he looked familiar, Nora was sure she had danced with him once—but the Faitoren did something that made one of them go down on one knee, and then he slashed heavily at the second's man's face, under his helmet. The soldier's jaw fell down, all the way to his collarbone. He screamed and gurgled. Broken teeth flew.

"Mistress Nora, this is no place for you." Perin, coming up behind her, his sword drawn, the tip stained dark.

No place for anyone, Nora thought, but all she said was "Where?" All directions were the same, a maze of men trying to kill one another. But Perin seemed to have an instinct for threading his way through the fighting. He took Nora's hand and they gave a wide berth to two more knights swinging swords, halted until several mounted knights had swept past, and then ran through an area where the fighting was sparser and wounded men had left mushy red trails in the snow.

"And the camp is just over there," Perin was saying when something came down like a curtain across their path.

"You again," Nora said disgustedly to Raclin, who gave her a jagged, insinuating grin and rattled his wings at her. She stepped in front of Perin with the unformed hope that the protection spell might safeguard him as well. The air was warm from Raclin's breath and smelled of burnt hair. Raclin himself—his long head, his yellow eye—kept swimming in and out of focus, so that it was hard to judge exactly how far away he was.

Then suddenly Nora's vision cleared, and Raclin looked startlingly real and close. Her heart sank as she realized what that meant. "I think my protection spell ran out," she said despairingly to Perin.

Behind her, a deep snarl that made her bones vibrate. She turned abruptly and found herself looking into the blank golden eyes and gaping, empty mouth of the Kavareen.

With an impatient swat of its paw, it batted Nora aside, then launched itself at Raclin. But Raclin, screaming in indignation, had already hauled himself into the air with a frantic flapping of wings. He circled low, hissing and baring his teeth. The Kavareen hissed back, gathered itself, and leaped upward; Raclin had to twist in midair to avoid the Kavareen's claws. He shot upward, still scolding. The Kavareen crouched on the ground, ears back, tail lashing, and watched him climb until he disappeared among the lowering clouds.

Nora got up carefully from the icy patch where she had landed. The Kavareen turned its glassy gaze back to her. She didn't recall being able to look at the Kavareen eye to eye. "My goodness, you've grown," Nora said, trying to sound upbeat and friendly. "Remember me? We took a nap together once." She saw with dismay that the creature's tail was still snapping back and forth. Its mouth opened wider.

This time, it seemed to Nora, the darkness inside the Kavareen was dense, crowded, full of lost, shadowy things. Aruendiel had said that it liked to eat whole cities; perhaps he hadn't been joking. A thin, wailing sound hovered maddeningly in her ears, like the whine of an unseen insect; she understood intuitively that, inside the dark mystery of the Kavareen, it would be a howling storm of trapped, desperate voices.

"Nora!" Then a string of fierce, unknown syllables.

The Kavareen shrank backward. Hirizjahkinis flung her arms around Nora. "Don't mind the Kavareen," Hirizjahkinis said, laughing. "He is excitable today, very greedy. I do not let him eat so much, usually. Nora, you found Aruendiel!" She hugged Nora tighter. "I did not believe it at first, when I saw him come. You did very, very well. That was not just good magic—that was you, your *kanis*, what is here." She made a fist and touched it lightly to Nora's sternum.

"Oh, Hirizjahkinis," Nora said, "I was so—" But Hirizjahkinis had already released her and was moving away.

"I must attend to Ilissa. We have turned the battle, now that Aruendiel is back. There he is, you see." Hirizjahkinis pointed into the thick of the battle; Nora looked for him vainly. "I want to hear all about how you freed him, later. He would only tell me a little." She called to the Kavareen— then called him a second time, more severely—and the two of them disappeared into the press of soldiers.

"Perin?" Nora started and looked around. There was no sign of him nearby. He'd been right behind her until the Kavareen came along—Nora was formulating a panicked thought in her mind until her eye fell on a pair of combatants at the edge of the battle line and she recognized Perin's helmet. She relaxed only a little as she watched. He seemed to be holding his own—no, better than that, the Faitoren was being forced back. She began working through the spell to confuse an enemy's sight.

Running footsteps and the clank of armor made her turn. A man in bronze ran staight at her, an axe lifted high.

Nora couldn't move. But somehow she was working the levitation spell. The Faitoren soldier bounced into the air. And hung there, legs pumping vainly. She almost laughed with relief.

He threw the axe. She began to duck, not fast enough.

A black flutter in the air, the sound of clanking iron. The spinning axe disappeared in a bronze flash.

Pumping its wings awkwardly, Aruendiel's iron bird landed heavily on the snow with another clank. Then it took to the air again, heading for the Faitoren.

Nora felt a light touch on her arm. "It is Mistress Nora, is it not? Aruendiel told me to look out for you." An older man, slightly stooped, slightly familiar. Aruendiel's old friend Nansis Abora, she realized after a moment, with relief and some pleasure. "This is no place for a young lady. Would you like to come back to camp with me? I have just been seeing to some of the wounded," he added, and she noticed his blood-streaked apron.

"I want to make sure that my friend is all right," Nora said, gesturing toward Perin. The Faitoren's sword blade had broken off; Perin had his own blade pointed at the Faitoren's throat.

"That boy there? He looks as though he's doing a tolerable job of taking care of himself, child, and Aruendiel won't thank me if anything happens to you while we dawdle here."

Nansis Abora had a small sled drawn by a pair of mules, in which he was transporting wounded men back to the hospital tent. To Nora's chagrin, he insisted on treating her as one of the wounded as soon as he noticed the bloodstain on the back of her wool cap.

"It's just a bruise," she said, but she had to explain about how she had been hurled across the room when Dorneng's spell exploded.

"Oh, yes, we felt the spell over here," Nansis Abora said, chirping to his mules. "Just a bump, though. Not enough to knock over a mouse." He nodded when Nora described the formula she had used; evidently he knew more math than Aruendiel. "Yes, the surface of a ball increases as the square of its radius," he said. "So, the bigger it grew, the weaker the spell."

"I was hoping it would break the Faitoren into little pieces, like the ice demon," Nora said. But Nansis Abora said that at some point the spell would be stretched so thin that it would dissipate entirely.

When they reached the hospital tent—Nora vaguely recognized the dog-faced figure painted on the outside, one of the healer gods—the magician made her lie down, despite her protests that she was fine, absolutely fine. From her corner, Nora watched Nansis Abora treat the wounded. First he had to determine whether their injuries were real or illusory. The white-faced soldier on the stretcher clutching his shattered knee was soon dealt with: Nansis Abora stripped away the Faitoren spell, and the man walked out of the tent looking as though he could hardly believe his good luck. The next soldier, an abdominal wound, was in a graver state, and Nansis Abora clucked as he examined him. Nora averted her eyes as the magician threaded a needle.

She must have slept all afternoon. When she opened her eyes, it was dark outside. Nansis Abora was occupied with another groaning soldier. His apron was completely red now.

Feeling a strong, urgent need for fresh air, Nora walked out of the tent. The lanes between the tents were full of soldiers and horses returning from the battlefield. She scanned them, looking for news. Had they won the battle? The men's faces seemed to hold nothing but weariness. Someone in the ranks burst into slightly hysterical laughter, then stopped just as abruptly.

One figure caught her attention as it passed from shadow into torchlight. A tall, dark-haired man, striding through the crowd, who drew her eye because he looked so positively *dashing*—there was no other word.

It was Aruendiel. The light had caught the unscarred side of his face. Nora got a quick glimpse of the rakish young man he had once been—his fine, aquiline features so handsome she almost felt shy. But that was only part of it. Aruendiel looked fresh, almost electric with vitality. His limp was invisible. Where was the decrepit old man of the morning? Aruendiel had been working enough magic for an army, that was obvious.

Nora had just formed this thought when Aruendiel looked in her direction. If he appeared startlingly young, she was equally shocked by the look of absolute desolation in his pale eyes.

"Lady Nora!" Perin's voice beside her. So he had survived the battle. She felt some tension disappear that she had not previously been aware of. She looked around again; Aruendiel was gone.

In her confusion, it took her a moment to notice the dirty bandage wrapped around Perin's right elbow.

"You're hurt!" she said.

He smiled. "A Faitoren tore my sleeve. Nothing to be concerned about. What about your head?"

She could not help smiling back. "Oh, that. Nothing to be concerned about. But the battle—what happened? Did we win?"

He looked more serious. "Well, the Faitoren are in retreat. We took about a hundred prisoners, a dozen dozen killed or wounded. Most of the rest are penned up on their own lands." There was no exultation in his voice, though.

"And the losses on our side?" Nora asked apprehensively.

"We lost about the same." Perin drew a breath as though to continue, then hesitated.

"Who?" At least Aruendiel was all right, she thought frantically. Or was he?

Perin's eyes were kind. "That witch Hiri—Hiris—the one we saw this morning. I'm sorry to bring you this news. You knew her."

"What happened?" Nora grabbed his hand in agitation.

"That dragon we saw, and the monster leopard—" he began. Nora listened with a sinking heart. Raclin had attacked a line of troops, and Hirizjahkinis had loosed the Kavareen on him. Raclin once again took to the air, but not before clawing the Kavareen across its flank.

The leopard recoiled. Whether from pain or confusion or sheer viciousness, it pivoted and pounced on the nearest living thing: its master, Hirizjahkinis.

"I was not close enough to see," Perin said, "but they say that the leop-

ard's mouth was like a cave. She was gone in an instant." Then the Kavareen rampaged up and down the lines, gulping down soldier after soldier,
human and Faitoren alike—and growing even larger.

"It was Lord Aruendiel who stopped the thing. He did something that
made it cower for a second, and he got it to vomit up a couple of soldiers."

But not Hirizjahkinis. The Kavareen leaped over a line of cavalry and
went bounding south across the marshes. Aruendiel and some of the other
magicians gave chase, to no avail.

"No wonder he looked so terrible," Nora said. Her heart felt like a wild
bird in her chest, trapped and frantic. "Oh, Hirizjahkinis." The brightness
that was Hirizjahkinis consumed by the Kavareen's dark—it seemed baf-
fling, too painful to think of. Perin said something about honoring her
grief. Nora was suddenly aware of the gentle pressure of his hand on hers.
She squeezed back in distraction, then dropped it. "I have to find Aruendiel. I have to—"

She went running down the line of tents in the half-darkness, straining
to glimpse Aruendiel's tall figure. The flickering light from torches and
campfires showed soldiers looking back at her with curiosity. Had he gone
this way? The farther she went, the more crowded the lane became; she
had to dodge and squeeze her way among the soldiers. A man with a lazy,
crinkling grin squinted down encouragingly.

"Do you know where I can find the magician Aruendiel?"

"Missy, you don't need a magician when you've got me."

After a while, she found herself on the other side of the encampment,
the noise and hubbub of the tents behind her, nothing but icy night before
her. A sentry gave her an odd look. With an empty feeling, her face wet,
she turned and slowly found her way to the hospital tent.

It was some comfort talking to Nansis Abora, whose blue eyes clouded
when Nora told him the news. "Such a sweet lady, always so lively. What a
pity! And a fine magician. Dear me, I must have known her for—how
many years?" He puzzled over that, splinting a soldier's wrist. "She came
with Aruendiel to Semr when I was still at court. Six dozen years or more.
Oh, this is a blow for Aruendiel, I'm sure."

"He looked miserable just now. Where is he?"

"Oh, he'll be in war council half the night, my dear child. They'll be
wanting me, too, even though I don't have much head for strategy. Poor

Hirizjahkinis! You know, I used to wonder why Aruendiel didn't marry her, although I never said anything to him about it. He was so obviously fond of her."

"I don't think she would have had him," Nora said carefully.

"No, perhaps not. He can be prickly, Aruendiel can. Let me see that leg," he said to the soldier.

Aruendiel did not appear that night, although Nora hoped he would. She spent the evening helping feed the wounded soldiers, those who were awake and able to eat. Many were sleeping; it seemed that Nansis Abora believed in the liberal use of poppy juice. Afterward, she had trouble sleeping herself, although it was the first time in almost a week that she'd had a bed of any kind and real blankets. Just that morning, she had taken Hirizjahkinis for a ghost. A few hours later, Hirizjahkinis had hugged her for saving Aruendiel. And now she was gone. No matter how many times Nora replayed the events of the day in her head, they never ended any differently.

The camp was beginning to stir when she heard Aruendiel's voice outside the tent. She fumbled at the flap and went out in a rush.

In the clear morning light, he was not the young man with the romantic good looks she'd seen the night before; he was not the dying old man she'd rescued; he was only Aruendiel, and the sight of him made her heart lighter, in spite of her grief. She came close, and impulsively she put her arms up to embrace him, but it was like hugging the trunk of a tree; she realized he was wearing armor under his cloak. With some awkwardness, she stepped away. "I heard about Hirizjahkinis."

The gray gaze flickered, then steadied. Aruendiel pressed his lips together. "Yes," he said. "She died bravely. It was a foolish accident, entirely preventable, but she died bravely."

"Oh—" Did it matter whether Hirizjahkinis died bravely or not? The fact that she was gone was monumental enough. Nora felt the sudden weight of the kiss that she had never given Aruendiel. "I'm so sorry," she said, clasping her hands. "I miss her, too."

"She was stubborn, she never listened to any prudent warning about the Kavareen. She treated it like her toy, her pet, her plaything—pure madness!" Aruendiel seemed ready to give full rein to his anger, but he checked himself and said more quietly: "She feared to face the Faitoren without it. Even when I returned to join the battle, she would not give it up."

"Aruendiel, I saw her yesterday afternoon, just for a moment. She was so happy that you had come, that you were alive."

"She saved me once and I could not save her in return." He shook his head violently, as though he did not want anyone to look too closely into his face. "And now we still have work to do. Your head—Nansis tells me you managed to break it open."

"It's fine," she said, but Aruendiel had put his hand on her shoulder to spin her around. Unwinding the bandage, he inspected the back of her head. She winced a little at his touch, but said: "I had a headache yesterday. It's gone now."

"It would be better for you to rest more," Aruendiel said, replacing the bandage. She turned and felt his eyes run over her, as though checking for other injuries. "But an army camp is no place to leave a woman alone," he said, "and perhaps you will be of service where we are going. You shall come with us to look for Ilissa."

The expedition to the Faitoren domain included some two hundred horsemen and nine magicians, including Aruendiel, Nansis Abora, and the man who she gathered was Euren the Wolf—slight, gray, forgettable except for his yellow eyes. Nora rode a horse bigger and livelier than she would have preferred, but she held on as best she could, a levitation spell ready in case she started to tumble off. They rode past the scene of yesterday's battle, where dead horses and broken weapons lay petrified on dirty red ice, and then south across the snowy marshland toward a line of low, dark hills. Perin rode up beside her a couple of times to exchange a few words. She tried to smile as she clung to the saddle.

After a couple of hours, the marshland gave way to fir-covered hills. A scout galloped ahead, then returned to direct the force through a small pass. Nora looked around curiously, wondering if she would recognize any landmarks. They had almost reached Faitoren land.

Nothing seemed especially familiar, though, until a warm gust of wind touched her face. She caught the dreamy summer scents of roses and fresh-mown grass. Looking up, she saw the red-roofed towers of Ilissa's castle, bathed in sunlight, not half a mile away, on the far side of a snow-covered rise.

"Mind this, Euren," she heard Aruendiel say, then felt the glancing edge of his spell, a wrench in her gut. The stone towers rippled, quavered, like heat mirages on a highway in August. And vanished. "You see?"

Aruendiel said to Euren the Wolf. "You saw how easily it came off, once I had the end of it?" Euren nodded, amber eyes hooded, then grinned suddenly. His teeth were very white.

That was how they entered the Faitoren domain, stopping now and then so that the magicians could strip away a clutch of Faitoren spells. Aruendiel was particularly thorough, undoing every piece of Faitoren magic he could find. A gold-and-ivory sundial became a gorse bush. The cloud of blossoms evaporated from the branches of a cherry tree. The scented breeze died away. Unexpectedly Nora felt a twinge of regret for the charmed, sweet beauty that, piece by piece, was passing away.

On the other hand, that statue of the two lovers that Aruendiel had just destroyed was dreadful, the girl smiling so moonily at the boy, who was just a little too gorgeous to be real. It was like a greeting card in stone. When you got right down to it, Ilissa had terrible taste—drippy, saccharine, juvenile. If she hadn't come up with such a horrible version of me, Nora thought savagely, maybe I wouldn't have minded being enchanted so much.

When they reached the site of the castle, most of the structure was already gone, but Nora thought she saw the balcony from which she had once spied on Raclin with a broken heart. Then it, too, trembled and disappeared.

What remained was a rough circle of snow-capped stones about the size of a tennis court. At the periphery were a collection of miserable huts—stone rings with crude roofs made of willow branches. As they approached, a small figure emerged from one of the huts. Nora recognized him by the tusks and the outsize, misshapen head. So it hadn't been a dream, Vulpin's transfiguration.

Vulpin looked up at the horsemen, his eyes settling on Aruendiel. He bowed.

"Where is your queen?" Aruendiel demanded.

"We have no queen," Vulpin said. "The one you are looking for—and her son—they are not here."

"Where are they, then?"

"We don't know. We have not seen either of them since we retreated here yesterday."

"Are they dead?"

"We don't know. Nor do we care. She is our queen no longer."

"What do you mean?"

"We served her loyally, but she led us into catastrophe and then abandoned us, so we have determined that we must rule ourselves."

"Rule yourselves?" Aruendiel exchanged amused glances with Euren and Luklren.

"Yes." Vulpin held his big head very high. "Yes, since there is no one else to do so. My compatriots have chosen me to parley with you, as the sole representative of the Faitoren people. I have their permission to sue for peace."

"Then you must lay down your arms in surrender," Aruendiel said, "and swear that you will make no more war on myself, King Abele, his liege lords, and any of his people."

"We will swear, those of us that are left."

"How many of you are there?"

By way of answer, Vulpin called in that language that Nora had never learned. The other Faitoren trickled out of the huts. There were perhaps a hundred altogether. "This is all of us," Vulpin said. "The rest you killed or captured."

Nora would not have recognized any of the Faitoren. None wore the fair, enchanted faces that she was used to. Nor did any of them much resemble each other. Some were the height of a child; others were gangling giants. A few looked bigger than they were because of their horns or their sail-like ears. Some had fur, some had feathers, some had scales, and some had all three. As a group, the Faitoren seemed to have stepped from the pages of some mad bestiary—not exactly human, not exactly animal, and some of them looked more like extraordinarily animated trees than anything else.

Moscelle—she recognized Moscelle by her eight eyes. That memory had not been a nightmare, either.

"What about the glamours you people normally wear?" Aruendiel demanded. "Why are you showing your natural faces?"

"We've agreed to do this, all of us," Vulpin said, showing more animation than he had previously. "The Faitoren are tired of wearing masks, of having to impersonate the dull uniformity of humans. Our own faces are nothing to be ashamed of."

"A matter of opinion," Aruendiel said.

"You would have stripped our glamours off in any event, the way you have been doing with everything else in our kingdom."

"Yes, and I will continue to do so until I have located Ilissa."

Vulpin held up his hands. "Then search as much as you like. She is no longer queen here. But please—I am appealing to your mercy as well as your honor, Lord Aruendiel—remember that we are a delicate race, and not accustomed to cold. If we might remake our dwellings—"

"How the Faitoren employ their magic will be a matter for discussion," Aruendiel said. "Your dwellings will remain in their current, unadorned state, for now. However"—an immense bonfire blazed up in the center of the large circle—"your people will not freeze in the meantime. And some of you have enough fur or feathers to withstand a little cold. Before our two sides can talk of peace, I must satisfy myself that your queen and her prince are not here."

"You have my word, and the word of all the Faitoren here," Vulpin said. "I suppose, however, that is not enough for you."

"No, it is not," Aruendiel said.

He and the other magicians spent the rest of the day combing over the Faitoren lands, gradually removing layers of enchantment. A velvet lawn turned into a lake surrounded by snowcapped mountains, which in turn became a crimson-sailed galley, then a string quartet playing Pachelbel's Canon, until it finally reverted to a patch of ground with a couple of fence posts sticking out of the snow. "Very careless, no sense of structure," Aruendiel observed.

A few times he asked Nora for directions through the Faitoren landscape, but she recognized only a few of the shifting locales. The one place she wanted to find was the iron-fenced graveyard. After the magicians had been at work for several hours, Nansis Abora found it under a tropical atoll. At least, he turned up a pile of iron railings. Ilissa must have found some non-Faitoren—Dorneng, perhaps—to tear down the fence.

But there was no sign of the graves or headstones, let alone the yellow police tape that Nora had seen there the last time.

"The gate's closed up," Aruendiel said, watching Euren the Wolf sniff the ironwork. "Otherwise, they would have gone through into your world, Mistress Nora."

"I didn't think it would still be open." She told him now about her abduction, and how Dorneng had tried to use her blood to make a new, permanent gate between worlds.

She could see anger hardening Aruendiel's face as he listened. When she had finished, he set off a string of curses like bombs. "I thought they took you as a hostage, and even then I was afraid they might kill you. If I had known what they planned all along—" He swore again. "I was a fool ever to trust Dorneng."

"Well, I was, too," Nora said. She was not eager to admit how gullible she had been, but felt it was important to set the record straight.

He frowned at her, but there was a flaw, something pained and helpless, in his usual severity. "I did tell you not to leave the castle, did I not?"

"Yes, you did. I thought it was Hirizjahkinis, and that you were sending for me."

"You should have known it was a trap. A good magician would have sensed, *smelled* the Faitoren magic—"

"It *was* stupid. So much of this is my fault. They would never have captured you—Hirizjahkinis would still be alive—if I hadn't been such an idiot."

"Yes, perhaps—but enough! I am hardly one to lecture you about falling into a Faitoren trap." Aruendiel shook his head. "I should have taken you with me, as you asked, Nora. Or I could have sent you elsewhere for safekeeping, found a way to hide you."

"Turned me into a geranium," she said faintly.

"Yes! Except that the weather is inhospitable for geraniums now." His face tightened again. "You said Dorneng was killed by an ice demon? It was too easy an end for him. That he would try to cut your throat in cold blood—I would like to—"

"Aruendiel?"

"Yes, Euren?"

"There is a cave nearby that we have not searched yet."

With an effort, Aruendiel collected himself. "By all means then, let us go there." He limped away at Euren's side. Nora, watching them go, had the odd thought that Aruendiel was just the slightest bit afraid of Euren the Wolf. Euren was one of the magicians who had brought Aruendiel back to life, she remembered, and she wondered if Aruendiel bore *him* any grudge.

She turned to find Nansis Abora beside her. "I beg your pardon, child. I could not help overhearing what you said just now about Hirizjahkinis. You blamed yourself for her death."

"Well, yes. I know, it's the Kavareen that killed her, but I can't help thinking that if Aruendiel hadn't been captured in the first place—"

"Oh, these things are difficult to predict," he said vaguely. "This comes up very often in my time work. So many factors in the causation of even minor events—but excuse me, you were saying that Hirizjahkinis was killed. I must correct you a little. I was considering this last night during the more tedious parts of the war council, and you know, being swallowed up by a demon like the Kavareen is a terrible thing, but it is not the same as dying. Or perhaps I should say that death is not inevitable."

Nora stared at him. "Do you mean that Hirizjahkinis might still be alive *inside* the Kavareen?"

"It is *possible*."

"So if we could get her out—?"

"Yes, yes. Of course, there would be difficulties. Finding the Kavareen, for a start. And then not being devoured oneself—that is always important."

This thread of hope cheered Nora to an almost unreasonable degree. Had she not sensed some kind of presence—voices, even—within the Kavareen? For the rest of the afternoon, as the party of magicians slowly moved through the Faitoren domain, she felt positively buoyant. When she caught sight of Perin with some of the other soldiers, she gave him a wave and a broader smile than she had shown him that morning; she wanted to tell him about Hirizjahkinis, but he was out of earshot, guarding Faitoren prisoners. He waved back at her.

At nightfall, Aruendiel called off the search. Ilissa and Raclin were nowhere to be found. He led half of the party to Lord Luklren's castle, a few miles away, leaving Euren the Wolf and a hundred soldiers to occupy the Faitoren lands; the other magicians would relieve Euren in turn, Nora gathered. Vulpin would be escorted to the castle the next day for peace talks.

Lord Luklren's castle was larger than Aruendiel's, but his estate seemed hardly more prosperous. The sheepfolds they passed were half-empty—more Faitoren depredations?—and when they arrived at the castle, Luklren's wife, Lady Nurkasa, came out to greet the guests with strained graciousness, obviously calculating fiercely how to feed the multitude.

Nora, wishing to be helpful, offered her services in the kitchen to Nurkasa, who seemed surprised at first but was glad enough to have another pair of hands besides her aged cook and two peasant girls. There was a flurry of frantic preparation—hams hauled out of the storehouse, stale turnips and cabbages being salvaged, soup boiling on the stove, a barrel of beer delivered from the tavern—and finally, very late, dinner was served in Luklren's great hall.

It was a raucous affair. From the far end of the long table, where Luklren and the cavalry officers sat, there were periodic eruptions of song—war chants and, later, obscene ditties about the Faitoren women. The magicians' end of the table, where Nora sat, was only slightly quieter. Aruendiel and Nansis Abora got into a long discussion of invisibility theory, heated enough so that Nansis said, "That's a bit much, Aruendiel," not once but several times. After several tankards of beer, one of the younger magicians, Uklin Bone, could not be dissuaded from transforming himself into a horse and urinating copiously on the floor. He was too drunk to turn himself back, and Fargenis Gouv had to find him a stall for the night. Euren the Wolf queried Nora at length about her trek with the ice demon to Maarikok. He was not so difficult to talk to, once you got used to his insistent yellow stare. The wolves, he remarked, also had chants that kept ice demons at bay.

The only incident that marred an otherwise exhilarating evening came after Nora got up to refill a soup tureen. The kitchen in Luklren's castle was located across a dark courtyard—where, to judge from the reek, some revelers had already followed Uklin Bone's example. Nora was returning through the courtyard with the full tureen when someone grabbed her arm. One of the cavalrymen, just finished with emptying his bladder. He mumbled something.

"Let me go this instant," she said.

"Don't be so stiff, girl," he slurred. "Everyone knows you're the wizard's whore."

Not again, she thought angrily. "I am *no* man's whore." The hot soup arced out of the bowl, rearing up like a snake, and splashed right in the man's stupid face. He yelped and dropped her arm, railing at her.

Another figure loomed in the darkness. Nora heard a blow, a groan, and the impact of a large, drunken man hitting the ground. "Lady Nora, are you all right?" It was Perin's voice.

"I'm fine, thanks." Nora tried to sound composed. "I'm just going back to the party. We're out of soup now, unfortunately."

"Ah, you threw it at him." He laughed suddenly. "Quick thinking. He deserved a soaking."

She hadn't thrown the soup—not the way Perin meant. But she had helped make that soup, and when she asked it, it did her bidding in a jiffy. Aruendiel would be pleased with how she used magic to get out of that particular jam.

The wizard's whore. Except, she thought, I can never tell him.

# Chapter 46

The peace talks lasted several days. Vulpin was willing to agree to almost any restrictions on magic practiced outside the Faitoren lands, but he held a firmer line on magic practiced at home. "We are magical beings," he said, clasping his stubby hands on the table. "We are willing to forswear magic for certain ends, but I cannot promise that we Faitoren will *not* do magic. Such restrictions would kill us."

Aruendiel was unimpressed by the last argument, but with some reluctance he assented to the eventual compromise: The Faitoren were prohibited from casting glamours on any living thing—including themselves—in their own domain or out of it. "So there will be no more hiding people in books or camouflaging sheep as ladybugs or disguising kidnapped young women, is that clear?" he growled at Vulpin. Yes, very clear, Vulpin said mildly.

As for reparations for the livestock that the Faitoren had stolen over the years—Luklren's main concern—there was less haggling. Vulpin agreed to a number only slightly lower than the one that Luklren first named.

The reason, Nansis Abora explained to Nora, was that both sides knew that there was small chance that the Faitoren would ever be able to pay the reparations. Almost any figure named would be essentially fictional. "Their land is very poor," he said, shaking his head. "And none of them is a real farmer, from what I can tell."

"But that's just asking for trouble down the road, setting up unrealistic expectations the Faitoren can't meet," Nora said. She was thinking of the Treaty of Versailles.

"I'm afraid you're right, my dear. As the dog said when he bit the serpent's tail, this will lead to nothing good. Well, neither side really has a choice. The Faitoren are in no position to argue—but really, what leverage do we have? We can't do much more to them, short of putting them all to the sword, and then the reparations will never be paid. At least Lord Luklren has had his claims acknowledged. But bad bargains like these," he added, "are why I got out of politics."

Nansis Abora was Nora's main source of information on the negotiations—filling her in when he came down to the kitchen in the afternoons for a goblet of hot sheep's milk and whiskey. If Aruendiel was not in the talks with Vulpin, he was closeted with Luklren or the other magicians, or taking one of the watches over the Faitoren. Nora spent almost all of her time with Lady Nurkasa, struggling with an embroidery needle. Perin came in a few times to visit, for which Nora was grateful, although under Nurkasa's eye, he talked only about the weather and his hostess's cousins near Semr, whom he knew slightly.

Sometimes Nora thought that she had enjoyed herself more on the frozen desert of the Ivory Marshes.

After Vulpin went back to the Faitoren to get their approval for the treaty, the magicians continued to meet by themselves—arguing about the new protection spells to install around the Faitoren domain. "Dull stuff," Nansis Abora said, although Nora wished that she could sit in. It would be a good part of a magical education to witness this kind of debate, and she was slightly hurt that Aruendiel had not included her.

Euren the Wolf had already left. "He wants to get back to his pack," said Nansis Abora. "He doesn't mind the fighting, it's the talking afterward that he can't stand."

Nora finally asked the question that she had been wondering about since meeting Euren. "Is he a werewolf?"

"Oh, no!" Nansis Abora seemed both horrified and amused by the question. "Not at all. No, Euren is a man—a man who prefers to live as a wolf."

"What is the difference?"

"There's a world of difference, my dear. For one thing, Euren won't bite you. Well, he did bite Aruendiel once," Nansis added vaguely, "but then he was provoked."

At the end of the third day Nora finally heard from one of Luklren's servants that the Lord Aruendiel would be pleased to have a word with her.

With relief she put down her embroidery needle and followed the servant. Aruendiel was in the room that Luklren called a library, although there were more weapons in it than books.

As she approached, the door opened and Vulpin emerged. He bowed. "Princess Nora."

"No one calls me that anymore."

"I wasn't sure who you were at first," Vulpin said. "You know, I never saw your real face before. I was happy to see that you recovered from your injuries."

"Really?" Nora said. "I don't recall you showing much concern before, when I was bleeding to death."

Vulpin's tusked face was masklike, but she heard him sigh. "It was difficult, you know. Ilissa treated us badly, too."

"She didn't kidnap you or marry you to her monster son, did she?" Nora demanded. Then she sighed, too. "Well, I don't want to stir all this up again. You were more decent to me than the others, and all of us are here to make peace, aren't we?"

"Yes." He paused. "There is one thing I was wondering about— whether you have any intention of asserting your claim to the Faitoren throne."

"What? My claim? You mean, because I was married to Raclin?" Nora laughed. "Gods, no! I have no interest in your throne. Your people are more than welcome to govern yourselves. But there's something I want to ask you, too. I still have Raclin's horrible ring on my finger, and no one can remove it. The one time someone succeeded, I almost turned into a marble statue. How do I get it off—without dying?" She showed it to him.

Vulpin shook his head regretfully. "That is Raclin's magic—the unitary ring. It is a sort of glamour, but not one of our usual Faitoren glamours. There appear to be only two rings." Seeing Nora's blank look, he went on: "Your ring and Raclin's ring are the same ring, and only he has the right to take it off your finger. The best thing to do, I think, would be to ask Raclin."

"He'd never do that."

Vulpin shrugged. "Who knows what Raclin might do. It is funny"— Vulpin nodded again in Aruendiel's direction—"*he* asked me the same question, about your ring. Well, good-bye and good fortune to you, Your Highness."

"You can stop calling me that."

With a flash of his old debonair manner, Vulpin said, "But you will always be a princess to me, no matter how long the Faitoren rule themselves." He raised his small hand and went down the corridor.

Nora laughed a little sourly and pushed open the door of the library. Aruendiel was sitting at a table near the fire, reading a scroll. Glancing up, he gestured for her to take a seat opposite him, then returned to the scroll.

After half a minute he asked: "And how are matters with you, Mistress Nora? The head you bruised, is it healing properly?"

"It's fine."

"And your health otherwise, and your spirits? You are keeping yourself sufficiently occupied while these damnable negotiations drag on?"

She thought he looked at her more seachingly than usual. "I'll be happy when we leave, but I'm fine."

Aruendiel grunted and took up a piece of paper from the table. "I have received a letter from Lolona, the Toristels' daughter. I had written to Mrs. Toristel to notify her that you had been found. It was Lolona who replied."

"Lolona? Is she at the castle?" Something in Aruendiel's tone gave Nora a feeling of disquiet. "Why didn't Mrs. Toristel answer your letter?"

"Mrs. Toristel is dead."

Nora stared at him, aghast.

"Yes, it seems that she suffered a constriction of the chest." He seemed to be trying to speak crisply, but his voice dragged. "She had had one before, a few years ago, but recovered. This one was more serious."

Nora closed her eyes and saw again Mrs. Toristel struggling in the snow, where Dorneng had flung her. A constriction of the chest? A heart attack, most likely. "What caused it? Was it because Dorneng—"

"It happened shortly after your abduction, as best I can tell from Lolona's account. She is not much better a letter writer than her mother was. Well, they did not have a patient teacher."

"Mrs. Toristel tried to warn me. She knew something wasn't right about Hirizjahkinis—I mean, Ilissa pretending to be Hirizjahkinis."

"I am not surprised. She was ever an astute judge of character."

I had only a handful of friends in this entire world, Nora thought, and that's the second I've lost. She took a deep breath. "This would not have happened if I had not—"

"If you are planning to take responsibility for Mrs. Toristel's death, I must preempt you. She was an old woman who was not in good health, who worked too hard for an exacting master, and that same master, who might have saved her, was absent, taken captive through his own foolishness. It is maddening, Mistress Nora, that I have spent several lifetimes practicing magic and yet that is no guarantee that I use it wisely or that it brings any good to me or those around me."

"You do a great deal of good," Nora said, more heatedly than she meant to. "And you do use magic wisely, more wisely—" She was going to say more wisely than he'd behaved in other areas of his life, but that sounded like faint praise. "Mrs. Toristel," she added, "admired you very much."

"Perhaps she was not as good a judge of character as I thought." Aruendiel sat in silence for a moment, his gaze unfocused, then glanced back at Nora. He cleared his throat. "I confess, I still do not quite grasp how you were able to free me. Algebra, you said."

"It took me a while to work it out," Nora said. In more detail, she told Aruendiel how she found him, figured out what sort of trap he was in, and then floundered by sheer luck into a way to enlarge his prison, even if she could not destroy it. Aruendiel nodded slowly as he listened.

She was not sure what to say about the wasted, white-haired figure in the dungeon, although she had an inkling that it was already less real and less fearsome for her than it was for Aruendiel. "I knew that once you could reach out and start doing magic again, you would be fine," Nora said.

Aruendiel said only: "I am grateful. It was a horrific imprisonment."

Then he remarked, more easily: "Ershnol the Silent was caught in a similar trap once. He escaped when a rat knocked over a candle and burned the building down. In my case, of course," he added, "it would have been more difficult to burn down that dungeon."

It felt familiar and consoling to be talking magic with Aruendiel again, after all that had happened since her last lesson back in his tower, the day they'd done the observation spell. She wished they were there now, safe among his books. How soon before we can finally leave this place and go home? she thought. There is no Mrs. Toristel to welcome us, now. That will be hard, very hard. But I'll have Aruendiel. And he will need a friend, he'll need me more than ever, with Mrs. Toristel dead and Hirizjahkinis dead or a prisoner or whatever has happened to her. And—Nora resolved suddenly—I will *make* him finish *Pride and Prejudice* with me, and he will see what happens with Darcy and Elizabeth.

"Now we must talk of different matters," Aruendiel said. "We must discuss your future."

"What is there to discuss?" she asked, surprised.

Aruendiel frowned. He looked at Nora without catching her gaze directly. "There are two things. The first concerns the young man who escorted you through the Ivory Marshes."

"Perin Pirekenies."

"Yes. I gather that you first made his acquaintance in Semr last summer. He has been to see me."

"What for?" Her first, uneasy thought was that this had something to do with the challenge that Perin's father had issued to Aruendiel. They were going to fight a duel.

"He would like to marry you. He has asked for my permission, since I have been your—guardian, in a sense. I have, of course," Aruendiel paused, "given my consent."

Nora wondered whether she had heard correctly. Aruendiel's face was composed and serious, as though what he had said made perfect sense. Finally, she managed to get a single word out: "Why?"

"I have given it careful consideration, and I believe this is a very desirable offer of marriage. I have made a few inquiries about Perin Pirekenies, and from all accounts he is an honorable man and a good soldier, and he stands to inherit an estate that, while not exceptionally large, will be adequate to support you and your children.

"His bloodlines are not unblemished, of course." A bitter rasp entered Aruendiel's controlled tone for an instant. "You may not be aware that he is the grandson of my wife and her lover."

"I figured that out."

"Ah. Well, his father was legitimately adopted by another relative, and the rest of the family line is entirely respectable. Despite the scandal involving his grandparents, he is connected to some of the greatest families in the kingdom. Given my own involvement in the matter, I could rightfully refuse permission for this match, but I am not inclined to do so. On the contrary, I must recommend that you accept his offer."

"I barely know Perin," Nora said. "I've spent a few days with him. And why would he want to marry me? I'm not a noblewoman or an heiress."

"He admits that it would be an unconventional match, but that does not seem to trouble him. He has taken a liking to you and is concerned for your welfare. He argues convincingly that the marriage will rescue you from the unfortunate situation in which I have unfairly placed you."

The conversation was becoming more and more surreal. "Unfortunate situation? What do you mean?"

"Perin Pirekenies," Aruendiel said impassively, "has pointed out how your name has been tarnished because of your association with me. It is commonly assumed, he tells me, that you are my mistress.

"You are young and unmarried—at least, you are absented from your husband—and I am a widower with an old reputation for being a libertine. It is no surprise that the world would jump to mistaken conclusions. I have heard such fools' talk from time to time, but never considered it worthy of notice. I did not think about the injury that such gossip would inflict upon you."

"Oh, please." Nora shook her head. "It doesn't mat—"

"It does matter, especially for you. You are in a more vulnerable position than most women. You have no family—not in this world, at least—and you are a foreigner. I have been remiss, keeping you under my roof all these months."

"Well, where else would I go?"

"Now Perin Pirekenies offers you a place to go. And," he went on before she could reply, "since I no longer have a housekeeper to be any kind of chaperone for you, it is all the more advisable that you marry Pirekenies."

"That's ridiculous."

"Pirekenies is quite serious."

"Then why didn't he ask me himself? Why did he talk to you about it?"

"He is acting in the customary way."

"And you agreed on my behalf?"

"Well, the final decision is yours. A woman should not marry against her will."

"Oh, thanks for that!" Standing up, Nora put her fists on the table and stared down at him. "What is *wrong* with you? Don't you know any better?" She was afraid as much as angry.

Aruendiel's face tightened. "I am trying to do what is best for you."

"You have no right to tell me who I should marry!"

"I am only counseling you. And if you had listened to my counsel the first time you married——"

"Oh, this is utter bullshit. You and Perin cooking up this marriage together to save my reputation—who cares about my reputation? Why would you go along with this? Why? It doesn't make any sense! A chaperone! Mrs. Toristel wasn't a *chaperone*. She didn't even sleep in the house—we could have been screwing like rabbits every night, and she would never have known!"

"Well, that is exactly the problem," Aruendiel said, his voice hard.

"What problem—what people think? Who cares? It doesn't matter."

"No, that is not true. I can tell you—I know how dangerous it is for a woman to be scorned, to be an outcast. You are a woman of independent spirit, Nora, and it is galling to consider these things. But I am not saying them to humiliate you. I am stating the reality of your situation."

"Who cares about that? You're a magician." Nora sat down again, but held on to the edge of the table as though she could draw strength from it. "So what if everyone thinks I'm a whore?" she said. The wizard's whore. "I don't mind."

Aruendiel's mouth twisted unpleasantly. "If you were married to an honorable young peer like Pirekenies, you would be safe from such calumnies," he retorted.

"I will tell you something that I did not say to Pirekenies," he added. "My wife's old estate, Lusul, is the subject of a legal dispute. I have a claim to it. So does Pirekenies, through his father, Lord Pireke—although their claim is inferior to mine. There are other claimants who could also trump the Pirekenies claim.

"I have never had any interest in claiming Lusul. But if you accept Pirekenies's proposal, I will exercise my claim and then turn the estate over to you and your husband." He pronounced those last words clearly and distinctly. "As a wedding present, since otherwise you will have no dowry."

"A wedding present," Nora repeated. It was hopeless. He was hopeless. "Aruendiel——" She looked at him pleadingly, but the ice in his eyes was unbreakable. How could he be so wrongheaded? No, she thought, her heart torn—it's me, I've been wrong all along.

Suddenly she was resolved. "If Perin wants to marry me, he can ask me himself. You can stay out of it, it's not your concern. And I wouldn't take Lusul as a wedding present. It didn't bring *your* wife any luck."

Aruendiel's eyes narrowed. "Perhaps not."

"All right, then. As long as we understand each other."

"You have made yourself clear."

"Fine." Of course, this settled nothing. If she didn't marry Perin, then what? Would Aruendiel bar her from his castle to preserve her reputation? She decided not to think about the possibility for the moment. "What was the second thing you wanted to discuss?" Nora asked roughly.

"The other matter, yes. It also bears upon your future."

"I can't wait," she muttered, but he ignored her and went on: "You were telling me a few days ago about your struggle with Dorneng and how he tried to kill you." Nora nodded impatiently. Where was he going with this?

"Dorneng was a traitor and a villain and a fool, but he was a good magician. Micher Samle taught him well. He had found a hole that led to your world—"

"Yes, I know, my ghost was supposed to hold it open. Otherwise it would close up."

"The hole is still there," Aruendiel said.

"How do you know?"

"I have detected it, and Nansis agrees with my observation. Either it has lasted longer than Dorneng expected, or it has re-formed in the interim. But the hole exists now."

"So I can go home. Is that what you're saying?" Nora looked at him half-suspiciously, as though he were offering her another affront.

"It's possible. The gap may not be large enough, or—as Dorneng feared—it might close up yet. But it is likely that, yes, you can return home, if you choose."

If she chose. She felt strangely flummoxed, paralyzed by the sudden opportunity to escape. On some level, she had come to accept that she would stay in this ridiculous, alien, hidebound, primitive world for the rest of her life. Otherwise she would have simply laughed at this notion of marrying Perin. And Aruendiel's blind stupidity, his callousness, his treachery—she could not even decide what to call it—would not be so scorchingly painful.

There was nothing to decide. She had been looking for this chance for a long time. Now it was finally here.

"Of course I want to go home," Nora said.

Aruendiel nodded. "Then we will leave immediately."

"Today?" Not even a night to think it over.

"The gap could close at any time. We must move quickly."

"Oh. Well, I don't have much to pack." There was nothing to pack, actually. At home she would have no need for the clothes she wore here. "I should say good-bye to Nansis Abora—and thank Lady Nurkasa—and I must talk to Perin. Tell him that I am leaving." She gave Aruendiel a hard look.

"Be quick about it," he said.

As the door closed behind Nora, Aruendiel remained seated at the table. His eyes moved over Lolona's letter one more time, but the words did not register. Pirekenies was on duty just outside the castle. Easy enough to work an eavesdropping spell to find out what foolishness he and Nora were talking—but no, he had no desire to know.

He could still hear Pirekenies's voice, annoyingly earnest. "Lady Nora—" Why did he insist on calling her "Lady Nora"? She had no such title, not unless someone like Pirekenies married her. "Lady Nora has told me that you have behaved honorably and respected her chastity, and I believe her." Absurd—why shouldn't Pirekenies believe her? Nora was as truthful as clear water. Although there was no reason for her to talk about such matters with this young idiot. She'd had a similar discussion once with Hirizjahkinis, too. Was the whole world so fascinated by what went on—or didn't go on—in his bed?

Apparently so, Aruendiel thought angrily, remembering the lout in the courtyard the other night, taking hold of Nora. *Everyone knows you're the wizard's whore.* The girl was too clever for him—she kept her head and magicked the soup all over the man. Aruendiel had seen it all from the top of the stairs. Then, before he could teach the thug a lesson, young Pirekenies knocked the bastard down first.

"But even if you have behaved correctly, sir, you must see what an awkward position you have placed Lady Nora in. To be associated with a man of your reputation—let's be candid—exposes her to constant ridicule and disrespect." Insufferable presumption, but the worst of it was, Aruendiel could not deny the truth of what the boy said.

He should have just bedded the girl. What had he gained from being honorable, when everyone assumed the worst? On more than one night, watching Nora's smile across the table, savoring her talk and the sweet chime of her voice, he'd wanted to suggest that they continue the conversation in his bed. Not that they would have done much talking. But he had held back. He would not copy that Faitoren filth, taking advantage of her helplessness. The fearful fate of a woman alone—any man's plaything—it would never be Nora's, if he could help it. And besides, Aruendiel thought with dry and bitter logic, what sort of lover would he make now, with his ravaged face and body? Nora deserved better. He'd been so careful, all those months of restraint, not even brushing against her. It was an evil joke that when he could finally lean against her—her strong, warm shoulder under his hand—he was barely alive, tottering out of that cursed dungeon a skeleton, a doddering wreck.

But far better for Nora to know him as he really was. And for him to know it too. It was too easy, when he was with her, to forget the burden of all his years, his broken body, the toxin of regret. He felt somehow restored in her presence, as though he'd found his true self again—but he knew it was an illusion. How swiftly all his power had disappeared once Dorneng trapped him in that chamber. And then the long slow slide into infirmity, exhaustion. He had given up, and then *she* was there. Holding hands with Pirekenies—he was almost sure of it, although his vision had been weak and the room full of mist.

The damnable irony of it. Kill a man and his ghost comes back fresh and young to torment you. She wasn't going to marry Pirekenies, though. That was some petty comfort.

Perin looked honestly shocked when Nora told him she would not marry him. She had started to feel sorry for him—had been thinking of ways to try to soften the blow—but the perplexity on his face made her angry all over again. As far as he'd been concerned, she saw, their marriage was a settled matter.

"Did Lord Aruendiel not say—"

"Yes, he did," she snapped. "Why did you have to bring him into it?"

"Well, it's customary—"

"That's what *he* said. Bullshit. This doesn't concern him at all. Not at all."

He seemed ready to protest, but then he said: "I'm sorry. The last thing I would want to do is offend you, Lady Nora."

"You can just call me Nora. I don't know who you think I am, but I'm not Lady Nora." After that she began to feel bad again. "Listen, Perin, I like you. I really do. Somehow you made trudging through the wilderness in the middle of winter with a soul-sucking demon and a soul-sucked would-be murderer seem not so terrible.

"But then you do something as boneheaded as asking Aruendiel if you can marry me. I thought you were different from most men here. I thought you were better than that."

Perin still looked perplexed. "You still don't see why this bothers me, do you?" she demanded.

"No, not really," he said. "But if you want me to ask you to marry me, instead of petitioning Lord Aruendiel, I'll gladly dispense with etiquette. You did tell me once that you were not a well-behaved young lady. I should have remembered that better."

"You should have! But it doesn't matter. I'm leaving, Perin. I'm going home. Back to my own world. There's a door that's open right now, and if I leave tonight, I can go through it."

"What!" Perin was skeptical, as he was about all things magical, and he tried for a while to convince her otherwise. Only when she told him that she had to return to her family did he abandon his protestations.

He even seemed ever so slightly relieved, Nora thought. Whether it was because her impending departure allowed him to save face, or whether he had had second thoughts about marrying her, she was not certain. Perin would be better off with a girl of his own kind, she thought, with a prick of regret. No doubt he would find one soon enough.

He did remark: "I think I prefer the traditional method of arranging marriages. Somehow it is less pleasant to hear you say no than it would have been to hear Lord Aruendiel say it."

The sleigh was waiting for her at the main gate of Luklren's castle. Nansis Abora was stroking the nose of one of the four horses, whispering something to it. He smiled at her as she approached. "I hope you don't mind me, Mistress Nora. I would like to help see you off tonight. It should be an interesting display of magic."

"Of course!" Nora said heartily. So there would be no chance to continue her earlier conversation with Aruendiel.

He came out a minute later, wrapped in his black cloak. "Finished your farewells?" he asked.

"Yes." She climbed into the back of the sleigh, followed by Nansis Abora. He helped her spread a sheepskin rug across her legs. Aruendiel took up a place at the front.

"These horses are a bit spirited, so we are not bringing a coachman," Nansis Abora said. "Aruendiel and I will take turns driving."

There was definitely some sort of swiftness-and-endurance spell on the horses, she could tell as soon as they started. Trees and huts slipped past like ghosts, dissolving instantly in the darkness. The wind in her face made her squint. Within a few minutes they had left behind Luklren's castle and the nearby village and were well launched into the wilder countryside. Aruendiel turned the horses east: Their route, Nora gathered, would skirt the southern border of the Ivory Marshes and take them back to the open plain where Dorneng had taken her.

Nora was not in a conversational mood, but Nansis Abora talked gently and persistently about cooking and gardening, asking her how both arts were practiced in her own world, so that eventually she found herself spending a long time trying to explain tomatoes to him. They did not exist in this world, as far as she could tell. Another reason to leave. After some time, Nansis Abora took up the reins, and Aruendiel moved back, next to Nora. They sat in silence. She thought of asking him some question about magic, just to get him talking, but what would be the point.

Now I'll never be a magician, Nora reflected. Not even a poor one. I'll never hear the rest of Aruendiel's story, of how *he* became a magician. She fought down sudden hopelessness, the urge to tell Nansis Abora to stop the sleigh. Home, she told herself, I'm going home.

After a while the moon rose, brightening the snow around them, and Nora saw that they were in the middle of a treeless flatland. Aruendiel leaned forward from time to time to give directions to Nansis Abora. In the intervals, he bowed his head slightly as though he were listening for something.

Suddenly, he shouted: "Careful, Nansis, you'll drive right into it!"

Nora's first reaction, as Nansis pulled the horses to a stop, was dismay. She wasn't ready. This notion of passing between worlds was more daunting now. How many things could go wrong? Aruendiel seemed confident enough, but even he made mistakes. Plenty of mistakes.

The magicians got out of the sleigh and walked a few steps away, talking in low voices. They seemed to be pacing something out. Slowly she unwound herself from the rugs and followed them.

"Here," Aruendiel was saying. "You can feel it. This coarseness in the air."

"Ah. It's not very large, is it?" Nansis Abora said.

Nora had thought of something disturbing. "Where does it come out on the other side?" She had no interest in being dropped into the middle of the Pacific Ocean.

"That's what you must control," Aruendiel said. "There will be a half second when you are literally between the two worlds, and you will have to choose where you will come out."

"How on earth do I do that?"

"The way you did when we worked the observation spell. Pick your path with intent."

"Oh, this isn't going to work! What if I can't get through—if I'm stuck in the middle?"

Aruendiel reached inside his cloak and removed a small coil of rope.

"Here," he said. "We will hold fast to you until you are through. Have courage, Nora. I would not send you into certain danger."

Feeling shaky, she tied the rope around her waist, then looked up at Aruendiel. "All right?"

"Yes," he said.

"Good-bye, my dear child," said Nansis Abora, smiling at her. She would have liked to embrace him—he had been so kind to her—but he only held out his palms to her to touch. She did so, then turned to Aruendiel.

He was holding one end of the rope, so he held up only one hand. She held her own palm against his and looked up at his face. In the bright moonlight, his face was full of shadows; his eyes glinted like stars. She saw more clearly now that his grim, desert quiet was a mask.

Nora managed to get out a few words of thanks. "Aruendiel, I—" She hesitated, stalling for time, waiting to hear what would come next out of her own mouth.

"Go!" he said sharply. "Now! Remember, you must move with purpose!" Roughly, he pushed her toward the hole in the air.

With purpose. Obediently, she moved forward, groping her way into something she could not quite understand. There was a moment of pure emptiness in the middle when she almost panicked. It reminded her of her first time on a ten-speed, pumping backward to brake and feeling the pedals spin uselessly.

Solid ground again, sunlight on her face. Ahead of her was her father's brown split-level, blissfully ordinary. Daffodils glowed under the maple tree. The front door opened, and her youngest sister came out, wearing a purple backpack, ready for school.

Nora stepped forward, but the rope around her waist held her back. She untied it as quickly as she could, then let it slip away into the air as she ran across the yard to her sister.

## Chapter 47

What to tell them, what they would believe, that was the problem. After the round of incredulous embraces, the jubilant phone calls, once her parents and sisters and friends had told Nora over and over again how glad they were to see her and how grateful she was safe, the questions popped to the surface as vigorously as divers that have been underwater ten seconds too long.

Where were you? What happened? What were you doing all this time? Why couldn't you at least call and let us know that you were all right? Do you know how worried we were? To Nora's dismay, a town police officer also came to take a statement, and reporters from the local stations arrived to do their stand-ups in the front yard.

It was clear enough to everyone that Nora had been through some sort of trauma. The scars on her face and torso had not entirely disappeared. The doctor who examined her diagnosed a recent concussion and signs of exposure. She was underweight, although otherwise healthy. She could not give a clear account of her whereabouts for the past ten and a half months.

Yes, Nora told the cop, she had left the cabin for a walk, then gotten lost on the mountainside. An animal had mauled her. A bear? She couldn't remember. She fell and broke her ankle. Some people found her, took care of her. They lived in the country. No telephone or electricity. Her step-mother examined the long-skirted dress she had been wearing and pro-nounced it hand-sewn.

The cop asked why she was wearing a wedding ring. No, I'm not mar-ried, Nora said. Yes, a man gave it to me, but it was sort of a joke. Then it wouldn't come off. How did she get to New Jersey? Someone drove me, Nora said vaguely. The cop pressed her for the names of the people she'd stayed with. Nora mentioned an older woman named Mrs. Toristel, who had died a few weeks ago. A heart attack.

The cop didn't buy much of the story, Nora could tell, but on the other hand Nora was no longer missing and insisted she had not been kidnapped, so he didn't seem particularly motivated to investigate further. He did ask her to spell Mrs. Toristel's name. Nora had to stop and think about the English transliteration.

"First name?"

"Margaret," Nora ad-libbed.

Her mother flew in from Richmond, and it was almost as bizarre as traveling between worlds to see her sitting in the kitchen of the old house in New Jersey again and drinking coffee with Kathy and Nora's father. No-ra's mother eyed the new kitchen wallpaper but said nothing about it. At dinner, everyone told Nora to eat more, she was too thin, and her father kept topping up her wineglass, although Nora was careful not to drink too much, because Kathy was watching her closely in case it was alcohol that had taken her away for so many months. Nora was also afraid of blurting out something so unbelievable that her family would take alarm. Bad enough that she'd slipped up and said how great it was to hear English again. Then she had to explain that the people who'd taken her in spoke some foreign language—no, not Spanish—a language she couldn't recog-nize. They spoke a little English, too. That was how she got by.

She withdrew upstairs when she could, and everyone watched her go, their fond eyes sharp. Lying in bed in her sister Leigh's room, exhausted but unable to sleep, she listened to the three adults talking, their voices wafting up like smoke. Her parents had never seemed to realize how easy it was for their children upstairs to hear almost every word they said downstairs.

They were talking about her, of course. Kathy was saying they could go by the hospital tomorrow to get the ring cut off. "She said she hates it but it's stuck on her finger."

They started discussing the ring and its possible significance. Listening to them, Nora began to see that, in a way, Raclin's ring was useful. It answered the most questions. Nora had gotten mixed up with some man. She'd lost her head and followed him into who knows what kind of life, and now, thank God, it was over. Opinion was divided as to whether Nora had come to her senses on her own or whether the man had dropped her. They also could not agree on what sort of milieu Nora had been living in, and whether drugs or motorcycles or unorthodox religious or political beliefs had been involved.

"She said she hadn't had pizza for a year." Kathy, bemused. "Could it have been some kind of radical, vegan, back-to-the-land group? And she looked as though she hadn't bathed for days."

"I could just kill her for running off, if I wasn't so happy to see her again. We are so blessed to have her back." Her mother, unable to resist bringing God into it.

"Yes, it *is* a blessing." Her father, trying to be gracious.

In the other bed, Leigh rolled over and sighed noisily, as if to signal that the conversation downstairs was too inane to sleep through. "It's so weird to think of Dad ever being married to your mom," she announced.

"Yeah," Nora said.

"You glad to be back or are you already regretting it?"

"It's good. Really good."

"How'd you get to be so thin? Was it drugs?"

"No!" Nora's turn to flop over in annoyance. "Why is everyone so interested in my weight?"

"Well, you look anorexic."

"I'm not that thin! No, I had to walk a long way, and I didn't have much to eat."

"Where were you walking to?"

"It was on the way home."

"And you don't have *any* idea where you were?"

"Not really. Somewhere in the mountains."

Leigh grunted dubiously. After a while she said: "They didn't find your body, so I thought there was a chance you were alive. But remains can skeletonize in a matter of weeks in warm weather—and animals scatter them—so I also figured that maybe they just missed you."

A sizable chunk of the books on Leigh's bookshelf were true-crime titles, Nora had noticed before the lights went out. That was new. "I'm really sorry. It must have been scary, not knowing."

"Well, yeah. Mom and Dad freaked. Not that you can blame them."

"I'm sorry," Nora said again. A car swooshed by outside, then another. She was going to have to get used to all this noise.

"The worst part is that they took it out on me. If I get home two minutes late, they're ready to call the police. Hopefully they'll ease up now since you weren't actually murdered. So, yeah, next time you flip out and run away, be considerate and text someone, okay?"

"Okay," Nora said.

The next morning, in the kitchen, she dropped her mug—after all those months without coffee, the caffeine was setting her nerves ablaze—and watched it break on the floor. Without even thinking about it, she started piecing the fragments together. And nothing happened. The shards did not cohere. She could not even say they refused to cohere. The mug was simply broken and remained so.

"Don't worry, it's just a souvenir mug," Kathy said, noticing how stricken Nora looked. "We got it when we took the girls to Disney World."

Later, Nora fished the pieces out of the trash and tried again. Nothing.

With each day, it was more and more as though she had never been away at all. Her mother went back to Virginia and only called twice a day. Reporters stopped calling. Her stepmother suggested that Nora see a counselor, but she was not pressing the point as hard as she could have. Nora herself could see the time was coming when she would not think twice about listening to music that came out of a box or taking an aspirin for a headache or driving along a street that was lined with signs and advertisements because pretty much everyone could read. She went so far as to let Kathy try to get the ring cut off at the emergency room, thinking that Raclin's curse couldn't possibly follow her to another world—although afterward she thought what a stupid chance to take, no one here would know what to do if she turned to stone.

Overall, she was readjusting nicely. Not more than a dozen times a day did she wonder what was happening back in that other world.

There was no way to calculate the time difference, of course. A few days could have passed there. Or months. But surely Aruendiel must be back at his castle. What was he doing now? Various images came to mind. Aruendiel leafing through a book in his tower study. On horseback. Wrapped in his black cape, moving with a jerky stride through snowy woods. Supping in the great hall, his gray eyes warming as he talked about magic. She could almost hear the rumble of his voice. But to whom would he be talking? And these were just recorded pictures in her brain. His real life was unfolding without her knowledge. She could only guess at its course.

She should have asked Aruendiel to teach her that observation spell, so that she could check in from time to time. But she couldn't work magic anymore, she reminded herself.

A small gray feather blew past her one day, as she was helping her father spade his tomato patch. She dropped the hoe and grabbed for it, but the wind took it out of her reach. As it disappeared behind a neighbor's satellite dish, her father asked what she was staring at.

Sometimes she wondered—just out of curiosity—about the magician friend of Aruendiel's who was supposed to be in this world. Micher Something. Micher Samle. But all she knew about Micher Samle was that he liked to transform himself into a mouse, and had once lived in a cave. Not much to go on, even if she felt like scouring the rodent-infested underground caverns of the world.

It was a trade-off, Nora decided sternly. She had her life back. Her family. The comforts of twenty-first-century American civilization. And English literature. Now she could lose herself in a novel again—any novel, not just *Pride and Prejudice*—and in a way, that was when she felt most at home. That first week, she went through one or two books a day, using her sister's library card. There was no particular logic to her choices, except that—Nora saw as soon as she considered it—they were generally realist novels, rooted in the observation of the here and now, nothing fantastical about them. She had no taste for anything but the most pragmatic of genres. When she finished a novel, she started another one right away.

She was close to the end of *Augie March* one afternoon when her sister Ramona, seeing how few pages remained, helpfully said that she could borrow any of the Harry Potters from Ramona's own bookshelf.

"No, thanks," Nora said absently. Lifting her hand to turn the page, she squeezed her sister's sock-clad foot. They were reading companionably at opposite ends of the leather couch in the den, Nora leaning against one arm, Ramona sprawled against the other.

"Why not?"

"It's a kids' book. I feel like reading something more serious, for grown-ups."

"Lots of grown-ups read Harry Potter. It's all about magic, you know."

"I'm aware of that." The books probably got all the magic wrong, Nora thought.

"So why aren't you interested?"

"I'm just not. Shh, I'm reading." Then—because it was still fresh and gratifying even to be able to be interrupted by her little sister—Nora looked up and asked: "What are *you* reading?"

Ramona turned the book over so that Nora could see the cover. "Ms. Kessenides at school said it was funny."

*Pride and Prejudice.* Nora sat still. "What do you think?" she asked after a moment.

"It's not laugh-out-loud funny, but it's funny," Ramona judged. "It's also kind of dumb."

"Dumb"—not a word Nora usually associated with Jane Austen. "What do you mean?"

"Well, it's so obvious that he's in love with her. And she doesn't even realize it until he actually asks her to marry him."

Nora cocked her head, pleased that Ramona was reading critically, not sure that she was reading carefully enough. "But he's so rude to her. And she doesn't get to hear Darcy say she has fine eyes, remember."

"When Noah Hurst poured his Coke into Janine Perez's locker, *everyone* knew that he liked her."

"Oh," Nora said. Sixth grade at Woodrow Wilson Middle School might be better preparation for reading Jane Austen than one might think.

"And Elizabeth's supposed to be smart!" Ramona said in a tone of grievance.

Nora took the book from Ramona and flipped through it. A much newer, sturdier copy than the frail paperback she'd left behind in the other world. Chapter 34, that was as far as she'd gotten with her Ors translation. She kept turning pages.

*How despicably have I acted*, Elizabeth Bennet cried—*I, who have prided myself on my discernment!* Elizabeth has just read Darcy's letter, and realized how thoroughly she has misread Wickham and Darcy. Her bad judgment about Wickham will cause mischief; her mistake about Darcy is potentially more costly, and only she will know why. Mentally, Nora put the sentence into Ors, then imagined Aruendiel reading it from her wax tablet. She was not sure she had used the right word to translate "discernment." Aruendiel would know. Suddenly she felt fiercely, shatteringly homesick for him. He was out of reach forever, for all the remaining minutes and days and years of her life. Oh, gods, she thought, what did I do? How could I not see how much—? *Till this moment I never knew myself.*

Ramona said: "What happened to that magician, Arundill?"

Hearing his name was a fierce electric thrill. Nora tried to look unmoved. "Aruendiel," she corrected Ramona, keeping her voice low. "He's fine." She hoped.

"Why didn't you tell them about him, about the other world?"

"They wouldn't believe me."

"They didn't believe me. But I'm just a kid. I bet they'd believe you."

"You told them about the night you saw me?" Nora had been wondering about this. Ramona had said nothing to Nora about a spectral visit from her and a tall, dark magician. Nora presumed she must have forgotten all about it.

Ramona nodded. "At first, when I told them, they got all excited. And then when I said it was magic—how you were visiting from another world—they got mad and said I was lying. I told them about the spell he put on Friday to make her talk, but I'm the only one who can understand her. They think she's just meowing.

"'Course, Friday doesn't really say anything worth listening to," Ramona added. "She just gripes about her cat food and says rude things about us."

"I've heard her." The day before, Nora had barely caught herself from responding, right in front of Kathy, when the cat made an acid comment about the size of Nora's feet.

"Really? That's good. I was starting to think, you know, that maybe my brain *was* making all this stuff up."

"No, it's real," Nora said reluctantly. Should she be saying these things to Ramona, who was already so prone to fantasizing? Was believing in alternate realities going to help her in sixth grade and the rest of her life? "It did happen, but you shouldn't think about it too much," she said stoutly. "Because we have our lives to live right here, in this world, and we don't need magic."

"Why not? You can still do magic, right? Arundill was teaching you, you said."

"I haven't even tried since I got back," Nora lied.

"What?"

"There's no reason to." Ramona looked incredulous, so Nora went on: "In that other world, they need magic because they don't have anything else. There's no science, no medicine. You wouldn't believe how much better things are here, really." To her own ears, Nora did not sound as convincing as she hoped.

"But that's so stupid! Aren't you going to go back?"

"Of course not."

"I can't believe you, Nora! You are so retarded."

"Don't say 'retarded.' " Kathy was strict on this point—no insults that slighted the disabled.

"Why not?" Ramona's voice rose on strong wings of outrage. "You were learning magic—from a magician—in a castle, and you decided to come back here to be a *Muggle*. That's the textbook definition of retarded. You know how lucky you were?"

"Not so loud," Nora hissed. Leigh was upstairs; Kathy would be home any minute. "I had to make a choice, Ramona. I chose you guys. I missed you. Everyone thought I was dead. When I was here that night, I saw how upset you were. Dad was drunk because of me. And now he's not drinking. So, yeah, I made the right choice."

"Oh, Dad getting drunk, that stopped months ago," Ramona said matter-of-factly. "Mom blew up over Christmas and he goes to AA now. They think I don't know."

"Oh. Well, that's good," Nora said, taken aback. "But I had to come back so that everyone would stop worrying."

"Well, yeah," Ramona said. "But I thought you came back only for a little while, to show them you were okay. I didn't know you were going to *stay*. Don't you miss that other place at all? Don't you miss the magic?" She was tensed, as though ready for Nora to deliver bad news.

"Yes, I do, very much," Nora said. She had to take a deep breath, the truth came out so fast. "I can't tell you how much I miss—everything." The magic. Aruendiel. Herself.

"I knew it! So you'll go back?"

"Oh, honey." Nora hated to say anything to spoil the glee on her sister's face. "I can't."

"What do you mean?"

"I don't know how. I came back through a door, and it's shut now."

Ramona's brow furrowed. "But no one said you couldn't go back, right, the way Aslan keeps telling people they can't come back? There's no *rule* that says you can't go back?"

"Well, no, but—"

"Arundill will help you get back." Ramona spoke with utter confidence.

"But I can't reach him. And *he* thought I should come back here."

"Why? That doesn't make any sense. I bet he didn't want you to go. And *you* miss him, too, don't you?"

By way of answer, Nora gathered her little sister in her arms and hugged her, the way she had wanted to the night when Ramona thought she was a ghost. She felt a little better, although embracing her sister did not crush the loneliness she felt. "How did you get to be so smart?" she whispered in Ramona's ear.

"I could tell from how he talked to you, that night, he likes you. A lot."

"I wish I'd been smart enough to see that."

Ramona studied her for a moment. "You have to go back," she said simply. "You'll find a way. We could go camping in those mountains where you got lost, and try to get back from there. Or, your ring!" She grabbed at Nora's hand. "It's magic, isn't it? That's why it broke the clipper at the hospital?"

"But not good magic." Nora jerked her hand back. That vile ring. How sickening that it was the only tangible connection she had to her other life. Her real life, she could see now.

But if this link survived, she thought slowly, there may be others. There might be other gateways. Going back to the mountains—I could try that. I've traveled between worlds twice now. I know *something* about magic. Surely I can find my way home.

Ramona was still fascinated by the ring. "The only way to get it off is if you cut your finger off," she was saying. "They'll call you Nine-fingered

Nora." Delicately she lifted Nora's ring finger and gave it a nip, her teeth clicking against the gold.

Nora thought of the expression on Aruendiel's face when she had once made a similar suggestion, and wondered again how she could have been so blind, stupid and blind, she who had prided herself on her discernment. But she only said, "No fighting, no biting," the way her parents used to when she and EJ were little, when magic was something you only read about in books.

What was it Aruendiel had said? Pick your path with intent. At least, she thought, now I know where I'm going.

AUG - - 2014